This is a very personal diary of the heart. This represents the voicing of my silent soul sounds. Therefore, this one is for. . .my eyes only.

This journal reflects the absolute truth as I recall it. . .no cloaks to shield places, events or. . .myself.

Soul Sounds

Mourning the Tears of Truth

Mary Summer Rain

HAMPTON ROADS
PUBLISHING COMPANY, INC.

For information write:

Hampton Roads Publishing Company, Inc.
134 Burgess Lane
Charlottesville, VA 22902

Or call: (804) 296-2772
FAX: (804) 296-5096
e-mail: hrpc@hrpub.com
Web site: http://www.hrpub.com

If you are unable to order this book from your local
bookseller, you may order directly from the publisher.
Quantity discounts for organizations are available.
Call 1-800-766-8009, toll-free.

ISBN 1-878901-33-8

12 11 10 9 8 7

Printed on acid-free paper in the United States of America

Our souls make mourning sounds and our eyes shed gifts of tears for you. We will miss you, dear friend. Forever will you remain within the depths of our hearts where your golden light will eternally live on.

(In loving memory of Art Reischmann, whose golden heart began shining upon the Spirit Horizon on January 2, 1992.)

Author's Introductory Statement

In the spring of 1991 I thought it might be wise to write down the events of my life. I wanted to have a personal record to review when I became very old and too forgetful of mind to remember. This was to be the recording of my private soul sounds that nobody else would ever hear.

But it was not to be.

I've been advised, by reasons spoken and unspoken, to have this very private diary published. This idea was not sanctioned by me until the very last possible moment because I'd thought no one else was going to be reading my words, and I'd written as honestly and outspokenly as I could throughout the journal pages. I'd recorded my personal thoughts, memories, and even confessions. In essence, this journal does indeed turn me inside out in respect to revealing my true thoughts and inner self to the public. But, as always, I abide by how I am guided; whether I will end up being chastised, ridiculed, embarrassed, or exposed because of the publication of this book is not important anymore. So then, dear friends, I give you my total inner being. I now bring my private soul sounds to your ears. I give you. . . .

THE JOURNAL . . .

BEFORE THE BEGINNING

Today's date is June 5, 1991. I'm beginning on page 47 of this record book because I've torn out the first 46 pages and ripped them to shreds. I did this because my family saw the recording of my life story as a bad omen which meant I was going to die. They falsely assumed I was driven to write my story for a reason: to leave a legacy behind me.

"I know why you're getting all your No-Eyes books written ahead of time and I know why you're driving yourself so hard to get your life story down on paper—you know you're going to die and afterward, we'll have your journal to publish!" my daughter Aimee cried. Aimee's deep concern then got Bill thinking too. He worried that I knew something I wasn't telling him. He kept saying that he couldn't live without me. And I could see the distraction this journal caused in his life.

So I ripped out the first 46 pages I'd recorded of my life. I shredded them in tiny pieces and left them in the kitchen "burn" basket for everyone to see.

When I was asked why I'd done it, I told them it was because they'd all assumed I was going to leave them. I also added, "It was a pitiful and depressing story anyway."

Yet I'm still driven to write the journal, so now I must take special care to do it in secret. I can only accomplish this by staying up when everyone else has gone to bed. The dogs sleeping in the living room know I'm here in the kitchen darkness. Jenny's cat comes to sit and watch me now and then. But my four-leggeds are the only people who share my secret—they're the only ones who know I've again begun my journal. This is how it must be—this lie—for everyone else thinks I'm staying up late to relax in solitude or do some leisure reading. This, I know, is the only way to allay the family's fear of my upcoming demise, albeit an assumed one.

Aimee's idea that this journal would one day be published felt utterly preposterous to me for several reasons.

One: I was doing it for myself and no one else. I wanted to remember the events of this last mission—I wanted to remember *all* of them when I was very old and things became cloudy in my mind. So, first of all, this journal is a very personal and private affair because it would record many, many events never revealed to the public. It would be meant for my eyes only. Secondly: When recalling what I'd written in the first 46 pages that I'd destroyed, it was very clear that my life was indeed a pitiful and deeply depressing story. Nobody would want to read such horrific events in one's life. Also, the "real" story wouldn't be believed. Especially things like the *real age I first began reading the philosophy and metaphysical books, and the presence of the Archangels. So my life story is not for the eyes of the public who may disbelieve my words.*

This is just for me and, because it's just for me, I must try to recall and record everything as accurately as possible. I will use real proper names of the actual people and places. I will try to remember everything just as it happened.

It will take me many nights to rewrite those first 46 pages and it will take me weeks to catch up to the date where I left this in 1991. But then again—I have the rest of my life to do it in and I strongly feel that I won't be "called back" until long after it's said and done, for I see myself as an old woman sitting alone in my porch rocker. . .just like No-Eyes. Why do I feel this way? Because there is some grand finale left to my destiny that has yet to manifest and the "timing" for it has not been revealed to me. There is The Knowing of some wondrous Starborn connection that will be known to the world. . .I yet have a part to play out.

And so I do dread the rewrite of my early years again, for, the first time I wrote them here opened many old wounds and stirred bad memories. But it must be done again, for I need to begin at the beginning.

Therefore, the secret journal of my silent soul sounds begins once again.

THE BEGINNING OF THE BEGINNING

I can clearly remember my life before entering into this earthly realm. It was so incredibly, vibrationally light and beautiful. I was among those I loved and who, in turn, loved me. We all worked together as one mind and one purpose. We were The Great White Brotherhood.

Although all members of The Brotherhood were united in the way of being completed ones who carried out God's will, we also had major divisions within the group. Some were messengers, some were light warriors, others were spiritual advisors to those completed ones who were serving physical missions. Some were protectors (these usually were the Archangels Gabriel, Raphael, Ariel and Michael), some were direct intermediaries between The Brotherhood division heads and God—who brought God's plans for specific missions required and current direction for various projects already in place.

It was always a great honor to serve God by volunteering for a physical mission or being asked to perform one. I had done so several times, but always loved returning to my main position as Record Keeper.

When the head of special projects approached me, I knew what was on his mind.

"We need you again," he'd said.

"Earth?"

"Yes. The Master sees a great need there. He wishes you to rekindle the ember again."

"But the others (the Starborn) will do that. It was foreseen and so deemed within the Plan."

"This is so, but humankind has strayed too far too fast. They will nearly destroy their planet before the Others' time is right. Humankind has fallen into the confusion and chaos

Belial has brought upon them with a silken tongue, coated with honey, and the people are believing his words."

"Surely they can tell."

"It seems not, for Belial has cloaked his minions in spiritual robes, and they do magic and speak golden words while giving out concepts contrary to the Precepts. The fervent Christians have become arrogant, religious sects are killing one another, and the self is becoming paramount in their minds."

"Who do you see is required this time?"

"You."

"As who? What role?"

"As a white one who is not white, as a native one who is not native."

"Then what will I be?"

"A messenger."

He nodded and gave me time to think.

Although he knew I'd never refuse a mission request, he knew I was so comfortable in my job. I loved being enclosed with all the books in the Great Record Hall. They were the etheric counterpart of physical books, and I was totally at home there.

To descend down the Vibrational Corridor for a physical lifetime was always a daring thing to do, because there was always the chance that the physical entity could incur karma. To accept an earthly mission was the least desired job possible.

Don't get me wrong though, these spirits accepting physical missions always had a great deal of help from their Brotherhood associates. They would serve as Spirit Advisors, and one or more of the protectors would be assigned to be a guardian—mine always seemed to be Raphael, who would present himself to me as a Shining Man of Light, or as himself.

I thought about the other times I had descended into the physical and I wondered at the wisdom of attempting the same type of mission again.

I went to the head of special projects with my concerns. "I brought the Living Light into the world and mankind destroyed it by distorting the Precepts to suit self. I brought the Ember Light back again and the native ones let it grow cold. How is it that I must do this again?"

"It is needed, for the Master does wish to once more have a messenger precede him. He feels great compassion for the chaos Belial had wrought with his Pretender ways and words. The Master wishes his voice to be heard as the final warning bell that tolls his coming so that those who hear and heed will open their ears, eyes and hearts to his messenger's voice."

"Will the light warrior again be my mate?"

"He is already eager to reenter."

"He always was prepared for a good fight," I said.

The head of special projects smiled.

I half-smiled as thoughts speared through my mind. "Why the odd ethnic aspect?"

"It is required to fulfill two native prophecies. One Anasazi and one Hopi. But," he cautioned, "this ethnic aspect will cause you much grief, for you will experience non-acceptance from both races. This is because your genealogy will have been tampered with for the sake of white propriety. You will have a fullblood relative who was given a fictitious French name. All evidence of native blood will have been eradicated from your family's historical records — this you will have to deal with. It will not be easy."

"It never is," I sighed. "So why bother with the native aspect at all then?"

"Because you will find you have a native mind, heart, and soul — it cannot be hidden or ignored — these will dominate your life and become the major aspect of your mission. You must walk the Way Between Races. . .the Shadowland."

I knew all about the Shadowland and it was a very difficult trail to tread because it presented so many additional problems and adversities.

I had other questions. "What will my name be?"

"At first you will be known as Mary Leigh, then, as your mission reaches its final stage, you will be given the native name of Summer Rain which you will make legal."

I knew the Record Book showed another physical life· as one known as Summer Rain, but I didn't realize that existence was to be the final special mission.

"Will the warrior also be a native?"

"No, but he will again be given the name of Joseph. He will be named William Joseph."

"Who goes first and when will we connect?"

"You enter first, he follows three months later when his selected vehicle will be prepared. You will connect when you both are 16 years of age."

"Who has chosen to be my Advisor and Protector?"

"Because this final mission has priority, the Intermediary (name withheld) will be your personal Gatekeeper and the Intermediary (name withheld) will be Joseph's personal Advisor who will speak through you. You're comfortable with these?"

"Oh yes, absolutely!"

"We decided the two Intermediaries would be best because they have a direct relationship with the Master and will better be able to direct your path for The Plan.

"Your Protector will again be Raphael, for he is very concerned with this final mission and sees many Sons of Belial trying to interfere."

"I will meet with Raphael to thank him for his concern."

"He loves you very much."

"As I do him."

And so it was that I consented to another descent which made my sixth mission into the physical realm. We had many serious meetings over this specific one where all involved were in attendance including the head of the light warriors, who was apprised of the various ramifications this mission would present for them. This project was foreseen to make them very busy battling the dark ones who would try their best at every turn to first: eliminate the messengers, and second: to foil The Plan to bring the Light of the Precepts back into the spiritual darkness that they wrought.

And so it was seen that my vehicle was prepared.

Raphael accompanied me down through the Vibrational Corridor and my being felt heavier and heavier.

I said my goodbyes to him. His light radiated.

"Fear not, Mary, for I will not leave your side until all has manifested according to the Master's will. You will know me from a young age. My presence will see you through pain of body, mind and heart. Go now. It is time."

I saw an infant being born. And, at 3:05 A.M. on December 12, 1945, I left my Brotherhood connection to enter the physical. It was a very heavy and confining space to be as the density and atmospheric pressure closed me in like a dark sarcophagus. . . and the infant's brain replaced my Knowing with a mortal nothingness—except when the baby slept and I was back unto my totality.

As foreseen, I was named Mary Leigh and I was the last child of Rita and Leo. Before me were two sisters. Elise was five years older and Barbara was nine years older. Three months later when the warrior of light (my counterpart) entered his vehicle, he too was the youngest, and like me, his siblings were also five and nine years older. We also had Polish surnames. We would attend the same school. We were born one mile apart and so lived our lives totally oblivious of one another until the appointed timing of our destiny to solidly connect.

The mother and father to whom I was born were not destined to hold together a family unit, but while I was very young, life was normal.

At first we lived on Mansfield Street. It was a two-family (upper and lower flat) house owned by my father's family. We lived upstairs and my ill grandmother lived on the first floor. The house was situated directly across from the massive complex and grounds of St. Mary of Redford Church and school. I was duly baptized there and would attend the school from the First through the Eleventh grade where one hour per day was devoted to dogmatic indoctrination by the Immaculate Heart of Mary (IHM) nuns.

When I was three years old, I used to love looking out our front living room windows to watch the priests and nuns walk the grounds. Their long skirts would swish about their feet and their robes gave me a comforting feeling.

Around the time when I was four, I'd visit my sick grandmother downstairs. I was somewhat precocious and would run into her room and spend time there. Sometimes I'd be allowed to stay as long as I wanted and, other times, I'd be shooed away. One afternoon I raced downstairs, but skidded to a halt outside her doorway. There seemed to be something different about the feel of the room in front of me, so I sneaked quietly up to her doorway and peered inside.

I froze in fright to see a real live ghost standing beside her bed. My wide eyes were riveted to its face. It was such a kind and calm face I couldn't seem to pull away from it. The ghost was a tall man. Light surrounded him. He gently raised a finger to his lips and I nodded with the understanding that I needed to be very, very quiet. He then gave me a sweet smile and I began to smile back when I saw smoke rising up out of my grandmother.

This was a truly fearful sight. I unfroze, turned tail and scrambled back upstairs as fast as my legs would carry me. I rushed up to my mother and told her about the ghost in grandma's room.

"Mary! *Shame* on you! That's a *terrible* thing to make up. Don't you remember that every story and lie you tell puts a big black spot on your soul?"

I shrunk back. "Yes, but there *was* a man down there. He had this bright light all around him and. . ."

"MARY! Stop it!"

"It's true! It's *true!*"

"Go to your room! You go get down on your knees and tell God you're sorry for lying!"

I went to my room, knelt beside my bed and looked up to the ceiling.

"I'm sorry, God, but I saw what I saw." Tears began to
fill my eyes. "Was that man an angel, God? Was he? Because he kinda felt like maybe he was. I mean, the light
around him was so beautiful and he smiled at me. That man
could *see* me and he smiled!"

When I came back out of my room, I guess I looked
adequately contrite because my tears were evidence of that—
but I knew better—so did God. And now at four years old, I
had a secret no adult would know, for I knew that from then
on, *my* truths were not theirs—*my* truths were considered lies.
After that incident I never saw my grandmother again. I was
told she was in heaven now.

That summer we moved into a new house that we had all
to ourselves. The address was 15370 Ferguson, and it was in
a nice neighborhood where big maple trees lined the streets.

My parents were so happy the day we moved in. My
sisters must have been in school because they weren't around
and I was alone with my mother and father.

They called out to each other from the empty rooms.

"I love you, honey!"

"I love you too, honey!"

Then I joined in while running here and there from room
to room. The only thing wrong with the neighborhood was
there were no other children my age. Because of this I kept
to myself, except for the times I'd visit with the adult neighbors.

When I was six, a divorced nurse moved in next door.
She had a six-year-old daughter named Marianne. Marianne
was very pretty with curly brown hair and green eyes. Marianne was a child model. She too was Catholic and was to
begin first grade with me at St. Mary of Redford school,
which was a mile away. I was so glad to have a friend I
told her about the Man of Light I'd seen two years ago.

"There's no such thing as ghosts," she'd chastised. "And
nobody *ever* gets to see their Guardian Angels! You better
stop telling stories like that because lies make big, black
marks on your soul and, if you have *enough* of them you
won't be allowed in heaven until you spend a hundred years
in Purgatory where they're *burned* off!"

I was enraged with a powerful sense to defend my facts.

"There are *too* ghosts and people *can* see their Guardian
Angels!"

"Can not!"

"Can too!"

"Momma!"

Momma came to the door and pretty Marianne spilled the beans. . .to an *adult*.

"Mary dear, we mustn't tell tall tales like that just to get attention. Your soul will be all black and I know you don't want that because the devil loves black souls—especially a little girl's black soul."

I was so frustrated my eyes filled with brimming tears and I ran home.

Marianne's mother thought she'd put the fear of God in me but good. Oh yeah, there was fear put in me alright, but it was the fear of speaking the truth! Now I knew I couldn't tell *anyone* about what I'd seen two years ago, or about how my feet got tickled at night by unseen hands, or about the soft voices I heard, or about knowing what was inside presents when I just laid my fingers on the packages. I couldn't tell anyone that I had dreams that came true or that I dreamed of a heaven much different than pearly gates and clouds.

At six years old I became a very quiet and seemingly withdrawn little girl. I withdrew into my own truths and let everyone around me live within their own spiritual lies.

Although this was my status quo, I never actually realized the difference between us (me versus the others around me), and never felt "different." I just knew that I had *proof* of *my* truths, while *their* truths were based on faith in what they were *told* to believe in. So I suppose I just accepted the reality of the two systems because I never, ever felt odd about what I secretly held in my heart. How could I, when I constantly had things verified for me time and time again?

On days when Marianne's mother drove us to school, I'd sometimes get talking about our religious concepts that we were supposed to memorize from the Question and Answer catechisms. "How come the Pope is infallible when popes have started wars and been ruled by kings?"; or, "If Jesus was a man and *saw* the devil in the desert, why can't all men see the devil's spirit too?"; and, "God's too merciful to make a place like Limbo, don't you know."

"My, my," Marianne's mother would say while clicking her tongue, "aren't we the little theologian!"

I didn't know what a theologian was, but it didn't sound good the way she'd said it. Later that day, Marianne said that her mother thought I shouldn't "think" so much about my catechism—I should just memorize it like a good little Catholic should—like she did. And so I stopped being a "little theologian," but *nobody* could stop me from thinking. . .thinking. . .thinking.

On a dreary, rainy day when Marianne was away on one

of her modeling jobs, I asked my mother if I could go across the street to visit a neighbor couple.

She said no and I begged. She said she just didn't feel right about letting me go over there because they were a strange couple. Woody drank too much and Tommy (a woman) was just plain not all there.

I begged some more and my mother relented.

Tommy was happy to see me. She was baking cookies and I joined her in the kitchen, where she began telling me another one of her "stories." These I was cautioned by my mother to never believe, especially after I'd relayed the awful story Tommy had told me about how her first husband was killed when he was on an expedition in Alaska. . .a herd of penguins sliced him to pieces with their flippers!

After hearing that one my mother wasn't too thrilled about having me go over alone to Tommy and Woody's place—even though it was just across the street.

But on this grey and drizzly day I felt warm and cozy in Tommy's luscious-smelling kitchen.

In the living room, Woody was playing with their German shepherd. The man sat in his chair and teased the dog with a leather glove.

I hated the mean growls I heard, and the dog was very large.

After Tommy gave me a generous sampling of her hot chocolate chip cookies, she thought I might like to go look through their new *National Geographic* magazine. She knew how much I loved to sit and study the beautiful photographs.

"Woody! Put that glove away. Mary's coming in to look at the new *Geographic*."

Suddenly the growling stopped, and when I entered the living room, Woody was nowhere in sight.

I spied the magazine next to Woody's chair. I also spied the dog still sitting in front of it. I wanted to see that magazine in the worst way, so I crept closer to the chair and eased past the dog.

"Nice doggie. Nice doggie."

He was statue still. Nothing moved but his eyes as he watched me sit down. And when I reached for the magazine I noticed the leather glove resting on top of it. It was all wet and slobbery and I was angry that Woody messed up the nice magazine cover. So I picked up the glove and moved it to my other side.

The dog went for it as it passed in front of his face—and mine. He got it, but he also got my face. Tommy was screaming.

"Woody! Woody! Come put the dog away! Bring me a wet towel!"

What commotion!

Tommy had my face pressed against her breast. She was smothering me with the towel.

"Call her mother! Then get the car out. We need to take her to our doctor. Does he have office hours today? *Hurry!*"

The dog was shoved in a coat closet. Woody called my mother and brought more wet towels. Tommy was crying.

Yet everything was as if I was hearing it through a great distance for, before me, stood the Man of Shining Light who held me totally entranced as he brought me into his warm, radiating light. He smiled and all other sounds and actions outside his aura were dulled. I was within absolute peace.

A shrill sound pierced my tranquility then — it was a siren. Policemen burst through the door. One of them said their boss's wife called to say his daughter was hurt.

Daddy's daughter? Was one of my sisters hurt somewhere? Which one?

Just then a big policeman scooped me up in his arms. "Jesus!" he'd muttered as the towel slipped from my face. "Give me a fresh towel!"

It was when Tommy returned to us when I saw her pretty blue dress was all wet. And when I realized the "wet" was blood —*my* blood, I looked to the Shining Man and felt totally removed from the event taking place.

Once in the scout car, the flashers came on and the siren wailed. What excitement! What a thrill to speed through red lights and watch all the cars move over for us.

All the while, the policeman holding me was gently stroking my hair and softly telling me it would be okay and not to be afraid.

Afraid? What was there to be afraid of? I was fine and *would* be fine too. I knew that because that's what the Shining Man of Light told me, and I'd learned that *he* never lied to me.

I was rushed into the emergency room of Redford Community Hospital, where Dr. Demitroff did a wonderful job with over 50 stitches to re-attach my left cheek.

The operating nurse talked to me the entire time. "Isn't Mary being good, Doctor?"

"Mary's the best patient we've ever had," he'd say. When all was finished, and I was sitting up on the gurney, my father strode in.

"Oh my God."

And by the look on his face, I knew I was a horrible sight to look at.

Once back home, I wanted a mirror but nobody would give me one. I was told I had to stay in bed and rest quietly for many days and not get upset about anything.

Naturally, the first thing I did when everyone was downstairs was to sneak into the bathroom for a peek at myself.

I wish I hadn't, for I was shocked at the deformed monster that stared back at me.

Tears fell down my face and stung my wound. I raced back to bed and never wanted to see another mirror for the rest of my life. I had truly become an ugly, *ugly* little girl.

During my many post-operative visits to the surgeon, I fell in love. Dr. Dimetroff was a very handsome man and his accent was music to my ears, for his big smile made me feel almost human again, and for the duration of my visit I didn't feel so ugly.

After several months had passed and I was back to school *sans* stitches, nobody acted like I was any different than I was before. But I knew that was only because the kids feared what the nuns would do to them if they made fun of me. And so I still felt very self-conscious about my ugliness, that everyone tried to hide their aversion for, but couldn't quite pull off as smoothly as they thought they did.

One day, after school, I had to attend a special Brownie meeting two miles away at Crary Public School. We were having a Boy Scout Troop come for a dance social. I wore my best dress. I remember it clearly. It was a brown and white check German style with puff sleeves and a solid brown apron bodice.

We were lined up and the boys came to choose a partner. A handsome boy stood before me and my heart fluttered. He looked at my dress and smiled.

My heart pounded.

He raised his eyes to my face and said, "Yuck!"

My heart shattered.

No boy would dance with me. Finally the scoutmaster took my hand and compassionately made up for his rude scouts.

"I guess we don't have enough boys for you girls," he tried.

"Guess not," I said, knowing it'd be rude to let him know I knew how rude his boys were being. But then again, I really didn't blame them either. How could I possibly expect anyone to dance with someone as ugly as me when *I* wouldn't even want to dance with me. I was a freaky little girl and that was that. Oh yes, this I knew for sure because a few weeks later, when Marianne and I were sitting on my porch steps, my sister Elise came out of our house and sat between us. Elise started asking Marianne about her last modeling job. It sounded fascinating and I commented on it.

"That really sounds like fun," I said.

Elise turned with a chuckle. "You'll never know, that's for sure."

I pretended I hadn't heard her. I pretended I hadn't been hurt by her meaning, which was, of course, that I was too ugly to ever be a model so I'd never find out how much fun it'd be.

Marianne also ignored the comment because she kept right on talking. But for me, I knew in my heart that I could never be beautiful—I knew I'd forever and ever be ugly. And so that's how I saw myself. . .even to this very day.

I was about the age of seven when great changes took place in our household. My father was now a big-time detective and began acting like one. He abhorred blacks, and I'd cringe when he called them "jungle bunnies." Sickening fights started when my oldest sister wore makeup (couldn't do that until she was 18), or dated (no boy equaled the height and breadth of father).

When my mother needed a hysterectomy due to excessive bleeding, my father took me aside to explain it.

"Women are *made* bad, Mary. Women are the *evil* ones. Your mother got sick because she was so evil, and all that blood was the bad coming out of her."

And I'd sit in my room. I wasn't only ugly—I was also evil and bad because I was a girl! Girls must be very dirty to have that bad blood come out of them. And I was deeply ashamed and mortified to be a girl.

I was right too, because for Christmas, I'd received a Madame Alexander doll, and when my father's partner came over I saw them making eyes and chuckling over the doll's developed plastic breasts. *That* sent a very clear message that women's breasts were something men thought funny and laughed at. I hoped I'd never have breasts when I grew up because I was ugly and bad enough already—I sure didn't want men to laugh at me too! So I hid my pretty doll on my top closet shelf. *I* thought she was too grand to be laughed at.

Another promotion came. Now he was Detective Sergeant and all his men called him "Sarge." One day I asked him where he'd gotten the scar on his ribs.

"A nigger stabbed me. I chased him into a dark building down in Boogey Town and he stabbed me with his long knife."

The next day I was talking with my mother.

"Mom? Maybe daddy doesn't like Negroes because one of them stabbed him."

"What?"

I repeated the story of his scar.

"Is that what he told you? He got that scar from an operation. He'd broken his nose playing football and they took a piece of cartilage from his ribs." I knew then just how bigoted my father was, especially when a Jewish family moved in on the other side of us. Oh, he was pleasant enough to Norman and Verna Merkin's face, but behind their backs they were little better or higher than the "jungle bunnies" he made up his lies about.

But I loved Mr. and Mrs. Merkin, not just because they were so nice to me, but because they had children. Patricia was called Patsy, Joanne was called JoJo and little Ronald was Ronnie. And together they would teach me what "Jewish" meant—the *real* meaning.

My older sisters saw and knew more of what went on between my mother and father, like the time they had his secretary and her husband over for dinner, and my mother had to pretend she didn't know my father and his secretary were having an affair.

I also hadn't known then that my mother had found a love note from the secretary in one of my father's shirt pockets and that he'd pleaded with her to give it back. When she did, he sneered and called her a "real stupid bitch."

So consequently, my sisters grew to hate my father and he, in turn, tormented them and turned to me because I was not involving myself. I became his favorite and, because of this, my sisters were often less than warm to me, especially when I'd go out on his new boat with him.

This boat was just a very small fishing boat that he pulled on a trailer behind our car. We'd go to Kensington Lake and spend the day there, usually ending up on the public beach for a swim.

One time when I was around 8, he lectured me during the entire ride out to the lake.

"You know, Mary, women just don't know their place in life. They were made to wait on men because they're inferior, they're not as good as men are.

"Women shouldn't be able to vote either because they just aren't smart enough to know what's what in life.

"Hey," he said, "I got a joke for you. Ready?"

I nodded.

"How come they always call boats a she?"

"I don't know."

"Because their bottoms are always wet!" Chuckle. Chuckle.

"I don't get it."

"You know, they always gotta be washing that bad blood off their bottoms."

I turned my head and looked out the window because I didn't want him to see my humiliation.

"Anyway," he continued, "women are just plain dirty. You're only a little girl, so you don't have to concern yourself about that now, but grown women are something else."

That day, when we were on the boat and I was sitting up front, I could hear him constantly pouring whiskey or rum into his "pop" glass. And when our day was done and he was strapping the boat to the trailer, I watched him urinate right through his swim trunks. I was shocked to realize he didn't even know he was doing it. He was that drunk. And my first thought was that *he* was the dirty one because *I* never did *that!*

On our way home that day, the honking horns and angry drivers didn't frighten me. Even though we were driving down a major highway (Telegraph Road) going the *wrong* way (against traffic), I was not afraid because I saw a shining angel leading the way in front of us.

When we got home and I told my mother all about my day at the lake, I was forever after banned from going there again with him—I was glad of that. . .not only because I hated his drinking, but mainly because my sisters would stop calling me a "daddy's girl."

When I was nine, and my oldest sister, Barbara, dated, there were terrible, terrible fights because my father belittled every boyfriend she had.

"He's not even man enough to carry my nightstick!" he'd taunt. And Barbara would sass right back until they'd get physical and she'd end up getting hurt.

All the while, my middle sister, Elise, and my mother would try to defend Barbara. I'd be up in my closet hiding and trying to keep from throwing up—and this was accomplished by the Shining Man appearing and surrounding me with his warming light.

Because of our weekly family fights, we'd become the neighborhood pariahs and no children were permitted to come over to play with me. So I was most often next door at the Merkin's house where I found the peacefulness of a real family unit. They welcomed me whenever I wanted to go over there. . .and that was a lot.

Verna Merkin took me on their weekly trips to the Jewish

market and I learned to love some of the specialty foods. The family never failed to save me some of the fancy candies associated with their holidays and I even spent hours and hours up in Patsy and JoJo's room studying their Hebrew with them. I was so proud of myself when the girls bragged to their mother about how good I was doing with the language. And later, I was fascinated at the synagogue when I'd been invited to their brother's Bar Mitzvah.

But what I liked best about being with the Merkin's was our weekly trips to the public library. Up until then, libraries were not a routine part of my life and I loved the smell of *all those books*! At first I checked out juvenile books on ghost stories and mysteries, but after a time I could find no books that held my interest and I asked if I could look around in the "adult" section. Verna said those books weren't right for me so I'd eventually pick something from the children's side.

Another new friend moved in down the block that summer I was nine. Her name was Janet. Janet was an only child and seemed to have everything—even her very own room.

One summer day, Janet's father drove her and me to the Cooley High School pool. I didn't know how to swim so I always stayed in the shallower end.

Janet got involved in a game and I got carried away with watching it because I soon found that I couldn't touch bottom and still keep my mouth above water.

I went down with my hand up. I came up for a moment, then down again where I saw my Shining Man of Light beneath the water.

I stared at him. He was smiling and his golden light spread out like wings to surround me.

We wavered together in a strange kind of dance. No sound came, just the underwater silence of we two dancing in golden, warm light. I wanted it to go on forever—but it didn't.

Screams and shouts disturbed the silence.

My chest hurt—someone was beating on it. I tried to keep the dance going and block out the noise. . .but I couldn't hold onto it.

I heard people crying.

My chest was being used as a punching bag.

Somebody shouted for the medics.

I looked around for my Shining Man.

Then I coughed. . .and coughed.

Everyone cheered. Everyone was rejoicing. . .everyone but

me, for my dance partner had disappeared and I somehow felt abandoned.

When my father learned of the incident I was forbidden to play with Janet again because "she was a spoiled brat with no adult supervision."

I never told anyone about my beautiful underwater dance. There was nobody to tell. Nobody.

During this time I'd become a "mind sore" in school. Every day we had one hour of religion class, and we had catechisms to memorize. These consisted of questions and answers that we had to know and repeat by rote.

Now I must say that I truly never intended to be a problem child when I was nine, but that catechism just didn't get it for me. I had so darned many questions—evidently, too many so I always found myself in the Mother Superior's office.

"Mary, all you need to know is right in your catechism. You're too young to understand anything else."

"But those answers are not answers for me," I'd say.

All right, dear, what is it that you want to know?"

Now we were getting somewhere—I thought—silly me.

"Well. . .I want to know why Jesus started a 'Catholic' religion if he was Jewish. And if Jesus was Jewish, why aren't all Jewish people Catholic? Or, why isn't the *Jewish* faith the 'one, true religion?'"

Mother Superior's cheeks reddened.

"Dear, Jesus began a religion he saw as being *more* true than the Jewish one."

"Then why did he die as a Jew instead of a Catholic? And if he died as a Jew, why aren't all *Jews* saved? What I want to know is if Jesus died as a Jew or a Catholic?"

"Dear, you wouldn't understand the answer."

"I could try."

"Do you have more questions, Mary?"

"Oh yes! Lots! First of all, Mary and Joseph weren't really turned away from the inn. See, the innkeeper and his wife and daughter already *had* a place all set up for them because they were *expecting* them. Also, the wise men didn't come *12* days later, they came. . ."

"Mary! That's *enough!*"

"But you asked if. . ."

"Return to your classroom immediately!" I scooted out of the office and wondered what I'd done wrong. Obviously I'd said *something* that upset her.

This was how I became a mind sore for the good nuns. I was considered precocious and overly inquisitive (much too inquisitive). So when the "priest" made his weekly visit to our religion class I saw the nun point me out. Now I would *get* somewhere, I thought—stupid me. Would I never learn?

After the class was quizzed on their catechism, the priest took questions. He avoided my wildly waving hand for as long as he could. Finally he acknowledged me.

"How come all the holy pictures of Jesus never have him in his black hair? He had *black* hair, you know."

"He did, did he?"

"Oh yes, and. . ."

"And just how do you know that?" the priest inquired of me. I shrugged my shoulders. "I'm not sure."

"Then perhaps you have a good imagination."

"Oh no, I don't spend time imagining things, but I just know Jesus had real black hair."

"And how about the Blessed Mother's hair? Do we have *that* right?"

"No. Her's was real black too. . .all the holy pictures and paintings have her in brown."

"And you 'just know' this too, I suppose."

"Yes, Father." The priest paced before the class in deep contemplation.

"What else do we have wrong?"

"We pray to the Blessed Mother, but she's not in heaven anymore."

The priest visibly flushed and the entire class sucked in their breath. I'd definitely gone too far.

"And how did you come by *this* information?"

"I don't know, I just. . ."

". . .know it," he finished.

Then the nun whispered in his ear.

The priest looked back to me. "Well, young lady, we'll not upset your parents about this, but I suggest you find other ways of getting attention from now on."

"Yes, Father," I said before meekly sitting back down. All eyes were on me. God, I hated the attention. I hated it so much I stopped asking questions and studied my catechism just like a good little Catholic child should—but inside. . .inside, the questions kept on coming.

This then was the singular impetus that, come hell or high water, I was going to invade the adult side of the library where I knew some of my answers must lie. And subsequent visits to the library proved me out, when I found some clues under the heading of Philosophy.

I wasn't sure what "Philosophy" meant, but who cared? I had an armful of great books and, eventually the librarian allowed me to check every one out. After a few week's time, she began smiling at my choices. "You sure you understand all this high-minded stuff?"

"Well," I admitted with a smile, "not all, but I get the gist of it and that's good enough for now."

At nine years of age I delved into the paranormal, metaphysical, Edgar Cayce, and different religious philosophers. (This, then, is a confession, for in my No-Eyes books, I listed this event as happening when I was a teenager. Who'd ever believe me if I'd told the truth of it? Who'd ever believed I'd done this reading when I was nine?)

And now I have another confession to clear off my past. . .

Although I dearly loved the Merkin family for all they'd done for me, I still held resentment in my nine-year-old heart for the loving family life my friends Patsy and JoJo had. I wanted to somehow make them feel a little of the terrible heartache I felt inside at having such a terrible family life.

So one day I found my chance and I took it.

JoJo and I were outside playing and she was admiring a beautiful caterpillar that was inching its way across the sidewalk. I got on my bike. . .lined up the front tire. . .and ran right over that bug.

Tears streaming down her face, JoJo screamed, "You did that on purpose!"

Of course I denied it, But when JoJo ran home, I'd looked down at that squashed bug—green blood all around—and my own tears began to flow. I'd done murder! I *was* bad! I *was* a bad, bad, *evil* girl! And that night I was so contrite, I knelt on stones for one hour with my arms held out at my sides, to do penance for the evil, evil thing I'd done. With all my heart, I hoped God forgave me.

Not long after that incident, a new friend moved into the neighborhood. Norma was real nice, but she was paranoid that all the other kids around were talking about her (which wasn't true). Norma had cerebral palsy, and walked in a halting manner with leg braces. Sometimes she'd fall and wouldn't let anyone help her up.

The other kids weren't too interested in Norma because they said they couldn't understand her slurred speech, but I had no problem once I got an ear for it. So I was the only one who went over to Norma's house.

I loved going over there, not only because Norma was a couple years older than me and was extremely intelligent, but because both her parents were professors and their home was *filled with books!*

Norma laughed at me for the way I'd thumb through their piles of scholarly magazines and books. Her parents found me "interesting." And I loved it most when the four of us would get into some pretty heavy discussions.

One day I found myself going for a ride alone with Norma's mother. We ended up on a university campus where I was going to be given "some tests." I was very nervous when we entered a tiny room with a mirror. I knew the mirror wasn't real and that made me more nervous, because I felt that I was ugly and didn't want people watching me.

After the tests were explained to me, Norma's mother asked if I had any questions.

I didn't.

After several tests were completed, I began to wonder if Norma's mother was playing some kind of joke on me, because she'd set her timer and I'd be done by the time she reached the door. I thought the tests were stupid and wondered if they were meant to evaluate my stupidity.

The Stupidity Tests took all afternoon and I was treated to ice cream when we were done. I never found out the results of those tests, but who cares? They were dumb anyway.

Between the Merkin's and Norma's house, I had plenty of opportunity for mental stimulation and my alone times at home were spent in my room reading my books to the point of devouring them.

One day, in late autumn, the entire neighborhood gang was playing on Marianne's porch. I was beating out a rhythm on my drum (I loved to drum). I got up, tripped, and fell on the drum stick. The knobbed top was stuck in my eye. I yanked it out and JoJo screamed.

"Mary! Your eye's all bloody!"

I raised my hand to my eye and checked the white angora mitten—it was soaked.

I ran home and banged on our door. My father rushed me to the hospital and wanted to know why I was always having "these bad accidents" around the holidays (for that's how it seemed).

Once at the hospital, while the doctor was examining the eye, I again saw my Shining Man of Light. I knew then that I was going to be fine.

On the way home, my father grumbled about my future eyesight.

"The man said I'd be fine," I said.

"Doctor's don't know everything," he growled.

But, of course, there was no way I could tell him that the "man" I was talking about wasn't the doctor.

At 10 years of age, I found a book hidden in the back of Elise's dresser drawer. It was entitled: *Love Without Fear.* My eyes bugged when I'd read how babies were made. Oh! How awful! How disgusting! I thought this because I'd remembered the day I'd seen my father wet his swim trunks and how dirty he was "down there." Now I knew for sure that there was just no way *I* was ever going to do *that* to make babies. . .I just wouldn't have any. . .I just wouldn't ever get married. Besides, men thought women were bad anyway.

So I'd made up my mind about boys and my future, and carefully replaced the awful book where I'd found it.

A year later my mother told me about what women did every month. I was 11.

"Do you want me to tell you how babies are made?" she asked.

"I already know."

"Okay," was all she said. And I wonder if she thought I really knew or if she thought I thought the stork brought them. She probably was just glad to not have to make the dreaded Birds-and-the-Bees speech, because she never checked to see if I'd gotten it straight or not.

Meanwhile, the fights in the house were getting worse and more frequent.

At 12 I became a woman and, for me, it turned out that *my* "normal" cycle was two weeks of massive bleeding with quarter-sized clots. Then I'd go six weeks in between. But I didn't know this was not normal and I was too embarrassed to say anything to my mother because, if this was "the bad" coming out of me, she would think I was extremely evil and bad. So I suffered through the events in silence.

And the family fights intensified still more. They intensified to the point where Elise would run out in the middle of the street and scream for someone to call the police and I'd run into my closet where my Shining Man would take up my consciousness into his peaceful light. Of course the police were always long in responding. Elise thought they probably drew straws to see which one had the awful job of responding to a "domestic violence" call at their "boss's" address. When they finally showed up, they'd come to the door with cap in hand and be so respectful and polite as they asked their boss if everything was okay. And they never had the guts to see if it really was. Wouldn't they be shocked to see my mother's face swollen and bruised and her neck reddened from the vacuum cord used in efforts to strangle her. Oh

God, how we all did suffer from one man's ego and bigotry. Yet every Sunday, there he was at Mass praying and singing God's praise.

And so it's really no wonder why I still question a religious belief system I was forced to believe in. It was no wonder that, at the age of 12 I was still a mind and soul sore for the nuns. Now I was developing a "chip on my shoulder" they claimed. I secretly disagreed—it wasn't a chip, it was a whole *tree!* I was plain angry at the blatant falsehoods I was told to believe in. Rarely could I hold my tongue in class. . .but I learned the wisdom of doing so. . . the hard way. (There would be only *one* outsider in my entire life who I could question to my heart's content; but at 12, No-Eyes was far into my future.)

One rainy day I took to my room to draw pictures. When I was done, I shoved them into my school folder.

At class two days later, I was called (again) into the Mother Superior's office. I'd wondered what heretical thing I'd done now. I didn't have long to wait, for the four nuns standing before me had their eyes riveted to something on the Mother Superior's desk—my drawing.

"Where'd you get that?" I asked in sheer surprise.

"Where you left it, dear, in the assignment folder you handed in yesterday."

Oh God, now I was in for it.

"What is this supposed to be?" asked Mother Superior.

"It's Jesus' face at the time of his death."

"Who drew this?" another interrogator asked.

"I did."

"Oh, come come, child. You're only 12. You couldn't have possibly drawn this."

"I did draw it." I was beginning to wonder why I ever bothered with the truth anymore—nobody ever believed my truths.

The nuns smirked. . .all four of them.

Mother Superior sighed. "What did you copy it from? I've never seen a rendition quite like this before. The eyes appear to look at you no matter from what perspective it's viewed."

"I didn't *copy* it from anything."

"Then, my dear, why the odd expression on the face?"

I was getting angry. I was ready to explode. Why couldn't these people just leave me alone?

"Because *that's* how he *looked!* I drew it from *memory!*"

All four sucked in their breath and crossed themselves.

Crap! I'd said too much.

Mother Superior stared hard at me.

I stared right back.

"Mary," she said softly, "please return to your classroom."

On the way there I berated myself for making such a stupid, stupid mistake. How could I have forgotten to remove the drawing before I handed in that damned folder?

However, the incident was dropped and I never saw my drawing again. Perhaps the dear nuns were beginning to see me as a "nut case" borne of a violent family background. Maybe they felt sorry for me. I didn't want anyone's pity and I certainly didn't care what they thought of my mind—I knew what I knew and *that* was definitely *that!*

At the age of 12 a great event happened—my father moved out.

You would think we'd have some peace at home now, but we didn't—at least not all the time, because now Elise would secretly wear Barbara's clothes. And Elise would come home from school and use Barbara's room (her record player, records, jewelry). And the fights between them could be like two wildcats.

After my parents separated (they couldn't get a divorce because the Church wouldn't allow it), my mother rented a calculator and a typewriter to practice for a job. Finally, after a few false starts in various positions she was hired as a medical secretary for one of Detroit's more prominent physicians. She had to walk a mile to her bus stop and then take a long bus ride to downtown Detroit where she had another long walk to her office building.

When she'd come home I'd run the massager on her neck and back. She'd be very tired, but she liked her job. And out of respect for her, my sisters' fights became less and less. Barbara now worked as a secretary at General Motors and, when Elise graduated, she'd take the bus down to Burroughs.

Now, at 13, I was pretty much left on my own. I'd come home from school, do my homework and fix my own dinner. My weekends were usually spent over at Norma's or next door at the Merkin's—but only after all the housework was done.

A new addition to our house was a collie/spaniel mix dog we named Mitzi. She was a great comfort to all of us. She'd know when my mother put on her white uniform that she was going to leave for work, and Mitzi would hide under my mother's bed. Mitzi was our pride and joy. I loved Mitzi with all my heart.

One evening I was out walking Mitzi. It was so quiet.

The stars were out and the maple leaves gently rustled. We'd come to a street corner and, out of nowhere, a car took the corner on two wheels. We were just stepping off the curb. I felt as though someone had pushed me back, for I'd let go of the leash and Mitzi was in the middle of the street. I heard her yelp twice as the car passed.

Mitzi lay still.

Mitzi was dead.

It took me a long, long time to get over losing my dog. I'd think about that black phantom car for many months to come because it haunted me. That night *had* been perfectly quiet. I *hadn't* heard the slightest engine sound of an approaching vehicle—it'd just suddenly appeared from behind us and took that corner at breakneck speed. The sound of its screeching haunted me like a black-robed banshee.

The few days following Mitzi's goneness, I cried in school and the nun took me out in the hall and chastised me for acting like my mother had been the one who died. I was to "grow up!" I bet she never loved anything or anyone in her entire life. Anyway, the entire incident remained a mystery that I spent many years contemplating.

When I was 15, a new family moved in directly across from us. . .a boy. His name was Bill (not my counterpart). Bill and I began spending time together. We'd go for walks, to amusement parks, to an occasional movie. I guess we were dating.

But he was Baptist and I was Catholic and my mother frequently cautioned me to not get too serious because the two religions would never, never mix.

Well, I did get serious and so did he. We talked about our religious differences, and I told him I'd give up mine because I had too many problems with it anyway. He couldn't believe I'd do that for him. He was impressed.

One of the things that attracted me to Bill was his mind; he was a brain. He'd left the public school system to attend MIT and we found much to talk about—except metaphysical matters. His great mind was closed to it, and this was very disturbing to me; yet we did get along so well otherwise.

His mother once told me that, when Bill turned 21, he'd come into a great deal of money. I'm not sure why she told me that but I do know she liked me and wanted to see us stay together.

This, however was not to be, for when I was 16, he decided he wanted to date other girls. I was devastated. I knew in my heart it was probably because I was ugly. And I cried for nights on end. Finally I decided boys weren't worth the trouble and heartache.

And we got another dog. We called her Sugar and she was all mine. I named her that because she was the soft color of brown sugar and had the disposition to match.

A month after getting Sugar, when I was in school, the girl sitting in front of me turned to the boy sitting beside her and loudly whispered, "Will you *stop* looking at my legs!"

I looked over to the boy in the letter sweater.

He looked back at me and gave the biggest smile.

I grinned back at him. His name was William Joseph and neither of us were ever alone again.

Although we'd attended the same school for 10 years, this was the first moment our eyes really connected. It was not love at first sight, it was more of a knowingness that filled the heart and soul. We each knew we belonged together. The love grew as the relationship matured.

And mature it did—a little too fast for my mother *and* the good nuns, for St. Mary of Redford was a well-disciplined school where nobody talked during class, class exchanges were conducted in single file and in silence, uniforms were worn by the girls, and boys wore white shirts and ties. And the way Bill and I did everything together as a pair rose many an eyebrow. Their false logic was: If Bill and Mary are inseparable, they also must be sinning.

Finally I was banned from seeing Bill.

Oh, no *way!* We were too much alike!

So I began sneaking out to see him. Yes I did. I was very clever.

We'd meet at the library and spend hours together. Our friends covered up for us. We'd talk for hours and hours on end about philosophy and metaphysical matters. He was so open and receptive to all I had to say. It was as if these contrary concepts were within him all along, and I just made him bring them up into the light of day so he could see them.

What joy it was for me, after 16 years of holding it all within my heart to finally be able to say anything that came to mind and have it agreed with!

So, on Sunday mornings, I'd slip out of the house at 5 A.M. to accompany him in his car as he made his paper delivery rounds. Then I'd slip back unnoticed until it was time for me to go to Mass where I'd meet him again.

Finally a neighbor saw us together and the game was up for us. My mother called my father and said, "You take her. She belongs in a girl's school!"

My father gloated in the fact that my mother couldn't control me. So as I was gathering the last of my things before he came to take me to live with him, my sister came up behind me and struck me over the head with a brass fireplace poker.

I was stunned for a moment, wavered on my feet, and then had to sit on the floor for fear I'd fall. I was dizzy. It's true what they say about "seeing stars."

My sister was shocked at her own reaction and fled upstairs to her room. Dizzily, I got up and staggered onto the front porch, where I awaited my father's arrival. My head cleared by degrees, and by the time he pulled up, I could cover my feelings of vertigo, though my head felt like it was split open and hurt so much I kept checking it for blood.

"You have a headache?" my father asked.

"A little one."

Then he saw blood on my finger, from touching my head.

"What happened?"

"Oh, I'll be alright. I just banged my head on the coffee table."

"We'll take a look at that when we get you home."

Home. I wondered where the hell that was going to be. All I knew was that he was driving me farther and farther away from Bill and I was churning inside. I was like a bubbling volcano ready to erupt with fury and anger. I was totally frustrated and, most of all, I felt the greatest and most painful heartache I'd ever felt. I was literally sick inside to be going away from Bill.

It turned out that "home" was just three miles away in an upper flat occupied by his "friend," Fran. He thought it'd be best if I stayed with her. So, that night, I slept in bed with Fran, and he curled up on the couch. I cried myself to sleep and the next three nights too.

My father still was spending his nights on her couch.

He must've thought I had a teenage mentality not to take note of all his personal belongings at Fran's place. His mistake was taking me for an idiot.

I'd managed to secretly call Bill before school to tell him to be sure to drive his car today—he was going to help me move out! I told him to meet me at the rectory—we were going to have a *talk* with Father Siefen.

Father Siefen was the favorite counselor priest of all the teenagers. He knew the score and understood teen problems. I was determined to lay it all out and get the priest's sanctioned blessing for what I had planned.

My father dropped me off at school. I walked in, continued down the hall and out the other side. Bill was already waiting for me at the rectory.

"What's this all about?" Bill nervously asked.

"Let's get inside first."

Father Siefen greeted us and took us into his office. He already knew of my family background and of my father's history of drinking and family violence. I told him about my mother not wanting me to see Bill anymore, but that we were so alike it was like cutting my arm off to be apart from him. I told him of the "sinful" living arrangement my father was forcing me to live in, because he was putting me up with him *and* his mistress, and I found the situation intolerable.

He agreed wholeheartedly.

"So what do you plan to do now, Mary?" the good priest asked.

"Bill brought his car to school this morning. I want him to take me over to 'their' place and move me out."

"I think that would be best, but where will you move to?"

I turned to his office window. "Over there. My aunt lives right across the street. She's a spinster and lives all alone. She'd take me in for now."

"You sure?"

"Positive."

"Alright, I'll give the two of you permission to move you out, but come right back here when you're done so I know everything went well."

We agreed, but first I had to stop at my locker for something. While we were at my locker, one of the nuns who'd forbid me to go outside at lunchtime (to keep me from seeing Bill then) spied us together in the hall. She stormed out of her classroom, habit flying like wings behind her, and demanded to know what we were doing *together* out of class and, wasn't I marked "absent" this morning? She tapped her foot waiting for my response.

Oh God, I didn't need this hassle. My insides were in turmoil as it was.

Bill explained the situation and that Father Siefen had already given us his permission to go ahead with it.

Sister Cajetan was horrified to hear I was now living with my father *and* his woman. She crossed herself and said, "Godspeed!"

And we were out the door.

All the way there I was sick inside. What if we couldn't pull it off? I had no house key. What if the crabby old landlady downstairs wouldn't let me in the door? What if my father forgot something and came back home and found us there? Dozens of possible scenarios were churning around in my head and my stomach reflected the fears.

Finally we pulled up and I knocked on the door. The crabby woman answered it with a frown as she looked Bill up and down.

"Remember me?" I began cheerfully. "I recently moved in upstairs with my dad and Fran. I got to school this morning and realized I'd left an important assignment at home and I need to get it. I don't have a key yet so could you please let me up?"

She was frowning as I was being sized up.

I smiled wider. "Please? It's very important."

The door swung open.

Upstairs I was trembling like an aspen leaf as I tried to hustle all my belongings into two paper bags (I didn't have much). I shakily scribbled my father a note telling him I couldn't tolerate living there under their sinful conditions and that I'd be at Aunt Cecilia's house (his sister's).

We scrambled back down the stairs, hastily thanked the squinting landlady and pulled away from the house.

Oh, relief! We'd *done* it! Now we had to get to my aunt's house and explain everything before my father got wind of our activities.

On the way there I was a nervous wreck.

"Bill, that landlady's gonna call Fran or my father. He already has wind of this."

"No, you're just scared, that's all."

"Yeah, I'm scared. He's scared me all my life, but I just know he already knows what we've done. Please try to hurry."

We arrived at my aunt's and she agreed to take me in for as long as need be. Then we ran back across the street to the rectory.

Once in the office I finally felt safe and breathed a deep sigh of relief. . .until. . .I saw through the window.

"There's my *father!"*

Father Siefen turned around and watched a man stride from his unmarked police car and race up my aunt's steps. The priest turned back to face us and saw the fear written all over my face.

"Looks as if God was with you two this morning. Don't worry, Mary, you're safe here."

"Now I am. I'm worried about later when I have to face him. He prides himself as being an ace detective and his 16-year-old daughter pulls a coup right under his nose and stays one step ahead of him. That hurts his ego. This is not going to go well with me."

He gave me his card. "Call me at any hour if you're in trouble or he threatens you. I'm right across the street from you now."

I looked at the card and took a little comfort in his words . . .still. . .he didn't know my father. Nobody did.

The three of us watched my father storm out of his sister's house and peel away in his beloved police car.

The rest of the day was like walking through Jell-O. I was numb to all going on around me. All I could think of was meeting my father face to face again and what would happen. I knew how angry he'd be. I felt like throwing up during each class I went through. I wished I could go home with Bill. I wished I could die, or at least be able to sink down in some dark hole and never come out again. Why was this all happening? Why? But then I knew the answer to that. It was all happening because I was being denied Bill. It was all happening because we were fighting tooth and nail for our destiny. . .a destiny we didn't even know about yet (at least not on a conscious level).

When I got out of school I thought I'd see his car parked in front of the house, but it wasn't. My aunt had a room ready for me. She'd moved into the bedroom where my grandmother had died so many, many years ago.

I couldn't eat dinner, I was so upset. Where *was* he? This waiting was pure torture.

I had the distinct impression that he was being very, very busy. He was involved in a lot of activity not related to work, but I couldn't seem to put my finger on it.

At 8:30 he showed up.

I steeled myself.

He came through the door and stared at me. "That was real smooth. My own daughter pulls one off on the expert."

He walked over to me. "Mary, you read this one all wrong. I could understand how you'd feel if Fran and I really were living together, but we're not."

My psyche prickled and stood at full attention. He was lying through his teeth.

"Honey, I want to take you and show you where I *really* live. You'll see all my things there."

My mind was working overtime as I realized then *what* his "activity" was that I'd picked up on before—he'd been late because he'd been busy *moving* all his things somewhere *else!*

"I'm not going anywhere with you."

His face reddened. *Nobody* talked to him that way. "Mary, I'm not asking, I'm telling."

"I'm not going anywhere with you."

"Oh yes you are!" And he grabbed my arm and pulled me out the door and dragged me down the steps.

It was a quiet night.

I screamed at the top of my lungs at the rectory.

"Father Siefen! FATHER SIEFEN! HELP!"

I was let go as if his hands burned.

"Shhh! Listen, Fran's over there in the car. Will you at least get in and talk to her?"

I looked over. There she was.

"I'll talk to her through the window *without* getting in."

"Fine."

Fran had a sweet personality and gentle voice. I had to admit that she was an older woman with grey hair and didn't at all fit the "mistress" idea. She talked to me for quite a long while and assured me that I'd been wrong about my father and. . .well, couldn't I at least give him the benefit of the doubt by visiting his real residence?

She'd sweet-talked me into the car with them.

When we arrived at his "residence," I almost laughed. It was some basement apartment of a private house. I spied the same articles that were previously at Fran's. They'd moved him in one big hurry.

"Take me back. Take me back to Aunt Cecilia's. You two must think I'm a real imbecile."

And they didn't even bother to argue anymore. They knew their little ruse hadn't done its job. So we drove in silence back to his sister's house.

Before I got out of the car, he said, "I'll make arrangements with Cecilia for your room and board. I'll check on you regularly and give you my charge card to buy some decent clothes. . .Fran noticed that your underthings are ragged. You can date whomever you want, just keep it reasonable. You give your aunt any trouble and you'll be in a girl's detention school faster than you can say 'fooled you, dad.' Goodnight."

"Goodnight."

Things settled down then. My aunt and I got along fairly well. She was in her sixties and wasn't used to living with anyone else, much less a teenager. She tried her best and I tried mine.

I used the credit card only once and I bought one skirt, one sweater and new underthings. I hadn't liked the comment he'd made about my clothes—what did he expect me to have on my mother's wage after he left us? Most all of my things had been my sister's hand-me-downs.

When I handed his charge card back, he'd asked me what I'd bought.

I told him.

He frowned. "How come you didn't get more?"

"I didn't *need* more." Quite frankly, I didn't want his money, not when he left his family with nothing but bills and a mortgage. During this time, Bill and I only saw each other in school if we shared the same class. I was still forbidden by the nuns to go out to lunch with my friends. But on the weekends, we made up for what had been denied us.

A few months passed and I decided to write a letter to my mother saying how sorry I was if I'd caused her pain. I told her I missed her terribly and that I wanted to come back home. I also told her how much Bill and I meant to one another and that, please, couldn't she accept our love?

A week later, when my father was over, my aunt handed him a letter.

He looked down at it. "This is addressed to Mary. Why are you giving it to me?" He handed my mother's letter to me.

I looked at my aunt and she lowered her eyes. I felt sorry for her, because she felt a loyalty to her brother who was paying my bills (and hers). I understood her traitorous act (kind of).

I took the letter to my room and tears fell as I read it. She too missed me and wanted me back home. And. . .yes! There would be no more hassles about dating Bill! I was free to date as much as I wanted, because I'd proved how much I loved him. She figured if our love could endure and survive my *father*, then it could probably endure anything.

My father was not sad to be rid of me.

I moved back home again. I guess everything we'd all been through was more than enough to finally say "Amen!"

I was glad to be home and Sugar was so excited she followed me all around. I'd gotten into the habit of taking her out for late evening walks. Unlike Mitzi, Sugar didn't need a leash because she'd stay at my side or follow close behind.

One autumn evening when we were out walking, Sugar took off after a rabbit (something she'd never done before). She chased it between yards where I couldn't go. And I walked the neighborhood for hours and hours looking for her. Finally my mother insisted I come in. She'd tried to placate me with the fact that Sugar knew where she lived and would come home when she was ready.

I couldn't sleep that night. I got up every hour to check if Sugar was on the porch, but she never was, and I had a terrible sick feeling in my stomach.

Before school the next morning, a neighbor at the other

end of the block called my mother to ask if Sugar was at home.

Mother explained that we couldn't find her.

"Well," the neighbor lady said, "I hate to have to tell you this, but it looks like Sugar was hit by a car last night and someone laid her up on our lawn. She's not breathing."

I was devastated and didn't want to go to school because I couldn't seem to control my grief. I had to go anyway.

Several times during the day I lost control. Once a nun pulled me out of class.

"What's all the tears for? You have a spat with Bill?"

"No, my. . .dog. . .died last. . .night," I said between sobs.

"Oh, for heaven's sake," she spat in disgust, "a dog's a dog. Get back in class and pull yourself together."

I turned on my heel and returned to class. Obviously, I thought, that was one nun who never felt the unconditional love of a dog.

Two weeks later my mother came to me and said that we need to talk. "I received a letter from your father today."

"Oh?"

"He also said he sent a copy of it to the school. Mary, he's accusing you of being pregnant."

"*What?*" I knew I had a little belly on me, but *come on.*

"I know, I know how you feel, but we'll need to prove him wrong, you know."

"Why do *we* have to prove anything? Won't it be obvious all by itself after a time?"

"Mary, do you want the entire school staff to be talking behind your back and giving you curious looks?"

"Of course not."

"Then we need to do something right away."

"Like what?"

"I've already made an appointment for you with an OB/GYN downtown for tomorrow. That'll settle everything."

So the next morning we got on the bus and neither of us said three sentences between us. I was dying of embarrassment for the exam itself and she was anxious for the verdict.

Finally she broke the silence. "Mary?"

"Yeah."

"You know they'll be able to tell if you and Bill have 'done anything,' don't you?"

"Yes, I know that." (But I really didn't. I was actually very naive about such things.) At the doctor's office they took a history and my mother was shocked to hear about the long and heavy cycles I'd been having since I was 12.

"Why didn't you ever tell me about this?" she asked.

"Because we didn't ever talk about this kind of thing. Besides, I didn't know I wasn't normal."

When I came out of the exam room my mother was beaming. A grin reached from ear to ear. We went into the doctor's office and talked for awhile. I ended up with a prescription to control my cycle. It was for Premarin and Progesterone. My mother came out of the office with the biggest prize—an official letter that stated that not only was her daughter "not pregnant," but she was also still a "virgin. . ." Oh how embarrassing! And copies of the professional letter went to my father and to the school! I nearly died.

But now the nuns were all sweetness and light to Bill and me, because we proved we were good Catholic teenagers and weren't sinning after all. I hated their prurient, suspicious natures. . . I hated how they loved to conjure up the worst scenarios and believe them to be true, then *treat* you as if they were. I hoped they'd suffered just a tiny bit of guilt for how they'd misjudged us.

The following summer I had to spend some time away from Bill. Barbara had married and her husband was stationed at Fort Carlson in Colorado Springs. My mother wanted to take my grandmother and me to visit them, and we took the train. We stayed a week.

I loved the mountains, but missed Bill so much I hardly noticed them, and I was glad to get back home again.

It was then I got the news that my mother had to sell our house. Oh, no!

She couldn't keep up with all the bills. We'd have to move into Grandma's upper flat in Dearborn—miles and miles away from Bill. And what compounded the situation was that I'd have to attend a public school for my senior year, and wouldn't be graduating with all my friends.

We moved, and I registered at Fordson High in Dearborn. On my first day, I got the shock of my sheltered life— couples were *holding hands* in the halls, and they were actually *kissing* by their lockers. The halls during class exchanges were total pandemonium and noisy with babble and laughter. The difference between the two school systems were like night and day. Or, more accurately, like prison and freedom.

My class load for that last year was heavy, because the public school system had different graduating requirements than the Catholic schools. So I took chemistry, physics, civics, American history, English comp, economics, typing, English comp II, and world history.

I loved going to my physics class, because the teacher

frequently interjected metaphysical aspects. Finally I'd come across a teacher who wasn't narrow-minded and was very refreshing to me.

One day the physics teacher announced that he was going to conduct an experiment on the class. He said he wanted us all to raise our hands.

We did. I sat in the front row and, when I turned to look behind me, all hands were up—something I hadn't seen since the eleventh grade.

The teacher then announced that now he was going to ring a bell and that when we stopped hearing it resonate we were to lower our hands.

He rang the bell.

My arm was getting tired. I heard whispers behind me and when I turned—nobody's hand was up—nobody's but mine. I lowered it.

"Mary, do you still hear it?" the teacher whispered.

"A little." Then, "It's gone now."

The teacher grinned at me.

A boy at the back of the room wanted to know what that was all about.

"I'll tell you at the end of class," said the teacher, before giving us an assignment to work on.

While I was busy with the assignment, I was becoming more and more self-conscious because the teacher kept looking over at me.

Finally it was a couple minutes before the bell and he stood before us. He had everyone's attention.

"What you all participated in was a psychic sensitivity experiment. The longer one hears the bell's resonance, the greater degree of psychic ability they're supposed to possess. And," he said, looking down at me, "we seem to have a highly psychic sensitive amongst us."

Thank God the bell rang because I hated everyone looking at me. And as I left the room a boy came up to me.

"Hey Mare, who's gonna win Friday's football game? Think I'll place a few bets."

"Save your money, Mike."

"Come on, who wins?"

"We do," I said to shut him up.

And, come Friday night, we did win. So on Monday morning, three more guys came to me wanting to know if our team's gonna do it again.

"Ask *them,*" I said, before walking away. And that was to be all my future responses because I could see how they'd make me into the school oracle if I let them. They just didn't understand these things—all they saw was the sensational aspect of it. . .not the real beauty.

One class I really hated was English comp II, because the teacher, Mr. Osterberg, always held my work up as an example. This was humiliating to me because I hated attention and people looking at me.

The day Mr. Osterberg announced that there was only one student in his entire senior class that could skip the final exam and still have an 'A' for her semester grade. When all eyes turned to me I could've just died. I wish teachers wouldn't do that to kids.

Trouble was—I enjoyed the class because I loved creating tapestries with words. I liked to "word paint." We were always given assignments to write on experiences or places and I would bring in all the senses. I did this for a reason.

Reason: One day, while riding the bus, I noticed a blind girl reading Braille. This young woman got me thinking about how much the blind miss in life—especially in books they read. Then I got to thinking about the deaf people who read and how little "sounds" are brought into books. So the more I thought about it the more I wanted to make a total sensual experience for them. I secretly tagged my writing style "double exposure," because I covered the sighted and the blind. It was also double exposure for the sighted readers too because they *read* the words, then had a *second* exposure through their senses of sound, extreme visuals, and feelings that reached out to "touch." Putting the scene *around* the reader like a warm blanket wrap came so natural once I began writing. It would be as if *I* were deaf and blind and wanted to "see and hear" the words. And so sound and color mixed with depth of feeling, as I wrote these class assignments, became my signature. Later in life—much later—people would wonder and ask me where I learned to write like I did. "You put the reader right into each scene." "You draw the reader into everything by wrapping the scene right around the reader." "Where did you get such a beautiful writing style?" And I should've said, "From a blind girl on a bus."

And so my final year in school was not so bad. I still dated Bill every weekend. We went on dates to St. Mary's sock hops and spent an evening with all my old friends.

One Friday night we went to enter the St. Mary's gym for the dance and a parent by the door stopped us.

"I.D., please."

This guy was definitely new because most all the parents knew me.

"I don't have one," I said.

"Sorry, honey, only St. Mary's kids get in here." I couldn't believe my ears.

"But I've attended St. Mary's for 11 years! I know everyone in there! All my *friends* are in there!"

"Sure, honey, nice try."

I was so frustrated to think this new parent wasn't going to let me in with all my friends just because he didn't know me that I fumed inside with a boiling anger.

"Shit!"

"Yeah, honey, and that 'public school' talk is *exactly* why you can't go in there."

What? What! Did this grown man really believe those sweet and oh-so-good little Catholic teens in there never said "shit" or swore? Was this parent that bigoted and egocentric toward non-Catholics? He was a lot dumber than he looked.

I was ready to roll right over this idiot when another parent came up and opened the gym door.

"Well! If it isn't Bill and Mary! How you two doing?" And he escorted us inside.

The door parent ran after us. "She's from a public school!"

"No she's not, Bob, she's from here," he said, staring down at the smaller man. "She just forgot her I.D. that's all."

"Well maybe Father Siefen should hear about this," the indignant doorman said.

Our adult friend scanned the gym crowd. He spied us talking to Father Siefen. "Yes, maybe you should go tell Father Siefen I've let in an undesirable from a public school. He's right over there."

The little doorman made a move to approach the priest when he saw that the robed figure was actually hugging the "undesirable," as if he'd known her for a long time.

After that incident I was fixed up with an I.D. card. I never knew where it came from and never asked either.

In the spring of 1964, a factory fire blazed two blocks from our Dearborn house. At night the flames looked to be only a few yards away. I feared the fire would spread—and so I grabbed the two most precious treasures I had—a photo of Bill and my prom dress.

But the fire didn't spread and I wore the dress to the St. Mary's prom. In June we both graduated and were now ready to make our way in the world.

My first official job was working for a CPA firm called Professional Management. They were located in downtown Detroit in the Broadway Theater Building.

My job was to type up monthly financial statements for our clients of dentists and physicians. It was a good job for a first one, but I didn't care for the long bus ride to and from my Dearborn location. The Oscar Mayer meat packing plant was situated on Michigan Avenue, and on hot summer days the smell from the plant was cloying and nauseating as it mingled with the bus exhaust and traffic noise.

Finally, one of my co-workers, Peggy, who also took the same bus I did, began driving to work. Since she passed right by my bus stop, she began picking me up and driving me home.

One day, after we'd left the underground parking lot and walked across the street to our building, we'd found our co-workers gathered at the office windows.

"Come see! A guy just jumped!"

Our office was only on the second floor, but the man who went out the window leaped from one of the top floors.

I wasn't prepared for the sight below me. The man's body was twisted and white matter was all over the pavement by his head. Blood flowed down the curb into a sewer opening. I couldn't believe the amount of blood there was. I spun away from the window and sat down at my desk.

Some of the CPAs were teasing me by giving me blow-by-blow accounts of what was transpiring.

"Here comes the ambulance. Oh geez, he's so broken up they can't lift him. Look! They have to roll him onto the stretcher."

As I sat there I blocked out their words. All I could think of was the man's timing. If he'd have jumped just two minutes earlier he would've landed at my feet. And I thanked God for getting me inside while it was happening.

That evening I couldn't abide being alone. Even though my mother was in the next room, I was afraid of being visited by the haunting face of that poor man. It took me many weeks to get over my first initiation into the Society of the Real World. It was a rude awakening.

Two weeks later, Peggy and I had to take the bus home because her car was in for repairs. We were walking down Woodward Avenue and were deeply involved in conversation, oblivious to the rush hour traffic. Just as we were about to step off the curb, I heard someone loudly whisper my name in my ear.

I spun around.

Peggy halted in mid-step to see why I'd turned. . .and a bus raced by us so close our skirts whipped around our legs.

Peggy went white. "We almost got killed! That bus would've run us down if you hadn't turned around!"

We stood there for a few more minutes trying to figure it all out. I couldn't explain the cause of what I'd heard. All I knew was that my name was called very clear as a loud whisper in my ear and I'd turned to see who was behind me. I recall having the subliminal impression (mental) of my Shining Man of Light, but the thought wasn't one I held on to. A few days later the entire incident was forgotten and neither of us ever mentioned it again.

I must digress now to cover a subject I've completely left out. . . which, I suppose, is only natural when one is trying to go back so many years in one's life.

The subject is my dancing. From the time I was four years old and my mother played the piano for Martha Heermans Dance School on Grand River Avenue, I was taken along to spend the day with her. I'd participate in all classes that I could fit into. This then was the root of my appreciation for classical music and ballet.

Later, when Martha went to records and my mother no longer worked there, I continued the dance lessons every year up until I got pregnant.

During high school, I was among the soloists of Martha's advanced class and, when she needed an operation, her advanced students took over the teaching by splitting up the lower classes between us. I had the classes that were scheduled right after school and I'd have to hurry from St. Mary's to open up the studio, record payments and then conduct the classes. By six o'clock another classmate of mine would show up to conduct the later evening classes.

The dance school was a mile from my house on Ferguson and, when I was having all the parental problems, I'd slowly walk home from class (after dark) and hope the Boogeyman would get me. Or, if it was raining, I'd walk slower, step in every puddle and hope to get pneumonia—I was so miserable during that time I just wanted to die because everyone was trying to break Bill and me apart. But I did love my dancing. I was always given the most sensitive and moving part of a music score as my part to dance because I "felt" it in my soul and, was told, had the gracefulness to also make the audience feel it. My favorite solo was to a violin rendition of "Ave Maria," and the audience ended up with tissues to their eyes. Today my toe shoes still hang in our room.

Martha was a wonderful teacher and lady. She never charged me for my classes (no matter how many I took a week—which was at least two) and she paid for all my costume material and the dressmaker fees because we couldn't afford the money. If my class was the last of an evening she'd usually drive me home and we'd sit out in front of my house in her car and talk about my problems. She even once offered to take me in until my problems smoothed out.

One evening, after she moved the studio to a new location on Puritan Street and we were the last to leave the building, we were in the car on the side street waiting for traffic to clear so we could pull out onto Puritan. (This was around 9:30 P.M. and it was very dark).

Suddenly we saw a large object hovering over the small bank across the street. We couldn't believe our eyes. We turned to see if the person in the car behind us saw it too, but it didn't look like it. When we turned front again, the object was gone.

Neither of us said a word. I think we were afraid to say what we were sure we'd just seen. We were deep in our own thoughts the entire way to my house.

Before I got out of the car, I had to voice something.

"Martha. . .did you see. . .?

"Yes."

"Do you think it could've really been a. . .?"

"I don't know, but I'll ask Charlie."

Her new husband was an officer in the Air Force and, for some unknown reason, I felt she'd get no satisfaction there.

I ran into my house to find my mother. "Mom! Guess what? Guess what Martha and I saw tonight? A UFO!"

"Right, Mary."

"We did! It was hovering right over the bank across from the studio. It was there one minute and gone the next! I saw it so close I could draw a picture of it! Here, let me show you what it looked like so you can. . ."

"Do you have homework? It's almost 10."

I shut up and went to do my homework. I had a lot of homework in the eleventh grade.

Next dance-class day I asked Martha what Charlie said.

She just gave me a frown and shook her head to indicate we shouldn't talk about it anymore. I figured that'd happen. But all the skeptics in the world couldn't convince me I hadn't seen a bona fide, real-life UFO that night because two days later the newspapers reported a "rash of sightings" and the artist's sketch was identical to what I would've drawn for my mother if she'd only given me a chance and listened to me.

So now I couldn't talk about my UFO sightings either. . . at least not to anyone but Bill, for I'd seen others in the sky while we were together.

Back to my job.

Professional Management moved out of downtown Detroit to North Park Court in the suburb of Southfield.

Meanwhile, Bill's parents and my mother were discussing our desire to get married. Although they both thought we were too young at 19, Bill's father had a personal reason to agree to it.

"Look how those two have fought us all to stay together. With the war in Vietnam, Bill's sure to be drafted soon. I couldn't live with myself if anything happened to him over there and I prevented him from having a little happiness in life first. The way I see it, they're going to make sure they're together whether we agree or not—it just seems like it's in the cards for them. I think we need to do this before he's shipped over there."

And so parental consent was given and my mother ceremoniously presented Bill with her wedding rings to give to me because he couldn't afford them.

I loved those rings because they were so unusual and like no other set I'd ever seen. The engagement ring was a tiny antique setting of a small flower with a very little diamond in its center, the band was plain silver. I was determined to do those rings right and I wore them with pride.

Three weeks before the ceremony, Bill's father took sick and was admitted to Providence Hospital in Southfield. The doctors thought he had TB, but it turned out to be lung cancer. We were all very worried about him.

Two weeks before the wedding my mother told me my father wanted to see me. He and Fran had moved into my aunt's house on Mansfield across from St. Mary's Church. They lived in the lower flat and my Aunt Cecilia was moved into the upper one.

I wasn't thrilled to go see them, but Bill said he'd go with me. My stomach was in knots just thinking about seeing him again, but go we did. After all, maybe he'd mellowed out some now that we were to be married.

We were welcomed with an over-enthusiastic greeting that immediately set me in a watchful stance. A wedding gift was presented—a Bible. Odd choice. We expressed our appreciation.

Then the bomb dropped.

"So, when's the rehearsal?" my father asked. "I guess I need to know that."

I knew what he was really saying but couldn't believe even *he* had the audacity to think it—especially when he hadn't offered to help my mother pay for the wedding. Surely with the way he'd treated me, he couldn't possibly think he was going to actually give me away in the ceremony.

"The rehearsal's a week from Thursday," I reluctantly admitted.

"Well what time? Aren't they usually held around six or so?"

"Why?"

"Well you wouldn't want me to be late, would you?"

"For what?"

"The rehearsal. Last I checked, the father of the bride was usually there to go through his part."

"Usually so, but not this time. This time the bride is being given away by her brother-in-law. Barbara's husband is going to play that part."

His face flushed with anger.

I continued. "How could you expect to be in my wedding when I haven't even heard from you in ages—except for the last time, when you accused me of being pregnant? You weren't there to give Barbara away, why did you expect my wedding to be any different?"

"I'm your father!"

"Maybe biologically you are that, but you haven't really been my father since I was in second grade."

"Why you dirty little snot! Get out of my house! And take your measly punk with you!"

I set the Bible on the couch. "I think you need this more than I do."

"Out!"

When we were back in Bill's car he tried to calm my frayed emotions. I was shaking all over and felt like getting sick. I'd grown up with violent confrontations and I'd get physically sick whenever they happened. He talked me out of the emotional state I'd exposed myself to.

"I don't understand him," I said. "How could he really expect to be in the wedding after how he's treated me? He nearly destroyed my self-image with all his sick talk about bad women. He nearly made me frigid with his evil women talk. If it wasn't for you and your long talks with me I'd probably be so screwed up I'd never have married at all. That man nearly destroyed me."

And so Bill, at 19, had the logic and reasoning and insight of a sage, as he analyzed the ego-mind and the chauvinistic personality that was my father. Bill should've been a psychologist the way he could see right through people's actions and words. Sometimes he would spend hours trying to ease me up from the darkness of the ugliness I saw myself surrounded with and existing within. Yet. . .no matter how many times he assured me I was not ugly, that one aspect became too ingrained in my psychological makeup.

Two weeks later, on October 16, 1965, we were married. The date was also his mother's birthday and a celebrated day called Sweetest Day.

After the reception, we went over to the hospital to visit his father. Everyone turned heads to see a Bride and Groom walk through the corridors. Even though it was a bittersweet visit, I did feel a little pretty that day.

For our honeymoon, we drove through the upper part of Michigan. The tourist season was over and we had the autumn roads to ourselves. It was so beautiful.

When we returned, we moved in with Bill's mother because she was all alone. My father-in-law was now in a hospital bed in his room in the house, and Bill was taught how to give him his shots—which was all anyone could do for him now. It was becoming more of a death vigil than anything else.

One day when I got home from work, I found out Bill had received his draft notice. He was given the MOS of Infantry, and I knew it was synonymous to his death warrant.

Bernie (short for Bernadette), Bill's mother, was in a terrible state. She needed Bill desperately. And one day, out of the blue, a colonel called her to say that her son was transferred out of the regular Army and into the Reserves because they needed more instructors—his MOS had been changed to Instructor, and he would not be going to Vietnam.

Bernie was relieved beyond words and so were we, but going deeper, I had an unknown knowing in my psyche that there was far more at work here than just some fluke-of-the-draw that shifted his name into the state-side Reserves. And when I contemplated on it I only received a strong subliminal impression that destiny had stepped in to alter Bill's course or, the course was altered for the reason of *insuring* his destiny. More than that was not made known to me at that time.

And so we both worked our jobs until we heard more about his orders. Meanwhile we enrolled in night extension classes in Psychology at the University of Michigan.

A few weeks later when I was at work, my mother called to chat. In the course of our conversation she mentioned that she'd talked to one of our old neighbor's—the mother of my old boyfriend, Bill. She said Bill had bought a $40,000 house on Gross Ile Island and that he even had a caretaker's house on the property.

My stomach churned and my neck prickled. Not because of what I'd heard, but because of what I'd *not* heard yet.

"I have to go now, mom. Talk to you later."

I hypnotically put the receiver down and stared across the office at my boss who was on the phone.

She looked over at me then hung up.

"I'm sorry, Mary, it's your father-in-law. You want me to take you home?"

"He's gone, isn't he."

She just sadly nodded.

After the funeral, Bill and I moved into his father's room, so his mother wouldn't keep going in there to grieve. She was upset with us at first, but then realized the wisdom of it.

I quit my job at Professional Management to stay home with her and keep her company. After a while, Bill's talks with her did some good and she decided to get out of the house. She got a volunteer job at a neighborhood Cancer Society office and her entire outlook began to brighten—she was returning to her old self again.

The change in her led to the idea that now was the time for me to look for work again.

I found a job at a printing company called Robot Letters. It was located on Puritan Avenue. My job was varied. I did lay-out work for customer's brochures, including the new Church of Scientology for Ron Hubbard, and Jerry Baker, who called himself America's Master Gardener. I typed up the Dealer Distributor Book for General Motors and did their presentation scripts for slide lectures. I'd work at the composition light table doing strip-ins, help stuff client's envelopes for mass mailings or work the collator machine. And I was sent to IBM School to learn how to operate their new Composer machine.

About this same time, Bernie convinced us that she was well enough to be alone and that we should be too. We looked for a place to live.

In the newspaper we found an upper flat on Ardmore Street that was only a few blocks from my job—I could walk to work.

We called the number and the renters of the lower flat answered. Nancy said she'd been getting calls all day and that the owner would be there at seven that night. She told us to be early.

We were there at six and couples were already waiting in their cars.

"Come on, Bill, let's go," I said.

"Go where?"

"In there."

"The landlord won't be here until seven."

"Yeah, and by then more cars will be here too."

"We can't just go barging up there and expect the other renters to let us in."

"Why not."

"Why should they? You tell me?"

I smiled. "Because this place has our name all over it."

"Oh yeah?"

"Yeah."

Before we knew it, we were being let in the front door. For an hour, we talked with Bob and Nancy who rented the lower flat. We got along like old friends and I loved their three kids. When the landlord arrived, we were introduced by Nancy.

"Meet your new tenants," she said. "They both work and they don't have kids or pets."

We were in.

Nancy showed us all around the complete house. I had sudden chills in the dank unfinished basement where I'd do my laundry, but other than that, we liked the place and furnished it with hand-me-downs from both mothers.

The Ardmore flat presented us with many frightening experiences caused from a haunting, and I don't feel the need to repeat them here, because they were detailed in *Phantom's Afoot.* Needless to say, we were destined to go through them.

During this time, Bill was away for his basic training in Fort Ord, California while I worked every day. When he returned, he went back to his job at Michigan Consolidated Gas Company where he worked in the Street Department. And to complicate our ongoing situation with the haunting incidents, the riots in Detroit began.

When Bill came home he'd tell me how his crew had to wear black taped hard hats while riding on their trucks with armed National Guardsmen as they drove through the worst areas of sniper fire. He had to shut off the gas in the riot area buildings. It seemed his life was on the line everyday, and he was tempting fate each hour. I hated when he had to work late into the night during those terrible times.

Finally the riots ceased and we decided to move out of our haunted house. Bill's mother gave us the down payment for a new mobile home and, when it was delivered from the factory to the residential park in the suburb of Warren, we were more than ready to move in.

So I quit my job and became an Avon Lady for the area. I was also working on becoming a mom, but that job proved to be the most difficult one of all—nothing was happening.

Eventually I went to an endocrinologist, who had me taking my temperature every morning. I explained to Bill that, when my temperature was up we had to make love at 3 A.M.

the next morning, and then I had to go see the doctor so he could evaluate the percentage of live sperm.

He was aghast.

"You mean we have to set our alarm, try to wake up and get romantic in the middle of the night?"

"You can handle it, honey, believe me, you can handle it."

"That sounds ridiculous!"

"Well it's that or else *you* go to the doctor's office and leave your own little sample."

He didn't take long to think that one over. "I guess we can handle the 3 A.M. thing."

And handle it we did, for the doctor said there were enough "live ones" left to repopulate the world.

But after months and months of this hassle, I finally told the doctor that I was going to leave it to destiny. I told him I had to go back to work because Bill had taken a second job and we still weren't making it. He thought that was a good idea.

So I went on interviews. Took buses here and there and couldn't find the right job. Then I went back to my doctor.

"I think I may be pregnant."

Bill and I waited anxiously for the test results. . .positive!

We were so excited, but now we had to make plans, because we couldn't afford to stay where we were. We couldn't bring ourselves to sell our mobile home, so we moved it up to a beautiful lakeside park in Port Austin (on the northern tip of Michigan's thumb), and we moved back in with Bernie until we could save enough money to buy a house. The Port Austin mobile home was used as a weekend and summer get-away, where we made good friends with the park's owners and the year-round residents.

Bill's mother had managed to get a bona fide job as a medical receptionist for an orthopedic surgeon. Bill worked all day breaking cement with a jackhammer and laying natural gas lines, and I stayed home trying to deal with Detroit's hot, humid weather and a pregnancy weight gain of 50 lbs. My feet would swell so much I couldn't even find a pair of sandals that would fit.

Toward the end of summer, in 1969, Bernie sold her house and bought a bungalow on Delaware street in Redford Township. I helped her pack up the house while she was at work and Bill did the heavy work when he got home.

A few days after settling in at the new house, Bill frosted my hair and I went to bed in curlers. At midnight, I got up to go to the bathroom and I didn't make it—at least that's what I thought—because my water broke just as I entered the bathroom. I called for Bill and he and his mother came running. We began timing the pains as I fussed over trying to dry my hair.

"I can't go like this!" I kept saying.

I was making Bill a nervous wreck. "You're about to have a baby! Who cares what you look like?"

"I do!"

When the contractions were two minutes apart, we left for Providence Hospital in Southfield. There was little traffic and we raced the entire way.

At 8 A.M. on the 2nd of September, I delivered our bundle of joy, and we named her Jennifer Ann. Other than being slightly jaundiced, our 5-pound daughter was perfectly healthy. We took her on our weekend trips up to Port Austin, where we spent many wonderful days on the shores of Lake Huron.

By the time Jenny was one and a half, we sold our mobile home for a down payment on a house we'd bought on Gaylord street in Redford Township. We fixed up the bungalow and managed to buy a few new pieces of furniture. We were just making the bills when I found myself pregnant again.

This time I went two weeks beyond my due date and Dr. Watts (chief of obstetrics) wanted to induce the baby.

I went in Providence Hospital at 10 A.M., March 24, 1972 and at 4:06 P.M. delivered another 5 pound-daughter we named Aimee Lyn.

Aimee was more jaundiced than Jenny had been, so we had to bring her back to the hospital a couple times for bilirubin checks—she was fine.

It was during this time when Bill had been transferred to an afternoon shift and was now working at a gas company substation that was closer to home. While he was in an office one night, his hair stood on end and he slowly turned to find the night guard staring at him. The guard's name was Mike and he was a university teacher moonlighting at the gas company. Mike wanted to know how Bill knew he was watching him.

"Bill, you feel very strong, psychically. Is that how you knew I was watching you?"

It turned out that Mike was very psychic and the two of them talked the entire night.

The next evening Bill called me to tell me he was bringing Mike and his wife over after work (1:00 A.M.).

The couple were interested in my large library of metaphysical books. We began doing psychic exercises and when Mike worked with me he was amazed at the protection he saw around me.

"It's just like she's sitting in God's hands! I've never seen anything like it!"

Eventually we had a falling out because Mike and his wife were preparing to establish a settlement in British Columbia. The main problem was when we refused to participate in a "high magic" ceremony.

Mike, who was very powerful, sent an elemental over to our house and everyone became very ill. When a vat of hot soup spilled on him at another moonlighting job, he accused Bill of doing it with *his* power. After that we never saw each other again.

As hard as Bill worked and as much overtime as he gobbled up, each week was getting worse and worse until we got to the point where we ended up each Friday with only $15.00 for the week's grocery bill. The only way out was to sell our house and look for something cheaper.

Our real estate man was Jerry Borregard. He and Bill were like old friends the moment they first met (later we were informed that they were brothers in one of their former lives).

While our house was for sale, Jerry took us out looking at places. Some gave me horrid psychic sensations, others I wouldn't even enter.

But one day Jerry took us to a farm house on Huff street in Westland. The property had an extra lot with it and gave the feeling of wide open spaces. A goat grazed on the empty lot on the other side of the house.

When we went inside, the place was very, very old. Every room needed painting and the basement had four inches of standing water. It was a nightmare. The only good thing about it was the price—$18,000. We left depressed because we loved all the openness of the land it had.

Meanwhile, our house sold and, although we had plenty of time to move out of our house and find another, I couldn't get that farm house out of my mind because I kept seeing it as it would look once I got my hands on it (I loved fixing places up).

So we went to look at it again and we bought it. When we took our mothers to see what we'd bought, we could see their shock. They thought we were crazy—literally.

But they soon changed their minds a few months later, for while Bill was at work, I'd painted and wallpapered the entire house—every room. Bill helped on every weekend and he even got his friend to bring over heavy equipment to grade the extra lot so we could plant grass seed instead of having a wild field of weeds. We had the basement waterproofed and the house and land ended up looking like a doll house right out of a child's fairytale book.

It was country, warm, and cozy. Bill even installed a free-standing fireplace in the living room. Oh, how I loved that house! It turned out to be absolutely serene. . .except for the small fact that Aimee turned out to be the direct opposite of Jenny. Aimee was hyperactive to the point that we finally took her to our family physician.

He asked me, "Who do you want the medication for, Aimee or mom?" We had Aimee on Ritalin for two weeks, and we couldn't stand that drugged look in her eyes. We took her off of it and I coped with her over-exuberance.

Shortly after Aimee was taken off her medication, I discovered I was pregnant again. We were doing okay financially and we were very excited. Maybe this would be "our boy."

On night, eight and half months later, I awoke toward morning to see my deceased grandmother standing at the foot of my bed. She looked so real—so solid.

"Mary," she softly said, "you are not who you think you are. You have much to do. You and Bill are not who you think you are. You both have a destiny to fulfill. This place will not serve that destiny. You must move to another state farther west, because you are really Summer Rain. Summer Rain is who you are."

And I fell back to sleep.

When I awoke to get Bill off to work, I told him of the visitation.

"Do you think it might have been a dream message?" he asked. I'd been having a rash of dream premonitions that were verified in the newspapers a few days after the dreams.

"I don't feel that it was a dream message, because this was so different—it was so real." Then I had a strange feeling come over me.

"Bill? I don't want you to go to work today."

"Are you afraid to be alone?"

"Yes."

"Because of the visitation?"

"No. The baby's ready. I'm going to go into labor today." Our doctor had warned me that this third one could come real fast, because Jenny was eight hours in labor and Aimee was six.

So Bill called work and stayed home. We made arrangements for Jenny and Aimee—Bill's sister would come to stay with them.

At 10 P.M. that night, labor began. We drove again to Providence Hospital and Bill settled in beside my bed.

But this was not to be a quick labor and we watched the hands on the wall clock move hour after hour.

My doctor came in at 7 P.M. the following evening—wearing a tuxedo!

"Sorry, Mary, but it's my anniversary and I never miss this one date with my wife." I'd been in labor for 18 hours. "You know my associate, Dr. Mackey, and he'll take good care of you. This one just seems to like it where it is, but everything looks fine."

"Happy Anniversary, Dr. Watts."

Shortly after Dr. Watts left, the resident ordered my water to be broken—that was delightful. Two hours later the resident ordered a heart monitor to be attached to me *and* baby —that was even more fun. But now Bill and I were getting worried because the *staff* was concerned.

When we were left alone in the room Bill said, "There's a volume control on this monitor, want to hear what it sounds like?"

I did.

He turned the knob and we smiled at the sounds.

BOOM-BOOM. BOOM-BOOM, went my heart.

BEEP-BEEP. BEEP-BEEP. BEEP-BEEP, went baby's.

"It sounds like a little rabbit's!" I said with a smile of delight.

That sound was so comforting to me because the head nurse kept coming in to read the tape readouts as if she wasn't liking what she was seeing on the baby's rhythm.

When she left the room I expressed my concern to Bill.

"What if the baby's in respiratory distress? What if they decide they need to 'take' it by C-section?"

But then the pains intensified tenfold, and I told Bill to help me get out of there (spirit exit). I could hardly bear much more.

Then my eyes widened.

"What's wrong!" he cried.

I reached down between my legs.

"Oh Bill! I feel the head!"

I must've said that louder than I thought, because nurses and the resident came running. One look and I was unhooked and wheeled away to the delivery room.

I got a quick spinal and was flopped over on my back.

"Fix the mirror!" I shouted.

And I watched Sarah Beth enter the world at 11:07 P.M. on September 23, 1975—after 24 hours of labor.

But I heard no cry.

The delivery team was quiet.

What was wrong?

"What's wrong?" I asked.

"Not a thing, Mary," Dr. Mackey said, as he brought the baby over for me to see. "You have a fine seven-pound girl.

"Is that blonde hair?" I asked.

"Yes, it sure is. Isn't she a real beauty?"

"Ohhh, she's a little doll."

"Mary," he said, "don't be alarmed, but she has a large wine stain on the bottom of her foot. It's called a birthmark."

I looked at it. The mark of Ra-Ta. "Yes, she sure *is* a beauty," I repeated. "We'd wanted a boy, but this little lady is 10 times better."

"Because she's a blonde?" he asked, knowing my other girls were dark.

I looked again at the deep purple on the tiny foot. "Yeah, the blonde hair comes from Bill."

After we returned home, Jenny and Aimee were very loving to the tiny new family addition and they always wanted to be by her.

Bill happened to take note of something one night. "Did you realize you're the oddball around here?" he said to me.

"We already know I'm odd, but what exactly do you mean?"

"We have two September birthdays and two March. . . you're a little out in left field with December."

"So does that mean we need to even it up with a December baby?"

"Ahhh, that wasn't what I was inferring."

I smiled. "I didn't think so. I think we're all set—at least for awhile."

So life was good. Bill was transferred again and was a stock controller at the gas company's main warehouse and I began to seriously meditate everyday while the girls took their naps. It seemed that each week I was attaining a deeper and deeper state that was accompanied by inner sensations that evolved into states of absolute openness of the pineal and pituitary gates.

One day Bernie called to say her sister had left a gift for me. Her sister was a nun in Chicago and had been up for a visit. It seemed that another nun had written a children's book that was illustrated by a Carole Bourdo. There were only 1,000 of these books printed and my Aunt Mary (Sister Marina) wanted me to have one for my girls. This was in 1976 and it was a cute book called, *The Observations of Orpheus Owl.* [Carole Bourdo and I would wait another 12 years before our destined connection would take place.]

Life looked bright for us until the gas company union went on strike. It was a long strike and we went through all our savings. Then we began selling our things. Then we had to sell the really important things like my flower wedding rings and Bill's rifles.

Bill took a job and I took in infants to care for, but we weren't making it. I baby-sat three infants, along with my own three. We were getting desperate.

Then. . .one night while we were sleeping, Bill was awakened by a voice that came from my lips.

"I am that I am."

"What, Mary? What'd you say?"

But I was sound asleep.

Bill sat up in bed. His spine tingled.

"*What?*"

"I know you as you have always known me. Your destiny has come into being and I will be with you to guide you through to it. I am your friend and Advisor—we are all of The Great White Brotherhood. It is time now to be about your chosen work. It is time to begin the beginning."

And Bill, realizing who he was talking to, was on a high like no other. He poured forth dozens of questions and had them all answered.

The conversation was continued for the next two nights after I'd fallen asleep. Finally the two agreed that I could be told about what was transpiring, because I couldn't imagine what had made the complete change in Bill—he was suddenly so happy and was no longer worried about all our problems. It seemed to me that he was walking on Cloud Nine and, for the life of me, I couldn't figure out why.

When he sat me down and relayed the entire happening and all he'd discussed with his Advisor, I was greatly surprised, but not incredulous because I was well aware of the conceptual existence of spiritual guides and The White Brotherhood.

It was explained to Bill that, because of my routine, deep meditations, I'd achieved the proper vibrational alignment for a solid communication to commence. The Advisor who had spoken through me and would give further direction was Bill's personal guide (the appointed Brotherhood Intermediary who was Bill's special friend in The Brotherhood. . .he was the Head Intermediary between God and The Great White Brotherhood and he was, in essence, in charge of making sure God's will was carried out by the various Brotherhood divisions).

We were informed that Bill's position on the spiritual plane was that of a high-ranking light warrior, and that I held the position of Record Keeper when not involved in a physical volunteer operation.

Our past-life personalities were revealed to us, including all physical incarnations we'd both volunteered for over the centuries.

My own personal Advisor served as my Gate Keeper, who guarded my psyche from being contaminated by any outsider influences. In other words, I could not ever be misguided, for only The White Brotherhood members were permitted to guide me and give insights pertinent to our specific mission ahead. My personal Advisor, in the capacity as my Gate Keeper, stands guard and will not permit any other entities near me. This singular aspect is why Mike perceived my strong aura of psychic protection when he was working with me.

We were informed at the outset that, because of Bill's Advisor's high position, he may frequently be "away" on other Brotherhood business, but *always* there would be someone of The Brotherhood Advisory Council to advise us. My Gate Keeper would only allow the highest members access to me.

Our mission would take a step-by-step approach to fulfillment, because the Sons of Belial were also aware of our work.

We were cautioned to be ever aware and watchful in our daily activities and to never place ourselves in a compromising position that would expose us to the Dark Side's advantage.

It was assured that soon I would be able to open the line of communication during the waking state and that this would never drain my energies nor produce any outward physical affectations while communication transpired. We were told it would be like sharing a park bench with someone else—I would remain fully conscious of all that was said during the communication transmittal.

And so I accepted this completely, for I was well aware of the concept. And, just as we were told, I was soon able to share my consciousness with Bill's Advisor without any shift whatsoever. It was as smooth as smooth gets, because only a very, very aware and spiritually-advanced individual would pick up on the difference between me talking and the Advisor speaking. Since he uses *my* vocal chords, there is no alteration in tone or quality—just an increased measure of seriousness is evidenced.

Our girls can tell by my eye intensity and the "feel" of the atmosphere around me when the Advisor is present, and they usually begin grinning and laughing with an inner excitement, for the Advisor is extremely friendly and accommodating with their own questions.

Our first step toward our destiny was to move further west. Because we were cautioned and also always encouraged to use our own free wills and personal choices, we were never actually "told" where to relocate to.

So we got out a U.S. map and, because we already knew of the coming changes, we looked at northern locations close to the Canadian border. We decided on Bottineau, North Dakota and sent for information on the region. It seemed like a geographically secure area and, if need be in the future, we could be in Canada in no time.

So Bill called our old friend Jerry and told him we needed to sell the house because we were moving out west.

When Jerry came over to the house, he couldn't believe what we'd done to the property. He said it looked like it came out of *Country Living* magazine, and that we should have no trouble selling it for double what we paid for it. And the "FOR SALE" sign went up.

Our family had adamant objections to our sudden plan. The two mothers couldn't understand why we wanted to sell our house and move out of state to somewhere we've never been. What will you do for work? Where will you live? You don't know anyone. All your friends and family are here!

My sister, Barbara, thought we were crazy, just plain crazy. And the mothers were incredulous.

But all the ranting and psychological mind games couldn't crack our firm resolve and determined path—we *were* going. The gas company strike was finally settled and Bill returned to his former job. Jerry brought two couples through the house and we had an offer on the table. The offer was for $32,000, but I also had to leave behind all my rugs and curtains. I was so upset over that, because the curtains in all three bedrooms matched the bedspreads. I was so tired of giving and giving and making sacrifice after sacrifice that tears came to my eyes as we were sitting at our kitchen table with Jerry.

The trouble was—we *needed* to sell right then because Bill had just gotten back to work and we didn't have the next month's mortgage payment. Curtains and rugs certainly didn't outweigh a foreclosure and losing everything. So we signed the offer.

The next thing we did was purchase a four-wheel vehicle as we were advised to. We bought a 1977 Blazer outright with a gas company credit union loan, which we paid off from the house sale money.

As moving day approached, we gave our Camaro to Bill's sister, who was divorced and on welfare with two young boys. Then we began selling off everything we owned except clothes, kitchen utensils, our bed, and the girl's toys. We also kept our record player and records. I could not part with my best books either.

So all furniture, color TV, washer/dryer, riding lawn mower, decor items, lamps, window air conditioner, etc. were all sold to neighbors and friends.

When moving day came, we pulled a small U-Haul behind the Blazer and nobody was there to see us off—after all, we were crazy. Crazy? I don't know, but I do know we were so very happy, even though we were headed into the future full of dozens and dozens of unknowns.

When we reached Bottineau and got into a motel for the night, we both were very unsettled. Over dinner, I had tears in my eyes.

"I feel sick," I said.

"Me too."

"This is not where we're supposed to be. Why didn't 'he' tell us that?"

"Because *we* have to make our own choices. We have to do some of the work too. They won't lead us around because it's *us* that has to use our inner feelings on most of these things."

I looked over at Bill. "They knew we wouldn't feel right here, huh."

"I'm sure they knew, but they also saw our psyches working too. They knew we wouldn't stay."

"Okay, so now where to?"

"Your guess is as good as mine." I thought for a few minutes. "We need to be farther west. . . and south. We need to be in the mountains. Colorado." My eyes brightened then. "Colorado. *That's* where it's all going to happen. That's where our cabin is."

He immediately loved the idea and that night we slept very sound because our sick feelings had vanished—we were going to Colorado to live in a log cabin in the mountains.

In June of 1977, we pulled into Colorado Springs and drove around looking for an apartment. Ashamed to admit being used to segregated Detroit and all its suburbs, we had a hard time locating the right apartment complex, because every one we tried we saw black children playing with white children and we just assumed we were in the "wrong" part of town.

Finally we stopped for dinner at Denny's on Academy Boulevard. The waitress noticed our U-Haul.

"Moving in from out-of-state?"

We smiled weary smiles and nodded.

"This is a two-job town, you know. Family can't make it on one paycheck here because of the military. You find a place to live yet?"

We shook our heads in unison as Bill responded.

"Can't seem to get our bearings, if you know what I mean." The waitress frowned.

Bill quietly explained our problem.

The waitress laughed. "You folks must be from out east somewhere. We don't have 'sections' here in Colorado because everybody lives together. You want a good school for these girls, you go up Academy to Templeton Gap (now called Austin Bluffs Parkway) and get yourself into the Foxfire Apartments. Grant school is just down the street—that's a real good school."

We thanked the waitress for her helpfulness. We thanked her over and over.

During dinner we kept expressing our amazement that here all ethnic cultures lived together and wasn't that wonderful— wasn't that just like someplace we should be.

After dinner we followed the woman's directions and located the Foxfire apartment complex. The "children's" building was full, but the manager saw we'd just come from Michigan, so he gave us a two-bedroom lower apartment in an "adult" building for $150 a month.

We unloaded the U-Haul, set up our bed and put the girls in sleeping blankets on the floor. We were exhausted and slept like babies that first night in our new home.

The next morning, we returned the U-Haul and had to pay an extra hundred dollars for the difference in our declared destination. Then we bought the girls small sleeping cots for their bedroom, put the Blazer bench seat in the living room for a couch, bought groceries, and unpacked the rest of our things.

The following day, we went to the Blue Cross/Blue Shield office to transfer our medical insurance from Bill's work—we wanted to be sure we were covered. Now we had to pay the two hundred per month out of our own pocket; but that was okay because, next, we went to the bank to transfer our huge $5,000 savings (which was going to be our land downpayment). The Blazer had taken most of our house sale profit.

When I called our mothers to tell the good news about where we'd ended up, they were very cool. My mother was in the hospital with an allergic reaction to a drug prescription, but assured me she'd be fine.

While Bill pounded the streets looking for work that paid more than minimum wage, I went through the telephone book trying to find him work. It was getting depressing.

Summer slipped by and no job. And our cabin savings was dwindling.

It was during this time that I thought of my father. He'd moved to Florida with Fran, and I thought I'd try to patch things up between us. I wrote him about our wonderful move and he made plane reservations to come see us and Colorado.

He loved Colorado, but hated our poor living conditions. He hated that Bill wasn't working (he was a bum who couldn't support his family). He hated the "jungle bunnies" and Mexicans who lived in our apartment complex, and he hated the fact that his beautiful granddaughters were (he was sure) going to grow up and marry "niggers." He called me "white trash," and his parting words to Bill were "buy her an ironing board." (I didn't have one.)

While my father was visiting, he saw Jenny and Aimee outside playing in the complex playground with two of our little neighbor girls (they were black).

He shook his head and made the most disgusting face.

"Mary, you should be ashamed of yourself. What kind of a mother are you to let your girls play with niggers?"

Well. . .Bill had finally reached his boiling point and really laid into my father. He really let him have both barrels about being so egotistical and bigoted. And why did he bother going to church every Sunday anyway?

And their verbal fight brought my old sick feelings back.

We were both relieved to see my father and Fran leave.

A week later, I received a scathing letter from my father that compared himself and Bill to a tall oak and a skinny, weak sapling. He again referred to me as white trash, and said he could just kill us for how we turned out.

The man was mad. Crazy mad, and I had nightmares for days afterward of him coming in the apartment and killing us all. But finally thoughts of him faded as we put our efforts into getting Bill a job. We ultimately had to drop our Blue Cross in order to economize what money we had left in savings.

A month later I had my third miscarriage (I'd had two in Michigan before having Jenny). Two months after that I'd had another and, because we were so saddened, the Advisor came to explain the reason why.

In all our previous lives (except for volunteered ones), Bill and I were always mates with four children. In other words, we always numbered six. In this volunteered lifetime, the same spirits wanted to join us again and came as Jenny, Aimee, and Sarah. But Number Six had been called back to God and, therefore, the destined spirit was not available—hence, no vehicle was required for it and the last two miscarriages occurred. For this volunteered mission, The Brotherhood wanted no lesser advanced spirit to participate.

When Bill heard all of this he was emotionally devastated and heartsick. He pined for Number Six and missed the spirit terribly. He cried and couldn't eat. He lost a great deal of weight. The situation hit him very hard.

Finally, The Brotherhood took compassion on his great grief and were given permission to "pass time" over Bill's heart while he slept. The following morning he was 98% better and could now deal with what he knew. He also made a decision—he was going to have a vasectomy. And he did.

While Bill was going through his emotional crisis, I looked for work. I was hired as a motel maid, but Bill could see the work was too hard on me. I quit and looked elsewhere. I was hired as a secretary at an architectural engineering company called J. D. Adams. I worked for the chief engineer and generally enjoyed my job, except for the times some of the men thought it was fun to "catch me alone" in a room. I finally quit after Bill announced that *he* had found work.

He had been hired at Looart Press (Current, Inc.) as a maintenance man on the night shift. This paid minimum wage, but we weren't finding anything better. His job was to maintain all the dozens of packaging machines used in the mail order card company.

Two weeks later, he told me about a young woman there who operated one of the machines. They'd got to talking on their lunch breaks and he found out that she too wanted a mountain cabin and the simple, natural life. When he began easing into his metaphysical beliefs, she was like a big light that went on and was all excited, and asked if she could she read some of our books?

So one day he brought her over to the apartment to meet me. Her name was Robin King.

Now we had a friend who loved to come over and talk for hours about spiritual concepts. Robin would often bring her cello and play for the girls. We took to each other as though we were family—*real* family of the spirit.

A month after connecting with Robin, I was standing at the bathroom sink and the room began closing in around me —I was going to faint.

I called out for Bill and he reached me just in time. I was out for several minutes and when I came to I was very ill. I'd had Toxic Shock Syndrome (before it was known as that) and spent a week in bed drifting in and out of consciousness. When I was awake, I was so weak and ill I didn't care if I lived or died. Robin stayed at my bedside whenever Bill had to go out. I didn't go to the doctors, because Bill was told by our Advisor that I'd recover. And I did, but now I was very depressed that we were having such a hard time of things. How could that be if we were here for a special purpose? And I'd stare at the mountains during the day and pine for their woods. At night, I'd stare at the stars and pine for home.

When I came out of that spell I had a great desire to write an illustrated psychic children's book. Never before had writing entered my mind; but now the idea consumed my waking hours and I felt driven to do it.

So we went out and splurged on a portable manual typewriter, and while Bill was at work at night and the girls were in bed, I'd write the book and draw the pictures.

One evening, when I was working on my new project, Jenny ran from the bedroom crying. She was holding her thumb. She'd done a cute somersault off Sarah's crib and broke her thumb. I was upset because we had no medical insurance now. I held her hand and pulled the thumb into place. Then I wrapped it and told her to give her teacher a note. I said Jenny had "sprained" her thumb.

A week later, the school called for a conference. Jenny was not performing at third-grade level and thought she should be put back into second. They also wanted a social worker to visit our apartment because I'd made the mistake of commenting that we had no TV. Evidently that signalled a "deprived" environment.

Well fine, I thought, go ahead and bring the social workers on.

When the woman came, briefcase and all, we had coffee and pastries. She noticed my shelves of "intellectual" books. She saw the girls' room full of books and games. I told her about my literary project, and she left shortly after without ever filling out her ream of forms. Seems Jenny wasn't deprived after all. That experience with school mentality was to be the first of many involving Jenny. One day it would come to the point when the so-called "learned educators" would cringe to see Jenny's mother stride down their sacred halls, and teachers would pretend they didn't see me, all the while, hoping I wasn't coming in to talk to *them.*

The following summer the apartment complex was taken over by new owners. They sent notices around that it was now going to be an "all adult" complex and all residents with children must move out.

I was outraged. How could people so heartlessly shove others around like that?

So I wrote to the newspaper—the *Gazette Telegraph.* I wrote because out of all the residents in the entire complex, we were the ones who cleaned up around the place whenever there was litter around. We *cared* about where we lived, and now we were being told to move elsewhere just because we had children.

In response I received several letters from landlords offering house rentals to us—but unfortunately, these rents were way beyond our means.

Then, out of the blue, Bill received a call from Empire Gas (a propane company) up in Woodland Park. The manager, Dan White, was going back to his former job up there at People's Natural Gas, so there was a manager opening at Empire if Bill was still interested.

He took the job and commuted up and down Ute pass.

When I was at a school conference for Jenny, I mentioned Bill's new job and that now we were looking for a rental in Woodland Park.

"I live in Woodland Park," the teacher said. "And my husband and I just bought a log cabin we need to rent out. It's up in Rainbow Valley if you're interested."

A log cabin? Up in the mountains? Was I hearing right?

The following day we met Jon and Donna Nelson at their house, and they drove us up through the winding road of Rainbow Valley. The little log cabin had two bedrooms, one bath, a small kitchen and a living room. It also had a one-car garage.

We fell in love with it and moved in on the weekend. This was our tenth move since we'd been married.

The cabin gave us so much peace, because it was so incredibly quiet out there. By day the birdsong cheered me and, by night the windsong sang through the high pines outside our bedroom window and owls would hoot and coyotes howled—all music to my soul.

However, I was not yet the mountain person I would later become—I was still a bit citified—and now I'm embarrassed to relay what happened one bright morning shortly after we moved into the cabin.

The entire family was up for breakfast. Bill left for work and Jenny and Aimee left for school. Sarah was now three years old and was in the kitchen with me when I saw something move on the floor. When I realized it was a mouse. . . I screamed. . . and ran to stand on the couch!

Sarah laughed at her mother's funny antics and, with the tiny grey creature at her bare feet, she twirled and twirled, long nightie billowing out as the mouse ran circles around her pudgy little feet. Sarah giggled and giggled at their dance.

And mother watched the Circle Dance of child and mouse from her "safe" place high on the couch. Thank heaven's that was *then*. I've come a long, long way since our first mountain cabin.   •

One day while Sarah and I were at home alone, I played music and she fell asleep for her nap on the couch. I'd bought a new record of music box songs and this was the first time I'd played it. I was sitting at my desk preparing to work on a novel I was writing. Suddenly a particular music box piece shifted my consciousness to another lifetime and I slipped back into the Sequanu of the 1700's.

When I came back into myself, I found a crudely printed letter in front of me. I was later advised that it was an exact duplicate of one I'd written in that life. . .shortly before I was killed. (I still have that letter).

In that life, I was the daughter of a Shoshone headman who had run away with a white mountainman (Bill). We lived in a small cabin of rough-hewn logs. I had three small sons and was also eight months pregnant with our fourth child. While Bill and his brother were gone hunting, I'd sit and practice my English writing. In this letter I commented on the beautiful music box Bill had given me and how I could feel the baby moving inside me. After Bill returned a few days later, he accidentally shot me in the back—Sequanu (my name) and the baby died. . .and a great love was tragically ended.

The music piece on my record was the same piece on the music box Sequanu had. I never again played the record. I threw it away.

Robin came to live with us in the cabin. I needed to go to work. I got rehired at J.D. Adams and would have to get up at five in the morning in order to make the long drive down to Colorado Springs.

Hank Danley, the chief engineer, found out I was a bookaholic and he'd give me his mailer newspapers from Hamilton Bargain Books, and I'd spend my lunch hours picking out books and filling in the order form (which I never sent in because I never had the money for extras like books). But it was fun just the same.

One day at work we needed to locate a specific drawing that could be found in any of five large boxes. Finding this would be like searching for a needle in a haystack and the job was given to me. I didn't want to do it because I knew it'd take forever and ever and I had other things to do. So I stood at the window behind my desk, put my head in hands and "went within" to locate the drawing plan.

One of my bosses noticed me and asked if I was alright.

"Oh, oh yes, I was just using my 'sixth'."

"Your what?"

"You know, the psyche." Then I strode out of the office into the storage room, rummaged down through one box and, a minute later, walked back in with the drawing.

"This the one we're looking for?" I said, placing it on my boss's desk.

He flushed. "How'd you *do* that?"

"Doesn't matter," I said, sorry I'd brought attention to myself.

And within 15 minutes the office was buzzing with what Mary did and *how* she did it. Twenty minutes later the company president strolled through my department, paused before my desk and said, "Having a good day, Mary?"

I said I was and blushed. He never came to talk to me before this. And I secretly swore to never, ever draw attention like that again because folks just didn't understand that it was natural to everyone. . .not just me.

That summer, all six of us went fishing at Rampart Range Reservoir. We'd been there about 20 minutes when I began feeling very strange. I was getting dizzy and extremely weak. I called out to Bill. I could barely stand by myself. He and Robin supported me as we all made slow progress back through the woods to our truck.

At the doctor's office in Woodland, I was diagnosed as having hepatitis and mononucleosis. I'd have to stay in bed for at least five weeks.

"I can't!" I said. "I have to work!"

The doctor didn't agree. "Okay, I'll put you in the hospital then."

"No! We don't have insurance. Okay, I'll stay in bed." And I did because I didn't feel like doing a damn thing other than that. I was very sick.

During this time I received no sick pay and Bill's income was not enough to cover our monthly bills. So he and Robin began selling our things again. They'd take our possessions down on Saturday mornings to spend all day at the Race Track Flea Market booth in Colorado Springs. I was most sad to see Robin sell her beloved cello and watch them take my grandmother's treadle sewing machine out the door. But they got $95 for the machine and a good price for the cello. At least that gave us a couple week's grocery money. I vowed then and there that, some day, I would buy Robin another cello.

When I recuperated and returned to work, everything was fine for a few months until they began laying off the older draftsmen and hiring boys right out of school. I was infuriated at the injustice of this. Also, two draftsmen had begun to think it was okay to come up to me when I was alone in a room and force their affections on me. I'd had problems with this in all my former work places, but I'd thought I'd escaped it here—I was wrong.

So one day, after another older draftsman was given his walking papers, I gathered up my personal things and left a note on my typewriter. I'd said I'd quit in sympathy with the older draftsman, when in truth, it was a combination of that *and* being shoved into closets.

When I got home, the septic had backed up into the bathtub. I never understood why landlords didn't take routine care of their own property. We moved out of the cabin and into a larger rental on the hill just above and behind the cabin. It was a beautiful spot because we could see around the valley. The house could be seen from the road to Cripple Creek.

Robin didn't move into this house with us, because she got married and moved to the Woodcrest Apartments in Woodland Park.

So we lived in the house-on-the-hill in Rainbow Valley and were down by two wage earners. I had to do something to help out. I hated the thought of working in another office again so I came up with the idea of starting a dance school in Woodland. Rent for studio space (it was very tiny) was only $100 a month. So I gave it a go.

Meanwhile our landlord decided to sell the house. We moved back down into our first cabin and things worked out—for a while.

The field mice were still there, but now we had a cat the girls named Kitty-Kitty. After she had two litters (on their bed with three little midwives present), the girls renamed her Mamasito.

Well, Mamasito turned out to be an excellent mouser. She'd catch the mouse, Bill would don his "mouser glove," and take the critter from the cat. Then he'd let the mouse out in the woods. (I wasn't scared of mice anymore.)

My dance classes were going well. I had one class with three pregnant ladies (one was Robin). I taught tap, jazz, adult ballet, pointe classes, and toddler beginners.

One evening on my way out of Rainbow Valley, I was alone on the road. Ahead of me, coming my way, were three small UFO's. I pulled onto the shoulder and shut off the Blazer engine. I looked at their straight approach through the windshield. I was so excited. I wanted to get out and wave to them, but was afraid I'd miss something or they'd vanish. The three vehicles sailed over the Blazer just as smooth and quiet as could be. When I got to a phone in Divide, to tell the family to go outside and look for them, it was too late. Sarah was very disappointed, because she'd wanted to go with me to the studio that night, but had decided to stay home with Bill.

Rainbow Valley and the Divide area were good regions to spy UFO's, for we'd seen several during our time there.

One afternoon our bachelor neighbor came over.

"I got a deal for you guys. I'm going to the Carolinas for a year to sell land on Hilton Head. I need someone to watch my house—live in it. You pay my mortgage of $200 a month, and I'll do utilities."

We couldn't believe our ears. Our friend had a very large house with huge glass windows that looked out on the valley and stream below. He had four bedrooms and a family room. Outside was a trampoline that the girls loved. So we moved into his house and brought our two dogs, Rainbow I and Sunshine with us (the cat was no longer around).

We loved living in the big house. The stream song from down below lulled us to sleep every night and we enjoyed playing in the stream and going for long walks. Horses in the valley wandered up to our door. The girls spent hours on the trampoline. Life there was good. For the first time, life was really good.

[I need to digress again because I realize I've again omitted something important.]

From the time Bill's Advisor appeared in Michigan, we'd been communicating on a regular basis (nearly daily). We were informed of our mission and were learning the higher aspects and concepts of spirituality as it aligns with the Precepts of the Law of One. We'd have very intense discussions that ultimately advanced to the stage of us carrying on a *three-way* conversation as I developed the ability to *consciously* share my psyche consciousness with the Advisor's. So all this time we were in continual communication with our Advisor. And while we were living in the small cabin, various members of The Great White Brotherhood began giving me information for a book to be entitled: *Autumn of Man.*

While we were in the small cabin, Bill went through a very long and black period of deep, deep depression. He'd come home from work, eat very little for dinner, and then go directly to bed. This was caused by his desire to be about his work and getting our own land and cabin, but never being able to afford it. He despaired at how long everything was taking. If it wasn't for his Advisor who continually talked to him, I fear Bill wouldn't still be here today. Finally he snapped out of it and took Acceptance into his heart. It was an extremely trying time for all of us because it lasted an entire year.

Sometimes I think people are better off not knowing about who they are and why they came because when you know all about those aspects, it makes it so incredibly hard to function in an everyday working world where society centers on such mundane things it *thinks* are important. When one *knows* the score, it's very, very difficult to have to be forced to wait for destiny's own prescribed timing. When one has all the facts and wants to be about his work—*waiting* can be pure agony.

As I said, life in the big house was really good.

Although I'd received dozens and dozens of publisher's rejection letters for my children's psychic manual and I'd filed the manuscripts away, I'd been also working on three novels and had some bites. Four publishers wanted to see chapters. I was encouraged and many of our Woodland Park friends now knew I was trying to be a writer. However, the two novels I'd written were becoming less and less attractive to me because I was shifting over to purely spiritual material. The novels were: *Only an Old Folktale* about a woman inheriting a Scottish castle estate occupied by an incubus; *The Aspen Affair*, about an Aspen maid and her misadventures; *The Cabin*, which I still intend to publish under the new title *Song of the Alpine Moon.* This last one is about a love that survives death—a love that is eternal.

But our life in the big house was good until. . .our friend showed up three months later. He said Hilton Head was "sweat city," and he couldn't stand the heat and humidity there.

So he was back in his home and we were still paying his mortgage. He expected to eat with us every day and I began feeling like his personal cook and housemaid.

Then one day he dropped the bomb.

"Those damn dogs got to go. I hate dogs."

I caught him laughing once after he'd given Sunshine a whole hot pepper.

We were devastated that we had to get rid of our dear dogs. Sunshine had been Bill's and he loved that dog. We all cried and cried when we took them down to the Humane Society.

After that incident, Bill and our "friend" had terrible words. Our friend decided he was going to sell his house and we'd better get *out!*

We talked it over and decided we'd try a major move to Upper Michigan. Marquette was woodsy and also by a large body of water Lake Superior. Bill had always wanted to live by water.

So we made plans. Bill gave notice at his work, and we sold everything—again. We sold the Blazer for an older pick-up with a camper on it and $5,000. We pulled a small U-Haul again and said our farewells to Robin and her new baby, Amanda.

I hated to close the dance school, but my example had given two other dance teachers the same idea, so when I left, my former students had other studios to choose from.

Our journey out of Colorado didn't begin well. The older pickup couldn't pull the U-Haul up out of the long, steep driveway of the house and we had to have a neighbor tow us out.

In Nebraska we got a flat and Bill pulled over by a corn field to fix it. After that, things went fairly smoothly. At night we'd all sleep in the camper at highway rest stops. This was in October of 1981 and when we drove through upper Wisconsin and into Michigan the woods were so beautiful. But we also noticed that people had stacks of entire tree trunks for firewood. This clearly indicated winters that were much worse than the Colorado ones we'd become used to.

When we reached Marquette we entered a cold rainstorm and stopped at one of the first motels we found. Immediately we got a newspaper and looked for a house rental. We found one that sounded good for $300 a month. It was located on Lakewood Lane.

This, we discovered, was out of town and followed Lake Superior's shoreline. When we entered the property there was a sign that said: Teepee Village, and we drove down a treed lane between cement tepees that had lofts and were rented out. At the end of the lane was a blue bungalow. Past the bungalow was Lake Superior—we loved it. . .we took it and moved in the next day.

We got Jenny and Aimee in school and Bill looked for work. He looked and looked. There wasn't even a gas station attendant's job available. Marquette was in a deep recession and nearly everyone was on welfare.

After a couple months our funds were dwindling, so we went to Social Services for assistance. We went for food stamps only—but before we knew it, the Social Worker said we'd be getting food stamps and $620 a month.

"What does that mean?" Bill asked her.

The woman smiled at us. "That's the amount of your monthly welfare check."

"We don't *want* to be on welfare. We only came in for *food* assistance until I get a job," Bill said.

The woman sighed. "There *are* no jobs here. You'll be required to attend job training classes and then you'll be placed on a government job near your home."

And that was that.

Bill was humiliated. We never, ever dreamed we'd be on welfare. Finally he was assigned work at Aimee's school, which was close to home. This job was in exchange for the $620 we received. It was more like an actual paycheck now. But we could not tolerate the situation of being on welfare. That winter we had more snow than we'd ever seen. The Advisors finished dictating *Autumn of Man* and I began sending it out to publishers.

By the middle of March of 1982, we'd had it with welfare and I'd had it with publishers—they didn't know their ear from a hole in the ground. What the hell were we *doing?* Our mission was a complete bust. We were sick of trying to accomplish our spiritual goal! Why'd we even volunteer for this if nothing was ever going to work out?

I sent *Autumn of Man* manuscript to one last publisher before we moved back to Colorado. I had my return address listed as General Delivery, Woodland Park, Colorado. The last publisher I held out a shred of hope for was Donning. If I received a rejection from them—that was going to be it! No more. No way. Our mission will have failed.

Although our Advisor had suggested Woodland Park again and told us there would be someone waiting there for me, I was losing faith because of all our physical problems, grief, despair, and suffering we'd experienced. Although we were told that all completed ones experienced this kind of adversity, it didn't help one bit to ease the pain and misery of it. It didn't ease it at all. Knowing the Dark Side was always pitted against us and knowing the Light Side was doing battles for us didn't help either. We were the ones experiencing the physical and it was no bed of roses.

So we were advised to return to Woodland Park, where the mission would commence via a new and powerful player. It was our choice to make the suggested move or go wherever we wanted. Bill and I both knew we really had no choice at all because we were *here* for one reason only. Why have a mission at all if you aren't prepared to listen and heed your Advisor's advice? So we toughened up, became determined once again and used our free will to choose to follow our Advisor's suggestion. Secretly I thought the "Woodland" connection would be that my manuscript acceptance that would be mailed there.

So, in order to have money to make the journey back, we placed an ad to sell the camper off the pickup. We got $150 for it and we packed our meager belongings in the bed of the truck (no need for a U-Haul now). We all piled into the cab of the truck and headed back to Colorado with Sarah on my lap.

As we passed the "WELCOME TO COLORFUL COLORADO" sign, John Denver's song "Back Home Again" came on the radio. Bill and I looked at one another and smiled. Maybe this really *was* it! And when I saw my mountains again, tears filled my eyes. I wondered how I was ever able to leave them and I vowed to myself I'd never leave them again. . .ever.

The only rental available was a tiny A-frame cabin off Twin Rocks Road. Robin helped us move in. We were extremely cramped, but we were back home.

The first night in bed I was visited by fears that literally made me sick. I worried about our finances. We only had $500 left after paying our first month's rent and deposit, and Bill had no job. I was so sick of being poor. I was sick of being sick with money worries. But I knew we would endure because, together, we were a team—we were warriors.

A month later, a real estate friend of ours located a larger cabin rental in town for $300 a month. The house was 306 E. Chester, and we fell in love with the rustic interior. We rented it with the help of our real estate friend who gave us the first month's rent free because the property needed major cleaning. The former renters had a horse on the property and there was even hay on the kitchen floor.

So we settled in the Chester house and I looked for work. I couldn't find anything and none of the three gas companies in town were hiring. We were getting desperate because we had no money for our next month's rent. We applied for food stamps and those were a true blessing.

Finally I saw an ad for a real estate secretary. I went for an interview and was hired the following week.

Meanwhile, because Bill couldn't find work, he began his own gas service business called Rocky Mountain Gas Service. He got his tax license and began advertising in the local paper. Soon he was getting service calls and referrals from all three gas companies who already knew his work. He was proud of his work and was efficient and thorough. He took calls from Cascade to Victor and put a lot of miles on the pickup. What he loved most about his work was the knowledge that he was helping people. And he had the perfect personality for the work because he loved being friendly and talking to folks. He'd always been very outgoing (so much the opposite from myself).

While his job was gaining momentum, mine was declining, for my boss was an egotist who went through secretaries like water. He never missed a chance to belittle or humiliate and this, in conjunction with more sexual harassment from the real estate agents, drove me to again quit my job. But now I had the beautiful opportunity to accompany Bill out into the mountains on his calls and I loved helping him and being his "go-for."

Then. . .I received a large envelope in the mail addressed to General Delivery. My last hope was dashed and I sunk into a deep depression. I took the truck and, through blinding tears, drove up into the mountains.

When I stopped, I walked into the woods and cried my eyes out.

"Why, God? Why is the Dark Side winning all the time? We've tried so hard to do everything that was asked of us. We've waited five years now and it's all been misery and disappointment and pain. Please, God, please help us!"

Then my scalp crawled and my spine tingled.

I looked behind me. There was nobody there.

But when I turned forward again, an old native woman was standing in the treeline. My destiny had reached a major destination point and my life had made a drastic change.

Much of my times with No-Eyes were recounted in my books. Those special experiences that were not revealed, like the magic we did and our times shared with the Starborn ones, will always remain within my heart, for as of this writing, these aspects are far from finished. My personal relationship with the Starborn ones is an ongoing situation that awaits a unified destiny to manifest according to The Plan and its predetermined time.

Robin and her husband began having serious problems called "communication." She returned to work at Loaf n' Jug convenience store and ultimately became manager. I watched Mandy all day and the baby-sitting income helped a great deal—especially when I took in two more infants. One was a policeman's son and the other was a teacher's daughter. So between my three babies and Bill's service work, we managed okay until he was offered a job at People's Natural Gas Company. So all my weekends were free.

Robin finally divorced. Her husband believed her beliefs were of the devil and that she was a lost soul. He became a born-again and bought a new Blazer and 40 acres of mountain land. Then he married his born-again friend and filled their house with material things.

Robin was left with their old 1973 Buick and Mandy. Robin wasn't into material "things"; all she wanted out of the settlement was her daughter.

And so Robin and Mandy moved in with us and between Bill's and Robin's days off, I always had a vehicle to take out to No-Eyes' cabin. I'd go whenever I could. . .on weekends, when Robin was home to baby-sit, when Bill was home, and in the evenings too. My *real* job now was to spend as much time as I could with No-Eyes, for she would be the ultimate vehicle to slip me through the battle lines. She was to also serve as the catalyst that would develop my own native heritage aspect that would have a strong bearing on my work. Although I knew I was destined to meet someone when I returned to Colorado, I was not informed it would lead to writing again, and when I discovered that fact, I fought it with a vengeance, until she made me promise her I'd do it. This was how she got around my reluctance to ever write again. But, other than taking notes on her healing ways, I never put pen to paper in the two years time I spent with her and her varied visitors.

At times she would slip in comments (or warnings) that related to what I could or couldn't write about in "them books." After a while I didn't need her clarifications, because it was very clear which subjects were taboo (magic and Starborn conversations during their visits), and which were okay (most everything else). The Starborn ones began visiting our home when we were living on Chester street in Woodland Park, but these were for observation only. The actual in-home communications didn't begin until much later.

When Jenny was in the ninth grade in Woodland, I began

having real problems with the so-called educators. When Bill and I attended the last conference for her, I was infuriated at the group ignorance I found.

In attendance were Bill, myself, Jenny's special education teacher, the school counselor, the school psychologist, and the district director for special education from Colorado Springs.

They wanted her to take gym in her tenth year. I said absolutely not, because she has poor motor skills and is humiliated to the point of crying when classmates holler at her if she doesn't know what to do (she didn't understand game rules). I emphatically told them that gym class only underscores a poor self-image for Jenny, and is definitely not productive to enhancing her development.

Well. . .okay, they supposed they could skip the gym class.

Then they listed her class schedule for the following year (tenth grade).

Somewhere in the depths of my brain, I could feel the mind preparing for battle with these people.

"I want to see the books for those classes," I said.

They went to get them.

I skimmed though several and then handed them over to Bill. He looked them over and passed them back. Now I was really hot.

"Those are excellent books," I said, throwing them off guard.

"We think so too."

"Tell me, we know Jenny's chronological age, but what mental age do you have her listed as from all her testing?"

They flipped through her thick file and the psychologist responded.

"Well there doesn't appear to be a mental age here."

"Then can you tell me at what *grade* level Jenny's comprehension is at?"

"Oh yes, she's approximately ( ) grade level."

Boiling was going on in the brain. Electrical sparks were cracking back and forth between the cells.

I stared at these "learned" people sitting before me.

"Then can you give me *one* sane reason *why* the *hell* you're giving *tenth* grade *texts* to a student who only has a ( ) grade comprehension and vocabulary understanding?"

They flushed and all looked at one another for an answer. These highly intelligent educators were dumbfounded to realize their obvious error in teaching techniques.

Finally, I broke the silence.

"Wouldn't it stand to *reason* that these special education kids should have texts *geared* to their comprehension and reading level? Surely there are lower-grade level history books!"

"Well. . .yes."

"So get some! Don't you *realize* that by making these poor kids struggle through *tenth* grade books they're not *learning* a damned thing? And on top of that you're psychologically *damaging* them further by making them feel *stupid*! Don't you see how you're *compounding* the problem?"

It was like a light went on. These people never even thought of that. And I was incredulous. That kind of gross stupidity on the part of people who are supposed to be educators made my blood boil. This was my daughter they were messing up and, when *my* family is being ill done too—look out! I'd never hesitated to stand up and defend my girls from injustices, and this was just about the worse case yet. It became a family joke when one of my girls said, "It's time to sic mom on the school again."

I've always kept a keen eye on the girl's school work and what kind of textbooks and lesson plans that were being used. Some had no educational value at all. Some teachers never really *taught*, rather opting for the "read the book and we'll have a test on it" method. Some teachers never had time to answer student questions. I always encouraged the girls to "ask questions" if you don't understand something—that's what the teachers are there for, but clearly, many of the teachers didn't know that.

So. . .it was agreed that the next school year, Jenny and her special education peers would have appropriate texts and also, she would be exempted from gym class.

When Bill and I left the meeting he squeezed my hand.

"I love it when you do that."

I smiled. "Do what?"

"Give'em hell."

"I knew you were loving every minute in there, but *you're* not the one getting a name for yourself around here. I can just imagine what these teachers call me."

"Mmmm, how about 'concerned parent?'"

"Nope. I don't think so. I think it's more like a witch with a capital 'B'."

"So what? If they're so stupid they need someone to show them what they're doing wrong then so be it."

"That's just it though, *they're* the learned educators while the stupid parents aren't supposed to know anything."

"That *is* the problem," he said, "they're finding out they're stuck with one parent who *isn't* stupid."

The following August when I accompanied Jenny to registration in the counselor's office, the special education teacher was sitting beside her.

This was not going to be good.

I steeled myself for another battle.

The schedule was the same as we'd agreed upon the previous June. . .with one exception—the inclusion of the gym class.

"We agreed that Jenny wouldn't take gym because of her gross motor coordination problem and her poor comprehension of game rules."

The counselor gave me a sweet patronizing smile that I desperately wanted to wipe off her smug face.

"Colorado law states that each graduate must have a required amount of gym credits."

"That may be, but when we had our evaluation conference with the district director last June, it was agreed upon that Jenny would be exempt from that. I was told this was done all the time for the special education students who were mentally handicapped. How can you now alter the schedule that the district director already approved?"

"Because it's state law."

I was fuming. "But we *agreed.*"

"I'm sorry, but Jenny *must* take gym this year."

"How about the text books?"

"Pardon?"

"The *text* books! Is Jenny going to be utilizing *lower* grade *text* books this year?"

The counselor looked to the teacher. They both shrugged.

"What *is* it with you people? What *is* your goal as educators anyway? You're just shoving these poor handicapped kids through their grades without even *caring* if they're learning anything?"

"Are you going to sign the schedule?" came the only response.

I signed the damned schedule. "You haven't heard the last of me."

And I left with my daughter. Poor Jenny. She understood most of what her mother was fighting for. She knew I was fighting for her, but the many details were not always clear in her mind.

School started.

Three weeks later, Jenny came home in tears because the kids in gym class laughed at her and called her stupid. She didn't know what to do with the ball when it rolled to her feet during a game.

The following morning I went to school with Jenny. She knew fireworks were going to go off.

I strode into the office and said I was taking Jenny out of school.

"You'll need to fill out an absent form."

"No, no, I mean to say I'm taking her *out* of *this* school."

"Oh, well then you need to fill out a transfer form."

"I don't think so. I'm not filling out *any* form. She's *not* transferring, she's just *leaving* this school."

"Oh, I see. Well then, you need to go to the counselor's office to clear her out."

We strode down the hall.

Counselor was out. I talked to the secretary.

"I'm taking Jenny out of school."

"What time will she return?"

"No, you don't get it. I'm taking her out permanently."

"Oh, then you'll have to go to each of her classes and have each teacher make sure she's returned all her books and. . ."

"I don't think so. Here are all her useless books," I said, slamming the pile down on the desk. "As of this moment Jenny no longer attends this school." And we walked out of the office and out of the school—forever.

Four days later I received a wonderfully supportive letter from one of the special education teachers who worked with Jenny. In a nutshell, he totally agreed with my bold decision and he admitted that the special ed kids were slipping through the cracks.

One week later, Robin hired Jenny at the Loaf n' Jug store and Jenny's self-esteem sky-rocketed, because she was doing things the school had convinced her she could never do. And, on top of that—she was earning wages!

Aimee was also hired to work after school and on weekends. All income was pooled in "the pot" for bills and household expenses. It would be this way as long as we all lived together.

Robin was transferred to Eagle, Colorado. She wondered if she should accept it or not. We discussed it. We'd been trying to relocate in the Glenwood Springs area for several years, but could never find a large enough house for the seven of us that had rent under $1,000 month. So we decided Eagle was a lot closer to our destined area than Woodland Park was, so she should go for it.

One weekend she made a trip over to Eagle and rented a tiny apartment in a converted garage. We helped her move in and Jenny joined her for a month before we could follow.

Robin located a rental house for all of us on Brush Creek Road and we made the move to Eagle in June of 1987.

Jenny and Aimee worked with Robin at the Eagle convenience store. We were finally doing well enough to put something in savings each week, but not well enough to replace either the old pickup or Robin's battered Buick.

While in Eagle, my second book was published and I had my first book-signings to do. . .Glenwood Springs, Vail, and Colorado Springs. I'd also been receiving readership mail since the first book was published in 1985.

I couldn't understand why people wrote to me. I was just here doing what I came to do—my job—I was no better than those who wrote to me. I had a hard time with it.

Behind my back, Bill had called Colorado Springs TV stations to inquire if they'd be interested in doing an interview of Mary Summer Rain, since she'd be down there doing a book-signing. One station set up a noon interview and I was furious. I was a complete nervous wreck. I told Bill I couldn't do it. I told him I'd be too sick to "go on"—I had a nervous stomach since childhood.

So we went to the Eagle clinic for something to calm my nerves. The doctor was real nice. He'd heard of *Spirit Song*; in fact, he ended up coming to my Glenwood signing.

He told me, "You don't want tranquilizers on your medical record. What I'll give you is Beta-blockers. He said concert performers and speakers took them to calm their physical symptoms of nervousness and stage-jitters. I walked away with a prescription for Inderal. It worked better than I thought it would.

When we arrived at the television station I was calm. We stood behind the cameras and watched the newspeople give the news broadcast. Behind us was the interview set. Bright lights suddenly lit up the set and the stage manager touched my arm.

"I need to tell you that your interview may be interrupted if they get Jessica out." (Jessica McClure was being rescued from the hole she'd fallen in). I said I understood. Then she said, "It's time to get into position now."

My stomach turned over.

Then she looked over to Bill.

"You can sit up there beside her on the couch if you like."

"No thanks. She's the author, not me."

Oh! That rat! Here he had the chance to be beside me and give a little support and *he* refused to go on camera.

I stepped up on the platform and let them affix the microphone to my dress. The cameras swiveled in my direction and the newsman positioned himself in the chair. He talked to me a minute to break the ice before we went on the air.

"Nervous?" he asked.

"That's an understatement," I replied.

"You'll do just fine, I can tell these things."

Then, before I knew it, he was talking into a camera and saying my name. I don't remember much after that, except, during the interview, I recall subliminally being upset that they neglected to tell me how to tell which camera was on; which to look into.

When the interview was over, the stage manager and production manager said I'd done a great job and that they'd love to have me back for future book releases. That was very kind, but I thought—fat chance.

Bill had been standing beside the cameraman the whole time and was beaming when I was done.

"Great job, honey, you looked great!"

I gave him the evil eye. "Chicken."

The following day at the Waldenbooks' autographing, another TV camera crew showed up.

I glanced over at Bill.

He was smiling. . .very sheepishly.

That was the first and last time I'd ever do a television interview.

Why I had to fight everyone over doing publicity I couldn't understand. It seemed that nobody could see my point of view. I didn't *want* to be in the limelight. I didn't *want* personal publicity. I never asked for it. I didn't come here for that. Couldn't people understand that I was just a mountain person and nothing more? I absolutely *hated* publicity. I didn't want my picture taken. . .I didn't want a microphone in my face. . .I didn't want TV cameras rolling. . .I didn't want *any* of it! I only wanted people to know No-Eyes. And just because I kept my promise to her didn't also mean I had to make a name for Summer Rain. *No-Eyes* was the name to be known—the *truths* were *all* that needed to be seen and heard. . .not the messenger.

Just because I wrote the books and shared the truths and my thoughts didn't mean I had to be a public personality. I was so adamant about that. I just wanted more than anything to remain in the background shadows where I belonged.

Aimee and Jenny worked at the Eagle Loaf n' Jug all summer and, in the meantime, had met boyfriends. Bill joked about the girls. "When they started working at the store, boys came out of the walls!"

Anyway, the girls really enjoyed their jobs and, when the school season was about to begin I asked Aimee if she wanted to go to the Eagle High School (which was located down the road in Gypsum) or if she wanted to continue working at the store and do home schooling (a choice for Colorado students). She opted for the home schooling. This was in the fall of 1987.

Meanwhile, our Advisors cautioned us that the house we were renting looked like it had a good purchase offer on it. That meant we'd have to move. However, the owners were not telling us this fact. Consequently, if we waited until the official word came down, we'd be forced to move in the middle of a mountain winter.

So Bill and I again journeyed over to the Glenwood Springs and Roaring Fork areas to try to find a rental. We were blocked. There was no room in the inn. We wanted so much to be over in our destined area, and because we were blocked every time we tried, Bill was quickly getting sour grapes on the area.

That hurt, because now he was thinking that maybe we should just return to Woodland Park, where it felt more like home (at least to him).

But I wasn't ready to move that far away from our ultimate location, so we compromised and checked out Leadville where the rents were cheaper.

The first real estate office we were guided to, we found Mary Hewlett, who had a rental house for $400 a month. It was located up on a hill overlooking the town. There were only two homes up there, one was the rental, one was Mary's. The rental was owned by another Mary, Mary Biggs, who was a nurse who had taken a position at Aspen Hospital and was relocating there.

The rental house had four bedrooms, two full baths, a huge kitchen with windows all along the wall that faced the mountain range, and a fireplace. We fell in love with it and we moved in just as it began snowing one evening in November.

Aimee's new boyfriend was an aware young man. He believed in the spiritual truths and the two seemed to be made for each other. When Eric informed us that his family was moving back to California, but that he couldn't leave Aimee, we offered him a home with us. So. . .in the Leadville house, we totalled eight.

Jobs were hard to come by in Leadville. Robin and Eric first got employment in a cafeteria at Copper Mountain Ski Resort. There was a bus that commuted the workers there, but many times they drove.

Then Robin secured a better job at the 7-Eleven store just

down the street from our house. Aimee was also hired there, and they continued on when Kum n'Go company bought the 7-Eleven.

I liked Leadville because it was an old mining town and the people there were so friendly. It was a poor town, but I felt that that was what made me feel so comfortable there. The school had an olympic swimming pool and resident membership was only $20 a year per family. We spent many winter evenings there.

A writer for *Omni* magazine came to see us while we were in Leadville, but nothing became of her day and night-long interview.

A lady spirit walked the rooms of that house, but she was friendly and never bothered us; in fact, she'd get downright playful at times. She had permission to be there in order to gain some deeper understanding she needed. She was not wayward.

The Starborn ones were also active there. It was in the Leadville house where their presence began to increase.

But the town was contaminated with lead from the mines.

Many of the children, when tested, showed elevated levels of the metal in their blood. Our dogs were not well there and, one morning, Aimee descended the stairs like a cripple. It appeared that, overnight, all her joints were painful—she couldn't even open the refrigerator door or pick up a glass of juice.

We took her to the medical clinic, and the doctor thought she had massive arthritis. He prescribed medicine that nauseated her.

I took her off of it.

Then he prescribed massive doses of aspirin and she got ringing in the ears.

I took her off the aspirin and cancelled all future doctor appointments. I put her on licorice, red clover, and yucca. We experimented with doses and combinations, and she began improving to the point where only her hip joint pain was left.

One evening the doctor called to ask why Aimee hadn't been in. Bill answered and handed the phone over to me. "You tell him," he whispered.

When the doctor repeated the question, I answered, "Because you told me there was no cure for arthritis and everything we tried didn't help—they only gave her additional problems."

"Well, yes but, I'd like her to see a specialist in Denver by the name of. . ."

"Doctor, I don't mean to cut you off, but I've put Aimee on herbs and the pain in all her joints has gone except for a little remaining in her hips."

Silence.

"Doctor? Are you there?"

"That's not traditional medicine," he said.

"It's traditional for Indians," I replied.

"Okay, if she gets worse, give me a call."

But I never had to. By the summer of 1988, Aimee was well except for occasional bouts with the hip pain and we decided a lower, dryer elevation would clear that up.

We tried the Glenwood area again—no luck. So in August we moved back to Woodland Park, in a mountain residential area called Ridgewood. Aimee's hip pain cleared up and never returned. She's been good as new ever since then.

Once back in our "old home" area we were welcomed by old friends who were glad to see us back. By now Bill was indispensable as my office partner and publishing liaison. He handled all the business end of talking with the various publishers, editors, book people, etc. He also kept track of print runs and stock for each book I had published. This left me free to answer my mail and meet with people. I also spoke at informal local gatherings when invited. So Bill's job (since Eagle) was to be my office helpmate. I couldn't have handled everything alone by then.

Aimee was doing home schooling and working part-time, and Robin got a job at a convenience store. My publishing monies were just enough to make the household expenses when added to Robin's income.

Off and on during her life with us, since her divorce, her ex-husband would drum up complaints and we'd have to pay her high attorney bills. Although Bill and I were happily married, we still had to continually deal with the stress, aggravation and expense of divorce. It was a constant irritant in our lives, but Robin was a dear friend who we wanted to help, and we loved Mandy as if she were our own (indeed, I'd been caring for her since she was in diapers).

During the time we were living in Ridgewood, a correspondent from Pueblo, who is a university professor, wrote me. He inquired about my children's book. I responded by saying that no publisher knew where to place it in my publishing schedule and that it was a difficult book to sell to editors.

Michael offered to set the type on his computer and he knew someone in Pueblo who could print it for us if I ever thought of self-publishing it.

We didn't have the money, but hoped to cover the printing costs with pre-orders. We did. Later we decided to go out on a limb (financially) and have the book done up proper with a full-color jacket. Ann Marie Eastburn was a reader who wrote me telling me of her art show in the Springs and that she'd love to have me stop by if I had time.

I thought I'd like to do that and, while Bill, Sarah, and I were downtown shopping, we stopped by Ann Marie's display. We connected and I spied a work of hers I thought would be perfect for the cover of the children's book. The artwork was of fairies and gnomes listening to a woodland storyteller. I asked Ann Marie if the artwork was available and she was tickled I was interested in it for a book. She offered it as a give-away. And so the children's book was produced as an official trade book, fancy cover and all.

Bob Friedman called us to say a woman by the name of Sandra Martin was interested in coming out to see me. She used to be a PBS producer and was planning on doing a 13-part series on the paranormal. He said she kept hearing Mary Summer Rain's name from people, so she wanted to come out and see me.

When Sandra came out from Virginia Beach, she had a friend with her. We spent several hours at our Ridgewood house, but talked little of her proposed TV series, other than she'd like me to be a part of it, and she just wanted to get to know me.

A few week's later, she called Bill and said that she wanted to try to sell a movie idea for *Spirit Song*. We needed to have a contract that gave her that right before she went ahead with her film company contacts. Her attorney worked on the details, but it never materialized on my desk. Sandra had decided to become a literary agent, and it looked as if I was to be one of her first clients.

At this time, our Advisors suggested that Bill and I take a trip to Norfolk to visit my publisher (we'd never met). We were concerned about the pickup making that type of long journey. We were encouraged to go, and assured that nothing major would happen. So we went and were glad we did. It took three days of driving 12 hours a day. Bill's eyes were bloodshot by the time we got there, but we enjoyed the trip and liked meeting everyone at Donning. They were more than a little surprised when we walked in, because we hadn't told them we were coming. That's usually the way we do things.

A week after our return home, Bill told me he had a severe pain in his back and I worked on it. The pain left, but then returned, and it was twice as bad. That evening I drove him to the medical center and he was vomiting with the pain—he had a kidney stone that was visible on x-ray and the doctor admitted him to St. Francis Hospital in Colorado Springs.

They gave him a shot and although it did little for the pain, he became more relaxed. I was going to stay the night with him, but he was so sedated by then, I decided to return home.

That evening, all the family psychically worked very hard on him. After the girls and Robin retired, I stayed up most of the night alternating on working on the stone and praying for him.

The following morning there was a thick mist around the house, and as I stood at our deck windows, a brilliant light speared through the fog. It grew and grew. I thought the sun was coming right at me (for this is what it looked like). My heart began beating faster, and I broke out in a cold sweat as I stood transfixed at the window. Then the light began to recede and I heaved a great breath of relief.

At the hospital, Bill was up and in the shower when I arrived.

"Bill? You okay? "

"Hon? That you? Boy, I feel great. Guess what? They came and took me for x-rays real early and they couldn't find the stone. Can you imagine that? The damn stone just vanished! Guess you know who got us a good spirit doctor, huh, Hon."

I handed him the towel. "You know the Dark Side did it, don't you?"

"Yeah, I figured they slipped one by our Guys, but we didn't take long to fix it, did we?"

"I'm just glad you're alright now." And so Bill drove himself home from his overnight stay and, luckily, his hospital expenses were paid by our medical insurance company just before they declared bankruptcy.

That evening, I stayed up late to work on *Earthway*. I took a break around 1 A.M., turned all the lights off and began meditating. A terrible thunderstorm began.

Thunder echoed, rolled and vibrated the house. Lightning was especially brilliant.

During one particularly bright flash I opened my eyes to see a grotesquely tall hooded figure standing before me. The evil power I felt radiating from him was terrifyingly real. I stared at him and into my consciousness came a booming voice.

"YOU. . .WON. . .THIS. . .ONE."

And he vanished.

I'd felt no personal threat from the Dark One, only incredible power. Later, our Advisor said that they allowed the entity's manifestation before me so I could gain a clearer understanding of what we were up against. The dark warriors were very powerful, but then, so are the light warriors.

In March of 1989, I received a letter from my publisher's parent company (a book printing company) which informed me that they had secured a new "distributor" for my books. This new distributor was also another publishing company. When I called Donning about it, they said there were major changes going on. Later we had serious suspicions that this distributor was not merely the distributor because, when Bill called my publisher to get stock figures on my books, as he does once a month, he was told that they no longer had any stock figures and that he'd have to call the "distributor" for things like that now. Something was beginning to smell bad— very bad.

In April, my publisher's parent company contacted us regarding a multiple-book contract offer. We were not interested in committing any more of my works, because our Advisors wanted us to decline all offers.

On the evening of May 2nd, the distributor himself called us and we put him on speaker so we could have a three-way conversation. Robin was sitting on the couch listening, too.

The distributor began talking book contract terms. He was interested in getting as many of my books as possible, and having them released twice a year.

We told him we weren't interested in his offer.

He upped it.

Still not interested. Then I mentioned my agent.

He became indignant and claimed we were trying to make a "whipping boy" out of him.

We were shocked at this attitude. Don't most authors deal through their agents?

This person does *not* deal with author agents.

The conversation ended abruptly.

The following day we received a letter from the distributor stating that we could no longer get stock figures from him, nor could we get any information that wasn't pursuant to contractual terms. Now we saw the light.

On May 10th, Bill called the distributor to try to reestablish a congenial working relationship, and the man said he would not give us any information, and that he doesn't want us wasting his time. Then he hung up on Bill.

On June 25th, Bob Friedman came to Colorado and spent the night with us. While Bob was at our house, he tried to make us understand his precarious position with what was transpiring between my publisher, the printer, and the distributor. He was totally removed from any of their goings-on, did not agree with the business decision, and was planning to leave and start his own company.

The mess my books were in was deeply depressing for me. From the time we first discovered that the distributor was far more than just a distributor, I was very upset. I felt he had literally ripped No-Eyes right out of my arms. I felt he'd kidnapped her from me after I'd worked so hard to shield and protect her essence. To me, my first four books were not ink and paper, they were the very living essence and sacredness of No-Eyes herself, and I was mortified I'd somehow failed her.

I cried and cried over what'd been done to her. I couldn't eat or sleep. I couldn't concentrate on answering my mail and couldn't write. What the three companies had done was literally making me sick and they were also preventing me from carrying on my work. I was so angry and hurt all the time—I just *had* to get my No-Eyes back!

We tried *buying* them back.

Maybe. . .if the price was right. Then, no, they wouldn't let them go.

Bill called my publishing company. "Who is the publisher there now?" There was none. "Who is the editor?" There was none. "Who is the publicist?" Who?

Then he found out that interested advertisers for my books were not to call the publisher, but to call the distributor instead.

Then Bill found out that my publisher was not accepting any more manuscripts. All of them that came in were sent over to. . .guess who? The distributor.

The next little surprise for me was to find my books in bookstores without my publisher's name on them. . .the *distributor's* name was there. What the hell was going on? And

I was furious! My publishing company wasn't even acting *anything* like a publishing company anymore. They couldn't give me any information on my books. And suddenly I felt as though I'd been sold down the river and sent adrift without even knowing it'd been done to me. I was an author with four books out, yet I had no publisher who could tell me anything about them. I had a publisher that was no more than a shell of a building with a few people moving around inside it. When I called the publisher to get some answers, I was told to call the printer, who said the distributor had all that information. When I called the distributor he wouldn't talk to me. And where was No-Eyes? WHO THE HELL HAD MY NO-EYES?

And I was getting nasty letters from readers because I wasn't responding to their letters. They were saying I was just like all the other authors—just out for the "big bucks and nothing more," and that "Summer Rain has lost sight of her purpose!"

Ohhhh, God! Dear, dear, God, what have I done to deserve all of this? Has no one *any* concern for *my* problems? My suffering. Do they *all* think of only themselves? Do they *all* now see me as some moneymonger? Oh God, what am I to do? Just what am I to do?

I was advised to not let the reader's comments hurt me, but that wasn't successful. I tried, but it didn't work. They hurt very badly. I never asked to be an Answer Lady. I offered to help people and I did for five years. Now I'm perceived by some as an egotist with no sensitivity, with only the thought of making money as my goal. Damn. I lost no matter what I did.

We thought of hiring an attorney to get my first four contracts back and we went to see one in Woodland Park. He clearly saw what was going on, but said we'd have a hard time proving it, because we didn't have enough hard evidence.

To compound our problems, our Ridgewood rental house was going on the market to settle a divorce. We had to look for another place to live.

Our real estate property manager didn't want to lose us and we were told to go look at a double A-frame. He said the house used to be a ski lodge and had been vacant for several months because the owners were over in Germany. We drove up 1,000 feet higher than the town and the area was heavily forested. When we got to the house, the view

from there was just beautiful, for the north side of Pikes
Peak was almost touchable.

The house had ski runs cut through the treed hills behind
it and the place itself was all knotty pine inside with a huge
stone fireplace that took up nearly an entire living room wall.
There were four bathrooms and two bedrooms, two lofts and
a mother-in-law quarters we converted into our office. There
was a large unfinished shop and a two-car garage.

We moved in on Sarah's birthday, September 23rd. Bill
and I took one bedroom. Robin and Mandy took the other,
while my girls split up in the two lofts (Eric had returned to
California).

By this time, people were always looking for me and trying to find my house. The place seemed like a good spot to
be in, even though we were only 10 minutes from town.

I rarely went into town anymore. Aimee and Robin now
worked at the City Market. Aimee was a cashier and Robin
worked in the Deli Department. They were frequently asked if
they knew Summer Rain, but on the whole, few people found
my house.

It wasn't that I didn't want to talk to folks or help them
out, but I just didn't see the attraction—I didn't ever see
myself as others did. So I stayed up in my mountains for
weeks on end and worked on my various projects and correspondence when I could.

In August of 1990, Bill made a routine call to Ingram (a
large book distributor) and inquired about how my books
were selling for them. The woman replied, "There's been a
good demand for them. We get inquires all the time, but we
haven't stocked any of Mary's books since January. She's
losing a lot of sales."

We were shocked. Literally shocked. Ingram *always* carried
my books.

After Bill did some in-depth checking with various book
people, he found out there was a little conflict between Ingram and the "distributor," so Ingram no longer carried any
of his books.

I was so outraged. No wonder people were writing, saying
they couldn't find my books!

Bill immediately called the printer to find out what the
hell was going on.

The printer said that the distributor won't sell his books to
Ingram because they don't pay their bills.

What a crock! Most of the nation's bookstores order stock
through Ingram. Would they do that if Ingram didn't pay

their bills to the publishers? So Bill told the printer to "get Mary *another* distributor!"

The following day, Bill talked to a Colorado Springs B. Dalton manager who has always stocked a good supply of my books. Rich told Bill that, when he attended the ABA and spoke to a representative of my publisher, he was told that they were bought out by the distributor.

I could endure no more. I was so desperate to get No-Eyes back I finally wrote the printer and gave him an ultimatum. He voided my first four contracts and returned them to me immediately, or I would go public.

He sent me a letter from his attorneys stating that there was nothing amiss.

I sent out my letters. I sent detailed explanatory letters pleading for public exposure and help. They were sent to the following: *Rocky Mountain News* (Tom Wolfe), *60 Minutes* (Mike Wallace), *20/20* (John Stossel), *Prime Time* (Diane Sawyer), *NBC News* (Tom Brokaw), *A Current Affair* (Maury Povich), and two Denver TV Stations who have investigative departments that claim to help the little guy.

And I only heard back from *20/20*. Seems John Stossel was on assignment, but I was assured they'd contact me whenever they did an exposé on the publishing business.

Shortly after that, we'd heard that some Donning authors were getting a lawsuit together—but I was never approached.

A few week's after I'd heard that information, the attorney for the authors called me. He asked if I'd like to join the lawsuit. I told him I'd love to join, and I did the same day.

I also sent him all the documents I had, and a chronological record of events we'd been keeping, including phone calls and verbatim conversations with the parties involved.

Now I was counselled to "not talk." In essence, the attorneys gently put a "gag order" on me.

We were also counselled by our Advisors. We were advised to "go along" with cordial relationships with the publisher and printer. In this manner, we were able to get our hands on the distributor's stock sheet and royalty estimate for *Phoenix Rising*, which ended up being an Exhibit in the brief.

In late September, friends from Detroit came to visit us for a week. Over dinner one evening, Bill and I were telling them the details of our publishing problems and how they were hurting us. . .emotionally and financially.

Our friends looked at one another. The man was just furious at how I was being duped.

Earthway was finally published, after a rough relationship with my editor. I had too much of the book to rewrite, and I wondered if it was worth it.

When I received my edited manuscript back from the editor at Pocket, I was furious to see nearly every line I'd written had been rewritten. Was I that bad a writer?

Then I had to completely redo the dream section. I had originally arranged the entry words according to subject matter such as Birds, Footwear, Colors, Animals, etc. But the editor said I need to alphabetize them. So I sat down and went through the entire section, picking out all the "A" words, then the "B" words, etc. I then handed the sheets to all the family members to put in alphabetical order. Once that was done, I had to retype the words and definitions all over again.

The Pocket editor also didn't like my astrology section; she said there was nothing different in it.

I explained that it was just supposed to exemplify the *fact* that the planets can and do affect us.

"But you've given your readers nothing different! Didn't No-Eyes have a different perspective on this subject?"

Oh yes, I thought, she surely did, but I was reluctant to include it. But the way the editor was acting, I knew it was time to bring out the Anasazi material. So I told her I'd give my readers "something different."

And when she saw the Anasazi Planetary Chart and detailed pages she loved it.

Then I had to fight to keep in the Earth Mother's Pharmacy section, because it didn't come directly from No-Eyes.

When I saw the jacket—I hated it because it was all *words* and no *feeling*. It finally grew on me, but I still didn't care for it.

And when the manuscript was finally agreed upon by both of us, I was greatly upset to get the bluelines and find *more* changes were done *afterward* without my okay.

Bill got along famously with the editor. He always seemed to get along with everybody, so he handled much of my business with Pocket. In the end though, the editor and I came to an understanding and she was eager to see my next book.

When I sent her *Daybreak*, it was 520 pages too long and she said they just couldn't do it unless I cut the book in half. . .maybe a *Daybreak* I and II would work. I didn't agree to that, because I knew it had to be one volume or nothing. And so the editor released her option, and I was free to take *Daybreak* elsewhere.

I was no longer associated with my agent now—with any agent—and it didn't appear as if I ever would be again, because I found it so much better to do my own talking and dealing, especially after the fiasco of mis-communication that went on with the five-book auction deal. (The former agent tried to sell a package deal that included my first four books, when she wasn't even sure we could get them back—which we couldn't.) Never again would I let another person do my talking, especially when I wouldn't be sure what was being said (or not said). Dealing on the basis of one-on-one directly with your publisher was the only way to lay everything out in a straightforward manner with no misunderstandings. This was the only way to conduct business for me. It was also clear that not having an agent greatly reduced the financial end of the business, but for me, the highest priority was keeping No-Eyes' integrity and presenting the books in a sensitive manner, including choosing my own book covers—*that* was my priority and, by doing this, I did trade off the high roller money for it. Ask me if I care.

Technically, my relationship with my former agent was never a bona fide author/agent one, as we never did sign a contract between us. We met that first day in our Ridgewood house because she requested a meeting about the metaphysical TV series she was going to do. We became friends and, because of her producer connection with other producers, she then became interested in trying for a movie of *Spirit Song*. She had her attorney draw up a contract for the rights, but we were going to revise it and we never did. So we never actually signed anything for it.

When she was out in L.A., she talked to Stephanie Kramer, who was interested in the project. Next, my agent sent the proposal to several screenwriters and they all said *Spirit Song* couldn't be done because so much of it took place on higher dimensions. What a bunch of pooh that was, especially with what the film industry can do now in the way of special effects.

So the film idea just died on the vine as my agent began leaning toward selling books to publishers. Her "agent" job just eased into her life and she wanted to sell my next book (*Earthway*) in a deal that included my first four books. But she was not experienced enough as an agent and so Pocket was upset with ending up with just Earthway and, consequently, my own relationship with the editor suffered because they blamed me too. How could they do that when everyone kept telling me to "stay out of the negotiations" and "authors can't get involved in this" or "you're supposed to let the agent do all the talking."

When the deal for *Earthway* was agreed upon, my agent finally sent me her author/agent contract to sign. She had changed our formerly agreed-upon split of 10 percent to 15 percent. Also I was under the novice impression that the agent got 10 percent of the *initial* sale or *advance* when they sold a book. I didn't realize they also got a percentage of every royalty check to the author.

I admit I was ignorant beyond ignorant about it, but in conjunction with how my deal was handled, I wasn't about to take that kind of an income cut on my writings.

Also the agent told me to "just sign Pocket's contract and return it." There was no *way* I was just going to sign a publishing contract without making changes, additions, and deletions! The agent didn't seem familiar with all the contractual clauses either. In essence, she was cutting her Agent Teeth on me because I was her first author. It was then I knew an agent—especially a brand new one—was not for me and we discussed it.

She then told me that she was disgusted with me because I hadn't pursued the legal aspect with my first four books. She also accused me of always stopping short of my goals, but she couldn't understand that I always had to follow our Advisor's advice every step of the way. If I had proceeded headlong with the legal angle way back then as she wanted me to (and gone against our Advisors), then I never would've gotten all the damaging evidence I did.

So our relationship ended. And when I'd done all my "marking" on the Pocket contract, the agent was in shock when she saw it. She called Bill and said that she didn't realize the author could do all that. She said she'd gotten herself more clients, and she just tells them to sign their contracts.

I then thanked my Advisor for suggesting I go it alone.

In the same conversation Bill had with her, he asked her how the TV series was shaping up.

"Oh, you don't have to worry about that project," she said, "it's moving along."

"I was just wondering where Mary was scheduled in it," he said.

"Oh, I never said she was going to be part of the series. No-no, I never said that at all."

I couldn't believe what Bill relayed when he got off the phone. The initial reason for her contacting me in the beginning was because of the TV series—unless that was just an excuse. But I didn't think so. I went to our files and searched through the file we had on our agent. Sure enough—there in black and white was a letter from her that talked about the series.

We were getting a taste of the publishing business and the flavor was extremely bitter.

With the money from the Pocket advance, we put some away for the IRS, paid our agent off, and the rest went into savings. Then we finally went down to Colorado Springs to buy a new vehicle. We were interested in a four-wheel. We were advised to stay with Chevrolet and also to pay cash. . . I had the money in my purse.

After getting "sticker shock," we realized that a four-wheel wasn't in the cards for us yet because we didn't have enough cash for one, but. . .just as we were about to leave the dealership, I spied a little red Geo Storm GSI. And I fell in love with it. We ended up buying it and the salesman's eyes popped out when I pulled the money bundles from my purse.

"You have it *all?* Right *there*?"

Now, whenever they see Bill and I browsing the showroom again, they ask me if they can hold my purse for me. It became a good joke, because normally I don't have more than five dollars in that purse.

The Storm, which I called Stormy, was great for us that summer because it freed the pickup for Aimee to take to work every day. It also saved us a lot on gas money because Bill and I were then traveling around the state taking photographs of scenery for my future pictorial book. The Storm was great on gas and it felt so, so good not having to worry about a breakdown on top of some mountain pass. In the fall we began to be concerned about not having a four-wheel drive vehicle. Stormy wouldn't be much use in the winter. So we checked our finances and discovered that a new vehicle was an impossibility. . .we just didn't have that kind of cash.

I loved my little red Stormy so much, because I could zip around in it and we'd never had a bit of trouble with it. But I told Bill nonetheless that we could probably get the four-wheel if we traded my Stormy in.

He was amazed that I'd even suggest it, because he knew how much I loved it. But practicality was more important, so that's what we did. And we drove away from the dealership with a 1990 All Wheel Astro Van.

Now it was Bill who had a vehicle he could really depend on—in all seasons, and it felt so good.

My hope is one day to be able to buy Robin a new vehicle of her own and replace that awful old Buick we keep having repaired. I'd like to take my next book advance and surprise her with a four-wheel Tracker or Blazer. That'd delay our land money, but she needs, and certainly deserves, a new and safe vehicle for her and Mandy.

I'd also like to get a Tracker to replace our old pickup, because Aimee needs a safer vehicle to take to work. If we ever manage to get the second Tracker, I already told Bill I'd call it "Rain's Tracker Jack." Bill then told our dealer friend about my plans for two Trackers and what I'd call one of them. Now every time we visit the dealer's, he says, "Mary! I got two great Tracker Jacks for you. Let me hold your purse while you go look at them."

And I always grin, "Sorry, Tom, but the purse is empty today."

I only had my little red Stormy for five months, but in that time, I received several letters from out-of-town readers who were traveling through town and spied me in it. They were not very kind. These people no longer wanted to meet me because "I'd turned flashy!"; and, "Is *that* what you do with all your money?"; and, "I saw you in that ritzy, red sports car. You're just *pretending* to be poor!"; and, "What a disappointment you've become!"

Is there no end to the prejudgments and false assumptions people make of me? For the first time in 14 years we're able to have a new, dependable vehicle, and people resent me for it. I don't get it.

While we were still in Ridgewood and the terrible revelations regarding my publisher were exposed, I had the idea that, if and when I got my first four book contracts back and took them elsewhere, I'd want them repackaged with brand new covers. There was a two-fold reason for this. One: I didn't like the covers of *Spirit Song* and *Phoenix Rising*. I thought the cover of Phoenix Rising was far too depressing, and it reminded me of a dismal swamp. The text material was dismal enough, and I wanted the cover to be more uplifting, to represent the final outcome of the changes. So I planned to redo the first four books whenever a new publisher did them. Two: I wanted to completely "cleanse" those books from any connection to my former publisher. I wanted them to be *re-born*, and rise up fresh and renewed. Right now I feel they're contaminated somehow. Also, when the public sees the new jackets they'll know the books were done by the publisher wearing the "White Hat."

Then one day, I was browsing over the magazines in a drug store in Woodland Park, and spied a *Southwest Art*. I glanced through it and locked onto a painting by Carole Bourdo. My spine tingled. This was the artist I wanted to redo my books.

When I found out she lived in Colorado Springs I nearly jumped for joy. I went home and sat at the typewriter to compose a letter to her. But then the words wouldn't come.

What if she thought it was bold of some nobody writer to ask such a thing of her? Who was I to ask a famous artist if she'd want to do my book covers?

I went over to Bill's desk. He was getting ready to make a business call.

"Bill? Do you think I'm being arrogant asking Carole to do my covers?"

"What do you mean?"

"Well she's famous."

"And you're a piece of dirt?"

I grinned. "You know what I mean. She's probably never even heard of me. Why would someone like her want to do my books? I think she'll think I'm some upstart writer who's being arrogant."

Bill sighed and shook his head. "Look, don't you get letters from all over the world?"

"Yes."

"Don't people try to find you and where you live at least a couple times a week?"

"Well yes, but. . ."

"Haven't you stopped going to town because a tourist is always there looking for you?"

"Well. . ."

"Does that sound like a piece of dirt? Doesn't that sound more like someone who's just a little bit well-known?"

"But I'm certainly not *that* well-known and I'm certainly not famous—at least not like Carole is. And I still feel as though I'm being bold writing to her like this."

"Oh God, honey, will you *can* your self-image for once and just go write the letter."

I knew I was upsetting him so I turned tail and went back to my typewriter. I tried not to sound overly inferior because then Bill would really rail at me.

A week later I received a package from Carole Bourdo.

"Look, Bill! It's postmarked Woodland Park!"

He grinned. "She was probably so excited about your proposal, she drove all the way up here to mail it."

I shook my head. "You never give up, do you? I told you, she probably never even heard of me."

"Open it," he ordered.

I tore the envelope open and found six signed prints of her work. But what amazed me was her letter. She'd just returned from a show tour and, on the way home, commented to her daughter that it'd be her dream to do a book cover for Summer Rain. And everywhere she goes people ask her if she knows Mary Summer Rain.

Bill was reading over my shoulder and when I looked at him he was giving me one of those looks.

I smiled. "I don't believe it. . .but she's *famous*! *She* wants to do *my* books? This is just incredible."

"No it's not. Your self-image is what's incredible. You keep thinking you're a nobody. . .a piece of dirt, but that's not the way the world sees you. When are you gonna wise up and realize how many people you've touched?"

"*No-Eyes* touched all those people, Bill, not me."

"Oh God, I give up."

I hugged him. "Sorry I'm such a pain, but I can't change me. Still love me?"

He grinned. "You're a bad girl, you know."

"I know. I'm bad."

"But I wouldn't change you for the world," and he hugged me back—he hugged me for a long, long while.

I wrote Carole back and explained the publishing mess I was in, and that whenever I got my contracts back we would get together about the new jackets.

Many months went by.

I was getting depressed and decided I'd have her do the covers for the two novels I had written. They weren't scheduled until a few years in the future, but I wanted to start getting my ducks in a row. I get restless if they're not all lined up.

Bill called Carole and we arranged a meeting at her home. I was so nervous to meet her.

When we arrived, she came out to greet us and she was so beautiful. The light around her was radiating warmth and beauty. I knew right then I'd chosen well.

We hugged one another and went inside. Her house was so cozy, it was filled with nature and native things. Her paintings were unbelievable.

We were offered tea (Bill hates tea), and I showed her my two novel titles and tried to explain my sketchy ideas for the artwork.

Carole was all smiles and after a half-hour, we were talking and laughing like old, old friends. We found out how much we had in common.

We both were from Catholic families. We both couldn't prove our native blood heritage (mine Shoshone, her's Blackfoot). We both had a Chicago church connection (my aunt was a nun there, she worked there). And there was one more "coincidence." When Carole went to a cupboard, she began telling me about a children's book she'd illustrated while in Chicago. It was called. . .

"*Observations of Orpheus Owl,*" I said. "I have that!"

Her mouth dropped. "*You* have one of these?" she asked, holding up the little book.

"Yes! My aunt was a nun in Chicago and when one of the people at the convent wrote a book, she sent me one for my girls.

"But there were only one thousand printed!" And then Carole too knew that we were destined to connect and work together.

The next time Bill and I visited Carole's house we brought Jenny and Sarah. Carole had just finished her gallery, set up in a separate building on her property, and she'd done a beautiful job.

In the center of the gallery was a couch and coffee table. When I saw that table I went nuts. It was a large bear on its back and three paws supported the glass tabletop. It was all carved out of a solid piece of pine by a man in Woodland Park. I imagine it was very expensive. I told her I was going to steal it some night.

That bear table became a joke with us. After we were all back in her house, she and I were laughing our heads off (we all were) when she admitted that she was so scared to meet me that first time. . .because I was so famous! She said she wondered what to offer us in the way of beverage, and naturally came up with tea. Now she always has Pepsi. And she didn't smoke in front of us that first time and we wouldn't smoke in her house. Now we are more open.

We laughed and laughed over how silly each of us had behaved, as we each thought the other was more famous than ourselves.

Carole said, "I remember telling my daughter that I'd give *anything* to do a Summer Rain cover."

"You said what?" I said.

She repeated it. And then I said, "You'd give *anything?*"

"Oh yeah!"

"Well. . .there's a bear table out in your. . ."

And we all laughed again.

But the business end of that visit was to give her the titles of nine books to create artwork for. She was thrilled.

I had a few mock-ups of my ideas for several of them and she liked them. She couldn't wait to get started.

When Pocket released my option for *Daybreak,* Bill immediately called Bob Friedman at Hampton Roads and asked him if he wanted it.

"Sure I want it, but I can't match Pocket's money."

"We know," Bill said. "Mary has a few terms though. She wants control of her cover art. She wants her book titles listed on a separate page in front of the book, and she wants to reestablish the same title type (script) as her first four books. She wants all her books to be consistent."

"No problem," Bob said.

"Okay then, work up your best offer and get it to us as fast as you can."

The following day Bob faxed us his offer. It was not as much as Pocket's advance for *Earthway,* but I didn't care about that, because I had nearly total artistic control and I need that in order to control how the books were visually presented to the public. That was so much more important to me than the money end.

Bob said he'd get the contract out right away, so I could work on it, and that he was scheduled to get out his spring catalog in a few weeks. . .it'd be great if he could include *Daybreak* in it with a mockup cover.

I thought that'd be great too, but I didn't want a mockup cover in the catalog. I wanted the real thing.

I called Carole.

She had the cover ready in three days. Could we run down and approve it?

When we got to her house and saw the cover, we were amazed that she'd created it in so short a time. She sent Bob the transparency and he loved the painting. We had the actual cover of *Daybreak* for Hampton Road's January catalog.

And I told Bob I'd decided to make Carole's work be a "signature" for all my books. He had no problem with that and thought it'd be a great idea. When Bill and I thought about it, we didn't think that had ever been done before in the publishing industry. Carole would end up having her artwork on nine of my 12 books. My children's book was already done by Ann Marie Eastburn, and I'd previously chosen another of her works for my *Ancient Echoes* title. Pocket, of course, did *Earthway.* Carole was just as excited as we were.

In November of 1990, I was struck down by a gallbladder attack. I had to have the organ removed and Bill was sick with worry that, for some reason, I wouldn't come back. Since this incident was detailed in *Daybreak,* I won't repeat myself here other to say that, when I was wheeled out of the recovery room and was met in the hall by Bill and the girls, I kept saying, "See? *told* you I'd be back." But although they tried to smile, their faces were very concerned—later I learned that that was because I *looked* so damned bad.

Because our insurance company went bankrupt, we had no insurance and had over $10,000 in medical expenses to pay. We had little in savings and Bill berated himself for getting the van for our twenty-fifth anniversary just the month before. He considered selling it, when a friend of ours offered to loan us the medical bill money.

I was so relieved to hear that, because I needed to recuperate now without having to worry about how we were going to pay off all that money.

Our friend was coming out that morning and I was happy to be having a visitor. Then she called Bill to say she was sorry, but she couldn't help us after all.

Bill was furious. I was worried. And he did something I never would've let him do if I'd have known about it—he wrote to 50 of my closest readers requesting a little assistance in our unexpected time of need.

We heard back from 10. Of the 10, some could help a little.

"How is it," he said, "that people expect you to drop everything and help them with their problems and answer all their questions again and again, but when *you* need a little something in return, it's a completely different story?"

He sat on the edge of my bed and I took his hand.

"Because that's why we came back, Bill. We're *here* to give help—not receive it." And I told him I wished he hadn't asked anyone for help. By then he wished he hadn't too.

But with the loving care of my doting family, I was back to normal energy capacity in five week's time and with the advance payment for *Daybreak* we managed the IRS payments, and a good portion of the hospital bill. The rest we chipped away at as best we could because Aimee and Robin's income was less than our monthly expenses and we had to draw from savings each month to make them. Land money was non-existent as of this date. But my readers thought we were all settled long ago with property, a big house, an office staff, and lots and lots of money.

Many of my readers send me photos of their newly-purchased land and, although I'm happy for them, I get a twinge of longing for the day when we too can afford our final "home."

One day I opened a letter that had more of these photos, and when I saw the log cabin and river and towering mountains behind them I just stared at them. If I could've drawn a picture of what I've always envisioned for us—those photos would have been it. One photo of the cabin was a winter scene, and there was a foot of snow on the roof.

I began reading the letter. It was from the former owner

of the property who said it was being rented—it'd been for sale for *eight* years and was located in a most beautiful spot. That was within our destined area of the White River National Forest!

The letter detailed the property. The log cabin had four bedrooms, two-and-a-half baths, living quarters over the two-car garage, a bunk house and shop, a small guest cabin right on the rushing river, a waterfall coming down the mountains behind the property and a stream in front from the waterfall—all on 20 acres. The place also had an Indian spirit guarding it.

The former owners also strongly felt that the spirit was "holding" the place for us (because it hadn't sold in 8 years). She also said that the mountain behind the property had a Phoenix shape on the side of it. My heart pined for the property, but when Bill called the correspondent in Grand Junction, he said he thought the owners were asking around $160,000 for it. That was way beyond our means and my hopes were dashed. Still, I couldn't get this property out of my mind, and when we asked our Advisor about it we were told that this was indeed one of our land probabilities because they all were occupied by one or more Guardian Spirits. When we asked why he hadn't told us about it, he replied that he just did (through prompting the correspondent to send us the photos).

Many nights I'd pull those photos out and envision us all there, especially those times when I'd be down and wondering if we'd ever be home.

At the end of May, Bill and I took a trip to try to find the property. We stopped in a particularly tranquil area and spent time meditating by a river —we had the entire area to ourselves that day. Clouds hung low and drifted silently between the towering pines. There was a High Sacred mood to the atmosphere, and we felt the strong presence of a great power in the area.

We continued down the road. My psyche was sparking. A moment later. . .there was the property with the river rushing beneath a bridge and the high waterfall cascading down the mountainside beyond the house. Clouds, drifting low, gave an immediate feeling of foreboding and I smiled at Bill.

"You feel it, don't you."

He said he did. "It's what's keeping buyers away. The spirit's doing it."

"Do you get beneath it?" I asked.

"Oh yeah, yeah. When I look at it all my former negative

feelings for the area are gone. I feel real positive about this place—it's right."

"And do you feel something beneath *that?*"

More intently, he scanned the mountains. I told him to center on the two mountains behind the property that were situated as a towering wall.

"Caves," was all he said. "Yes, caves."

"And do you get an association with those caves"?

He gave me a very serious look. "The Starborn ones."

I smiled wide.

On the long four-hour drive back to Woodland Park, I talked of my plans to build a sunken kiva (an underground ceremonial room) with a domed top on our property. I wasn't interested in sweat lodges nor medicine wheels, as everyone else was—I always knew I had to construct a large kiva. And when I saw that property, I also saw the finished kiva back by the base of those mountains near the waterfall.

Because of my increased contacts with the Starborn ones, I knew that my books were not my only ultimate destiny—they were rather the stepping stones to it. And this destiny involved the Starborn ones. So when we received the identical impressions upon seeing the Marble property, I knew why I'd been so driven to complete the book series so long before their scheduled publication dates. I now had all 12 complete, yet *Daybreak*, the sixth, was just released.

This fact underscored the approaching time for my true destiny to commence. But. . .I had to be settled first, and now I feared the chosen property would sell before we had the money to purchase it, for we were advised never to mortgage our land. . .we had to pay cash, so it would be ours . . .free and clear. . .forever. I would not receive that kind of money from my writings, but our Advisor said that a lawsuit settlement *would* bring it. How ironic that thought was. How ironic it would be that the publishers who stole No-Eyes from me would also be the vehicle to return her and provide the means to take me home. How little we see the good ends that can ultimately come from bad. If this proves true, without negative probabilities interfering, then the Advisors were certainly very wise by cautioning us to be patient and play dumb with the printer and distributor for so long, because, during that time, we had indeed amassed a ream of evidence against them.

And so we wait for the attorneys to redo their brief again. We wait still longer for the suit to be filed. Patience is wearing thin these days, for now I have the feeling we're in a race to get a settlement before the Marble place sells to someone else. Although I know that, if it does, there are alternative properties for us that will serve just as well. It's just that I haven't *seen* those, so they're not as close to my heart as our chosen spot is.

It's very hard being on a starvation diet and have someone waft chocolate cake under your nose. We'd been waiting to get on our land for 14 years—that's a long, long time to starve for something we could now see before us and actually taste. . .and that made this current waiting time all the harder. This is why I'd pace the darkened house waiting for my Starborn connections to appear again. They knew how anxious I was to get on with things, but alas, *I* knew it was useless to force the issue before the destined time had manifested. But I paced anyway. . .I always wanted to discuss it one more time. . .just in case things had changed—as they've been known to do.

The Starborn ones began their physical contact with us when we lived in the house on Chester in Woodland Park (after moving back from Marquette).

I'd had contact with them with No-Eyes at her place, but it was on Chester that they began visiting us. This contact was not two-sided, for they would seem to appear out of the corner of our eyes and then not be there when we looked straight on.

Then one day, when Jenny was sitting in the living room, she looked up and saw a white face looking back as it peered around the kitchen archway. It scared her and she looked away, but when she looked back it was gone. The same thing happened to me also on several occasions and, believe me, it makes your hair stand on end and your heart begin to thud.

Then, in Leadville, the manifestations were more of a strong presence (other than the lady spirit). This presence gave one the immediate visual of their appearance. Several times when I'd be up late with just the oil lamp burning on the kitchen table and the house was dark, the white face with large dark eyes would peer at me from around the doorway. My heart would skip some beats and I'd break out in a cold sweat, but I'd keep on writing my rewrite of *Phantoms Afoot.* It'd do no good for me to run to bed and pull the covers over my head, because they'd appear there too. So, little by little, they were breaking us in to their presence.

In the Ridgewood house (the one Bob Friedman stayed overnight in), our visitors became more active.

One night, around 2 A.M., when I was up working on *Earthway,* I subliminally heard our wooden deck blinds clank together. This was a sound that didn't compute, because the glass sliding doors to the deck were shut and locked. The only way the wooden curtains could clank together was if they were being opened or moved. Nobody else was awake and the dogs were sleeping soundly at my feet. I'd heard a sound that was, it seemed, impossible. So I ignored it and kept on writing. . .until. . .out of the corner of my eye. . .I saw a tall white figure move from the blinds to behind the free-standing bookcase that separated the kitchen from the living room.

My skin crawled. I *knew* one of them was standing behind that bookcase.

I set my pen down and walked to our bedroom. I left the stove light on all night.

And so it was that each manifestation was more bold than the one before it. This was to ease us into an acceptance of their physical presence. The night Bob Friedman slept at our house I hoped they wouldn't manifest before him, because it's very terrifying at first and I didn't know how strong his heart was.

And so I was eased into a comfortable acceptance of them.

When we got to our current house, I went to bed one night, but tossed and turned so much, I went back down to the living room and settled on the couch. Rainbow was asleep on the floor beside me. I covered myself with one of my Indian blankets and fell asleep. Aimee and Sarah were asleep in the front loft right above me.

What stirred me from my sound sleep was the sound of our front door opening. But, subliminally, I knew that couldn't be, because Rainbow would've been raising hell with an intruder. And I drifted deeper into sleep. Then something else woke me. . . my blanket was being removed. Unseen hands were raising it at my feet and shoulders.

I sat up and called for Sarah, but no sound came out my mouth. I didn't remember anything after that.

When Sarah got up for school the following morning and Aimee got up for work, they came downstairs and was surprised to see me sitting up on the couch.

"Mom, they came again last night. The fresh air smell was real strong and I could've sworn I heard the front door open but the dogs weren't barking."

Then Aimee sat beside me. "Sarah's right, mom. They did come. Last night a bright light woke me up. It was shining right through our windows. At first I thought it was headlights reflecting off the glass from a passing car, but then I realized they usually don't shine that high up in our loft.

That light was shining *down* into it. That's all I remember because I fell right back to sleep."

"Well," I said, "the front door did open last night. I was on the couch because I was too restless upstairs. The sound of the door woke me but I dismissed it because Bo wasn't barking. But then the blanket was being lifted and I screamed for you, Sarah. That's all I remember. God, it's so clear."

And that was the beginning of *our* visits to *them*.

When I told Bill about it, he asked our Advisor if it was real or a dream.

"It was real," came the answer. "You're being eased into your destiny."

So now Bill wanted to "go for a ride." He said he planned to sleep on the couch that night.

"You think it's a magic carpet or what?" I teased. "If they want you it doesn't matter where you're sleeping."

He grinned. "Humor me."

So that night he followed through with his plan. I got ready for bed and came back down to kiss him goodnight.

"How come you got all your clothes on? You're not going to sleep very well in your jeans."

"Hey, I'm not going for a ride in my skivvies!"

"Oh, but it's alright if *I* do. For God's sake, all I had on was my *birthday suit* beneath that robe!"

He grinned. "Poor planning."

"Hope they drop you." Then I kissed him. "Happy flying."

When I awoke the following morning, I had the strong impression that he too had gone for a ride, but he said he was so anxious that he was awake nearly every hour or so.

"It doesn't take them but a couple minutes," I said. "I'm sure you went."

Then he admitted to his strange experience.

"I was awakened by movement. . .of my own body. I was levitating off the couch and all I can remember is thinking, 'This is *neat!*'"

"Well, why'd you say nothing happened then?"

"Because I thought maybe I was dreaming. I was awake so much I couldn't justify the experience as being real."

The Advisor confirmed a visitation.

Later that day Aimee came to me and said she'd seen the bright beam of light shine down through her windows again last night and wondered if I had any disturbances during the night. Then I told her about Bill's experiment. She thought that was nice that Dad went too.

Not all the Starborn manifestations were for the purpose of personal communication. They'd be in the house at night for various other reasons.

One night Aimee got up to go to the bathroom and took sleepy subliminal note of a bright beam of light that speared right down through the ceiling and floor. Her thought was, "Oh, they're doing something again," and that was that. She returned to bed.

I seem to be the only one who's had conscious contact with them. And it's developed to the point where I wait up for them to come and talk. And so this brings the issue up to date. Now they and I seem to be at an impasse, because I want us to move forward with what we're here to do and they say, "It's not time yet."

So as of 2:30 A.M., June 23, 1991, I can sit up writing in this journal with complete confidence that I will not be visited—at least not for the purpose of conversing about The Plan—because lately, all we do is go 'round and 'round about it. I think they're avoiding me. . .what else is new.

But they're still here just the same. Evidence of this was made clear when, last month, our neighbor's house burned to the ground. It happened in the middle of the night when sounds carry so easily in these quiet mountains. Fire trucks, water trucks, firemen shouting and bellowing to each other . . .yet. . .all seven of us, including the two dogs *never heard a sound*, even though our bedroom window and deck doors were opened.

Normally Rainbow and Magic go crazy if they hear the slightest noise outside—especially at night. I felt like a fool when the fire investigator came to interview us for the owner's insurance company. What could we say? We all slept through the whole thing. Our Advisor informed us that the Starborn ones kept us all asleep so we wouldn't be alarmed by the neighbor's fire. Our house was being protected, so there was no cause for us to know what was going on.

Still. . .neighbors looked askance at us when we had to admit we hadn't heard a thing and had slept through it all.

"The *trees* were on fire!" one neighbor said. "How could you *not* know that it was burning so close to your house? The fire trucks were making a racket. The entire neighborhood was up!"

What could I say? What could I do but shrug.

"Guess we're real sound sleepers."

But in our hearts, it was comforting to know how well we were watched over. The incident just became another situation that underscored our proof that we weren't imagining things. Our happenings were real because *they* were real. The Starborn ones were our friends. . .they were definitely real!

The filing date for the law suit has been delayed five

times and each time was agonizing for me, for every moment that No-Eyes was held hostage by the distributor and printer was a moment that I felt I'd failed to protect her.

When the filing date was postponed the third time, I'd written a letter to the attorneys stating that, if it wasn't filed within the next week, they were to file on my behalf separately, or remove my name from the suit, so I could then try to go public again.

When I'd found out my four contracts were sold to the distributor for one dollar, the pain of it was increased a hundredfold. Was that all my No-Eyes was worth to these people?

Although we were advised that all would be filed in due time, the day-to-day stress was taking its toll and I think I aged at least a hundred years because of it.

During this waiting time, Bill called the printer to request the return of my children's manual negatives (we wanted to be sure we had them in our possession and out of his hands by the time he was served with his summons).

The printer asked Bill if we were dissatisfied with the price we were paying. Bill said no, but we just wanted the manuals done locally—in Colorado—to save on shipping and freight costs.

The printer agreed to send us our negatives, and then commented that he'd still like to keep doing Mary's future No-Eyes books. They were interested in anything I had. Bill nearly choked when he heard that, but he recovered well, and said that Mary had already made other arrangements for her next book.

When we received the children's book negatives back, it felt so good to have them out of the printer's hands. I only wished that I also had No-Eyes too.

Bill called around trying to locate a local printer for the manual and wasn't having much luck until he called C & M Press in Thornton, Colorado, who gave him a reasonable price quote for having 1,000 copies done. We couldn't afford to pay for more than that at one time. Also, C & M Press said they'd ship the books directly to our front door via Best Ways freight company for free—no freight charge. So in the end, we'd get the books done for about the same price that "the printer" was doing them and they'd be produced right here in Colorado. That was a big load off my mind.

Bookstores and book distributors were still calling us at Lodestar Press, trying to get the children's book for their stores and warehouses. I realized I could've sold thousands of them by now by making them available through bookstores around the country, and I was losing out on a lot of money just because I wanted to make them special by autographing them to each child. I compromised sales and, ultimately, our income, because of this, but I still wanted to personalize each manual.

We have no staff in our home for Lodestar Press. I open all the mail and when we receive book orders, Bill and I don all the hats needed to get the books out. He keeps the records and makes out the envelope addresses, and I sign and package the books. He takes them to the post office the following morning when he picks up our mail.

We have no high-tech facilities—no computers for mailing lists or ordering record keeping. Bob Friedman keeps hounding me about putting my manuscripts on disk, but we don't have a computer and I'm not about to get one either, especially when all my manuscripts are already typed up and ready to go. I'm a simple person and not technically inclined. I hand-write all my manuscripts. Then I type them up. After they sit for a few months, I'll go over them and do a rewrite to improve clarity, descriptions, or add things I'd left out. Then I do a final typing of the complete manuscript. When that's done, I read it over carefully to proof for errors and typos. I fix them. And then the manuscript is put to bed in my file cabinet until its scheduled year of publication comes up.

I do get plenty tired of my books by the time they're published, because not only have I already gone through it four times before I send it to the publisher, I have to go through the editor's editing of it. Then, when it's set in type by the publisher, I have to check through each word and comma of that typeset (galley) form. Then the galleys go into bluelines and I have to proof each word and comma of the bluelines, because those negatives are what the final book is printed from. So by the time one of my books appears on the bookstore shelves, I've gone through it at least seven times. Whoever said "writing isn't a real job" obviously never tried it. When I got my first bluelines I was living in Eagle, and I thought I'd go out and soak up some sun while I proofed them. Wrong. What soaked up the sun was the photo-sensitive paper. . .the pages started turning a dark blue! I ran in the house like a swarm of killer bees were after me. There sure was a lot to learn.

When we decided to go ahead and self-publish the children's manual and establish Lodestar Press in our home, Bill subscribed to the magazine of the publishing industry, *Publishers Weekly*. This was not a good move. Now we saw how much money many "first time" authors were making, and it especially pained me when these "first novels" were explicit sex or murder and crime stories. I felt the beauty of No-Eyes was smothered by the public's base, prurient interest. And when the *Publishers Weekly* put out specialty issues where No-Eyes' material should've been included—she never was. There was an issue on Natural Healing Books, but *Earthway* was never mentioned. There was an issue on Native American books, but No-Eyes was never mentioned (that was the distributor's fault because *he* held those books). There was an issue on metaphysical books; again No-Eyes was never mentioned (again the distributor's fault). . .and an issue on New Age and Prediction Books—no mention of No-Eyes (the distributor again missed the boat).

So reading through the publisher's bible each week was deeply depressing for me, because it was as though No-Eyes didn't exist. It was as though having 400,000 books in print (mine) meant nothing at all and made no waves anywhere.

Pocket had a beautiful opportunity to latch onto the general public's new heightened awareness of the Earth with *Earthway*, but they had no foresight, no general advertising, nothing but a couple of ads in two New Age magazines—when the public at large was so primed for it. And when I receive reader's letters saying they can't find *Earthway* I get very, very upset.

So as it stand right now, when I get my first four contracts back from the law suit, I'm planning on taking them all to Bob Friedman at Hampton Roads, even though Pocket already offered $80,000 for them if I take them there. Why would I turn down $80,000 and sell all four to Bob for less? Because he truly respects No-Eyes and my purpose. He also understands my deep feelings about how I want the books presented, and gives me the artistic (cover art and type style) control. Bob also doesn't fool with altering what I need to say—all his editing is strictly punctuation, typos I've made and missed in the proofing, and fine-tuning of the prose. Being able to say *what* I need to say and having the freedom to say it *how* I want to say it is a high priority to me. Being able to present No-Eyes as she needs to be presented (in my perspective) is priority to me. The mega-bucks are not priority—and that's exactly why we're not settled on our land yet. But to go about it in any other way would be to personally sell my integrity and self respect—it would also be selling No-Eyes out. These books are a part of my heart because they're about No-Eyes, who was definitely a part of my heart. I have an intense inborn need to protect her essence, and will do whatever I must to hold firm to that goal.

If I must remain poor to do it then that is the result of my own choice, but I'd never, ever resent that choice, even if it means never getting our land. People just don't understand how important these books are to me. They just don't see that I perceive all these books as being the living essence of No-Eyes herself. . .they are pieces of my heart. . .fragments of my soul. . .our soul sounds.

And they don't see me cry myself to sleep at night for want of her touch again. No one knows how badly I still ache for her physical presence. Although her spirit is frequently beside me, it's just not the same, and my heart bleeds when it pines for the old days. Oh God, how I *miss* you, No-Eyes! Why couldn't you have stayed just a little bit longer? I don't even have Many Heart now either; at least we could've shared our memories of you together. Oh, I feel *so* alone. . .so, so alone without you.

I need to explain what I meant by what I wrote last night. When I say I feel alone without No-Eyes, I mean the "special relationship" we shared and the one-of-a-kind bond we shared that was so unique and rare between friends. I have so few friends—Bill too. We've always seemed to be loners throughout life. We've had friends—but not real ones that share an unconditional friendship. . .except, of course, for Robin.

Robin was always there for us, just as we've always tried to be for her. She felt a great pull toward us right from the beginning, and that came from deep within her spirit, for she too came back with a mission to again be a helpful friend to us. She had been of the Essenes and, in biblical times, was there to assist us as we played out other roles. When she met us in this life, her soul memory engaged and knew the three of us would always be closely associated.

And so that has come to pass, for she was in a position to give Jenny and Aimee jobs to help with our finances and, whenever Robin lived with us (which has been most of the time), she always unselfishly gave of her own income to the "pot," so household expenses could be met.

It can't be easy for a grown woman to have all her possessions in one room all the time instead of having her own place, but we, in turn, provided the nice homes for her and Mandy to live in. Robin always has her laundry done for her, meals provided, car insurance paid, medical expenses, and attorney fees paid. She never had to worry about a babysitter for Mandy either, because Mandy was a part of our own family and my girls were always like her older sisters. So it was an equally synergic relationship. Her added income al-

lowed us to be about our work and she, in turn, had everything taken care of for her. The only aspect regarding Robin
that I regret is that she does want a lifemate, and she's never
been able to connect with one who is spiritually aware of the
truths and not into the "materialistic" or "ego" side of life.
She turned 36 last May and my heart breaks for her aloneness. She is such a sweet and good person.

Robin is one of the reasons I hope our chosen property
works out, because she and Mandy could then live in the
guest cabin by the rushing river. To have her own place and
still be on our property with us has been her dream since we
first connected in 1977. And I still hope to buy her a new
vehicle (Tracker) to replace that horrible Buick she's been
forced to drive for so long. Although the car's upholstery is
falling apart and we always have it in for repairs, we all
make a joke of her "junker"; but rarely does she complain
about it because she knows we just can't afford a replacement right now. For her last birthday we were planning on
surprising her with a Tracker with a big bow on it, but my
hospital expenses got in the way.

When I said I felt alone before, I didn't mean to make
my family sound like they weren't supportive or a comforting
factor in my life because they are—they're the lights of my
life and have deep compassion for the long struggle they've
watched their parents go through for the sake of a spiritual
mission.

Jenny will be 22 on September 2nd and, despite her learning disability, has been a complete lifesaver to me because
she manages our entire household of seven people. She cleans
the house, does all the laundry, plans menus for the week,
does the grocery shopping and cooking. This has allowed us
to concentrate on our work eight to 10 hours each day. In
turn, we pay her each Friday for all her work. Jenny really
can't work outside the home because she gets too frustrated
in a job situation and would think nothing of "telling her
boss off" (this lack of attention to social etiquette is part of
her disability). But my heart breaks for Jenny too because she
frequently talks about when she's married and has children of
her own. As a caring mother, I want her dreams to come
true, but am concerned about the right "aware" young man to
come along for Jenny. He will have to be a very special one.

All my girls want to live in separate cabins on our property with their own husbands, but it will take the "right" young
men to also want that. Aimee, now 19, has had several false
starts with young men. She has been totally disgusted with
them because they've either been too into themselves, want to

party all the time, or have been too materialistic. Only one was spiritually aware and they'd met in Eagle.

Eric was perfect for Aimee. He was "aware" and artistic (an artist). They were going to be engaged and when Eric's parents moved back to California, he couldn't leave Aimee. We took him in because he was all alone and young (18). They were so right for each other and were so happy.

Eric lived with us in Leadville. In *Phantoms Afoot* I gave him the name of "Mike." Then, when we moved back to Woodland in the Ridgewood house, he came there too.

But Eric began missing his family and, when his dad came back to Colorado to do some hunting, Eric went along with him. When Eric returned home he dropped the bomb on us—he was going back to California with his dad.

Aimee was heartbroken and so were we, because Eric had become the son we never had.

A year later I received a letter from Eric. He was in Vallejo, then San Jose, going to college to get his art degree. He told me how sick at heart he'd been for hurting Aimee and said he still loved her.

Last February, he wrote again and said he needed to come back to talk to Aimee because she was still in his heart. He said he'd done a great deal of growing since he'd been away and now knows who he is.

Aimee would have nothing to do with Eric when I told her he wanted to talk to her.

"I hate him. He hurt me so bad."

"But Aimee," I said, "until you two have it out, until you shout and argue and say it all face-to-face, how can you ever see what's there under the hate?"

She listened.

"Aimee, you *need* to face Eric. You need to get all that hate out by screaming at him. Then you need to get all the hurt out by crying with him. Only then will you be able to know what's left.

"Eric needed to find himself—to *know* himself—before he really knew what he wanted in life. Now that he's done that he sees he still loves you after all this time. And most important of all. . .you need to see if you still love him."

"I don't," she said.

"Aimee?"

"I won't see him when he comes."

"Yes you will. You *need* to. You need to get it all out."

"No I don't."

"Why don't you?"

"I just don't."

"You say that because you're letting the hard shell of hate hide the flame of love you suspect you still might have."

"Well he deserves to hurt too."

"And he did, Aimee, he still does hurt. Don't you think he blames himself all this time for being the *cause* of your hurt? Aimee, you know our Advisor said that Eric was one of the possibilities for you this life. And I know that, deep down, you still love him. Don't you think it's only right to resolve this thing? I would never force a relationship, you know that, but you two need to resolve this one way or another before you both can be completely free to know your own hearts. Are you afraid to do that, Aimee?"

"Afraid to do what?"

"To know your own heart. Are you afraid to face Eric, cry and see what's there when all the nasty words have been said?"

Silence.

"Aimee?"

"Yes"

"You still love Eric, don't you."

"Maybe."

And that finally said it all. Not only for me, but mostly for her.

Meanwhile, we're presently waiting to hear again from Eric. He was planning on moving back to Colorado, so I give him time to make his arrangements.

So Aimee has had relationships since Eric left, but she's been so disappointed. Personally I see she's secretly comparing them all to Eric, but none of them are coming close. I do pray these two work things out—they were so right together.

Now Aimee's thrown her energies into joining the Woodland Park Volunteer Fire Department. She's always wanted to work in the medical field or something comparable where she's in a position of helping people. She works eight hours a day as a cashier in the grocery store and then goes to training classes at night. The other firefighters think the world of her and tease her because she's so petite. Her full bunker gear weighs 70 pounds, but Aimee only weighs 90. But they say they need small firefighters, so she's trying real hard to pass all her tests.

Yesterday she surprised them by handling the fire hose that had 125 p.s.i. of water shooting out of it. Soon she'll be tested on ladders and, at the end of July, will have her big test in full gear at "the tower" where the real "burn" is to take place.

Last week, while she was at the fire station, a call came

in from Search and Rescue. They needed help to find two little lost girls in Woodland Park. Aimee went out with the crew and helped search. They found the girls and Aimee came home just glowing with her "high."

I was very concerned when Aimee first asked me if she could join Search and Rescue or the Volunteer Fire Department because such work places one in very dangerous situations—not only that, but she's very aware of the Dark Side taking advantage of such times. But I knew Aimee desperately needed something worthwhile in her life—the dating aspect was a complete bust for her. I could see her restlessness to be *doing* something helpful, so I talked Bill into letting her join.

We can't keep our kids in a safe basket all their lives and we have to go about whatever we feel is part of our purpose (and theirs) no matter what the challenge or danger that purpose presents. Aimee felt drawn to the firefighting, even though she's a 90-pound china doll. Now her restlessness is gone and she's happier than I've seen her in a very long time. I still have a mother's natural concern for her, but on the other hand, I don't worry. She must be free to walk her destiny and I pray her guide and the Light Warriors will walk beside her—more I cannot do.

Sarah, 16 this coming September 23, 1991, is my little nature sprite. She's an animal lover and woodswalker. Sarah is incredibly shy, but beautiful with thick blond hair down to her waist. Sarah has a main fault—she thinks she must be a real loser because she's never had a boyfriend. Bill keeps trying to tell her that boys will shy away from an extra pretty girl, but she's not quite buying that one.

Tomorrow is her last day of driver's ed class. She was a nervous wreck driving down in Colorado Springs and on the interstate but her instructor said she did fine.

Robin has been letting Sarah drive her Buick to practice in. Robin's car has been the "training car" for Sarah (Aimee too when she was learning to drive). Bill's nerves got frayed when he took Aimee out to learn to drive when we were living in Leadville. Aimee drove up our steep hill, made the turn and drove right into Eric's car.

But Sarah seems to be more mentally centered than Aimee was at that age (remember, Aimee was the hyper one when little). Sarah gets mostly "A's" in school and is an excellent artist. She really liked Eric because they both were interested in art and woodswalking, while Aimee is the typical "girl type" who can't even hammer a nail. . .but she sure can wield a fire hose now!

Sarah too has reached the age where she wonders if there will be a spiritually-aware young man out there for her. Our Advisor has assured them all that they would connect with their mates after we were finally settled. Still—it's a concern for them and I can certainly understand it, especially when they see Robin still waiting and waiting for her Mister Right to come along and she's 36! All of them know that they'll be living in separate cabins on "the land," but the waiting game can get to be a very boring game to play.

[Note: Now the re-write of my journal has finally been brought up to date. I will continue with the night-by-night entries.]

June-July, 1991

6-25-91, Tuesday

If the weather's nice Thursday, Bill and I are planning on taking Jenny and Sarah on a little trip over to see our chosen property. We haven't done anything (family-wise) during summer vacations in seven years and we thought a little two-day trip to the Glenwood area would be nice. Robin and Aimee have to work so they won't be going. During the trip I'll take advantage of the journey by taking more photographs for my pictorial book—hope the weather will be good for us. I'm excited to be over in that area again. The area's such a strong Power Point—especially our land there. Oh, *please* God, don't let anyone buy that property before we have the money for it! Please?

6-27 through 6-30-91, Thursday — Sunday

We didn't leave for our trip Thursday morning because there were clouds over the western half of the state. They cleared out Friday morning and we were on the road by 10:15.

Our first stop was the rushing stream above Turquoise Lake just west of Leadville. Sarah came with me back into the woods while Bill and Jenny waited in the van. Jenny's not a "woodsy" person because she has an aversion to the crawly ones.

Sarah had her little Kodak Instamatic and I had our two Minoltas. We took some great shots and, if they come out half as beautiful as the real thing was, I'll be happy with them.

We headed back to Twin Lakes for our journey over Independence Pass which ends up in Aspen before going down Highway 82 into Basalt.

The motels in Basalt were all full so we went into Carbondale and stayed in the newly-built Days Inn. That night the girls and Bill took advantage of the pool and jacuzzi—I don't wear bathing suits so I sat outside the pool area and watched the Roaring Fork River rush by.

The following morning we were greeted by mostly cloudy skies and I was very disappointed. We'd come all this way expressly for my pictorial photos. Since the sun peeked out now and then, we decided to go ahead into the green valleys and hit the mountains too. These are both beautiful regions, but the cloudy skies dropped a damper on my photo session — I took pictures anyway and got a few good shots of some high waterfalls.

By the time we'd gone all the way around the Ruedi Reservoir and past Meredith, it was getting late. Sarah had taken a few photos of me taking my pictures. The family seemed to think one of the photos might be nice for the back of the pictorial book —I wasn't enthused about that idea at all.

Originally we'd planned to stay over just the one night because motels are so expensive, but I could see that Bill was just too tired to drive all the way back to Woodland after driving so many hours, so we stayed one more night and he was sound asleep long before the girls were.

On Sunday morning, the skies were cloudless and I wished we'd had the money to stay over another night so I could retake my photographs. We compromised. Bill said he'd stop anywhere I wanted on Independence Pass. He regretted that offer because we stopped a *lot*.

We arrived home around 1:30 in the afternoon. I'd taken six rolls of film. Sarah had taken three and Jenny two. This pictorial was getting very expensive to create, but these were the final photographs I'd need to take—these would represent the Season of Summer in the book. I already had the photographs for the other three seasons. I just hoped they'd be good enough to make a photography book from. . .I'm by no means anything more than an amateur and I'm counting on Grandmother Earth's incredible beauty to make up for any errors I may have made. I pray my inexperience and clumsiness won't make her portraits look bad.

When we got home, Sarah put all our things away, Jenny did up a load of laundry and Bill and I got right on the mail that was stacked on my desk.

Bill called John Nelson (a Donning author who was working closely with the attorneys) to see if there'd been any new developments. John told Bill that one of the authors was still dragging her feet and holding up the filing of the lawsuit. If this is postponed again (past July 3rd) I'm going to have one royal fit!

Aimee was very glad to see us when she got home from work Sunday evening. She told us that she felt very alone with us gone for two nights. Then her eyes brightened with great news—she was scheduled to go up on Pikes Peak with the firefighters when they had to standby for the Pikes Peak Hill Climb (a professional auto race up the mountain) that was an annual July Fourth event.

Bill and I are still a little nervous about Aimee's new-found special interest, but we said we were excited for her and hoped she'd not only be careful, but have fun too. She has to be up on the mountain at 2:00 A.M. because everyone has to setup and be in place before the officials close down the mountain highway for the race. I knew how much she's looking forward to this and hope she has a great time.

Rainbow must've really missed me while I was gone because she followed me all around the house after we got back from our trip.

It's late now, Bill and the girls are in bed, but Rainbow's lying at my feet beneath the kitchen table—I think she's very content right now. How wonderful and warm a four-legged person can make one feel. Their *actions* are so much more sincere than any words could ever be.

7-1-91, Monday

Today is Monday—a heavy day for mail—and I received an enormous floral arrangement from a correspondent congratulating me on the publication of *Daybreak*. What a sweet thing to do! But he really shouldn't have spent so much money! It always makes me uncomfortable when people spend money on me.

Bill called the attorney today and was told they weren't filing the suit on the third after all (Postponement Number Six). They're now looking at Friday, the fifth. Somehow I didn't have the royal fit I thought I'd have—guess I'm finally getting used to the legal delays. There's nothing I can do about this ongoing situation, so I can only go with the flow (as Bill always tells me). Trouble with that is, whenever he says that, I "see" a river with *boulders* to crash into. Seems his "flow" is never a smooth and easy one.

We had a huge pile of mail today, but only two manual orders. I'm beginning to wonder if it was worth all the trouble we went through to provide it.

One of today's letters was from a woman who says she was Jesus in a past life. I'd like a red cent for everyone who's said that. This lady wrote me once before and, because

I didn't "recognize" who she was then (and now) says I'm only out to sell books and am a charlatan. God, I wish these fruitcakes would leave me alone. I never asked for this abuse, all I came to do was shed light on the truths and, because I don't meet with everyone, I'm then some phoney. Give me my land and let me just go home in peace.

Another letter today was from a lesbian who railed me up one side and down the other because I'd explained the karmic ramifications for homosexuals in *Daybreak*. Now I suppose all these people will denigrate Summer Rain because they didn't like hearing the "law" of it. My truths are fine and beautiful *until* they hit home—*then* they're a crock. It seems that *Daybreak* has created a reverse effect than the one it was supposed to. The book was for the purpose of "answering" the public's questions so I wouldn't keep receiving so many duplicate questions. Instead, readers now see the great variety of questions I get so they think it's fine to write more and more. The questioning has only increased! I cannot respond to them all. I just cannot.

This evening, around sunset, we had a very black sky. I went outside to watch the cloud formations and was presented with something I've never seen before. From a very large black, flat cloud, long rays of light speared up from it. It looked just like the sunset rays except that this was in the *east* and the sun had just set in the west and, between the two, were completely black clouds. It was a beautiful sight to see. It looked just like daybreak rays spearing up from the dark cloud. No rays could be seen beneath this huge cloud— only coming from *within* it. I took a few photos of it, but anyone seeing them would think the sun was behind those clouds—it wasn't. . .something *else* was.

So between the morning's floral bouquet and the evening cloud display, the legal delay and nasty letters were negated. Nature. . .my saving grace.

Last evening, after my prayer and meditation hours, my Starborn friend appeared. We talked for two hours and I not only felt much better, but also received an explanation for the rays that speared up from the dark storm clouds. My encouragement comes in many ways and in many forms. For this I am eternally grateful.

Bill took my rolls of film in today and I hope we have the money to pick them up when they're ready. I really get excited looking through each set of slides when I get them back. Some of them surprise me, for Grandmother Earth sometimes presents me with her "best side." When this happens I know it's *her* and not me who's created the beautiful photograph. I hope people will enjoy the pictorial book because I think it will be a pleasing visual of beautiful Colorado to be picked up and looked at over and over again. These mountains are so sensual—I want to share them with everyone in ways other than words on paper. I just hope the pictorial can be produced so the public can easily afford it —that's always been a big concern of mine.

When we were out at Beaver Lake, I captured photo shots of a mother duck paddling across the water with eight ducklings in a line behind her. They were so cute. I'm anxious to see if those photos came out well enough for the book.

I think the "Spring" section is where I'll place all the flower and animal shots. Right now most of the meadows and pastures are blanketed in a variety of colorful flowers. I could spend hours lying on their fragrant patchwork quilts, but I have no time for that anymore. Perhaps when I'm old or when some other author replaces me and Summer Rain fades from memory, I'll again have time for my frequent unions and communions with nature. Until then, I keep adding my thoughts to *Pinecones and Woodsmoke* (my last book). Perhaps then I will be forgotten and no longer be sought out. Perhaps then I will hear the nature spirits call me back into the woodsmoke from whence I came. Who knows? My destiny leads and my spirit follows its voice. More I cannot do. My life is not my own. . .my life belongs to The Purpose. There is no more "I" or "me". . .only an agent of The Plan. That's all I ever see in the mirror anymore.

Today I received a letter from one of my native readers who regularly writes to me. He is an elderly man and, when I find correspondence from him in the packet of mail, I set the letter aside to read in the evening when I'm resting. I'd sent him a copy of *Daybreak* because I knew he didn't have any extra money to spend on books. In return for my gift to him, he sent me two pair of feather earrings. The native way is always a gift for a gift and he keeps to that traditional custom.

Now that he has been reading the book, he had some strong comments to make regarding the Native Chapter. It got him thinking on the mindset of non-natives who are in the position of making laws. He expressed his concern over a newly-proposed law that may take away native rights to own bear claws and eagle feathers. He couldn't see how this could happen or what right another race has to ban the native people's traditional use of these items. He commented on the fact that he'd been trying to let the Past rest in its grave, but, when non-natives continue to place more and more restrictions on the Indians, he finds it hard to set aside resentments.

I wrote my native friend back and tried to soothe his newly-opened wounds. I hope I did some good.

Today I was also gifted with a very sacred symbol by the son of a native medicine woman. The package had warnings on it: FOR MARY SUMMER RAIN ONLY - CONTENTS SACRED TO HER PEOPLE!

When Bill brought me the package and I held it, my heart skipped a beat. I could smell the contents even before I opened it. The fragrance was of a "wild one." It was a scent I knew and loved, but never, ever dreamed of having. Inside the carefully packaged envelope were two of the most beautiful eagle feathers I'd ever seen. They were resting on sage.

Tears fell down my cheeks.

My soul felt so peaceful and free as I caressed the feathers to my face.

Now these Sacred Ones rest in a glass cabinet where my most treasured possessions lay: owl feathers and owl wing bones, an Anasazi pottery shard, an Oriental jar containing my gallstones, a Chinese box holding locks of my girls' hair, dried roses from Bill, a turquoise corn maiden carving, an authentic medicine rattle and skull-cracker, ashes of a deceased friend, obsidian earrings, a hummingbird's nest, a baby chipmunk skull, a set of 40 Tribal books (each signed by each tribe's Chief), and other special native and natural treasures.

Last week we were informed by our Advisors of our "second" mission. We were told that it was to commence *soon* (which could mean any time in the future), and that our "first connection" would be in contact with us. We were informed that our "Spiritual" mission was now complete (because I'd finished all the books) and that the new one was to be a "physical" one—to help feed and clothe the needy and homeless. I loved it. I couldn't wait to begin. So many people just *talked* or *wished* or *thought* about helping get rid of hunger, but few actually *did* anything about it. Now we were given a new mission to be really active in feeding and clothing the needy and homeless and I was straining at the bit to begin.

And. . .today I received a letter that sent chills up my spine. It was from our new mission "contact!" But. . .*already!*

The bottom line was that we now could begin helping a great deal of people—right now! This just tickled me to no end to think we might be able to do this on the Q.T. I get the biggest high out of helping people without them ever knowing it's me who's helped. Guess I have a gene of Santa

Claus in me or maybe Robin Hood. Well anyway, I sure hope this thing pans out.

I've not mentioned this correspondent's name nor the organization she's connected with because, in order to pull this operation off, neither of us can allow anyone else to know what we're doing for the less fortunate. What a great, great idea this person has!

It seems to Bill and me that the "timing" for our destiny has speeded up because quite a few pieces of the puzzle appear to be dropping into place as the right timing for their manifestation comes to pass and the picture the pieces are making is so beautiful. Even the letter I received today was perfect timing to plan everything out. I'm getting so excited!

7-2-91, Tuesday

Tomorrow Bill and I are taking Jenny and Sarah on another day-long photo session to Cheyenne Mountain Zoo in Colorado Springs.

I want to include some Rocky Mountain animals in my photography book, but, so far, only have a buffalo, ducks, and chipmunks. I regret that I can't get close enough to a bobcat or our mountain lion or bear to say, "Dear four-legged friend, please stand still so I can take your picture." Ah yes, man and his gun has prevented that from happening—at least for now.

Aimee's been moody and distant lately. I must have a long talk with her to see why. I think she's nervous about all her upcoming firefighter tests and the tower qualifying test. She's usually such a sweetheart. Also I have the feeling she's worrying about ever finding a spiritually aware lifemate—she's not the kind to be content being alone. I feel this has been on her mind a lot lately.

We haven't heard anything back from Eric. He was supposed to move back to Colorado this summer and resolve things with Aimee —maybe that's on her mind too. We'll talk.

Received one children's book order today, maybe this wasn't such a great idea. We thought mentioning it in *Daybreak* would help spread the word on it, but maybe folks just aren't that interested in enlightening their children like I was. What a shame to miss such a beautiful opportunity to reopen their young minds to the beautiful truths. What a pity.

Finally got around to doing our Lodestar bookkeeping for the month of June. I usually have each month's expenses recorded on the last day, but we had so much mail after we got back from our photo-taking trip I couldn't get to it until today. I was surprised when I added up all our Post Office receipts. Postage expenses for June were $207.00. I sure wish my correspondents would remember to include a stamped envelope for my response.

Got a call from a Woodland Park shopkeeper who said a group of women were looking for me. My friend said they were insistent to the point of being rude. I apologized to my friend. She shouldn't have to put up with that. I wish my readers were more considerate, especially to people they don't even know. I still don't understand why folks want to see me. I could comprehend the attraction if I was famous or some film star, but I'm just Summer Rain. The people in town treat me like a neighbor next door—why doesn't everyone else do that too? Who am I supposed to be anyway? Can't folks see that I'm just another face on the street and nobody more special than they? I think Aimee will explode the next time someone comes through her cashier line and asks if they can see her mother. The last time that happened the spokesperson for the group said, "Well, my *dear,* we've come all the way from *Germany* just to meet your mother."

Aimee kept her cool, but felt like telling them they should've written first and that "her mother" gets people coming here from all *over* the world looking for her.

I was proud of how Aimee maintained an air of courtesy, even if she was itching to slug the woman for her patronizing stance.

When I was meeting with everyone who asked for a visit with me (for five years), the one or two-hour meeting was almost always extended. Several times people would locate me in a restaurant, sit down at my table and request "a moment" of my time. On eight occasions, this one moment lasted six hours. But every time I would accommodate all their many questions and help them with their personal problems, never once did any of them ever inquire if *I* had other matters I needed to attend to that day—luckily for them I didn't. And so, because of this, I don't go to town anymore—which is perfectly fine with me.

Today the Pikes Peak racers qualified and I awoke to the sound of roaring engines going up the mountain. From our front deck we look directly across at the Peak and the highway going up it. On race day (the 4th), we can sit outside and hear the engines roar and see their dust as they cover the hazardous, twisting course. Only a mountain valley separates us.

The man who keeps our pickup and Robin's Buick in shape is usually the winner of one of the race divisions.

Went to the zoo but wished we hadn't. The feline cages were too small and it broke my heart to see the big cats pacing from one side to the other. In fact, most of the animals didn't seem to have adequate space for their habitat. Seeing the eagles and falcons caged gave me an ill feeling. Guess it wasn't a very good idea after all.

Sarah would catch my eye and her entire face showed a mixture of disgust and rage. We left without using up my roll of film—these were not what I had in mind for my book.

Bill wanted to make us feel better so he surprised us by taking us to Red Lobster for a nice dinner. We didn't discuss the zoo.

We arrived back home at three and Robin had our mail on my desk. There was a big stack. Bill wanted to get right on it, so he began opening the envelops looking for manual orders (he processes these). He read a letter and said, "You're not going to see this one."

"Who is it addressed to?" I asked.

"You."

"Then I'll see it."

"No, it's the most rude one you've ever gotten."

"I won't shatter, Bill. Let me see it."

And it was rude. The writer (who didn't have the nerve to sign his name) called me egotistical, out for money, conde-scending, and accused me of comparing myself to a god. Trouble is, the writer's entire premise was in serious error, because he totally misunderstood the word "enlightened." This was clearly evidence of a broad lack of comprehension of the simplest terms and spiritual concepts. All this writer had to do was memorize the meaning of enlightenment from any dictionary in order to gain its true definition. Instead, he had some half-brained New Age idea that the word meant "one who existed on the Seventh Plane with God—one who can create worlds." Therefore this person thought I was saying all that trash about myself! My goodness, with so many people not knowing the true definitions of the most basic spiritual terms, no wonder the world's so screwed up! Anyway, the letter didn't bother me one bit, because its author was so obviously confused and had very little spiritual comprehension.

7-5-91, Friday

John Nelson called today. Seems our lawsuit won't be filed today after all—maybe by next Friday. I'm beginning to lose track of how many postponements this is—the seventh, I think.

7-6-91, Saturday

Last night I shouldn't have left the garage doors open for Aimee because, when she came home from work at 11, she found our two garbage cans tipped over and everything was scattered over the garage. Our local bear had visited us again. Aimee got Sarah up and they both cleaned up the mess so their dad wouldn't have to deal with it in the morning.

One of our correspondents today wondered if it was wrong to keep the purpose of her path before her at all times. I wrote back to commend her on what she was doing.

These are very critical times and those in the White Brotherhood do not fool around—they're *very* strict. They have no patience for people who play mind games, snow themselves, or rationalize their actions through defense mechanisms.

People just don't realize how important things are—how *serious* —when the Great White Brotherhood is actively involved. People think this Group is just existing somewhere doing their thing and "that's cool." But then when these same people get *themselves* involved with The Brotherhood then it's "Whoa! They're too strict!"

But dammit! *That's* how it *is!* There is no room for mind games or procrastination! God doesn't touch you to direct you. . .and then you say, "Okay, but *after* I do this and that first." That attitude *will* not and *does* not get tolerated by the Brotherhood. Why is it that everything is fine with people until the time comes to face their own truths and destiny? Isn't *truth* what it's all about here? Do people want our real help or not? They say they only want to do God's will, but do they? They certainly are not committed to doing God's will when they have to attend to their own will first! Do people even know any more what a commitment is? Have we lost that too? A commitment doesn't mean it works just when the sun shines or when the road is smooth or when there are no barriers. A commitment must still overcome darkness, barriers, rough roads, adversity, heartache. Commitment doesn't mean beans if there's always sunshine, laughter and party time. Commitment must experience tears and pain, struggle and suffering. Otherwise it's nothing more than a word in a verbal mind game one play with self!

Oh, my dear father above, I should've remembered how hard it would be to be back here. I just should've remembered. There are times I think people *believe* in The Great White Brotherhood, but that belief is only in the title—the words—not the *living* entity those words represent. When I receive this correspondent's letter that clearly exemplified her strong commitment to her path it was very heartwarming, because we've seen so many others taking the easier path of the self's ego.

7-7-91, Sunday

Last night an energetic raccoon tipped over three of my flower planters on the front porch. Petunias and dirt were all over. I hope the curious little critter satisfied his curiosity. Robin helped me set things to rights and, if the little fellow does it again, I'll be out of flowers for the rest of the summer.

Today, being Sunday, Bill can attend to projects outside the office because our phone doesn't ring all day like it does during the week. So while I spent the day at my typewriter answering the longer letters, Bill and the girls crumpled up four storage boxes of my correspondence letters and spent most the day incinerating them in our wood stove. I don't really know why we were hanging on to them in the first place. They took up a lot of space that we don't have.

Tomorrow when Bill goes to town for the mail he's going to pick me up some wood stain so we can make picture frames for two posters I bought. One is of wolves in snow, the other is a sunset scene of Stonehenge. I love it when we're working on projects together. I remember when we'd bought the old-style topper from one of our friends. After we'd gotten it on the pickup bed, we needed to build a back for it because we had no tailgate. That project was our first carpentry attempt, and we had to figure out how to make a back to it, plus a door with a lock. When we were done we'd managed an airtight job. That was what allowed us to eventually go out and spend nights in it during our "clearing" journeys.

Later on, when we weren't doing as many, we put an add in our local paper for a "free pickup topper." A man and his

son came out to our Ridgewood house to see it—he was so
excited about it and they offered to pay Bill something. Bill
wouldn't hear of it, he was just glad someone could use it.

Hope our mail isn't too heavy this week so I can work
with Bill on the poster frames. Seems we just don't get to
do anything any more but work at our desks. Our last phone
bill was $300. When I promised No-Eyes I'd "do the books,"
I had no idea how personally expensive they'd become. I
need to get Bill away from that telephone—maybe I should
take it off his desk! Maybe our chosen property has no
phone lines! Wouldn't that be heaven. But alas. . .it does.
Guess it's not quite as remote as I'd really wanted it to be.

7-8-91, Monday

Bill received a call from Moving Books, a distributor.
They'd been getting a lot of requests for my children's
manual, and wanted to stock it. Bill had to explain that it
was only available through us, because I wanted to autograph
each one. The distributor understood, but was disappointed all
the same. I'd like to know where all those "requests" are
coming from because they sure weren't showing up here! Orders were dribbling in. So far, mentioning it in *Daybreak*
hasn't seemed to help. If things don't pick up considerably, I
think, once we're out of stock, we won't have any more
printed. If folks really don't care about it I may as well
discontinue it. After all, it was because of their requests that
we put it together in the first place. Well, maybe it's too
early to tell yet; *Daybreak's* only been out a couple of
weeks.

One thing that amazes us is that *Spirit Song* is still out-
selling all the other books in the series. We're real happy
about that because it means more and more *new* people are
finding No-Eyes. It tickles me every time I hear that that title
is going in for another reprint. They did the eleventh one at
the end of June.

Bill and I went over to the lumber yard and got everything we needed to make six poster frames (Jenny and Sarah
decided they needed frames for their posters too). So after I'd
cleaned up all my mail, we got right on it and now that
they're all made, I'll have to find time to stain them (hopefully tomorrow).

Today I was so excited to receive a follow-up letter regarding the woman who connected with me about our new

mission. The Brotherhood sure doesn't believe in any "breathers" between our mission projects!

Anyway, it looks as though we'll be able to coordinate our efforts. What tickles me so is the fact that this woman (now a friend), must remain unidentified in order for her to "supply" us and remain anonymous. Oh God, I'm so excited! This is just like one of the old, *olde* days! This is such a wonderful project, I can't wait 'til we have the money to get settled. Secrets are such a kick, especially when you end up helping people. I get such a high from that. Look out. . .Robin Hood rides again. . .he's back! Ha! If people only knew. Oh, it's going to be just like the olde days again.

This project is going to be a hell of a lot of work, but so what, huh No-Eyes? That's what we came here for. I bet you had a hand in bringing all this together for us—you're still a busy little elfin, aren't you. I do love you so.

Bill is just as excited about our new project as I am. All of us are going to have such fun doing this in secret again.

I sure hope this lawsuit gets filed this week and it gets settled fast. I couldn't bear it if it dragged out. *Before,* I wanted to be settled on our land so I could finally feel "home," but *now* I want to be settled so we can get busy on our new project! Just thinking of doing that again makes me giggle. Thanks Guys for a great, great new mission. It's a beautiful gift to us. We will do our best by it. . .promise.

As I'm writing this, there's some critter scratching at our kitchen door that's six feet from me. At first I thought we'd left one of our dogs outside, but Rainbow's at my feet and Magic's up in Sarah's bed. The cat's pacing and hissing in the living room. . . she's not fond of the woodland wild things. She did the same thing when our bear came around. Well, whatever critter it was has decided I'm not letting him in. I would've turned on the outside floodlights to look, but they're so bright they shine into all the upstairs bedroom windows and I don't want to wake anyone at 2:00 A.M. Cat settled down now.

7-9-91, Tuesday

Got up early so I could stain the six poster frames. They turned out just right—real rustic-looking, just how I like them. I'd picked out wood with knots and bark—the more natural-looking the better.

While I was processing the mail today, Bill got a call from John Nelson. Seems one of our lawsuit authors just remembered how she'd lost out on some money that another publisher offered her for her books and, now—at the Eleventh Hour—wants to incorporate this amount in the brief. Bill was furious.

"What's this woman been doing all this time that she doesn't have her case together? She just now remembers this past offer? John apologized. He'd been helping a few of the authors and, evidently, he'd been a little too helpful because every time one of the authors adds anything to their case, the brief has to be altered to include it.

While I was sitting on my porch this evening watching a beautiful sunset and offering some prayers, a neighbor lady came by to say a bear was on her deck last night. We talked for a while and I joked about the bear and the "scratching" I'd heard at our kitchen door the night before. She was frightened, so I kept it light to make her feel better. She actually began laughing over it.

I shed light on a perspective she never viewed.

"After all," I'd said, "*we're* living up here in *their* territory. It'd be different if we were in the city, but all these homes up here were built in the mountain woods. *We* encroached on *their* lands, so there's bound to be coexistence with them."

She hadn't realized how extensively this little community of scattered homes were surrounded by miles upon miles of nearly virgin woods where bear, cougar, elk, deer, and other mountain wildlife abound.

A bear romping across the roads in front of your headlights at night was certainly not uncommon. Neither were the herds of hundreds of elk and deer that journeyed from meadow to meadow just after twilight.

I think my neighbor lady is not a mountain person. We don't know each other's names (which is not rare for mountainfolk), but we all know we're here for each other in an emergency. Mountainfolk live in the more remote mountains because they don't like cities, they resonate with the serenity of nature and the quiet solitude, and rarely enjoy socializing. . .but they'll always rally to a neighbor's time of need. Just because we don't party and socialize, doesn't also mean we don't care about one another.

I responded to 25 letters today and will spend a couple hours in meditation when I finish up this entry—that is, I will if Buttercup doesn't start hissing at our bear again. . . and especially if she starts "growling" again. Never heard a cat actually growl like a dog—until we got this strange cat.

Maybe she thinks she's a dog. Yeah, she's probably creating her own reality. . .that was *definitely* tongue-in-cheek.

I came out of my meditation at 2:30 A.M. and awoke to a pouring rain. Lightning flashes speared through the dark living room and thunder vibrations reverberated through the house. One particularly brilliant flash illuminated my Starborn friend who was seated in my reading chair.

"You gave me a fright, "I whispered, not wishing to wake anyone up (though no one ever did when he was here).

He apologized.

I stood and went over to the ottoman in front of my chair. I sat down.

"Your people really should adopt our ways since you're here."

He smiled. "If we 'knocked' on every door we needed to enter do you really believe we'd be given entry?"

I smiled back. Then glanced over at the illuminated VCR clock.

"Well, not at 2:32 in the morning, anyway. But you know you're welcome here so why don't you give me some warning before you just 'appear' out of the blue? One of these nights you're going to give me a heart attack."

"Your heart's just fine."

"Not if you keep this up, it won't be."

"You worry too much."

"And you're changing the subject. You know I've been waiting for you and you know why."

"Yes, I know and we've been over and over it. Why can't you leave it alone? Why must you continue to force things that are not yet destined to be?"

"Because I don't understand *why* there has to be a 'right' time for this."

"Doesn't matter if you understand or not. All must and will unfold according to The Plan—destiny, if you will."

I looked my friend in the eye.

"But it's so simple. . .you *have* it and I *want* it. Tell me again why you can't give it to me. You know our reasonings are pure."

My Starborn friend sighed as I once again reviewed my old logic.

"Look, a couple inventors here have the right idea but their devices need a lot of refinement, both in size and design. When Bill and I talked on the phone with one of them, we realized he was no longer the one to bring the device to the world because One: he traded humanitarianism for profit and Two: he went off the deep end with his spiritual beliefs.

So why does that have to be the end of the golden chance for the world to have the energy device?

"I was so excited that night when the idea came to me. I envisioned *giving* these refined devices to everyone! That way, people could personally convert all their electrical appliances themselves and, when they stopped using up electricity, the Power Companies would be suddenly obsolete! It's the 'little people' who could make it work and turn the energy moguls OFF!

"I don't see why this can't begin right now. You have the devices already. Just give us a supply or show Bill and me how to make them, so we can begin to anonymously distribute them with directions for their use.

"You know notoriety wouldn't work here. If the money and power people knew who was giving these devices away we'd be dead inside of a few days. Why can't we do this anonymously? Why can't the pollution stop right *now?* To think of all the *ramifications* that would have is so astounding! Why can't we *do* this?"

"You've asked that every time I come."

"Are you still going to give the same answer?"

He nodded.

I sighed in frustration. And it was frustrating trying to argue with a Starborn One. They were much like The White Brotherhood. Both knew The Plan and both knew the Rules of Destiny, for timing played a paramount role and could not be forced before its appointed manifestation date. What I had proposed to them was "admirable" and "selfless," they'd said, but it still represented a gross "force on time" which would upset The Plan.

I'd been so excited when I'd first had the idea that would circumvent the other inventor's sluggishness with their devices. I'd been so excited with the idea of *giving* the refined device to everyone. I thought my Starborn Ones could supply us or else show us how to make them. We'd then secretly assemble them and anonymously distribute them. But I was shot down the very first time I voiced my idea.

Now I had another question for my friend.

"Do you still have the *other?*"

"Yes, we have it."

"And you'll still show it to me when we're settled on our land?"

"We promised you that you would see it then."

"And it's still part of my destiny?"

"Yes."

"You're very active in our chosen area, aren't you?"

"You've sensed this while there. You don't need me to verify this for you."

"I want very much to get over there, but we can't without the lawsuit settlement. I'm fearful the property will sell before we have a chance at it. It's so perfect in many ways."

"You mean for your new mission project."

I chuckled. "Yes, I should've known you'd know about that."

He paused before asking, "What other way is this property so perfect?"

"Because you're all there."

"And?" he pushed.

"And because that's where the 'other' is."

A few moments lapsed before he spoke. "Why do you feel we have the 'other' somewhere in your world and not on our own?"

I smiled. "Because here is where it belongs. I can feel it."

"Then why not beneath the Seventh Mesa?"

"I told you, I can *feel* it over there near our property."

And I told him about my very powerful desire to build a kiva back at the base of the mountain by the high waterfall. I told him of the special visions I'd had that gave sacred reasonings for the kiva.

He made no comment, but his new expression said much in the way of his silent confirmation.

He couldn't stay longer this time and we made our usual goodbye greeting.

The *other* is none other than a prophesied Tablet.

It is now 4 A.M. and I must get some sleep. If Bob Friedman calls early and someone tells him I'm still in bed he'll think I'm one lazy so and so. But I'm still very disappointed (and irritated) that Bill and I can't do this "energy device project." I just can't reconcile the reasoning, yet I know both The Brotherhood and The Starborn ones can see so much farther than I. And so I must, as always, respect and abide by their vision. . .again and again.

Oh, if people only knew the half of what I have to deal with—if they only knew. Well. . .then again, they probably wouldn't even believe it. Nope, I'm sure they wouldn't. Thank God all this writing is just for me. I laugh when I think of what a flap this journal would make if it was ever seen by anyone, huh, No-Eyes? You're the only one who peeks over my shoulder. Goodnight, No-Eyes. I love you.

7-10-91, Wednesday

When I awoke this morning I was feeling very down. For some reason my thoughts were on our finances. Every month we had to take money out of our savings in order to make our monthly living expenses, plus take out $1,000 a month to pay on the hospital bill. At the rate we were going, we'd be out of money in three months. Out. . .zip. . .No more. And I awoke with this on my mind.

My Donning royalties are due in September, but I'm uncomfortable with what they may try to pull once they're onto the lawsuit. I've made no royalty money from *Earthway* yet and, although the German rights have been sold for that book, Pocket deducts the amount from the original advance and I won't be seeing any money from that sale.

It seems so futile to be still waiting to get settled after 14 years of hoping for it. And here we sit still waiting —still scrimping from one month to the next and worrying about our savings going down to zero in a couple of months —then what will we do? Probably sell the van.

By the time I'd showered and cooked up another week's worth of dog food (ground turkey and rice), I was feeling much better, because all that time I realized that we'd always been taken care of—especially when situations were tightest and getting down to the "desperate wire."

While Bill and Sarah were in town going to their chiropractic appointments and getting the mail, I'd nailed the six posters to their stained frames and was surprised to see how nice they all turned out.

Bill returned with the stack of mail and I began going through it while he was busy at his own desk.

I'd opened and read a nasty letter. . .then a second nasty one. I was beginning to wonder what all our work was for. I was quickly losing faith in my work and also faith in mankind.

The next letter I opened put me in shock. . .*real* shock. It came from a woman I'd never heard from before. She wanted me to please accept her "small" gift in appreciation for all we'd given her. Enclosed was a check for five thousand dollars! My eyes were so unbelieving I thought I must've read the amount wrong. But no, I hadn't, for the amount was fully written out.

Tears came to my eyes. I couldn't believe this woman's generosity. No one had *ever* done anything like that for us —never. . .ever!

"Bill?"

"Mmmm," he mumbled from his desk.

"A woman just gave us a check for five thousand dollars."

"Cute, honey, real cute."

"Bill, she gave us five thousand dollars," I softly repeated.

He shot up out of his chair and was at my desk in a flash.

"Oh my God, Mary!" he said, looking at the check. Tears welled in his eyes as he tried to read the lady's short letter. . .no strings, now or for the future. The gift was just a small gift of love, for all we've done and gone through.

I was so deeply moved I couldn't talk for the crying.

Bill called the woman to express our deepest appreciation for her goodness. He almost lost it on the phone, because he was getting choked up.

During their conversation, the lady told Bill that just that morning she'd prayed we'd accept her gift. Her prayers were answered.

Our prayers were answered once again too, and my faith in humanity had been fully restored—not because of the amount of the check, but because someone *cared* enough to do that for us. We still are in a state of semi-shock and can hardly believe it. I get misty every time I think of it. Now we'll have enough to carry us through and still pay the hospital. Now we won't have to sell our van. There are a few diamonds out there after all. I could probably never make this lady realize how much her "gift of love" meant to us. So few people have truly understood our purpose and what we've endured for it, and when real help comes to us from the depths of someone's heart, we are deeply moved.

7-11-91, Thursday

I awoke with a dream of scud missiles with nuclear warheads. It disturbed me.

Today is eclipse day. I'm amazed at the general public's reaction to such a natural event. The news programs showed masses of people making spectacles of themselves over the celestial occurrence. They reminded me of a very primitive race.

While the eclipse was at its zenith, Sarah and I were out in the mountains gathering wild strawberries. I think we ate more than we brought home. They were so sweet and luscious.

I received a letter from Dian Zimmer, owner of the Phoenix Rising Gallery in Cripple Creek. When we were there a month ago she invited me to participate in an art show for Charles Frizzell (a famous Victor artist). Dian thought a Summer Rain appearance and book signing would complement the artist. At the time, I really loved the idea, because I'd always admired Charles' work and, just last week, his wife, Shawn, had ordered a children's manual from us. I'd originally wanted a particular painting of his on the manual's cover, but figured he was too famous (and expensive) to approach. Later, I'd seen Ann Marie's fairy painting and knew her's was equally right.

Dian's letter was to inform me that we'd reached the final decision date for the appearance, because she needed to print up the announcements. Bill called her and said we had too many things in the fire right now to commit to a scheduled date.

Carole Bourdo has the new artwork for the *Phantoms Afoot* cover done and I can't wait to see it. When she's back from her tours we'll go visit her. We also have a surprise for her. The last time we were at her house I presented her with a copy of *Daybreak*—right off the presses. Bill took a photo of her and me with the book and I had an enlargement made of it for her. Artist and author with their first creation. I know she's going to be tickled with it. I love surprising people.

I'm also going to send Bob Friedman an enlargement because he loved Carole's work and thought I'd had a great idea to use her art on all my book covers as a "signature" of my work. I'm sure he'll enjoy having a photo of us together with the first book we *all* collaborated on.

I thank Brian Many Heart for leading me to Bob, for he's gained a deeper respect for my work and purpose, and the creative freedom he gives me would not be found in any other publishing house. I pray that the No-Eyes series gives him a good foundation for his new company and that he's very successful with it. Bob's new crew at Hampton Roads is top-notch in spiritual awareness. . .for this I thank God.

Today, among my new letters, I'd received two from people who'd never heard of me before, but bought *Daybreak* because they were drawn to the beautiful cover. I'll have to be sure to tell Carole and Bob that. They'll be pleased to hear it. I'm convinced that Lady Destiny has brought the three of us together—publisher, artist, and author—for the purpose of perpetuating the truths in the traditional manner of sacredness. This has been one aspect of The Plan that came together smoothly.

Later. . .

Tonight after everyone was asleep, I went out into the woods. There was heavy cloud cover and the mountains were darker than usual. The atmosphere was dense and heavy like a shroud that weighted the air and muted sounds. Yet it was a comforting sense to me,—like a blanket to cover with.

I walked for a while then sat on a fallen tree. I could feel No-Eyes near and I carried on a one-sided vocal conversation—her responses coming into my mind as soft and clear whispers.

I missed her so.

I told her how alone I often felt without her and how hard life had become since the books had been published— meaning the shouldering of people's problems and expecting to be their personal "answer lady." I'd never asked for any of that, but somehow I'd become the sounding board for thousands of people who never realized what a burden they were giving me.

Yes, I was here to help to keep "the light" shining and, yes I said I'd answer letters, but people don't realize that most all the answers have now been given in the six books. How is it that they don't read what they read there? The message has been given. All the words have been given. There is no more, yet the letters increase almost daily. How many ways can I say the same answers over and over? Everything has already been reduced to their lowest common denominator. Clarity in its most simple form—yet the questions still keep coming.

Is it because I'm still here for them, No-Eyes? Is that why they're not looking within for their answers? Have I become a crutch for them?

What happens when I move on to our new mission and leave the correspondence days behind? Will they then think I no longer care about them because they don't understand the workings of Destiny and how one moves along from one aspect of it to another and another?

Ohhh, No-Eyes, I do wish my trail had been more private as yours was. You helped and taught, but still had your solitude. I don't want to be Summer Rain any more, I just want to be a nobody. I want to return to the woodsmoke again. I want to just be a faded memory in the back of peoples' minds. We have endured so much pain trying to help people and still many do not see or hear. How is it that our suffering has worth and is justified?

Help me, No-Eyes. Help us to endure and shoulder what we must, for we will continue to walk the trail that has been laid out before us. You know we will walk its length no matter how weary we become. If we didn't—we'd have failed our purpose for coming again and, neither of us could live with that, once we returned to spirit. We couldn't face our Brotherhood companions if we failed. So we'll walk the designated path. All I ask is for you to remain at my side. You give me such comfort and encouragement. You are my light at the end of the tunnel.

Keep shining, my sweet friend, I need to see and feel your heartlight burning bright beside me.

When I walked back to the house, our two garbage cans had been ransacked by the bear. Robin had just come home from work and she pulled her car around so the headlights would give us some illumination. Sarah heard us and got up to help clean up. We put on surgical gloves and spent a good 15 minutes cleaning up the mess that was scattered about. The garbage can lids were all dented in and bite marks were in food containers. This is one hungry bear we have around here. Some great "watchdogs" we have! Rainbow and Magic *and* Buttercup never sensed our wild visitor, Sarah said. Good thing this was rubbish night and the bear found better pickings than me, for I was deep in the woods tonight.

Tomorrow is Friday and the attorneys are supposed to get the lawsuit filed. This will be interesting, yes? We're down to three working days left to do it in before the Statute of Limitations runs out. Why does *everything* in our lives go right down to the wire? It's a wonder we don't have ulcers. . .or drink. . .or throw in the towel.

What a life. Sometimes we can't believe we actually *volunteered* for all this! Were we a couple of dummies or what? Well. . .I know that's not true, but sometimes, sometimes. . .
.

7-12-91, Friday

Last night when I went to bed the "fluttering" sound came again. I've not mentioned this before, but, for the last four nights Bill has heard it just as his head hits the pillow and, when I come to bed many hours later, I too hear the sound just after my head hits the pillow. It sounds just like wings and only lasts for a minute or so.

At first we thought there was a moth on our window, but after extensive searching, no moth was found.

During the day today Bill told me that he felt a "presence" in our room last night as he laid in bed. He didn't recognize the essence; he said it was different from our Advisors and the Starborn ones. He admitted to being uneasy because of the unfamiliarity of it. Then, he said the fluttering began for a minute or two.

When I checked on the source of the presence, we were told that three native medicine men in Arizona sent spirit helpers to protect us. . .the "fluttering wings" sound is often a manifested audio aspect of these particular entities.

We were glad to hear the reason for both phenomena and especially pleased to know of the caring that came from the native elders so far away. We were grateful and psychically thanked them for their efforts. Now when I go to bed tonight I'll *thank* the entities instead of telling them to "go to sleep!" as I did last night.

Bill called the attorneys today, but they weren't available. Their secretary said the suit was not filed because of an addition that was being written into the brief. So then, where were we?. . .oh yes, Postponement Number Eight. This thing had better not get bungled. If it does, people will finally see Mary Summer Rain go public because the first person Bill will call is Oprah Winfrey! I would even offer up my shyness to make No-Eyes' captivity a very, very public affair. This thing is so far down to the wire I can taste the metal.

Today I received a reader letter that requested information on how to order a catalog of Carole Bourdo's artwork. This is a prime example of how people read but do not read. I purposely featured her address in the back of *Daybreak* so people would see it. When the *answer* is right in front of someone's face I still get asked the question.

UPS made a delivery to the house around six o'clock. It was Carole's transparency of her work called "*Old Woman of All Seasons*," which will be the cover of my next book, *Whispered Wisdom,* the pictorial.

Every time she paints a new cover for one of my books, she sends it to Fine Print to have the transparency made. They, in turn, send one or two to me so I have the cover work with my manuscript. Then when each book is ready to send in and contract for, I have the entire package to give to the publisher. Because I myself have control over the covers, I also have the responsibility to pay the artist. At first, when we initially visited Carole and we discussed her doing the books, I told her what I could afford to pay her. I know it was far below what she would charge for creating a book cover, but she just smiled and said it was fine. I just love that lady so much and her work certainly expresses her spirituality and the sacred manner in which her work is created.

When she begins a new work, she sits and waits for spirit to take over and guide her. What a lady.

While we were there that day, Carole was very upset over new legislation that Ben Nighthorse Campbell introduced. In essence, anyone "claiming" native heritage *without* the papers to prove it would be slapped with a hefty fine. To me, that's pretty discriminatory, because many, many native and part-native people cannot prove their native ancestral heritage, including Carole's own Blackfoot ancestry.

She called me one day all upset over this and said this would even affect famous artists like Bert Seabourn who, by the way, certainly has the classic native facial features.

I told Carole that maybe the law would "Grandfather" those artists and authors who were already established in the public eye before the law was signed. She hoped that was so, because she'd been given her Blackfoot name in a sacred ceremony on the reservation and I personally know how much she treasures that heritage.

This law seems very racist. How could any other ethnic race do what Campbell is proposing? What if one *had* to prove they're French in order to *say* they were? I'm part French but I certainly have no papers to *prove* it, other than my grandfather's name of Regnier (Ren-yea). I'm also part German, but how does one prove that? Birth certificates don't ask for nationality other than if one is born alive or not. Driver's licenses don't distinguish what nationality one is either. This law blatantly discriminates against the thousands and thousands of "part" Indian people who may or may not cherish that native part of themselves.

So where does that leave people like Bert, Carole, and me? In limbo? In an eternal Shadowland where we're not welcome, and will be penalized if we show and live by our native hearts? After all we've done to bring appreciation for the Native culture to the public?

When Silvereagle wrote me last time he railed and railed over *another* piece of legislation he heard about. He says the "whites" are now going to make it a law that states: "If you don't have black hair and brown eyes you're not an Indian." He was hopping mad at that and I sure don't blame him. The entire thing shows gross ignorance because. . .not all native people had black hair. . .some had red!

Ohh God, you can call me back any time now. At least "over there" I don't have to show *papers* to prove who I am!

7-13-91, Saturday

Went down to Colorado Springs and took the girls. We needed some office supplies from Biz Mart and then made a few other shopping stops.

Aimee didn't come with us because she had to work. After work every night, she likes to go over to the fire station for extra classes. Last night she didn't get home until 12:30. She said they were going to let her drive the "big rig". . .but she chickened out.

Robin had the day off and was alone, since Mandy was at her dad's this weekend. Rob spent half the day trying to put a new trunk lock on her Buick because the old one wasn't working—sure wish we could get her a new vehicle. Anyway, I think she enjoyed her day alone. It's a rarity when you live with six other people all the time. We always try to give each other space—but it's not always possible.

Tomorrow is Sunday and I'll spend the entire day responding to all the letters we picked up today on our way downtown.

One letter was from a Florida lady who'd knitted me a beautiful shawl last summer and, last week, I'd finally had Bill take a picture of me wearing it. Tomorrow I'll answer the questions in her letter and send the shawl photo with it—I'm sure she thinks I've forgotten all about it by now.

Aimee's nervous about performing her fire tests at "the tower" in a few weeks. She has to be in full bunker gear and climb a ladder into the burning building. She's fearful about the dark side causing an accident. I had a long instructive talk with her regarding her negative thoughts and how her fear could hurt her. She has to give powerful positive thoughts and visualizations directed toward this event. We practiced together as I talked her through the entire "tower" experience.

Aimee is very powerful. Her mental energies are very strong. Her worst enemy will be fear if she allows it to take over—she must always *instinctually* bring the *positive* thoughts to the forefront. I'm helping her to make that her first reaction to any threatening or dangerous situation. Her protection shield is strong like iron, but one fearful thought could melt it like butter. She knows that and I pray that knowing will save her one day. I will request our Advisor to send a specialist to accompany Aimee while she's going through her tower exercises. That will be her greatest hurdle; after that, her own guide will suffice.

Please watch closely over Aimee. She's so tiny, so pretty and so loving. I'd die inside if anything happened to her. She's giving the Dark Side the ultimate opportunity, but she's doing it to help others because she cares—please make that overbalanced in her favor—please make that count for something that deserves a little more than the usual protection she's given.

7-14-91, Sunday

Sunday night, everyone is asleep and my Starborn friend just left. He says I must *not* talk about our future mission that we've been given. He said all reference to it must be *stricken* from this journal. I didn't understand that because I'm the only one who will ever read it. But, as always, I will do as advised and obliterate all referenced lines that deal with our new mission. I will not be specific about it from now on. Henceforth our secret work will be referred to as "Wellspring" and, the lady who is involved in it with us will be called "Link." I must have some reference words for these because I'll be mentioning them in the future.

7-15-91, Monday

Had a ton of mail today.

Attorney tells Bill that they're filing tomorrow.

I need to spend some time in the woods. People's problems are weighing heavily today.

Sarah went driving with Robin, and when she came back, she spent the afternoon roaming our mountainsides, gathering flowers to dry. Wish I could've gone with her. Sometimes, she comes over to my desk, takes my hand and pulls me outside just to see a cloud formation or to stand in silence with her to listen to the elk bellow. She's such a little Mountain Spirit—her sensitivity is so heartwarming to me. She's the only one of the three girls who loves nature and love to be out in it. Jenny's afraid of bugs, bears, and the dark woods. Aimee never was into nature.

There's a cougar in our neighborhood now. I forgot to mention that I heard it the other night when I'd gone out into the woods.

In the mail today I received a drawing from a six-year-old girl who I'd signed a manual to. I tacked her artwork on the wall above my desk. That little drawing made my day. . .and I sent her a thank-you to tell her so.

Tonight I will devote my hour of prayer to the little ones of the world.

7-16-91, Tuesday

Bill called the attorney's office and their secretary said they were in conference making more changes on our brief. These attorneys are giving me more grey hairs. Think it's time to take a walk into the woods and. . .not come out again.

Later in the day, when Bill was talking to a friend about the projected monetary damages involved in the suit, our friend said, "You'll be able to buy any piece of property you want with that kind of money."

Ahh, but the friend did forget two little things called the attorney fee and the IRS. . .each taking a third of our final settlement. The one-third of that settlement must be enough to get us our land and a couple new trucks.

This morning I told Bill that, if we ended up with enough money I was planning on "giving" Bob my first four books to publish. As long as he agrees to re-package them with Carole Bourdo's artwork, I find little reason to ask for an advance for them. I want all of No-Eyes in one place. She needs the right home.

When Bill initially contacted Bob regarding *Daybreak,* Bob said he'd never before offered a contract without first seeing the manuscript. When he faxed us his offer, he said that "this was a first." Well, I'd like to give Bob another first—that of getting four books for *nothing!* And I do hope we'll be able to do that, but only if we can, otherwise it will have to be business as usual. I'd like to see Hampton Roads make it big, because when Bob first left Donning to start the new company, I heard derogatory remarks from people who had no faith in him. I have faith in him and I'd like nothing better than proving those people wrong. I'm still so grateful he initially accepted *Spirit Song.* Even though Many Heart foresaw its acceptance by Donning, Bob still had the free will to alter that prediction—but he didn't. And now I may have an opportunity to really show my appreciation and I'll do it if I possibly can. It is native tradition to return a gift for a gift. This I try to keep to. . .one way or another.

I must remember to remind Bill to call Link tomorrow. We have some logistics to iron out for our Wellspring project. Hopefully we can begin immediately to implement it. What a kick this is going to be. This project is truly a Godsend—for *many* people. It's going to be hard for me not to write about it.

7-17-91, Wednesday

Well, well! Guess what finally made its way into reality today? The lawsuit was filed in the Virginia court. Our attorneys decided enough was enough and went ahead and filed. The brief, with Exhibits, is nearly two hundred pages, and we'll be receiving our copy by Federal Express.

Next step is for the attorneys to hire Process Servers for the Defendants. Then they have 30 days to respond, but we don't expect to hear anything from them until the first part of September. Court date will be approximately six months from the filing date. If the publishers don't want to settle out of court, we're looking at a trial sometime in January. There's no way we can drive for three days in the middle of winter to be present in Norfolk for a trial.

Sure would be nice to have our property as a Christmas present. . .especially since last year there *were* no presents under the tree.

Well, I pray that the light warriors make all end well. I will be doing much in the way of participating on many levels to add my own energies to this end. Bill too (and the girls) will assist in this effort, for their individual powers have worked pure magic when they've joined forces in the past.

Bill tried calling Link twice today, but her message recorder was on. He'll try again tomorrow. We're very anxious to begin Wellspring. It will take up most of our time, but we're all geared up for the new mission we've been given. This is something the entire family can actively participate in and they're looking forward to doing their part.

The publicist at Hampton Roads, Vernon Turner, called me today and wanted to know if I'd be willing to do a one-hour live radio interview for a Nebraska station. I told him no—no live interviews. Then we compromised by coming up with a taped interview after first being faxed the intended questions. Vernon then suggested that maybe we could do an interview together and send out the tape to interested radio stations. I was open to that.

But I shouldn't have been, for later that evening I was strongly "advised" under no uncertain terms was I to do an audio tape with *anyone!* God, I hate this.

So I typed a letter to Vernon and Bill will fax it to him in the morning. I told Vernon I can't help the restrictions I must work under and that it'd be best if he publicized my books "as if they were published *posthumously*" as if I were dead.

The Advisors (and Starborn ones) do not want Summer Rain in the public eye (or ears). That's fine with me, but it plays hell and havoc with one's book publisher. I'm really sorry I'm such a royal pain in the backside for them, but I just cannot go against my advisements. They (publisher) may as well think of me as being dead, that way they'll not be tempted to try to set up interviews.

Some wonderfully thoughtful correspondent sent us a gift of a roll of stamps today. I sent back a thank-you card with a note, but I know folks can't really imagine how much we appreciate that kind of help. Postage is one of our biggest office expenses. It's not only my readership correspondence that eats up stamps, it's the mailing of the manuals too. We have an exceptional friend in Victor, Colorado who sends us stamps every month as a "gift of love."

Bill worked his behind off in the office today. Seems he was on the phone all day. It was one of those crazy, wild days when the phone never stops ringing.

Sarah helped us out in the office. She typed up a letter for Bill and then typed the new correspondents' names onto the mailing list. After she finished that, she filed their new index cards away. What a help she was! Of course we couldn't accomplish all we do if Jenny didn't free me up by taking care of three laundry loads a day, all the housework and the meal preparation. I've noticed that I haven't mentioned Jenny much in this day-by-day journal, but she's *really* the one who makes our work possible. Thanks, Jenny. You're a real sweet-heart. We appreciate all you do. Of course, you already know that because I tell you that every night before bed, huh honey?

Love ya lots. Goodnight, Jen.

7-18-91, Thursday

We received the filed brief today and it looks real good. Finally the ball has begun rolling and we'll see how far it goes.

Bill faxed Vernon my denial for the taped radio interviews. Got a return fax that accepted my position, but opened ideas for "print" interviews. Faxed back to Vernon that he should just proceed with book publicity as though I was dead. Told him to "take a break and file Summer Rain away."

Bill finally made audio contact with Link tonight after dinner.

They discussed preliminary work and options, and we decided to begin with a trial-and-error testing sequence until the operation gets fine-tuned.

I cannot continue beating around the bush and playing word games while trying to write about Wellspring. This is just ridiculous.

Wellspring is our new spiritual mission. Link is in a position to supply us with many goods that include perishable and nonperishable foodstuffs, first-aid supplies, clothing, bedding (blankets and sleeping bags), and other miscellaneous items.

She wrote me with the intent of my suggesting a needy organization to donate and distribute these to. It *just* so happened that one week *before* I received her letter, we were given our new mission to help the needy and homeless. When I received Link's letter, my spine tingled, for I immediately knew she was to be our mission connection. She would supply us with the goods and we would be responsible for their distribution to the needy.

Wellspring turns out to be the perfect name for this new project. We will warehouse Link's shipments here at home, and when we're settled, I want to have a Lodestar Office with Wellspring housed in the back where the needy can come to help themselves to whatever we have that they need. I'd like to have this established somewhere in our new geographical area. Our private property will be no good for this project.

The entire family is very excited to begin this new work. We know what it's like being on food stamps and welfare—it's a personally humiliating situation. If we can alleviate someone's physical suffering and help them a little with extra food and such, that will make us so happy. And if I get enough money from this lawsuit we'll be sure to have left-over funds to rent or buy a building to house the Wellspring warehouse. Oh God and the Powers of Light, please make everything fall into place.

Now I'm definitely in deep doo-doo for writing the specifics about Wellspring. Now our Advisors and my Starborn friends will be upset with me. I wouldn't be surprised if they erased the ink on these pages just to teach me a lesson in Obedience, but regardless, this is *my* private journal and there aren't supposed to be any more secrets kept. If they don't want our mission recorded in black and white then they're welcome to dematerialize these pages, but I'm at least going to go ahead and record the events of our project. Sorry Guys, cut me some slack and humor me.

This evening a stray dog found its way to our porch. Sarah's heart went out to it and since we couldn't shelter it inside with our two dogs, we laid a rug down in the corner of the porch where the A-frame roof comes down. Sarah fed it oat cereal and two dog Milk Bones. She covered it with an old blanket.

We all felt bad we couldn't bring it inside for the night, but it's warm and sheltered now. In the morning, Bill will call the Teller County office and give them its license number. Then we'll be able to call the owners to come pick it up. I'd be so sick at heart if Magic or Rainbow was ever lost overnight. . .they're "family" through and through. I hope this little fella doesn't wander away during the night. When I last checked, he was all curled up beneath the blanket. He appears to be well cared for and. . . *DAMN!* I wish my "friend" would stop "popping in" on me like that—scares the bejesus out of me! (He'd appeared at my side while I was writing about the stray dog). Seems he came to discuss what I've written about Wellspring—they must be reading over my shoulder (which wouldn't be the first time they snooped).

Anyway, he explained why I wasn't allowed to write about our new mission before. He said there is a small percentage probability that this journal will one day reach the eyes of the public and they didn't want hoards of people *thinking* we had a warehouse of supplies *on our land.* But now that we've already evolved the plan by relocating the storehouse somewhere else, they see no problem with me writing about it. Why didn't they just say that in the first place? 'Course I know the answer to that one—*we* have to do a good measure of our *own* thinking and problem-solving with each specific mission.

The only thing he cautioned me about was to never record our "connection's" real name or where she gets the supplies. So for this journal, she will remain "Link."

The Starborn and I talked of other matters, including the publicity situation with Vernon that arose today. He still adamantly concurs with our Advisors that I *must* remain out of the public eye and do no personal publicity of any kind. This is still fine with me, but it puts me in a continually awkward position with my publisher. I can't very well come right out and tell Vernon or Bob, "the *Starborn ones* don't want me doing radio or print interviews." Jesus, they'd think my elevator finally stopped going all the way to the top! There's no *way* they'd buy that.

So I remain stuck between a rock and a hard place. I suppose Bob thinks I'm "one tough cookie," but the *truth* would probably be worse to bear than that. God, if people only knew what my everyday life really involved. . .if they only knew.

OH-OH, Bill just walked into the kitchen. Now I'm *really* in deep doo-doo.

Forty minutes later. . .

He's gone back to bed. Seems he couldn't sleep so he decided to come downstairs. His eyes bugged to see my journal half filled. I told him I *had* to do this, but did it in secret so he wouldn't think I was going to die.

He said he already knew I wasn't going to "go back" in 1994, because his Advisor had assured him that my death date probability was now down to Zero.

So. . .what a relief for me, because now I don't have to hide this journal and lie about what I'm doing at night. That made me feel real uncomfortable with guilt—guess I'm a lousy liar.

I told Bill what our friend said about our having Lodestar and Wellspring in our new area. He was extremely doubtful about having enough funds for that, but knew that if that was the right direction for the mission, then something would turn up to make it so.

Bill went back to bed.

I closed my journal and followed him up.

7-19-91, Friday

After I got in bed last night I couldn't shut my mind off. It was spinning. Churning out thoughts.

The idea came to me that if we had the Wellspring warehouse behind the Lodestar office, wouldn't that also be a good place to assemble the free energy device? I made a mental note to again plead my case for the project the next time my friend popped in on me. Of course if he knows what's on my mind (and he usually does) he'll probably avoid me for a while. We've really had some falling-outs over this issue.

Another subject I thought about while lying in bed was what my friend had said about the possibility of this journal getting out to the public. To me, that's ridiculous. I'm not saying it's impossible because I've witnessed too many impossibles become possibles; what I'm doubting is the probability of it. I think that's so remote that I'm not even going to consider it. This is *my* book. These are *my* soul sounds . . .sounds nobody can or will hear but me.

Another thought that speared into my mind was of Many Heart. What brought him to mind was a little something my friend had let slip, and I put that together with what he'd said about the Starborn being active around our chosen property along with what Many Heart himself told me about seeing him again when we were settled. Conclusion: Many Heart *does* have a Starborn connection!

It took me a long, long time to finally fall asleep last night.

Mail was heavy today. Sixteen people wrote to say how much they loved *Daybreak* and how much they learned from it, and one woman wrote to say I don't know anything. She sent me a Shamanistic Class brochure to "enlighten" me. The purpose of this was supposed to teach me how wonderful and right shamanism is for people to get into. . .but the $500 price tag on the brochure only hurt her case and underscored mine. There are times I think people just use no logic whatsoever, and their ability to reason appears nearly nonexistent. Case in point is this woman who sends me something that clearly proves my point instead of hers.

Another letter today flatly informed me that my dream symbol interpretations in *Earthway* and *Daybreak* were all wrong. But the letter that most disturbed me was from a woman who needed clarification about books being "supposedly" written by beings calling themselves Intergalactic Commanders. I told this poor woman that these were pure fiction and that they're not written by the entities who are claiming authorship. This information came to me via my Starborn friend who was greatly upset by this group. In addition, one of these so-called "alien" authors claims to once have been Jesus. . .not true, for that entity is now walking the earth in *human* form and is remaining anonymous—so too is St. Germain whose name is also being used by another of these "alien" authors. I felt great compassion for this woman who is confused by so many pretenders. It used to be only discarnates who were being channeled and writing books, now it's alien beings who are popular. What crap. And I get upset when "my friends" don't pop in on these phonies to personally tell them so. But their response is always the same—"we cannot interfere yet." Good thing I'm not one of them, because I'd probably be a renegade alien going about appearing to the pretenders and telling them to *cease at once!*

Nothing riles me more than to receive letters from good folks who are trying to step through the New Age muck and sort out the truth from all the stinking garbage. Sometimes I feel so defeated—so useless—like my voice is mere butterfly breath beneath the roaring din of the pretenders. How can I possibly do any good when I feel like one drop of rain water falling into a polluted ocean? My words are lost to the roar of the collective pretenders. And I feel so diminutive—no more than a weak squeak. This then weighs heavily on my heart, for I'm here for the sole purpose of bringing the Light of the Way. Yet, though I'm continually told that my mission is going well and that all the people have to use their free wills and own awareness to *see* that light, I'm still disheartened when so many are still being duped by the pretenders. It's almost as if my truth is harder to believe in than theirs. But it's all so simple. . .so beautiful! *God* is the answer. . . the Way! The God Essence *inside!* But no, people have to follow the lesser, more interesting phonies who are aliens, or "Jesus," or St. Germain, or Geronimo, or the so-called ones that proclaim themselves as the "Elite of The Great White Brotherhood Hierarchy!" Oh God, even my Brothers of our beautiful realm are being impersonated. When will these poor people come to their senses?

Thank God for the little things that come to brighten and uplift my day. Sarah brought me a bouquet of fresh-picked wildflowers in a glass of water and set them on my desk today. I set down my letters and took time to smell them and admire the blossoms. She has that closeness and special sense that tells her I'm feeling defeated. She hugged and held me for awhile. For a 15-year-old, she has the awareness and comprehension of someone of great age. She is a comfort to me.

And when Jenny notices I'm feeling the weariness of the battle, her little hugs mean the world to me because she doesn't quite understand all the high philosophy, but only knows when mom's sad.

Right now Aimee's too wrapped up in her own life to notice anything. She's constantly on the go and not here enough to sense anyone's deeper feelings, or keep up on what's been transpiring. That's okay, she's at that age where the separation begins and her own path materializes.

Today I also received a gift. It was a beautiful Indian rug. What saddened me was the letter that accompanied it. It was from a man who hadn't received my last reply to his letter. I hate it when my letters don't make their destination. Tomorrow I'll get right on a response to him.

Bill talked to Bob and, after they discussed business, Bill told him he had a surprise for him from Mary.

"Oh?" Bob said.

Bill laughed. "It's nothing bad. Mary just told me to tell you not to be so suspicious. She says I can now tell you that when we get the first four contracts back she wants to *give* them to you—no advance. . .just new covers and delete or change the photos in *Phantoms.*"

Silence. Then, "You just made my day! No. . .you just made my *month*!"

When Bill told me what Bob said, I got all warm inside. I love making people happy.

Goodnight, Bob.

7-20-91 Saturday

Received a good-news letter from Claire Zion at Pocket today. They sold the Spanish Rights to *Earthway!* Now that book will be in Spanish and German. It seems so strange seeing my books printed in a language I can't even read, but it's a great feeling knowing how far No-Eyes is reaching around the world.

We had another one of those "war thunderstorms" again this afternoon and, for the first time, Bill felt held back from watching it on our porch. It was horrendous, with powerful lightning and house-shaking thunder. Just after I unplugged everything in the house, a bolt of lightning crackled down nearby. You could actually hear it. A moment later our neighbor called to ask if all our electricity was out. We were still fine, but they were completely out and the woman thought their house had been hit. No wonder Bill was forewarned to stay inside this time.

Our neighbors are from Los Angeles and have only been in Colorado for two years, but they're going back in a few months. They say you can't make any money here, so they're returning to make the "big bucks." What a shame folks put such priority on those big bucks. They'd rather give up this mountain beauty and security for money and L.A. I suppose if that's where their mindset is, they should go back to California. We have a bumper sticker here that says: DON'T CALIFORNICATE COLORADO! And that means "love the mountains—not the money."

I forgot to record the outcome of that lost dog we sheltered. It's name was Petey. He belonged to a rancher family down the way, who owns over 180 acres just before our mountain community. The grandmother drove up here to get Petey and she was very glad to get him back. We were likewise glad to know that Petey had a loving and caring family to return to.

Bill and Sarah spent the day cleaning out the large shop area between the house and garage. We needed to make all the space we could to accommodate our Wellspring supply shipments. Tomorrow Bill will call the Woodland Community Cupboard (an organization that supplies free food for the needy) to see if they'll accept and be able to accommodate our fresh perishable foodstuffs from Wellspring. The clothing we receive will go to another free distribution center in Woodland called The Clothes Closet. This is a place where needy people just come in to take whatever they need without any charge or paperwork involved. We used the Clothes Closet when the girls were little, now we have the golden opportunity to be on the "pay back" end, and it feels damned good to be able to do this.

When we get settled and Wellspring can have a real home, we're planning on canvassing supermarkets for contributions. The more food we can supply through Wellspring the better. I cannot put into words what this new mission means to me. For years, the plight of the homeless and hungry have weighed heavily on my heart and I've felt so helpless, with no way to alleviate their suffering. And now our new direction veers off onto a path with that very purpose in mind. Feeding and clothing the poor will fill my cup to overflowing. How balanced were our missions. First the spiritual aspect was our purpose and, now that I have all the 12 books written, I'm free for the next phase—the corporeal one. No wonder I was so "driven" to finish all the books long before their publication dates. It was for the purpose of freeing me for our next mission! Now I'm so glad I listened and crammed 12 years of work into only six. It was not because

I was going to die (as my family feared), it was because I had so much more to do. . .and I can't wait to get Wellspring a real established home for people to start coming to. Jeez, I'm getting happy shivers just thinking of it.

Bill is still dubious about us having the warehouse building, but I'm sure we'll get enough settlement money for it. I have complete confidence this project will manifest just the way it's supposed to.

This thought brings to mind a friend of mine whom I've never met, except through her letters to me. Jeannie has been trying to get financial backing to purchase the huge Redstone Castle for a spiritual center. If she can accomplish this, she offered one of the estate's houses to us. At the time, I didn't see us there. I only foresaw our land. But now, with the Wellspring project I wonder if a stronger connection down the line isn't in the offing. Last I heard from Jeannie was that she was still in California working on investors. The upkeep on the castle for annual maintenance was around a million dollars. We're talking about a huge estate, huge operation, and huge expenses for her project. She even tried to interest Shirley MacLaine, but some secretary wrote back that the lady already had many other projects going and couldn't get involved in any more. Maybe that's just as well. Jeannie was very disappointed, but I told her only the right people will respond to her project, and that she really knows it shouldn't be any other way.

Well, I haven't been advised if we're to connect projects, but it seems like more than a coincidence that both of us are currently looking at the tiny town of Redstone. I really have no ambition for Lodestar or Wellspring to be housed in the castle, but perhaps the area will be able to accommodate both our operations as separate entities. Actually, Redstone is no more than a narrow country road winding between the mountains and the Crystal River. It has no traffic lights, no grocery stores, and no schools. Redstone is more of a "place out of time". . .just my style.

What do you think, No-Eyes? Am I getting warmer? You don't have to answer that one.

Goodnight, No-Eyes.

7-21-91, Sunday

Had another terrific thunderstorm today, in fact, we had several that came one after the other. The family joked about the Light Warriors really kicking butt today—it's about time. The power was intense.

Spent the entire day answering letters.

Sarah had written Eric six week's ago and mentioned to-day that she hadn't heard back. It has been a long time since I've heard from him—maybe he's changed his mind about clearing things up with Aimee. That'd be too bad, because she'd broken up with her last boyfriend and was primed to meet with Eric. Oh well—what will be will be, I guess. In matters of the heart, there's no telling how things will eventually turn out. Right now the way Aimee's thrown herself into this firefighting activity, she's really not into relationships because of her full schedule. I'm lucky if I see her a couple hours of each day.

Tonight's a good night to have a long meditation period. I'll probably be gone into it for at least an hour, so I'll end today's entry now.

7-22-91, Monday

Today we received our first supply shipment for Well-spring. I was amazed at all the food and the variety of it. It took me four hours to sort and repackage it for distribution. Wednesday Bill will deliver our boxes to the needy.

Next week we'll be receiving boxes from Link that contain samples of all her available items. We'll try to streamline our shipments after we get a better estimate of what's available. We can already see that this is going to be a lot of work, but it sure is worth it.

Rainbow hasn't been feeling well lately. She's getting cat-aracts and can't see as well as she did before. She has arth-ritis and also is having more and more digestive problems. The vet said she's aged about three years beyond her chron-ological age because of her hyperactive system. We hate to see her limping around when her joints are stressed—which is almost always, due to her high-strung, protective nature. Bill and Sarah are taking her to see the vet tomorrow, to see if we can't do more for her in the way of easing her problems. None of us want to put Bo to sleep, but we'd rather endure *our* heart pains than to see her endure *her* pains. Poor Rain-bow, we'd always told her she'd be able to run free on our land. . .that was 10 years ago and she's still waiting.

Jenny called us to come see the bear today. It was loping alongside our house.

7-23-91, Tuesday

Bill wouldn't let Sarah go with him to take Bo to the vet. He came home alone. His eyes were filled with tears. He'd held Bo's head while the sleep shot took effect.

The vet said it was the best thing we could've done for Rainbow.

When Bill came home it was drizzly and a heavy fog drifted down the mountain to surround our house. Even nature shared our mourning today.

Although all of us went around all day with red eyes and we each had our own private bouts of crying, Bill was hardest hit because Rainbow was more his dog. He'd always tell her how he hated fencing her in every time we rented another house and he promised her (at least once a week) that as soon as we had our land, he and her would run and run together. . .and when they got tired of running, they'd just walk through their woods together.

Bill had an extremely difficult day. I can't imagine how one heart can take so much ripping pain. First it was the heartache and worry over my operation which tore him apart. Then it was the rejection of all his months of help for our lady friend (which really stabbed at his heart), and now the loss of his dog. He is totally shattered. He says he cannot live with such searing heartache. He says now he cannot keep his promise to Bo and the land means absolutely nothing to him now. He doesn't care where we live, or if we ever have our own place. Even our new project is meaningless to him right now. He feels he's a complete failure because he couldn't get through to our former friends. He is totally devastated. Extreme heartache can do that.

So I spent the day comforting, talking with and holding him. He'll come through; it'll just take time for his heart to heal. He's so loving and caring. What a cruel joke it is that the most ripping and searing pain is caused by love. How utterly ironic that is. Deep love can be so bitter.

At twilight tonight Sarah called me to the front windows. There were some strange birds at our birdfeeder. When I looked, I called Bill to come look at the new birds. We held each other and watched 12 large doves perch on our deck railing. Never before had these birds been seen around our house. It was clear the 12 were not what they seemed. It was clear they had come as a sign for Bill. And he was comforted.

Rainbow, you were a brave soul. For nine years you protected us with no regard for your own life. For nine years you gave us all your love, companionship, and comfort. You were a brave little warrior and you chose a good day to die. You were a true Buffalo Heart.

Goodnight Rainbow, we will never forget you. . .always will your spirit remain in our hearts.

Now I will spend the rest of the night in prayer and powerful spirit work to help the other Brothers in healing Bill's heart. More pain he cannot endure—this I know. I will also call for my Starborn friend with the hope there is something he and his associates can do for Bill. . .they're very good at blocking out selected memories. Perhaps they will do me this one personal favor. I will desperately try.

7-24-91 Wednesday

I stayed up until 3:30 A.M.last night. All the house lights were off except for the two oil pots that were burning on the fireplace mantle.

I alternated between prayer, meditation, and just plain thought-talk to the powers of light. The entire time was spent on Bill's behalf.

Bill was up at dawn as usual, only he woke up frisky (something that doesn't happen when he's heartsick) and that was definitely a good sign that he'd been helped during the night. I was so happy he was feeling better.

During the day he admitted to only a couple twinges of heartache and commented that he must be getting some "big time" help from our Advisors.

Then I told him what I'd done last night and how long it took me. He was concerned.

"That means you were in bed only a few hours before I woke you up this morning. Why didn't you tell me and I would've left you alone?"

I smiled. "I wouldn't have ruined your mood for all the tea in China. Besides, I went back to sleep anyway."

Later, he and Sarah delivered our first Wellspring box of food and they both felt real good about it.

The worker at the Community Cupboard couldn't believe our big box was filled with food and he was so overjoyed by the contribution. He wanted to know Bill's name, but Bill told him he wanted to remain anonymous and that we hoped to be making regular donations.

"God bless you, Mr. Anonymous!" he said.

Now I think Bill's interest in our new mission has been renewed. He returned home with a big smile on his face. Later in the day he talked about our future Wellspring warehouse after we're settled—I knew he'd bounce back. Thanks Guys for helping him so much.

Tom, our UPS man, delivered another supply box from Link. When he banged on our front door, it was eerie not hearing Rainbow bark and charge through the house. It was a strange feeling not to have to defend a visitor from her.

Our second delivery wasn't food; it was items of a different nature that we knew we'd need to help the homeless. These will serve the Vietnam vets who are "cave dwellers," living in the mountains of our future area. These items were sleeping bags, medical supplies, blankets, heavy yellow rubber raincoats, and winter clothing.

Bill called Link and talked to her for two hours. He gave her a priority supply list of five categories and this helped her a great deal. Now she knows what to concentrate on. She is also lining up other possible suppliers for us.

When Bill got off the phone, he reiterated his conversation with Link. He's getting more and more into it. And we discussed how we could solicit store owners and managers in the Glenwood and Roaring Fork region, once we were permanently settled over there. Even the convenience stores throw away edible and usable goods —I know because Robin and the girls worked in them. If we could pick up damaged goods and day-old or broken packaged foodstuffs, we'd be able to keep our Wellspring warehouse going and still maintain good distribution. In the meantime, all food deliveries we receive while we're still here in Woodland will go to needy families we know and to the Community Cupboard. The nonedible items we'll store and move with us. I just wish we were settled right now so we can really get set up and official. . .we got *work* to do!

7-25-91, Thursday

Worked on correspondence all day.

It was cloudy and chilly up here at 9,500 feet. Bill made a fire in the woodstove to take the gloom out of the house. This seems to be The Summer That Never Was.

7-26-91, Friday

Someone sent me more printed material on the Alien Command Group. Somebody's making a ton of money off the gullible public and it turns my stomach to see so many being misled by a few totally unscrupulous schemers who fabricated their own little version of Star Trek. God I hate having to live in this phoney, ego-filled world. Come, my friend, pop in and take me for another ride a much *longer* one this time.

The living room is dark except for my oil pots burning low on the fireplace stone mantle. Wood is crackling in the woodstove. It was another chilly day today. At 6 P.M. it was only 45 degrees out and all afternoon we had terrific thunderstorms. It's been a "Seattle summer" here this year. I'm not complaining though, because the wet woods have been a real blessing—no forest fires—but the weather has been so out of character. I'm used to seeing deep blue skies all summer long.

This evening I took out my enameled Chinese box from the glass cabinet and looked at the treasure within. I held the white quartz stones I'd collected from around No-Eyes' cabin. After I'd reminisced awhile, for some reason I thought of the comment someone had made about Summer Rain just out to make money, and I smiled at that thought as I caressed the white stones. Out to make money? If that were true I'd certainly have already made my first million by "selling" these white quartz stones "from her property." COME ONE. COME ALL. COME GET YOURSELF ONE OF THE VERY STONES NO-EYES WALKED ON! Oh God, how can anyone think I'm only going through all this just to make money?

This morning I got to thinking about the lady who'd gifted us with the large check. Good grief, I still can't believe such generosity. We'd paid off my hospital bill with it and she'll never know how much she unburdened us.

Anyway, I sat down and typed her a letter to again express our deep appreciation and I chatted with her about our lawsuit and our new Wellspring project.

But I needed to do more. I needed to return her gift with a gift of my own, but had nothing to give her. Then the idea came to me to send her a complete set of signed books. I only had a couple left of two titles, but this was the only gift I had. I included the children's manual and Bill packaged up the seven books. He mailed them priority mail when he and the girls went back to town for their chiropractic appointment. I hope she's surprised because she certainly pulled a good one over on us.

I missed Rainbow today. I missed the way she used to sit next to my reading chair, put her chin on its arm and just stare up into my eyes. We'd have a private staring contest, at least that's what it'd looked like to an observer—actually, it was so much more than that. I miss her big brown mahogany eyes. I miss her sleeping under my desk. I miss her love. I will never get a replacement for her because loving hurts too much. Loving can be very painful. Someone once said that it was better to have loved and lost than never to have loved at all. I don't believe that opinion, for how does one miss what one never had or experienced? How is it one would miss the deep heartpain that accompanies love? And so, because of this, Rainbow will stand alone and never be succeeded by another. I love to love—I do not love love's pain.

Tomorrow Aimee has to be downtown in Colorado Springs at the fire practice tower. She has to be there at 7 A.M. So far I'm feeling alright about her test, and hope I'm not being blocked as I've been in times past. Tonight I will stay up again all night to pray and converse with the Light Powers. Aimee wants to do good on this test, but will also know in the back of her mind that she's providing the dark side with the perfect opportunity to strike at us. I can already clearly envision the tower area surrounded by both forces ready to do battle over Aimee. I've seen this before and it's a powerful and truly incredible sight. I realize how utterly paranoid this would sound to an outsider or an unaware person, but they just would never grasp or begin to understand the reality of these intense situations. If they only knew. If they *really* only knew. Well. . .someday they will. Yes, someday they certainly will and what a horrendous shock that will be. Their awakening is only going to be that much harder when it comes knocking at their door—they're going to think it's Halloween, or at least try to create that reality. . .but it won't work. No, it won't work at all. And then they'll be totally unprepared. Well, I've done my best to bring the reality of the Dark Ones to light. If people still don't want to believe— if they still want to hang onto their flimsy straws, then I can do no more than accept their choice, the end result will be their's to deal with and try to face.

I'm grateful my new mission has given me a trail that leads far away from the New Age community. To continually see so much utter garbage was like trying to hold your nose while swimming through a shoreless cesspool. I cried many tears over what I saw and heard there. Anger too was felt. Now, thank God, I've been given the Gift of Purpose that takes me far away from the Pretenders and onto the path that leads to the honest poor and hungry—*that* I can welcome like a breath of fresh air. . .like a wellspring of pure mountain water. At least the poor and needy people I help will see me and my heart in their true light. At least *they* will never say that I'm doing what I'm doing "for the money." I've finished my "soul work" and the phonies called me phony. I wore my soul on my sleeve and few saw it there. Now I will place my soul back in its tabernacle and replace its vacated sleeve position with my heart. Literally, I now harken to the Autumn Spirit's beckoning call and walk back into the woodsmoke of my pine-filled woods, for there awaits my trail to the Wellspring that gives to me new life and purpose.

Tonight a full moon rises. . .how fitting. I will go out and be renewed by its light while I pray for the misguided ones.

7-27-91, Saturday

Oh Guys, thanks so much for being there with Aimee today. She felt her Guide real close and even caught herself giggling in her face mask because of her Guide's closeness.

Aimee did well on the ladders and the roof. When it came time for the four trainees to enter the burning tower, the man in front of her made the mistake of spraying water before he should've and ended up with steam and backsmoke in their faces. He screamed for everyone to back out. The instructor shouted for them to "FIND ANOTHER ENTRANCE!" and . . .only Aimee grabbed the hose and ran with it to another entryway, charged down the stairs and faced the blaze. She wondered where the hell her backup was. Finally the three come down the stairs behind her.

Aimee did make a few mistakes. When she grabbed the hose she was supposed to check the nozzle setting and two more things that I forgot, but above all, she showed she had the guts to go get the job done! Yeah! Aimee! Although she had respect for the roaring fire, she did not shirk her duty. All the trainees were in full bunker gear with masks and tanks. Aimee says it can seem hard to breathe and that some of them panicked and needed oxygen. Overall, she felt good about the tower test and now she tells us she's going to go with three others to observe an autopsy. She wants to know and understand more about the human body—she feels if she observes an autopsy she'll be able to handle accident scenes better. I agreed with her, but also warned her that an autopsy will never prepare her for the massive amount of blood she may see at an accident scene. Cold reality is what she's preparing to deal with on this job, and so that is how we must discuss its aspects. She understood what I was telling her because, last week, a trainee accompanied the fire truck to an accident where a car crossed lanes and hit a motor-cyclist. The trainee lost his lunch due to the fatal head injuries of the cyclist.

Aimee knows exactly what she's getting into and I don't have enough praise for her—especially when she's not even going to be paid for putting her life on the line. She's a petite grocery store cashier who will have a second life as a volunteer firefighter and EMT. Way to go, Aimee! God bless and watch over you.

One aspect of Aimee's new project that Bill and I find amusing is how many male firefighters are knocking themselves out to help teach her. They see her as some tiny China doll and fall over themselves trying to help her study and make the grade. Due to Aimee's brave performance today, these big and burly men have also been shown that they'll be able to depend on her when the chips are down. They know they need little people on their team, because many times someone is needed to get into small spaces or under things a big person can't handle. Anyway, Aimee's not hurting for male attention right now, and I think it just may be possible that Eric waited a few weeks too long to make his move. I wouldn't expect her to wait forever for him. . .life goes on.

A city person has a residence up here in this mountain community. She left her patio door open and. . .in strolled bear. I thought it was hilarious, but I guess she didn't. Maybe that sounds cruel or unsympathetic of me, but if you want to live up in the high mountains, especially ones that are surrounded by such a large near-virgin forest as our area is, you'd better be aware of the wildlife and the new rules you live life by. If we left our doors open we'd have everything from chipmunks and raccoons to black bears rummaging in our cupboards. Who knows, maybe that cougar would even venture to the door. . .five have already strolled down the Woodland Park streets this summer. . .I surely wouldn't doubt they'd come around the houses way up here.

Bill is still missing Rainbow a lot. His Heart Center seems to be open extra wide these last couple of months. He's been extra sensitive and he's not liking it. We'll have to work on making an adjustment on that Gate.

Mandy's down in Penrose with her dad this weekend and Robin just walked in from a date. She said the mountain lion was into the trash behind the grocery store around 9:30 tonight.

"Funny you should mention him," I said, before telling her about how our neighbor had a visit from Yogi.

She thought it was funny too. Maybe I'm not so cruel after all, either that or we've both got a warped sense of humor. Seriously, all of us know there's no Yogi or Pink Panther out there. Bears and cougars can be a real threat, and we all are on our toes when coming home after dark or are out in the woods during the day. It was broad daylight when the bear romped alongside our house the other day.

As predicted—the wildlife is becoming unpredictable.

Goodnight, Yogi. Sleep tight.

7-28-91, Sunday

It was finally a normal summer day and the family went down to Colorado Springs for a shopping day. We don't go down there more than twice a month, or only when it's absolutely necessary. There are no clothing stores in Woodland (unless you care to count the one high-priced women's store), so we go down to Target and Walmart for things we need and usually stock up on regularly-used items such as lamp oil, shampoo, Pine Tar soap and general medicines that are so much cheaper downtown.

We had a nice day and went to Denny's for lunch. When we returned home at 6 P.M., we found a dead rabbit in the dog yard. Magic had been in the house all day, but she'd chased it when we let her out. Sarah discovered it about a half-hour later and called her dad outside to see it. We all went out and, after Bill buried it, he brought our attention to a new visitor that was clinging upside down to the house above the back kitchen window. A tiny bat, head down and wings folded, instilled high interest in the girls who'd never seen a bat up close before. Last I checked, the little critter was still clinging to the house. The wildlife has certainly provided us with some interesting moments lately.

This evening Bill and I danced to one of our songs, "True Love Ways" by Buddy Holly. What a shame his career was so tragically cut short.

Goodnight, Buddy. . .wherever you are.

7-29-91, Monday

It was a beautiful Colorado day today. When Bill and all three girls went to town for their chiropractic appointment I asked Bill to bring back some wild bird seed. Lately the doves, chipmunks, and squirrels have been raiding the feeders. I've gotten to the point of filling the feeders then spreading the rest on the picnic table and deck so they can all feed at once. Everyday for the last week it's looked like a Bambi film. . .even the bunnies come to feed.

I worked on answering letters all day. In the afternoon, Pete from Hampton Roads called and told Bill they'd had a call from one of my readers who wanted to know where they could get my two novels. I'd mentioned them in *Daybreak* as being two of the 12 books I had ready to go. Evidently this reader misunderstood and thought they were already published. Actually, I really would like to get two books out each year because this new mission will be taking up all my time and the new path leaves little time for the former work. The new purpose came five years early—I believe that's because they urged me to hurry with the completion of the 12 books. Now that they're all written, I no longer feel like a writer as that part of my work is already behind me . . .yet people will still perceive me as an "active" author for five more years. This is a strange situation to be in and I feel we'll soon have to inform the public that my new purpose came early and that I can no longer be available to answer their letters. That aspect of my mission has already passed. Due to *Daybreak's* format, people are seeing how many questions I've responded to and now more and more people are feeling freer to write with *their* questions—at a time when I need to be gearing down to the stopping point.

I can't help it that They arranged our new mission so close on the heels of *Daybreak's* publication. I must be about my work whatever it is and whenever it evolves into other aspects. Actually, my "spiritual" purpose has been completed and ended, even though the rest of the books will still go on being published. In the meantime, I have another path to walk and I guess I'm going to have to make that known through a new information letter to my correspondents.

If this is how we'll remedy the flow of continued questions, I don't feel free to expose what our new purpose is. It
will be difficult to precisely word our information letter so
feelings aren't hurt. After all, we won't be deserting them,
we'll just be helping the public in a different manner.

All the important words have already been said and written. All the questions that are coming in now have already
been answered in the books published so far. People think
they still need me, but they really don't. I feel like I'm
becoming a crutch for many of them because they already
know the answers to their questions —they already know how
I'll respond—but still they want the reassurance of hearing it
from me. They don't need that. They need to begin trusting
and having strong confidence in their own answers and decisions. And, I can give them that by finally halting my responses. To some, that will seem cruel, and I suppose, I'll be
called more nasty names, but I came here to accomplish more
than one mission, and now I'm being called to another one.
That brings to mind a concept I never covered—that of an
individual having more than one or consecutive missions.
Everyone asks what their purpose is—never what *are* their
purposes (with an "s"). More often than not, people do have
more than one reason for being here—they do have multiple
missions that are arranged to follow one after the other. I'll
have to remember to include that thought into my last book
(which I'm still adding to as ideas come to mind). Maybe, if
I got enough money from the suit I *can* get two books published in one year. I could make this happen if I forfeited
the advance money for each of them. I certainly don't want
or need to drain Bob's new company if I don't really need
the money. Yeah, I like that idea—wouldn't *he* be surprised
if it really came about!

Right now I feel caught between the proverbial "rock and
a hard place" because of my situation. The public believes
I'll no longer be available *after* the twelfth book is published
when, in actuality, that event has already arrived and I don't
know an easy way to make it known. It will be hard for
people to understand. This has happened so fast. The Brotherhood wasted no time in having our new mission connection
contact us. I had to act on that and accept our new direction.
To refuse would've been absolutely *unthinkable* to both Bill
and me. We are being overburdened right now because we're
trying to actively work on the new Wellspring mission while
still carrying on the former spiritual aspect via correspondent's
letters and responses. We must find a way to ease out of the
latter. I think getting the rest of my books published as soon
as possible will be a great help. . .waiting five more years

seems ridiculous and, in the end, unnecessary. Besides, I know my readers would love it.

Another aspect that troubles me is what to do about the children's book. The way I see it I have three options. We can keep paying to have it printed and distribute it ourselves by mail order through our Lodestar Press; we can sell it to another publisher to publish and distribute (but then I'd no longer be able to personalize them); or we could discontinue the book altogether (which would be a shame). We don't have to decide on this right now, but as our current stock diminishes, we'll need the funds for another reprint and, depending if we have the extra money available for it, that will force us into a final decision. This book was conceived of "for and by children," I'd hate to deprive them of the book's important spiritual concepts that they need to grow on. I suppose it does turn my stomach that "money" has to be the determining factor here. That seems sort of sickening to me. I treasure the letters and drawings children have sent me after receiving the book—they're so touching and mean so much to me.

I need to get away. I pray I won't have a ton of mail tomorrow. . . I need to renew myself in the woods and be close to No-Eyes. I'm wearing myself out trying to answer everyone's letter and also work on Wellspring too. If I could clone myself I would. Tomorrow I will make it a point to spend at least a couple of hours in the forest.

7-30-91, Tuesday

Link called to talk to Bill. She has a shipment for us of 300 pounds of supplies—100 pounds of it is food. They're going to try to meet somewhere to transfer the shipment. I knew there was an ulterior reason for our getting that van, there's no way we could do this project without it.

I had a lot of letters come in today. I never had time to get out to the woods. . .somehow I knew that's how it would be.

7-31-91, Wednesday

Worked all day on correspondence. I had Wellspring work I needed to do. Tomorrow I must turn the correspondence over to Bill, so I can get out of the office and give my full attention to our shipment. I'm spreading myself too thin by trying to keep up the former mission when it is already finished—trouble is, folks don't know that yet and my heart still goes out to them. How does one say the door is now closed? I find I don't have the heart to do that yet, so I will keep it cracked open for as long as I can. I fear Bill will slam the door for me if he sees it's too much of a drain on me to carry both jobs. Nothing gets him riled into action more than me being stressed or overworked. He's like a mother hen. Can't really blame him after the worry and grief he suffered over my operation. Poor Baby was deathly afraid I wasn't going to come out of my anesthesia, even though I promised him over and over that I'd come back. In fact, first thing I said (rather woozily) when I was wheeled out of the Recovery Room and the family was all around me in the hall was, "See? I *told* you I wouldn't leave. I *told* you I'd be back." But later they told me I looked really bad at that moment, but all they cared about was that I *had* kept my promise—I *had* come back. And anyway, what *was* I supposed to look like after having a major operation an hour and a half before? I'm no great shakes to begin with, and I probably did resemble death warmed over when I was wheeled out of recovery.

Anyway, I know Bill couldn't handle another incident like that, so he dotes on me all the time. Even the girls get worried looks if I seem overtired or work too many hours on the correspondence. They too think it's time to shut the door so I can devote all my time and energies on the new mission. But they're not as close to the correspondents as I am. They don't truly understand how hard it is for me to make that break you know must be made. But tomorrow I must give the mail over to Bill because I cannot work on Wellspring and also spend 12 hours on letters at my desk.

In the mail today we received a sympathy card from our vet. We thought that was very kind, but it did bring renewed tears. Rainbow was such a loving family member—the heart-pain over her goneness is incredible. Never . . .ever. . .will I bring home another cute irresistible puppy again. Bill had actually asked me if I now wanted to get a blue-eyed Husky pup (something I'd always wanted), but I told him no. In fact, I told him that the next time I saw some little kid sitting next to the grocery store door with a box of cuddly puppies, I was going to force myself to look the other way. Both Rainbow and Magic were "free" give-aways outside the grocery store. I took them home with me. . .but never again.

Last month Aimee came home after work one night with a black kitten which had a clubbed foot. I wanted to keep that little one in the worst way and my heart went out to it. One of the hardest things I ever had to do was to hand that little ball of fur back to Aimee and tell her to return it. She had the owner's address—but she also had a bag of newly-bought kitty supplies out in the pickup. But Bill's allergic to cats; he's been doing real well with Jenny's cat, but two would be just too much and I think Aimee already knew that, but couldn't resist the handicapped kitten. I cried when she took it back an hour later. A mushy heart is hell to live with, still. . .I wouldn't trade it for any other kind.

The day after Aimee returned the kitten, the owner came through Aimee's check-out line and said that the kitten was placed in a good home with loving people. Aimee was comforted by that, but we both still wished its home could've been ours.

August, 1991

8-1-91, Thursday

I managed to stay out of the office and work on Wellspring. When Bill brought the mail home he carried in a huge box from Kim Firebear Brennan. She and her husband Leo were so appreciative of my mention of their book in *Daybreak* they sent me gifts of both their handicrafts. Leo made us a beautiful Dreamcatcher, a simple gorgeous Prayer Smudge Feather and a very unique antler centerpiece on wood which I placed on our coffee table. Kim sent a delicate feather and bead barrette (to hold back all that long hair, she said) and also another unique native Face Plaque she called "Rain Dreamer Woman." She said it was the first face she fired, and made it as her personal inner vision of No-Eyes. The old woman has long grey hair with feathers and beads. It's so beautiful. We placed it on our stone fireplace mantle and I arranged the grey hair to look like it's blowing in the wind.

My goodness! Kim and Leo didn't have to do anything like that. I never in my wildest dreams ever imagined getting such gorgeous gifts from them. I was just so tickled! It really made my day. When I found myself going back again and again to look at and touch their gifts, I couldn't help thinking that they're too fine for me because I can feel how much of themselves they put into their work.

Goodnight Kim. . .Leo. Thank you for gifting me with so much of yourselves.

8-2-91, Friday

Bill again processed all the mail today while I worked on Wellspring. There is so much to do that involves sorting out the shipments and especially rationing large packages of food (like flour and rice) into smaller family-sized zip-lock bags I had to buy for this purpose. Food and supplies have to be distributed and packed into separate delivery boxes. Clothing has to be sorted. Sleeping bags have to be washed. Medicines need to be divided up into family assortment packs. It's a lot of work, but I love doing it. Can't wait 'til we're settled and can have warehouse shelves to store all this stuff and keep it in an organized manner for people to come and take what they need.

John Nelson called and talked to Bill. Seems he heard that the printer called Bob Friedman to see if he wanted to buy Donning. Sure. . .I bet he'd love to unload it on someone else when there's a lawsuit pending against it.

Bill also talked with Bob this morning. Hampton Roads just ordered a reprint for *Daybreak*. Also Bob wanted to know if I'd like to write an article for ARE's *Venture Inward* magazine.

Told Bill nope. There were several valid reasons for that answer and Bob accepted my decision.

Besides, I didn't relay this, but with my present frame of mind I'd probably write an article entitled "Hocus Pocus," about how the public is paying to be duped. Who'd print something like that anyway? The truth would offend too many subscribers, yes? Although I did once toy with a book title by that name. It was going to be a New Age exposé geared to the Christian born-again segment of society. On the surface it would *appear* to be a New Age cult-basher book, but on the *inside,* it would've been the *truths* these Born Agains need to see. In the end I decided not to do it, because they wouldn't get it anyway. I'd played with several titles for this book idea. One was the *Hocus Pocus.* Another was *The New Age Pied Piper*; or *The New Age Exposé.* Of course there were other possibles like *Everything You've Always Wanted to Know About the New Age—A Christian's Guidebook.* But, as I said, I shelved the whole idea and wrote *Daybreak* instead. I suppose I wanted to concentrate on helping the believers instead of trying to make a dent into the hard-core skeptic arena. Priorities always come first with me. I made a good decision because it was one I never lost sleep over.

It was another grey and rainy day. We had the woodstove going to chase the chill away. Can't ever recall such a wet and cloudy summer—that's just not like Colorado. This year she's been very much out of character. 'Course our Advisors would probably say we would've had a string of bad forest fires if the season had been normal. So then, I stoke up the woodstove and don't complain.

I reexamined the gifts Kim and Leo Brennan sent me yesterday and came up with a word that describes how I feel about them. . . treasures. . .pure treasures.

8-3-91, Saturday

Woke up this morning to the sound of rain falling in the woods. Bill had been up long ago to begin his day in the office. As I laid there listening to the gentle rainfall I thought about the ARE article Bob suggested I do and I was worried he'd be upset with me for declining. I think I'm a difficult author for a publisher to cope with. I apologize for that—I truly do, but I can't help how I'm guided.

When Bill came home with our mail, he also brought me a bouquet of daisies with one red rose in the middle—he's so thoughtful. His thoughtfulness brings to mind something he did for his birthday last March and I'd forgotten to include it in my journal. All he wanted was to buy me a "real" wedding ring set because I'd been without one for 14 years. We went down to Manitou Jack's in Manitou Springs and I found a set made of Colorado gold. . .a small diamond was set in the center of a flower and the matching band had two leaves curled on either side of the blossom. He also found a Colorado gold band with leaves engraved on it. He was so happy we'd found rings we liked so much and that was all he wanted for his 45th birthday—'course he still received presents anyway. . . we girls don't listen to him when he says "no presents."

Although this is Saturday, Bill called Bob at home (something we normally don't like to do), but he wanted to be able to talk without business interruptions. Bill explained to Bob about our new Wellspring mission, and that I was basically done writing. He explained about how I'd been busy working on the supply shipments. Bob was surprised to hear of the new mission we were given. He didn't say too much about it, so I'm not sure what he thinks of it. Hopefully he understands that new aspect also.

During their conversation it somehow came up that my twelfth book was going to be my last. Bob seemed to have not realized that. I guess he thought I was going to continue writing until I was 90 (or something). Now that he sees I have all 12 written, he better understands how I can say that that part of my purpose is over. So over all, the conversation was good because it clarified our position of where we are now and where we're headed. I've always been one to operate with all my cards on the table, so there are no hidden

or secret aspects about a relationship I share with someone.
Bill is the same way. I was glad Bill made the call (even
though it probably invaded Bob's personal time at home).

Thanks for understanding, Bob. You're one in a million—
even though one Mary Summer Rain does make life difficult
for you.

Goodnight, Bob. Bless you.

8-4-91, Sunday

The day was grey and pookey again. Bill wanted to go
out for Sunday breakfast but I didn't feel like it. I'd been
fighting off a virus that had my lymph nodes swollen and
one hell of a canker sore on my gum. Mornings were worse
until my treatments began working. So we had a light breakfast at home, then drove to town to do a few errands and
pick up a Sunday paper. When we came home, Aimee told
us that her bosses at City Market were giving her a hard
time about scheduling her off for her firefighter classes. Bill
was upset, because he thought employers were supposed to
make allowances for those workers who do civil services for
emergency purposes. I have the feeling Aimee's being un-
necessarily hassled. There've been other instances where one
employee (who calls himself "the King") never misses a
chance to make sarcastic comments to her about "how lucky
she is," or "you don't know how easy you have it," meaning
he thinks she's spoiled by living in "such a *rich* family."
How mistaken people can be when they make such erroneous
assumptions about others.

I didn't have a good day today. It was one of those days
when I desperately wanted to go buy a one-room cabin somewhere in the middle of a forest and never come out of it. I
get so tired of problems and money worries and the eternal
"waiting" for our land. Living through days like these seem
endless, as if I'm running in a dream, yet never getting anywhere, and I scream and scream for help, but nobody hears
me because no sound comes out my mouth. When I have
these days I call them the "Dark Nothings." I also get the
strange inner feeling that there is no tomorrow and I see and
feel no future. . .only a dark nothingness ahead. And so this
uncharacteristic sensation drives me to the radical desire to
run out and buy any little miner's shack I can afford just to
get away and finally have a small measure of peace.

But then I feel guilty because no one but me could live in
such a tiny place. . .where would my family live? Separately.

Is that what I'm subconsciously saying I want? I can't believe that, because I know I couldn't live without them. I get
these "cabin" urges because I'm so damned tired and worn
out from the years of waiting and I get so desperate for
some kind of movement that I get irrational ideas like buying
a miner's cabin just to buy "something." There's been many
a time I almost took our savings and drove over to Glenwood to "find" *anything*. These large houses we're forced to
rent are draining our savings every month. Many times I've
approached Bill with the idea of buying a small cabin for
just the four of us—Aimee could get an apartment in town
close to her work. Same with Robin and Mandy. That's the
only way we could afford something because it'd have to be
small. He never minded the idea of Robin and Mandy having
their own place because that's only natural, but he never
could come to terms with splitting up our own family unit.

And so all my various ideas were always shot down.
There was never any way we could force a move until we
had the money for a place large enough for all of us and
that wasn't coming until destiny deemed the Time was right.

So today was another one of my "Dark Nothings" that
made me feel stuck in a forever-limbo, with no future. It was
an imprisonment I could not escape from, but must learn to
endure.

Robin called from work to say her car died half-way into
town and she hitched a ride. She called to have it towed to
the service station. I'm so sick of these crummy vehicles always needing something I told Bill if her Buick needed
something major we were going to junk it. She can use our
van to go back and forth to work in. This is getting ridiculous—how much more are we supposed to suffer? We
have important work to do and all we seem to have are
problems—one right after another. Com'on Guys, stop letting
the bad guys get to us so much. Are you forgetting we're
stuck down here with human minds and tend to get just a
little frustrated and depressed? Help us out here, will ya?

Well. . .I can't write any more tonight. It's 3 A.M. and
I'm going out for a walk in the woods. . .damn the bears,
cougars, dark fog, and all. With the way my aura's spiking
right now I don't think a wild thing would want to come
anywhere near me! And that's a fact.

8-5-91, Monday

Had a real bad morning. Aimee and I got into a horrendous argument about her not getting enough rest. Last time she got into this kind of schedule she contracted pneumonia. I just care, that's all.

So I sat at the kitchen table with a piece of toast while Magic sat beside me and begged for a bite.

Then Bill came in and started in on me for not taking care of myself. I was in pain from a mouth virus that affected the entire left side of my face. He wanted to know why the hell I wouldn't go to the doctor's. I kept telling him that there's nothing a doctor could do for what I had, and that it just had to run its course.

Between my words with Aimee and him railing at me I tossed my toast to Magic and began to cry. "I can't stand living here anymore. I need some peace!"

Even with that outburst he still mumbled behind my back about me not taking care of myself. I left the kitchen. I was going to make today the day I left to find my peace somewhere.

While he and the girls were in town I was going to pack a few things, take most of the savings and go find something over by Redstone.

But after they left and I sat at my desk, my eyes were drawn to the family pictures. . .I couldn't really leave them. Besides, the only vehicle left for me to use was the old pickup, and I just knew it'd be my luck for it to quit on me half-way to Glenwood, because I was too upset and my vibrations would affect the damned engine again. So, in the end, I remained a prisoner of time and did my best to bear the intolerable confinement of non-movement.

When they returned, Bill said he stopped off at the medical center to talk to Dr. Mitchell about my canker sore and swollen gland beneath my chin. Bill said the doctor said there's nothing they can do about those common viral ailments but try to ease the pain until they run their course.

I didn't say I told you so—I didn't have to. He should've known I'd be doing everything possible. I was doubling up on Vitamin C's, A's and Ginseng, plus applying golden seal and taking Tylenol, but he acted like I needed to see a doctor. He knows antibiotics are not used for viruses, so why bother going to a doctor? It seems lately that whenever I say "white" he says "black." I noticed this in the last six months and really don't know why it is. We've always shared the same opinions until recently when he's been softly challenging things. I think he's just frustrated with the long waiting and this lawsuit, and it's his way of getting his frustrations aired.

While they were gone this morning, Link called to talk to

Bill about setting up a meeting point to transfer 300 lbs. of goods. This was the first time I had spoken to her. I said, "Hi! This is Mary." But she just said to have him call her back. She must've been in a hurry. I wanted to tell her how much this project excited me; instead, I told her I'd have him call her as soon as he returned.

When Bill came in, he returned her call. They're meeting in Deckers at 3 P.M. tomorrow. Sarah and Jenny want to go with him and I'll stay home to hold the fort down. When they return with the supplies it'll take me all evening and most of the following day to sort and repackage the goods. Then we'll make our deliveries to the needy.

Bill also called Carole Bourdo this afternoon. She'd just returned from a tour. She's been displaying *Daybreak* with her artwork and people have been going nuts over it. She had a mini-cassette recorder, and told the people they could send a message to Summer Rain if they wanted to. They were thrilled, except for the executive man in the business suit who was too shy to speak to me on tape. Carole is sending me the tape and recorder to prove to me how many people "love" me as they come to her shows. I always thought she was just pulling my leg when she said that about what people say of me and, when she said she was going to record their comments to prove it, I still thought she was kidding me.

Even though I receive so many wonderful letters, I still don't perceive myself as being loved or famous—that just never computed in my own mind. It's like people are really talking about someone else (maybe No-Eyes), but certainly not me.

Robin drove her car home after work tonight. The shop couldn't find anything wrong. Either our Guys fixed it or else the problem was a temporary one due to all the rain we've had. Whichever it was I'm very grateful, because we need her vehicle and would be very much hard-pressed without it.

I'm feeling better tonight. Maybe our Guys performed brain surgery on me during the day, but I'm ready to continue persevering. Maybe it was because I filled the birdfeeder and while I was outside, I held out a handful of seed and a dove came down from the pines to take my offering. That really made my day. It perched right on my hand. Then, later in the evening I watched Sarah play hide-and-seek with Magic and it was so funny to watch, because Magic is a real hunter with a nose like a bloodhound. She always finds Sarah.

When Magic got tired of the game, she picked up her ball and brought it over to me. She'd put it in my hand and, if I didn't do anything with it, she'd nudge it or pick it up and drop it back in my hand, as if to say, "Hey, you big dummy, get with the program!" If everyone's too busy to play with her, she'll play ball all by herself. She picks it up in her mouth, drops it and catches it again when it bounces up. Some days we can hear that ball bouncing in the house for hours. Never saw a dog who knew how to bounce a ball the first time she saw one.

Magic missed Rainbow a lot. Bo treated her like a baby. Bo washed her ears and they'd lay together while Bo washed her coat like a cat would wash her kittens. So we've been trying to make up for Rainbow's goneness by showering Magic with extra love, attention and playing time. She seems to be doing better now. It still seems so strange to us not to have Bo charge to the door barking when someone knocks now.

When I'm finished with this entry I will stay up with just the mantle oil pots burning. . .I'm receiving strong impressions from my Starborn friend. Or maybe I'll go walk the foggy woods to meet him there. Either way, he'll find me.

8-6-91, Tuesday

I opened my journal tonight to record this date's entry and found a cartoon character drawn by Sarah. She's so in tune with me. She'll leave little drawings or notes in my desk drawers or taped to my typewriter. Usually they're there to cheer me and make me chuckle, or else they're there just to say "Hi" or "I love you, mom." And, during the school year,

I'd leave little drawings and notes under her breakfast plate so she'd see them in the morning. Not many 15-year-olds do that kind of thing with their parents.

Anyway, I did chuckle at her drawing when I opened my journal tonight.

Last night I did go out into the woods as planned. It was around 2:30 A.M. and was very foggy and damp. I walked through the forest for a while, then sat on a tree stump to meditate. I don't know how long I was in that state, but when I came out of it I wasn't alone anymore. My friend was sitting beside me and we talked for quite a while. We talked more while he walked me back to the house. The things he said gave me encouragement and greatly eased my waiting time. He made me see that I really *didn't* want to take that "one-way" ride with Them.

Bill and the girls met Link in Deckers as planned. They came back with five boxes of supplies and I got right on working on sorting and repackaging them. It took me four hours to complete the job, but we ended up with some great assortments of food.

The non-food items are being washed and stored for our future warehouse. These items are more for the homeless people we'll be helping in our new area. We're washing and airing out dozens of rain-gear and sleeping bags. Jenny has been my main helper with this task. We're also receiving shipments of medical supplies, which we're not doing anything with until we get enough to make up separate boxes of individual items. At that time we'll be organized enough so we can make up more individual kits that contain a good assortment of what we've got in stock.

Earlier today, I packaged up my next manuscript (Book Seven) *Whispered Wisdom*. I looked over all 105 slides for the photographs and was satisfied with my choices. Everything is all set to send in to Bob. He knows my next one is the pictorial, but hasn't asked to see it yet. I won't bug him about it, because I don't want to seem pushy.

My "friend" had an interesting idea last night. He asked me if the book (pictorial) was all I was going to do with the photographs.

Guess I wasn't being too swift in the brain department because I asked him what else *would* I do with the pictures?

He smiled. "Try a 'Four Seasons' note card set. Or a calendar. Maybe posters of Colorado entitled 'Land of Visionaries.'"

"My goodness, I never thought of all that."

"I know," he softly replied.

Then I frowned. "But I don't think Bob would go for that sort of thing."

"Why not? It'd sell."

"Because all that sounds very expensive to produce. Bob has to watch that. Don't forget, his company is only a couple years old. I need to help him wherever I can, not *cause* him more expense. I've got a vested interest here too, you know."

"I know. That's why I suggested what I did."

"Then are you telling me you see these products doing good if we did them?"

"Why would I suggest them otherwise?"

"I don't know. I mean I believe what you say, but Bob is very, very cautious. I don't think I could sell him this idea of yours."

"Mine? You'd tell him *who* the idea originated from?"

"Probably not, huh?"

He just shook his head.

"I think he'd believe me," I said.

"You know that's not the point."

"Yeah, I know. . .I'm not supposed to talk about you yet."

He smiled sympathetically. "I wouldn't object if you said that 'a friend' came up with the idea."

I shrugged. "I don't know, that sounds kind of corny to me. Maybe I'll just leave it and see what happens when the time is right."

"Why?"

"Why what?"

"Why leave it? Products like these take planning if they're scheduled to be available the same time the book's released."

"I suppose so, it's just that Bob's a little hard to read sometimes. If it wasn't for No-Eyes and the Advisors. . .and you. . . I'd have a hard time knowing where I stand. Sometimes, when I talk to people, I think they don't like me."

"I know. And you know that that's not true, don't you. You know that feeling stems from your childhood. Just because some people don't voice their real feelings doesn't mean that they don't like you—and it certainly doesn't mean that you're free to misinterpret unvoiced attitudes."

"You're chastising me again."

"Only because I care about you."

Silence.

Waiting.

"My childhood really messed me up in some ways, didn't it."

"Let's just say that your self-image was fractured in the process."

"Yeah, fractured, I like the way you put it. Still. . .you'd think I'd be over all that long ago. After all, I'm 45 years old."

I chuckled. "Know what?"

"What?"

"Even now, when I talk to people, I feel like I'm so inferior to them. I feel like I'm just a dumb mountain woman and they're world-wise. And I especially hate it if I have to go into a fancy place—God, I feel so small. I'm lucky if I know the dinner fork from the salad fork!"

"You think that's important to people? Do you really think they care?"

"I don't want to talk about me anymore. I hate talking about me. How'd we get on this dumb subject anyway?"

"You introduced it when we were talking about your conversations with Bob and other people. Remember? You said some people were hard to read and so you thought maybe they didn't like. . . ."

"I remember," I said, cutting him off. "Sorry I brought it up in the first place."

"You should be, because it's all wrong. You've got to get over that inferior image you have of yourself."

"Well . . . at least with our new mission nobody will expect me to do anything other than giving food away. I'm much more comfortable staying in my own element—behind the scenes."

"Yes, you're happiest there. That's one of the reasons we care so much about you."

I smiled at my friend. "Yeah?"

He chuckled. "Yeah." I looked into his eyes, eyes I'd come to love. "Thank you for caring so much for me. Thank you for accepting me the way I am."

"Mary," he whispered, "the *way* you *are* is the reason we met in the first place. You and I wouldn't be walking together in these woods if you weren't what you are."

There was a lump in my throat. I couldn't respond to my friend's final words. We walked back to the house in a warm companionable silence.

8-7-91, Wednesday

Bill and the girls made our food deliveries this morning. I spent all day working on Wellspring while Bill processed the mail. With this new mission, there are more and more days when I'm completely out of the office and never get to see the mail at all. If there are children's books for me to sign, I do them up after dinner. In the late evening, I then have some quiet time to read the day's correspondence that came in.

Our property manager called to say the owners of our rental house are in town (from Germany) for a couple days and want to visit, to make sure certain repairs were done by their contractor. They'll be here before noon tomorrow and won't be too happy to see the roofing job that was done this year.

Woke up this morning and found my mouth virus completely gone. Wonder if my "friend" had anything to do with that while I slept last night. He probably wouldn't admit it even if he did, because he knows I don't like it when "they" come during the night and do things we never remember in the morning. That was okay in the beginning, but we're long past that stage now. Well. . .guess I could overlook this one time because I sure am grateful to be relieved of all that pain and gland swelling. Thanks, Guys.

It was so beautiful out today I couldn't resist sitting out on our front deck for about an hour. The sun shone from an incredibly blue sky and the wind whispered softly through the high pines all day.

While I was out reading, five tiny chipmunks scampered about the deck the whole time I was out. I'd thrown seed and nuts over the porch in the early morning and the critters were still cleaning them up when I went out. The little fellas didn't mind my being there and they scampered about my feet. One brave one even ran up my chair and right over me. But I temporarily scared them when I laughed—one critter tried to see if my bare toe was edible—it tickled when the tiny paws came upon my foot. Luckily for me he never got his taste test. Anyway, all five were back in a flash and I so enjoyed watching their antics for that sweet hour of rest.

Sarah solved our mystery of the empty birdfeeder. Everyday we had to fill that thing, and although seven kinds of birds were feeding from it, it shouldn't be completely emptied in one day.

She called me to the front window. "There's our thief," she whispered.

A squirrel was sitting up on the feeder and having a real messy pig-out.

I went outside and walked right up to the feeder. Squirrel and I were going to have a talk. Squirrel and I were nearly eye to eye.

"Hey, little fella, don't you know this seed is for the feathered ones?"

Little Fella just looked at me and cocked his head.

"What say we make a deal? How about I put some seed and nuts in the corner over there and you can have it all."

Little Fella blinked. He sat up. He began nibbling on a kernel of corn. We were nearly eye to eye by now.

"Did you hear me? You're eating the *bird's* food. You're going to have to get down and leave this feeder for them."

Critter finished the kernel, looked me in the eye again and scampered to the ground.

I went inside and grabbed a handful of nuts and seed. When I returned to the deck my little four-legged friend was sitting up, forepaws held in to tiny chest. . .waiting *in the corner* of the porch! Twilight Zone time? Naw, I thought, just weird coincidence. So I knelt down and emptied my hand and he began to stuff his little cheeks. None of the family saw the squirrel up at the birdfeeder for the rest of the day. Now I have to remember to keep their restaurants separate and well supplied.

Still. . .the way that squirrel stared eye to eye with me, I could swear he understood exactly what I said to it. Maybe this was the beginning of what No-Eyes had said about me and the animals relating in the future like friends. When I think about the dove that ate out of my hands the other day and, today, how the chipmunks played at my feet (and *over* me) and the squirrel's eye contact, I dare to hope her words have come to pass. However, I wouldn't want to push my luck. . .I think I'll wait a while before I test this "new communion" out with the cougar and Yogi.

8-8-91, Thursday

Our house owners didn't show up until after dinner because they had car trouble. They seemed pleased with how we were caring for their house, but were very upset with the roofing company. It was good to finally meet our landlords and have them meet us. I think they're going back to Germany with a more restful mind over who's been living in their house these last two years. They want to stay in Vandenburg for another three years, but may be back for good next summer. If that comes to pass, we'll hopefully have our own property by then. If not, we'll be forced to move into another rental.

8-9-91, Friday

Early this morning, Sarah and I went into the woods to gather wild raspberries. Mmmm, so good and big this year. I think we again ate more than we brought home. That was okay though, because the rest of the family doesn't care for them as we do. . .they prefer the wild strawberries we picked earlier in the year. It felt so good to get back out in the woods during the day—even if it was only for an hour or so.

Received Carole's tape cassette and recorder in the mail today. When she was in Washington, D.C. for her art tour, she told people who saw the *Daybreak* book that they could send me a message on the tape if they wanted. Six people "talked" to me and my eyes misted as I listened to their words. I was so touched to actually hear how much No-Eyes and the books have affected people. The comments the people made and hearing them speak my name left a lump in my throat. I guess I'm a lot more sentimental than I thought I was. Why should hearing those people bring tears to my eyes? I think the answer lays with my current dilemma of being in between missions. Hearing those people makes me realize how much I still care for everyone and, because I still care so much, how can I ever stop responding to their letters as I'm supposed to now? I think that I cannot do it. I will have to attempt both missions as long as I can. I must remain open and available to the public until Wellspring takes over in an all-consuming manner. Those people on the tape sounded like they really liked me.

Maybe Carole was guided with her idea to do this, so it would help me to justify doing both missions at once—or at least continuing the first one a little while longer.

Several people have written saying that their Waldenbooks or B. Dalton bookstores can't get *Daybreak*. That's pure garbage, and I can't figure out what the bookstore clerks or managers are doing when the major book distributors have the title in stock! I get so upset whenever I hear this from people.

Some bookstore clerks look up my titles in their *Books In Print* volume and then have the nerve to tell their customer that my titles aren't listed, which means they're out of print. *All* my titles are constantly being reprinted, so that never happens. I think bookstore clerks either don't know how to look something up, or else they're just plain too lazy to take the time. What other reason could there be for a clerk to say my books aren't available when they always are? None of my titles have ever been out of print. This business can be very disgusting and certainly disappointing much of the time.

I'm going to go into the living room now where it's dark except for the two oil pot flames flickering. I will pray for two hours for all my readers. . .I only wish I could do more for them. When I'm done, I'll go upstairs to bed and rest my head on Bill's chest. I have a great need to be comforted this night. His heartbeats give me the most tranquil warmth I have ever known.

8-10-91, Saturday

I worked all day on Wellspring except for a couple hours when we all went to town for the mail and to go to the Mountain Arts Festival.

Link called in the late afternoon to arrange another supply pickup for tomorrow. We have plans to go to Carole's house to see her new *Phantoms Afoot* artwork, then we need to do a little shopping. In the morning we'll finalize the schedule for all of this after Carole calls to let us know when her company is leaving.

This evening, Harry Glover called to arrange a visit at our house on September 16th, after his seminar lectures are finished in New Mexico. We told him we didn't see a problem with that date and that we'd call him if something came up that we couldn't alter for him. For some reason, when Bill told me the date, I felt something would interfere, but couldn't imagine what, so I told him okay.

Aimee spent the day with her fire department practicing vehicle rescues with the Jaws of Life. They practice on junkyard cars and learn how to break out windshields, open doors with the equipment and cut through roofs. She was very excited to tell us all about it when she came home around 7 P.M. She really loves every minute of it. Next month she'll be on-call and will be sleeping overnight at the station, or at one of the firefighter's houses in town. She's also scheduled to be on-call during November and January. I've stopped worrying about her because worrying is a waste of good energy. I leave her care in the hands of the Powers That Be

. . .and destiny. However, being a mother, I still hope and pray that nothing bad happens to her. I love her so much.

8-11-91, Sunday

We did our shopping and were at Carole's house by 1:30. I gave her about 12 jackets of *Daybreak* and a copy of a photo Bill took with her and I holding the first book we'd worked together on.

Link arrived there an hour later and we transferred the boxes of food from her truck to our van. Afterward we all visited with Carole until 6:30.

It had been sunny and warm all day at Carole's, but when we were outside her house watching some eagles and antelope, dark storm clouds were covering Pikes Peak, and we knew our house was getting plummeted with rain again. It must've been some terrific storm because our dirt roads were soaked and filled with ruts from rain run-off.

After we were home, it took me a couple hours just to sort and repack the canned goods. Tomorrow it will take me most the day to repackage the flour, seeds, dried fruit, and pasta. This shipment was great and I can't wait to deliver it.

Forgot to mention that both Bill and I loved Carole's new art for Phantoms. It gives one the feeling of eeriness. I think Carole is very in tune with my material because she's definitely producing perfect cover art for them. She is some lady.

8-12-91, Monday

Terrible mail day today. Bill came home with an armful and I had no way (or time) to take care of it. Our kitchen had boxes of food that took up every available space and I spent the entire day sorting everything out and repackaging it for distribution. We ended up with 187 lbs. of food this time. I'm so happy doing this work—there's a real sense of satisfaction that it brings.

This evening, after dinner, Bill and I discussed the problem with me not having the time to respond to the mail any more. We finally both agreed that the time had come when I was *forced* to close the door on that aspect of our former mission. Although I knew this was true, I had a difficult time severing an activity that kept me connected and in touch with my readers. Yet we had no alternative. So I went back into the office and composed an explanatory letter to my future correspondents. This detailed the reason I could no longer respond to their letters and I hoped, in my heart, that they truly understood. I would never want to hurt anybody's feelings or have them think I'm abandoning them, but clearly, all evidence points to the fact that my spiritual counseling days are over. I must now give my full attention and time to the new mission given to us. Starting tomorrow the new letters will be going out. I suppose I'll receive some nasty letters back, but I cannot ignore my course. If some folks are offended, it simply means they have not grasped the concept of Destiny and all its ramifications.

I have decided to continue to open and review all our mail—I just will have no more time to lend to replies. This will be a difficult transition for me—yet it is one I must make.

Tonight we gave Sarah the choice of returning to high school or staying home and doing home schooling like Aimee did while working part-time. Sarah opted for staying in school because *we* finished and got our diplomas. That was fine with us, but we hate seeing her get so stressed out during the school year. She's so conscientious about her grades and has a royal fit if she doesn't get all "A's." In the back of her mind, part of her wants to stay home to help in our office (as she'd been doing all summer), and also assist with Wellspring because she knows we'll need extra helping hands with that after we're settled and we have a fully operational warehouse to run. But right now her feelings are to return to school, so we support her one hundred percent. I just wish school wasn't so stressful for her. My heart goes out to her, but I'm also proud that she chose that course despite the stress she knows it will bring.

8-13-91, Tuesday

Spent the day on Wellspring delivering our food.

8-14-91, Wednesday

Errand day. Went down to Manitou Springs to get Mandy's birthday presents.

Bill dropped me off at a new used bookstore in Woodland Park. Felt like I found Paradise Lost, and walked out with two grocery bags of books for 15 dollars.

A therapist at the chiropractor's asked Bill if he still did "ghost-busting" work. Said a patient had a problem with an

Indian man that various people were seeing in her Florissant home. Bill told her to tell the woman to write us. Don't think it will come to much, because my first strong impression was that the spirit isn't wayward—it has permission to be there. . .we'll see.

One of our bears was caught by the State Wildlife people who transported it down to the southern region of Trinidad. Wish they would've left it alone. Now we have a couple smaller ones left.

Stay out of sight, guys!

8-15-91, Thursday

A close friend of ours called today and, in our conversation, she asked if we were flooded with children's book orders. When she heard my response, she couldn't understand it. I told her it might be because people don't want to take the time to order something, especially if it's sight unseen. She thought maybe my idea to personalize it by autographing it wasn't as good an idea as having it available in bookstores where people could see it and buy it right then. I think maybe she's right, but I'd just wanted to make the book special by signing it directly to the child receiving it. Well, when our stock gets down to around one hundred books we'll have to make a final decision about what to do.

I've been feeling bad lately about our land sitting for sale and here we sit not being able to buy it. It's all just so terribly frustrating. And if we don't get our money until winter, how do we look at property that's under three or four feet of snow? Tonight I again approached Bill about going now to secure the land with a lease option, but he says no way because then we're locked in to a top-dollar asking price, instead of a lower cash offer. Right now I'd pay that top dollar just to secure it and *be* in it. Dammit, we have things to do and lots of needy people to help. Why the hell can't we get on with it? These last months of waiting are giving me a head full of silver hairs!

I need to talk to my friend. I knew he has ways of seeing the future, but I also know he usually is very closed-mouthed when it comes to aspects I want to know about us. He tells me so much about what we'll be doing and our future interactions, but he tends to leave out the in-between details. Maybe he can't relate to time as I have to experience it. Maybe he doesn't compute what "waiting" means. I really think his conception of linear, earth time is much like our

Advisors. . .nonexistent. When they say "soon," that could mean in two days or two years. We learned that real quick and we had to word our questions very carefully in order to get precise answers. I'm going to stay up tonight and call for my friend to come for a talk. . .I need some information. . .I need some answers.

8-16-91, Friday

Although I got the same answer—timing—other information was freely given about a "third" mission that would come when Wellspring was fully operational. This third mission is so incredible, so fantastic, some would even call it miraculous. Now I have much to contemplate. And tonight I will spend three hours in prayer. I must pray my heart out tonight.

8-17-91, Saturday

Our mail was heavy today and although we're sending out the new information letters, it still took Bill until dinnertime to process those. We just can't seem to get around spending so much time in the office. We still have to make out index cards on the new correspondents, and Bill still needs to keep adding them to our mailing list because people are expressing their desire for that. I suppose after readers received Hampton Roads' special discount offer for *Daybreak*, they realized the value of staying current on our list. Seems just the job of keeping up with people's changing addresses adds a few hours to Bill's office day. Oh well, that's something we'll probably always have to maintain. . .until the twelfth book is finally published.

I thought I had a good idea this evening. I asked Bill if we could go ahead and buy the house for Lodestar and Wellspring, so we could live in it until we could afford to purchase our chosen property. My thinking was that the Wellspring house would be quite a bit cheaper than our land. I suggested that it would get us "over there" a lot sooner and when we bought our land, the warehouse building would be exclusively Lodestar office and Wellspring warehouse.
No go.
He reminded me that even if the warehouse place was cheaper, we still needed more money for a downpayment. He

brought up the fact that we only had so much money and still needed to buy two new vehicles.

I hate it when we're always held back by finances.

Then he wanted to know what I had in mind for this "Lodestar" office I kept talking about.

I explained that I wanted our office out of our home, because we never seemed to stop working when it's only a room away.

He bought that, but knew there was more. "And?" he asked.

Oh boy, here it comes. "And I want to be available to people. I want them to be able to come to Lodestar for a consultation or to pick up a children's book if they want one."

Silence.

Waiting.

"Consultations," he repeated.

"Yes."

"People just walking in off the street will be able to see you?"

"Yes. . .if I'm there at the time or not busy with someone else."

"You planning on having some sort of conference room there?"

"I thought that'd be nice."

"Of course there'll be no charge."

"Of course not."

He thought about all that. "If you open yourself up for that kind of public availability, how much time do you think you're going to have for Wellspring?"

"Wellspring comes first because that's our current mission. I don't know, I haven't thought out the logistic details yet. All I know is that I want to have an office where I'm available to people. I couldn't do that while we just had everything in our house, because we were cautioned to keep our home location private. But this way. . . our home will be completely separate. See?"

He did. . .kind of.

"Boy, I don't know about this hair-brained idea of yours. I'm not at all crazy about it. . .there's so many kooks out there."

"Honey, it's something I really want to do. I feel bad enough that we've had to discontinue our letter responses, but down the line I'd at least like to make myself available to people. Maybe on a reduced time schedule like two or three set days a week would work."

"And what if Wellspring becomes the full-time job it's predicted to be? What then?"

"Then I could reserve only one day a week for walk-in conferences."

He sighed. "You're really dead set on this, aren't you."

I smiled my special smile.

He grinned back. "Now I know you're determined. Well, tell me this, how do you refuse your walk-ins who come on days you're in the back working on Wellspring?"

I frowned. "Do you always have to give me more problems?"

"No more than those you're going to have to deal with because *that's* one that *will* come up."

Now it was my turn to sigh.

"People will just have to understand that I'm trying to work on two missions at once. They'll have to realize that I *have* to stick to the reserved conference days. . .otherwise they're hampering my second mission."

"And you really believe, after all the people we've dealt with in your correspondence, that people will honor and respect that?"

Silence.

"Honey?" he pushed.

"I'm hoping that that's the *least* they could do because I don't have to be making myself available at all."

"Some people have been awful demanding of you, honey. Some just don't take no for an answer."

"They'll have to if they come on an unscheduled conference day. Above all, I have to attend to Wellspring; the needy, the homeless and hungry people come first now."

The discussion ended there, but I knew my plan didn't settle well in his mind. He was worried sick that some nut would do me grave harm if I made myself available as I'd planned. Yet I also knew that his own solution would be to join me in all private conferences—not as a co-consultant necessarily, but to be my guardian. And that was fine with me because we'd found that most people enjoyed talking to the both of us.

So. . .although I couldn't manage to get us over to our chosen area early, I at least laid out my plan for the Lodestar office. And even that won't materialize unless we receive enough settlement money from the lawsuit, which, by the way, we've heard nothing about since it was filed nearly a month ago.

8-18-91, Sunday

Bill and I went to the Fossil Inn in Florissant for break-fast. We hadn't gone anywhere alone together for many weeks and it felt good to get out, if only for a couple hours. We never breakfast in Woodland Park any more, because too many people look for me in the restaurants there. In order to bypass this situation, we'd started going to Florissant instead. No one ever bothered me there and we became "regulars" every Sunday morning for quite a while. But since last May we'd been too busy, and only went about once a month all this summer. We just don't ever get out any more.

We thought it was so cute when one lady correspondent sent us a $20 bill with a little note: "FOR YOU AND BILL TO GO OUT FOR DIN-DIN SOME NIGHT." What a sweet-heart she was. We went out for breakfast instead and really appreciated it.

Last night, after I finished writing in my journal, I went out into the woods. It was around 1:30 A.M. and the sky was dark with drifting clouds.

I prayed for a long while and, afterwards, my twinkling light companions flitted around me in friendly communion. Oh, how these Little Ones do lift my heavy heart. Their antics never fail to bring a ring of laughter, as I break the solemn silence of the night surround.

When a Little One alighted on my finger and another on my shoulder I stood and waltzed them around the forest, while their companions followed and joined our Dance of the Fairies.

My personal comforts come in many forms. . .forms many others would call mysterious and mystical; yet to me, they are all so normal and common to my everyday life.

Sometimes I wish all people could commune with these Bright Entities as I do, at least then I could be more open and sharing with the public But since that isn't so, I must keep my routine relationship with various entities to myself . . .just as No-Eyes and Many Heart did.

When the Little Ones winked away, my friend appeared. Seems he either overheard my discussion with Bill regarding my Lodestar office plans, or else he was reading over my shoulder as I wrote last night.

He says it's not *in* "the Plan" for me to be available to the public and I asked him if we could *put* it in The Plan.

He spent a great deal of time explaining why it wouldn't

work. There were more than a few reasons. And, although I saw the logic, was still greatly disappointed.

The Plan calls for Wellspring only. This operation will be open to the needy three days a week. We are to maintain our Lodestar office in our home. This, he emphasized, was because we needed to cooperate on the Third Mission on our land with the Starborn Ones.

As we talked, I voiced a concern I had about our land location that came from a dream last night.

"Last night I had a dream that our land was underwater. It flooded because the mountain came down during an earth tremor and all the rocks dammed up the river."

"That was not a dream," came the soft reply. "Last night we brought you aboard to show you some future scenes, but we saw that you did not bring accuracy back with you, so I needed to come this night to bring clarification."

I sat down on a log.

"Please, do clarify, because I've been upset all day over this."

"What you were shown were slight earth tremors that loosened the composition of the region you call (withheld) Mountain. This rock slide does indeed block the road and the river. However, you didn't also recall that it happened in late autumn when the river is low, and you also didn't recall that the dam and road were *cleared* before any major flooding manifested."

I sighed a great breath of relief. "Next time you guys want to show me something, will you *please* not do it when I'm asleep. We discussed that a long time ago. I thought you agreed. . . ."

"Yes, we did, but you were up late enough as it was and we had to take our opportunities when they come."

"So why was this future scene so important to show me now?"

"Because you yourself knew of it. And we saw doubts forming regarding your chosen land location. We had to deter those."

"I never expressed any doubts or. . . ."

"Yes you did."

"Only in my own mind and you've been in there again."

He smiled his funny smile. "Just as I've caught you in mine."

"Sorry, I guess by now we've become pretty in tune, huh?"

"Remember what No-Eyes would tell you about that?"

Now it was my turn to smile.

8-19-91 Monday

I'm beginning to be concerned about all I'm recording in this journal. Maybe this wasn't such a great idea after all. When I opened it tonight and re-read some of the entries, I wondered about the wisdom of revealing so much of my private life. Even Bill doesn't know about all my communions with my "friend" and, in a very deep way, I want him to be an active partner in that aspect. But I'm told that his part will come later and things are as they should be for now.

Yet. . .on the other hand, I strongly feel the need to write everything down. My friend keeps encouraging me to continue. He insists there's a reason why I felt compelled to initially do so. I don't know. Maybe for posterity's sake. I certainly hope to God it's not because it'll be published someday, because I've said far too much about too many things.

Well, whatever his reasons are for prompting me on, I think, just in case, I will cut down on writing about some of the more mystical aspects and communions I have. . .nobody would understand them anyway. In fact, now that I think about it, I shouldn't have written about my dance with the Little Light Beings Saturday night. Oh well, that's fairly mild I guess. At least it is compared to a lot of the other things that go on.

This was a typical Monday for mail—a ton of it.

Received my first royalty statement from Hampton Roads and was surprised to see that I'd already earned off a little over half of my advance. *Daybreak's* only been out two months. I sure hope this keeps up.

So far, my correspondence from those who've read the book has been very encouraging. Many folks are shocked at the kinds of rude questions and comments that came from my readers. Yet most admit that I've managed to give them a very helpful volume that really helped them expand their knowledge and understanding. That pleases me, for I'd felt, for a long while, that a good straightforward Question and Answer book was definitely needed. I'm glad it clarified so much for so many.

It was our Advisors' suggestion to do a book based on my readers' questions and I'd been keeping a running list of their questions for a book, but as the lists got longer and longer, I realized I'd amassed plenty of them on separate subject matters and I began adding reader's personal comments and opinions (the good and the ugly) too, because they represented various public opinions regarding No-Eyes, the material, and me. I wanted to share those with my readers to give them a flavor sampling of the sweet and bitter letters I receive. Most agreed with the sweet sentiments and, likewise, most were outraged over the bitter (rude) ones. In this manner I was able to share my mail with the public. In the end, I'm glad I did because, although some readers admitted that they had to get accustomed to the new format (Q & A), they quickly found themselves so engrossed they couldn't stop reading. And that's probably the best compliment an author can receive.

I went with Bill and the girls to town today. While I was in Ben Franklin I found two treasures. . .baskets! I love baskets, especially unusual ones, and these were half price! When I came out to the van with my "find" Bill rolled his eyes and laughed at my obvious joy. I have a real passion for unusual baskets and I held those two all the way home . . .I was just so tickled to have found them. Bill says it's a good thing that the little things make me happy because we'd be in a world of trouble if I had expensive tastes. Well. . .I do love Persian rugs. . .but finding baskets make me just as happy.

So, over all, today was a wonderful day, especially since Bill and Jenny had something to cheer and whoop about this evening. . .the Denver Broncos won their football game. Who cares if it was only a pre-season game—Colorado takes their team *very* seriously. It's Jenny's dream to go to a Bronco game. . .maybe some day.

My "friend" says not to worry. . .Gorbachev will regain his position of power. He also told me that "settlement" talks for the lawsuit would begin before the end of September. This I wasn't expecting and was thrilled with the encouraging news.

8-20-91, Tuesday

This afternoon I asked Bill when he thought I should send my next book to Bob. I told him about the idea of creating note cards and such to go along with the pictorial, although I didn't say who the idea came from.

He liked the thought of offering other items with the book, but he too thought it would be too expensive for Bob to do. Yet, because of production time needed for a photography book, he didn't think sending it in now would be too soon for a Spring '92 release date.

I told him I was thinking along the same lines and I typed up a cover letter for the manuscript, while Bill prepared the FedEx box. I hope Bob doesn't think I'm being pushy, but usually after one book is released, we soon begin communication on the next one.

When I was actively taking pictures for this book, I'd asked my "friend" if he could give me "something special" to put in it. I was hoping for a presentation of his vehicle, but knew deep down that that wouldn't be permitted. So instead, he cloaked the large vehicle in a cloud one evening, hovered just above the "eastern" horizon close to our house and gave a spectacular display of *moving* light rays that speared up from the *bottom* of the cloud.

This photo is in the Summer section of *Whispered Wisdom*, and to most, it looks as though the *sun* is behind the clouds. When in reality, the sun had already set moments before in the west. I think if someone was exceptionally aware and observant, that particular photo would strike them as being special.

Anyway, I did explain that shot to Bob in my cover letter because I think he believes in "them" and I wanted to share the background on it with him.

Bill will mail my package out tomorrow and Bob should receive it on his desk after 3 P.M. on Thursday. Sure hope he likes the book and photos. I always have a fear that each book I send in won't be liked by the publisher. Guess I just don't have much confidence in myself or my own work.

I also included a slide Bill took of me taking a picture. This particular photo was taken on Independence Pass. I hadn't planned on including any more photos of me on the back jackets of my books, but my girls and Bill wanted this one used because they loved the idea of a photo of me taking the pictures. I included it, but told Bob not to enlarge it any bigger than the size of a regular snapshot. The photo I sent Pocket for *Earthway* was blown up so much I hated it.

So *Whispered Wisdom* will now be in Bob's hand to accept or reject. Hope he doesn't wait too long to give me his answer. An author usually waits on pins and needles to hear how a publisher likes their submitted work. . .at least I always do. At least nobody can accuse me of being egotistical, if anything, my fault lies in the opposite direction of being too full of self-doubts when it comes to my work. Oh well, I am what I am. Yes?

Tonight we watched the Soviet upheaval on television. Although it is a terrible event, I told Bill I still saw much beauty in it because of the way "the people" were revolting against the takeover. I saw this as beauty because a couple of years ago the people would've been led as silent lambs—too fearful to utter a whisper in opposition. But watching them fight passionately for their freedom and democracy was truly beautiful.

Another thought crossed my mind as I watched the world-shaking event. I realized that the grave situation did not pale our Wellspring project. Sometimes great events or others' problems can make events in one's own life pale by comparison, but the feelings I held about our new mission were actually strengthened by what I was observing on television. In fact, it made me feel all the more devoted to feeding the needy and homeless. I think this is because now we're involved with the "physical" aspect of people's needs, and, to me, I saw an equation that correlated to the physical aspects I was watching tonight. . .especially when the Soviets themselves are experiencing such a horrendous food shortage problem.

I have some very strong feelings about what's transpiring in Russia. I feel Communism will completely fall and envision the people themselves toppling the Marxist statues. I will have to get this verified with our Advisors or my friend.

In the mail today I received two beautiful letters from the Rosebud Reservation. Both appreciated my work because I'd refused to tread on Sacred Ways. Both honored me for not trying to speak of the Unspeakable. And one of these asked me to pray for the reservation people—especially the children.

When this entry is finished, I will slip out into the dark woods and spend a couple hours in solemn prayer for the children of all reservations. I wish I could do more, but my Prayer Smoke is all I have to give. I will be so happy when we build my Prayer Kiva on our land. I know I'll spend many midnight hours there.

It is 2:20 A.M. It is time to go outside.

8-21-91 Wednesday

Last night a wonderful thing happened! While I was offering up my Prayer Smoke in the woods, I felt a new presence nearby. It was of an essence I'd never before felt, yet there was an undeniable companionship felt.

Through the shadows cast by the waxing moon, I saw the

entity lying down. He was observing me in a most casual manner.

My spine tingled the moment I realized it was our mountain lion. I felt momentarily threatened. Then the feeling passed as quickly as it had come. Elation filled my being, as I softly whispered a "Welcome to my Prayertime." Soon I was again engrossed in my Prayer Smoke.

I don't know exactly how long I prayed, but when I'd finished, my companion was nowhere to be seen. I'd been so involved I'd never heard him leave. Yet he'd been so close I could hear him breathing and shift his weight and move his forepaws in the brush. But never did I hear him take his leave. Oh No-Eyes! How wonderful that you lived with this unworldly relationship with nature every day! Did *you* bring the cougar to me? No? He came of his own will? It's happening? It's finally happening? My heart is so full I feel it will surely burst!

Not an hour passed this day when I didn't smile at the warm thought of my companion's presence last night. Oh, how I wish I could share this with Bill, but if he knew I went out in the woods so late every few nights, he'd have a fit. I cannot tell him. His worry over me, his increased protective nature precludes revealing my nightwalks. Hopefully he and the girls will not find out about them until after my kiva is built and he'll feel more comfortable with me being in a protected enclosure for my midnight Prayertime.

As it is I frequently don't sneak up to bed until around three or four in the morning and I must be careful not to sleep in too late or appear too tired the following day, for fear I'll evoke his attention to my late hours and outside activities.

I regret this temporary ruse, but I also understand his greatly intensified protectiveness. That operation really scared him to death, and now he watches over me like another Guardian Archangel. It doesn't really confine me. I just have to readjust my activities (the frowned-on ones) to when he's asleep. I don't fear these night woods and neither should he, but then again, he would perceive me as being "alone" out there—where I view it as *never* being alone. That has been proven to me too many times.

And so I have another reason to want to be settled: my sheltered Prayertime Kiva and Bill's comfort over my being safe from harm in it. . .and also, I will feel relieved to pick a right time to confess my nightwalks and Prayertimes in the woods that I've been doing all these many months. Secrets between us have short lifespans. Yet this one must live strong

until we're settled, for my Prayertime is the breath of my
life. . .I cannot live without it.

My feelings about the Soviet situation were confirmed on
television before I could even ask if I was right. He did
come back to power. He was on his way home shortly after
I had feelings he was. The beauty I saw was correct, for in
the end, it was the people's love of freedom that the usurpers
never counted on. I only wish they also had eyes to see *who*
had begun the reform to free them in the first place—instead
they turn the coin around and blame him for things not progressing fast enough. The people seem not to understand that
the switch from Communism to Democracy and free enter-
prise is a monumental undertaking, and must endure adjustment periods while sorting things out in the act of striving to
forge ahead. Yet in their collective impatience they become
forgetful and end up persecuting the savior who came with
the mark of Ra-Ta. Will history never stop repeating itself?
How many times must societies make the same mistakes in
order to learn the same lessons history already taught — over
and over, again and again.

This clarifies my own understanding of my Starborn
friend's perspective of us, because when I see this happening
it makes me feel like I've come to live on a planet populated
by children who can only learn their lessons through repeti-
tion. Indeed, now when I observe this firsthand, it serves as
verification why earth humanity has kept its forward progress
in such a regressive state. It gives clear evidence why these
people of earth are so primitive when compared to the advanced level of their Starborn relations, who learn quickly
from each mistake made. How agonizingly slow the progress
is when an entire civilization must repeat and repeat the same
mistakes in order to finally retain the lesson of it.

And so that is the perspective of the Starborn ones, who
view Earth ones as children quarreling over whose toy is
biggest and best (as in comparing the many religions and
spiritual beliefs). The Starborn know there is but one list of
Precepts, yet how embarrassed I feel down here when everyone around me is still arguing and calling one another names
over their separate beliefs.

Oh God, it's five minutes after midnight and Aimee just
called me. She's at the fire station and said the ambulance
and police are up at a house in our subdivision. Seems
there's a man with a gun held up in a house and another
person is reported "down." The house isn't far from me—just
down the hill through the forest. Aimee wanted me to be

aware of the situation, because she knows I'm always up so late. She says she won't come home until she gets the "all clear" on her beeper radio, because she has to drive right by that house on her way home. Wish Rainbow was still here.

But then this is just another example of what I was writing about before Aimee called. These people are so violent! So irrational! Even my mountain woods offer no respite from their threat.

When Aimee called, before she said goodbye, she told me she'd worry about me until she received the all-clear. I reminded her that worry never altered anything—it only makes the worrier sick. Then she said, "When are we moving?"

Trouble is: there's really nowhere on this planet we could go to insure our safety other than OFF of it. And that truth really sums up this civilization I'm trying to work in. It makes me pine for my peaceful relations more than anything else can. I'll be so relieved to be among them again once we get settled. To have them so close all the time will be a true and warm comfort. I'm certain that if people heard me express such sentiments, I'd be severely chastised, but when one has lived among the Loving and Peaceful Ones, being down here is a monumental adjustment. The general mind-set and violent tendencies are aspects one never reconciles, and it's a constant battle to persevere in the midst of it all. Earth. . .the Eternal Elementary School.

Oh Raphael, please never stop giving me strength. I do so appreciate your advance presence before me. I imagine you're tiring of the job you've taken on. Thank you for your unfailing protection and love. I think of you so often and, sometimes, I wish you'd give some of these people a peek at your glorious beauty—I think a few *real* miracles wouldn't be out of line now. I know you've shown yourself to a select few, but maybe you could increase your favors just a little. This world really could use the sight of your magnificent light.

8-22-91, Thursday

Bill and I spent the entire day down in Colorado Springs doing errands and buying Jenny and Sarah birthday presents.

It was one of the rare times we went down there and didn't get headaches from the bustle and vibrations of the city. We actually managed not to get stressed out from all the crazy drivers. In fact, we almost enjoyed our day away from the office.

When we returned home around 7 P.M., Sarah said we'd

had a "Good News" fax from Pete at Hampton Roads. *Daybreak* had made Number 19 on a book distributor's Top 100 Bestsellers List. That really made me feel good.

At 12:30 last night, Bill got up because he couldn't sleep and I stopped writing in my journal to talk to him. He says he feels on-the-edge.

I know what the problem is but, unfortunately, the solution isn't as easy as defining the trouble. He's always had a steel trap mind when it comes to details and heightened awareness. And that's exactly what the problem is, because he ends up expecting that same level of awareness from everyone in the house. Therefore, he's doing everyone's thinking and attending to their business to make sure all details are covered. No wonder he gets so overloaded that he feels on-the-edge.

I told him he can't expect others to attend to details like he does. He can't babysit everyone. He's got to ignore more and not pay so close attention to what everyone's doing all the time. He can't constantly be reminding people to be aware.

His major problem is with Aimee, and the very late hours she keeps every night. She's rarely home before midnight and he's concerned about her getting proper rest.

I reminded him that she knows all about that. I reminded him that she's almost 20 and that he can't think of her as if she's 12. He has to let go more.

Then he confesses how worried he is about the firefighter work she's doing. He says she's giving them open opportunities to injure her and, through that, hurt us.

I didn't exactly agree.

"Honey," I said, "you have to let her choose her own career. She's too old to say 'you can't do this or that.' You can't choose her career for her and you can't keep her in a box either."

"But she's giving openings for the other side."

"Is she?"

"Yes."

"Bill, you and I both know how strong the Dark Side is. If they really wanted to get to her they could do it any hour of the day or night. They could have a robber choose her cashier line in the store; she could have a bad accident in the pickup. . .anything. They don't need her to put herself in any dangerous situation in order to get at her. So why try to put her in a box? Whatever her destiny is you have to let her be free to follow her guided path to it. You *have* to give her space. You *have* to let go."

"But don't you care about her late hours? You used to worry about her fire work."

"Sure I did, but I've come into the right perspective on it. And, sure I care about her late hours, but she's too old to babysit, Bill. She's her own person now. She's old enough to be out on her own. Just because she wants to remain with us doesn't mean that she's still 14.

"I care about her. I care about what she does, but I don't worry anymore because she must be left to be her own individual—she can't be that if she can't make her own decisions. She's not a schoolgirl anymore, honey."

Silence.

"Right?"

"Well, yes."

"So I suggest you leave her be and allow her to be her own person. You worry way too much about things that have to be allowed to play themselves out. Worry only gives you added stress. And don't always be taking on other peoples' details for them. God, Bill, we've got enough of our own work to handle. No wonder you're getting burned out. Will you try to ignore more around here?"

He said he would.

We waited up for Aimee to come home. We waited until 2:15 A.M. Our neighbor's trouble was a violent dispute that erupted during their party—some party. I don't think I'd like to be invited to a party where the police attend, and the party-goers end up in the hospital.

I forgot to add something to Tuesday's entry so I will record it here. . .we were all home that morning. Robin had occasion to go into our bedroom for something and discovered the attic door was opened. This door is located at the head of my side of our bed and leads up stairs that tunnel the entire length of the house. At the top of these stairs is a trapdoor that lets one out onto the flat part of the roof. This house is literally full of hidden doors set in the paneling. There are large hidden cubbys and spaces everywhere behind the walls. If anyone entered our house through the roof trapdoor, they'd descend the steps, push open the door and find themselves in our bedroom. This door is *never* opened.

Last Tuesday Robin said she found it open. She left it as is, because she was afraid Jenny's cat had snuck up into the attic and she'd need a way out. When she came back downstairs, she found Bill and me busy in the office so didn't want to disturb us over the opened door.

About an hour later, Aimee was upstairs with Magic when the dog's ears went up and she whined. Aimee said she was acting the same way she does when she plays Hide-and-Seek with Sarah. . .but Sarah and Mandy were downstairs.

Aimee followed Magic into our bedroom and she whined just before Aimee *heard the attic door slam shut.* (It has to be *forcibly* shut to be tight.) Magic raced over to the door to sniff and whine. Aimee never thought to open it either.

Bill and I didn't hear about the incident until Wednesday morning. Everyone's first thought had gone straight to the Starborn Ones, yet they usually shunned daytime activities. Another reason we all thought of "them" was because Magic acted like it was playtime with a familiar friend instead of displaying her "attack mode" as she does with complete strangers. The scent she picked up was definitely a familiar one to her.

8-23-91, Friday

We had a ton of mail to process today. While I was doing that, Bill did some house chores he had lined up. One of these was to install two hook latches on the top and bottom of the attic door.

I thought that was funny.

"That won't stop them, you know. Those little hooks will raise so silently we won't even wake up."

"I know that, but I'm not worried about 'them.' It's *people* we need to keep out and those little latches will do just fine."

I agreed with that and went back downstairs to work on the stack of mail where I opened our first complaint letter regarding the new information letter we started sending out on the thirteenth. This lady was extremely irate and totally disappointed in me because I can no longer respond to my correspondents.

I knew that would happen—I just knew it. Even though our letter asked people to "please understand," they just don't. They immediately make all sorts of false assumptions like, I'm straying from my purpose (they don't even *know* my purpose), or I don't care about them anymore, or I'm being selfish. If they only knew how many hours I spend praying for them. Oh well, if I've learned one thing from all of this, it's that there's no way I can please everyone. Besides, I didn't come here to please anyone, I came to get certain jobs done and that's what I must remain centered on.

Another correspondent today had six single-spaced typed pages of questions. She'd read *Daybreak,* yet still asked some of the same questions I'd already answered in the book.

Haven't heard back from Bob on the *Whispered Wisdom*

manuscript yet. I was hoping I'd hear today. Maybe he does-n't like it, or thinks the photos aren't good enough to make a pictorial. I'm sharing my private woods-walking notebook in that pictorial and if Bob thinks my thoughts are not appro-priate I guess I'll trash the whole idea. After all, it was Many Heart who told me No-Eyes wanted it done—at least I gave it my best shot. Still. . .I can't see our Advisors letting us spend so much time and money on the project if there was a strong probability showing for it to be rejected in the end. Maybe Bob just wants to spend more time looking it over and going through the slides. Or maybe he hasn't even had time to open the package. I'm not his only author and I shouldn't be so anxious that I act like I am. Now I feel that I was pompous for expecting his comments so soon. . .a later acceptance is far better than a sooner rejection.

Link called Bill this evening and she'll have approximately 15 boxes of supplies for us. They plan to meet near Deckers again on Sunday. I'll sure have my work cut out for me when he gets back home with that shipment.

He told her she was welcome to come all the way up to the house, but I think she feels like she'd be disturbing our privacy if she did that. She's more than welcome, but I know it'd make her trip quite a bit longer than if they just rendez-voused at a half-way point. I sure am thankful for Link—she has a good heart and has listened to her inner guidance to connect with us the way she did. So far, our association has produced some very happy smiles and full stomachs. What a kick this mission is!

Goodnight, Link. And many blessings to you.

8-24-91, Saturday

This was not a heavy mail day; only 32 letters. When those were processed, I helped Bill and Sarah reorganize our supplies. We'd had five large boxes of our original first edi-tion manuals that we had to move out of the way. Those consist of 210 children's books that we don't know what to do with. People aren't going to want to buy those after we issued the new ones with the full-color jacket. A friend of ours knows an officer of Science of Mind. Bill left a mes-sage for her to call us back. We're hoping he might want the books to distribute to the children of their branches. I hope something can be worked out because I'd sure hate to have to destroy all those manuals. . .there's no way I'd put them out in the trash.

Tonight I will devote an hour of prayer for a correspondent who requested my prayers.

8-25-91, Sunday

This was one crazy day. Bill and Sarah were supposed to meet Link at South Platte north of Deckers at 10:30. At 12:30, Bill called me to say he can't find her. He said he's back in Deckers and, if Link called, tell her where he is.

Bill called again some time later wondering if Link has called. She hadn't. He said he couldn't wait any longer and was coming home.

Link called about 10 minutes later, and I told her Bill was on his way home and did she want him to head back out to Deckers. She decided to drive into Woodland Park and would call me when she arrived.

Bill called from town to see if Link called. I told him she was headed into Woodland Park and he said they'd wait.

Finally Link called me from town and I told her where Bill and Sarah were waiting for her.

For a connection that was supposed to happen at 10:30, it was 3:30 when both vehicles pulled up to the house.

After 15 boxes of food were unloaded, Link told us about the vision flashes and dreams she's been having about her rendezvous with Bill. She has dark feelings about them where a very tall man with dark hair is always waiting for her to arrive at the meeting place. She dreamed of a river scene where two horses were connected to her truck and she got shot in the leg by this man. She also dreamed that she and Bill didn't make their connection.

Today Bill had the feeling he should take my small handgun with him when he left for their meeting (something he's never done before). Today Link said their meeting place was exactly the same as her dreamscape, and there also were two loose horses that hung around her truck the entire time she waited for Bill. . .and today they never connected (Bill never arrived).

When Link realized her dream was a premonition, she left the meeting place by the river to make other arrangements.

While discussing this with her, I emphasized how anyone helping us with our mission, or anyone that becomes actively involved in our mission is a target for the dark side. Her psychic visions were generated from her Higher Self as a forewarning of this fact.

Because Bill had the gun with him today, that evidenced

verification that he could've been involved with a dark one in defense of Link, but because she didn't continue to wait by the river, events were altered. From now on, they will not rendezvous in secluded areas, but rather use parking lots of towns where enough people will be around.

I'm sorry this is how it is. I'm sorry those who come into our circle are threatened. Maybe that's why we're so reluctant to open the circle to anyone who's not specifically destined to connect with us.

Last week someone shot Carole Bourdo's dog. It's going to survive, but it caused her much heart pain. That kind of thing has never happened in her area before.

After Link left our house, the girls helped me sort and repackage the food. It took us three hours. Bill and the girls will deliver the boxes tomorrow morning. Bill gets a kick out of what the recipients call him. . .Mr. Anonymous.

I'm thinking we should make Wellspring Mission an official non-profit project, but there's so much red tape involved with that. I once filled out the non-profit 501c Forms for The Mountain Brotherhood when it was first going to be a spiritual center. I'd sent everything in and received back a notation that all was in order, but where were our monies expected to come from and how much income was expected? Monies? How could I project that? So I never followed through with the finalization of it. Now I'm wondering if we should again try to make Wellspring Mission non-profit because, in actuality, we get absolutely no benefits ourselves from the project. It'd be nice to be able to solicit donations so we could buy some foodstuffs we're not getting from Link. I'm going to have to give this more thought. My additional concern is added paperwork or IRS records that I have so little time to devote to. My time just cannot be sapped by the red tape and extra record-keeping required of non-profit projects.

Tonight there's a beautiful full moon. When it first rose above the horizon the enormous orange orb silhouetted the tall pines. I wish I knew how to take a proper photograph of that—all my beautiful moon shots were duds. First I learned that a tripod was necessary. After I used that, the pictures still made the moon seem too far away—even with my 400mm lens. When I looked through the camera lens the moon filled the entire frame, but when the slides came back it looked far away. Oh well, I'm all done with my pictorial book photos now, so I suppose it really doesn't matter.

I'm going out into the silvery woods now. I'll walk awhile then sit and pray for Link's continued protection. It's 12:45 . . . I should be back by two or so.

8-26-91, Monday

Bob liked the book! He said the photos were beautiful!

Bill called Bob this morning before I was even up. They talked about *Whispered Wisdom.* Bob's considering having duplicate slides made in case anything happened to the ones I sent him. He also wants to do the book in an 8 1/2 x 11 format in order to do justice to the photos.

Oh, what a relief he liked it all. The only problem is that he wants to release the book *next* October because he sees it as a gift book for the holiday seasons. He said he's interested in releasing another one of my books this spring. That means I'd have two published in one year. That's definitely a problem because my set schedule of books had *Whispered Wisdom before* my others. I can't seem to figure out which of my other four books would fit best for a spring of '92 publication. This would probably sound ridiculous to most, but my dilemma is that none of the other books seem to fit in before the pictorial. I'm not at all comfortable with any of them in that scheduling slot. This is an awful oddity that's come up. I just never dreamed this situation would arise.

I'm going to wait up tonight and call for my friend. Maybe he'll have some counsel. Maybe this opening manifested because he has a book in mind for me to do, although I personally feel it's way too soon for *their* book, but what do I know. . .they're always changing things on me. Not that I mind because they can foresee what's required at any given time much better than I can.

I hope he comes. I hope he already knows the situation and has an idea ready. His logic is impeccable. I can't wait to hear his thoughts on this. This is gonna be great!

Two hours later —

This was not great. I could've waited to hear his idea. I hated it. We clashed on every reasoning count. He explained that *Whispered Wisdom* was moved to October for a *purpose*—that of making an "opening slot" for. . .my *journal*! I was outraged. Truly outraged.

"Do you have any idea of the intimate matters I've written about in that journal?"

"Yes," he calmly replied. "You've written of your life and I'm well aware of those events."

"Well yes, but why in God's name does *everybody* have to be aware of them? Can I not have *anything* to hold onto just for me? Why must I have to tell *all?*"

"Because the time has come for it."

"Is 'timing' the answer to *everything* around here?"

"No, but then you already know that."

"I don't believe this, I really don't." I paced before him. "You *knew* this was going to happen all *along,* didn't you. You *knew* the pictorial was going to be shoved all the way back to next fall and that's why you suggested the note cards and posters. . .because there'd be plenty of time to *produce* them! You *knew* there was going to be an opening slot for my journal!"

He didn't answer.

"*That* answers a lot of questions. Your silence says that's why you told me to alter Link's name and why you didn't want me *saying* certain things I was ready to write about. Oh," I sighed, "this is just great. . .this is royal."

"It will be great," he said.

"That's not how I meant it and you know it. No. No, I can't do this. That journal was always meant for my eyes only. I wouldn't have written *half* that stuff if I had *any* inkling that someone *else* was going to read it. Your idea stinks. It's just not fair to me. In fact, it's borderline cruel."

"Is it?"

"Yes!"

"Is it cruel to show your heart? Is it cruel to expose your pain. . .your trials?"

"For what *purpose* though? Those are *my* pain and trials. Those are my private thoughts. . .very private thoughts. I don't see what they have to do with anyone else."

"You don't?"

"No, I don't."

"You would if you stopped to think about it. You would if you saw past your anger. . .your. . .self."

"Oh, now I'm being selfish. You think I'm only thinking of *myself* here?"

"Aren't you?"

Silence.

Waiting.

"People will see me as being egotistical if I publish that journal

He frowned. "Why do you say that?"

"Because it's all about me, that's why."

"Is it?"

"Oh God, sometimes talking to you is just like talking to No-Eyes.

He smiled. "I know." Then, "Mary, over all, what *is* your journal about. . .*besides* you?"

"It's all about *struggle* and *adversity* one encounters upon their destined path! It's about *not giving up* no matter *what!* It's about *why* we're all here." Then I sighed with the realization of my own words. "It's not really all about me at all, is it?"

"Yes, in a subliminal way it is, but only as a 'vehicle' . . . a story 'character' that gets a meaning across. Is the character or the *meaning* of a story more important?"

"I see what you mean. Still. . . ."

"Still?"

"Still, I never, ever intended to share so much of myself with the public."

"Share?"

"Did I say that? Yeah, guess I did, huh. Well. . .after this nobody can ever say I didn't share enough of myself."

"It will be the greatest give-away you could do for your readers. Mary, you'll be bringing them right into your very soul."

"My soul," I whispered.

"Mary, they *need* to see how destiny works. They *need* to know you better."

I looked into his eyes. "They know me."

"Do they? Do they really? Don't many of your letters make reference to what a mystery you seem to be to them? An enigma?"

"You know they do."

"Then *shed* the mysterious cloak for them."

"I'm not wearing one."

"Doesn't matter. They think they perceive one."

"Oh, God."

"Exactly."

Silence.

Waiting.

"Do you have any idea how hard this is going to be for me? Do you have *any* idea?"

He nodded.

I just sighed and shook my head. "If I do this, can we make a trade-off? What about this?—I agree to publish my diary and you give us the makings of the free-energy device. That's fair enough."

"True. But let me propose a counter-offer. What about this?—you agree to publish your journal because it will help a great many people."

"That's not even fair."

"No? How about this then?—you agree to publish your journal because it was 'asked' of you."

"That's *definitely* not fair."

"But it worked, didn't it."

"It worked."

He smiled.

I grinned.

"Sometimes I think you're hiding No-Eyes' *twin* under that funny-looking skin of yours."

He smiled wider.

"You're pretty funny looking yourself."

And our heated discussion ended as many did. . .with us teasing each other about our otherworldly looks.

8-27-91, Tuesday

I spent the entire day at my typewriter. I had another job to do now on top of everything else. I began a new manuscript and gave it the same title as my journal. . .*Soul Sounds*. As if the story wasn't pitiful enough to write it the first time, now I had to do it all over again on a typewriter. I finished 74 pages and photocopied them for Bob to see.

Bill had called him today to tell him that my private journal had to be the book to fill the spring publishing slot. Bob sounded leery. He's got to realize that I've committed the book as being my "next work."

So I wrote him a cover letter trying to explain the forces at work here. This is not frivolity. I'd put everything on the line here.

In the evening, we discussed it further. Now that Bill had read the cover letter to Bob, Bill also knows about my late-night hours I've been keeping. He now knows about my going out in the woods so late and also the visits from my "friend." He wasn't at all upset—just asked me to be extra careful. What a pleasant surprise that was.

As our conversation deepened, he expressed concern about using people's real names. He worried about being sued by someone. I reminded him that everything I'd written in the diary was plain *facts*. How could someone sue the truth?

"Yes, but people could object to you making those 'facts' about them a public matter."

I saw his point and we decided to ask our attorney about the legal ramifications of one writing an autobiography that named names.

Then Bill had other concerns. The more he talked, the

more I doubted my decision to do it. And that upset him because he too felt the journal was right for the time slot.

Finally I'd decided not to do it, and I told him not to mail the partial manuscript to Bob in the morning. After all, why should I expose my entire life. . .my most private thoughts and experiences to strangers?

Before he went to bed tonight, he kissed me and held me for a long while.

"Promise me something?" he whispered in my ear.

"Promise me you won't rip up your journal or Bob's package? Will you just think about it a little more?"

I promised.

So after I'd stayed up for a few hours of contemplation, I had my final decision. Why expose my entire life to strangers?

And I whispered, "Because it was *asked* of me."

I left Bill a note to go ahead and mail the package off to Bob in the morning.

It just occurred to me that this has been one hell of an example of how things change hour to hour around here.

Goodnight, Guys. Hope you know what you're doing this time. As usual. . .you can count me in.

8-28-91 Wednesday

Again I spent the day typing from the journal. I'm not even a quarter way through it. Bill and Sarah handled the correspondence for me again.

Our attorney called to inform us that all parties named in the lawsuit have now been served and those in Missouri requested a month's extension for their response. It was granted because of the long length of our brief. By September 25th, we should know what kind of response they're going to give us.

Eric (Aimee's ex-fiance) finally called today. He and Bill talked for nearly an hour. Eric still wants to iron things out with Aimee, but he needs to save money for a car, then have some savings with which to move back here. He plans on coming in December. . .we'll see. Funny thing though, before Aimee left for work this morning, she asked me if I'd heard from him. I told her I hadn't, since the last time he and I talked was several months ago. All that time goes by and then they each ask about each other on the same day. Wonder if that's some kind of sign.

While Bill was talking with our attorney this morning, he asked if it was legally all right to mention the names of the three publishers who breached my contracts. He told the attorney I was going to publish my journal. The bottom line was to avoid names even though the facts are a matter of court record now. This was because the publishers could still legally hassle me if they wanted to. I haven't typed up to that part yet, so I'll have to remember to make adjustments and leave out all their names and companies. That may end up coming out in a confusing way.

Received a letter from a woman who tells me No-Eyes prefers to be called Bright Eyes. Good grief, she needs to read what I said about that in *Daybreak!* She needs to realize that No-Eyes no longer clings to that identity. She has chosen the more comfortable aura of her totality—her total spirit. Now she has a beautiful speaking voice and no longer speaks with the clipped native accent. People who send me their "channeled" messages from No-Eyes don't even know the glorious transition she's undergone. How can people continue to fool themselves so completely? Worse yet, how can they also try to fool *me* into believing *they're* channeling *her?* Especially when she's by my side so much and speaks so eloquently now—except when she tells me to have compassion for those who are deluding themselves in her name. That I have difficulty doing.

Earlier in the week, a reader wrote Bob at Hampton Roads. They faxed us her letter. She was so sweet and her words really were timed well. She wanted them to get more of my books out—more than one a year, that is. She said I was no Stephen King because, while his books may be entertaining—mine were life-saving! Little did she know that 1992 just may be the year we get two of mine out. Two a year is fine with me, because then they'd all be out by the fall of 1994 instead of 1997. Wouldn't that be great?

We had nine children's book orders today. . .broke a record! I love sending those out because, for every one that goes out, another child will grow up with the truths. Now *that's* what I call rewarding.

A bookstore in California called us today. They got our number from the listing of publishers. I think it's funny when they don't realize they're talking to Bill or me. They think they've connected with some employee of Lodestar Press. Somehow they don't actually make the connection. During dinner tonight, Robin answered the phone and it was another bookstore. They had no idea who they were talking to, but when bookstore owners do make the connection, the conversation becomes quite lengthy, and Bill usually enjoys those because he's so outgoing.

We're going to have to make a decision on the children's book soon. With an IRS tax payment due next month and the money it takes to have a reprint done, we won't be left with a comfortable buffer in savings. If my Donning royalties (due Sept. 15th) come in, we should be able to swing the reprint, but I feel a problem coming.

Bill mailed Bob the first 74 pages of my journal book this morning. Hampton Roads should have it by Monday. Sure hope he sees it as being a good book for the 1992 spring slot. We definitely have a major problem if he doesn't. Come on, Bob, be daring. . .go for it.

I just noticed something. I've written tonight's entry with no thought of it being read by others. That is a surprise because after I decided to publish this thing I was concerned about if I'd alter my natural thoughts in it—it never even crossed my mind tonight. Guess if I have something on my mind I'm going to go right ahead and say it. That's what this book's all about.

8-29-91, Thursday

Bill called Bob this morning to let him know the beginning pages of this journal are in the mail. Bob asked if No-Eyes was in the book. He seems to feel she's who the public wants to read about. But when you think about it, only my first two books were totally about No-Eyes and every book after that was devoted to different subjects, like Many Heart, wayward spirits, health, reader's questions. My prime mission for coming again was not to write exclusively of any one personality, but to bring the truths to light. No-Eyes was the Player who made that mission possible. And so I have continued on to finish it with the rest of the series. After all, my very first effort on this path was directed toward the little children. . .long, long before I met No-Eyes. My writing genre is not No-Eyes, it's Spirituality. And, I believe, that's where the confusion arises.

Today I spent at my typewriter. I never realized this diary would make so many typed pages. Maybe this book will be a lot longer than I thought it would be, especially since I'd like to carry it through to the end of the year. . .hoping some of our plans for the future will be finalized by then.

This evening Bill and the girls met Link at an alternate location to pick up another shipment. They returned home at 9 P.M. and Robin and I helped unload. This time we got sleeping bags, wool blankets, and three large boxes of clothing in addition to the many food boxes. This shipment will take me several days to get ready to deliver. What pure joy this mission is!

8-30-91, Friday

Bill called Bob this morning and, among other things, they discussed my diary. Bob's still concerned that I'm "crossing over" with it. In other words, he perceives it as a subject matter or genre shift out of the No-Eyes realm. Generally, a cross-over book doesn't do as well as the author's former type of material because it's so different in content and readers recoil from it. But what could be more "different" than *Daybreak* was?

While they were on the phone, I could hear Bill's end of the conversation while I was sorting out the clothing boxes in our office. I kept trying to tell Bill to convey an important aspect to Bob, but Bill wasn't listening to me. . .what else is new. When he got off the phone, I told him what I wanted to say and he said, "Why didn't you tell me that?" I give up.

So I faxed my thoughts to Bob and underscored the fact that my "genre" is spirituality—not No-Eyes. And that my books reflect that spirituality in "different forms." I hoped my letter helped to dispel his crossover notion.

Later in the day Frank DeMarco of Hampton Roads called me to say he'd read the journal pages I'd sent in. He loved them. He sees the book as "the bridge" from No-Eyes to Summer Rain. Guess that settles the crossover dilemma we had.

I split my day between typing up the diary and sorting the rest of the clothes for deliveries tomorrow. I still have seven boxes of food to sort through and repackage.

8-31-91, Saturday

Bill and Jenny went down to Colorado Springs. We needed some office supplies from Biz Mart and Jen needed some new shoes.

While they were gone, Sarah did laundry and I spent the day typing up my diary. When they returned home, Bill brought in a stack of mail from the post office. Sarah began pulling the correspondent's cards. If they had no card in our file, she made one for them.

The last letter I read was addressed to Rainbow. Seems a lady was outraged at our information letter she received, and decided writing me was no good; so she wrote to Rainbow. What's the matter with people who do that kind of thing? Our letter is clearly apologetic about not being able to respond anymore and asks them to "please understand" that we have to follow our guidance to move on to new missions. I don't know how much more clear or soft we can make it.

I certainly didn't appreciate her inferred sarcasm. I didn't appreciate her stab at being clever. I wrote her a one liner back: "Your letter was not amusing—Rainbow's dead." Is there no limit people will go to?

Bill was upset when he saw how the lady addressed her envelope. He's quickly becoming disgusted with people like this and is glad we've been given other work to concentrate on.

This evening, after dinner, I got right on sorting the boxes of food. Jenny loves helping with this project and I'm sure she'll be spending a great deal of time working in our Wellspring warehouse when it's all set up. Tonight I decided to add to the name because, while Jenny and I were talking about it as we worked with the food, I automatically called it *Wellspring Mission.* When I heard the words I loved the sound of them. Wellspring Mission is so apropos because it truly will be a "mission" in *both* senses of the word.

Later in the evening, Bill's sense of protection kicked in. He'd been reading the typed journal pages for the purpose of proofing them—not only for typos, but also for accuracy for event chronology (he'd caught a few out of order and I'd had to retype several pages to correct them, but I find I still have a few misplaced events. It's not easy getting it all exact from one's birth).

Anyway, he's adamant that I don't publish the precise location of our land and Wellspring. He says we (especially me) need some peace on our land and, if I write where we'll be, we'll never have that privacy we both so desperately need.

As far as Wellspring Mission is concerned, he reminded

me that I shouldn't publish where that is either, because it's only for the local needy people to know. What he didn't realize is that my "friend" told me the same thing about our land, but *he* didn't see a problem with saying that Wellspring may be in Redstone.

I saw their points and had to retype many pages, because I'd detailed our land so precisely that a blindfolded child could find it.

We ended up with a record month for the children's book. I guess I hadn't given it enough time. As long as I receive my September royalty check we've decided to go ahead and have more manuals produced by the new Colorado printer. Eventually, when we relocate, we'll have an address change for Lodestar Press, but to take care of that we'll just have new address stickers placed over the Woodland Park one in the manuals. Having our mail forwarded for a year will take care of the interim slack.

A week ago I was beginning to get another canker sore and Bill was the one to determine it was due to hormonal alterations, because it appears to be connected with a certain point in my cycle. I began taking four Vitamin B-6's per day and the damned thing halted its nasty progress, regressed, and vanished in three days. What a mind! What a guy!

September, 1991

A busy day for a Sunday. I typed from my diary and worked on the letterhead for Wellspring Mission. We won't put an address on it until we're settled. Since it's a not-for-profit project, we're going to try to solicit donations of supplies for our warehouse. We currently have 70 families in Woodland Park who are needy.

Today I also filled out a Viking Office Products order form for Lodestar printed envelopes. This, I found, will cost us less than buying blank envelopes and separate address labels as we've been doing. I also had to order another 500-page journal because I'll have this one filled by the end of the month. I plan on keeping these hand-written journals even though the contents will be published in book form. I feel the need to save the originals.

Bob sent me two novels he published through his Hampton Roads publishing company. He wanted my opinion of them. *Ezekiel's Chariot* by Dana Redfield (a Denver author) was a humorously entertaining tale. . .a delightful story. The second novel was *Living Is Forever* by J. Edwin Carter. Had I known about this book when I'd written *Daybreak,* I surely would have included it in my book listing as "*must* reading," for many, many truths were woven throughout the story of the cataclysmic changes and aftermath. This one was truly "inspired" by many unseen Forces surrounding the author. The ISBN number for this book is: 1-878901-00-1.

This morning when we went to town for a Sunday paper, we brought Jenny along to pick out her birthday cake. Tomorrow's her big day (22) and she just about drove Bill nuts checking here and there for just the right cake.

Jenny's birthday is extremely special to her. She even bought balloons. She loves big celebrations and is just like a little kid about them. She wants to go out to Pizza Hut for dinner, so we'll do that. Also, Aimee has plans to take her and Sarah downtown to go roller skating on her birthday. That's something Jenny's been wanting to do for months. Aimee's current young man from the fire department is going to drive them all down, and then they'll come back up to meet Bill, Mandy, and me at Pizza Hut for dinner. Afterward it'll be back home for presents and cake and ice cream. That will be our Labor Day celebration.

Bill's been keeping numbers on how many letters I get each month from "new" correspondents. Since *Daybreak* was released they tripled—this doesn't even count our repeats from former correspondents. . .these have doubled. It's a wonder either of us get anything else done around here.

This afternoon Bill and Jenny watched the first official game of the NFL season. I think I went deaf during that game. The Denver Broncos won by a high score, and the screaming and stamping. . .and barking was enough to rattle the walls. Magic even ran around the house with a Bronco football in her mouth. Broncomania is alive and well in this house! Jenny would think she'd gone to heaven if she ever met John Elway.

9-2-91, Monday

Until 3:30 in the afternoon, I worked on typing up the diary. We had to leave for Pizza Hut to meet the girls. Jenny said she had a great time skating and loved her sister's birthday surprise.

When we returned home, they blew up balloons while waiting for Robin to come home on her dinner break from work. Once she arrived we lit the candles, sang the song and waited. . .and waited. . .and waited for Jenny to make her wish (which we already know is for us to move to Glenwood because Jenny loves it over there). Finally the candles were blown out and the presents were dug into.

Jenny's a cinch for gifts. . .anything with kittens on it is purrrfect. She received a music box with kittens going up and down on a teeter-toter; a kitten statue, laser picture of a kitten, kitten sweaters and tee shirts. She even received kitten flannel sheets with pawprints all over them. And, of course, friends and relatives send money in their cards. Jen had a great day.

Happy Birthday, Jenny. I love you, honey.

When I'm done with this entry, I'm going into the candle-lit living room to spend an hour or so praying for my readers. I may not be able to respond to their letters, but that doesn't mean I can't still help them in other ways.

9-3-91 Tuesday

Spent the day processing a double stack of mail after the long holiday weekend, then did errands.

During the late night hours, lightning flashed and thunder rumbled, but no rain. It was very eerie.

9-4-91, Wednesday

Bill and I drove over to Alps Printing to order our new letterhead. Bill picked out purple ink. We were going to have matching envelopes done, but when Georgine asked us the address for them we just looked at each other. . .we didn't have a final Wellspring Mission address yet. It was at that moment that I realized how fast things were moving for us. We explained about our plans to move to the Glenwood area, where we'd establish the Wellspring Mission warehouse. Georgine said they could still handle all our printing needs via fax and UPS. So we just ordered the letterhead for now. We think it's going to look real nice because we kept the Lodestar star on it. That way the connection between the two divisions remains intact.

Sarah starts school tomorrow and she's very excited. We're going to miss all the office help she's given us over the summer months. Magic's going to miss her too. Sarah seems to be her favorite person of all of us. . .I come in second, so Magic will probably follow me around all day and lay under my desk. She'll have to be satisfied with second fiddle—at least until four, when her favorite comes through the door.

9-5-91, Thursday

Spent the entire day typing up the journal pages. By the time I proofed for typos, I was signing children's manuals at 9 P.M.

Bill missed Sarah's presence today.

"Gonna have to get me a secretary," he said around noontime.

"Just make sure you get one that *types*," I teased.

"Guess I can handle it, but the pay sure is lousy."

"Yeah, but look at the *benefits* you get! In fact," I crooned, "isn't it about time for your bonus pay?"

He turned from his desk and grinned wide.

And we left the office unattended to go upstairs to "discuss" it.

He was right about the pay.

I was right about the benefits. . .they far outweighed everything else.

Before Bill went to bed tonight, he expressed deep concern over a specific section in my journal, with regard to a conversation that could present a problem. This discussion was between us and another couple. Bill wants the conversation entirely deleted. I'm on the fence about it. I think I'll leave it in the manuscript for now and discuss it with Bob after he reads it. I'd be interested in hearing his opinion. However. . . I think Bill may be right. I'd recorded the conversation because I never dreamed anyone but me would be reading it. And, when I typed it up, I didn't necessarily think anything more about it, because it was just one of many conversations that took place in my life. . .nothing more, nothing less, but looking deeper at it, I can see where problems could arise. I don't particularly condone altering any of my journal entries but, in this case, I may have to delete one altogether.

Tonight my Prayer Smoke will be offered for a special request from one of my correspondents. It will be quite involved and I expect it to last nearly two hours. It's 12:45 A.M., so I'd better get going.

See you in a bit, No-Eyes.

9-6-91, Friday

This morning our phone was ringing at 7:30. Bill was in the shower and I was still in bed trying to open my eyes. Luckily Robin was up, as she'd gotten Mandy off to school. Pete from Hampton Roads had a fax for us. Moving Books' bestseller list now had *Daybreak* in the Number 2 spot. This was good news, but I wasn't awake enough to fully appreciate it at the time. Four hours of sleep isn't getting it. Don't know what else I can do though because the dark, silent midnight hours are the only undisturbed times I have the proper solitude for my Prayertime and communions. I've become a nightwalker who also must be up to walk the morning hours. Bill suggested I go back to taking naps after dinner, as I used to do when I was up late writing the first few books. At that time I also had to rise early to get the girls off to school. I think I'm going to have to go back to that because, right now, the face that looks back at me from the mirror in the morning resembles one that's participated in a sleep deprivation experiment. . .the luggage has luggage.

Shining silver strands are sprouting from my head. I'm going to leave them. Why try to hide the real me? I've earned every last silvery one and, as my friend said, I don't need any cloaks.

Bill processed the mail today while I typed from the journal. I've finally worked my way up to the current date, so now I'll only have to type up the entry I wrote the night before. This will free up my day for concentrating on other obligations that I've gotten behind on.

Haven't heard Bob's opinion on those first 74 pages of the journal we sent him. Frank DeMarco loved them, but we're still waiting on Bob. . .he's the one who signs the contracts.

Aimee won't be home at all tonight. She's on-call, so she'll be sleeping at the fire station. Next week she begins her four-month EMT training. This will be extremely valuable—not only for the present, but for future use too.

The Woodland Park High School instituted a new Absence Policy this year and it's got me riled again. Seems a child's illness is "unexcused" unless they return with a doctor's slip. Eight of these unexcused absences and the child forfeits all credits for that semester.

What they're *really* saying is that they've taken away parental rights to make an educated judgment call regarding their own child's illness. A parent should have the right to keep their child home if he/she is ill, and that decision should be respected by the school. What this policy says is that the school doesn't *believe* a parent who says the child is sick. So they make the parent spend unnecessary medical expenses just for colds, flus, or stomach upsets. I don't think so. Nope.

There's no way I'm taking Sarah to a doctor for a bad cold or stomach upset. No way. And if this school dared to take all her semester credits away because of eight days lost due to flu, I'll test the constitutionality of their "policy" in a court of law. . .*after* I take her out of school so fast their heads will spin. Who are they to take away my right to judge my own daughter's illness? If I call in to say she's sick then, dammit, she's sick! I don't need any doctor's note to verify my judgement. This is just going too far. We're losing so many rights it's downright scary. Our individual rights are being chipped away a little at a time and, when I see another chisel aimed at another of my rights, I get very defensive. We're losing the right of free speech. . .the right to protect ourselves (bear arms). . .the right to a dignified death and to have personal and private control over our own bodies. *No one* has the right to interfere with these. Sarah and Bill joked about making sure mom didn't see the school "parent night" announcement in our local newspaper, for fear Rambo Mom would attend and deliver an animated display of outraged attacks on "the policy." And, by God, I surely would too if it hadn't been for the fact that the school's getting a lot of flack anyway about this from other parents. I'm going to wait this one out a bit.

A while back, Bill thought he made a cute joke that everyone but me thought was funny. We were watching the Leona Helmsley story. . .*The Queen of Mean.*

During a commercial break, Bill says to me, "Man! After seeing *her*, you look like the Tooth Fairy!"

He called me Leona for about a week after that. He was only teasing, but is it my fault I turn into a raging bull when I see injustices? *Someone's* got to fight for rights. . .especially when it involves children! If nobody does anything or stands up for what's right, what will we have left worth leaving our children?

My Starborn friend never called me Leona. He has his own way of terming my ingrained passion for justice. . . "spirited," he says. But then he, probably more than anyone, understands the complete totality of spirit mind it's generated from and, from that level, he says, it's an equitable response.

Rambo Mom? Damn right—every kid should have one because then every kid could stick out their chests with pride and say, "*My mom cares!*"

Whew! How'd I get on that one? Oh yeah—school policy. Look out school, somebody's. . .*watching.* . .you.

9-7-91, Saturday

It felt good not to have to spend all day typing up the diary. When I finished, we went to town for the mail, and I browsed through City Market's and Ben Franklin's paperback rack. It's a sad commentary on our town that every bookstore which tries to establish itself ends up failing. So every couple weeks, I accompany Bill to town on a Saturday and look to see if I can find anything new that interests me. It's not very often I do. It's a shame the people of Woodland Park aren't bookaholics. Having a B. Dalton or Waldenbooks store up here would be heaven, but I satisfy this craving by ordering from the Barnes & Noble, Postings, and Hamilton catalogs that come through the mail. You can take away the book-stores, but I'll still find a way of getting to the books.

We came back with a stack of mail and I helped Bill go through it. Three letters last week and two today requested my suggestion for a "right" meditation book. Seems people are confused and don't know which one is best or right. I was remiss not to include the title of the *only* one I recommend to folks. Hopefully I can remedy that oversight by listing it now.

Meditation by M. E. Penny Baker
Doubleday, 1973   *[NOTE: This book is out of*
ISBN: 0-385-00984-4   *print and unavailable.]*

This volume is the most accurate and comprehensive one I've found and is based on the Edgar Cayce readings. I've had my copy for a very long time and hope it's still in print—if it's not, the public needs to demand its resurrection.

Aimee participated in a "controlled burn" today. The fire department razed some sheds and old cabins just off Trout Creek Road and Highway 24. Aimee got initiated when the veteran firefighters dunked her in the water tank. Guess she's one of them now.

Bill surprised me this evening by softening his former ad-amant stance on the possibility of lease-optioning our chosen property. Yet when we discussed it at length, we realized we still wouldn't be able to swing the monthly lease payment on it.

Then I suggested maybe we could at least buy a place in Redstone for our project. We could live there just to "get us over there" before winter. Nope. It wouldn't be big enough for all of us. So we dropped the entire issue because every-thing we came up with brought us right back to square one. As my friend so aptly reminds me, "Nothing works when it's *not the time for it.*" Yet I can't help wondering what's *really* blocking us—is it really timing? Or finances? When you rea-son these together, it results in a conundrum that equates to the old chicken-and-egg question. Will the *right timing* mani-fest only when we have enough funds? Or will the *funds* manifest only when the timing is right? Which generates the impetus for which? Which the forerunner? I'll say this much . . .I'm not going to lose sleep over this one.

I'm going to go meditate now.

Two hours later. . .

My friend says, among other things we discussed, that my paradox was worded wrong and that my answer would be clear as crystal if I had done it right.

Right.

He clarified it. The word "because" denotes the forerunner term for a "reason." Therefore, my clear as crystal answer is this: We will have the funds for our land *because the time is right.* "Time," he reiterated, "is destiny's Twin Ruler. The same cannot be said of money."

And that took care of that.

"So," I smiled, "which came first, chicken or egg?"

"You know that one. You tell me," he said.

"Chicken."

"Oh?"

"Chicken came first."

"You sure you don't want to think a little more on that one?"

"Chicken."

Silence.

"Chicken," I whispered.

"Why?" he whispered back.

"Because *God* created all the animals. The animals *then* produced the offspring. . .eggs. Chicken first, egg second. Easy."

He deferred a nod of recognition, but then cut me back down.

"Your original conundrum, or what you *thought* was one, could've been just as easy if you would've given a little deeper thought to what destiny is and how it works."

"Thanks. With one hand you pat me on the back and with the other you shake a stick at me."

"Balance, my friend, always *The Balance* must be maintained."

I sighed. "That's very difficult to do down here."

"We realize that."

"I think you do. No, let me start over. I think you *think* you do, but *living* every hour—every single moment—here is a lot different than just *knowing* about earth life. I mean, between the two there's a world of difference."

"Yes, different world."

I smiled. "You took that literally."

"It is."

"Yes, but only for a little while longer."

"Only until then, yes."

Silence. I was deep in thought.

My friend's voice was soft. "You worry about including our communions in your journal."

"Yes, among other things I've written of."

"You're uncomfortable with your decision?"

"I'm never uncomfortable doing what's asked of me, no that's not it. I'm uncomfortable with outcomes—the end result of it."

"This is because we are not No-Eyes."

Silence.

"Yes?"

"Yes, I suppose that is the bottom line. Most of the conversations between her and me were okay to publish, but between us. . .well, I just don't feel real good about that."

"You're not introducing a new issue here. Many books are published about us."

"But this is real. This is me."

"You?"

I moaned. "Ohhh. . .I'm not wording it right again. It's not just the 'me' that's at issue—that's not it. I guess I can't explain why I'm uncomfortable recording these times together."

"Is it as simple as having wanted to keep our relationship an unknown? Quiet? Private?"

Our eyes met. "You're getting closer, but I still can't put my finger on it. It's more of a deep inner feeling that I can't seem to voice. I'm having trouble finding the right words to express it."

He touched my hand. "How about 'bond'. . .our unique bond. That's the feeling you're scared to reveal."

"Am I wrong to feel that way? Is that being selfish?"

"No to both, but it's expected because it's natural."

"So? Why am I scared to reveal this one aspect of my life?"

"Don't you know? Don't you really know?"

I couldn't voice what I really knew.

He did for me. "Could it be that you might be revealing more of the 'who' of you than you ever planned to?"

And I never voiced my answer for the lump that was lodged in my throat. At that moment I hated my decision to make this journal public. I *hated* it. I may as well be living in a glass house—no. . .a damn *fish* bowl!

9-8-91, Sunday

Finally had a day where I could catch up on my personal correspondence and reading.

Our local newspaper has been running articles about the gambling that's going to begin in Cripple Creek in October. That town has been torn up half the summer as they renovate the old buildings to convert them into gambling halls and casinos. I hated to see so many of the little shops gone— even the bookstore sold out to the investors.

Five new state police cars were added to the two that always seemed to suffice. This is in anticipation of the increased traffic flow through our area.

Housing costs have gone up. Rentals are scarcer. And I think this region will no longer have the "little mountain town" flavor I so loved. I have the feeling that our *timing* is getting closer.

For the last month I've been reading *The Philosophical Scientists* and *Ideas and Opinions* (this one by Einstein), and I finally got to finish them. How wonderful to be able to spend an entire day reading.

9-9-91 Monday

We had quite a lot of mail today, and I helped Bill by opening the letters, reading them, and making out the cards. Two letters were unsettling.

One was from a woman who called me a cynic and said I was the only one she knew who lives in the past and bemoans the historical fate of her people. She wondered why I couldn't be "accepting" like all the other peaceful reservation people were? It was clear that this woman never delved into the native issues that have to do with their ongoing problems and legal battles, for then she would surely have discovered that the reservation people are not idly sitting back. . .they are doing battle still. This woman's reading must be extremely limited, for many current books on native issues define their current tribulations and the people's passionate determination to rectify the ongoing wrongs done them. She needs to hear the tape cassette called *Tribal Voices*.

The second letter that bothered me was from *another* woman who is claiming a past life as Jesus. She even listed all her former life identities, but not one of those entities were *any* of Jesus' former life entities. This saddens me so. What can people like this be thinking? What is it they hope to gain by such grave self-delusions? Tonight I will devote my two Prayertime hours to people who are deluding themselves in Jesus' name, for I know how these ones cause my Father pain.

In contrast to the above, the rest of our correspondence today was very uplifting and served to balance out the negative aspects of our mail. I'm very grateful and deeply appreciative of those who express how much No-Eyes and Many Heart have helped them. Even though I've not the time to respond to these people, their kind and loving words are always brought into my heart.

Autumn approaches with soft footfalls through our woods. Aspen branches here and there have already turned to gold with Autumn's breath upon their leaves. Air, crisp now, fresh as newfallen snow, greets me each morning. Soon woodsmoke will scent the forest and I shall be called forth to join in the new celebration, for Autumn Spirit and I are then united, and we will dance to the thundering drums that ignite our primal twin souls. In wild freedom will we give our sacred Thanksgiving as we dance through the fiery red and gold flames of the ceremonial fire. Yes, truly the red and gold leaves are Autumn's sacred fire, and the mountains themselves send forth a powerful drumming that only the soul can hear.

Autumn. . .nature's most wild native celebration, so full of chanting voices, strong cadence and colorful costumes. Autumn. . .

9-10-91, Tuesday

Bill had to stack a cord of wood today, so I spent the day in the office alone and processed the mail. One letter in particular brought tears to my eyes. It was from a 59-year-old lady who wrote of how I'd changed her life. My eyes misted when she said I was the "wind beneath her wings." Those words really hit me—touched me—because I don't see myself as affecting people in such a monumental manner. All the correspondents today were sent our information letter with a handwritten personal response at the bottom. Whenever I do have time to work on the mail, I still try to keep the connecting door open by writing a specific response at the bottom of each reply. I will do that for as long as I can.

Aimee came to inform us that the fee for her Emergency Medical Technician training is due and Bill gave her the $406 for it. Her first class is tonight and she's very excited. She's also on-call at the fire department (where the EMT classes are held) so I won't see her until late Wednesday night.

Bill finally talked to Bob and got his opinion on the beginning journal pages. . .he liked them! They discussed how
they thought my diary would do and Bill wanted to pin down
the spring '92 release date for it. Bob said he'd get back to
him in a few days. I don't want Bob's financial consideration
to hamper his decision, so I need to let him know that the
advance for this book (the journal) may be the last one I
need. If I can forego the advances for the rest of my books,
I'll be glad to do so, if that will get my readers two of my
books a year. I think I'll fax that thought to Bob tomorrow
morning so he can take it into consideration.

This evening, Bill, Robin and I were sitting in the living
room having a discussion about our future plans and we were
updating Robin about what's been transpiring day-to-day in
the office. Bill mentioned to her that he told Bob I was still
writing every night in my journal and that they'd better watch
how they behaved or "Mary will tear us to shreds." That
comment reminded me of the "Rambo Mom" and "Leona"
incidences I'd included in the diary. I never told Robin or
Bill that my Starborn friend calls me "spirited," but he had
made that initial comment during a conversation we had after
I'd recovered from my operation. This would be a good place
to explain that.

After the surgery and my girls were walking with me
around and around the hospital halls, I'd made a comment to
them that "trying to get any sleep around here at night was
impossible because the night shift made so much noise it
sounded like a *bowling alley* in the halls. It's party time
every night," I'd said.

Well, one of the night staff heard that and I was *in for it*
then. That night was like slipping into the Twilight Zone,
because their professionalism vanished and I experienced such
uncharacteristic humiliation and childish acts of abuse from
the staff, that I nearly called the administrator at midnight.
These "professionals" even began ringing my bed phone to
harass me. Finally I had to crawl on the floor behind my bed
and unplug the jack. They were giggling and laughing out in
the hallway, and I felt they were all possessed.

I swore I was *leaving* that place in the morning. I would
not spend another night in that hospital! So at 1:30 A.M. I
wheeled my I.V. stand over to the sink. Got a bandage out
from the cabinet, ran the cold water and placed my wrist in
the sink. . .I pulled out my I.V. line. I was going *home*!

When the day shift came on, my nurse was outraged over
my state of distress and determination to discharge myself. I'd
only been operated on two day's ago.

I'd been crying from the unbelievable absurdity of it all.

"Tell me all about it," she demanded softly.

"It's been so noisy around here at night nobody can sleep. They play a radio out there (nurse's station outside my door) and run up and down the halls. They do something that sounds like they're bowling and nobody can sleep. One of them overheard me telling my daughters about that.

"Then late last night I began having terrible stomach pains and I requested medication to relieve them. The night nurse told me I needed to walk more."

My nurse shook her head. "You've *walked* more than any other patient on this floor!"

I finished my story. "So I told her walking wasn't helping and could I please have some Mylanta or something. She gave me a suppository, and when she went back to the station I could hear them giggling and whispering about it.

"When I was in the bathroom, one of them came in and pretended to spray Lysol around the room. He said, 'Whew! We need some air freshener in here!'

"Then when I was back in bed curled up with the sharp pains, I heard sounds coming from the next room that sounded like a horn of some kind. God, they were imitating someone passing gas and I couldn't believe it. Then my phone started ringing and ringing. Nobody would be on the other end when I picked it up. So I crawled out of bed and got on the floor to unplug the phone jack. Then pulled out my I.V., because there was no way I was spending another night in this place. The way they were acting was so out of character for professionals, it was just like they were all possessed. I'm going home."

Bonnie was very upset over this. "Have you had any *pain* medication all night?"

"No, and I don't need any either. I just want out of here."

She brought me two pain pills and hung a new bag on my I.V. stand.

"Bonnie," I said, "what's that for?"

"This is your antibiotic."

"But I've taken my line out."

She was so upset over the incident, she forgot I'd done it.

"Dr. DePinto's not going to like this."

"Does he have to know?"

"Oh dear."

"Bonnie, I'm going home this morning."

"I think he wants you to stay another day."

"I'm going home if I have to sign myself out."

My nurse left the room while I got dressed and waited for my family to arrive. In the hall at the nurse's station I could hear the Head Nurse giving hell to the night crew. I only heard bits and pieces.

"You can't *treat* famous people like that!" she'd said.

Famous? She must be talking about someone else. Anyway, my doctor was down in surgery, and they had to phone him about the crisis situation. He told them to have any physician on the floor sign me out.

When Bill arrived, they again called down to my surgeon —he'd just finished an operation. He and Bill talked and my doctor was furious. He wanted *names*. I had none. What patient bothers looking at everyone's name tag right after they'd had surgery?

I was so glad to be home in my own bed again. And because I'd pulled my I.V. out and was going to sign myself out of the hospital, my "friend" said, "*that's* the spirited Mary I know!"

I didn't know about that, all I knew was I was not going to spend another night in Demons-R-Us! I remember one nurse asking another if maybe the "patient" was "imagining" things from morphine effects. And the other nurse reminded her that the "patient" had requested the morphine be *discontinued*. I did, too. When I began seeing the wall swirl and the chart holder begin sliding down the wall, I said "no more morphine." So I was not hallucinating the uncharacteristic antics of that night staff. Even my roommate, who slept the sleep of morphine through that night, admitted the next morning to the head nurse and, later to our surgeon, that yes, each night sounded like a bowling party was going on in the hall. Frankly, I was outraged that patients just out of surgery could get no sleep or decent rest. But the cruelty I was subjected to for saying anything was just plain mean—it was truly like being caught in the Twilight Zone. And for *that* I had to pay $10,000! Well, at least my surgeon was exceptional. A week later I sent him a copy of *Earthway* and signed it to "To my Medicine Man with the Magic Healing Hands." Credit had been given where credit was due.

Several months later, we'd received a notice from a billing company that we *must* pay the *full* balance of the hospital bill or else it was going to *collections*!

What? WHAT! We'd been paying them what we could every month. They knew we had no insurance. Now I was *really* "spirited!" And I sat down at my typewriter to tell the whole sordid story to the hospital administrator himself. By return mail we received his reply. He apologized for the "inexcusable staff performance" and that "the incident was being investigated." We were told to call the head of billing to set up a comfortable payment schedule—we wouldn't be receiving

anymore Nastygrams. I shouldn't have paid—I should've sued
—but that's not my way. . .I just wanted to forget the whole
thing. Amen!

9-11-91, Wednesday

Before Bill and I worked on the mail, we revised our
Lodestar information letter. For different reasons, we were
each uncomfortable with the one we worked up in August.
This new one better explains our new mission and it leaves
our door open for correspondents.

Bill faxed Bob my note regarding my future advances and,
when Bob later called about a magazine that was doing a
Daybreak article, he said he'd call us Friday to discuss the
journal.

A woman wrote to express concern over an abortion she'd
had years ago. She was wondering if her actions created negative karma and if she would have to reconcile with the spirit
that awaited her fetus' vehicle. I told her no to both. Abortion is a free will choice, and does not create karma for the
woman, because there is no spirit dwelling there yet. Spiritually speaking, abortion is not a negative action that directly
correlates to any of the Precepts. This then is why no specific karma is involved. The spirit intending to occupy the
aborted vehicle immediately returns to the Record Hall and,
with counsel, re-evaluates its various alternate options available.

I'm extremely upset when I receive letters from women
who've been told by a psychic or channeler that the spirit of
their aborted fetus is crying for its "mommy." Don't they
know that these spirits are not babies? Don't those "psychics"
know that incoming spirits are the sum total of *all* their experiences and are, overall, intelligent *adult* entities? And these
are *psychics?* The terrible psychological harm they're doing is
causing many women irreparable damage. Abortion is not
looked upon as a "favorable" decision, but then again, it's not
condemned either because it's viewed as an individual *free
will right* of each woman to weigh her life, physiological or
psychological, circumstances. Clearly, the spiritual aspect of
this issue sides with the current pro-choice perspective. We
need to be very careful when governments and religions begin
interfering with an individual's right to make free will choices
such as these. No government, no religious leader has the
right to tell a woman she can or cannot have a baby.

Harry Glover, regional director for A.R.E. and a friend, called us tonight to say he couldn't make his September 16th visit with us. We were disappointed, but also know there'll be other visits down the line. I knew something would interfere with our meeting.

The last time Harry was here, Jenny cooked a wonderful baked chicken dinner. While we were eating, Jenny's cat kept reaching up to paw Harry's leg. . .seems he'd been secretly slipping her a few chicken tidbits and she wanted more of his supper. It was very humorous to see because he couldn't get rid of her once he slipped her that first piece. He seemed to enjoy sharing with Buttercup, and we, in turn, enjoyed seeing his joy.

My dear sister, Elise, wrote me a long letter. She and her husband are selling their Shelby Township home in Michigan so they can move into their newly-built cedar home near Asheville, North Carolina. I'm very excited for them—they deserve the best.

I'm all the family Elise has left; the rest of them disowned her because, in their minds, she married the wrong man. How is it that some family members aren't happy unless they're trying to manipulate their relation's lives? Why can't they be happy with their *own* lives and leave other's alone to live theirs?

Elise is getting ready to write a book about the issue of family manipulation and vindictive families that gossip and slander each other. She's using her own personal history as the case in point. She's calling it *Family Secrets*. Last year she was toying with the idea of writing her story with the theme of family violence entitled *Brass Knuckles*. I told her I liked that title because our father always left his own brass knuckles on his dresser top every night, with his service revolver and badge.

My oldest sister still thinks I'm the Mother of all Nuts so we haven't corresponded in years. But she and my mother are very close, so they have each other as family. And with me being out here in Colorado, I try to stay out of the gossip and slander going on back in Michigan. Elise finally came to the realization that she has to move out of state in order to escape all that misery.

My mother and my older sister don't believe in my truths. My mother just avoids the issue altogether. Whenever I send her a copy of one of my newly-released books, she doesn't comment about the content. . .only how well I write. And that's fine with me.

Well, I'm just so glad Elise will be moving far away from the constant gossip. . .she deserves some peace with her husband, who treats her like a queen. They're so happy together, and I dearly love them both.

Goodnight, Elise. Goodnight, Charlie.

9-12-91, Thursday

I helped Bill with the mail until 1:30 when a heaviness came over me and I couldn't seem to stay awake. It was such an uncharacteristic sensation for the middle of my day, I felt almost as if I was being "called" to another dimension where my spirit was needed. So I went upstairs, opened my bedroom window wide so I could hear the wind through the pines, and slept until four. During that time, I'd been in conference with my White Brotherhood associates on their familiar level. No-Eyes, a shimmering essence now, was also present at this meeting.

I was updated on events of The Plan that were foreseen to be shifting somewhat toward a more secure direction. This, of course, directly involved Bill and me. Our future location was one of the major issues, for a strong probability was beginning to manifest that would severely alter our course. Wellspring Mission was still solid, but its ultimate location was not. I was apprised of the alternates and advised to remain "open" for confirmations that would be forthcoming during my conscious state.

Other aspects of our work were covered, including our Third mission involving my Starborn friend and his associates. This facet of our meeting included representatives of that group. Afterward, with the information I'd gained, deeper logic and reasoning was brought back to the awake-state consciousness. And for that alone, I'm most grateful.

Aimee had a day off today and spent most of it studying her EMT books. It means a lot to her to pass this course and become certified.

She brought home some medical equipment catalogs and Bill and I will go through them. We've always planned to have well-stocked medical supplies for the future, and now seems to be the time to get whatever we think we'll need.

Writing about the medical supplies brings to mind something else. Last year a fan of No-Eyes met with us at Tony's Garden Cafe (formerly Godmother's Kitchen) in Woodland Park. He was a cardiologist, who was planning on moving his practice here to Colorado because of the beautiful way I'd described the state. During our conversation, the doctor told an amusing story. He talked about one of his hospital interviews in Colorado Springs. The woman interviewing him wanted to know why he chose to relocate in Colorado. Well . . . he said something about weather and climate and the beauty of the mountains. He told us he couldn't very well say, "because of how Mary Summer Rain described it."

Later in his interview when they were more relaxed, Summer Rain and her books did come up. The interviewer had read them and our doctor friend smiled, "*that's* what *really* brought me here."

The interviewing physician grinned back at him.

"Now I do understand. That explains why you came here."

Our cardiologist friend was very pleased he'd connected with another No-Eyes reader.

Later in our conversation with him, after I'd told him I'd asked to be taken off the morphine after my operation, he said he wished he'd known I was in the hospital. He does a great deal of hypnosis for pain. He said I would've never needed that morphine if he could've visited me. Now he tells me. . .oh well.

He called us last month and said things are going well. He wants to take us to a celebration dinner when (and if) the law suit settles in our favor. He also said he'd like to help us with our Wellspring Mission project too—but he needs to get more established first. I imagine it's hard for a physician to leave an established practice and relocate to another state. It means beginning all over again as far as a patient base. We were glad to hear things were progressing well for him.

Our correspondence contains a large percentage from the medical field. . .surgeons, psychiatrists, dentists, and nurses. At first that really surprised me, especially after several psychologists wrote asking personal advice from me. After awhile I realized that they were people too—they were on the seeking path like everyone else, and soon a reader's profession made no difference to me.

It's very, very dark out tonight, but I'm going to spend my Prayertime in the woods. There seems to be a mood to it tonight that is almost eerie. I want to experience it. I already know my friend won't come, so I'll be left alone with my smoke offering.

Tonight I heard about a two-hour-old infant found alive in a paper bag. . .in a dumpster—it broke my heart. This night my Prayer Smoke will rise for the purpose of helping to alleviate infant abandonment. It will be a hard two hours.

9-13-91, Friday

Received two beautiful cards in the mail. No questions, no name-calling, and no chastising. . .only a sweet "thank you." Neither correspondent left traceable names or return addresses; they only signed their first names. Such simplicity touches me.

One letter today exemplified how devastating the "create your own reality" junk can be. This woman was in her forties, married with children, and thought she was a total failure because they were still "renting" a house. She had bought into the false New Age concept and, when she couldn't "create" well-paying jobs, increased money flow, or their own house, she felt like a total failure. Then she read *Daybreak* and was relieved and renewed. She realized the concept she'd believed in was self-defeating and could now live with her restored self-image. Then when she read that we too were still renting—that frosted her celebration cake! I'm so glad that *Daybreak* has helped so many people. I knew it was a much needed book. I knew the need for a straight-talk question-and-answer book was there. I knew it would fill a wide gap, but never did I realize how wide a gap it was. *Daybreak* may indeed have been the book that broke from my usual format, but it's already proven its value to the public. It has proven, at least for this author, that book format plays second fiddle to content.

Bill has not yet learned his lesson of guarding his spiritual heart. He has again involved himself in private counseling. He cannot seem to be able to say no.

Now, one of his clients said her husband asked her why she's always talking to "Bill" and not to Summer. I hear the beginning strains of jealousy here and neither of us need that . . .not again. Robin's former husband was so jealous of us, he began telling townspeople that we were taking her away from him and that *Bill and Mary* were the cause of their divorce. Trouble was—he told these things to the wrong people. Everyone *knew* us and told this guy he was barking up the wrong tree. When his accusations got back to me, I unloaded all over him and warned him I'd sue him for slander and defamation of character if he didn't stop spreading lies about us. He did stop, but then we began being harassed by his born-again friends about how lost our souls were.

Anyway, I don't need jealous husbands building up false assumptions in their heads. I can't help it if Bill is a natural born counselor. It's his inherent nature. These people need to know one of his favorite sayings, "I live with *six* females. Even our dog and cat are female! I need *another* woman like I need a *hole* in my head!" I think there must be some terribly insecure husbands out there to even *think* Bill would or could threaten their marriage. These men are not thinking with their spirits; their thinking is all in their pants. They can't see how far beyond that kind of behavior Bill is. They just don't know Bill and they can't have any idea of the incredible love he and I share. We don't need someone else's jealousy to invade our lives—we've got enough problems as it is. I just wish there was a way for him to rein in his constant need to help everyone. Maybe I should set up a Lodestar counseling office with *him* behind the desk. Ahh, but that won't happen because we've been told that that idea is not an aspect of The Plan. Still, I wish he'd not be so inclined to stick his heart out the way he does because, every time he does. . .someone runs it through with a sword. If I don't protect him—who will? But when I try, he says, "Why can't I do the things that make me feel good?" And I sigh.

Today was Friday the Thirteenth and Jenny reminded us of that tonight.
"Today is Friday the Thirteenth," she said spookily.
"So?" I replied.
"So it's scary."
"What scared you today?"
"Nothing."
"So?"
And she giggled. I think she got the point.

Today was also Elise and Charlie's wedding anniversary. I'd sent them a cute card on Monday. Hope their day was filled with loving. If I know them half as well as I think I do—their day was filled with exactly that.

We waited all day to hear from Bob. We were going to discuss his decision on the journal. He never called.

This had been a high-anxiety day. One filled with frustration at every turn. Tomorrow's got to be better. Who knows, maybe it'll snow. That would definitely make *Bill's* day! Me? I'd at least like to see the rest of Autumn before Winter blusters in. It snowed a blizzard up on Rabbit Ears Pass near Steamboat Springs today. I'm not ready for that over here yet. I've got some serious dancing and chanting to do with Autumn before I do any dancing with a snow shovel. And that's a fact.

9-14-91, Saturday

Bill, Jenny, and I picked up our mail and went down to Colorado Springs for a day of errands. The day went well, but all the traffic and store crowds did unsettle me somewhat. I'm always relieved to be heading back up through the hills of Ute Pass to home again.

When we arrived home, I got right on the mail while Bill worked on some other household projects that needed attention. Today's correspondence seemed to all be wonderful letters—a few were very touching. I didn't have time to write responses because by the time I finished reading the letters and making out new cards on them it was 8:30 P.M. So I set them aside on my typewriter and, first thing in the morning, I'll finish up with my replies while Bill processes the children's book orders we'd received.

One of the letters was from a bookstore owner who wrote requesting information on my next book. He's been doing well with *Daybreak* and wanted to know the title of my seventh book, when it would be published, and who the publisher will be. I can't respond to that letter until we hear from Bob. . .hopefully on Monday.

We're also waiting to see if I'll receive my Donning royalty check (due on the 15th). We've been holding off getting the children's book reprinted because of this check. If it comes this week we should be okay.

Last night, before sleep overtook me, I thought about the conference with my Brotherhood associates. Their advice and new information led me to some pleasant speculation regarding our future location. Now, because of this probability that may alter our course from Redstone, I'm again entertaining hopeful thoughts that our original area-of-choice will be a viable one. This is the one Bill and I initially discovered while traveling to a wayward spirit region south of Eagle—this being the region most of my readers missed the mark on, because they only took it halfway to Sylvan Lake instead of continuing on up to the Frying Pan River. My soul belongs up there. My heart yearns for there. And yet, my mind dares itself to again place too much hope that we will be there. Instead, I know that whatever property is open, available and affordable to us when the timing has come will be what's right and destined for us. To perceive it in any other way would be wrong, for we're not here to go where we *want* to go, but rather wherever we're *supposed* to be. Individual wants are not woven into any spiritual mission or plan. Indeed, such aspects *have* no individual bearing at all, because everyone involved moves toward creating "the whole" that, in turn, produces the beautiful culmination of *The Purpose.* In truth, we are not separate individuals, but rather we are the "cells" that work to maintain the health, maturity, and long life of the Body of the Purpose. In this light then, a cell that veers off course to go its own way becomes a malignant cell that has rebelled to contaminate and destroy The Purpose.

Since we've reworked our Lodestar letter to better clarify our new mission for the needy, readers have been offering to volunteer their time and energies to help with it. But I cannot accept their offers because we don't have the room here for more people to be involved. Also, I feel, more hands involved with this kind of work eventually prevents the needy from benefiting from *all* the goods.

Just as in the old days when the government gave goods to the Indians, the middlemen (agents) passed little of it on to the intended recipients. I see this so much in today's non-profit organizations, where most of the incoming donations go for "administration" expenses rather than the needy they were intended for. I'm not saying that any of my readers who would help us with this project would pocket donations or take goods for themselves. No, I'm not saying that at all. What I am saying is that the more involved in the process, the more overall expense there is. The more involved, the less goes out to the needy. So less is better. This is our personal mission and we will be the only middlemen involved. I've already decided that any overflow of donated goods will be sent to reservations for distribution as they see fit. Although Wellspring Mission may not have any overflow of supplies or clothing because we won't be operating like a Goodwill that has a purchase price on goods. Wellspring Mission will truly *be* a mission. It will offer *everything* as a give-away. And that's what makes me so happy about it.

I smell snow in the air tonight. There's that scent of crisp and rarefied air that precedes the coming snow. Winter Spirit this way comes, but harken One-in-White, you're playing an unfair hand, you're placing a "force on time," and that is not allowed.

Go back White Spirit, let Autumn sing her song. Let her dance her dance to the drumming mountain thunder. Have respect for your Autumn Sister and honor her glorious essence as only you can do.

9-15-91, Sunday

Winter Spirit was absolutely rude. He paid me no mind when he awoke me this morning. Sounds of sleet lashing against our bedroom window brought me to the frosty glass at 5:30. Peering out, my heart fell to the ground as eyes rested upon a two-inch blanket of white all around. Disgusted, I climbed back beneath the quilt and tried to shut out Winter's uncouth behavior.

By 10:30, Autumn had regained her foothold and chased away every last remnant of the White Invader. Deep blue skies were bright. Sun glistened through gold and red-orange aspen leaves. Autumn held the day and I wondered if this year we were going to witness a game of Tug-of-War between these two Season Rulers.

When I came downstairs this morning, I found that Bill had been into early mischief. He'd completely rearranged his side of our office by adding the 3 feet x 5 feet typing table and extra typewriter to his work area. He'd also moved two large file cabinets to another spot. He wanted to know what I thought of it.

I looked around the converted mother-in-law quarters.

"There's a lot more space in here now," I said.

"Yeah, we'll be needing it for our supply shipments. And now I don't have to go over to the other side of the room to type up the mailing list. Everything's right here within reach."

I glanced from his office area to my own neat one, then back to his.

"Aren't you a little cluttered?"

He grinned.

"No. But now you sure can tell who does all the work around here, huh? Your area looks too neat."

Now it was my turn to grin.

"I guess you're right, honey. It's plain to see *you* do all the work and," looking back at my desk, "I do all the thinking."

He laughed at that one, but knew how to get back at me with one better.

"Did you see my note on the kitchen table?"

"I haven't even been in the kitchen yet."

"Go get your coffee."

He was too anxious for me to see this wonderful note of his. It had to be some wisecrack about something.

And it was.

Merry Christmas! Let's put up the lights!

I crumpled up the nasty note. He knew this early snow had upset me.

All day, as I worked on writing responses to our correspondents, he'd walk through the office humming Jingle Bells.

I put my headphones on and blasted my deskside tape player.

Around 9:15 P.M. he opened up our kitchen blinds, hummed the forbidden tune again and flicked on the outside floodlights.

"*Ta-da!* Jingle bells, jingle bells. . ."

Enormous flakes were falling.

I got up out of my reading chair and, slowly, with deliberate stealthful steps, crept toward him. My mind kept goading me on and on with one tempting command—*kill! Kill the Christmas Hummer!* Closer. . .closer I crept up to his exposed back.

"Lights?" I said in my best Renfield, "You want to see *lights? I'll* give you lights. But not before I punch *your* lights out!"

He swung around and we playfully wrestled.

Magic came charging and barking to save me.

And the house was suddenly in an uproar.

Finally Bill held me and, in the darkened kitchen, we looked out the picture window to watch the silently falling snow.

"It is pretty, isn't it, honey," he whispered in my ear.

"Yeah, it is. But it's way too soon. If this keeps up, the frost will wreck the autumn colors. We had little summer this year, I'd hate to have no autumn."

"We did have autumn."

"What do you mean?"

"Remember the two beautiful *days* last week? That was autumn. What's the matter with you, did you miss it? Jingle bells, jingle bel. . ."

I swiftly turned and pretended to smack him.

Magic barked and charged.

And, outside, the snowflakes grew bigger.

There were only two good things about this day. Autumn chased the Winter One away during the day, and the Broncos won their football game.

The bad thing was. . .the Winter One also won.

Mother Nature seems to be making up new rules because, this time, she's definitely off-sides. Com'on Autumn, get in there and pick up her fumble! Pick it up and run with it! Let's hear that Rocky Mountain Thunder for Autumn!

This wishful thinking isn't getting it. . .I'm going to bed.

Afterthought: I guess I really shouldn't smother Bill's joy. He loves Christmastime. He's like a little boy then. He gets so into doing the decorating, especially stringing tons of lights around the house. . .inside. He loves converting the living room into a magical fairyland of lights. For three weeks out of the year he manages to leave all the heavy aspects of our work behind and immerse himself into the real Joy of Christmas. He gets so anxious that the girls expect him to say (the day after Thanksgiving), "let's put the tree up!" And usually we do because Christmas is very special to all of us. But. . . this is only September. . .he's really reaching to grab a little bit of joy. Conclusion: He must be desperate for joy. Resolution: he needs some joy. Ergo: I will take him to my "upstairs" office and we'll see if we can find a little joy there for him.

9-16-91, Monday

The nation's highest paved road is here in Colorado and it received a foot of snow yesterday; with the drifts, they had to close the entrance to Trail Ridge Road. No such problems by us though. Today was a little chilly, but it was a beauty to look at. When Sarah and Mandy left for their school bus this morning, it was only 30 out.

This was a full day for me. The correspondence took many hours to process and I handled that while Bill attended to other aspects of our work. One of his many errands was to pick up more Lodestar letterhead and also the new Wellspring Mission stationery we'd ordered. We were pleased with how it turned out.

John Nelson called this morning to inquire if I'd received my Donning royalty check. I told him Bill was in town picking up our mail and wouldn't have the answer to that until he got home. I assured him Bill would return his call.

When Bill came in the office door with an armful of mail, I asked him about the check. . .no check. My spirits fell. Don't publishers realize that we authors *depend* on those semi-annual checks? Publishers and editors get their regular weekly wages but we have to budget *six months* between paydays! Then, if you should inquire about your overdue check, you're made to feel like a beggar with cap in hand asking for the world. This is not fun. It's often downright humiliating just trying to get what's due you. . .when it's due you.

Last August I was supposed to receive a royalty statement from Pocket Books for *Earthway*. Did I get it? No. I don't know, I really don't: There's got to be a better way. Sometimes I envy Robin and Aimee, who come home with their checks every Friday. They know exactly how much those checks will be for each week and can count on them. Too many grey areas and variables exist in publishing. An example I've run into is the advance payment that's divided up. Half on "signing" the contract (that's not too hard to fudge with) and half on "acceptance" of manuscript (easy to fudge on). "Acceptance" to some publishers means as soon as they receive it, read it, and say "okay, let's polish it up now." "Acceptance" to other publishers may be interpreted differently, and mean "*after* it's all polished to our liking," which could take months if the publisher leaves it on his desk until he's damn good and ready to go through it. This last leaves the author waiting and waiting and waiting for the second half of the advance money. Ohh, the stories I could tell. They would surely open up the public's eyes to the things that go on in the publishing business. Big name companies do *not* mean the best. Likewise, small publishing companies do not mean the worst. Personable friendliness, open communication, and author consideration are far more desirable than having a big-time name printed on one's book as being the publisher.

Received a letter today with 23 questions regarding the specifics of Gateway Healing Treatments. The correspondent must not have read *Daybreak* where I clarified that the patient "chooses" which aspects to utilize in treatments. It seems clear that a patient could not combine *all* Gateway aspects during one treatment session. If someone only wanted to utilize the incense, nature sounds, and visualization aspects, that would be fine. But to try to incorporate every aspect at once is too much.

Bill's been concerned about the late hours I've been keeping. Last Friday he came home with some new B-Complex Vitamins that are taken sublingually (beneath the tongue). They're called *PerfectB*. Taking these vitamin drops sublingually is compared to a heart patient who needs to place nitroglycerin tablets beneath their tongue. The medication is quickly absorbed by the bloodstream as an injection, instead of going through the stomach, liver, and digestive tract. The recommended dosage is 2cc per day. . .one in the morning and one at night. I found that the 20 drops that make lcc can be easily held by a one-eighth measuring teaspoon. This makes it much easier than counting 20 drops in your mouth and prevents contamination of the vitamin nozzle. The entire family has been taking these new sublingual Vitamin B-Complex, and each member has noticed a big difference.

Today we waited to hear from Bob about publishing *Soul Sounds* —this journal. He never called.

It's a magical crystal clear night. It's cold and crisp. I'm going out to share my Prayer Smoke with the Woodland Spirits. Tonight our smoke will rise for the hungry. . .the homeless.

9-17-91, Tuesday

In the mail today I received a letter from a woman who suggested I read a book written (or channeled) by an alien being. I do deeply resent these suggestions, because it shows how little people know about me. Why in God's name would I be interested in some trumped-up, secondhand "channeled" alien information when I regularly communicate with my Starborn friend face-to-face? Besides, what's even more infuriating is that the channeled alien material isn't even correct!

If I talk to the person who was once known as Jesus, why would I be interested in phony "channeled" Jesus messages or want to physically "connect" with the people (and there are dozens) who are claiming to have been Jesus? People must really think I'm either dense or a real push-over. Either that or they don't believe I know what I know. This last is a serious miscalculation on their part.

This may sound extremely arrogant of me, but dammit, when one comes down here for a volunteered mission from the Great White Brotherhood and is in regular communication with them, that individual is more than outraged when people send "channeled" Brotherhood messages. To me, it's absolutely absurd. Especially when the channeled messages contain *no* correlations to what's *really* transpiring within the Brotherhood.

The same applies to the so-called "alien" messages. What utter ridiculous *nonsense* these channelers are purporting to bring through from them. It's nothing but pure crap! And I get so upset because it's like having to stand back and watch an errant child continue to lie and lie and not be able to do a damned thing about it. When I personally talk to the Star-

born ones, how else am I to feel when I see all the false
messages and experiences being given out to the public. . .
and to me? Have these channelers lost all their personal integrity? Have they no shame or sense of guilt? They have
even suckered in some very intelligent people who, in turn,
spread the false messages through seminars and mail order
products. Ohh, dear God, I do not want to be down here any
longer. I'm just a minnow swimming in a sea of sharks. My
voice is too small and I'm being drowned out by the din of
the swelling tide. It's been too painful to witness. People accuse me of being judgmental, arrogant, and call me a clown.
I've endured their hatred and cruelty for nothing. Please,
please take me home. Please give us just enough to get that
little cabin in the peaceful woods. This has gone on long
enough. The ridicule has lanced my heart. They will not listen. Please, Father, just take us home now.

Waited for Bob to call. A week ago last Wednesday he
told us he'd call us on Friday regarding the journal. This is
Tuesday and he still hasn't called. Bill gets very upset when
people don't do what they say they'll do. In the morning
he's going to call Bob and ask him if he wants the journal
or not. Yes or no. If yes, send the contract for it. If no, we
take it somewhere else.

I don't know why, but I'm going to spend my two Prayertime hours tonight for the Message-Givers. . .so they may
speak true. I know what great power prayer wields, perhaps
this silent sacred Way of mine will accomplish more than my
public voice and written word has, for this manifests on a
finer level that journeys far above the dense din of mankind.
Perhaps my tiny Spirits of Light will join me in tonight's
effort, for they do seem to love adding their sparkles to my
rising Prayer Smoke. They usually come when I'm particularly world-weary.

9-18-91, Wednesday

We received a letter from Paris, France, today. The lady
said she knew of many people there who would love the
No-Eyes' books if they could only read them. She'd already
translated some of the *Spirit Song* chapters and wanted to get
a French publisher interested in doing the books.

What a wonderful idea she had. However, I had to tell her
that nothing could be done about it until I had my first four

contracts back in my hands. I told her I would let her know as soon as that happens.

Another correspondent's letter today was very interesting to me because she'd found an authentic native pipe with beaded sheath in her great-grandmother's trunk. She had a curator check it out, and it's a circa 1880-1890 Dakota Sioux. This lady did a prayer ceremony over it with some friends and wants to know what was best to do with it.

I told her that this particular pipe cannot be sold nor given to a museum. She cannot "use" it either, for if she does, it will attract several native entities that were connected with it. I told her to respectfully wrap it and place it in a sacred (or secure) place in her home. This pipe is *extremely* special. She will know what to do with it. Her spirit will do the guiding.

Our attorney called Bill and informed us that the defendant's attorneys want to meet with our attorneys at their office in Norfolk on Friday. We were told this was a very encouraging sign that meant they want to "know what it will take to make this thing go away." We needed to give our attorney a settlement figure. We did. As with any financial negotiations, the starting figure is always high, because they'll be a compromising aspect as time progresses. We don't want the bank—only what we know will cover our needs (property and two vehicles). We're not looking to set ourselves up for life here. If this thing went to trial, the punitive and mail fraud damages alone would be astronomical. So. . .Friday it begins. Hopefully it will be the beginning of the end of the years of misery and stress this has caused me. I'm so very anxious to have No-Eyes back in my arms again. I'm so excited about that my arms are nearly shaking in anticipation.

Still waiting for Bob to call about the journal.

A friend called Bill this evening to inform us that *Publishers Weekly* magazine had an article about our lawsuit and the illegalities that transpired. Now I wish we'd re-subscribed, but our friend said he'd photocopy the article for us. I suppose if the defendants' names are published in the industry bible, I shouldn't be reluctant to name names in my personal journal. The way I had to alter that on my typed pages is confusing to the reader when I say the "printer," the "publisher," and the "distributor." Bill seems to think part of our settlement agreement will be "mum" for the authors.

This evening, while I was sitting in my reading chair and

Bill was on the couch going through the newspaper. He called over to me.

"Honey? Listen to this. There's a guy who wrote a book about the most wonderful man he's ever met."

"Oh?"

"Yeah. The author met him in Florida and says he's Jesus. He's even including a tape with the book and; get this, for so much money a minute, you too can call a phone number to hear Jesus' voice as he reads bible passages."

Steam began rising from my head.

"Why'd you tell me that? You know how I feel about my voice being smothered like that."

"I told you because you've got to realize that it's not how many phonies you stop that matters, it's how many people you and No-Eyes have *helped.*"

Silence.

"Know what?" he said.

"What."

"Even when I was a kid I remember hearing of this person or that one claiming to be Jesus. You can't stop people's delusions. You've got to see that. Asylums are filled with *hundreds* of Jesus Christs. Add to that all the ones who are walking the streets, and then add to those the ones who claim to *know* one of these Jesus characters and, before you know it, you could populate a small country with them all."

"Jesusland," I whispered under my breath.

"What?"

"Nothing."

He peered over at me.

"What's the grin for?"

"When you said there's enough Jesuses to populate an entire country I got an immediate visual of that."

"And?"

"Seems it'd be a pretty violent country."

"How so?"

"Think about it. If they *all* claim to be Jesus, they'd be fighting over who was the *real* one."

"That's an interesting outcome."

"It's logical. But what's even more interesting is that the *real* one wouldn't even *be* there because he's not *claiming* that biblical identity now."

"Well," he said, "now do you see why things like this article shouldn't upset you so much? There's always going to be imposters and impersonators . Whether they're claiming a Jesus identity or a White Brotherhood one or a Starborn one is irrelevant. These people are just a fact of life down here.

There's no way you're going to stop their claims, so let them roll off your back."

He did have a point.

"You missed your calling," I said.

"I did?"

"Yes, you did. You should've been a psychologist."

He shuddered. "I may have the logic and reasoning for it, but sure don't have the heart. I've had all I can take of that counseling business. I took my shingle down after that last episode."

"Seems like it went back up tonight."

He grinned. "Only for you. . .only for you."

"Poor doctor," I cooed, "you only have one patient?"

"You bet! She's a real challenge. She's almost more than I can handle!"

I frowned. "Am I really that difficult?"

He smiled kindly. "Yes."

I gave an exaggerated pout. "I'm bad, huh."

"Very bad."

"Then I can change. I'll be good."

"Nope."

"Nope?"

"Nope, because then you wouldn't be you. I happen to love you just the way you are."

"You *like* bad?"

"No."

I sighed. "Have you been taking Circle Dance lessons from No-Eyes?

"Maybe."

"Now *you're* being the difficult one."

"Nope."

"Nope?"

"Just stickin' to the facts."

"Is that a fact."

"Yep."

And I left the dance floor before it turned into an all-nighter that'd make us both dizzy.

It's cold and very foggy out tonight. My Prayertime will take place in the dark living room where the woodstove sends out the wonderful sounds of crackling wood and the two oil pots on the mantle cast soft flame light down through my sacred moments. The Prayer Smoke will rise this night for a correspondent's special request that I received today.

9-19-1991, Thursday

Answering correspondence took up most of my day. Bill seemed to be on the phone all day. Every time he hung up from one call the phone would ring before he could do anything else.

Bob does like the journal and he's planning on it being a Spring 1992 release with *Whispered Wisdom* (the pictorial) coming out in the fall of 1992. For the first time I will be able to give my readers two books. We don't know if that two-per-year schedule will repeat itself the following year, we'll just have to see how well this trial went. That's okay with me. The important thing is we're going to at least try it.

Bill also talked a couple times to our attorney today. We gave him our bare-bones bottom-line settlement figure. Bill also informed the attorney that we hadn't yet received our Donning royalty check and perhaps the attorney would like to bring this to Walsworth's attorneys' attention in their meeting tomorrow.

Jyoti Walsh wanted to give us a thank-you gift for mentioning her astrology service and Starshine Essences in *Daybreak*. She offered to do a free chart on one of us. We decided it should be Bill.

Today we received the chart and cassette tape that went with it. Incredible! When she projected his "intense transition" forecast for the end of 1991 and the summer of 1992 she hit the nail right on the head by predicting a major "relocation and building" period. She is very good at what she does.

Bill's too tired tonight to call her (he worked 'til 10) so he's anxious to phone her tomorrow evening to thank her and also inform her of Wellspring Mission which she predicted as a 1992 "major social project" he'd be heavily involved in. Also predicted for 1992 and 1993 was an "incredibly strong and intense new relationship" (this, of course, is when Bill's Starborn activities will commence), but Jyoti had no way of knowing that kind of detail.

This evening I finally made time to season my new cast-iron skillets. The process took an hour. Aimee tries to hide my "old-time" cookware and speckled graniteware whenever company comes to dinner because she keeps calling it "little-house-on-the-prairie-ware." Whenever I remind her how much I like those old-time pots and pans she gives me an exaggerated sympathetic look, pats me kindly on the back and, playing geriatric nurse, says, "Com'on now honey, it's time to take your medicine." She thinks mom's nuts to like those old-time utensils because she likes all the newest designs in gourmet cookware. I asked her how her classy kitchen was going to fit in with her very Victorian chintz, lace, and flowers decor of her own place when we're settled. Well. . .the *kitchen* would be the only room out of character, she concluded.

Our decor? A little of this 'n' that. We're very Bohemian with our eclectic furnishings, because we buy whatever strikes our fancy, whether or not it fits in with anything else we have. When visitors walk through our door they enter a blend of native American, Egyptian, and Mountain Man decor with lots of books and plants and baskets thrown in. Oddly enough, the overall effect is quite warm and "interesting," although I suppose some people would be a mite uncomfortable with all the skins and furs I have around. They wouldn't know they all came from roadkill. And the kitchen is all country, with flowers in Mason jars and old-time glass penny candy canisters holding our herbs, nuts, and seeds. And, of course, the cast-iron and speckled graniteware. Naw, Aimee can have her shiny gourmet contraptions. . .I'm very much at home with my little-house-on-the prairie.

Today I received a beautiful hand-carved Talking Stick from a native man who's been writing me. This looks similar to a regular walking stick, but has the additional use of assisting in Spirit Helper communications. He carved my name on it. It has two Herkimer diamonds embedded in it and the top carved face has eyes of brilliant blue stones. There is much more to it that I will not detail.

Last month this man also sent me a native flute he made. It has a wonderful, clear sound to it. In turn, I sent him three of my books because he loves to read and can't get out that much.

This man wishes us to go to him where he lives on the Colorado reservation for a specific purpose, but we cannot because that purpose is not *my* purpose. It's not in The Plan. I personally feel very bad about this situation, but on the other hand, I must be about our given mission and he really doesn't understand that. It makes things so hard when you care so much about people's feelings. I hate turning this man down, but I cannot do otherwise.

Oh crap! Kitty's got a mouse. . . .

. . .Whew! She let me take it from her. I returned it to

its hole in the living room moss rock wall. The tiny critters have several openings. Good thing I know them all. Trouble is. . .so does Buttercup. She tried eating the first little grey field mouse she caught in our office, but it didn't agree with her, so now she just likes to catch and play with them. That's not good either, because they get injured that way— that's even a worse fate for them. So whenever any of us catch her with one we take it from her and return it to its hole. I wish she wouldn't do that, but we also realize the behavior is nothing more than natural instinct. In the spring, when moth season hits the mountains, she's constantly in her "Stalk-Attack-Eat" mode. Crazy cat drives Jenny nuts when her kitty does all that extra "snacking." Jenny hates bugs, especially moths and crickets (crickets because they can "*jump* on you").

I suspect we'll be real busy with our supply shipments soon. Our main contact has been out of town for the last two weeks and I'm anticipating a call in the next few days—then we'll have our hands full again and may have to forego the correspondence responses during that time.

There are two correspondents I need to pray for tonight and will try to spend on hour on each. It's 1:34 A.M., so I need to end this entry now.

Goodnight Bob, thanks for taking the journal.

9-20-91 Friday,

Bill called Jyoti this morning to thank her for the astrology chart and tape. He told her he'd like one done on me and asked her how much it will be. She said there's no way she'd take money for doing my chart so Bill thanked her for her give-away. . .except that we'll send her payment anyway —even if we have to do it anonymously in cash, because Jyoti is a single mom who really needs the money right now. We know how much time she puts into her chart work and there's no way we'd ever expect her to give us two freebies. That just wouldn't be right.

After dinner, Bill called Carole and informed her of the change in my book schedule. He explained how the new spring slot came about and the diary that was going to fill it. She had to know about all of this, because we suddenly had an unexpected book cover for her to do. I don't think she realizes that, when all my books are published, her artwork will be on 10 of them.

When I got on the phone with her, I went into more detail about how this journal was going to totally expose me —my private life and thoughts. I explained how this book was going to be the giving of my entire being to my readers and it needed a cover to symbolize that.

She asked me what I had in mind and I told her.

"I want one like the one I fell in love with at your house —the one you had hanging in your hallway—the old woman holding out her pipe. Only you'll need to make it a younger woman with black hair. I also want a couple well-placed tears."

She thought the idea sounded perfect.

"Do you also want the animals in the background?"

"Yes, just like the other one."

"Okay, I'll get right on it Monday morning and call you when it's finished." Then she had another question. "Do you want this picture wrapped around the book like *Daybreak*?"

"No, let's make it full front cover. I don't want it broken up. Let's make it all on the front like your work for the new *Spirit Song* and *Phoenix Rising* ones are. The publisher's production department can choose a complementary color to carry around the back."

She liked the idea.

This evening Bill contacted a correspondent who's been writing us for a long while. This person has made all the intuitive connections regarding our past-life identities and has planned to bring his family out to Colorado to look around for a possible future relocation. The couple will be here Wednesday with one of their sons. They'll be at our house for a few hours and we'll give them some specific areas to look at. They're coming at a beautiful time of year, for the aspens are turning the mountainsides to a brilliant gold and red-orange.

It's early, 11:40 P.M., and Sarah is outside listening to an elk bellow. The fellow is real close in our woods tonight and I'm going to go join Sarah. Later—my Prayertime will be for Carole. She's such a grand lady.

9-21-91, Saturday

Our attorney never called us back after his meeting with

Walsworth's attorneys yesterday, so Bill called John Nelson to see if he knew what transpired.

It was not good news. The defendants asked for another 30-day extension. The attorneys said their clients were willing to make up the authors' lost royalties, but they insisted on "retaining all contractual rights."

This caused a slow burn inside me that soon became a bubbling volcano. We gave them *another* 30 days? They insist on *keeping* our contracts? And where is my royalty check? If I don't get that we cannot reprint the children's manual. That check was due on the 15th and, dammit, I'm going to rattle a lot of cages if they don't send my money. Walsworth's accountant told Bill on Monday that my check was for nearly $9,000. I need that semi-annual pay-check! How do they expect us to live without our checks? I am so fed up with Walsworth and Schiffer I'm ready to try anything. I've even toyed with getting the other authors to-gether to picket in front of Walsworth, Donning, Schiffer, and his Whitford Press. Perhaps we need national publicity now. Maybe we need to call Oprah. I'm getting to that exploding point where something must be done. These people have had No-Eyes long enough and, for their attorney's to say that they *insist* on *keeping* her. . . *God*! Their *audacity*! I *will* get her *back*!

At one point in these last few years of incredible stress I even wrote to the famous cowboy lawyer in Wyoming, Gerald Spence, who represented Imelda Marcos. I pleaded for him to help me get No-Eyes back. I'd heard he was one of the best and most powerful attorneys in the country and that he championed the poor and underdog. I fit both categories. He wrote back and said he was in a small firm and couldn't take on my case.

The Denver *Rocky Mountain News* and Denver's television news investigative departments turned deaf ears to my plight when I tried to get some help. Now a friend in Virginia tells us that the Norfolk newspaper won't publicize our problem either, because one of the editors there had a book published by Donning. National news programs didn't care either, yet this is a big story. . .12 authors are suing *three* publishers for 12 million dollars! Yet no reporter can smell the news. None of them care, because these authors don't have names like Stephen King, Robin Cook, or Danielle Steele. We're just the little guys who don't merit their time.

And so nobody knows of our plight. Nobody gives a damn that these publishers have taken our books away from us.

Monday morning we're getting on the phone to our attorney with two questions for him. What do you have to do to get Walsworth to release our royalty checks? and, Can we *talk* about our case with outsiders? If we can publicly talk about it, I'm going to do it. I'm so frustrated and fighting mad, I'd gladly override my nervousness and shyness in a minute to tell everything to Oprah. . .on television! Yes, I *would*! My Warrior Gear has definitely kicked in. To champion No-Eyes I'd move mountains!

I must get off this subject now before I get so riled up again I'll end up pacing the living room all night.

Link called early this morning to tell us she had another shipment for us. At 12:30, Bill and the girls drove for an hour and 15 minutes to their meeting point. When they got home I immediately began my work on the food. Two hours later, I was done and ended up with eight boxes to deliver on Monday. This was a nice shipment, because it contained some beautiful apples, oranges, and potatoes. The potatoes were huge—they looked as if they were home-grown. Our recipients are going to have a real treat this time.

Today was a gorgeous "Blue Day." That's what I call days that have that brilliant deep blue to the skies. I cannot resist going outside on these magical high Colorado days so, while the family was gone, I took Magic with me into the woods where that incredible blueness gave a striking backdrop to the bright yellow of the quaking aspen leaves.

When I sat down in the forest, Magic lay beside me. When thoughts of my legal problems speared my mind and I began to quietly cry, Magic licked my tears. As frustrated and defeated as I felt, that little four-legged person brought to me an incredible feeling of comfort and love. It swelled my heart. Her sensitivity and gentle nature made mankind look barbaric. Her genuine concern over me made me laugh and that brought a responsive bark. She wanted to play. We got up and, on our way back, I let her romp free through the woods. And when we went inside the house and I returned to my desk to proof through this manuscript, Magic curled up at my feet. She didn't leave the spot until the van pulled up three hours later. Such a comfort. . . such a love. She had actually helped me to feel better this afternoon and I was deeply grateful for her powerful, good medicine.

Tonight my Prayer Smoke will rise for those who hold No-Eyes captive. I will pray for a miracle—one that warms and transforms their hearts of cold stone.

God, No-Eyes, I'm so sorry. I'll get you back. I *promise* I will.

9-22-91, Sunday

This day was spent catching up on odds and ends we never seem to get to during the week.

At 3:00 P.M. we all went out for a birthday dinner for Sarah. We celebrated it today, because she'll be in school all day tomorrow. There were 16 candles on her cake. She's our "Autumn Child."

Her gifts were a unicorn statue, a family of dragons (statues), a movie video she's been wanting, a book of the Robin Hood film, a cassette tape player and a puzzle and bookmark from Jenny. She also received cards with money from family, friends, and Robin. She had a great birthday and, before she went to bed, she had to do the puzzle.

This afternoon, before we went to dinner, Sarah finished her homework. The assignment for her Mythology class was to utilize nine gods and goddesses and create a new myth about the ending of the Old World and the fate of the Modern World. She created this story in an hour and I was amazed at the finished product. Maybe she'll be a writer some day. No, she says she wants to be an artist. I support that choice all the way—as long as she never has an agent and always handles her own marketing.

Bill's been a little disgusted with our van lately, because it gets so full of dust in the back interior. We travel a lot of dirt roads up here. We took it back to the dealer once to have the cargo doors tightened, and that helped, but we still seem to be getting dust inside. He's also been thinking that we'll need a vehicle with a larger engine, because of the many mountain deliveries we'll be making for Wellspring. These thoughts have been coming from his Advisor.

So last night we discussed the idea of trading the van in for a full-sized Blazer. He strongly feels prompted to do this, but did express that he really likes the anti-lock brakes on all four wheels of our van. Their performance in last winter's snow was incredible.

I asked him if the Blazers had that and he said only on the rear wheels. Then I suggested he stop at the store and pick up a new 1992 automobile magazine. He got one today and there was a new Blazer with anti-lock brakes on all four wheels. Now he's getting excited about going through with this trade, because it represents one aspect of our life that will have come full circle—we came here in 1977 with a 1977 Blazer and we will move to our new area in 1992 with a 1992 Blazer. This holds special significance for Bill, because we've been advised that all our aspects are converging into one—all aspects are leading up to the ending of our 15-year journey to completion and finalization. We are supposed to have gone full circle sometime in 1992. . .the date that's always been given as our "final" year to be settled.

And so it would be reasonable to end with the vehicle we began it all with. This has only been one little sign that's manifested for us. On the whole, the many pieces have been dropping into place—one at a time—for the last three years. Now the process has escalated so much we can finally see the final picture these pieces are making. There is only one major puzzle piece we need to obtain and. . .our attorney holds that one.

I sure hope we get that royalty check soon. After all that's been done us, I think it's beyond belief for them to withhold my check on top of it. It smacks of kicking someone when they're down. Yes? Please don't kick us again. But if you do, you ought to know we'll still get back up on our feet again, because our strength is greatest at the 11th hour. If a warrior's horse is maimed he will rely on his *own* legs. If a warrior's lance is broken he will fight with his *hands*. If a warrior's hands are cut off he will fight with his *mind*. As long as we have legs, as long as we have hands, as long as we have minds. . .we will fight, for our power shields have not been touched. Our Ghost Shirts will prevail. We are Buffalo Hearts.

9-23-91, Monday

My friend waited until my prayers had concluded before he popped in on me last night. In a way, I was glad he did, because we ended our long conversation with a subject that'd been bothering me lately. It concerned a deep emotion of mine.

He'd opened up the issue with a comment on the most recent development with the legal problems.

"You're handling it well," he said.

I looked into the blackness of his eyes.

"That's a strange way to describe rage. This last incident with my missing check has my insides whirling like a Kansas twister. I feel like a volcano ready to blow and you call that 'handling it well?'"

"Your term is all wrong."

"Again?"

He smiled. "It's not 'rage' you're feeling, it's outrage."

"Same difference."

"No. It is not. Rage is out-of-control anger. It signifies an irrational mind. Outrage, on the other hand, is generated from a rational mind as a reasonable response to an injustice or action committed against the Precepts. Coming from you, extreme outrage is an expected and natural response. You've had this throughout your entire life and evidence of it goes back to your youth, when people criticized your truths. Remember the powerful outrage you felt back then?"

Oh yes, I thought, his words rang true. When I tried to get answers from the good nuns and priests I'd become so outraged at their patronizing responses and sarcastic ridicule I wanted nothing more than to push them or scream at the top of my lungs.

"Yes, I remember."

"And all the times while you were maturing, and throughout the years of experiencing the trials and obstacles of your purpose, the outrages were there. Why else did you fight for Jenny's rights with the schools? Why else did you rid Woodland of the scam business? Your outrage got a corporation to put fans in for its employees. Your outrage—every single time—was to champion the underdog or battle an evil. Can you not see where I'm going here?"

"There's more?"

He patiently waited.

I spun my wheels while he watched. Then I shrugged.

"I guess I'm not sure what you're getting at."

"I want *you* to get at the *reason* for this history of outrage you've had."

"Isn't the reason as simple as my hating to see injustice? Isn't the reason that I simply can't abide it?"

"No. That's the resulting *effect* of the reason. What is its *cause*?"

"I'm very tired. Do you know how long I've just been praying? This isn't fair to bring me into a deep philosophical discussion at this hour of the morning. . ." I halted my complaint, because his mind had sent me a powerful vision of a charging horse with a warrior astride.

"Warrior. A warrior. Warriors get outraged very easily. I've always gotten outraged easily, because, inside, I'm a warrior."

He grinned wide.

I sighed. "Thanks for the vivid clue, but I don't feel much like a warrior."

"That's precisely how a warrior *should* feel."

"Don't talk in riddles, I'm too tired."

"No riddle. Mary, a true warrior sees an injustice, immediate outrage is the natural response and swift action follows; all done without a single thought applied to what has transpired. So then, the warrior has inherent warrior responses without any conscious perception of same. This then is the singular mark of a true warrior. This then is why you react the way you do."

"I understand the premise, but. . ."

"If my words were not true of you, why then did you write what you did in your diary a few hours ago?"

"I'm sorry, I don't remember."

"You were outraged over not receiving your due earnings, your check. You wrote your most inner feelings that the outrage generated. Do the words 'warrior,' 'shields,' 'Ghost Shirts,' or 'Buffalo Hearts' come to mind again?"

"But those were just my ways of expressing how I felt inside." My eyes met his. "Yes," I softly said, "that's exactly how I felt. It's how I feel all the time."

Several silent moments passed between us before he sensed the time to finalize his visit.

"And so I came to dispel your concern that perhaps you weren't living up to the spiritual standards of your station. I came to assure you that you were not slipping out of that mode. Rage is not in your makeup. Outrage is. Outrage is, because it is what true warriors *feel*."

I'd been staring up at the tiny flames of the two oil pots on the mantle while listening to him speak. So soft was his voice—so gentle and kind—that a tear had escaped my eye. I turned then when I felt him touch it.

"I'm scared, my friend," I whispered, "I'm so scared."

"All will be well. It is time."

"Please release me from this. People aren't ready. Oh, please, you're so special to me."

He smiled so sympathetically. "As you are to me."

"Then let me keep the journal sacred. Nobody knows about us. Can't we keep us a secret?"

"Are you fearful of more ridicule?"

I bowed my head and slowly shook it.

"All I know is that I feel a Great Nothing that causes this fear I have. It has no name. No face. No form nor essence."

"Ahhh yes, your 'Great Nothing' again. That Blackness, that Dark Void you frequently sense in times ahead." He paused a moment before continuing. "You have a great fear of making your journal public. This fear is generated from an Unknown you call Great Nothing. You term it this, *because* it is an unknown. Now, could this unknown possibly have the name of Notoriety?"

The word didn't seem to fit at first, but the more I

thought about it, the more fitting it became. "I guess it sounds right. That could be the face and form I'm fearing. But you see, we're so special. Our friendship is a sacred thing to me, and that kind of sacredness is not broadcast near and far across the land. It's held gently, reverently, here," I said, touching my heart, "inside."

He'd heard my racking soul sound then. "Yes, my sweet friend, here, inside. But our long friendship and what we say to one another, our quiet nightwalks in your woods, our relationship, is but one star in the heavens. It is minuscule."

"Minuscule? It has meant the world to me."

"You misinterpret the meaning. It is minuscule when *compared* to our relationship, our activities that are to come."

"Yes. Yes, I do realize that, but that's then and this is now. Now *this* is what we have, and I fear to share it, though it be minuscule in your eyes. What we have will not be minuscule to others."

"But it is time," he whispered. "After the twelfth month of this year you will write no more of us. . .no more of you and me. All that follows will be what you can hold as truly sacred."

My heart was aching. "I don't. . .want to. . .do. . .this book."

"We know." A long silence passed between us.

The only sounds heard were the crackling and snapping of the pine logs in the woodstove. "But. . .I will," I whispered, "I will."

"We know," he whispered back. And again he reached out to gently touch my cheek.

I didn't include last night's conversation for the public—I wrote it down for me. This is my journal and I wanted to make sure I never forgot the words that passed between us that night. I wish with all my heart that I could blank those few pages out—make them vanish so nobody could read them but me. But since I can't, I will try to forget my fear of them and continue my entry.

Today was a beautiful triad. It was the beginning of autumn (a perfect Blue Day). It was Sarah's 16th birthday. And it ends with a gorgeous full moon that has flooded our woods in bright silvery light.

Since we don't have any idea when my royalty check will arrive, we sent Walsworth a Notice of Demand informing them that they're in "default" of my four contracts. The legal jargon of the letter isn't germane for this journal, but the bottom line is that if they don't "cure" the situation in 90 days, my contracts are legally terminated (technically, of course). Yet I wrote them a similar letter when the contracts were initially breached and they flatly ignored it. So big deal. I go by the rules but they make up their own. Go figure that one.

We had a lot of mail today. I worked all day processing it in and Bill worked on processing it out. One letter was especially great news. A couple of week's ago, we received a request for the manuals from a Canadian couple who operate the Sundance Trading Post in Rockwood, Ontario. Bill wrote back explaining that we no longer distribute to Canada, because of its new tax on U.S. mail-order books coming in to that country. But he said we had two hundred of the first edition spiral-bound manuals that we didn't know what to do with. So Bill offered these to the couple at a great discount.

Today we received their check and order for one hundred copies. If they sell well they'll take the other hundred.

We boxed them up and Bill will take them to our UPS outlet in Woodland in the morning. I sure am glad someone wanted those. We receive a lot of Canadian requests for them and I'm happy we were able to accommodate this time.

Re-reading tonight's entry made me realize that I no longer need to fear that I'm falling victim to an earthly negative—rage. Thanks to my dear friend, I understand the reason why I'm so frequently outraged over things down here. Now when my family teases me about being Rambo Mom I won't feel guilty any more. I think I could've messed myself up real good if it hadn't always been for the saving grace of my destined helpers this time. Our Advisors, No-Eyes, Many Heart and now, my friend, have always—always—kept me from falling victim to my own over-scrupulous conscience. They never allow an error in reasoning to mar my course.

So now I've one less aspect to concern myself with; however, I do still retain concern over this journal.

Thanks, my friend, thanks for caring so much. Tonight you were again the wise and gentle, gentle man I've come to love. When I first met you at No-Eyes' cabin, I never dreamed our connection would eventually contain so much depth.

Goodnight, my friend.

9-24-91, Tuesday

Mail was light and I finished it early. This freed me up for other things I've been letting slide.

I was able to enjoy a brief walk in the woods. Autumn is nearly at its peak now. The colors are vibrant and at the height of the celebration. With the moon so full, this night is perfect for my communion with the nature spirits. I have a strong feeling the four-legged ones will join me this night. Perhaps the cougar. Perhaps the large elk herd. I know two things. One: I will commune. Two: I will not write of it. Goodbye.

9-25-91 Wednesday

Bill met our out-of-town friends in Woodland at 10 this morning and they followed him up to our house. They hadn't cared for Colorado Springs, but the drive on the dirt road up to our house and the magnificent view we have of Pikes Peak from our deck was quite another matter.

We spent a couple hours in our office and Bill showed them our two possible land areas over by Glenwood Springs. He marked the travel route on one of our new Colorado Highway maps and they were going to head in that direction when they left. We got along with this couple we'd never met before. The feeling of comfort led to easy laughter between us. I hope they have some good feelings about the areas we suggested to them. They would be most welcome as our future neighbors and friends. After we bid them farewell around noon, Bill returned to town to pick up our mail. Upon his return, we worked in the office until dinner time.

Good news! The royalty check is being released. Now that we know the income is coming, Bill called our car dealer friend to check on getting Robin a Tracker. I thought they were around 10,000, but we found out that the price would be closer to 14, and that was more than we could spend now. I was greatly disappointed. Seems we're always just short of being able to swing things. So now we'll have to wait until I receive some initial advance money from *Soul Sounds* (this journal).

I was excited to receive Carole's artwork transparency for the new *Phantoms Afoot* cover this morning. Once she does *Dreamwalker*, I'll have the first four books ready to repackage when this lawsuit is settled. I think they're going to make an impressive and eye-catching set.

Carole had also enclosed a note informing me that her artwork for *Soul Sounds* should be finished tomorrow or Friday. I can't imagine how she does these things in only three days—amazing, truly amazing.

When she's done she'll call us and we'll drive down to her house to see and approve it. If there are any alterations I want done she'll do them. I already know one aspect I will want her to add —a few silver strands to the native woman's black hair. . .just like mine, because the cover is supposed to symbolize me holding out the pipe as a sign of offering myself to my readers. I wonder what kind of title Carole has given this piece of art. She called the *Phantoms* one *The Unveiling,* because the foggy mist looked like a mystical veil to her.

Tomorrow Bill is going to pick Sarah up at school, so she can take her driver's road test. Since the school demands a doctor's note in order to "excuse" an absence, our chiropractor already made one out for her—there's more than one way to get around that craziness. In fact, our chiropractor thought the school's absence policy was ridiculous and he told Bill that whenever Sarah was out with a cold or stomach upset, he'd be more than happy to cover for her with a "doctor's" note.

One of our Denver television news stations gave coverage to a new book by an author who's claiming to be from Venus, and my blood boiled. You'd think with all my outrages that I'd have a terrific high blood pressure, but when I had my operation and the nurses kept taking my blood pressure their eyes would shift up to mine and I'd just smile. They'd take it two or three times, because my normal pressure is around 90 over 40. I think they thought I should be dead with that low of a reading.

Anyway, this news broadcast infuriated me, not only because of the silly issue itself, but because they'd publicize that kind of garbage, yet give no recognition to a real local visionary like No-Eyes. Where's the rhyme or reason anymore? Where the justice? Ahh, well, I'm getting used to it by now. I'm getting accustomed to the ugly fact that "newsworthy" means *sensationalism* and not. . .sensitivity.

No-Eyes, to me, you *were* sensational! And still are.

Forgot to mention that Bill did ask our attorney on Monday if "Mary could publicly talk about our case." John Hart said he felt inclined to release me from the unofficial gag order, but wanted to think about it a while longer. He said he'd get back to us.

But now that my check's being released, I'm prompted to shelve the Oprah idea. I strongly feel that our Advisors and my "friends" want me to hold my tongue—at least for now. So I'm going to follow my inner feelings on this thing and not upset the apple cart. Outrage is one thing, but damaging my case, because I can't hold my tongue is quite another. My outrage must find another vent. My warrior instincts must be applied in a constructive manner. I must choose another weapon and it will probably be one no one can see or hear, for that particular one is the most power-filled one of all. No-Eyes knew several lesser-known shamanistic ceremonies. I think now is the time to bring these into my heart and mind once again. I only wish I had my kiva for these, but I'm going to count on the nature spirits out in the woods to help me contain the power within my sacred fire circle. Tonight, beneath the bright silver moon, one of these high ceremonies will be performed.

9-26-91, Thursday

Bill spent 13 hours in the office today. He began it early with business calls and faxes. In the afternoon he negotiated my *Soul Sounds* contract with Bob and, all evening, he reviewed the royalty statements I'd received for my first four books. He found a gross error that caused the check to be over five hundred dollars short. Bill plans on calling the publisher's accountant at seven in the morning to straighten it out.

Sarah took the road test for her driver's license and passed with flying colors. She'd been driving Bill to town in the van all summer and he never even got nervous with her behind the wheel. She's glad that's all over now. So are we.

Our friends never made it to the Glenwood area. They decided to take in some local color in the Woodland Park area. They're leaving tomorrow and plan to head out to Frisco, Colorado, and then catch the Interstate back through Denver and home to Ohio. They've had beautiful weather and I pray they have a safe journey home.

Cripple Creek has really got Gold Fever now. The gaming halls are furiously trying to reach their October first deadlines. Our local paper is advertising the various establishments; Diamond Lil's, Phenix House Gaming, Johnny Nolan's Saloon and Gambling Emporium, The Mother Lode, Virgin Mule, The Black Diamond, The Ore House, and Bronco Billy's, to name but a few.

Friends of ours own the Phenix House Gaming, and a lady who works at our chiropractor's office has taken a job as a cocktail waitress there. Things are getting crazy around here already and I'm not looking forward to October 1st.

Bill expressed that, after the casinos have been open for a week or so, he'd like to go see how the town has changed. That might be fun to see how our friends are doing with their third business venture. Maybe on October 16th for our 26th Anniversary we'll mosey in and out of the new saloons and gaming parlors that once were craft shops, bookstores, and home cookin' eateries.

Tonight my Prayer Smoke rises for our friends' safe journey home. Perhaps Raphael will give them an assist as he has for other visiting friends I've requested safe journeys for.

9-27-91, Friday

Bill called Carole this afternoon to confirm our meeting at her house tomorrow. He told her that we were going to stop to have the first half of my manuscript photocopied on our way there and did she have a title for her painting yet? I needed one for the copyright page of the book.

Carole said she hadn't thought of one and asked him if I had any ideas. He told her I did— "A Gift of Tears." And she loved it. So, in the end, I was surprised that I was the one to title her painting. Once I okay the artwork and then receive the transparency of it, I'll send it to Bob along with the photocopied half of the manuscript. He suggested it be done piecemeal like this so they can begin the manuscript scanning and setting it in text pages. This will speed the process, because I'll still be writing nightly journal entries until December 31.

I'm not in too good a mood tonight. Generally I feel the weight of many of our problems, and I'm disappointed we didn't end up with enough money to get Robin a new vehicle before winter. Between Donning's royalty check we just received and the payment schedule Bill worked out with Bob for the journal's advance, we still can't swing it now. And on top of that, this journal is getting me down. It's cold outside tonight, but I need to go into the woods.

Two hours later —
A heavy blanket of clouds shrouded the starlight and a gentle breeze rustled the aspen leaves and chilled the darkness around me. I walked until I was warmed, then sat beneath a grandfather pine. My thoughts were many, so were the frustrations. And soon I began to silently cry.

A hand gently touched my shoulder.

I looked up into my friend's eyes.

"Leave me be," I said.

"I want to help," came the soft voice.

"There is no help when the timing's not right. I just want to be alone out here. Can't I ever be alone? Can't I ever go off into the woods without you guys watching me on your screen up there?"

"We watch, because we care. We wish to protect. We desire to insure that which is to be—our future together."

I patted the forest floor.

"Sit beside me for a while. I'm sorry, my friend, I'm sorry I was rude."

"Not rude—honest. It is, because of who you are that the solitude is sought. This we understand, perhaps even more than you yourself." He touched his finger to the corner of my eye. "Your thoughts are sad."

"Yes," I said, looking out into the darkness. Then I shivered.

"You're chilled."

"I'll be okay."

"*Now* you will," he said as the air around me began to warm.

He'd done this before so I wasn't surprised. My only comment was, "Thanks."

"I know how hard the waiting is for you."

"Do you?"

"Yes. Fourteen years have passed and still all of us tell you to wait longer. Out of all of us, you two are the ones who are forced to live the earth time—among the violence, the misery, and the ignorance. We do know your pain."

Again his whispered words touched me, for he had a great well of compassion within him that frequently brought tears to my eyes.

"Tonight you cry, because you've been asked to give the gift of truth."

I wiped my eyes and nodded. I couldn't talk, because I couldn't seem to stop crying..

His soft voice was soothing to my ears, heart and soul.

"You still don't want to speak of me—of us. You still don't want to write it, do you."

I shook my head.

"Your tears are for the truth then. Mary, look at me. Do you fear your tears of truth?"

I turned my face to his and, through the flowing tears, looked deep into his eyes.

"Fear them? No. No, my friend, I. . .mourn them. I'm mourning my tears of truth. I'm in mourning for the sacred gift of my secret life that I must offer. I. . .mourn the. . . loss. . .of a relationship I. . .treasured."

He touched my chin.

"We will always have this relationship. It will grow and deepen."

Silence.

"It will become so much more entwined."

"But never. . .will it be. . .mine. . .again," I whispered. "Never will it be that sacred secret I. . .held so dear to my heart. Once people know—it will never be the same again. It will have turned into a truth told through tears. And for that. . .I have found myself. . . in mourning.

"Let me have my sacred moments. Allow me my solitude. Permit my mourning of the tears of truth to expend its pain, so I may be healed."

My friend stood then.

"I will leave the warmth ray here until your mourning is done. We will not watch."

"Thank you," was all I could manage to voice.

And when he left, the mourning began.

9-28-91, Saturday

Sky of azure. Stained glass coins reflecting translucent lights of orange and gold. Living crystal trees shimmering, laughing with Ra's tickling touch of light.

A Blue Day it was. It was an incredibly brilliant Blue Day that smiled back at me when I awoke this morning. And, in heart and soul, all was well once again.

At 10 this morning, while I was typing up last night's journal entry, Sarah came running over to my desk. In an excited whisper, she told me there were deer just outside our office. I had the heavy inside door open and just the screen door separated us from the outside. The deer were so near we had to mime to each other for fear our voices would frighten them away. There were four doe and a young buck munching on the woodsy undergrowth in our yard. What a thrilling sight! What a magnificent gift this was!

I hurried to load my camera. It still had the 400mm lens attached and I took an entire roll. Some photos were shot through our office window and some were shot when I eased out the door and slowly approached the deer. Oh, what beauties they were! I can hardly wait to see how these photos turn out. If I end up with a couple exceptional ones, I'm going to send them to Bob to include in the pictorial. How truly thrilling it was to have those four-legged brothers so close to our house. They were so close we could hear their munching sounds.

When we lived in the Ridgewood house, the elk would bed down at night in the thick undergrowth in front of our front windows, but here, the deer had never before ventured this close to our house. And in broad day-light! I felt truly blessed and my heart was full of joy.

After the deer moved on down through the woods behind our house, Bill and I left for our trip to Colorado Springs. Our first planned stop was to mosey around the Daniels Chevrolet new car lot—just out of curiosity, of course. But when we pulled up and parked, a brand new 1992 red Tracker was staring us in the face. There was only *one* on the lot and it was nowhere *near* the $14,000 quote we'd been given by another dealer. Was this a sign or what?

Bill and I looked at one another. Dare we? And we both started talking at once. We went over and over our money figures. If we really tightened our belts and pinched a little harder on those pennies, we could do it. We were getting excited at the prospect. But then I expressed deep concern over Bill's plan to trade the van in for the full-sized Blazer. That would now be out of the question if we got this Tracker for Robin. Bill said she *needed* a new vehicle and that need came first.

From the dealership Bill called Robin.

"Do you have a preference between an automatic or 5-speed?"

She was so taken off-guard she hardly knew what to say. Finally she admitted that she had no preference.

Then Bill asked, "Are you tired of red?"

"No, but what's going on?"

"Come down to Daniels right now. We'll be waiting for you. There's a little red Tracker that's anxious for you to test-drive it. If you like it. . .it's yours."

Since it would take Robin a good 35 to 40 minutes to get

down from Woodland Park, Bill put down a deposit to hold the Tracker while we buzzed across town to have my manuscript photocopied. When we returned, Robin had just arrived. She said she was in a state of shock and that she was so excited she didn't know what to say. I told her that didn't matter, because I knew how she *felt*.

Our salesman was busy with another customer so he told Bill to go ahead and take Robin out in the Tracker. I waited behind. When they returned, Bill was all smiles and Robin was still in semi-shock. She reminded me of someone who knew they "weren't in Kansas anymore." She definitely had that dazed Land of Oz look.

"Well?" I asked her.

"I love it, but I can't believe this is happening."

We hugged. "Merry Christmas," I whispered in her ear. "Let's go sign those papers."

We arranged to pick the vehicle up next Tuesday on her day off.

Later, when we were all back home in the evening, Robin told us that when she was driving her old Buick back up the pass to home, she cried the entire way.

Bill and I left the dealership and headed up the Interstate toward Carole's house. I can't express how wonderful I felt inside. My heart was near to bursting with joy. We'd waited so many years to replace our friend's old beat-up Buick and now we'd finally managed to do it for her. What a kick! If I was a billionaire I'd have a field day *every* day. Bill felt the same way. He was glad we decided to do it.

So we were riding an emotional high when we reached Carole's house and I excitedly told her all about the big mischief we'd been up to. When I calmed down a bit, she asked me if I was ready to see the journal painting. I was.

She took my arm and led me over to her table. When she held up the painting I froze—literally froze.

"That's me!" was all I could say. Then tears flowed. "Oh God, Carole, it's *beautiful!* It's incredible!" And we hugged one another for several sweet moments. Then, when I turned to Bill, he too was misty-eyed and we hugged each other too.

"Carole, I don't know how you do it, but you've captured the totality of everything this journal symbolizes. You've even placed a buffalo over my heart. . .it's just so incredible." And I told her of the journal entry I'd written about being a warrior. . .being a Buffalo Heart. Truly, her spirit heard my soul sounds the night I wrote those words and, looking at her painting sent psychic chills through me, because of the eerie correlations that were so beautifully represented. She even informed me that she was strongly drawn to the purple color—no other color *felt* right. And. . .she *already* had silver in the hair!

As soon as I saw the painting I'd immediately recognized my own likeness, but she made me look beautiful. I didn't know she was going to paint me. That was a very special give-away.

Carole was greatly relieved I liked it so well. She was a bit fearful of my reaction, but my tears said it all. I told her that people are going to see that book cover and be immediately drawn to it. People are going to buy it just for the cover.

"Will there be art prints available of this?" I asked.

"Oh yes! Just like the *Daybreak* cover. People can get your cover art for themselves if they want."

I smiled and turned to Bill.

"I'll have to make sure my readers know that.

"I'm sure they're going to want my book cover art—especially *this* one."

He wholeheartedly agreed.

This day I mark as: The Day God Smiled Upon Us.

This night I will mark with my Prayer Smoke in Thanksgiving for all the blessings we've received this day. Even the Autumn Spirit and the four-leggeds brought us gifts. And, for these, I feel like the richest person in the world.

9-29-91 Sunday

Wave after wave of gunmetal clouds rolled into each other like angry breakers crashing against a stone seawall. It was a grey, chilly day. No deer came to play and birds stayed away.

It was a good day to spend at my desk where I worked on responding to Saturday's mail. When I finished, I went into the living room where Bill had a crackling fire going in the woodstove. Selecting a new book off my library shelf, *The Novel* by James Michener, I nestled down in my wing chair and spent the afternoon in his Pennsylvania Dutch countryside.

It was one of those deeply comforting days when the outside dreariness is shut out by the inside warmth and tranquility. It was one of those days when one found oneself dozing off, book in hand, to the soothing sounds of the hearthfire.

It was one of those rare, restful days.

9-30-91, Monday

The entire day was spent responding to reader's letters while Bill was on the phone all day.

We'd found out that one of the largest book distributors in the west, Gordons (located in Denver), has been bought by Ingram. Bad news, because Ingrams is not stocking any of my first four books. This is solely because those books are no longer published by Donning, and Ingram isn't dealing with Schiffer's books (mine included). Does this now mean that bookstores will no longer be able to order my books from the Denver distributor anymore? If so. . .Schiffer is truly killing them.

Bill put in a couple calls to Ingram in Denver. One of the buyers is going to call him back tomorrow. We may have a major problem developing here. This we don't need. . .seems the dark side is taking every opportunity in suppressing No-Eyes' voice. But this is just a small skirmish they may have won. I have a strong feeling that, when the battle dust settles, No-Eyes is going to be the one warrior left holding high her lance and shield.

You will rise up to be the victor, No-Eyes. Your voice will ring out loud and clear. Your victory chant will echo around the world, for, like your beautiful spirit, your truth cannot be killed. Though our enemies may have struck a coup on us, I can feel their strength weakening. Their warriors are tiring. Yet ours are just beginning, for we have a powerful new Spirit who rides with us. And this Great Spirit has never lost a battle. Not one. He lets His opponents wear themselves down with attack after attack and then—He leads His own strong warriors in for the Final Charge. We're circling them, No-Eyes, and they don't even know it. I hope our enemies are practicing their death songs. I hope their bad medicine man has already foreseen that soon it will be a good day to die.

My heart has also been heavy these past months, because Aimee has chosen not to bring her problems to us. We've always been able to talk about everything. Bill and I would spend hours upon hours talking with her about things that bothered her. Yet it seems that ever since Eric left, she has kept her male relationships to herself and has greatly distanced herself from us and family. Now she seeks advice and consoling from other women friends, and this pains us. She will still come to me for answers from our Advisors and she still comes to me for her dream interpretations, but her personal problems are taken elsewhere. She knows her current young man is not one destined for her, but refuses to face that fact. It hurts a mother (and father) to see their once close child choose to seek comfort somewhere outside the home. We're told that she knows she'll get the truth from us and, right now, she really doesn't want to hear it. So instead, she gets subliminal comforting from others who don't have all the known details of her destiny and life circumstances. We understand that. . .still. . .it does hurt. She has a great need to have male companionship and be loved, so naturally she clings to each relationship that comes her way even if she knows, down deep, that the current young man is not destined to be "the one." She seems to have a hard time keeping the right perspective with these relationships, because they can never be kept light and carefree. We see that she's looking high and low for another Eric, but she won't ever admit that and closes her ears to the sounds of that truth. We walk the fine line between offering to talk and seeming to be interfering. So we leave the decisions up to her.

Bill gets upset when she takes her problems elsewhere, because of who I am, especially when her chosen counselors know her mother is Summer Rain and they have read all my books. He thinks that reflects badly on me and the relationships we have with our girls. But I don't totally agree with that, because even psychiatrist's children have problems that are not taken to the parent. Each young adult must follow their own feelings. I just hope, one day, she will again turn her heart back to us. Maybe after she faces Eric again the hardened shell will shatter and her searching heart will again be at peace.

It's a crystal clear night. That is where my Prayer Smoke will rise. Tonight it will be reverently offered for the opening of Aimee's heart eyes.

October, 1991

10-1-91, Tuesday

Bill drove Robin down to Daniels Chevrolet to pick up her Tracker. She was excited and ended up picking up Mandy and Sarah from school so they could ride in it.

We discussed what to do with her Buick and decided to give it away to a poor family. It certainly is better than nothing.

Tomorrow Bill's going to talk to the man at the Community Cupboard food donation center (where we deliver some of our shipments). This man says some people have to walk there to pick up their food. I'm sure it won't be hard to find someone for Robin to sign the title over to. We were told we could probably get five hundred for it, but why?

A correspondent blasted me today for what I said in *Daybreak* regarding ascended masters. She sent me an oversized sheet that was full of underlined and circled text from an organization that claims origins from these so-called masters. There were photographs of them with the founder (how convenient, yes?). That would be comparable with Lodestar putting out pamphlets with a group photo of Jesus, Abraham, Mohammed, Buddhah and *me* all sitting together. What garbage.

At the bottom of this photocopied page was written instructions for me to "see pages 209-210 of *Daybreak*," where I explain the *truth* regarding this issue. I guess this correspondent was attempting to "teach" me something. She cut out her last name from her return address label—that didn't hide her identity. I found out her name and sent back her sad spiritual propaganda with notations added to it. She is, of course, free to believe whatever she chooses, but I came down here for the express purpose of bringing the truth to just such issues. And *Daybreak* represents that fact. We receive enough New Age and spiritual junk mail to keep our woodstove hot all winter long.

Since Bill was gone most of the day and he had our Post Office Box key, I couldn't pick up our mail. I did our month-end bookkeeping and caught up on various office projects I'd let slide during the week. Then I went outside to read on our deck. It was a glorious sun-drenched autumn day and I finished reading *Foucault's Pendulum* by Umberto Eco. What an apropos story this author wove. I found it so like the spiritual Pretenders that currently lug their soap boxes around. This tale was concerned with bragging about the esoteric secrets and knowledge one knows, and the terrible karma that "comes back around" for the lies. So, so indicative of the New Age today.

Not long ago, Bill bought me a stuffed animal that represented the same theme. I have it in our bedroom. It's a Garfield in a sheepskin and he's holding a shepherd's staff. Of course Garfield is displaying his usual wide grin. This time it says, "Fooled you!"

Ah yes, so many still being fooled. So many following the ones in sheepskin. I've given out the words of truth—I cannot do more. People choose that which they want to believe—contrived photos and all. That I cannot change. . .I must accept.

Gambling began in Cripple Creek today. The saloons and casinos are going to be open daily from 8:00 A.M. to 2:00 A.M. There were so many people there, long lines snaked out onto the sidewalks with folks waiting to get in and try their luck at the slot machines and Black Jack tables.

The evening news programs gave full coverage of the opening day gaming in all three mountain towns. The two others are just west of Denver; Black Hawk and Central City. We're not looking forward to this coming weekend when traffic on Highway 24 is expected to be heavy with curiosity seekers and gamblers heading out to Cripple Creek.

Robin's little red Tracker looks so cute next to our van in the garage. She still can't believe it's really hers. I imagine she's excited to go to work tomorrow so she can drive it. Before she went to bed tonight, she again expressed how much she loves it. Yet, to us, it's nothing more than she deserves. It was just a little late in coming, but it came all the same.

Because we got Robin the vehicle, we're forced to hold off on a children's book reprint until after I figure our taxes in January. There's no way I'm going to leave us short of our IRS payment. I just hope we don't run out of the books in the meantime. If the orders continue at the rate they have been for the last month, it's going to be a close call.

A very thoughtful lady sent us our first donation to Lodestar for Wellspring Mission. We bought fresh fruits and vegetables to give away. Our incoming shipments mostly consist of canned goods and dry staples, so purchasing those fresh foods was a much welcomed variety addition for our recipient families.

I'm antsy to get a real warehouse established. In a way, I wish They hadn't given us this mission until after we were settled —still. . .whatever we can manage to distribute in the meantime serves to help alleviate someone's troubles. I guess giving a little help now is still better than doing nothing.

Tonight my prayers will be offered for the poor families we help, and especially for those we haven't been able to get to yet.

10-2-91, Wednesday

It was a heavy mail day today. The first three letters I opened were from people who said—in various ways—that I was only out for personal notoriety and that No-Eyes was a charlatan.

I put the letters down, left the rest unopened and walked out into the woods. It was a magnificent autumn day and I didn't return until after dark.

10-3-91, Thursday

Today's mail—unopened on my desk—piled on top of yesterday's.

I spent the entire day dancing to the thundering drums of the mountains. Autumn spirit and I entered our world of nature spirits where my soul was filled with the joy of our celebration ceremonial dance. My entire being was totally absorbed by the sacred unions, and our magic held back the petty words and the hurtful cruelty of humankind. For these two days the magic filled me—every living cell of me—and it infused my veins, my bones, with a new and potent power.

I returned around suppertime, but after everyone was in bed for the night, I went back into the woods where we finished our ceremonial magic beneath the clear starlight. I didn't return to the house until 3:30 A.M. I love the midnight magic most of all. I love the midnight mountains—such powerful entities come to commune then. And they are the ones that know my heart.

10-4-91, Friday

A cold front descended upon us during the night and, this morning, I awoke to a shroud of grey clouds that drifted around our house like lowland fog.

Bill had left the house at 5:00 A.M. to take the van down to be serviced at the dealers. Before he left he stoked up the woodstove and the house was warm and cozy by the time I came down into the office. My desk was piled with two day's worth of letters and I got right down to business. Magic curled up beneath my desk and didn't leave her spot until I was done.

When Aimee went to work she took Jenny in to do her Friday grocery shopping. Bill was going to pick her up on his way back up the pass. Robin was at work. Sarah and Mandy were in school. At home it was just Magic, Buttercup, Shadow, and me.

I stocked the woodstove, lit my mantle oil pots, and burned some cedar incense. When I looked out the front bamboo blinds, thick clouds were lowering down the mountains like a heavy curtain. On the deck, birds were looking for food—the feeder was empty. Donning a jacket, I picked up the seed bucket and went outside. Tiny snowflakes were falling here and there as if they were undecided about making a full-fledged appearance or not.

While I was filling the feeder, I turned to face a newcomer. A grouse was not 10 feet away watching me. I spoke softly to it and welcomed him to our home. It took a couple steps closer and listened. Being new to my deck restaurant, he then walked off to stand a few feet away beneath the pines. Smart move, for he'd made himself so camouflaged he was nearly invisible. Yet my practiced eye could clearly see him.

When I went back inside I watched through the blinds. Steller jays, grey-headed juncos, doves, snow birds, and chickadees came to feed. Then, tentatively, the grouse eased out from his cover. I smiled at the little fellow as he finally joined the others, for as was my habit, I'd thrown seed all around the ground as well as fill the feeder. If I didn't do that, the greedy jays would hog it all.

Once I was satisfied that everyone was feeding and getting their fair share, I busied myself in the kitchen. It was a good day to dry apple rings and orange rinds for my favorite "apple 'n' peel" potpourri mix. While those were drying in the oven, I made homemade applesauce on the stove. Magic watched in high anticipation while her nose sniffed the deliciously fragrant scents that filled the kitchen. She had to settle for a Milk Bone or two. That seemed to satisfy her.

Link called this afternoon. She'll be bringing us a food shipment tomorrow around noon.

Received the contract for *Soul Sounds*. I scanned it and found a couple things that need to be changed. Bob had the date for the manuscript delivery set for November. That can't be, because I'm going to be working on this journal until the end of December. Generally the contract was nearly identical to *Daybreak's*. Tomorrow Bill and I will go over it line by line.

Bill called the man at the Community Cupboard about a possible recipient for the Buick, but he couldn't help us. Then Bill called Social Services and never got an answer— guess they're closed on Fridays. He's going to try the churches next. The man at the Community Cupboard suggested we place an ad in our local newspaper. No way! Every teenager in town would be calling us for a free car.

Our Ohio friend called to talk. She and Bill conferred for two hours. She and her family have been wanting to relocate to a western state. They were thinking of Montana, but appeared to be drawn to Colorado. That choice must come from within themselves.

Tomorrow Robin's taking Sarah and Jenny down to Colorado Springs to do some shopping. They get to ride in the new Tracker and they're looking forward to it. Mandy's at her dad's this weekend. When he came to pick her up tonight, she couldn't wait to point out their new truck.

When everyone's gone tomorrow and before Link comes, I plan on making up some orange clove pomanders that I roll in spices. They make wonderful country scent hangings for use in any room of the house. If this cold, dreary weather keeps up, I'll soon be in my apple pie baking mood. Having the woodstove fired up seems to bring the homebaked mood upon me. Fresh bread sounds good. . .maybe butter-topped braided bread. And maybe some blueberry muffins too.

We talked with Aimee for two hours tonight. She finally

admitted some things she's been shoving away. We hugged her and told her how much we love her. I think her heart eyes opened a little. I know how hard it is to face things that want to stay hidden and she grew a lot tonight. She's going to be okay. She's got a lot of thinking to do now, but she's going to gain and advance with it. She's quite a brave young lady.

By the way, she passed her second EMT exam. Soon she'll be at the mid-semester point. It's going faster than she anticipated it would.

It's very dark and cold out tonight. The clouds are hanging low around the house. I'm going to don my ghost cape (hood and all) and walk these mystical woods.

I've not written of this special cape that covers me from head to heel. I don't think this diary is ready to receive the words I'd have to write about it. Some magic and power must remain untold. . .at least for now.

Goodbye.

10-5-91, Saturday

Bill and I had errands in Woodland. While he went over to pick up our mail, I roamed the grocery store to gather ingredients for making apple pie.

When we returned home, I went through the mail. One woman had made me a beautiful pair of earrings. One large envelope had 20 nights of dreams for me to analyze, and another reader sent me photocopied pages from someone's latest message of her planetary claptrap. This skeptical reader wanted my opinion because she couldn't quite swallow the idea of Doorways being activated and human Anchors around the world. I minced no words in clarifying and agreeing with her inner higher self-perception. She also didn't like the fact that the brochure said, "send donations." Sure am glad *some* folks are using their intellect and looking a little harder at these cult personalities, especially those purporting to have alien connections or messages.

After I finished up in the office, I had about an hour to work on making my orange and clove spice pomanders before Link arrived with our shipment. We unloaded all the boxes in our office and then the three of us sat in the kitchen and talked for four hours. I thought it was more than interesting that some strong impressions came to me while we were conversing. Link appears to have a time frame similar to ours for relocating. Not only is her timing close, but her targeted geographical region also approximates ours. I see an overview of several roads converging at a specific time next year. I see how pieces are dropping neatly into place one and two and three at a time. Things are pulling together in such a physical manner now that I can actually see where it's all going to meld into the whole.

After dinner, when the girls got home, I completed the work on our Wellspring shipment. I prepared eight boxes of food for Bill to distribute Monday morning. Again we're able to supply fresh fruits and vegetables in addition to the canned goods and staples.

Later —
I waited up for my friend to join me this night. I had some questions for him and I knew he knew that.

I left the house in darkness except for the oil pots burning on the mantle. The woodstove was well stocked, so I wouldn't have to bother with it while he was here. At 12:34 P.M., he made his appearance, and after our greetings he got right down to business.

"You have questions that are not questions," he said softly.

I smiled. "That's true, but I'd like to gain a deeper understanding of the 'whys' of the subject."

"These are the same as the reasons we previously discussed. They do not alter. People do this for monetary and personal gain. Greed. Fame."

Well I knew all that already, so I began with specifics.

"What does 11:11 mean to you?"

"Absolutely nothing. There is no direct connection at all. We do know of 11:11 through our observance of what some humans have contrived it to be. In actuality there is no connection to us whatsoever."

"And. . .January 11th, 1992?"

"Constellation alignment. That is all."

Silence.

"Mary, the human mind does tend to choose a celestial event to place esoteric or alien significance to. Doing that does not make it real."

"So I've observed. Many New Age personalities are already fighting to be the dominant prognosticator for that particular date and it does remind me of cavemen looking at a falling star and proclaiming it to be magic."

"Mary, you know us well by now. You know there are no 'doors' to be opened—no mystic vortexes or openings. You know we have no human 'anchors' established around the planet. There are none of these things happening, nor will they happen. You also know why certain humans feel the need to broadcast such tales. Isn't the important factor here that *you* know the truth of it—of us?"

"No."

"No?"

"No. The important factor is for the *public* to know the truth of it—of you. Their heads are being filled with wild fantasies far beyond science fiction. Can't you make your mass appearance *now?* So many people believe in you, but the sickening part of it is that so many pretenders are leading them way off base from your reality. How can you sit back and let that happen? Don't you care?"

"We care. And we've been over and over that."

"Yes. I know, it's not time. But why can't one of you or a group of you appear to these pretenders and set them straight? I can't imagine how you can let them say whatever whim comes to their mind about you and lead so many astray." I sighed. "Doorways. Commanders. Anchors. Keys and Legions of the Archangel Michael. Oh, poor Michael. They're even bringing him into this sham. Come on! And to deepen the perversity, these people even have the gall to *tell* the public to send in *donations* to their trumped-up group." I peered over at him. "Why are you smiling? I'm *serious!*"

"Oh yes, serious. I know that."

"Then stop smiling. Do you see *me* smiling over this?"

"You should be. You should be because you know we view this kind of thing as humorous human folly. It is the human aspect that wishes for the ridiculous and then strives to make it real for themselves. There are always those who will devise the absurd and claim singular knowledge of it. This then makes them big, yes? This then makes followers lining up behind their 'big knowledge.' Oh yes, these ones are as an amusement to us."

"It's *not* amusing!" I flared. "While you cruise around laughing at the idiots down here I have to *live* with them. I work my tail off trying to straighten people out and you think it's 'amusing' to see others bend them in knots with their fabrications."

"Mary."

"Silence.

"Mary?"

"What?"

"We—you and I—we're going to settle that, remember? We're going to set everyone straight about us, and all those imaginary alien commanders and personalities will be exposed then. Isn't that what you want?"

"Not really. I'm not out to 'expose' anyone, I just want the lies to stop. I get very upset when I see so much corny information being given out about you. It just turns my stomach, it really does.

"I know there will come the time when we set things to rights. I know that, but you've got to realize how hard it is for me in the meantime to tread water amid all the garbage floating around me. It's not at all amusing to me. It's extremely frustrating." I looked deep into his eyes. "My friend," I whispered, "we've done all we can do. If I send the rest of my books in to Bob, will you. . ."

"No."

"You're rude not to let me finish my request."

"Perhaps, but you make a request I cannot grant you yet. When we've completed our work together, then and only then will the time be right for me to take you and your family for that long ride. Mary," he said softly, "you both came for The Plan. You would not want to abandon it now when it's so close to finalization."

I sighed. "No. . .but. . ."

"This is the last battle, Mary. It's all so close. Can you not endure for a time longer? I think you can. I think you will. That is one of the reasons we connected long before necessity made it so. Our companionship has served to encourage and strengthen your resolve, has it not?"

"Yes. Oh yes. Our friendship has meant so much to me, and I know it will mean a great deal to Bill too when he becomes more involved with you. Yes, you have increased my power and I do understand what you're saying.

"Times become so frustrating and difficult down here amid the confusion of people's minds, but yes, I will endure—both Bill and I will see this through."

Then, for a long while, we spoke of how things were progressing with my friend's activities and how aspects were materializing regarding our eventual mission together.

I loved hearing him speak of these things because they represented a time to come when true understanding of the facts of their purpose would come to the people. It represented a clearing out of all the fallacies that people were being led to believe of them. And that was certainly an uplifting event for me to look forward to. For now. . .it gave me enough encouragement to endure the dark age I often felt I was forced to live within.

After my friend left, I spent an hour offering up my Prayer Smoke for myself—so that I would continue to have the strength to accept the pretenders and the temporary harm they do.

It is 3:43 A.M. I'm going to bed. I'm very, very tired.

10-6-91 Sunday

It was a glorious autumn day. Deep blue sky. Cloudless. Gentle breeze. A real gift.

By 9:30 in the morning, I was in the office typing up last night's journal entry. When I finished, Bill walked in the door from his trip to town for the Sunday paper. He'd stopped at the Post Office and brought back two letters that were put up late Saturday. I opened them and found both to be extremely encouraging. One woman wrote to say "thanks for changing my life," and the second lady had one major criticism of me. "You let your rude readers hurt you," she wrote. "When you get nasty letters you need to tear them up and forget you ever saw them because you've been a light that guides so many people."

Yes, she was right—about the nasty letters, I mean. And those include the ones my friend and I had talked about too. I need to disregard all the pretenders that have previously caused me such deep pain and heartache. And, thanks to the compassionate help from Bill and my friend, I believe I can do that now. I seem to have crossed a threshold of tolerance—acceptance—where my newly acquired perspective has acted as an insulator around my heart. The time will arrive when the world is shown the indisputable truth and that will be the time some will smile and others will seek to hide their faces. I will smile. Oh. . .how I will smile.

While Bill and Jenny tuned in the Bronco game, I began to put an apple pie together. The living room was filled with a mournful silence. The game was not going well. It was not a pretty sight.

Bill gave up on it and grabbed my *Soul Sounds* contract and joined me in the kitchen to go over it line by line together while the pie baked. We made some changes and were done when the pie was. Tomorrow he'll mail the contract back to Bob. I'm still waiting to send in the first 426 manuscript pages until I have Carole's cover art transparency to send with it. I think Bob's really going to like it. We think it's fantastic.

Sarah took her homework out in the woods this afternoon. She goes quite far to a special place she found. Bill always makes her take her mace with her whenever she goes off into the forest alone.

When she returned, she had an excited tale to tell. After she'd reached a thickly forested part of the woods, she heard crunching sounds behind her—like creeping footfalls on the fallen aspen leaves. She stopped to listen and the sound behind her stopped. When she walked on they began again.

Finally she stepped behind a wide aspen tree and waited. No sound came. She waited and waited without moving a muscle. Then the crunching began again. One step . . .two . . .three and four.

She eased her eye around the tree and faced a buck. He froze and stared back at her. And they communed while she sent him strong visuals of friendship bathed in a warm pink light. The deer flickered his ears then and began to casually munch on the undergrowth. The two remained near one another for a long time before the four-legged one began to wander off. This union filled her with a joy she found hard to contain. I doubt much studying was accomplished after that. Sarah would be in Seventh Heaven if she could spend her entire life in the woods. She often reminds me of a young No-Eyes.

Sarah said that, while she was out in the woods, she was sickened to hear rifle shots. Our mountain residential area is protected from all hunting so the four-leggeds seek protection here, but just outside its boundaries is a large acreage ranch where the owners hunt the deer and elk that cross their land. Sarah is going to have to start wearing my red jacket when she journeys out into the forest from now on.

One of the occupants of the ranch is a young man who rides Sarah's school bus, and he derives great pleasure in telling her about the squirrels, rabbits, and deer he shot. And Sarah calls him a cannibal. Usually these two are fairly good friends, but she really gets riled when he gets talking about his latest kill.

Throughout my day today I thought a lot about the discussion I had last night with my friend. Various parts of our conversation echoed in my mind and served to reinforce the new feeling I had toward our mission and all the separate aspects of The Plan.

I caught myself grinning now and then when I realized that some of the New Age material *would* seem amusing to my Starman, especially the alien information that's being spread around. And when I viewed it all from his perspective it certainly did seem ridiculously funny. I only wish more people laughed at it instead of taking it seriously.

Our girls are well aware of the issue of Time and how it relates to our Advisors' perspective as compared to our own. This evening, after I told them about last night's talk with my friend and how we must "endure for a time longer," Sarah had a joke for me. It went like this.

A man asked God how long a million years was to Him.

"A second," God answered.

Then the man asked, "How much money is a million dollars to You?"

"A penny," God said.

So the man asked God, "Can I borrow a penny?"

"Sure," God said, "in a second."

And that pretty well sums up what we've been dealing with for 14 years. Time and money are abstracts to the Powers that guide us, yet these are very real and frustrating realities that we must deal with and work around every day. It's very difficult for me to be continually *thinking* on *their* level all the time while *living* down on this one. My mental and physical is rarely in the same place. And that's why I so desperately need valuable moments of respite from our work. Woodswalking, baking, reading, taking an hour out to make an orange 'n' clove spice pomander; all serve to ground me and revive my perspectives.

My family frequently tells me I'm getting too serious because I'm always thinking "way up there," so I need little moments here and there to bring me back down to earth again.

I know I can be a real drag at times, especially when someone says something funny and I'll remain deadpan because I'm too engrossed in my thoughts. But so many ideas are always coming to mind and I have the responsibility of giving them my full attention because many times they're advice or guidance or new revelations. Other times they're simply some philosophical thought that I need to go write down in my woodswalking notebook.

Yes, I know I think too much. Sometimes my mind feels like a racing engine. Thank God for my woods that slow it down to an idling purr. Grandmother Earth's spirit is very, very soothing to this one and I do offer her my Thanksgiving gratitude, for she has saved me many times from overheating.

Tonight my two hours of Prayertime will be for my readers who have greatly encouraged me through their beautiful give-aways of kind words. These ones can never know how much their supporting sentiments mean to me.

10-7-91, Monday

Under blue autumn skies I helped Bill load the food boxes in the van. He and Jenny went to town to distribute them and I returned to our office where I typed up last night's entry.

A phone call interrupted me. Jennifer, from the Community Cupboard, wanted to talk to Bill. She told me that when he dropped the food off an hour ago, she forgot to tell him she had a recipient for the Buick. I told her how pleased that made me and she gave me the person's name and address. It seems a nurse with small children fled an abusive husband in Nebraska and came here a week ago to live with friends until she can get back on her feet. She has no job yet and she has no car. Perfect!

When Bill returned he was excited to hear about the possibility and he immediately called the woman. He set a delivery time and a few hours later, he and Robin filled up the Buick, washed it and delivered it. The woman was so happy to have transportation. She was smiling from ear-to-ear. On the way home, Robin and Bill felt wonderful inside to be able to help someone out like that.

We had quite a lot of mail, and by the time we were done processing it, Jenny called us for supper.

During our meal, we got a call from the fire department. Aimee had asked them to inform us that she'd been called out on a structure fire. A house in the Tranquil Acres mountain community was burning to the ground. Aimee's beeper had gone off at work and she responded.

Later she called us and was very excited. The house was a total loss and nothing was left. Her final job at the sight was to walk through the rubble and uncover the hot spots so the others could hose them down. This had been her first official big fire and she said she was so glad to have gotten the experience. She's somewhat concerned that City Market's manager will give her flack about leaving work. I can't imagine his doing that, because Teller County (which includes Woodland Park) has no regular paid firefighters. Every fire that breaks out is tended by all volunteers who get called in from their jobs. Day or night these volunteers need to be available at a moment's notice. No fires would be put out if the volunteers couldn't leave their jobs, or if they'd be fired if they left. I think if Aimee's boss's house was ablaze he'd be pushing her out the store door to go help save it.

Just finished reading *Castle Eppstein* by Alexandre Dumas this afternoon. Interesting ghost tale. When I replaced that one back on my library shelf I took down *Freedom In Exile — The Autobiography of the Dalai Lama.* I don't watch television except for a few special programs during the week like 20/20, 60 Minutes, PBS Specials, and the nightly newscasts and I can't just sit without my mind spinning. . .so I read and read. This grounds me and gives me needed relaxation time. Because of this favored pastime, I continually order books from catalogs, and I keep a stockpile of unread ones on my shelves so I'm never out of new titles to read. I tend to get agitated with withdrawal symptoms if I'm out of books when I need one. Oh, how I love books! If I ever had to go back into the workplace, I'd surely get a job in a bookstore or book warehouse or book *something.* Bill once told me that I was addicted to books. He said I don't just read them—I inhale them.

Apple pie's all gone. Guess someone inhaled it. I wonder who? Far be it from me to point the finger and name names, but I suspect it was someone who wears cowboy boots.

There is a new moon out tonight. The sky is crystal clear and the stars are sparkling like polished jewels on black velvet. Beneath these twinkling lights I will let my Prayer Smoke rise. Tonight's whispered words will be offered for the lady who now drives a 1972 red Buick. Also, prayers of Thanksgiving will be spoken in gratitude for Aimee's protection that was given this night.

10-8-91, Tuesday

Autumn was a regal lady today.

While going through our mail, I came across a letter from a woman who asked where she should send packages for Wellspring Mission. This surprised me. I guess it never dawned on me that any of my readers would wish to contribute goods, and the lady's offer was quite unexpected. I told her Parcel Post to my box number would suffice for now. Later, when we're settled, we'll be receiving deliveries directly to our warehouse address. It appears that this new mission is taking off all by itself whether we're ready for it or not.

Maybe we should go over to our chosen area and rent something just to establish an address there. No, that never works —we've been through that a dozen times already.

I feel we've now got the cart before the horse and I'm impatient to make a reversal correction. That can only be accomplished by a relocation and there's no way we can swing that right now. Oh, this interminable waiting for the "right time" can drive a person batty. I feel like a racehorse waiting for the gate to open. I'm ready to charge forward. I'm primed to run. . .but the gate is stuck closed.

What a nonsensical predicament. Well. . .I know there's sense to it because the timing has to do with two aspects; getting enough funds to purchase our land and warehouse and having the "right" property open and available for us. Still, the nonsensical part is the cart being before the horse when the horse is eager to run with it. Methinks "They" need to adjust their clocks to correspond with *our* timing. Right, No-Eyes? You know how anxious we are to get Wellspring Mission established. You know how we're chomping at the bit to get it going. Maybe you could go talk to the Big Guys about this. You're a very persuasive lady. No-Eyes, please see if you can do something to speed this up.

This is Fire Prevention Week and Aimee is with her companion firefighters over at the Woodland Elementary School, giving talks and demonstrations. She's the one who keeps dressing up for each class while her co-firefighter explains all the gear they wear. She said they need to have the little kids hear the sound their breathing apparatus makes because it's been known to actually scare kids caught in fires and they've tried to get away from the incoming firefighter. The kids thought Darth Vader was coming after them.

Today, in one first-grade class, Aimee said she placed the headgear on and when the oxygen was turned up, one kid began to cry hysterically. The teacher calmed her and brought the student up to Aimee where she could touch and see Aimee's face through the face shield. Aimee talked softly back to her and the girl's fear faded into a smile.

Later, the firefighters went to join the kids on the playground and the little ones gathered around wanting autographs penned on their hands. Overall, Aimee enjoyed her instructional day at the school. When she was finished with the elementary level, she strode over to the high school and, with her gear on, asked the office lady which class Sarah was in. The woman's mouth dropped open. Aimee loved it. She got Sarah out of her Psychology Class and they talked in the hall for a few minutes. Sarah said that when she hugged Aimee goodbye, she could hardly find her beneath all her gear.

I went out to walk through the woods this afternoon. I took a basket and gathered pinecones. It felt wonderful to be out in the forest with the sun rays streaming down through the high pines. I could've stayed out for hours and hours, but I had to get back at my desk. So far we've managed to answer letters and fill book orders the same day we receive them—even if it means working until seven or eight in the evening. This is true, of course, except for the few days when certain letters have driven discouragement into my heart.

When I returned to our office Bill grinned wide. "You look so cute with your little basket of pinecones."

"Cute?"

"Yeah, I mean with your knee-moccasins and that long skirt—it looks so native-like."

I put down my filled basket and kissed him. "Thanks, I needed that." Then, "any earth-shattering calls come in while I was out?"

"I wouldn't say earth-shattering, but you're going to like it. Fine Print called to say they're sending Carole's transparency overnight. We should have it tomorrow sometime."

I squealed with delight. I'd been so anxious to have the family see this extraordinary painting.

I know I've yakked a lot about this particular piece of art, but I can't help it. It's just so beautiful! Not because it's a painting of me, but because the entire thing is so incredibly attractive. It has a magnetic quality. . .it's magical. Go ahead, dear reader, look at the cover of this book. Is it not soul stirring?

Oh Carole, truly your native heart has heard the mournful drumming of my own. How else could you have seen so clearly into the depths of my soul, for your hand was guided to paint what your spirit eyes saw there. You have transformed my soul sounds into color and given them form. You have exposed my raw soul that does willingly offer its gift of tears. You have honored me, Carole. In a most sacred manner have you honored me.

I am saddened that I have no return gift for the one I received from Carole. So then, tonight's Prayer Smoke will rise in hopes that my readers themselves will honor Carole back a hundredfold by their desire to have a print of "A Gift of Tears" of their own.

10-9-91, Wednesday

I managed to spend a few hours outside this afternoon. It was a magnificent day to soak up the forest energy and watch the feathered and four-legged ones come for the food I brought for them. Squirrels and chipmunks ate from my hand while the birds hopped around to partake of the seed I scattered about.

Just as I walked around the side of the house, Tom, our UPS man, was approaching our front door. He had the transparency. Excitedly I signed for it and ran inside to show Jenny. She thought it was beautiful. When Sarah and Mandy came home from school they finally got to see the famous painting I'd been telling them about.

Mandy's mouth dropped. "That's *you*, Mary!"

And Sarah looked at it for a long time because she wants to be an artist. She can't get over the fact that Carole creates my book covers in just three days. Sarah would love to spend time at Carole's house to watch her work and learn from her. Unfortunately, Carole's on the road a lot and we have to catch her between tours to commission our book art. Her goal is to stay home and paint, so she's trying to ease out of the tours and into mail order through her catalogs. I think it won't be too much longer for her to reach that goal.

Tomorrow Bill will send the manuscript and transparency to Bob. He'll receive it before noon on Friday.

I'm having stronger and stronger impressions that certain people are going to be connected with us and our work in the near future. I can't tell these people that yet, because they have to follow their own spirit voices and use their free wills without our interfering in any way that would influence them. It's interesting for us to sit back and observe the workings of destiny and timing. When we watch the unfolding process in other's lives we gain a deeper understanding of how it's always worked in our own lives. It isn't quite the same, of course, but the identical laws apply.

Bill has been in close contact with these people and he can see how their decisions are bringing them in closer and closer to our circle. I could write down and record the outcome right now, but I don't feel that'd be playing fair. I think that would somehow detract from their idea that their decisions were their own. Just because I know a future outcome in someone's life doesn't also mean that I can voice it before their final decision is made—that would constitute interference, because they'd never be sure the deciding outcome came from *their* free will or from what *I* said. Did all that make sense? It did to me.

Two hours later —
Just returned from my Prayertime in the forest. The cougar watched again. He just lay down and watched. There's something unnatural about him—maybe supernatural is the word I'm looking for. He's not quite real, then again, he's not quite a spirit either. I've the strong feeling I've got a shape-changer here. . .a friendly one. I will get this verified as soon as possible. Whatever—whoever—it is. . .I have no fear of it and there's no threatening aura given off. For some reason it's been allowed to join me during my more sacred ceremonies. It watches my magic, yet I feel a welcoming emotion toward it. My power is not impeded nor diminished by it's presence. In fact, now that I've thought more on it, this cougar *increases* my power. I've never had this happen before, and am now very anxious to ask our Advisors who it is, for now I do know it's a who. . .a powerful who.

10-10-91, Thursday

Before I came down into the office this morning, Bill had already called Bob to inform him that he'd be receiving *Soul Sounds* tomorrow.

"You'll have the first 426 pages," Bill said.

"The *first* 426 pages? Is this another long *Daybreak*?"

Then Bill explained that I'd anticipated the total manuscript page count to be between six and seven hundred. That seemed to be a relief to Bob. Then he said he was getting married on Sunday. He added that he didn't say anything to us before this, because he knew we couldn't make it anyway. Then he told Bill he'd probably take the manuscript with him because he'll be gone for a whole week.

We had a fair amount of mail today and quite a few book orders. A bookstore owner in Montana called to say they hadn't received their shipment. Bill checked on it and he'd mailed it nearly a month ago, so he told her we'd put a tracer on it.

Usually we fill book orders the same day we receive them and they go out the following morning. People rarely have to wait two weeks to receive them. Hearing that an order didn't make its destination upsets us, because out of nearly two thousand we've mailed out, only one came back damaged and none were ever lost—until now. We really appreciate it when bookstores order these children's manuals for their customers, because we can't wholesale them and it takes a very special bookstore owner to go to that kind of trouble when they don't make anything from it. Quite a few owners regularly send in orders when people request the book through them. They just include a slip of paper with the children's names their customers want the books autographed to. Some bookstores send us the customers' checks or else the bookstore pays us and they get reimbursed by their customers. It's worked out real well this way.

Tonight my Prayertime will be for a correspondent I received a letter from today. She had a special problem and I told her I would pray for her. I will do this first because afterwards, I'm going to journey far away without leaving the house. This will take several hours.

10-11-91, Friday

This may be a long entry. Much has happened today.

I awoke to a beautiful morning. If it hadn't been for the aspen trees that are nearly bare now, I'd surely think it was summer. The air was warm and the gentle whisper of the breeze brought with it the fragrance of fertile earth. Above, the sky was like looking into the depths of a glassy sea. No whitecap clouds disturbed the calmness, no wispy ripples marred the tranquil blueness. All day long one had the mystical sensation of being within the core of a rare and precious jewel.

Although we had much mail, nature's sweet song reached my soul through our opened office door and I left the stack of letters on my desk.

I filled the birdfeeder, scattered nuts and seeds around the deck and reclined on a lawn chair to soak up the wonderful mountain energy.

Soon I was surrounded by wee four-leggeds who scampered about me for the nuts. Soon a myriad of colorful feathered ones were peeping, chirping, and squawking around the porch. For the first time, I witnessed a lark bunting come to feed at my table. She was a real beauty and I mentally welcomed her. The Stellar blue jays get upset when I fill the feeder and then stay outside. As big as they are, they're more skeptical of my friendship than the tiny chickadees are. Those big blue boys will sit perched in the pines and squawk their heads off at me, while the tiny juncos are already bravely feeding. I tell the jays that I'm not the one keeping them from getting their fair share. I tell them to get rid of their fear of me and that they know I'd never harm them.

They then go silent as if they're listening. Soon one, then two, and another and more hop to the ground and inch closer to the seed. Actually, it's better for the little ones if I do remain outside for a while because those Stellar jays are real uncouth eaters who hog the dining table. When I'm out there, the little ones come right away and begin to eat while the jays sit in the trees shouting obscenities at me in hopes they'll shoo me away. I can almost hear the little ones chuckle.

I stayed outside most of the day. The sun felt so good and energizing, the soft breeze had such a wonderful fragrance. I felt I was getting inebriated with the richness of nature's powerful nectar. Days spent drinking my fill were few and far between lately, and I gave myself over completely to it.

Around four in the afternoon when the sun began to lower, the autumntime chill returned. I left all my little nature companions then and went back into the house.

Bill had spent the day in the office with phone calls and he'd also processed the mail for me. He said another reader had sent a gift for Wellspring Mission. I don't know why this still surprises me, especially after receiving one previously, but I was truly delighted. Bill also said that another correspondent was preparing a box of clothing to send.

When we worked up our information letter about Wellspring, we did it with the sole intention of informing our correspondents of our new mission that we were now involved in. We did this for the prime purpose of explaining why we may not be able to write responses back to their letters. Never had it crossed our minds that people would want to donate goods and money to Wellspring. And when those first offers materialized, they really threw us off, because I then worried if people thought we were soliciting contributions—and I didn't want to give that type of wrong impression.

We reviewed the wording of our letter. It still sounded good to us, because its intent still sounded as if it were more of an apology than a solicitation letter. We left it as is. Still, I'm amazed that people wanted to contribute to our work. Am I that naive? Stupid? Cynical? Well, whatever I was (or am), my heart goes out to the kindness we've been shown.

This early evening I pulled a new book from my shelf
and got comfortable in my wing chair. With feet up on the
ottoman, I began to read a novel entitled *Fools Crow* by
James Welch. Before I had the first chapter read, Bill came
over and sat on the ottoman.

"Can we talk?"

I closed the book, looked about the living room and noticed we were completely alone. Everyone was upstairs. Robin
was in the shower, Sarah was reading in her room, and Jenny was playing a card game with Mandy in Robin's room.
Aimee was at the firehouse.

"What's the matter? You seem down tonight," I said.

"Ever since that fiasco with our former friends, ever since
we got burned so bad, I haven't felt like myself."

"I know," I sympathetically agreed, "I feel like they ripped
a part of you away." I put down the book. "You need
friends, Bill. That's a very deep and inherent part of your
being. When those two relationships ended so tragically, it
was like a part of you was missing—gone."

He looked at me with soulful eyes.

"Is it so wrong for me to want to help people?" he asked.

" No, but. . ."

"You know what it is?" he said, cutting me off. "It's my
spirit. My spirit has this incredible compassion toward other
spirits. It wants to do all it can to help another spirit advance. That's just what it feels like, because it kicks right in
before my mental can hold it back."

I thought on that. "I think you're right. On the outside
you're an incredible extrovert to begin with, but when you
add the spirit's compassion and great desire to help, I can
see why you get so deep into friendly relationships."

He sighed. "But then you tell me that's wrong to do because I'll only get stung again. It makes me feel like my
judgments are all wrong."

"It's not your judgment, honey, it's your heart that gets in
the way. I'm trying to protect your heart. I just don't want
you getting hurt again. God, Bill, I couldn't stand to see you
go through that kind of ripping pain again. I just want you to
allow our friendships to develop naturally without getting so
involved too quickly. When you counsel some of these people, your heart is in every second of it. Bill, you give your
all and sometimes that's too much to risk."

"I know. I know, but I can't seem to counsel any other
way. Especially with people who are starting to be good
friends and have their future linked to ours. Those people are
real special to me."

"And me too. But will you try to keep your heart gate cracked open a little instead of swinging it wide?"

He said he'd try.

"Something else has been bothering me a lot," he added.

"Shoot."

"What's *really* blocking us getting settled?"

"Timing." He laughed sarcastically.

"Bullshit. That's bullshit and you know it. Are you going to tell me that us getting settled hasn't had *any* right time in almost 15 years? This is plain nuts for us to still be waiting for a place of our own."

"We've never had the money, Bill."

"Look. We're not a couple of Bozos here. We *volunteered* for God's sake. . .literally. Our Guys could've gotten us settled a long time ago if they wanted to."

"They tried, remember? It's just not the right time."

"Okay, let me put it another way then. We came specifically to do a job, right?"

"Right."

"In essence, that job's for God, right?"

"Yes."

"So why doesn't God help out his helpers a little, so their job isn't so tangled in earthly problems?"

I smiled. "You want a suitcase of money to appear in your closet?"

"It wouldn't be the first time we've been saved by the appearance of a few newly-arrived bills in my wallet."

"But *He* doesn't *do* that kind of thing. It's like we're the warriors out on the battlefield and He's the General in his headquarters tent. He gives us our orders and we go carry them out. He isn't going to kick stones out of our way or give us motel lodging along the way. We're here for the purpose of the battle, not easy street."

Silence.

Waiting.

He looked over at me.

"That's it! Damn! Fourteen years of wondering why we're not settled and we finally get the answer."

"Answer?"

"We screwed up, honey. We screwed up royally."

"We did?"

"When we volunteered for this—when we were still up there —we should've made our land *part* of the deal. . .the purpose. We didn't and it's not. Our purpose—one of them— is to enlighten the people to God's precepts. . .not get comfy, cozy settled. Don't you see? We can carry out our purpose from a tent if we had to. Getting settled is secondary, like a motel on the battlefield. It's not even connected with our purpose—it's not in the deal so it's a *want*, not a need."

Silence.

"Right? Agreed?"

"Yeah, it makes a lot of sense."

"Okay," he said, "if you could alter your perspective on this and we moved around like nomads while carrying out our purpose, could you shed the idea of being settled? Get rid of your sense of urgency to do so?"

"Mmmm, that's a hard one because one of my main reasons for having our own place is to have something—some security—to leave the girls in case anything ever happened to us. I want them to always have a home."

"Well. . .anyway," he said, "that's why we're not settled yet. If it was part of our purpose we'd have been all set years ago. So now we're forced to wait for the right time for it. And that time seems to be going right down to the bare wire."

"Is it wrong, selfish, to want to be settled then?"

He thought a bit on that before responding. "Maybe it was before. But with our other two purposes it'll be a necessity. We need a permanent base near our Starborn connections and we need a permanent base to establish the Wellspring Mission warehouse.

"The first purpose—getting the truth out through the books —could've been (and was) done anywhere, because we did move around while doing it, so timing to be settled was not relevant. But *now*, because we'll *need* a permanent location the *timing* for it is nearing, and so is the lawsuit action and all the other aspects we're seeing dropping into line."

"Well," I sighed, "we certainly could've been saved a hell of a lot of grief and frustration if we knew that from the beginning."

"You kidding? If our Advisors had told us, when we first came here, that we wouldn't get that log cabin for 15 years, we'd have been incredulous. The length of our struggle would've been too hard to imagine, to endure."

"No. No, we just wouldn't have been *waiting* for it everyday for the last 15 years, that's all."

It was about at this point in our conversation that we heard a helicopter in the distance.

"Must be Flight For Life," Bill commented.

We were about to resume our discussion when I noticed the sound of the helicopter was getting louder. . .too fast. . . way too fast. It sounded as if it was heading straight for us at great speed. I had a shiver ripple through me and I ran to the front door, threw it open and raced out into the darkness.

Bill was right on my heels—but in those lost seconds. . . missed the sight I'd witnessed. It all happened so fast.

When I opened the door, the odd helicopter was nearly touching our roof peak. It was huge and had red and green lights. About 15 feet in front of it and off a little to its left, was a speeding ball of light—it looked like a star right above me. In front of the ball of light, an *unlighted* object sped ahead. There were three in all.

I ran out further on the deck to watch the flight of the three airborne vehicles.

The unlighted object banked sharply and soared off to the right. It climbed swiftly out of sight. The ball of light sped straight ahead while the military helicopter chased it. Then the ball of light rose vertically and distanced itself high in the sky. The helicopter was left in the dust somewhere beyond the treeline, where we heard its sound fade away.

We watched the ball of light hover in the sky. Now it looked very much like a star twinkling blue, red and green. We watched it hover for 20 minutes before it vanished from sight.

We had witnessed a military helicopter chase two UFOs directly over our front deck. All three flew directly over me at such a low level, I remember subliminally thinking I could reach up and touch them. I also remember having the split-second thought that the enormous copter was going to clip our roof.

Sarah had run downstairs and joined us on the deck when she saw the copter pass in front of her loft windows. By the time she got out far enough to where Bill and I were standing, the ball of light was high in the sky. As the three of us took turns watching it through binoculars, Sarah said, "Look! There's another one!"

It was behind us hovering above the treetops. It was a distance away but had the same blue, red, and green lights. It hovered for several minutes and then moved erratically up, down, and sideways back and forth (like a cross). It hovered a couple minutes and went up, then down out of sight behind the treeline.

Meanwhile, the original one we'd been watching was still there. Then—it just wasn't, as if all its lights blinked out. The show was over.

When we came back inside, Bill was more than a little irritated that he hadn't made it outside in time to see the ball of light and the unlighted vehicle pass above the deck. . .all three were traveling incredibly fast. It reminded me of a Top Gun dog fight.

Bill was beginning to feel a little left out, and that's ex-

actly the reason I didn't want him reading my journal entries.
This damn thing has revealed too much—even to him. Although he realizes he'll be involved with the Starborn ones in
the future (on our land), he'd like a little one-on-one right
now. I can't blame him for how he feels so I'll spend some
time tonight asking my friend if he couldn't visit Bill tonight
. . .or sometime soon. We'll see what happens with that.

Robin and Jenny finally came downstairs to inquire what
all the commotion was about. They'd heard the helicopter
buzz the house. I explained all I'd seen and told them I
could kick myself for not running out a few seconds earlier,
so Bill could have seen that ball of light. Then I grinned.

"I would not be surprised if a couple military-type characters knocked on our door tomorrow. I wouldn't be one bit
surprised if they said, 'You didn't *see* anything last night, did
you.'"

They shook their heads in understanding.

I then said that if any military appeared, that I'd respond
with, "Last night? You mean that Flight For Life helicopter
that went by?" Because if I said I saw a military helicopter
chasing two UFOs, this journal would never see publication
. . .and that's a fact.

The reason we're probably the only people in the neighborhood to witness the event is because our A-frame was
once the ski lodge, and it sits atop a semi-cleared hillcrest at
the highest point in the community. It sits in the middle of
11 acres while all the other homes are down the mountainsides in the trees. So when the three vehicles sped through
the air they nearly clipped our roof.

From the back of our house we look way down on Woodland Park which can be seen between the hills below us. In
front of us is Pikes Peak. I'm sure one of the helicopter
pilots saw me run out and watch, because it had just gotten
dark and the light from our opened front door would've
backlighted me real clear—probably Bill too.

What a great night! Though having UFOs around is nothing new to our normal nights and days around here, having
the military chase two of them was an exciting variation.
Now I was ready to double kick myself for not having my
camera at the ready. You can bet I do now!

10-12-91, Saturday

Didn't get to bed until after 3:00 A.M. and arose early this
morning to take a shower and get ready to attend the open
house at Aimee's fire station. We took Jenny and Sarah along

with us and, when we arrived, Aimee proudly gave us the grand tour.

First we were shown all the various training, conference, and communication rooms. When Aimee stood before her gear in the apparatus room (where the rigs are parked) she pulled her fire pants and boots down off the shelf above her name. The boots were already tucked inside the pantlegs and Sarah stepped inside them and pulled up the suspenders. She said it felt heavy and Aimee reminded her that she didn't even have the jacket on, or the helmet or the SCBA tank on her back. Sarah then groaned and stepped out of Aimee's boots.

We walked outside where all the rigs were parked in the sun and Jenny was eager to sit up in the seat of the largest one. She got a kick out of that. And when Sarah sat in the driver's seat, her dad embarrassed her by not letting her out until she pulled the horn rope above her head. Her fair complexion turned as red as the truck when everyone in the firehouse jumped and turned heads her way. Sarah needs to be a little more assertive and her dad has been known to help her along—whether she likes it or not.

Aimee was very thorough in taking us around. She showed us all the various equipment compartments on the fire trucks and then let Jenny wear the SCBA oxygen tank on her back. Jenny immediately leaned far forward to compensate for the weight of it. She thought it was funny, but couldn't imagine how her tiny sister could climb ladders with it on.

Smokey the Bear arrived and delighted the little kids. About that time Aimee had to leave for work, so we kissed her goodbye. We then dropped Sarah off at a friend's house in town, where she was planning on spending the day decorating their Sophomore Homecoming float. Jenny stayed with us while we picked up the mail and then she and I roamed a few stores. She was looking for whatever caught her eye and I, of course, was looking for books. I didn't find anything good. Still. . .I ended up with a great find from the grocery store —a beautifully-painted mallard duck planter with a pothos plant in it. Since Saturday morning is my one and only day away from the house, I can usually find a little something to bring back home with me.

I worked on two day's worth of mail while Bill went back to Woodland later to pick Sarah up and keep their hair appointments. By the time they returned, Jenny had supper ready and I'd only processed one day's mail, which is okay, because I still have tomorrow and Monday to finish it before we get another wave of letters.

I'd received a package in the mail today. It was a wonderful gift of braided sweetgrass from a medicine man in Canada. I placed it in my glass cabinet with the rest of my sacred objects.

This evening I sat in my reading chair and tried to stay with Fools Crow and his adventures, but my head kept bobbing. I'd only had a few hours sleep last night and the woodstove sounds lulled me into a deep state of cozy peacefulness. Although the television was on a few feet away from me, I'd learned to completely tune it out while I'm reading. This evening it didn't even keep me from dozing in my chair.

It was a quiet night—no military dog fights.

I've decided to leave out the recording of some of my frequent mystical journeys and experiences from this journal. Instead, I've been recording them separately and will include them in my last book, *Pinecones and Woodsmoke.* I can't say when that will be published, because that will depend on how many of my books we continue doing a year. However, tonight I'm going out into the dark and still woods to do a little magic for the benefit of my four-legged relations' protection. This date is a sad one, for it marks the opening of *The Hour of the Hunter.*

Two hours later —
I'd gathered my sacred objects into my medicine bundle and donned my ghost cape. Taking my owl wing bone off the shelf, I held it safely in my hand while quietly slipping from the house.
The forest was very black, but the sky above was clear with the flickers of a million candle flames. It reminded me of a great cathedral filled with the dancing flames on hundreds of votive candles. Oh yes, this, with the hushed silence of the woods, gave way to the high solemnness of a sacred ground, for this night I sought a very special place I'd found deep within the forest. There I would encounter many nature spirits and also join the physical presence of a sleeping elk herd. And, as anticipated, this did come to pass.
When I silently removed each object from my bundle, prayers were said over them. Setting each one in its proper place before me, the ceremony began. It took a long time.
Eventually the mountain lion made his powerful aura felt and, above me in the bare aspen, the owl perched to softly hoot beneath her breath—as if in reverent whispered prayer.

Together, the cougar, owl, and I, joined our spirits' essence in bringing forth the spirit helpers who would manifest a living circle of protection for the majestic four-leggeds who were represented before us.

When I finished uttering the final words, I sat and watched over the small elk herd. So beautiful they were—so magnificent. Their innocence was as a light in the darkness. And I was so moved by their gentle nature, through mist-filled eyes I wished I could physically follow them wherever they went and be their personal protector. The horrid thought that any one of these beauties could be shot rent my heart asunder.

After I had carefully replaced the objects back into my bundle, I held the owl wing bone and stood. I whispered a final farewell to the sleeping ones and, while walking back through the forest, heard the comforting wing beats of my special companion as she followed me. Behind me, the undergrowth crunched. Cougar, too, accompanied me home. Truly, the night mountain woods was home, for nowhere else did I feel so completely comfortable and protected. . .nowhere did I have so many beautiful and powerful companions. Nowhere.

10-13-91, Sunday

I worked on the mail most of the day while Bill spent his time on the phone counseling several people. These sessions of his can run as long as two hours per person.

Between his calls, Michael from Windows of Light bookstore called to inform us that Sarah had not located a copy of *Dreamwalker* by Whitford Press. He and Bill talked for a bit about my next book—this journal.

Then Bill called one of my favorite places in Manitou Springs—Valhalla, which carries some wonderful native items in addition to my books. Bill asked Joe if he had any Whitford Press copies of *Dreamwalker*, but Joe didn't.

After a couple more calls, he located one that our Ohio friend has, and she's going to mail it to us so we, in turn, can send it to our attorney with the other three titles.

Jenny and Sarah spent three hours in the woods this afternoon. When they returned, Jenny showed me her great nature finds. She had some particularly pretty white quartz stones and feathery fern leaves.

The evening was uneventful, which is a rarity around here, and I spent it reading.

Tonight my Prayer Smoke will rise for all my readers.

10-14-91, Monday

While Bill and the girls were in town taking care of errands and keeping their chiropractic appointment (they go in one room as family. . .but not me, because *nobody* fools with *my* bones), I worked at my desk finishing up the remainder of our mail. I had just sat down in my reading chair when they returned. Bill wanted the two of us to go down to Manitou Springs to the Valhalla shop.

"I forgot we need to replace the Whitford *Dreamwalker* copy that Kristi's sending us. It wouldn't be fair to make her buy another one."

"You go. I don't feel like going out of the house today."

"Oh com'on, you know how you love that place."

"That's just the problem, I see too many goodies there."

"Please come with me," he said, on bended knee.

"You ham." So I tried to make myself presentable and we left for Valhalla.

When we got there, Joe wasn't in. Instead, his lovely wife, Monika was. She's only been in this country for nine months and this was her first day alone in the shop. Her heavy German accent was enduring and she was surprised to see Summer Rain and Bill walk in. She said her Joe would be so disappointed that he'd missed us, because he'd wanted to meet us for a very long time. He was good friends with Carole Bourdo and carried much of her artwork in his shop.

Monika called Joe and Bill talked to him. It was okay to exchange two of his *Dreamwalker* copies for the one *Daybreak* we brought with us. Then Joe talked with me for a while.

When I hung up, I asked Monika what that beautiful Indian music was that she had playing. She said, "Following the Circle."

"That's one of Dik Darnell's," I said. "Someone sent me a copy of it but I accidentally erased it." Then I told her that I was not technically inclined, and that me and machines didn't get along at all.

Monika pulled a new tape from their display and said, "this is for you."

I was floored. And when she said she couldn't read my books, because they were English I was delighted.

"I have German language copies at home. I'll bring them to you."

My intent wasn't quite clear to her.

"You mean gift them to me?"

"Oh yes! I'll sign them to you as a return gift for the tape you gave me."

She couldn't hide her joy.

Then I told her I'd sign any of my books that she had in the store. She had two of each, but none of *Earthway*. I signed them while she disappeared into the back room.

My mouth dropped when she reappeared with about 30 more books!

Evidently Joe has good sales with No-Eyes' books. We'd noticed that *Daybreak* was the only book displayed among the native items in the front shop window. Shop owners like these are truly appreciated.

After our business was concluded, I browsed around the shop. Bill wanted to buy me some anniversary presents.

I picked out a buffalo jaw with rawhide and native beads hanging from it, a 14-inch woodland mother troll holding a baby, and a deer spirit medicine stick (for when I go into the woods to pray for the deer and elk's protection). Oh. . .the things I saw in that shop! I wanted the walking stick with the antler top. . .and the wide-eyed native baby in the elaborately decorated cradleboard. . .and the beautifully painted and beaded buffalo skull. . .and the heavily decorated medicine rattle. . .

What marvelous things Joe and Monika have at Valhalla! But what Bill bought me was far more than I deserved and I was so tickled with his gifts.

On our way back up the pass we decided to return there tomorrow to drop off the three German copies for Monika. Joe will be there then and we'd like to finally meet him.

When we returned home, our wood delivery was piled in the garage. The whole family joined in the task of stacking it in the shop. This house has a monstrous woodstove that takes tree trunks and won't completely shut down. The heat in the chimney vent gets so hot it warps and melts the two dampers Bill has to keep replacing. The massive stone fireplace opening is so big, three or four people could lay down in it. Of course it's all bricked in now, but the draw on that massive flu is incredible. During the cold weather the stove eats a cord of wood a month. And at one hundred dollars a cord, our heating expenses really rise. Bill thinks we should replace the wood eater with a used Fisher stove, because then we could regulate the air and shut the thing down if we wanted. He's probably right. We had a Baby Fisher in our kitchen on Chester Street and that little thing held banked coals all night long. Well, we'll have to see how the budget goes.

Tonight my Prayertime will be for Bill's continued protection and health. I don't know what I'd do without him. . .I'd be lost. . .truly lost. He's so good to me.

10-15-91, Tuesday

Before I made my appearance in the office this morning, Bill had already talked with Frank DeMarco at Hampton Roads. Bill asked him if he'd seen the *Soul Sounds* transparency. Frank said that he had and that he liked it except for the tears. Tears is what it's all about. I guess he didn't realize that. His response sure burst my bubble. I'm guilty of expectation when I was anticipating people sharing my excitement and love for the cover. I should know better by now, because every time I do that, I get disappointed.

Bill, Jenny, and I headed down to Valhalla around 10 o'clock. Joe and Monika were happy to see us and Joe ushered us upstairs to show us the work they've been doing to convert the vacant living quarters into their future gallery. I could easily visualize what it's going to look like when it's all finished, and it will really be a wonderful addition to their shop.

When we went back downstairs, I gave the three German books to Monika. She was so pleased to have them. As Bill conversed with the two owners, Jenny and I began to mosey about the shop. I spied a native wing fan, but couldn't afford it. Then my eyes rested on a perfect beaver skull and I was very attracted to it. That one I could afford, so I picked it up and placed it on the counter. When Bill went to pay for it, Joe took a one-dollar bill from Bill's hand and said, "sold." We tried arguing with Joe but he'd have none of it.

"Well," Bill smiled, "with Mary's birthday in December and then Christmas, we'll make up for it in your shop, there's at least a dozen things that've caught her eye."

And we all laughed at that, because we knew it was true. Come Christmastime, he and I would be back in Manitou again.

We visited with Joe and Monika for a couple hours and then picked up our mail once we returned to Woodland. Because of the "unmentionable" holiday yesterday, our mail was heavy and I got right on it when we got home.

There were seven book orders that I processed first for Bill so he could record them. A few readers had detailed dreams for me to interpret (which I don't do), and the rest were general except for three.

One of these was a horrid eight-page Summer Rain basher. This correspondent had so many hateful complaints about me her pen was swung like an axe. By the time she was through, there wasn't an inch of my skin left that wasn't in ribbons.

This woman said if I wanted to know the truth I needed to read Lynn Andrews, because my books were comic books compared to hers. She said that I was a big egotist who was trying to teach those who knew more then me. And I knew absolutely nothing about native ways (she was white).

Well, I could handle all that, but she trampled upon my heart when she said that I made fun of an old blind woman.

Make fun of my No-Eyes? Me? When?

I don't know. I just don't know what motivates people to be so downright *mean* to another—especially one who says people come from all over her state to hear her spiritual advice. This woman also sent me brochures from an organization that teaches the "truth," but charges from $200 up to $6,000 for their enlightenment. Where is this woman's head? What's *really* eating away at her? How can such utter cruelty come from the lips (pen) of someone who's also supposed to be teaching spirituality to others? This is definitely someone in possession of two distinct faces here. She speaks with a split tongue. I would cut my own tongue out before saying the things she said to me to anyone else.

When Bill read the letter he immediately knew that this woman "charges" for her "truths." He was the one who wrote back a response to her.

People like that are scary, because their intense hatred makes them seem more than a little insane.

The last two letters I opened put good medicine on my open wounds.

One was a letter that was short and to the point. The heartfelt sentiments penned by Ron and Betty brought tears to my eyes. The beautiful things they said pieced my heart back together and made me whole again. And I taped their letter above my desk to refer to whenever the mean ones came in again.

The second application of good medicine came from a native man who was an AIM member. He sent me a long Prayer Tie. His words of appreciation soothed my injured soul. How interesting it is that not a single cruel and hurtful letter has come from Natives.

Although the last two letters I opened served to heal me, still there seemed to be a powerful thunderstorm raging in my heart. Although it was made whole again, I felt the raining torrents falling unrelentingly.

I sat for a long while at my desk. I was just sitting, thinking strange new thoughts of an unusual vision that entered my mind of me taking off and walking across the Arizona desert toward a mesa. The emotion that accompanied this vision was one of peace.

This setting is out of character for my usual deep woods preference. Was this sudden vision brought on by a subconscious desire to escape and walk far away from the mean people? Was it a symbolic representation of walking toward a place of true peace? All I know is that it came of its own volition. It felt like I was walking home. I left my desk and went outside. Today I'd worn my long skirt and knee moccasins again and I took to the deep woods behind our house. I needed nature. I needed to walk the softness of Earth Mother's breast and feel her pure spirit through my soft soles. I walked for a long time; sometimes thinking, sometimes just absorbing her incredible healing essence. And I found myself hurting inside for the absence of No-Eyes' physical presence. She would have the words I needed to hear. And I began to cry, but immediately took a deep breath and forced back the tears.

In the worst way I wanted to drum. I wanted to sit alone out there and drum and chant until I was no longer in the woods, but somewhere far away in another world. This I could do with abandon in my special place that was in the deep near-virgin woods outside the perimeters of the community, but here, neighbors were too close and I couldn't have that sacred aloneness I needed for one of my magic Drumming Journeys.

When I returned home, I sat for a long while in the warming sun that bathed our front deck. My thoughts then were to disconnect our phone, close our P.O. Box and leave no forwarding address. . .and move away to some faraway state, like the coast of Maine. This was not to escape, but to take radical measures to find a small measure of peace. The cruel and hurtful letters act like I've set myself up as some anointed guru or high shamaness. Don't they *read* what they read? Are their hearts so hardened that they can't *feel* mine? Have their spirits no way to pierce through their conscious shell? How is it that I, a simple mountain woman, present such a threat to people? Why am I called so many horrid names? How can I possibly hurt anyone when my nature is that of a newborn fawn—shy, quiet and gentle?

These thoughts and personal questions wove through my mind as I sat in the warm autumn sunshine. The solemn pensive mood was stirred only by the soothing kiss of Wind Spirit's breath upon my cheek. It lifted the strands of my hair as if to gently stroke my head in comfort. This I did notice. This I gave thanks for.

I'm going out in the woods now. It's 1:00 A.M. and the Wind Spirit is calling my name. I can hear it through the pines. I can hear the dry aspen leaves blowing around upon the ground. The moon appears to have half waned and it is a beautifully clear night. I will wear my warm Deer Spirit Robe, take my Deer Spirit Stick and join the four-leggeds, for they speak no cruel words—only welcoming ones.

10-16-91, Wednesday

Autumn Spirit gifted us with a perfect Blue Day for our anniversary. Not a wisp of cloud was seen in the sky of cobalt blue and I knew there would be no way four walls would confine me this day.

By the time I came downstairs, everyone had left for town and, while I typed up last night's journal entry, I took several business calls that came in for Bill. When he and Jenny returned, I was ordered into the kitchen until I was called back to the office.

Bill came and held my hand.

"Close your eyes until I tell you to open them," he said, leading me over to my desk. He sat me down and then pressed the PLAY button on my tape player. *Unchained Melody* began to play and I was told to open my eyes. Before me was a beautiful bouquet of purple flowers and a box of candy with his card. Tears streamed down my face and we hugged for a long while.

Jenny then gave us two red rose buds with her card and Robin had left us a flower arrangement. Aimee had gifted us with a miniature rose plant. Our 26th anniversary was perfect in every way.

Shortly after the gifts were given, we got down to business—or so I thought. Bill shooed me outside so I could enjoy the day without reading any nastygrams or having to be confined in the office. He wouldn't take no for an answer and, while he took the mail over to his desk and began making his first return call to David at Ingram, I left him to do what he does best and went outside where I spent the afternoon picking dried flowers and seed pod weeds.

Twice while I was sitting on the deck playing my native

flute for my feathered relations who were feeding there, Bill came out to tell me good news from his calls.

David at Ingram informed him that they'd continue stocking my first four books at their Denver warehouse and also, he was going to make sure all their other outlets around the country stocked them. That was definitely great news to hear. (However, he called back later and informed us that he'd made a mistake, that Ingram does not and will not carry any of my first four books because of a disagreement with Schiffer.)

The second time Bill came out was to tell me of a "discovery" he'd made. He found out that Schiffer upped the price of *Dreamwalker* back when a reprint was done, but my royalties had been based on the old (lower) cover price. He'd been talking with the Walsworth bookkeeper who, by the way, has been very open and straightforward with Bill. The accountant admitted what a headache this was becoming, because now he had to go back and recompute the royalty figures all over again. We were never told that Schiffer increased the book price and, evidently neither was Walsworth's accountant. Was it a fluke that Bill uncovered it today? I think not. At any rate, he placed a call to our attorney because this incident constitutes another valuable piece of solid evidence against the defendants. As more time passes, more and more nails are added to the coffin. You'd think those publishers would want to settle "yesterday" before any more discoveries are uncovered against them. Yeah, Bill! What a clever agent you are!

After I came back in the house around four o'clock, Bill showed me a cute letter from Emese, an eight-year-old young lady. It was so sweet. She'd also sent me a photograph of herself and I tacked it up on my wall beside my other readers' kids' pictures. Later in the evening, I sat down and wrote Emese back.

Just before supper, the UPS man brought me a package from someone I hadn't heard from before. Inside was a beautiful lotus light. It was very unique and I hadn't seen anything like it before. The woman it was from said it represented the "light" I bring to people. How nice that was. It really touched me. I placed the lotus light on a corner shelf of our breakfront in the living room and, in the evening, it gave off a beautifully warm glow.

At suppertime, Jenny had to refrigerate Bill's anniversary meal. A client called at 4:30, and he wasn't off the phone until almost seven o'clock. He gives people everything he's got. I'd wanted to take a walk with him after supper while it was still light out, but when he hung up the phone, the moon was up. I was a little irritated.

"Did this person know it was our anniversary?" I asked.

"Yes, but I told him it was okay."

"Well, did he know you missed your dinner?"

"No, I wouldn't tell somebody that. Besides, we got a lot accomplished and that makes me feel real good. We really needed to get some things cleared up."

"I was going to surprise you with my gift while it was still light out. I was going to take you to my special place in the forest."

"Oh honey, can't we still go?"

"It's dark out now. There's only a half moon and you've had nothing to eat."

"So? I'll eat later. Com'on, you can still show me where you go at night."

He slipped a jacket on and I donned my serape. We walked down the dirt road. Hand in hand, we talked in lowered voices. He commented that this had been a great anniversary for him, because he'd felt good about all he'd accomplished today, and also because the weather was so beautiful.

Many of our previous anniversary dates had involved going out to dinner in cold and snowy nights. We'd agreed to be home-bodies this year and we were both glad we did.

"Hey," he said, "how much farther is this place of yours?"

"Oh. . .a bit," I smiled, leading him off the road to enter the semi-lit forest.

"I had no idea you went so far at night. Can't you do your thing closer to home? Like maybe in the woods behind the house?"

"Nope," I said, looking around.

"What're you looking for?"

"I was hoping cougar would join us. You remember what I told you about him."

"Yeah, but that's okay. He can skip tonight."

"He will."

"How do you know?"

"Because you don't want him here."

We traipsed through dense woods and Bill was concerned as he glanced around.

"I don't think it's a great idea for you to go so far away at night. . .not alone."

"Nothing will happen to me, don't worry."

"How can you be so sure?"

I stopped in my tracks and glanced into the silver-dappled wood. Pines were swaying. Leaves blew across the ground. Rustling sounds were heard from here and there.

"I'm sure, because the Unseen Ones watch. The spirits always walk with me. I'm never alone."

He scanned the forest.

I smiled. "We're almost there. This is so good, isn't it? You're the only person I've brought here. I hope you know this is a very special present." And we reached the moonlit clearing surrounded by high swaying pines and a stand of bare aspen.

I knew he felt the power of it as he slowly panned the perimeter of my special forest.

Within the circlet of moonlight, I slipped off my serape and spread it out like a blanket over a bed of leaves. I sat on it.

"Come lie with me. Now I want to give you my anniversary gift."

It was a gift from me that had no Giver—no Taker. It was a gift that was equally shared.

And so the moonlight fell full upon us to bless our union while the Spirit of Autumn smiled with her own gift of a perfect Fall night. . .one made for two who were lovers. . . still.

Much later when we returned home and he took his jacket off, I grinned at him and pointed to his shirt.

It was hanging out. He smiled and tucked it in.

About an hour later, *he* grinned and called me over to him. "Seems you're looking a little like your new woodland troll doll," he whispered while pulling a twig from the back of my hair.

Embarrassed, I looked over at the girls who were watching television. They hadn't seen Bill pick out the tell-tale twig. But had they noticed it in my hair? Well, no matter, they're well aware of the amorous mischief their mom and dad get into. They're certainly used to it by now, because, with so many people in the house, it's been pretty hard to hide those impromptu "frisky" moments of ours.

10-17-91, Thursday

Bill and I went to town to intercept our UPS man in the McDonald's parking lot. We wanted to pick up our *Dreamwalker* copy from him so we could prepare and send our material to our attorney FedEx overnight. If we waited for the regular UPS delivery to our house, it'd come too late in the afternoon and we'd miss the time for the FedEx pickup.

Leaving McDonalds with our package, we headed out to

the Fossil Inn for breakfast. It'd been a long time since we'd gone out there but the waitress still remembered our special orders. It was nice getting out for a few hours.

From the restaurant we headed back into Woodland to pick up our mail—which was quite a large stack—and once home again, we got busy on preparing the attorney's requested material. We'd been concentrating so much on gathering up Whitford copies that we'd forgotten he also wanted to have all book reviews and publicity articles for my first four books.

It took me a long time to photocopy all the articles and write-ups from my files and, by the time we were finished, Bill got to the FedEx dropbox with only 20 minutes to spare.

Since it was another treasured Blue Day, completely cloudless and warm, I again spent the late afternoon playing my flute on the deck. Actually, I only had about an hour and a half available to me, but still it felt wonderful to be out in that warm autumn afternoon sunshine. I can feel the impatience of Cold Maker. He's anxious to make his entry and hold center stage, so with every Blue Day I'm gifted, I feel I'm being rude not to at least spend an hour outside in receivership of the gift.

While I was outside, Bill began to process the mail. He told me we'd received a letter from a woman who wanted to contribute food to Wellspring. He also raised his brows and informed me that another correspondent wanted her name taken off our mailing list, because I didn't tell her which publisher to send her manuscript to. This lady was outraged to receive our Wellspring information letter. Oh well. You're damned if you do and you're damned if you don't. I'm beginning to think that trying to keep the door open for reader correspondence while being involved in our new mission is a "no win" situation for us. Even though either Bill or I try to include handwritten responses to people's questions at the bottom of our information letter, it doesn't seem to be enough for people. When our very best efforts fail, that tells us that we're knocking ourselves out for nothing. Sometimes we're back in the office after supper and we don't close up our desks until 10:30 when all the day's mail has been responded to.

Tonight my Prayertime will have to be postponed. I'm very tired. I'm going to go to bed on time tonight and fall sleep listening to Bill's heartbeats.

10-18-91, Friday

A Blue Day greeted me again this morning and the air held a hint of Frost Maker's chilly breath.

While Bill took Jenny grocery shopping, I responded to yesterday's mail that Bill logged in but never answered due to the late hour.

Link called. She's got another shipment of goods which she's going to deliver to the house tomorrow. She's become a good friend and we're always glad to see her—whether she has a supply or not. The last time she was here, I was making potpourri and orange 'n' clove pomanders. She said she went home and made some too. Tomorrow she's bringing me some lemon verbena leaves from her plants. She tells me they make fragrant ingredients to add to potpourri mixes. I'll try them in my special blend.

Our attorney called this afternoon and told Bill we'd sent him a great package. He was also pleased to receive the *Dreamwalker* price increase discovery that Bill uncovered. The two talked for a while about the case. We're looking forward to the 25th, when the defendant's attorneys respond again.

In the mail today our children's book orders broke a record—12 books were requested and sent out. I'm still concerned about having enough funds to cover our January IRS payment if we do a reprint before then, yet I've the feeling we'll go ahead with one anyway and hope for the best.

Also in the mail was a pouch of tobacco from a native elder in South Dakota. What a heart-warming message that sent me. Tobacco is a native gift that symbolizes deep respect for another, and I was deeply touched by his sentiments.

All the other letters were good ones. There wasn't a mean one in the bunch. *That* was a welcomed breather!

We also received the Roaring Fork Area Home Magazine we sent for. There were about six homes for sale in Redstone and I pined for the timing to hurry up. I want a Redstone address to give my readers before this journal ends on December 31st. But I also know that's a slim probability. It's not impossible, just not probable. I so much want to go buy one of those Redstone properties on the Crystal River, but yes, I know . . .*acceptance* is the operative word I must live by. Sometimes that can be a dirty word that one would prefer to avoid. Yes?

This evening I began a new book entitled *Mountains of the Moon* by William Harrison. It takes place in 1854 and details John Hanning Speke's and Sir Richard Burton's journey to discover the source of the Nile. It's interesting to learn how expeditions of this kind are riddled with politics and ego.

Bill had a lengthy telephone conversation with Beverly Ford, who owns the Spiral Circle bookstore in Orlando, Florida. They talked of many aspects of our work. Beverly was surprised to find out that the public could purchase prints of my bookcover artwork from Carole Bourdo. I'm going to have to be sure to spell that out at the back of my books. Also Beverly asked Bill if Carole had greeting cards available. He was pleased to say that she had beautiful ones that came in boxes. I hope she'll eventually have cards with my book cover art on them—not, because they're *my* book art, but, because that artwork is so beautiful.

Beverly also spoke to Bill about our children's book and he told her we'd send her a sample copy with order forms for her customers. That's such a tremendous help to us when store owners do that.

Sarah just returned from her Homecoming football game— they lost, but she still had a great time. Last night she went to the big bonfire and had a lot of fun.

She brought home her art project from school this afternoon, because she needs to work on it over the weekend. So far it's beautiful. It's a large poster-sized work of a native elder which will look just like the original photograph when she's finished. I'm planning on framing it with our rustic homemade woodwork when she's done; of course she doesn't know that yet. She's got real potential as an artist, I just wish she had a real artist to apprentice with. . .everyone's seeking a teacher, aren't they.

Aimee came home with the bad news that City Market is cutting down for the winter season. The cashiers are the first to be laid off, because they make the most (Aimee makes over eight dollars an hour). Yet it really bothers me that the store manager hired in a friend and then began cutting the cashier's hours. That doesn't make sense. She's been bumped down to part-time and some days she's scheduled for as little as four hours. Tim, who does the scheduling, told Aimee that she just might find herself scheduled to work the nights she has her EMT classes. Why are these bozos being so vindictive toward her about the medical training she's trying to get? City Market's like a real-life Peyton Place soap opera.

Anyway, this cut is not good. But at least she'll have more time to study her EMT textbooks, and go on runs with the Woodland Park Ambulance Service. They'd accepted her written request to go along as Third Rider on their calls. So maybe this cut in her hours has a bright side after all.

I also forgot to mention in Tuesday's entry that Aimee had arranged to go down to Penrose Hospital in Colorado Springs. Since she's a firefighter and also a First Responder for rescue calls, she wanted to see the Penrose Burn Unit.

During her day there, her mentor told her there were quite a few job openings at the hospital for someone with Aimee's experience. She said that most jobs that Aimee could apply for would require the Nurses Aide Course. Aimee immediately wanted to take it, but I helped her to see the logic of concentrating on finishing up her EMT first. She wants to work in a hospital. That's her ultimate goal. Bill and I told her to finish up the EMT which ends in January, then, if we don't have a replacement four-wheel vehicle for the pickup (which she uses daily), we'll let her use the van to commute down the pass to her Nurses Aide Course and, if hired, a job.

She's so anxious to work in a hospital, she wants to do it all at once, but I told her a medical student can't operate until he goes through all the steps in becoming a surgeon. She *sees* the goal. She *wants* the goal and. . *forget* all the middle! Oh, how I can relate to that! I kidded her about it.

"How'd you like to know your goal was a mountain cabin and then had to wait over 14 years for it?"

"I'd go crazy. I'd never last." And that answer pretty well depicts Aimee's inherent hyper-energy that's still very much a part of her. She's a real go-getter and if anything gets between her and her goal she's going to run right over it. She'd *force* things. . . or at least try to. We give her encouragement and a lot of credit for knowing what she wants to do. She's only 19 and her purpose is so clear to her.

She'll obtain her goal, because that's just the kind of person she is. She's got my fighter—warrior—instincts. With her inner power, she'd make a formidable psychic opponent. Her mind power, when centered, is incredible—just incredible—and I have to help guide it whenever she's overly upset or angry at someone. Her psychic creative capacity is something to be reckoned with, but she also has equal control of it.

Lately, she tells me that her visions now come when her eyes are open. This is an indication of ability advancement. She explained to me that, when the vision occurs, her being is actually *in* it and she has complete understanding of its meaning. But a millisecond later when the vision vanishes and she's back into herself, she often loses the comprehension. I explained that that was normal until she developed more. I likened it to dream recall—sometimes they could be remembered and other times they couldn't, but with diligent practice and longer experience time with them, the recall ability naturally strengthens.

While I was writing about Sarah's art project a few minutes ago I had a chilling sensation of deja vu. We moved before she could finish a big art project in school. It can't mean this present one —that's obvious—so we'll have to see if we actually do move during the school year and, if so, will she be in the middle of an important art work?

I'm extremely energized tonight. I'm going out into the woods to do a Smoke Journey after I offer my prayers for Maxine (a correspondent today who I feel drawn to pray for).

Goodnight Grandfather. Thank you for the tobacco. You have honored me in a most sacred manner.

10-19-91, Saturday

By the time Link arrived with our shipment Bill and I had finished processing the mail. Jenny and Sarah helped unload and I was glad to see fresh fruit and vegetables again. Our recipients' eyes light up when they see those. Other boxes contained canned goods such as tuna, vegetables, and chili. And there were the dry items like unbleached flour, powdered milk, cereal, oatmeal, and several varieties of pasta.

We left the boxes stacked in the office while Bill and Link went for a walk and I busied myself in the kitchen helping Jenny prepare dinner. We were going to grill the salmon that Carole Bourdo's daughter caught in Alaska. Jenny wasn't sure how to cook it, and she needed some assistance. We'd been given slabs of salmon that I had to cut into steak-sized pieces.

We were glad Link stayed for dinner. Usually she only stays until four o'clock, but we were enjoying each others' company so much she didn't leave our house until almost nine.

Our conversations covered many subjects and she told us about her Starborn experiences. We then relayed the one we'd had several night's ago involving the UFO chase. Although we discussed these incidents freely, I didn't mention the close relationship I had with my "friend." Eventually we talked about our mutually chosen relocation area and I commented that the Starborn ones were very active over there. She seemed to know that already.

We enjoyed having Link spend the day with us and the more time we spend together the deeper and clearer our connection becomes. When I showed her the Redstone sale properties in the Home Guide she tried to talk Bill into "going for it"—now. He laughed and said that we were ganging up on him. Well, can't blame us for trying.

The vision came again today. It came while Link was talking about her visit to a kiva on Old Oraibi. This time I was walking toward the mesa in the light of a full moon. I was carrying something in my arms but couldn't tell what it was. The visual flash was gone before I could glean more information from it. The one strong impression I did receive was that I'd been walking across the desert for a long time and was finally nearing my destination.

I don't know what this new vision means yet. Perhaps its meaning is being kept from me until the right time arrives for it to be known. Sometimes that's the way of them and I accept that. It is very strange though. My walking alone across the treeless landscape is a foreign scene for me to imagine myself in, yet twice it has presented itself to me. So clear it comes. So distinct. So solid and sure.

My Prayer Smoke will rise this night for all those dwelling on reservations. . .everyone. My prayer will be for *their* prayers to be answered.

10-20-91, Sunday

After a leisurely breakfast at the Fossil Inn, Bill and I drove into Woodland to take care of a few errands. While in town, we checked the mail and there was a package for me from Silvereagle. I opened it as soon as we returned home. He'd sent me some home-grown tobacco. It smelled wonderful. What a sweet brother he is.

I spent the day dividing up our Wellspring Mission shipment from Link. We ended up with 12 boxes of food for Bill to distribute tomorrow morning.

The rest of the day was devoted to making up another batch of potpourri. Link had given me much more than the lemon verbena she initially told me about. Her gift of fra-

grant plant cuttings also included lemon balm, rose-lemon ger-
anium, pineapple sage, French lavender, and lavender cotton.

First I spread pine wood shavings out on three cookie
sheets and soaked them with orange juice from fresh oranges.
I dried these in the oven so the orange scent was absorbed
by the wood. These then went into a large mixing bowl
where they were blended with nutmeg and cinnamon.

Next I dried all the plant cuttings from Link and tossed
those in with the shavings.

After slicing apple rings and drying those, they too went
into the mixture (at least whatever was left after my girls
were through grabbing and eating them warm off the cookie
sheets).

By then it was 9:30, and I'd run out of time to dry the
orange and lemon rinds. That will have to be done sometime
during the week when I can sneak out of the office. Even so,
already the blend has a great fragrance.

Sarah worked on her native face art piece all day. She
sequestered herself in the office and was bent over my drafting table for hours on end.

Aimee was home from work today and finally caught up
on some much-needed sleep. After dinner, she studied her
anatomy books.

Jenny had a leisure day, except when tensions arose during
the Bronco game—we won.

Around seven Sarah asked me to go outside with her, because there was something she wanted to show me in the
woods. She had Aimee's stethoscope in her hand and I knew
what we were going to do. We were out in the dark for 40
minutes listening to. . .trees. What fun! We could actually
hear the blood-flow (sap), and each species of tree made a
distinctive sound that distinguished it from others. I told her
we'll be able to get louder and more active soundings in the
spring, because the aspens were real slow right now.

After we came back inside, Aimee had Sarah lay on the
floor so she could feel and name all Sarah's bones. Magic
wasn't sure what Aimee was doing to Sarah, because the
patient kept laughing each time she was touched. Finally we
had to put Magic outside to stop her from barking at the two
on the floor.

Around nine o'clock, Bill called me in the office where
he'd been working at his desk. He had pieces of papers with
figuring on them all over. He'd been making calculations to
determine if it was feasible to do another reprint of the chil-

dren's book. He had computed costs of production, mailing supplies, postage, what we had in savings, and the projected IRS bill for January.

The rate of incoming orders had tripled in the last two months and our in-house stock was down to less than 200. We decided to get a reprint of 500 done as soon as possible. We wanted to do a printing of 1,000, but didn't have the money for that many books. Bill's going to call his contact person at C & M Press tomorrow morning to reconfirm their last estimate and make sure all they need from us is the jacket negative and two books to produce the text from. When that's taken care of, we'll send out the material and get this thing into production again.

I stayed up late reading. Now I'm going out for a walk in the woods. It's 2:30 A.M. Lately I've been feeling as though I'm more a part of the forest than a house with walls. When I'm out at night I feel like an extension of the woods. . . there's a deep inner and warm sense of belonging felt. It's a comforting familiarity—like coming *home* after being away for a long, long while.

10-21-91, Monday

This was a heavy counseling day for Bill so I processed all the mail. He'd brought it back later than usual, because he'd made the food deliveries first.

In the mail was my natal chart and explanatory tape from Jyoti Walsh. There were a few unusual aspects revealed on it but what I found interesting—amusing—was the fact that I had no earth element aspects at all. . .anywhere. That fit, I commented to Bill. It fit right in, because I'm really not of the earth, meaning that that specific element is no longer an aspect of my true beingness. And, interestingly enough, that's precisely why I have such difficulty accepting that beingness as part of the earthly civilization. The spirit essence of nature and those dwelling on the finer dimensions (such as nature spirits and helpers) are far more comfortable to me than what I see of the earth peoples' violent and egocentric natures. I can't help this attitude, for it's an inherent perception generated from long experiential spans within the finest dimension and highest vibrational level. I would like to write more of this explanation but this journal is not the place for it. Perhaps January's entry will be the proper time and place for it to appear.

We received a UPS delivery. A friend sent us six rolls of paper for our fax machine. What an incredibly thoughtful gift that was.

Bill received a fax from our friend in Denver. It was a full page ad from Sunday's *Denver Post*. Big money was put behind big headlines about *The Rapture* coming in October of 1992. Bill put the fax on my desk. I took one look at it and told him (nicely) to get that sheet off my desk!

He obliged, but not without comment.

"We'd better hurry up and get our land, because we only have 12 months left to enjoy it."

I gave him one of my *"can* it" looks.

"Oops. Sorry," he grinned. "But look! If we send to this organization we can find out how to be *saved* next October!"

"You had to rub it in, didn't you."

"Yeah, I couldn't resist. The words, they just came out all on their own."

"I noticed they have a way of doing that sometimes. You really ought to teach them a little discipline."

"Nah," he shrugged, "they like to see you get riled. Do you know how cute you look when you get riled up?"

I rolled my eyes. "Go back to your desk, Bill. I think you need to pick up the phone."

He frowned. . .just as the phone rang. He hated it when I did that.

The evening was uneventful and, after everyone was in bed, I read until Aimee came home at 11 o'clock. We talked for an hour and a half. It was good. She'd come to understand some very complex psychological mechanisms various people were using on her and, ultimately, themselves too. She's disgusted to finally see that so many people play mind games. She correctly perceived those as an incredible waste of time and energy. And she was right.

I'm not going outside tonight. My Prayertime will be spent in the candlelight of the living room. It's 1:15 A.M. and I will whisper words of gratitude for Aimee's new inner sight. I'm so sorry she hasn't yet found a meaningful relationship that hasn't involved mind games. But she will. . .she will.

10-22-91, Tuesday

My eyes opened this morning and were drawn to the window where a skeletal aspen was starkly silhouetted against the brilliant backdrop of another perfect Blue Day.

I awoke from a dream of No-Eyes and a tear fell from the corner of my eye. It disappeared into the pillowcase as I laid watching the aspen bones sway before the sweet breath of Autumn's gentle spirit.

"I miss you, No-Eyes," I whispered as another tear slipped from my eye. "Oh God. . .how I miss you."

I tossed back the quilt and padded over to the deck doors to draw open the curtains. Yes, the sky was again an endless sea of blue that one could so easily dive through fathom after fathom. It was a magnetic deep. It was Merlin's magical mirror where visions were reflected. It was a great and wondrous gift.

A mountain chickadee landed on the deck railing. My eyes met his and he cocked his head at me as if to say, "Don't be sad, all of nature is happy today."

I smiled at my tiny winged relation and he flew away then to glide and dance with the Wind Spirit.

I was truly grateful for the magical Indian Summer days I'd been gifted with, and that renewed appreciation did swirl within me and encircle my heart like a healing mist.

I backed away from the glass doors and, with a lighter soul, began my day.

While I was showering, Bill came in to say that Carole was on the phone. The California company that makes tee shirts of her art wanted to do the *Daybreak* painting. Carole wanted to know how I felt about that. I said I thought it was a great idea and also wanted Bill to ask her if she was going to have greeting cards of the book cover art too. I thought that'd be great. He said he'd ask her and went back downstairs to the office to finish his conversation with her.

When I came down for coffee in the kitchen, I noticed a not-so nice odor. It was strongest in the furnace room off the kitchen where we keep our winter coats and boots. I knew that smell and told Bill that there was a dead mouse in the furnace room somewhere.

He and Jenny moved everything and searched it thoroughly. They found nothing. It must be under the floor or in the wall, but I wanted to be sure.

"Did you check all those boots?" I asked.

"Yes," he assured, "we checked the boots."

"Did you put your hand all the way in to the toes of them?"

"Yes. . .no bad omens there."

He said that, because, the morning of my gall bladder attack last November, he and I were going out for breakfast. It was a snowy day and when I slid my foot into my boot my toes hit something. . .a dead mouse. Kitty had chased it, injured it, and it had run into my boot to hide. . .to die. Because of what happened to me that evening, we later chuckled over it all starting out with the bad omen of the dead mouse in my boot.

I know there are omens and portents, but sometimes they come in doubles to cancel each other out.

An example of this is when Bill and I first drove up to this house to look it over before renting it. The first thing I took encouraging note of was the *blue* door. That told me the occupants of the house would be protected.

As we walked around the outside of the house and were standing in the back, I looked up and a psychic shiver rippled through me. Not two feet above my head was a dead blue jay. It had been strung from a tree branch with a wire through its head. It was grotesque, because it'd been done by human hands as a warning. It hadn't been done more than a couple of hours before we arrived.

Bill reverently took it down and removed the wire. He buried it while I silently said sacred words over it. We've since been advised who the murderer is. This person does not like coming into (or even near) us or our home. Whenever he can't avoid coming here, his eyes never meet mine. He knows. . .and he's afraid. We never told our girls that this man was the one who impaled the blue jay, but we didn't have to. Although they probably never made the actual connection, their psychic senses made them automatically recoil from this individual. They just didn't like his dark vibrations.

The first time Aimee met this man, after he left, her eyes shifted to mine and she shuddered.

"Oh, mom!" she grimaced.

"I know. I know," was all I said.

"Do you think he sensed the shield I put up?"

"Definitely. He definitely sensed *all* our shields."

This man now avoids us like the Black Plague. He does anything he can to get out of coming to this house. That pleases him. That pleases us. We have enough dark ones to deal with. We're just glad that this one knows and *feels* what he'd be up against. He's not quite a full-fledged warrior. The first day our eyes met, his got as wide as saucers and he stammered. He would never again look me in the eye.

I got on this issue by writing about omens and how they can actually cancel out each other when they're presented in multiples. The blue door canceled out the dead blue jay. Although, seeing that awful sign did send a shiver of subliminal trepidation through me at first. But I felt good about the house even after getting inside to examine it further and discovering all the hidden panel doors and cubby rooms between the walls and false roofs. Before we actually moved in, Bill and I did our routine Clearing and Blessing Way ceremony. When we began them, heavy and dark vibrations were felt. After we opened all the hidden doors and went from room to room, the house was as clear as an untouched crystal. And so has it remained ever since.

Sarah has an interesting way of describing our home's vibrations.

"Mom," she frequently says, "when I come home from school and walk through that front door I feel just like a warm blanket has been wrapped around me. . .it feels so calming to come here."

Amen.

In our mail today I received another Kitaro tape from Charlie, who has corresponded with me for a long while. We got on the subject of music when he'd asked me if I'd heard any music by Kitaro. I'd responded by telling him that I didn't get much time to browse around the stores for music I could write to and, when I did try a new tape I thought I might be able to work to (Yanni), it always ended up not being right, because it'd be wild or irritating to my spirit. For my work I required soft, soft music and it was hard to find.

Well, the next time I heard from Charlie he'd sent me a Kitaro tape. I loved it and he's since sent me five or six of them. The one he gifted me with today is beautiful and brought tears to my eyes. This probably happened because of the melancholy mood I'd awakened in, yet these tears were healing ones and I was very grateful for Charlie's sense of timing.

As I was processing the mail while listening to the tape with my earphones on, Aimee came up and tapped me on the shoulder. She'd received a fire call on her pager and had to leave. A brushfire was burning a mile from us. Four hours later she called to say the fire was out and that she was going to stay in town for her EMT class.

After finishing the mail, I went outside to absorb the wonderful sunny vibrations of autumn. I filled the birdfeeder, sprinkled bread pieces and nuts around the deck, and spread out the leavings from my apples when I'd made the potpourri mix.

Reclining in the lawn chair, I was halfway on my journey

into the sun when a psychic shock jolted me back. A black dog the size of a small bear was licking my face. What a sweet greeting it was. This dog was enormous, yet it was clear she was still a pup and wanted to play. And so we played and ran and laughed in the golden autumn sunshine.

Tonight my Prayer Smoke rises for Charlie. It will also carry whispered words for Michael with the blue eyes and beard who I heard from today.

10-23-91, Wednesday

I came down to the office this morning and found out that Bill had already talked to Bob Friedman at Hampton Roads.

"Get your coffee," Bill said to me, "then we have to talk about the journal's cover."

"Now what?"

"Just go get your coffee and bring it back to the office."

I did and he told me about the problem Bob saw with the artwork—no room at the top for title and it needed to wrap around to the back.

Bill had already talked to Carole about it and she, in turn, personally discussed it with Bob. Carole is going to get right on it, because she's going back on the road and will be gone until the middle of December. She called us back to inform us that she's going to fix it two ways and have two transparencies done so Bob can choose which will work best.

After all that was settled, I sighed and turned my chair to face Bill's desk.

"So. After all the problems I just heard about, did Bob tell you if he liked the artwork?"

"I'm sorry, yes, he liked it a lot."

"Good." And I turned on my typewriter to begin typing my journal entry. I also needed to type up a short piece I wrote last night for *Pinecones and Woodsmoke* entitled "Many Bones Watching." This was about a vision I had that taught me how to make Ghost Bones that were hung in trees and on Trail Marker Sticks throughout one's property. These Ghost Bones, when created in a sacred manner while saying the power words over them, contained spirit energy to watch over one's property and protect it. No-Eyes brings me native way teachings such as this. In this manner my higher ceremonial instructions are maintained and advanced. Sometimes she'll send the visions and other times she'll come to me in the physical when I take my owl wing bone with me into the woods. During these special times the large great horned owl manifests itself.

No-Eyes comes as one of my spirit totems; the other, she recently informed me, is the large mountain lion who comes as my male totem aspect to balance my instruction and to also provide protection for me while I'm out in the forest at night. Never had I realized how three-dimensional an animal totem spirit could be until my cougar started showing up. Now he is a very welcomed companion.

Neither did I realize how clear communication can be from a spirit totem. Of course this was due to my never having given the subject much thought before now. But a true animal totem is like communing with an animal who possesses incredible magic and speaks with a human tongue. This has been my experience with my cougar. I feel his presence beside me now whenever I walk alone among the shadows of the midnight woods.

What still amazes me somewhat is the fact that I never did a vision quest for the purpose of receiving a personal animal totem. I never gave the issue more than the surface thought of knowing these spirits were fact. I never even desired an animal totem for myself. Yet there he was one night . . .and every night thereafter—always my shadow—always my teacher and protector. And I feel truly blessed.

Bill, Jenny, and I took a trip down to King Sooper's grocery store on Uinta in Colorado Springs. We went for pumpkins and Indian corn. I also found a book.

While we were at the shopping center, I noticed a new Hobby Lobby shop had moved into a vacated department store. I had to investigate. So, while Bill waited in the van, Jenny and I went on an adventure.

She found two treasures—baby Indian corn (she likes tiny things) and a kitten calendar. I found treasures too—bittersweet and two unusual baskets for five dollars each.

I also discovered that the art section carried Bob Ross instruction books and paints. He's an artist who's on television every Saturday, and Sarah tries not to miss his hour show. Now I know where to go for her Christmas shopping this year.

When we were walking toward the van and Bill spied my little baskets, he grinned and shook his head.

I smiled wide. "Look! I found *treasures* in there! And I only spent 13 dollars!"

Jenny and I climbed in and I excitedly showed off my wonderful finds. He grinned.

"That's nice, honey." He's obviously not into baskets.

Bill then aimed the van across the parking lot to Radio Shack. "Mind if I look for a scanner?" he asked.

"You don't have to ask me if you want to look for something."

We'd previously talked about getting a scanner to listen for fire calls when Aimee's out on a run. We both agreed it'd be a good idea to have one. So, while we were right there, we went into Radio Shack to look around and see what they had. He found one he thought would serve our limited needs and bought it. Now *he* had a "find," but wouldn't ever admit it. Still, I knew he was happy to get it, because it would be a connection to Aimee whenever she was out on a fire, ambulance run, or rescue call.

Aimee now wants to observe a birth. Soon her EMT class will be centered on emergency delivery procedures and she's very excited to get into that phase of instruction. I'd asked her if they were going to be using a teaching model and she said she didn't think so. Too bad, those things are great. It'd be wonderful if one of her ambulance runs was for a birth and she could observe and perhaps assist. Maybe that'll happen for her.

This afternoon while Bill was in Woodland, I received a call from Jane at C & M Press regarding our children's manual reprint. She was going on vacation next week and was tying up some loose ends.

I confirmed with her the materials we needed to send them and told her the print run would be for 500. Then I said we'd send everything in when she returned to work in November. Hopefully our present stock will hold out until the new shipment is delivered. We always get an increase in orders around the holidays.

It's midnight. I just went out the kitchen door to sense the night. There's a clear full moon high in the sky and I smell the approaching breath of Cold Maker. He is very near.

When I came back inside, my Owl Spirit Bone was nearly rattling with anticipation on the cabinet shelf. The wind is beginning to blow and I hear the hooting voice calling to me. Okay, No-Eyes, I'm coming. I'm coming out now. You're going to wake the entire neighborhood!

10-24-91, Thursday

Cold Maker came to say hello this morning. When I opened our bedroom drapes snow was falling on top of a two-inch blanket of white. That was okay, because, last night beneath the autumn full moon, owl, cougar, and I celebrated a wonderful ceremony where farewell chants and songs were given to the Autumn Spirit. The new Season Ruler in robes of white is now welcomed to my woods. His presence this morning brought a smile, for he'd respected my sacred time alone to bid goodbye to his predecessor.

Bill and I had to leave for town at 10 o'clock to keep some appointments we had scheduled. We didn't return to the office until after lunch, when we began processing the mail.

We had 14 book orders. Ten of these were from the Spiral Bookstore in Orlando. We're beginning to get orders from bookstore owners who want to have a stock of the children's book in their store. I autograph each one of these. This situation was a surprise to us, because we can't discount the books. These bookstore owners pay full price and get reimbursed when their customers purchase the copies from them. The store people just want to make them available through their bookstore. And we see that as a beautiful Give-Away of Sharing. It takes a very special bookstore owner to do something so selfless like that for their customers and. . . for us.

I had a long talk with Sarah tonight. Her feelings were badly hurt by something someone casually said to her on the school bus. It had to do with a school course she was taking and the person's comment came out as a put-down. An apology was made to her as soon as the boy realized he'd hurt Sarah's feelings. . .still, the pain had already been inflicted.

It's hard to teach teenagers the lesson of ignoring the comments of peers. Young people at that age are so sensitive. And, trying to instill self-worth in them is an ongoing parental duty.

By the time I was finished I had her laughing over the incident and she'd realized how she needed to look deeper into the comments at the reasons that generated it.

Sarah hears her own drummer and sings her own personal song, but sometimes she needs to be reminded and encouraged to not let the beat and words be drowned out by her peer's group song that keeps repeating the old refrain, "don't be different—follow the crowd."

Eventually Sarah was again reinforced when I told her that someone who wants to be an artist does not waste time taking the same courses as someone who wants to be an engineer. She has to keep her eyes on her *own* path and disregard all wasteful and fruitless trails.

"If you were going to be an accountant," I asked her, "would you spend time on courses in chemistry?"

She smiled with that. "No. That'd be a waste. That'd be a stupid move."

"If you were going to be a secretary, would you take courses in anatomy or woodshop?"

She grinned wide. "Mom! Come on."

"If you were going to be an artist, would you take courses in auto shop?

"Her smile faded—then she giggled.

"See?" I said, "see how silly it is for you to feel inferior just because you're not following the crowd's choice of courses? They'd be a waste of your valuable learning time that should be devoted toward that of your own goal. Right?"

"Yeah. That'd be like delaying my path progress."

"I couldn't have said it better. So, next time someone criticizes your choice of courses, what are you going to do?"

"Not let it hurt me."

We hugged each other and Sarah went into the office with her art portfolio. She set up the drafting table, put earphones on and, for the next two hours, made great progress on her art project. I wish there was an art school nearby that also offered high school graduating course requirements. We'd have her enrolled within the blink of an owl's eye.

Another tidbit of food for thought I gave Sarah to chew on was the fact that college graduates were now finding it hard to find jobs. I pointed out the current status of white collar executives who were losing their jobs and finding themselves in unemployment lines while her own 19-year-old sister was making almost nine dollars an hour as a cashier. Suddenly people with years and years of college can't support themselves anymore in society, but Aimee could and she graduated from. . .home schooling.

The lightbulb flashed on then, because Sarah had this ideal drilled in (from school educators) that you wouldn't amount to beans if you didn't go to college. What a pile of propaganda that is! Not only is it demeaning and destructive to a mentally slower teenager, it's also damaging to the brighter students who can't afford college, or choose a career that doesn't necessitate a college degree. I told Sarah that she could quit school tomorrow if she wanted and, if she did that, I'd make sure she studied with local artists to get her training.

No. She wanted to stay in school. That was fine with me, but I told her that she has to stay centered on her professional goal so she won't continue to be hurt by any comments or college talk from peers or teachers.

She said she'd try. I can't ask for more than that.

I just wish people would leave others alone so they can follow their own path. I see so many people criticize another's path or life decision. So many trying to manipulate others. And those who are desperately trying to follow the words of their own sacred song are continually having to block out those of others around them who are shouting a different tune in their ear.

Sarah came to some deep realizations tonight. I just hope she keeps them strong before her.

Tonight my Prayer Smoke rises for all those who try to stay true to their paths in spite of their surrounding adversities and distractions.

Bless you all.

10-25-91, Friday

This morning I was able to type up last night's journal entry before Bill and I were due in town for my dental appointment. On November 5th (just before the new moon, of course), I'm having major oral surgery done.

Bill's already worked himself into a worrisome dither over this surgery and, although he knows I always have a team of "special" doctors around me at such times, he cannot help being deeply anxious until he's reassured of the actual positive outcome. The thought of any fluke happening that would cause him to lose me is so deeply ingrained in him (from the one lifetime when he prematurely lost me through the shooting accident), that no amount of pre-op reinforcement alleviates his anxiety. The moment he helps me out of the dental chair when it's all over will be the first moment he can take his real breath of relief.

I know this from experience, because, five years ago, when I had major oral surgery he paced the waiting room like an expectant father.

During today's appointment he made sure I was going to be on antibiotics a day before the surgery, and that I was going to receive the eight-hour anesthesia (Novocain) so I could ingest soft foods afterward to prevent the severe nausea I experienced after the surgery last time. At that time the doctor told Bill to force me to eat. When I did, the nausea subsided and soon vanished altogether. So this time Bill's covering all bases.

After we left the dentist's office we picked up the mail. I noticed we'd received a large envelope from the lady who'd previously cut me to ribbons and Bill had responded to. This time she'd sent booklets on Astarta, or something, and included a long, long second letter penned with her sharpened axe. Even Bill got sliced up this time.

Neither of us bothered to read any of her material or letter after we'd skimmed the first few lines. Bill dropped the deranged rantings in his waste basket and said, "Bye-bye." We're finally taking our readers' wise advice and trashing the trashy letters without reading them though. We don't need it, nor do we have time to waste on incoherent rantings and hateful mail.

The UPS man delivered a box of clothing that a correspondent sent for Wellspring Mission. I was very excited to receive her generous surprise.

Another thing I'm happy about is that our UPS deliveries are now coming in the morning instead of six o'clock in the evening. This is because they've added more routes and deliverymen due to the increased business in Cripple Creek since the gaming casinos opened.

Aimee called this evening to tell me bad news. City Market is bumping her down to a four-dollar-an-hour job as a caddy. What crap. The store gave wage increases to the employees in order to prevent their vote for a union last year. Now that the vote was a tie and didn't make it, management is literally taking the raises away by bumping the higher-paid cashiers down to lower paying jobs in-store.

I told Aimee and Robin to tell management that I'm putting all their shenanigans in my book. There's nothing here that isn't absolute truth and, if these people have any sense of integrity at all, I would hope the exposure of their little games would curb them. I'm so sick of seeing greed in the business place. I'm so disgusted with the almighty Profit God that's worshipped at the expense of offering human sacrifices in expendable employees.

This is one screwed-up world and I eagerly await the hour of God's entrance into it.

Today was the day our lawsuit defendants' attorneys were to respond. I heard they were to file their response brief in the Norfolk Federal Court.

We waited to hear from our attorneys, but received no call. Bill placed a call to their office and they were out. We waited for a return call—none came.

John Nelson called us to see if we'd heard anything. He and Bill talked for a while about the case.

This evening Sarah and I watched the video of *The Good Earth*. She has to do a literary critique on the book for her literature class, so I wanted her to get a clear visual sense of the story before she took the book from my shelf to read.

It was golden time spent together, as we talked about it while viewing it. Aimee had been at work. Jenny wasn't interested so she'd been reading in her room and Bill had been on the phone in the office the whole time. Rarely do I get the living room to myself like that and it was the perfect opportunity to have concentration time centered on Sarah's project. She thought it was a tragic story. At the end, her comment was, "It makes me feel bad I let the little things bother me. Those people had *real* problems."

"Don't feel bad," I said. "The important thing is that you recognized how many blessings you have to be thankful for."

She hugged me then. I hoped she considered one of those blessings to be her mom, because that's just what her misty eyes conveyed.

Jenny did our weeks worth of grocery shopping today and prepared a wonderful dinner. God, I wish I would've been as good a homemaker as she is when I got married. At 19 I didn't know how to plan menus or cook. I got frustrated, because there were no cooking instructions on soup cans and I boiled the contents without adding water or milk. And Bill would smile kindly as he ate my mushy meatloaf with a spoon. That was definitely an early sign he was a brave warrior. He still tells people about that horrid meatloaf.

But Jenny does warm my heart. She's come so far and is so full of love. Her cat, Buttercup, doesn't give any of us the time of day. With Jenny though, it's a very different story; she follows her around the house, sleeps next to her pillow, and perches on top of the refrigerator to watch Jenny cook dinner. The incredible love that cat has for Jenny attests to the deep tenderness and capacity to love that Jenny herself has. I've never seen a cat express so much attachment and show so many expressions of love to a human like Buttercup does to Jenny.

Tonight my Prayer Smoke will rise for all the countless blessings I've been given. I'm so grateful for the gift of every one.

10-26-91, Saturday

We heard more disturbing news from Aimee's work and our Midnight Raider gear kicked in. Before nine o'clock in the morning, I'd begun to work on an information flyer for the public. The eye-catching headliner was "Blowing the Whistle on City Market." Below that were eight points listed.

Meanwhile, Bill and Aimee and Robin prepared to go to town for a powwow with City Market's management. Robin, being the quiet person she is and never having been actively involved in one of our Champion of the Underdog escapades, didn't look too thrilled to confront the opposition. The last thing I reminded them about as they were going out the office door was to be sure they told the managers that I was writing about them in a book.

By the time they returned I'd had the original copy of the flyer all ready to photocopy for distribution. As I listened to them recount the meeting, I began to boil inside. They'd not mentioned the book I was writing. They said that Aimee was offered a position in the General Merchandise department for five dollars an hour (four dollars an hour less than she's making now). A.J., the department manager, came in and when Bill asked him if Aimee would be allowed to take off for a fire call, A.J. said "absolutely *not*! She'd be severely disciplined for that!" So much for Aimee working in *his* department. . .and so much for A.J.'s house if it was burning.

Aimee's only other option to stay on with 40 hours was to be demoted to being a caddy at four dollars an hour (a five dollar an hour pay cut). All three were told the cuts came from the main office in Grand Junction.

The managers said Aimee was a good worker and one of their most efficient cashier checkers, but, because she wasn't one of the top four checkers with the highest seniority, she had to be cut from that job and bumped to another position with a lower pay rate.

I asked some specific questions of Bill, Robin, and Aimee. Did they bring up such and such? Did they question the managers about this illegal practice or that incident? They hadn't and I was angry they didn't pin the managers down and catch them with those important points. The bottom line now was that our flyer was not the next move to make and I was disgusted. I filed it away and began typing up my journal entry. Everyone knew I was upset and they left me alone while they continued to discuss Aimee's work options at the store. It was decided that she should take the caddy position where her higher seniority there would assure her 40 hours of day shift that would allow her to be free for her evening EMT classes. There is no way I would've agreed to Aimee working under A.J., who calls himself "the King."

Overall, I was greatly disappointed how the entire scenario went down, and Sarah was eager to go out tonight to help distribute the flyers around town. After all, the last time we did that she was in diapers—she hates it when I say that, because a lot of events Bill and I talk about, she'll ask, "When was that?" And we'd say, "Oh, you were in diapers then." That's kind of become a joke between us now.

Bill talked to John Nelson today. Bill told him about my journal and how I write about everything that happens each day.

"You're in the journal, John," Bill chuckled. "She writes about our business day and who I have conversations with."

"Oh-oh," John said, "I'd better bake her some cookies so she'll be good to me."

Bill laughed. "Yeah, I told a few other people that they were in the journal too—I was hoping that'd keep them on good behavior for the duration."

"Is it working?" John asked.

"No."

I didn't do mail today. When Bill returned with it after their store meeting and I'd heard the outcome, my heart wasn't in it. I won't process the mail when my mood is bad, because that's not being fair to the correspondents. So Bill did it all today.

He showed me one letter though. It was from a woman in Colorado Springs who is nearly blind. She wanted to know if I'd permit the Library of Congress to do Braille or recordings of my books for the blind. Well, on the initial copyright form that's filled out and filed with the Library of Congress, I always check the "Blind" box that gives my permission for such rights. So that grant is given before my books are actually published.

I spent the evening reading. I really wasn't into the book and found myself re-reading paragraph after paragraph. I kept thinking about this morning and all the injustices in this world's society. I wanted to disengage my being from it. I wanted to walk into my tiny one-room cabin deep in the woods and close the door. . .forever.

Tempting thoughts subliminally disrupted my reading. Maybe I should take some savings money and drive over to Redstone and rent something—any little old place. . .now. Then thoughts of my dental surgery negated the former idea. That singular event would anchor me to Woodland Park for at least three more months until the entire dental process was complete. So now I was tied down here until February. It didn't look like there was any way we could secure a Redstone address before this journal ended in December. The only way it could be done was if we somehow came into extra money, bought a Redstone house and had Robin and Mandy reside there until we could follow. And that was definitely a very, very slim probability.

Heard the Florida lottery is up to 94 million. That amount doesn't even register with me. Can't imagine that much money. Ah, but how wonderful it would be to be able to have an unlimited fund like that to keep our Wellspring Mission warehouse filled with a continuous flow of goods. Then it surely would be a wellspring. What a dreamer I am . . .always visualizing the most optimistic possibilities . . .always. I set myself up for plunging disappointments when I do that, but there seems to be an inner valve mechanism that prevents me from turning into a pessimist. I suspect this valve is in place to prevent me from giving up. Therefore, each time I'm disappointed, I pick myself up again and strive onward. But it's interesting that there have been times when I wasn't sure I wanted to do that—preferring to stay kicked on the ground, to wallow in my misery. Yet I never actually carried out that urge, because the mind always took over by shouting, "What a dumb thing to do! You'd be wasting valuable rebuilding time! Get up! Get up!" And I would. No lying in the battlefield dust for this one. Keep on fighting! Drag yourself to your feet and trudge onward. . .always onward. And I would. Again and again I would.

My Prayertime tonight will be for the winners of the Florida lottery, that they may use their new wealth in a spiritually wise manner.

10-27-91, Sunday

Yesterday Bill and I didn't have a very good day so he decided to begin this day with breakfast at the Fossil Inn. On our way there my eyes almost deceived me, for perched on a fencepost was an eagle with wings spread wide to the sun. It looked like it was warming its wings. It looked like a statue and reminded me of the winged Isis statue we have.

The odd pose was so unexpected to see, we were past it

before the reality of it registered in my mind. I asked Bill if he'd seen the eagle on the fence. He hadn't. And within my being, I felt as though I'd been given a very special gift.

When we arrived at the Fossil Inn, we were told to go right in to our special table in the back. Helga, the hostess, came over and began telling us about some people who had come over from Germany to meet me. They never made the expected connection, but had a wonderful time making good friends with Helga.

Now these people are back in Germany and have recently married. Helga asked me if I'd do her a big favor. She wants to send this couple a copy of *Earthway* signed to them by me. She thought she could drop the book off at the City Market deli and Robin could bring it home for me to sign, Helga would then pick it up there again. I told our friend that I'd be glad to sign her wedding gift and that people frequently left books for me to sign with Aimee or Robin at the grocery store.

While the Bronco game was on (we won, by the way), I went outside to walk in the afternoon sun. I felt I needed to do this. I felt it would be a final day to gather wild dry plants and just enjoy the autumn sunshine. For 40 minutes I sat beneath a bare aspen tree and let the sun warm my being. I was a little sad to sense a finality to autumn while I was out.

All evening Sarah worked on her native portrait art project while I photocopied the next section of the journal manuscript. I'd typed up over another hundred pages and needed to send them to Bob for editing. When I'm done with the November entries I'll send those pages in. When December's are done the manuscript called *Soul Sounds* will be finished. The journal won't be, though—that will go on and on.

Aimee spent the day at the fire department. She works at City Market tonight from six to 11 (not exactly eight hours, is it). When she popped in at dinner time, she announced that she'd put in an employment application at the police department for dispatcher. She hates working at the store now, because of all the cuts they've made and how she's hassled there about her EMT classes. She's groping for a way out. She grasped without looking at what she reached for, because a police dispatcher job will not allow her to take off evening hours for her classes. I wish she had a little more patience and had waited to apply for this job after her classes were finished in December.

Bill and I said nothing negative about what she did. She's frustrated enough as it is without us adding lack of support to her decision. We hope all works out for her and she can juggle a new job with her other responsibilities.

I wrote four pieces tonight for the *Pinecones and Woodsmoke* book. They were descriptive essays of a few of my mystical experiences. These have increased lately and, if truth be told, there are times I feel very much like No-Eyes. I don't mean the deep wisdom of her—I mean her private experiences with other dimensions and through nature's magical windows.

There were wonderful heartwarming times we spent together when she'd talk softly and most reverently of her journeys through "vibrational shifts." These magical stories of hers held me enrapt for hours on end. Yet. . .now the deja vu feeling chills my spine as I find myself passing through the same shifts at times. Mostly these have taken place quite unexpectedly, while I've been out alone in the deep woods. Sometimes it happens in broad daylight. And a few of these magic moments are recorded in my final book.

I've had vision flashes lately that depict two scenes. They are separate from each other.

In one vision, I'm walking alone across the desert toward a mesa with a bundle in my arms.

In the other vision, I'm very old and walking alone in the woods behind my small cabin.

Do these visions that come unbidden represent different times of my own future? Or are they not literal, but rather symbolic holograms of something else? I don't have the answer to those questions now and, those who do. . .aren't telling. Nor have I asked about them, because these visions are only for me to decipher. I must come into my own knowing of them and, when the time is right, I will.

Cold Maker is coming. He's very close. There is something I must get done in the woods tonight and I feel tomorrow might well be too late. There is one out there that I must commune with.

When I return, my Prayer Smoke will be for Bill. Tonight I need to ask for a special favor on his behalf.

10-28-91, Monday

I smiled when I looked out the deck doors of our bedroom this morning. White all around. Snowing on top of a sparkling three-inch blanket. Cold Maker had made his grand entrance.

By the time I came downstairs, Bill had already left for town. He'd taken the pickup in to have the two spare new tires put on. He also needed to get sandbags for the bed of the truck and buy new chains.

At 10 o'clock I left for my dental appointment. The roads were icy beneath the snow and at the bottom of Bluebird Hill going into town, cars were in ditches. I thanked God for our all-wheel van that handled so beautifully on ice and snow.

Bill returned home shortly after I did and, while he and Aimee put the new chains on the pickup, I started on the large stack of mail. We had 16 book orders and 30 letters.

John Nelson called to tell us about the defendant's response. They're trying for arbitration instead of a court trial.

Our attorneys are going to file for a hearing for a trial determination, because we want this thing to go to court. We also were informed that the defendants were going to offer an initial settlement. We're not holding our breath for this first attempt to appease us. They don't appear to have any conception of the personal misery they've caused us authors, especially me, because of how I've viewed them stealing my No-Eyes away from me.

So, in a couple weeks we'll know how the court decided, and whether we'll be going to a court trial or not. With the fraud, conspiracy, and mail fraud charges, we're confident the judge will rule in our favor for a trial.

Things are beginning to move along now. After living the hell of this situation for so long it's like a cool breeze that soothes the parched soul.

Bill and I worked in the office until 7:30 P.M., when he and Jenny got into the Monday Night Football game, and I roasted the seeds from the pumpkins Jenny and Sarah had carved earlier.

It was a cozy evening. Woodstove was crackling, the oil pots were burning on the mantle, good roasting smells from the kitchen and snow falling outside.

Robin said her little red Tracker did just great on our icy roads. She said it felt wonderful not to have to worry any more about winter driving. Earlier in the day, when Bill passed her on our winding mountain road, he said the Tracker looked like it was really holding the road. He said it looked real nice. I'm so glad we got it for her. It tickles my heart every time I see Robin pull away from the house in it.

She just loves it so much and still comments that she can't believe it's hers.

It's midnight now and it's 4° outside. I'm going into the woods to welcome Cold Maker to his season. I will wear the reindeer robe and take my Deer Spirit Stick. These are necessities for the medicine ceremony I must perform tonight. The Prayer Smoke will rise up through the snow-covered pine boughs. How nice it would be to have the kiva during this bitter season. Yet being out in the open has an inherent attraction and special mood that no other setting offers. I must go and gather the sacred objects for my medicine bag now. Timing is important.

Goodnight, No-Eyes. See you in a few minutes.

10-29-91, Tuesday

It was cold and snowy all day.

When Bill came back from town with the mail, I was relieved to see it was light for a change. Charlie (the gentleman who sends me the Kitaro tapes) sent me a copy of a Native American newsletter, *The Drumbeat*, that had a beautiful write-up of Summer Rain and her books. The native organization wrote that I had honored them by listing them in *Daybreak*. I was so surprised to see the article, but felt their expression of appreciation wasn't needed. I'd listed them because I was moved to do so as my only way of showing my gratitude to the People of No-Eyes' homeland for all she'd given to me. When a reader requested my recommendation for a native organization to send donations to, my heart naturally followed the trail back to No-Eyes' people. If our lawsuit goes well I will do more for them than just writing of their needy conditions. After all No-Eyes had done for me—and so many others—the very least I can do is to help her people in any way I can. These may not be her specific people per se, but they are of her native state and region. That's close enough for me.

Aimee called us from the fire station this evening to tell us the good news she's been so anxious to hear. She passed her mid-term EMT exam. Yeah, Aimee! Before she left for class tonight, she asked me what her score was (she'd taken the exam several night's ago and wasn't getting the results until tonight). Everyone around here treats me like their own personal oracle. I'd answered her by telling her that she did pass, but wouldn't give her the actual score, because I wanted her to be surprised. She thought the score was going to be much lower than it was, and I knew I'd spoil it for her if I told her beforehand how good she did.

Aimee has some cockamamie idea in her head that she's not as good or smart as others, because she did home schooling instead of regular high school. Little by little this idea is shattering and tonight's mid-term exam score will certainly have worked to further crack that false impressions, because her score was higher than some older adults who took the test with her. She's no dummy, that's for sure!

We also had good news regarding Aimee's work. Looks like she won't be bumped down to a caddy after all. She's going to transfer to the bakery department and, because of her overall seniority, won't have to take hardly any cut in pay. That was definitely great news.

Things sure change from day to day around here. In fact, it's a family joke when we begin to make any kind of plans that have to do with our future, because the Advisors are always watching ahead and then giving us alternate routes at each stage of carrying out a plan. I don't know how many times we've had to inform the family of "Plan Change Number Six or Ten or One Hundred." At first it drove Robin crazy but after she saw how many times our plans would've gone awry if a change *hadn't* been made, she eventually came to accept these as being a normal operational mode for us. Living with us can be very interesting at times. The "unexpected" becomes the norm. *Our* normal life would definitely not be considered "normal" if judged by the conventional, established pattern of the general public. But as someone once liked to say. . . "what so!"

I'm advised not to go outside tonight, so I will offer my Prayer Smoke in the living room candlelight. The smoke will rise for all the native people of Minnesota—No-Eyes' homeland.

10-30-91, Wednesday

While I worked on the mail, Bill was busy at his desk revising our flyer. I wasn't having good feelings about it and was becoming uneasy. Then, just about the time he was done, the message came through loud and clear.

"You can't do the flyer, Bill," I said.

"Why not?"

"We're advised not to do this one. The warning is real strong. There's negativity—a blackness—all around it."

He turned in his chair to face me.

"Dammit. Is that coming from you or Them?"

"The bad feeling's coming from me, the warning's coming from Them. Their words were, 'don't do this one.'"

"Why the hell not? How come everything I want to do gets squelched?"

"Retaliation. We can't do this one, because there'd be retaliation. That's what they see."

"How can there be any retaliation if nobody knows where the flyers came from?"

"That's the point—people will know. And don't ask me how. All I know is they say people will know it's us."

"So what?"

I just looked at him and he didn't say anymore.

The rest of the day didn't go well after that. Bill was in a black mood and everyone pretty much stayed out of his way. He respects our Advisors' warnings and advice, but that doesn't also mean we always like what we hear. Regardless, we always follow their wise suggestions, especially the warnings.

UPS delivered a package from a correspondent in South Fork, Colorado. She'd knitted four winter hats for our Wellspring Mission recipients. They were nicer than the ones one finds in the store. Jenny wanted to keep the pink one and I said, "No way. These donations aren't for us to use—they're for poor people."

Today I also received a letter from a Lakota man who is a Pipe Carrier. He requested advice on a few personal concerns and I wrote him back.

There were some interesting questions in our mail today and I responded to all of them.

Tonight, after my Prayertime, I will prepare for tomorrow. Halloween may be for the little ones, but there have been years in the past (like last year) when some "big kids" take their candles, incantations, and psychic games a little too far . . .in my direction. You'd think they'd know that whatever they send out will ultimately return to them. I'm going to make sure it does.

10-31-91, Thursday

Bill got up at 4:30 in the morning so he could have the van down at the dealer's in Colorado Springs. It needed some warranty work done, and he had a list of errands to do while

he was down there. When he returned home in the late afternoon, he had a stack of mail for us to process.

I'll have to wait to respond to the letters until tomorrow,
because we worked on the new book orders until 9:30 at
night. More and more orders are coming in daily, and now
we're to the point where we're questioning whether or not
we made a wise decision to self-publish them ourselves.
Some nights I'm still signing them until very late.

Bill and I discussed the situation after I told him I felt it
was getting to be too much to handle with all our other
work. We'd received inquiries about the book from many
bookstores across the country, and one of the major national
book distributors had contacted us to say they've been getting
a lot of requests for the children's book. And Joe, down at
Valhalla in Manitou Springs told us he could've sold at least
80 of them this summer if he'd had them in his store.

So Bill and I reviewed the pros and cons of our situation
and decided to put out feelers regarding having a regular publisher take it over. In the morning Bill will call Bob to see
what his interest would be and what would be involved in
the transfer to his company. I'm not saying this is what
we're going to do—we just want to check out our options.

Aimee spent the evening riding around town on one of the
fire trucks and passing out light sticks to the little goblins,
witches, and ghosties that were Trick or Treating.

It was a cold night for the little ones and, when Robin
brought Mandy home with her bag of goodies, I went
through it for her. This has been an annual routine for me
each Halloween night. I psychically check each piece of candy by holding it for a second. This is how we've always
sorted the good from the questionable. It's too bad it has to
be done at all, but such is our society and we work around
it as best we can.

We're sensing some changes coming. Both Bill and I have
had feelings that our direction has been slightly altered. We
have ideas what these might involve, but I'm not going to
voice those aspects now.

Tonight my Prayer Smoke will rise for a special request I
received today from one of my correspondents.

November, 1991

One of those weird days today.

When I got up I came downstairs, went directly to the living room couch and slept for two hours. I thought it was just me that felt so sleepy I felt drugged, but Robin was draggy and so was Bill. This had happened before. It's a psychic residual effect from extreme protection given us by the other side. The only way to explain it is to liken the protection given us to a heavy, thick cloak. Actually it's a psychic force field that surrounds us and creates a strong repelling aura. This aura does not drain our energies, but rather is so protective it's like being a babe asleep in its mother's arms. The effect on our physical system is one of complete embryonic security, comfort, and warmth which, in turn, acts as a powerful tranquilizer would. In order for the other side (our Advisors and others) to manifest this particular force field around us, there must've been some powerful negativity directed toward us last night. I don't care to know from whom it came—the fact that the attack failed is all that matters.

Needless to say, because of our extreme tiredness today, yesterday's mail (and today's) did not get answered. We handled the necessary phone calls and processed the book orders. By late afternoon my head had cleared enough to do our month-end bookkeeping for October.

During the day, Bill had called a CPA in Woodland to ask him a couple tax questions we had that came up while I was recording our October expenses. I needed to know if we could somehow deduct the Tracker we bought Robin. . .we couldn't. That answer and its full explanation brought up another question that involved gifts to us. That answer was far more agreeable than the one to our first question.

When Bill later went to town to pick Sarah up from school for their chiropractic appointment, he stopped by the CPA's office to pay him for the phone consultation. While there, Bill slipped in one last question we had about our charity project. The answer was, "No, you can't say it's a not-for-profit project unless it is legally registered as such."

Okay. . .so now we use our Wellspring Mission letterhead as woodstove fuel and rewrite our information letter. There's no way I'm going through all that non-profit red tape and separate bookkeeping. I just don't have the time. So even though we don't personally gain a red cent from our project or the gifts given to it, we're officially a business—and unofficially we're non-profit. And that's fine with us. We'll keep it all on a Robin Hood scale. . .just like the olde days.

Another call Bill made today was to Bob, to inquire if he'd be interested in taking over the children's book. Yes, he was interested but was concerned about the size of the book (which translates to a high production cost). Bob thought maybe a 6" x 9" book would be more feasible. He'd look into it.

We didn't agree with the smaller size, because kids use the book as a coloring book. For that, the larger size is perfect. Bob also had some concern about how well the book would sell on the open market. We had no such concerns because of the feedback we'd received from bookstore owners around the country.

Overall, we weren't encouraged by what we were hearing. I think it was at that point when we decided it might be better to keep self-publishing it after all.

This evening, while Bill was in the office with a conference call, Sarah, Robin, and I watched the *Fantasia* video I'd ordered. Sarah loved it and was especially interested in the artwork that went into the film. Aimee was at the fire station—it was her night to sleep there and be on-call for medical rescue calls. Jenny wasn't interested in the video and went to her room to watch television. Mandy was at her dad's.

By 10 o'clock Bill was still in conference on the phone. He's doing it all over again, but I can't say anything. How can I deny him what's so deeply inherent in him to do? Yet I'm the one that has to pick up the pieces and put him back together again whenever his more involved counseling relationships end up bad. He just puts far too much of himself in them. He's told me that people have told him that they sense a wall around me, and that which is behind my eyes is well guarded. That's true for several good reasons, the lesser being a natural stance that says, "experience has taught me to know a friend as well as my enemy—otherwise I get hurt by both."

But Bill. . .he's so open. . .so exposed. Especially his vulnerable heart. Yet because I love him, I must let him be his own self. To do otherwise would suffocate him and his spirit.

In this vein, Sarah said something to me the other evening that really shocked me. We were talking about the journal I was writing.

Very thoughtfully she said, "I never realized you were such a softie inside."

"What do you mean," I asked.

"Well. . .I was reading your typed journal pages for the book and you're really so sensitive inside."

"Sarah!" I smiled in sudden amusement, "You *live* with me. You know me better than anyone does."

"Yeah, I know, but I see so much of your assertive side and how you're always fighting for this or that and defending us. You don't go around telling us your most private thoughts like you're writing down in the journal."

"For instance."

"Oh, like when Aimee's out on a call how you work to protect her, how hurt you are by mean letters you get, and all the people you pray for. I never knew you prayed for so many people."

I took her hand. "Prayers are usually a private affair, Sarah. I only mention them in my journal because it *is* a record of my daily activities and thoughts. Why should I bother writing in it every night if I'm not going to be straightforward?"

"But it's going to be a *book*. People are going to read those private thoughts." She had a point.

"Well yes," I said, "but if I wasn't honest in the journal the Advisors would not want it published. If they'd foreseen me altering my entries after I found out they'd planned it to be a book, they never would've made that decision in the first place."

"So you *have* to write everything down?"

"No, Sarah, I don't *have* to do anything. I do it because I started the journal for a reason—a personal one. It's still my personal story. . .written for me. I still want to record everything because I want to remember it all. And now, somehow it doesn't even enter my mind that others will read what I write each night. When I sit down at night it's just me and the journal. I don't know," I admitted, "maybe it just hasn't sunk in that people will read it. I'm not sure I care anymore. I agreed to do it and that's that. I guess I don't think about it now." Then, "We kind of got off the subject, didn't we."

"Not really," she said. After a moment of thought, she said, "Mom?"

"What, hon."

"I'm glad they want your journal published."

"Oh? How come?"

"So people will see past the warrior." She hugged me then.

I whispered in her ear. "Do I seem that hard on the outside?"

She whispered back. "You're a warrior, mom. That's what people *see*. Now they'll *feel* what your *heart* is."

Yes, I thought, now they'll hear my soul sounds. And I wondered if that was good or bad.

I kissed Sarah and thanked her for being open with me and sharing her thoughts.

She kissed me back and told me not to worry about people knowing the inner me.

I smiled on the outside. . .inside she got me thinking again. Do I really appear so hard on the outside? Is my warrior aspect so visible that it completely hides the sensitive softness within? Is *that* why people think me a Tough Cookie and would rather deal with Bill? Is the real me that protected?

It's 11 o'clock at night and I'm back into my full awareness now. Actually it returned just before dinner. Bill seemed to perk up then too. Robin went to bed early and so did Jenny and Sarah. I think they're still a little wrung out yet, but they'll be good as new in the morning. These "special effects" usually only last for a day.

Thanks Guys for watching out for us. I don't need to tell you how deeply grateful we are for all the ways you express your love.

It's 3° out and snowing heavily. It's so beautiful. Bill's still up and I'll wait 'til he goes to bed to begin my Prayertime. This night it will be spent in Thanksgiving for all our Protectors—they don't have an easy job.

11-2-91, Saturday

I awoke with a clear message from our Advisors. Now we could proceed with our flyer. Bill would receive that bit of news well. Especially after we'd found out that the one manager at City Market who anointed himself "the King," filed a false accusation against Robin. She was written up because the King had observed her talking with other store employees during work hours. Well. . .Robin is their Store Employee

Representative, so she's *supposed* to be available to her peers when they have questions on store policy or management.

Robin's boss, Tony, really stood up for her when he went to management. He asked them what the policy was for her position as rep. Is it against store policy for the employees to talk to their representative during work hours? Management scratched their heads. Seems there are no such rules spelled out. So then, why is the King trying to get Robin written up on an infraction of a non-existent policy? Oh, how the sharks do circle those who defend the poor employees. Maybe they see Robin as a trouble-maker for giving the workers information with which to defend themselves and fight back.

At any rate, the Midnight Raiders were given the green light. They were fired up again.

When Bill and I went to town, we had to go to City Market to pick up some soft foods to have after my dental surgery next Tuesday. While there, we visited the deli department, where Robin waited on us and helped us choose some offerings there. She gave us a taste test (customary procedure with undecided shoppers) of a few items I thought might appeal to me after surgery. Neither Bill nor I had really taken a good look at the deli department after they installed it several years ago and we were impressed with the variety of foods. I chose the Cherries Jubilee jello and the Chinese Chicken Peanut preparation. The chicken was done to such a flavorful turn it melted in my mouth. Just the thing for someone trying to eat with a mouthful of stitches.

Then Robin came out from behind the counter and asked me a favor. Seems a deli co-worker was a big fan of No-Eyes and asked Robin, "Is that Summer Rain? Can I meet her?"

I met Mandy and hugged her. We spoke for a few minutes and discovered this was the woman who is also a paramedic and is coming out to our house this month to help Aimee with her "practicals." That means testing on various accident scenarios and how one goes through the right medical procedures.

I told Mandy how grateful we were that she was helping Aimee out, and that we'd see her in a few week's up at our house.

Later Robin told us that Mandy had felt speechless and stupid talking to us. That always surprises me because she certainly didn't appear that way to us.

Robin also told us that, while we were in the deli, a woman who works in the meat department saw us and suspected who we were. She'd told Robin that she wanted to meet us, but was afraid to. Do I look like an ogre or what?

Wouldn't people laugh to know that I'm more shy to meet them than they are to meet me! That I feel totally tongue-tied and stupid when they compliment our work and the books! Half the time I don't know what to say back to them and I feel like the Mother of all Klutzes. I guess face-to-face compliments embarrass me. I'm so pleased and tickled to hear how No-Eyes has touched folks and changed their lives, but when those words are spoken to me personally I somehow feel they're misdirected. Maybe that's all part of this anti-publicity thing I have. Who knows? All I do know is that I'm very uncomfortable in public when people know who I am and come up to me. Maybe a blonde wig would help. . . just kidding.

Anyway, after we were done shopping and got in the tail end of a long check-out line, we noticed the grim and grumbling faces of the other customers. Bill went up to the cashier manager and gave him a piece of his mind—arms waving and all. The recent demoting of so many checkers was not making for contented customers.

It was about that time when I spied "the King" walk by. I told Bill to stay with the cart and I followed his majesty. I called to him.

"I think it's time you were told that you're in my next book," I said.

His face flushed while he listened to the rest of my words. "You and the other managers are all in the book. This store and all the shenanigans that go on here is better than a soap opera. Anyway, you and all of Woodland Park can read about it next April when the book comes out."

"That's wonderful!" he said. "I hope it sells a lot of books!"

What a Ninny, I thought. But then I noticed he made one hell of a beeline to the stairs. . .right up to the office. Maybe these young store managers will stop harassing the employees and reps if they know their pettiness is being made public. It's hard to tell, but I did want him to be made aware of the fact he was being written about in a book. Legally, his answer was a very positive one—he had voiced no objections whatsoever.

When we returned home with our pile of mail, we dug into it. Then we revised our flyer. The initial one was addressed to City Market's president. Three days after that's mailed (on Monday) one copy each will go to our two town newspapers. If no corrective measures are in evidence after that, they'll go on the windshield wipers of cars parked in the grocery store lot.

We don't go into action for petty causes or insignificant company infractions. We go into action when *many* employees of a company are being dealt with in an unjust manner. We always get our facts straight before making our move. This time we not only have personally witnessed dozens of complaining customers, but have also heard the complaints of many employees who have the inside information. All of our charges on the flyer are valid and can be proven. So. . .we'll watch and see what happens now.

While going through the mail I was surprised to read that a correspondent wants to give us a computer as a gift. I didn't know at first how to respond to that so I talked it over with Bill. He said he'd been thinking about that lately, because our system of keeping the mailing list was so time-consuming and since we'd been trying to find ways to cut down on our time in the office, he'd toyed with the computer idea. He said the computer could be his responsibility and that he thought he'd enjoy his work more if we had one.

I haven't responded to the woman's offer yet, but will when I sign her children's book tomorrow. Right now I don't know what I'll say. A computer is a very expensive gift and it seems I'm unsettled about accepting something like that.

Over and over again people keep telling me that my perspective on accepting gifts is wrong. They say I'm supposed to understand a gift-giver's desire to help us or their inner wish to offer something in the way of expressing a thank-you to us. But the way I see it is this: Why should I accept gifts for something I promised No-Eyes I'd do? Oh, this is all very complicated for me to deal with. I perceive it as *No-Eyes* being the one who helped so many, and she's gone. I know what folks tell me and I do understand their viewpoint—I really do. Yet I cannot shut out my own view that speaks so loud and clear from within me. If I refuse gifts, then I feel that maybe I've hurt someone's feelings. The native way of this issue is to always give a return gift for a gift received. If people feel I've given them a gift through the books, then native tradition says I must accept their return gift to me. However, it was No-Eyes who really gave them the gift of her wisdom. . .not me. I think I sound like a crazy woman. Yes? Well, I can see the problem rests with *who* people think changed their lives. *They* believe it's me, while *I* believe it's No-Eyes. And there lies my dilemma of not wanting to hurt anyone's feelings. How did I get myself into such a mess?

Link has a delivery. We decided the weather's too bad to

make a connection. She said she may send it UPS. We've got so many things going on now it'll be difficult finding the time to work on it, especially when I'll be out of commission for several days next week.

Tomorrow we're going to be working on getting everything ready to send to the printer on Monday. Bill will have to take the over-sized negative package in to town to the UPS station. We need to get this off before my surgery. Our remaining stock of the children's book is dwindling each day and holiday orders are already coming in. We're cutting this reprint dangerously close and we hope we don't run out before the new shipment arrives. Financially we're sticking our necks out, but we couldn't disappoint kids either. We must have books for those who order them. I'd feel really bad if we didn't and had to return orders. Maybe Bill could keep track of book orders on a computer too. Oh God, there I go again. What to do. . .what to do.

Tonight my Prayer Smoke will be for clarity of mind over this silly gift-accepting confusion I have. Maybe the Powers That Be will take pity on my simple mind and straighten me out. They know I will trust and abide by their answer. Whatever the response is, it will finally put me out of my misery over it.

11-3-91, Sunday

We began our day with Sunday breakfast at the Fossil Inn and when we returned home, began to finish responding to Saturday's mail.

By one o'clock Bill came over to my desk and reached for my hand.

"Let's go snuggle," he said.

He got no objections from me and we went upstairs. We snuggled, made love, snuggled some more until we fell asleep in each other's arms. I awoke at four o'clock and, while I dressed, my sleepy mate opened his blue eyes.

"Guess we needed a nap, huh honey," he said.

"Guess we did."

Then he got up while I returned to the office. I wasn't back at my desk five minutes when Big John from Victor called. Although my head was still a little fuzzy from my nap, I enjoyed talking to him. I told him about the dental surgery I was having Tuesday morning and he said he'd burn some Frankincense and Myrrh at that time for me. What a sweetheart he is. Every month he gifts us with stamps. Bill and I have planned a drive to Victor to visit him, and every time we tentatively planned the drive, something would come up. I'm determined to go see Big John around the holidays and bring him a Christmas present. I will make it a priority after my mouth has healed enough to permit half-way decent articulation again. That feat takes a few weeks to accomplish.

I'm all prepared for the surgery. I didn't have any mental or emotional work to do. I'm not scared and don't even have any anxiety over it. It's something that needs to be done and I just want to go do it and get it over with. The only aspect I've applied energies to is psychically preparing the teeth and gums through vivid visualizations. This helps a great deal. I'll do the same afterward for post-operative healing. When I did this before after oral surgery, the dentist said my healing was about three week's ahead of normal time. Having a wisdom tooth that's deeply embedded down in the bone extracted won't be much fun, but neither will having the other seven teeth extracted at the same time. Eight pulled at one shot will put me down for a couple days.

After I spoke with Big John, I worked on signing the 14 books that had been ordered. After I finished those, Bill and I prepared the jacket negatives to send to the printer. Those are no little photo negatives. They're four-color separation negatives of four sheets measuring 2'8" x 3'9." They had to be protected in a strong cardboard portfolio type of packaging for secure shipping.

By the time we finished, the Bronco game began and Bill vanished from the office to join Jenny in the living room. Sarah kept me company while working on her art at the drafting table.

My next project was to respond to two women who wrote us. One wanted us to accept occasional gifts for our Wellspring Mission and the other wanted us to accept her offered gift of the computer.

I sat at the typewriter and, in both letters, explained my dilemma over gift-acceptance, and how I'd prayed last night for an answer to clarify my perspective on the matter. The bottom line was that I told these ladies that we'd gratefully accept their kindness and, although I still felt a mite uncomfortable, I apologized for that and explained the new perspective would naturally take a little time for me to get accustomed to.

Aimee had her first day in the new Bakery position. When she called this evening, she said she liked it a lot. Her boss is nice and spent several hours teaching Aimee how to decorate cakes.

When Robin came home from work tonight, she commented that Aimee was smiling every time she saw her today. Aimee hasn't smiled at work for a long time. Robin also told us that Aimee came over to the deli with a sign made of icing. It said: "Hi Deli! Love, Aimee." The deli workers, including its manager, Tony, think Aimee is so cute. Her little sign was received with laughter and appreciation.

Tonight Aimee's on medical rescue call again and we won't see her until tomorrow morning. Lately Bill's been letting her take the van to work and keep it overnight, because it's so much safer in this snowy weather than the pickup. Aimee loves driving the van. She said she never realized how easy it'd be to handle. I agree with her, because when you're behind the wheel, it's no different than being behind the wheel of the little Storm we had. That amazed me the first time I drove it, because I thought it'd feel like driving a tank. Shame on me—I was in the no-no state of expectation. Tsk-tsk, Summer Rain, you should know better.

After I responded to the last of the mail, I spent two hours boxing up the medical supplies we'd accumulated from the incoming shipments from our suppliers. We'd had them scattered around the office and I needed to get them boxed up and stored away. I didn't turn the office light out tonight until 10:30.

The name of Big John Fuller will be whispered as my Prayer Smoke rises tonight. He has a few medical problems and he's such a sweet soul. I'm ashamed of myself for not visiting him yet. So, until we do. . .I will pray for him.

11-4-91, Monday

After my Prayertime last night, my Starfriend appeared. It had been a while since we last spent time together and I was beginning to miss him. I hope he sensed that. He doesn't miss much, so he probably knew what was in my heart.

He didn't stay long, yet our conversation covered several subjects relating to some of our current activities. It was also verified that a few aspects of our future had been altered just as Bill and I had suspected through our individual inner feelings.

Although my friend's visit was not one of his usual

lengthy ones, it was long enough to cover some very serious matters.

This morning I accompanied Bill to town to help with the errands we had. When we returned, we dug into the mail and spent the rest of the day processing it. I signed 14 children's books and cleaned up all the odds and ends that required my attention. I didn't want to leave any extra work for Bill to do while I'm laid up for the next few days.

He's a basket case. He's worried sick about my surgery tomorrow morning. I can't wait for it to be over so he can finally relax. His anxiety has been building and building for the last few days. I feel so sorry for him. I know he subliminally senses the carryover grief from losing me once before, and anything that may threaten my health or could possibly endanger me in any way is a source of great anxiety for him. By 11 o'clock tomorrow it'll be all over and he can breathe easy once more.

I doubt there'll be an entry for tomorrow's date. I'll return to this journal just as soon as my "private doctor" lets me.

So this night I pray my prayers for my beloved William. I will pray for a quick surgery with no complications so his pacing-the-floor time will be kept to a minimum. I couldn't ask for a mate who could love me more than he does. There's no one on earth who could even come close to matching the depth of his love. Love—how utterly painful and bitter it can be for one whose cup is full. Goodnight, honey. You'll feel a lot better tomorrow. I promise.

11-5-91, Tuesday

It's one o'clock in the afternoon. I kept my promise. . . Bill's breathing easy now.

At three o'clock our dear friend, Art, called from New York to see how I was. He had been praying for me.

Tonight I pray Thanksgiving prayers for all those who prayed for me and surrounded me in protection. Then I must give serious work time to healing my gum tissue.

11-6-91, Wednesday

I'm feeling awful. I have a slight fever, but I'm being a good patient and eating as much as I can.

Bill talked to Bob Friedman. The people at Hampton Roads have been trying to come up with a promotional idea to encourage my readers to take advantage of a pre-publication offer for *Soul Sounds*. They wondered what we thought of offering the public a free print of the cover artwork. That's out, because Carole will be selling her artwork prints separately. She has her art copyrighted and we can't just make copies of it to give away. I think a replica of the book jacket might be nice. Well, I'm sure they'll come up with something good.

At seven o'clock Bill brought me six children's books to sign.

It's nine o'clock and Bill just fixed me a baked potato (sans skin). My diet has been dramatically altered. When I'm done eating this gourmet meal, I'm going to read until my eyes droop and I fall asleep. Hopefully I'll get up tomorrow and be more active. I'll still have pain, but I'd rather be busy than lying in a bed all day and having people wait on me.

Before I begin reading, I'll do my work on visualizing the gum tissue completely healed.

11-7-91, Thursday

I didn't get up today as planned. My private doctor gave orders to stay in bed, because I still had a slight fever. The right side of my jaw is still swollen and very tender. Generally, I would've done better if I didn't need that embedded wisdom tooth pulled. There are moments when my right ear feels as though it's about ready to explode, but overall, I can tell I'm much better today than I was yesterday. Tomorrow I'll definitely get dressed and out of this damned bed. I hate being down.

Aimee passed her First Responder exam and was voted into the Fire Department as an official member. She's no longer a Probationary member. She was told that she could now get her Fire Department license plate and flasher lights for her pickup. She's very excited and her parents are very, very proud of her accomplishments.

The flyer that was sent to the president of the grocery store chain opened a Pandora's Box. The Woodland store was in such an uproar today, it was like a bear had knocked over a beehive. The officials from the main office called in the store manager from his vacation and a big powwow (inter-rogation) went on all day. Robin was called in to the office and was there for two hours—longer than anyone else, be-cause she's the employee rep that everyone comes to.

The feeling we got is that management is fearful employ-ees are going to want another shot at getting the union in. Management is still trying to cover their behinds by claiming the job cuts were made because of the state of the economy, yet in a newsletter they state they're building new stores and profits are being maintained. . .a little contradiction here. And it's this contradiction that Woodland Park's newspaper report-ers need to investigate.

Bill called Bob and explained why the art print for Soul Sounds couldn't be used as an incentive give-away. . .Carole will have prints of *A Gift of Tears* available for sale through mail order from her personally. So a poster was decided upon. A poster of the book's jacket will be used as a give-away with every paid pre-publication order sent in to Hamp-ton Roads.

Sarah had a half-day of school today and, when she came home, she went for a walk in the woods. She was very excited as she burst into my room to tell me about the gift she'd been given. A group of deer shared her presence in the forest. They took note of her and then began to calmly munch on the undergrowth. This made her feel especially good, since her friend on the school bus told her of the huge bull elk he'd shot the day before.

Speaking of that incident, Sarah had a question about it.

"My friend said his family eats everything. They don't waste any of the elk or deer meat. Does that make it okay?"

I smiled. "Sarah, there's only two reasons for killing the wild ones," I said. "If someone lived in the wilds—off the land, or if all the grocery stores were empty." I rose my brow. "Your friend lives 10 minutes from a well-stocked gro-cery store. There's no reason to hunt our four-legged relations and kill them for food when there's plenty of meat on the market shelves." That sounded right to her because it clarified the issues between "quantity eaten" and "necessity." One was an *excuse* to kill while the other was a *reason.*

Before I fall asleep tonight, I will again center my mental and psychic energies on healing my gum tissue.

11-8-91, Friday

Awoke this morning with my jaw screaming and my ear ready to explode. We've got to settle that right nerve down.

Bill called the dentist and he wanted to see me at 10 o'clock. I showered, dressed, and ate a mushy breakfast of scrambled eggs with cheddar cheese melted in.

By the time we reached the dentist's office, the pain was totally under control and, before he examined me, Bill inquired whether I should be on Motrin to control the inflammation of the nerve. That was a good idea and a prescription was written for the stronger strength drug.

After my mouth was thoroughly examined, the dentist looked at me and shook his head.

"I'm amazed, really amazed at the amount of healing that's gone on in just three days."

I loved hearing that. I smiled and pointed to my head.

"I guess all the mind stuff I've been doing has paid off."

Having read most of my books, the doctor just grinned. "Keep it up then, because you're doing a great job."

And next Tuesday morning I get the stitches out. I wonder how much more "amazing" healing I can manage by then? Of course I wouldn't be so arrogant as to take all the credit, not when so many other wonderful forces have been at work.

I was actually feeling rather good when we returned home and I wanted to dig into the stack of mail. Before I could sit down at my desk, Bill had other ideas and booted me out of the office. I was to do nothing but sit in the living room in my reading chair or. . .go back to bed. Phooey! I plopped down in my chair and curled up with a frivolous novel. Around two o'clock I moseyed upstairs and snuggled down beneath our quilt for a little nap.

After a mushy dinner, Bill told me that Bob had called to see how I was. Bob also let Bill know that they were going ahead with the poster idea, and asked Bill if he could photocopy our mailing list for them. I can work on that tomorrow (if Doctor William will permit me that activity).

Bill also brought me the mail to read. He'd already processed it all.

A woman wove me a beautiful strip of native beadwork

with my initials in the center. That was very touching to me
and I admired all the intricate work that had gone into it.

One letter that I thought was interesting was from a correspondent who works at the NBC Studios in Burbank. She
was wanting to help with our Wellspring Mission and came
up with the idea of placing a box labeled Wellspring Mission
at work so employees could drop off discarded clothing items.
This lady said she could ship everything to us.

My goodness! Truly I never imagined that so many of my
readers would want to personally become involved in our new
project. This totally unexpected situation has been a public
response that surprised all of us in the family. We never
even considered the possibility of others wanting to be a part
of our work. But what a beautiful surprise it has been! In a
way, it makes me giggle to think we have so many "helpers"
out there who are helping us help the needy. It makes me
feel that our little Family Circle that was involved in this
special mission has gently spread out in a wide ripple to
include many good souls in the project.

We received a note from Eric today. He expects to arrive
in Woodland Park on December 13th. Aimee says she's not
interested. That may be, but Aimee knows Aimee still must
have it out with him all the same. If she doesn't, it'll never
be a part of her life that she can close the door on. It'll
always be something that was left unresolved and my girls
know better than to run rather than "facing" something to the
finish.

Heard a national newscast anchorman say on television tonight that President Bush said that "we are not in a recession."

Oh. . .get *real*, Mr. Bush. I think you can't talk the struggling public into your own little reality. Wishing isn't going
to put food on our tables and give us jobs. Incredible. . .just
incredible. So many hurting and in such misery, and there he
stands saying it's not real. I wonder if he has some New
Age books in his closet?

Tonight I received a phone call from a friend of ours who
is a physician interested in alternative healing. He'd recently
gotten his hands on a small machine that healed all manner
of illnesses through the use of vibrations. This utilized the
varying frequency rates that correspond with those of the disease. . .just as No-Eyes spoke of with Gateway Healing. But,
my friend cautioned, the machine was illegal according to the
FDA, and condemned by the AMA and National Cancer In-

stitute. If he used it he'd be breaking the law. . .but he was
undaunted. He was going to go ahead and follow his spirit's
lead on this thing.

After I hung up the phone, I thought about all the secrets
there were and how many professional people were confiding in
me. Then I picked up my pen and wrote of all those secrets.

What a sorry world mortals make,
Where so many are on the take,
And can be bought for a price,
With a throw of loaded dice.

Secrets. . .so many secrets.

Folks don't see the things I see,
When many mortals confide in me,
Nor can they even begin to guess,
How many things that are suppressed.

Secrets. . .so many secrets.

But no one sees the secret world,
Around the mortals that unfurls,
And so they miss the blackened shroud,
Because their heads are in the clouds.

Secrets. . .so many secrets.

Then so another page is turned,
And still no one has learned.
What a sorry world mortals make,
When so many are on the take.

11-9-91, Saturday

The day didn't begin well. Mornings are the worst time
for me in respect to my pain and I have to eat something
before I begin my medication. Bill wanted to fix me breakfast, but nothing was turning out, because he wasn't in a
good mood. He burned two pancakes and the third attempt
was mushy inside. Between that, all his swearing, and my
pain, I told him to go take his shower and I'd fix some
scrambled eggs.

I fixed the eggs, but he still hung around grumbling and
slamming things around in the kitchen. It hurt to eat and he

was upsetting me. I began to cry and I put my plate on the floor for Magic.

Bill finally went back upstairs. He'd been extremely on edge —stressed out—lately, because of a culmination of things. Our finances, the law suit, problems at Aimee's work (she'd just been cut to 16 hours a week), counseling complications, etc., all placed a personal burden on his shoulders and he'd been on edge for several weeks. This, with the added tension my surgery had put on his nerves made a very short fuse and frayed nerve endings.

On his way upstairs, he barked at anyone who was unfortunate enough to cross his path. He'd been like this for a while now and, although we all understood the reasons for it, that knowledge still didn't make life easier to cope with.

While Bill showered, I typed up the journal entries I'd written while in bed. When he came back downstairs he was clearly making a noble attempt to start the day over.

We took Jenny to town, while Sarah stayed home to finish her art project that's due Monday. I'd wanted to explore the new Hallmark shop and I found three little treasures—squirrel and chipmunk Christmas tree decorations. The main reason for going to Hallmark's was to get a birthday card for our friend Art and to pick up more thank-you note cards that we use in our correspondence.

When Jenny and I went back to the van, Bill had a Bad Boy look on his face as he held up a bouquet of purple carnations and baby's breath.

"I'm sorry for this morning," he said.

My eyes began to mist and I kissed him. I know the tremendous pressure he's under as the Main Warrior and Chief of our small clan. His responsibility is incredible and he takes it very seriously.

Jenny leaned forward and kissed her dad.

"That's okay, daddy, even if you *did* make me cry this morning." Jenny's very straightforward and not at all reticent to speak her mind. But then that's our Jenny and we're well accustomed to her ways.

Our next stop was the grocery store where Jenny and I browsed the deli and seafood section. We had to pick up some pastrami, and I spied the deviled shrimp. That'd be a real treat for Bill, I thought.

When we arrived back home, he grinned in pleasure as we had our lunch and he thoroughly savored the rare treat of a fresh shrimp cocktail. Of course I tried to ignore what he was eating as I sat and mashed up my own mushy repast of macaroni and cheese.

The rest of the day was spent working in the office. It

was the first day I worked at my desk. After I helped process the mail, I got busy with catching up on the correspondence that had backlogged on my desk. It was a big load off my mind to clean those up because I hate having work left undone and waiting for me.

We worked until dinnertime and my eyes tried not to attach themselves to the over-stuffed pastrami sandwiches, cole slaw, and potato salad everyone was enjoying. I had to concentrate hard on my own plate of mashed up baked potato and sour cream. It was very good, but I sure would've loved just one itty-bitty bite of that tender pastrami.

After dinner Bill returned to the office where he began photocopying our mailing list for Bob to use for the *Soul Sounds* pre-publication offer.

I went to bed at 10:30, leaving Bill and the girls in the living room engrossed in an Eddy Murphy video Aimee had brought home from work.

In our darkened bedroom, I opened the drapes to the deck doors and turned on the floodlights. Sitting with my legs crossed before the glass, I watched the falling snow and contemplated the incredible beauty of this winter mountain night. I wished I could be out dancing with Snow Maker, letting him wrap his crystal white garment around me. These thoughts faded into prayers that were so intense that I eventually lost myself within the warm aura of the Power that accepted both my prayers and my humble essence.

11-10-91, Sunday

This was one of those rare and treasured days when nothing needed our immediate attention and all the office work was caught up. I think people call this "relaxation." We're not real familiar with this state of being.

Bill was in a good mood and brought me breakfast in bed. Magic and kitty followed him into the bedroom and they parked themselves in strategically calculated positions that would best serve their intentions. Magic knew her golden eyes would melt my heart as she looked up at me, and kitty was within a paw's reach of my plate as she settled herself next to me. It was very comforting to have these two furry companions for company—even though I knew their true reasons for being there was more out of their love for their stomachs than for me. Still. . .their cute antics warmed my heart and made it smile. It was a good way to begin a new day.

Bill occupied himself by doing a few odds and ends-type things around the house and I snuggled down in the reindeer robe on my reading chair to finish *Journey Across Tibet* by Sorrel Wilby. This was a beautifully descriptive account of a young Australian woman's trek across 1,900 miles through some of the highest and exotic regions on earth. I love reading of these personal journeys. Without realizing it, I'm transported across the world to walk as a silent companion beside the author to see what they see and to share their adventurous spirit.

While the woodstove crackled and flames on the oil pots radiated an aesthetic sense of coziness and tranquility throughout the room, I journeyed from one friendly Tibetan nomad village to the next, totally absorbed in my new surroundings until. . .football kickoff.

Jenny and Bill had settled themselves before the television. I hadn't even been aware of the increased activity and their excited preparations until the Bronco game was suddenly blasting, the house began to tremble with Rocky Mountain Thunder, and Magic barked and ran around and around with a Bronco football in her mouth. My far-away journey had been shattered and I'd been sharply jerked back to my own wild world of Broncomania. By the way, since others will be reading this, I probably should explain what Rocky Mountain Thunder is.

At Denver's Mile Hi Stadium, the fans in the stands begin to stamp their feet. As the activity spreads from one section to the next, the growing sound resembles rolling thunder. At home, when a great play is made by a Bronco member during a game everyone watching joins those in the stands and the house shakes with Rocky Mountain Thunder. In turn, this signals Magic to bark and take up her football to run around and around the living room in her shared enthusiasm.

We didn't win the game this day—lost by one point—but a tremendous amount of stress and tension was released and that ain't all bad.

Toward the end of the game, Jenny fixed dinner and I amazed myself by actually managing to eat (very slowly and carefully) the topping off two pieces of pizza. I couldn't manage the crust underneath, but what I did eat sure beat the baby mush I'd previously been forced to ingest for so many days. This had been the first meal I didn't spend eyeing other people's plates. I was totally content.

Afterwards, Bill and I snuggled up together on the couch to watch a true-story movie staring Judith Light. It was about a woman who slowly poisoned her husband with injections of arsenic, and then attempted the same with her daughter. After the movie we discussed the psychological mechanisms of the woman's mind.

We retired shortly afterward and I left the journal to be filled in in the morning. After we snuggled for a while and Bill turned over, I prayed until I fell asleep. The special prayers were for our clan Warrior known as William Joseph.

11-11-91, Monday

Before I could step into the shower this morning there was a knock at the bathroom door—there stood Bill with my breakfast tray. I scooted back into bed and again was surrounded by my furry companions.

It was another good day. No mail today, because it was Veteran's Day. Although our office work was practically nil, we'd received a UPS delivery from Link. I had four enormous boxes of supplies to sort out and spent most of the day working on those. We ended up with a little over 260 lbs. of food for Bill to distribute on Wednesday.

Sarah's "photo-real" art work was due today and she was nervous about her final grade on it. There was more detail she wanted to bring out on the native man's face, but time had run out. She's such a perfectionist when she's working on her art projects, and she works slowly and precisely.

When she came home from school she was all smiles. Her art teacher had praised her portrait and held it up to the rest of the class as an example of where they should be. The teacher embarrassed Sarah by telling the class that she had real talent and an eye for art. He wants to keep her project to enter into various art shows throughout the rest of the school year. She was so thrilled, because she expected him to criticize it for not having every detail shaded in. Poor Sarah, my heart goes out to her, because I can relate to her feelings and fears of not being liked or not doing well enough. Yet for someone with as little art training as she's had, she's really very good. Today was a big boost to her confidence and self-image.

The manager of cashiers at the grocery store offered Aimee a midnight shift position. Respectfully she declined, but she felt more like telling him what he could do with his suggestion if that was all he had to offer her. Although the bakery department just laid off three people, and Aimee doesn't get many hours, she still enjoys working in that section of the store.

We were talking about this situation this evening and I'd casually mentioned an ad I'd seen in our local paper. Our friends in Cripple Creek who own the Phenix Rising Gallery and the Phenix Gaming House were advertising for casino help.

Jokingly I said to the family, "I know! Why don't we move to Cripple Creek and we *all* could work in the casinos!"

To my surprise, Aimee, Robin, and Jenny responded in kind. "Yeah! Let's do that!"

Whoa. *Me* dress up in a *dance hall* girl outfit? And I grinned wide as I expressed that very thought.

"No way," Bill laughed. "No way at all."

My wheels were spinning as I grinner wider.

Bill didn't like the looks of it.

"Whatever you're thinking, I don't think I like it," he growled.

"Oh," I said, "I was just visualizing how nice it'd be to work where people are having a good time and laughing. That'd be such a change, don't you think? Especially from Aimee's depressing work environment."

Everyone agreed with that aspect—that *one* aspect. But nobody wanted to actually move to Cripple Creek. Sarah said, "no way" to the Cripple Creek school. And that squished the whole idea.

Later in the evening I caught Bill grinning to himself. I eyed him. "Now what're you thinking?"

"Oh. . .I was just picturing you parading around the casino in one of those frilly little saloon girl outfits and how shocked people would be to know where Summer Rain was working."

"It's not a very apropos visual. Still. . .it might be fun to work in a happy atmosphere for a change."

Bill's brows shot down in a sharp and decided vee.

"And just what do you think our Advisors or your Starfriend would think of that brainy idea?"

I shuddered.

"That's what I thought, too," he said. "Case closed. We struggle on until we know how this law suit gets settled, then we'll see if we all need to go out and get jobs somewhere."

"In Cripple Creek? "

"Honey," he sighed. "If They can't see their way clear to finally get us what we need to get settled and do our work, then I don't much care where we live anymore. The point is—we need to live—we need to get on with our lives and support this family. The time is almost here when we won't be able to live on promises anymore. . .time will have run out on us. . . and, depending on where we are when it does, that will be our deciding factor.

"The Plan and all its aspects won't mean a damn if we're not provided with the means to carry it out. If we're not, then we have to all go get jobs so we can at least get a little place of our own. We've given it our best shot and done everything asked of us, but we can't print the damn money we need."

There wasn't anything left to say after that. Time *was* running out and we both knew it. We could *feel* it. It haunted our days and nights. The dark aura of the thought caused us continual stress as its approaching deadline crept nearer and nearer each day.

11-12-91, Tuesday

Last night Bill and I had difficulty sleeping. I'd had enough pain medication to sweep me away on a warm wave of deep sleep, but I laid awake for hours. I could feel Bill's alertness too. From downstairs, I could hear Magic getting on and off her bed—a couch in our office just beneath our bedroom—she too was restless with some thing felt.

In the morning, Bill asked me if I'd had a good sleep, and I told him I didn't think I did sleep—much. Then he described the dark shapes he'd seen in our room during the night. He never felt threatened in any way, only a detached state of psychic observance was present. He said he felt as though he was seeing the various forces that are around the outside perimeter of our protective circle trying to break through it.

As I write this entry I'm uneasy. Everyone's in bed. The living room to my left is dark except for the two oil pots burning on the mantle.

Kitty just ran upstairs to seek Jenny's bed and Magic keeps nudging my elbow. Her ears are plastered back and her tail is hidden between her legs—she's scared.

I keep peering into the dark shadows to my left as though something is drawing my attention, but all appears normal when I look. It's not my Starborn friend—he doesn't play games or frighten our pets. I'm trying to rub Magic's head to comfort her while I write this. I think she'd crawl upon my lap if she could.

We had a triple stack of mail today and both Bill and I worked until dinnertime on it. After our meal, he watched the news while I returned to the office to sign the children's books that were ordered today.

One letter I was excited to receive was from my sister Elise. She and Charlie are leaving Michigan on the 16th to drive to their newly-built cedar home in North Carolina. She'd sent me progressive photos of how their house was coming along during the building stages and it looks so wonderful. The woods come right up to their back deck. I was literally tickled to get her note that they were finally leaving. How perfect to be able to be in their new home for Thanksgiving and Christmas—what a great holiday present! I wished we could've somehow been there on their porch when they arrived. I would've loved to welcome them and help them settle in. Elise gave me her new address and telephone number. I immediately made out their Thanksgiving card and hope it will be the first piece of mail they receive at their new home. I'll call them on the 17th hoping it's the first phone call they receive. I'm just so happy for them. I know they're going to love it there.

Elise also wrote that the last time they were down there, they were invited over for coffee at their new neighbor's house. They got talking about books and Elise said that her sister was a writer. The new neighbor had read *Phoenix Rising*. That tickled me too, because earlier I'd written Elise to tell her that a nearby Asheville store sold a lot of my books and that she wasn't going to be able to get away from me. Now her new neighbor has even read one of my books. I'm sure that surprised her, because, before she'd come to Colorado to visit us last year, she and Charlie had never realized the extent of my readership. After Bill showed them our mailing list they were somewhat amazed.

The temporary dental appliance I have in my mouth has caused some raw gum and teeth pain today, but I tried to hide it from Bill. If he had his way he'd keep me on Percocet until I was completely healed and my teeth didn't cause any more discomfort. I don't think I'm very expert at acting, because I've caught him watching me several times today. When he'd ask how I was doing I'd say okay. When he got more specific and asked if I hurt I'd say just a little.

Magic just ran into the office and up the stairs. I can hear her scrambling up on Sarah's bed in the loft above the living room. She's probably trying to get under Sarah's quilt.

Now I'm down here alone.

Our general mood today was dampened somewhat by what

Bill had said last evening about Time and us getting settled. It seemed that whenever we discussed that subject it always served to darken our outlook for a few days, because it recalled all the struggles we'd been through and reminded us that we weren't through with them even though we were bone tired.

There it is again. . .in the living room shadows. There's something there.
My protection just tripled itself around me.
Damn, this is creepy.
No threat felt.
I'll keep on.

All day today our phone was on the fritz. It'd ring with only a quarter ring and when we'd answer we'd hear a dial tone. Sometimes the light on Bill's desk phone would be on. This light indicates a "phone in use" signal such as our kitchen extension, but nobody would be using it. This irritating problem persisted all day. Other times we'd pick up the receiver and the line would be completely dead.
Bill had Robin see if our neighbors' phones were out too. She'd gone to five houses and nobody was home at any of them so we couldn't verify if it was a regional problem with the lines in our area.

Now I hear a whispering from the living room. I peered up toward the loft to see if maybe Sarah had her light on and was soothing Magic—all is dark. I walked through the darkness to the front stairs and listened. . .no sound was coming from her room.
On the way back to the kitchen I walked through icy air —right in front of the hot woodstove.
My protection felt solid.
Now I know who's here.
I'm going back into the living room. I must get this over with.
Raphael. . .stand behind me.

An hour later —
I'd gone into the dark living room. He was there—in the corner—standing his full height. The black aura wavered about him, yet no flame reflection from the oil pots illumined any part of him. He was like a Black Hole that sucked even firelight into his vile being to extinguish its life.
In a voice that was deep, deep, he spoke.

"Where is Raphael? Where is your Michael? I see none of your precious archangels here to shield you from me now."

I said nothing, while I split consciousness between his presence and my protection.

Behind his cowled hood came laughter.

"You. . .are. . .*alone!*"

That wasn't true.

"Ahhh. . .so you do not believe me. Shall I prove it to you then?"

"Yes."

He sighed. "I've not come for games. I've come to offer you an alliance."

Silence.

"Are you in pain, my dear? I can take all your pain away. You know that, don't you. Does Raphael or any of your *protectors* do that for you?"

"I don't expect them to. . .that's not why they're here."

"Here? Here?" he said, looking about. "Where?"

"It won't work. You can see them all as well as I can. You would never be allowed in this house if they didn't allow it, so. . ."

"Allow? *ALLOW?*" His angered tone then dropped off suddenly. His voice became softer—almost a creamy whisper. "I can give you your *land*! I can give you all the *money* you would ever need or *want*! Would you like to buy your *property* next *month*? Be *settled* like your *sister* is in her brand new cedar house in the *woods*?"

"Get out of my house," I said in a return whisper. "Get thee gone."

"Ohhh, we slip back into our olde tongue? How clever we are."

"We are not *we*. We will never be a *we*."

"No, not yet. Would you like to take away people's misery? *Heal* them? I could make that possible for you. Think about how much *suffering* you could ease by just *touching* the sick! I could even give you the *energy* device you've tried to plead for from your *friend*! Now. . .you want to stop all pollution, do you not?"

"Yes, yes I do. I want to heal people and I want to stop the suffering too. You know all my desires—land and being settled. How is it you do not offer what I desire most?"

"Most?"

Silence.

Searching.

Waiting.

"You are a greater *fool* than even *I* had anticipated! You will *regret* your decision. I would've preferred you on *my* side!"

A blinding ray of laser light flashed out from behind me.

And the leader of the Dark Warriors had vanished.

I slumped in prayer. For 30 minutes I prayed, then returned to my journal. I was reluctant to record what had transpired for fear it would reveal too much, or perhaps damage my integrity, but the sweet voice that came from behind me prompted the entry to continue. This, *because* of integrity. Just as the hand of Abraham was stayed, mine is urged to move across the page.

I've done as asked yet I've omitted some of the verbatim words that were spoken this night between the Dark One and me. These were words relating to a past identity of mine that I prefer to remain untold. The words and the identity are not germane to the meaning of what transpired tonight.

I'd be lying if I said I wasn't shaken by the encounter. Not just because of the Dark One's vile aura, but I'm becoming more and more outraged that he appeared for the reason he did. Playing on my most wanted desires! *Bribing* me! Why, the whole of all my accumulative *lives* would've been forfeit. Did he not know I'd think of that? And how was it he knew not my greatest wish at that moment? How was it he knew not that, more than anything in the world, I wished him gone? "Get thee gone from me" repeated over and over in my mind until finally he heard.

My Father, is it truly possible this one can be fooled after all? Is that what I needed to learn from this vile lesson? Is that why he was allowed to come so close? So I could see? Know?

Father, I'm confused. How is it he knew not the heart and mind of me? How is it he knew not where my allegiance lay? Wouldn't he already know I couldn't be bribed by material things or use healing to turn myself over to evil? How is it he didn't really know me? Is this a flaw in his nature or a fault in my thinking? I must gain clarity on this for it does confound my mind.

Raphael, for the first time in this lifetime I have witnessed the might and glory of your powerful sword. If I live to be an old, old woman, never will I forget what my eyes have beheld this night. The vision of it will be with me all my days.

Thank you, Raphael, for standing tall behind me this night. Thank you for being there. . .again.

11-13-91, Wednesday

By the time I came downstairs, Robin had helped Bill load the boxes of food into the van. Shortly afterward, he and Jenny took off for town. It was going to be a busy morning.

Their first stop was to drop the food shipment off and one of the recipients exclaimed, "Oh, here's Bill Anonymous! We're so grateful for all you do." They found out his first name, because "Bill" is on the front of his jacket—he'd forgotten about that.

Next they picked Sarah up from school and took her over to the orthodontist's where the Happy Day was celebrated— her braces came off. And what a beautiful smile she has now.

Afterward, all three walked next door to keep their chiropractic appointment. Sarah had brought the good Dr. Dave a cartoon she'd cut out of the newspaper. It depicted *hunters* running from buckshot. . . a Rambo *deer* was shooting at them.

Dr. Dave had mistakenly mentioned going on a hunting trip down near Durango, Colorado and Sarah had read him the riot act. But today he told her not to worry, because, more and more, he just likes getting out in nature and is losing his desire to hunt.

Sarah was dropped off at school and Bill and Jenny came home after their final stop at the post office. They went into the kitchen to have lunch while I sat at my desk to start my office day.

For once the mail was light. There was an envelope from the school. It was Sarah's report card. Way to go, Sarah! Six A's and one B!

The rest of the mail was general comments and questions except for two of them. Both the sender's names and addresses got the special treatment of being recorded on a special colored index card and the letters themselves were placed into our "Negative" file. We keep track of the crude, abusive, and deranged-type letters. One of these was from someone who took the time to hand-write 12 pages of something neither Bill nor I could make head nor tail of. We couldn't tell if the correspondent loved or hated my books, because it appeared to be both ways.

The other name that received the special attention was a reader who sent me two photocopied sheets from some publication regarding "Curly, Larry, Moe, and student" "Ascended Master" propaganda again (with photo of the Phoney Four).

This kind person also went nuts circling and underscoring the text passages—which still do not represent the truth of the issue.

I cannot imagine why these people waste postage stamps sending me their junk mail. Do they delude themselves into thinking they're "teaching me the *truth* of the matter?" God Almighty, what I'd like to say here to get across the proper comparison cannot be written without revealing who Bill and I once were. But *people*, please *do* wake *up!* PLEASE!

Tonight Jenny prepared a delicious fresh fish dinner and I could eat all of it. What a treat that was and it surprised me, because my teeth hurt like hell.

After dinner when I was in the office bathroom doing my routine saltwater rinsing, Bill came in and picked up my dental appliance. He silently examined it for several minutes and then asked to see my mouth

"You've got some bad sores in there," he observed, "they're all raw. No wonder you're in constant pain."

I didn't say anything back. I'd had a mouthful of saltwater and was swishing it around. I watched him again scrutinize the appliance.

"Mmmm," he mumbled, setting it down before he left.

I peeked out the door to watch him disappear into the shop. He reappeared with his electric drill in one hand and a sanding disc in the other.

For 45 minutes he alternated between sanding my appliance and checking my mouth. Finally he rinsed it off and had me put it back in my mouth. My eyes widened—no pain!

He was incredulous.

"I can't believe you wore this thing for a week and never realized it needed reshaping. I can't believe your pain was that simple to alleviate. I never thought to check it before now, but you're the one going around suffering with it. God, honey, I feel awful we didn't do this right from the start."

I hugged him. "You devil," I grinned, "you took my pain away!"

He laughed at that one.

"I guess after last night you could say the devil made me do it. Who needs him anyway? What else can I help you with?"

I smiled. "Ohhh, I'll think of something."

And I did.

The house has a deep tranquility to it tonight. Kitty is sound asleep, curled up in my reading chair, and Magic's sawing wood on her couch in the office. The woodstove is crackling and the twin flames of the oil pots are casting a warm glow through the living room darkness. Shadows are dancing over the moss rock walls, inviting me to whisper the preliminary chants of my Prayer Smoke. It is a good night to pray. I have so much to be thankful for. The mixture of cedar, Myrrh and Frankincense will be especially sweet this night as the fragrant smoke rises to the house of my Father.

11-14-91, Thursday

Bill and I went into town. I had a dental appointment to have my stitches taken out. Everything's looking good and I had no pain today except for a little general soreness with that temporary appliance sitting on top of healing tissue. I'll have to wear that until around the first of January because it keeps my teeth from moving.

Didn't have much mail when we picked it up and, after we stopped at the hardware store to buy more wild birdseed, we headed home.

Shortly after lunch, Bill and Aimee headed down to Colorado Springs. She needed to be fitted for her Fire Department uniform and Bill surprised her by taking her over to Laytons to pick up the portable red flasher he'd ordered for her pickup. She was so surprised, because her dad kept telling her we didn't have the extra money for her flasher. She'd had to put up with a lot at work lately and Bill wanted to give her morale a boost—something to be happy about.

I spent the afternoon with Jenny, but since she was one-minded about getting certain things done around the house (she's extremely regimented and quite a perfectionist Virgo), I didn't disrupt her routine. Instead, I kept the woodstove full, watered all our plants, and filled the birdfeeder. Afterwards, I curled up in my reading chair with a new book while Magic settled herself beside me on the floor. I nodded off a couple times. It was so restful in the house. It's vibrations are a soft, wavering type that exude a complete calm and comfort to those dwelling within.

When Bill and Aimee came home, I was called outside. There stood Aimee next to the blue pickup with a bright red flasher going 'round and 'round on top. She was all smiles. She's really into this fire and rescue work—it seems to fulfill a great need she has to help people. I never would've guessed that our tiny, petite daughter would ever choose to do that kind of work. Sometimes when I look at her the visual of a fragile China doll subliminally flashes through my mind; but she's one determined young lady and can be quite a scrappy little fighter that holds her own. I think maybe the little wolverine is her animal totem. If one is smart. . .one does not mess with a wolverine!

Bill handed me a few pieces of mail he'd picked up from the post office on the way back up the pass from downtown. One was this month's Home Guide from Glenwood Springs. I quickly looked through it. I knew the Real Estate Company that had our Marble property listing and I was hoping to see it still for sale. I saw it alright. . .they'd subdivided the acreage. The main log house was now only on three acres with no other cabins with it. What a terrible disappointment. Oh well. When the time is right for us to purchase something I'm sure there will be just the right piece of property available for us.

Toward the back of the Home Guide, I spied another piece of property I wanted (only a dream though) and the price had been reduced. It is called the Diamond J Ranch and is located above the Ruedi Reservoir. It has a main log lodge with nine guest rooms, a full-service kitchen, and 12 guest cabins on 27 deeded acres plus 200 acres of National Forest Permit Use behind it. And. . .ta-da. . .it's not $1.2 million anymore—it's only a paltry $995,000. Okay, let's break open the piggy bank and go buy it. Sure, Summer Rain, only in your dreams. . .only in your dreams. That "piggy bank" wouldn't even get you a one-room miner's shack right now.

Another piece of mail was one juicy and satisfying piece. The day Bill had sent our Midnight Raiders flyer to the president of the grocery store chain, he'd also sent one to the man who was in charge of organizing the union vote last November. So the union also got a flyer.

We'd not heard anything back and were beginning to wonder how our flyer was received and what they would do with it. Well. . .the employees of City Market got a little pamphlet from the union and inside. . .on page two. . .was a reprint of our flyer! How sweet it was to see what had become of it. Now the City Market managers are really in a sweat and, Robin tells us that, next Wednesday the Big Boys from the main office are coming to the Woodland Store for a pow-wow. . .again! Our little flyer is making a lot of people scramble and sweat over the possibility of a new move to have another union vote in the store.

So far, the two newspapers in town who each received our flyer have remained "mum" on the issue. Of course, the grocery store does place a lot of full-page ads, yes? Truth or money, that is the question. Isn't that usually what it comes down to a good part of the time? Hands get greased and mouths get shut.

I thought up several very meaningful and to-the-point cartoons I might have Sarah draw up for the flyers that get distributed to cars in the grocery store parking lot (if it comes to that). Sarah's all fired up. Remember. . .she was in diapers when her mom and dad last did a major raid, so she's anxious to be active in one with us. What a little minx she is.

Aimee had classes at the Ambulance Barn tonight, but she's not on-call at the fire station. Bill had her take the van (with her new flasher, of course), because Snow Maker is coming. The weatherman's forecast was for 20 inches between tonight and tomorrow. Bill's all excited over this. Good grief, if that forecast comes true, he's going to want to put the Christmas tree up again—or at least string the lights in the living room. He's like a little boy with this "snow" thing. Well, that's fine with me; every man should let his Little Boy come out to play at least once a year and what better time than Christmas? However. . .please, Bill, *please* don't put the tree up before the Thanksgiving turkey is cooked!

My Prayer Smoke will rise tonight for a correspondent's special request that came in today. I will also say a few words that may make Bill happy when he looks out our window in the morning. Snow Maker can lend a hand for this one.

11-15-91, Friday

There was snow this morning, but not the 20 inches that were predicted. Snow Maker is doing a slow dance along the Colorado mountains and has decided to waltz around the southern hills before he does his Mazurka over Woodland Park. That's okay, as long as he shows us his fancy footwork, we can wait a few days to enjoy the extravaganza.

A few days ago, a correspondent sent us a gift of $50 for Wellspring Mission, and I cashed it today to buy fresh fruits and vegetables, and some warm winter wear for our recipients.

Afterward, Bill dropped me off at home and he took Jenny grocery shopping. I got busy on the mail and Aimee announced that the UPS man had just dropped off three large boxes. I told her to bring them in the office, because they were probably clothing donations for our Mission and we'd sort them out later. She'd lugged the boxes in.

"Mom, I don't think there's any clothes in these. I think it's a machine of some kind."

"Machine?"

Good God. . .the computer!

I'd just opened the top flaps of each box and it looked as though we'd had a computer, a WordPerfect keyboard, Star multi-font printer, joy stick, monitor, and a 6-outlet surge protector.

I had to sit down. I knew nothing whatsoever about computers but felt awed at what was before me. . .this was somehow very, very special.

After a time, I returned to the mail. One letter was from one of the two people who sent the computer. She explained that it'd been "built" for our own specific needs and the telephone number of its creator was listed at the bottom of the letter. We were to call him and he would "walk" us through assembly and use.

I didn't know what she meant by "built." Maybe that was another term for "loading." So I put the letter with the boxes and resumed work on the mail.

Aimee had been studying in the kitchen while I was alone at my desk. I had my cassette music playing and cedar was burning. The mood was set and I didn't even realize it, for the letters and cards we received today were deeply moving . . .deeply.

All of a sudden I was overcome with the feelings of love from my readers. It was like a tiny pinpoint of warm, rosy light had ignited somewhere in the world and it grew and grew as it traveled from one of my reader's hearts to another —collecting the love. When it reached me, it touched me like a huge fragile bubble that burst in shimmering sparkles of pink light throughout my being.

And I was overwhelmed with the tremendous feeling of love. I broke down and cried. I cried great tears that fell and fell.

"People *do* love me," I whispered through the sobs. "They really do."

Never before had I actually "felt" that deep love that's out there for No-Eyes and us. Today it came barreling down on me like a runaway train. . .and it hit me square in the heart with its powerful force.

I turned to look at the boxes on the floor. A computer. A real computer. How is it we are so blessed with that kind of unconditional love from these two people?

Turning back to the letter I'd been reading, I saw that I'd smeared the ink with my tears. And again. . .I could not hold them back and they fell in a stream from a long-closed floodgate that had finally burst open—free.

By the time Bill and Jenny returned, I was decently composed. When Bill saw the computer I'd unpackaged his own eyes misted. He too felt the love of good souls who cared so much for us.

After dinner, Bill called the lady who sent the computer letter. He told her how grateful we were and that he was sorry, but Mary was too emotional to speak to her right then. She understood.

I felt like a fool. I wanted to talk to her in the worst way, but every time I mentally rehearsed the "thank you" part, the lump came in my throat and I knew I'd begin to cry. Maybe that sounds like a real baby, but no one's ever done anything like that before for us and I was just so deeply touched and appreciative.

Bill spoke with the woman for two hours, while I listened in the background. When he hung up he said that the lady and her gentleman friend (clearly a computer genius) had wanted to do this for us. Bill said another package was coming with disks, printer ribbons, books and games. He said the computer itself *had been built especially for us* by this man. It was already loaded with a data base, WordPerfect, Print Shop, Banner, and other menu items such as Questions & Answer. The menu was entitled "Phoenix Light." Bill also said the computer has two different disk-style drives, plus the 40 megabyte hard-drive, which the man will upgrade to 100 if we need it. I couldn't believe what I was hearing.

When Link called us while Bill was telling me about our new computer, he began to tell her what we'd received.

She laughed. "You guys got a million dollar computer in front of you and you don't even know it!" She knows computers and was absolutely incredulous that someone would personally "design" and "build" a computer for us. She said this man must be a genius. It would seem so, but to me—he was one kind and bright soul.

About 20 minutes later, the Genius himself called us. Bill

told him we were going to have a friend (Link) come over in a few days to help us with the computer.

"No you're not, Good Buddy," the man said. "You're going to assemble and work it right now."

Bill's face went white.

"Maybe you need to know we're a couple of computer dummies here."

"Not for long," he said. "Get Mary on the line." And the Genius talked one of the Dummies through the assembly of all the components. The Genius had the Dummy run the Banner program.

"Which daughter is around?" he asked me.

"Sarah's right here," I said.

"She's the one who likes art?"

"Yes, she's very good." I looked over at Sarah and she was turning red. She was afraid "the man" was going to want to talk to her or, heaven forbid, have her *do* something on the computer too.

The Man said, "I'll send her one of the art programs. Put her on and we'll have her run through Print Shop now."

I handed the phone receiver to Sarah and her face went white.

"Me?" she mouthed to me.

I nodded. She thanked the man for the wonderful gift, and they talked for a few minutes about her interest in art. Then his instructions began and she created a greeting card from Print Shop. She was laughing and having a great time.

Then he spent another 45 minutes with Bill showing him various things.

When the Genius asked to speak to me again, he inquired about Aimee's and Jenny's interests. When he heard about Aimee's firefighting and medical training he mentioned a biofeedback program, and perhaps her learning acupuncture. He also talked about programs that utilized special glasses worn by the operator. He said we were going to have a lot of fun.

He's going to call Monday night to walk Bill through the process of putting our mailing list and index-card information on a disk. Then his lady friend will call another day to instruct me step-by-step on how to run my manuscripts through the WordPerfect program. They also want to work with each of the girls in turn.

I'm very concerned that these two wonderful people will run up tremendous telephone bills with all this teaching they want to give us. Bill expressed this to the Genius and the man brushed it off and told us not to let it concern us.

Still. . .these two gave us an unbelievable gift from their loving hearts and I don't want them going to greater expense.

We were on the phone nearly three hours tonight—that's going to be an expensive call on our new friend's phone bill. I truly wish they lived closer than Michigan. . .like maybe next door?

Bill is so excited over this computer. He feels a spirit connection to our gift-givers and truly enjoyed the Genius' marvelous outgoing personality. I don't think I can remember when Bill was this excited about anything. His eyes are actually twinkling.

11-16-91, Saturday

Mail was heavy today. I'd received a letter of invitation from Shanti Toll from Celebration bookstore to be a keynote speaker at the Colorado Springs Metaphysical Fair. It's a three-day event held twice a year. I respectfully declined and stated my reasons, but added that we may be interested in having a booth for our children's book and also, because *Soul Sounds* is due to be released at the time of the fair, perhaps we could arrange a booksigning through Celebration.

Bill brought home a box of computer printer paper from town this morning, and he was so excited to set it up and experiment with it. Sarah typed a letter on the computer and they printed it out. Then she went to the Banner program and played with that, but neither of them could get a printout to take place. . .we need a lot more lessons.

This evening Bill called the lady who sent the computer. I was supposed to talk to her too. I waited at my desk for Bill to finish his conversation. I waited. . .and waited. . .and waited. After an hour had passed and he was still gabbing, I went outside to shovel the 9 inches of snow that had accumulated on our front deck.

It was a beautiful night. The snow was light and as fluffy as goose down. The deep silence intensified the sound of falling snow and I wished I could go right then for a long walk in the woods. But I was waiting for Bill to tell me it was my turn to talk to our Giftgiver. I was anxious to thank her. I also wanted to tell her we need to concentrate our instruction time on teaching Bill how to transfer the mailing list, instead of my learning WordPerfect, because all of my manuscripts were already typed up anyway.

A minute after I stepped back inside and shook myself

off, Sarah tells me daddy wants me in the office. Oh good, now I can properly thank our generous benefactor. I raced through the house and when I entered the office, Bill was at his desk—no phone in hand. He'd hung up.

I was irritated he'd gotten yakking (as usual) and completely forgot that I was supposed to talk too. Oh well. I went back outside and shoveled our back porch and the office porch.

What Bill had wanted to tell me was that our computer-giver had done an astrology chart on both of us. She'd said that 1992 showed major changes in both charts. That's interesting, because when Jyoti Walsh did our charts she said the same thing.

I feel it has to do with the 14-year cycle we're coming out of. We came here with our mission 14 years ago and now we've been feeling certain aspects coming full circle. I suspect that 1992 will bring several major changes for us.

We heard that the "King" at the grocery store has been playing up this flyer mystery to the hilt. Today he's been going around to the employees announcing that "they may be getting a letter from the union!" Ooooh, the mystery deepens and the plot thickens. There's something invisible afoot and nobody knows what. . .or who.

I need to correct an error I made in respect to the "King's" position at the grocery store. He's not an official manager, he's a department head. I guess there's a distinction between the two.

Tonight my Prayer Smoke will rise for a correspondent who wrote me today. He's serving a life sentence in a prison and has been greatly helped by No-Eyes' wisdom.

After my Prayertime, I'll don my reindeer robe and walk beneath the sparkling snowfall within the hushed silence of the forest. This is a good night for a communion with nature.

11-17-91, Sunday

Bill talked with our computer lady again today and she showed him how to do a business letter through the Word-Perfect. He had a good time. It seems that, lately, he's not in a good mood unless he's talking on the phone to someone or having someone come over. It's an irritating situation, yet most likely stems from having a diversion from our daily problems. His outgoing personality is naturally drawn to others because he's very personable.

I called Elise at her new telephone number and wished her a "Happy New Home!" She and Charlie are so very happy. While we were talking, the movers pulled up with their furniture. She said living in the woods was so serene and last night they heard owls. I'm so happy for her.

Jenny watched the Bronco game alone today, because Bill was working the computer. I joined Jenny during the second half of the game to help her cheer the Broncos on to victory.

In the evening, Sarah showed Jenny how to create a card on the Print Shop program and Jenny had a lot of fun.

We had two feet of snow today.

Bill was in a bad mood all afternoon and evening. I want my friend to come and take me for a one-way ride.

11-18-91, Monday

Bill contacted the union representative this morning to inform him that an outsider had sent the flyer. They talked for a while about the problems at the grocery store. The rep said that they'd been contacted by other employees and that the union thought our flyer was great.

Shortly after Bill hung up the phone, Aimee called from work. She was upset, because her boss read her the riot act. She'd gotten in trouble for staying late to get all her work finished. What do they expect when so many workers were cut from the department? Aimee gets hollered at if she doesn't finish her work and clocks out on time, and she gets read the riot act if she has to stay later to finish it. Go figure. The bottom line is that they want the same production out of three employees that it took six to do. It's a real sweat shop there now and the Midnight Raiders are not going to stand for it. Get me riled and just watch what happens.

Bill told Aimee to tell her boss that she can't be expected to do the work of three full-time people on her five-hour shift and, if that's what's expected of her, then she's going to the Labor Board. Unfortunately, she didn't repeat her dad's words to her boss, but Bill's ready to burst in there with all verbal guns loaded like Lethal Weapon. He's ready to let loose.

We're doing a second flyer that we'll distribute to cars in the parking lot on Saturday. This will not only open the town's eyes to what's going on at the grocery store, it will also let people know that their two newspapers were informed of the situation and chose to do nothing about it. I wanted to personally picket the store but my family wouldn't let me. . . spoil sports.

Bill called Bob to tell him the exciting news about our computer. Bob was amazed that our computer friend actually got *me* to assemble it. I think some people have the impression I'm like a Pit Bull sometimes. Does that mean I have an unrelenting determination or a donkey-like stubborn streak?

Speaking (or writing) of Pit Bulls reminds me of Bill's behavior lately. His mood hasn't been the best so, today I snitched the little Tasmanian Devil Jenny recently got at McDonalds and placed it smack dab in the middle of Bill's desk. When he saw it he chuckled.

"What's this?" he asked with a smile.

"That's *you*," I replied with a smile. "Thought you'd like to see a visual of your recent mood."

"Cute, honey, real cute. Mind if I keep it?"

"Ask Jenny, it's hers."

Jenny let him keep the little devil on his desk. Hope he doesn't think it's cute. He probably thinks it reminds him of me! Good grief, aren't we a pair. The Pit Bull and the Tasmanian Devil! Guess we're well matched after all. Yes?

Today was the first day I had no mouth pain. I awoke with none and was truly surprised that not one twinge showed itself all day. I actually ate Jenny's taco dinner (minus the shell, of course).

We now have three-and-a-half feet of beautiful sparkling snow on the ground. We had someone plow out our driveway around noon, but by dinner time there was another foot to shovel.

Tom, our UPS man, came at 7:30 P.M. He said he'd been stuck in someone's driveway for three hours and had to have a tow truck get him out. I was surprised he made it all the way up to our house.

Tom brought us three packages. Two were clothing donations for our project from a correspondent, and one box was from our computer friends. They'd sent the instruction books, disks, printer ribbons, games, and two additional programs. Why is it I have such a hard time dealing with the generosity of these two people? Is it because we've always had to sweat blood for everything we obtained in life? Is it, because we've never had things "given" to us before now?

When our computer friend called us tonight and offered to

scan my manuscript for us, I told him we'd have to pay him for that. I just didn't feel right accepting more of his generosity. I didn't have prior experience with this and was afraid I'd get too near the line that distinguishes "gift-accepting" and "taking advantage." When someone is *so* generous that they want to keep giving, isn't there a point when the recipient should begin declining?

I didn't express all of this to our friend, but when I mentioned payment for the scanning, he kindly informed me that there were all kinds of "payment." He spoke of karma as being part of his reason, and there was no way I could argue with how one chose to balance that out. I'm new at this gift-receiving thing so I need to learn and grow into the right perspectives of it. I hope I don't make too many mistakes along the way. I have no problems with people's gifts to our project, because those gifts go to the needy. My problem is with me or *us* being the recipients. But I'm trying. . .I'm trying.

Bill was in a lot better mood today. He was fired up to take on the world and the snowfall made him happy. While he waited for our friend to call us tonight, he sat at his desk in the darkened office and turned the outside floodlights on to watch the snow fall. If he said it once he said it a hundred times.

"It's just beautiful. It's so beautiful."

And it was. It had a very tranquil effect as the light caught the dancing sparkles and the miniature crystals spun and drifted with each new shift of Wind Spirit's breath.

Snow Maker. . .giver of shimmering beauty—pure and full of inner peace.

My Prayer Smoke rises for two people tonight, two who live far away, yet dwell so close to our hearts. For B. and J.—many blessings to you, my friends.

11-19-91, Tuesday

Bill, Sarah and Jenny left the house early this morning. Sarah had an 8:30 orthodontist appointment down at his Colorado Springs office. There was no school today, because of all the snow. We had to have the driveway plowed a second time. At $25 a shot, I think a snow blade for the van might be a good investment.

Received a fax of Hampton Road's promotional announcement for *Soul Sounds*. Bob wanted us to look it over and get our opinion. Looking at it brought home the fact that my private journal really was going to be read by many. I experienced mixed feelings. When I called Bob back I told him they'd done a good job. The jacket of the book is quite beautiful and I'm sure many of my readers will want a poster of it. Hampton Roads is going out of their way to give my readers special treatment; maybe that's because Hampton Roads is a very special publishing company.

When Bill and the girls returned home, I was handed the mail. There were two book orders and only three letters. The small amount was quite a rarity. Two of the letters were actually cards and one was the first Christmas card of the season. How nice it is to be thought of during the holidays. Although I can't respond back to each Christmas card we receive, every one is passed around for the family to read and is saved for the duration of the season. They are gifts in themselves.

Bill talked to Link and, because she lives alone, invited her over for Thanksgiving dinner. She'll let us know.

The manager of the grocery store told the bakery department head to "write Aimee up whenever she doesn't finish all her work." Poor kid's so frustrated trying to do the work of three people and not being given the hours to do it in. She can't even have eight hours allotted to her.

She had the day off today and she spent it studying her medical books. Later in the afternoon the union rep called her and he told her that none of the other City Market stores that are union stores are having hour cuts similar to the Woodland Park store. She'd expressly asked him if they were, and his answer was what we'd expected. He also informed her that three more store employees called him to complain about their Woodland Park working conditions. Things seem to be heating up.

Aimee also told us that the bakery was told to make up extra pies for display tomorrow—when the Big Boys are coming in for inspection and conference with all the department heads. What a false show they're getting. Too bad I can't picket tomorrow.

Aimee sees the current bakery situation as a no-win scenario, because they're going to ruin her good work record with unfair write-ups. If her meeting with management tomorrow doesn't bring some satisfaction, she's going to switch to being a caddy just to save her performance record. If she's forced to do that, her pay will be cut in half.

On a whim, I told Bill that maybe he should call our Cripple Creek friend Dian Zimmer to see what her Phenix casino pays its employees. Since Aimee's not yet 21, she couldn't work in the casino proper, but she could be employed in other positions, as many of the establishments have attached restaurants.

Bill did place the call, but Dian wasn't in and was supposed to return his call. The Police Department also called Aimee today for an interview for their dispatcher job. She's going to keep that so she can get the employment particulars. There aren't a lot of job opportunities in this mountain town. It's no ski resort and people only pass through it on their way to somewhere else—usually points west like Cripple Creek or ski resorts.

Thinking about Aimee's terrible work conditions and how unfairly she's being treated makes me wonder why such a sweet young lady who works hard can be so mistreated by an employer. The answer rests with much of Big Business, where all the little guys—the workers who *keep* the company running—get treated like expendable pieces of machines. . . throwaways. It doesn't matter how good one's heart and soul is, because Big Business can't see those. All it sees is dollar signs.

Do I sound bitter? I'm not bitter, I'm angry that so many are hurting now. I'm furious over the overall gross injustice of it all. Bill even said this afternoon, "Even if Aimee quits tomorrow, I'd still try to go after them for what they're doing to their people."

I went over to him and wrapped my arms around him. With my head on his chest, I whispered, "let's go far, far away where nobody can find us."

He smoothed his hand down my hair.

"I know, honey, if we had the money I'd take you away in a minute."

Did that sound like we want to run away—escape? No. No, no, that sounded exactly like two people who desperately need to find a small measure of peace somewhere on this crazy planet they came to. It sounds exactly like two people who need to get the more base elements of this society out of their personal lives, so they can be about their work without the many extra irritations that are wont to plague their days. The continued cruelty I see done by neighbor to neighbor is an abomination to my spirit and a torment to my mind. And my heart is again pierced with swords of sorrow.

I am not bitter. . .I'm merely in pain.

So all I can do is pray to my Father so He may hear my spoken words that rise in pleading whispers upon my sacred Prayer Smoke. This night I don the reindeer robe, take my medicine bundle out into the silent snowy woods and walk with my spirit ones beside me. Together, the owl, cougar, and I will join as one in a special ceremony of transcendental prayer.

11-20-91, Wednesday

We spent the day organizing our strategies for the Midnight Raiders. For this Bill had to speak to several people. He called the police chief of Woodland Park to check on where we could and couldn't pass out flyers; he called one of the local attorneys we use on occasion to check on Power of Attorney to represent Aimee in meetings at the store; and he contacted Mario, our postmaster, to inquire about permission to pass out flyers at the post office.

Had five cook pans placed around on the office floor, because the snow's melting through the damn roof. I tried to tell our property manager last summer that the roofers were doing a lousy job. Now, whenever it rains or we have snow melt, we *still* have to dodge the floor pans. And we pay $650 a month rent for this? I don't think so—no way, José.

Received a letter from Eric today. He had his first art showing in California and sold several creations. He's also doing native figures he calls "Guardians." He stopped making the kachinas, because he didn't feel that a white man should be making them. Eric has finally accumulated the funds to move back to Colorado and expects to be here around December 11th. This is going to be interesting. Yes? I sure do hope these two can resolve things.

Robin took the girls to the movie theater in town tonight to see the new Michael J. Fox film. They had a good time.

While they were gone, Bill and I watched the two computer videos our friends sent. I felt like the Mother of All Idiots. I'm so technically illiterate I have to have Jenny start the VCR whenever I want to watch a video. . .now *that's* dumb! Although Jenny has a learning disability, she seems to have a real knack with machines, while her mother sits in front of a dual cassette component and screws up every tape she tries to record. Jenny takes pity on me and comes to save the day. The last tape cassette I tried to record for someone I ended up erasing the original. I'm out of my element in this Age of Technology. . .I'm an Ancient Times soul and it shows.

Bill's working on the computer now. He, Sarah and Jenny are creating our new flyer from the Print Shop program. They write what they want to say through a machine and I'm writing what I want to say with my hand. I can't seem to do it any other way, because nothing comes between my spirit, heart, mind, and body. . . all four must be integrated elements of all I write. The heart opens wide as my spirit flows through mind to hand before the flickering flame of a kerosene lamp. In the dark of night when all is silent my spirit is free to speak in hushed whispers that quietly manifest themselves upon the page. This is the way it must be, for this is the way it finds form. . .the only way.

11-21-91, Thursday

Aimee's meeting with management, with Robin as her representative, went well. Although management was told by the main office not to allot any training hours to new people in departments, it was decided to give Aimee five to seven days training in bakery. Other problems were ironed out and, overall, the meeting was well worth the effort.

After Aimee came home from the meeting, we had to turn right around and go back into town. She had an optometrist appointment and we had errands. She didn't need glasses. The doctor said overwork and stress was probably tiring the eyes. Aimee was glad to hear she has 20/20 vision, and there were no problems.

Our next stop was to drop her off at the police station for her dispatcher interview. Several of the policemen already knew her through her fire and rescue work and also had come to know her by going through her checkout line at the grocery store. They were glad she applied and so was she— she was hired. So now she has to find hours in the day to be at the police station to observe the dispatcher for training. She doesn't get training pay and the actual job is only for every Thursday. This means she'll work the job on one of her days off from the store. The police department knows she has a regular job, and also is doing on-call nights for the fire department and finishing her EMT training at the Ambulance Barn, so they told her not to worry if there was ever a conflict, they'd cover for her.

Aimee's very excited about doing this Thursday job. Good grief, she's a firefighter, a First Responder for medical emergencies, an "almost" EMT and a police dispatcher! Aimee! How many more ways can you help people?

When we returned home, the real estate maintenance man, Mike Newsom, and his son, Steve, were on our roof. It's leaking at a spot just outside our bedroom deck. We now have eight pans in the office and the carpet's getting soaked. It even began running out the fluorescent light fixture. I sat at my desk to begin processing the mail and I was serenaded by the sound of rain in the room. What a joke.

Aimee was in the office with me when the three men came back downstairs. All the while we talked with Mike, his son and Aimee were eyeing one another (I don't miss much). I have to admit that he's a handsome young man.

While we were talking, Bill mentioned that Mike never knew I was a writer until they got discussing it while up on the roof. It turns out that his son was at college near Durango and they studied my first two books.

"Oh-oh," I said. "Did you pick them apart?"

Steve grinned. "We had to write articles on them and send them to the reservation people to get their opinions on how much was true."

"And?" Bill prompted.

"Most of it was," came the verdict.

"That's better than telling me 'most of it wasn't!'" I smiled. I would've liked to find out what parts were thought fiction, and how one could possibly come to that conclusion when they weren't there, but Bill began to talk about how I hate publicity.

After they left, I smiled over at Aimee.

"He's cute," I said.

"I tried not to be obvious," she grinned. "He looks Indian, doesn't he."

"Maybe a little." Then, "I think you like his native warrior looks."

Now she grinned wider.

I was right.

Sarah's Psychology class spent the day down in Cañon City at the State Penitentiary. Aimee left to pick her up at school at 3:30, but the bus was almost two hours late in arriving. Aimee went instead of Bill because he was in conference with two friends who were going to pass the flyers out at our post office on Saturday morning.

By the time Aimee got home with Sarah, she barely had time to eat a quick dinner and be off to the Ambulance Barn for class. It's been a hectic day for everyone.

An out-of-state friend who Bill had been counselling called while Robin was filling us in on the morning's store meeting. When Bill finished his call and Robin wrapped up our up-date, Link called. She wants to come down from Denver on Saturday morning to help distribute the flyers. We'll be glad to see her. She also accepted our Thanksgiving dinner invite. We were glad about that too.

At 10 o'clock, Bill called our computer friend, Bill, to take him up on his generous offer to scan one of my manu-scripts—*Soul Sounds*. Of course, I won't be finished with it until December 31st, but he could get started on the 600 pages I already have typed up.

Our friend, Bill, also wants us to photocopy our mailing list to initially enter all the names and individual addresses onto a disk. It will save Bill a lot of time.

Our friend asked us if we could get Bob Friedman's birth date figures. He and Jan feel that Bob has a greater connec-tion to us. In other words, there was a "reason" Brian Many Heart suggested that I send my first manuscript to Bob. Clearly, as I've already stated in this journal, I do firmly believe Bob was a designated Player in The Plan for our work this time around—just as No-Eyes and all the others were. When the timing's right, the different players enter on cue.

Anyway, Jan and Bill have done charts on all our family members in an effort to get an overview of how we're con-nected. Following this logic, they'd be interested in seeing how Bob also fits into the pattern (astrologically speaking, that is).

Although our Marble property had been abruptly deleted from The Plan, I can feel a strong magnetic pull of other aspects being drawn nearer and nearer to the core of our circle. The clock is ticking so loud I can hear it. The pen-dulum is swinging back. . .tick. . .and forth. . .tock. And new players are being brought forth to manifest themselves according to their destined moment of appearance.

I sometimes find myself deep into thought about that beau-tiful Marble property. I recall how I'd envisioned the kiva over by the waterfall and I'd hear the sounds of the rushing

Crystal River in my ears. I'd been assured that the place had indeed been one of the possibilities for us and hoped in my heart that it would be saved until we could afford it. Yet there was an aspect about it that I always refused to examine—Bill and Sarah thought the place was eerie. . .they had dark, unsettling feelings for it. Yes, the log house was old and dark-looking in the shadows of the pines surrounding it, but that didn't also mean its aura was menacing. That's what they felt though. And they could never seem to push that perception away.

My conclusion is that the property was right for me, but not vibrationally right for them. This would appear to be a contradiction if our Advisors saw the place as being one of our destined land locations, yet I feel certain my family's vibrations would've been altered to align with the property. The Advisors have managed that simple feat more than once.

So the only other alternative for the place being removed from our access is a negative probability that began to show up for it. Tonight this has been confirmed for me.

I'm so appreciative of how They look out for us and orchestrate elements in our life, yet it can also cause temporary disappointments too. We're used to these Plan changes, because they're an integral part of The Plan itself. That part is called Protection.

Tonight is a full moon. The forest snow is shining silver. I'm going out once more to offer up my Prayer Smoke. The words of prayer will be whispered for a special request from Louise in British Columbia. The special request has a name . . .Rick.

11-22-91, Friday

We had another full day. Bill, Jenny, and I went to town. After I was dropped off at Dr. Eric Helland's office for my dental appointment, Bill and Jenny went over to the chiropractic office to see Dr. Powell. Then Jenny did her grocery shopping while Bill came back to check on me.

When he walked in the dentist's office, Eric told him I was in his office participating in a stress test survey. I was nearly done filling out the forms when Bill came in, so he was offered coffee while he and Eric went into the lab to talk of our Raider project.

Dr. Helland was again amazed at how well my gum tissue was healing (two to three weeks ahead of schedule). I was glad to hear this, because it meant that the whole process would be completed that much sooner than originally planned.

After we left Eric's office, we picked Jenny up from the grocery store and went over to Mail Boxes Etc. to photocopy 1,000 copies of the flyer. They were running a November Special for 2¢ a copy and that saved us from having to go all the way down to Bizmart in Colorado Springs. On Monday morning we'll go back there to copy my typed journal pages and mailing list to send to our computer friend, Bill.

A correspondent had sent us a $50 check for Wellspring Mission so I cashed it and, before we left town, bought some winter coats from the new Goodwill store. I picked out various sizes for men, women, and children. When we got home, we added them to the clothing boxes we have ready to distribute on Monday.

We picked up our mail and headed home.

The rest of the afternoon was spent on the mail and I didn't get to sign the book orders until after dinner.

All evening the phone rang. Link called to confirm the meeting point tomorrow morning. I told Bill to tell her to dress warm. It's only 5° in Woodland Park now and it's supposed to remain cold for a few days.

Aimee called from work to talk to her dad, then asked to speak to me.

"Mom! Guess who stopped by the bakery to see me?"

"Are you kidding? It could be anybody."

"Mom. . .you know. Guess."

"Ahhh, could it have been your warrior?"

"Yes! And he's going to come by again when I get off at nine!"

"Ah-huh, what'd I tell you? I knew there was something going on between you two. I could feel it. You two had sparks flying from your auras yesterday."

She had to go then. She was really excited and I was happy for her. She needs some Happy in her life right now. I just hope she doesn't give all her heart away too soon again. Her love life has dealt her some devastating blows.

This evening our UPS man delivered a gift from a correspondent in South Fork, Colorado . They'd sent us a smoked turkey from their own smokehouse. Bill and I were absolutely floored. It looked delicious! People's kindness continues to present us with surprise after pleasant surprise.

I received a communication from Kim FireBear Brennan today. Her letter was somewhat distressing because it had to do with how some of the local people were treating her two young girls. It appears that most of their neighbors are Mormons and Kim's girls have been subjected to some verbal abuse because of their nativeness. She has talked to the school teachers, but nothing seems to effectively stop the teasing her kids receive. Kim had decided to turn to home schooling and, since I home schooled two of my own girls, she wanted some basic information on the process.

My heart goes out to her and her little ones. Having a child's heritage ridiculed is a painful heartache for a parent and a cruel attitude to direct at a child. Kim made the right decision to remove her girls from that kind of environment. They will learn much better at home and thrive in their school work by being surrounded by their heritage and the love of both Kim and Leo. This is one solid example of how the more things change, the more they stay the same.

The night is once again flooded in silver light. The woods are so incredibly silent I feel as though I've stepped into a soundless Christmas card. I'd gone outside earlier while Bill was on the phone and I knew my Prayer Smoke would rise up through the snow-laden boughs later on.

And now that time has come. The smoke will rise for Ray and Barb Pruett of the Chinook Lodge and Smokehouse. Their kindness touched our hearts.

11-23-91, Saturday

Raider Day.

Bill left the house at 7:30 in the morning to prepare the rendezvous point for our Raiders, who were to meet up with him.

Link came from the Denver area and one man backed out because he was fearful of repercussions. The other man showed up. Because we were now one Raider short, Bill took up his position at one of the post office exits. Link and the other man covered the other exits.

After a few hours of handing out the flyers, Bill called to say Link had passed one out to the City Market store manager and he told her she'll be sued for using the store name logo on the flyer. But when I cut the name out of their ad, it had no notice of trademark or registration after the name, as other brand names do. Link was completely unruffled, and made no comment as she handed the flyer to the next car driver leaving the post office.

Next thing we knew, a City Market assistant manager was out in her car with a camera taking a picture of the Raiders.

Aimee called me. Her beeper went off. She heard a transmission to the police department—a couple people were making complaints about people handing flyers out at the post
office. Aimee heard that a police car was dispatched and I
told her not to worry.

Bill called and said a police car pulled up at the post
office, with its lights flashing. The officer went inside to
speak to the postmaster, who was neutral to what was being
done, because we were on private property and not the post
office property. The policeman got back in his car, turned off
the flashers and quietly drove away.

A short time later, Bill said another policeman drove by
and smiled and waved to him. Seems the police had no problem with the Raiders today.

Aimee then called from work. She was very upset. She
said the manager was blaming her Teller County Fire Department for the flyers because one of the people passing them
out had a Teller County Fire Department jacket on. What a
crock. Bill has a blue jacket that looks like a policeman's
jacket. There's a flag on the shoulder, but certainly no fire
department emblems.

The manager called one of the fire department officers and
read him the riot act. The officer didn't know what was going on.

Meanwhile—back at the post office—the Raiders were going full hilt. For three and a half hours the three Raiders
remained steadfast and endured the 12° temperature.

Finally, at 12:30, the post office closed and the Raiders
came home. When they walked in the door, they were
greeted by a round of cheers.

As Bill and Link were telling us how receptive people
were to the flyers, Aimee called to say that the store manager told her that her dad was going to hear from the main
office on Monday and that they *will* sue. Was that supposed
to scare us?

I told Aimee to calm down and that there can always be
repercussions expected, but not to worry—everything was going to be okay. She was worried because we'd used the store
logo and they were going to sue us for copyright (trademark)
infringement.

"Look Aimee," I said calmly, "they had no posted trademark or registered notice after their name. All they can legally do is threaten us with action or have their attorneys send

us a notice of infringement and warn us to desist use of it. . .which we did already. Don't worry! Besides, we don't have any money or property for them to go after anyway."

She seemed reassured.

After we warmed up the Raiders and fed them, Link and Bill played with the computer while I processed the mail.

We'd planned another town raid this evening to hit car windshields "on public property," but I was receiving a warning message to alter the flyer by inserting a different type font for the store name.

I voiced the warning message and told Bill and Link we needed to alter the flyer.

So he and Link went to Print Shop on the computer and selected a bold type font. They printed it out and I pasted it over the no-no logo. Then I ran off 200 copies.

At six o'clock, Jenny, Sarah, Bill and I bundled up. Link had to head back home to Denver. Sarah was excited to finally be on a real Midnight Raider raid. Jenny was unsure, so she stayed in the van with Bill, while Sarah and I did our thing around town.

At one of the places we stopped, I had the bejesus scared out of me. When I touched a windshield wiper a shrill alarm went off and lights flashed. My old heart can't take that kind of thing anymore. Sarah and I raced for the van and we were "outta there!"

By the time we'd gotten rid of about 50 flyers, Jenny felt braver (maybe a little left out of the fun perhaps?). The last two stops we made, she got out to help. When we all got back in the van, she said that her legs were shaking.

"You cold?" I asked, knowing that wasn't the reason.

"No! I'm nervous! Will they check for fingerprints?"

I laughed. "Jenny, you've got *mittens* on."

"Oh yeah," she smiled back.

Then we headed home.

Isn't it ironic that the police chief knew what we were going to do, the attorney knew, and the postmaster knew, yet none of those official men expressed one legal objection. One policeman who drove by the Raiders even smiled and waved at them. The Raiders were breaking no law. And 96 percent of those receiving the flyer, after they'd read the first few lines, made comments similar to, "it's about time!" Yet City Market says we're going to be sued? For what? The Raiders were nowhere near their store property. The Raiders were exercising their free speech right. The logo had no notice of registration posted on it, and store management always brags that "the customer is always right!" Well we were very unhappy store customers and now we get sued for voicing our displeasure with them? We get sued for free speech? For trying to be an advocate for oppressed workers? Come on. Ralph Nader can speak out about the auto companies and other corporations and products, what makes City Market exempt from dissatisfied customers complaining or being vocal with their town neighbors? What are they trying to keep swept under the carpet or hidden in their closets? Huh? Huh? Is this society owned by Big Business which runs roughshod over anyone who attempts to bring a small measure of justice to workers? Has this society allowed Big Business to actually *threaten* those little guys (Joe and Jane Public—you and me) into meek submission and subjugation? Do we have free speech in this country or do we not? Is this a true democracy or is it a "sound-good ideal" that covers up a paper tiger? What the hell is our Constitution for if it can't be exercised?

Well, Monday should prove interesting if nothing else. I'm not going to lose any sleep over these bully threats because I have other priorities on Monday—delivering warm clothes to the needy.

Aimee was late coming home from work. She'd been out with Steve. Bill and I waited up to talk to her at 12:30 when she came in.

She's taking a lot of heat for our activity. Employees and managers in the store are ignoring her or giving her crusty looks. Poor kid had absolutely nothing to do with what we did. Her manager, Les, keeps saying her dad's going to be sued. I think he'd better stop saying that to people because he has no idea who he's dealing with. It can all end right here and now, or they can sue us. If that happens, I'll guarantee these people that it will turn out to be a national media event. Do they want that? Are they that stupid?

Aimee's boss at the fire station called her in. He said that the department didn't want any bad or controversial publicity. She was steaming angry and full of fire. It hurt her that the department was being falsely blamed by the store managers who mistook Bill's jacket for a fireman's. She told her boss she had nothing to do with it, and that she's not responsible for what her parents choose to do.

After we hear from City Market main office to see how they're going to chastise (or try to punish) us for trying to help the workers, I'm going to write a letter to the editor to both our town newspapers to tell my side of the story to the townspeople. Aimee told us we'd riled a hornet's nest. People were coming into the store and asking the cashiers and other employees what was going on. . .but of course. . . the workers were too afraid to say boo.

Bill's a dynamo. I've never seen him so cranked up. He'd finally been given permission to come out from "behind the scenes" to actually participate openly and be vocal against injustice. . .before, we always had to use extreme caution and remain anonymous. His energy level is off the scale. His adrenalin is pumping at a double-time rate. He's primed for the battle. I see now that his full Warrior aspect has been freed. What a *sight* it is!

As a side thought to this situation, I wonder at the store manager's aggressive reaction to the Raiders and having the truth come out. If I were him, and had so much pressure from the main office to cut employee hours so drastically, I'd welcome public pressure placed back on the main office. I'd see the flyers as "help" for my situation instead of a threat. Yet the first thing he did was accuse the fire department and then threaten to sue Bill. Go figure.

Dian Zimmer from Cripple Creek finally called us back. She said the only job opportunities for a 19-year-old like Aimee would be office work, waitressing in one of the casino restaurants, or being a bartender's assistant (making sandwiches and such). Dian mentioned that Cripple Creek was planning on having a full-time paid fire department in the spring and that it sounded like that type of work was more in line with what Aimee was looking for.

I told Aimee what Dian said and her eyes lit up like sparkling stars before she frowned with an afterthought.

"But I'd have to live in Cripple Creek. I couldn't live that far away from you guys."

"Aimee," I smiled, "if we don't get a decent settlement from our publishing suit, we won't be trying to get over in the Crystal Valley region anymore—we may just buy a house in Cripple Creek Mountain Estates and all work in Cripple Creek. I don't know—we can only do what we can do with whatever we're given to work with. It really doesn't matter anymore."

And that's exactly where we sit right now. Our Wellspring Mission can be established anywhere we are. That one aspect seems to be a major component of all our projects.

Bill's Little Boy is beginning to show. He's excited to go down to King Sooper's grocery store in Colorado Springs tomorrow to "get his *Turkey*!" *Nothing* interferes with his Turkey Day!

I bet you anything that, when Link is over on Thanksgiving, that damn *tree* gets put up! Bill's definitely in *that* kind of joyous mood. Between the turkey and the snow. . .well, he's acting very, very huggable.

11-24-91, Sunday

There is a 20-pound turkey in the refrigerator. Bill, Jenny and I went downtown as planned and Bill was anxious to pick out his Thanksgiving dinner.

When we came back up the pass to Woodland Park, we had to stop in at City Market to pick up a couple fresh-made pizzas from the deli. We didn't cross paths with any managers and the employees treated us with courtesy. However, there were only a few cashiers working and the lines were still long.

Once home again, I typed up last night's journal entry and packed up our clothing boxes for distribution in the morning when we go back to town to buy turkeys for the needy. Link had given us some money for Wellspring, and we're going to add to it and use it to make sure some poor folks have a Thanksgiving dinner this year.

For the remainder of the evening, I tried to concentrate on a book, but couldn't lift myself out of my melancholy mood. I kept thinking about "going home." Visions of a two-room cabin kept invading my thoughts. My mind drifted back to No-Eyes' cabin and I finally came into a full understanding of why she stayed deep in the forest, for I too have reached that same inner level of. . .need. I, like No-Eyes was never meant to fit in society. I, like No-Eyes, find nourishment for the soul within the shadowed depths of a quiet, sun-dappled wood.

11-25-91, Monday

Bill and I distributed our clothing boxes this morning after we finished our early errands. He dropped me off at Mail Boxes Etc. to photocopy the first 623 pages of the journal I'd had ready. While I was doing that, Bill did our banking, went to the chiropractor and picked up the mail. He also had to meet Tom, our UPS man, at the McDonald's parking lot at 9:30 to pick up the children's book jacket proof for the reprint. It looked good and we turned it right around and sent it back within the hour.

Our next stop was City Market where we picked out 10 good-sized turkeys to donate to needy families for Thanksgiving. Oh, what *fun* that was! Doing that shopping was the highlight of our day. What a kick it was to drop them off for our recipients.

Well. . .while we were in the grocery store we received a few side-glances from some employees, but nobody said anything about the flyers. Everyone now knows it was Aimee's dad who passed them out—after all, the assistant manager took his picture, as if that was supposed to put the fear of management in him.

It's so interesting to hear the rumors that are flying around the store. The latest one is that Aimee's dad photocopied the flyer from the union pamphlet. That's okay. That shows they don't really know *who* the heck made the flyer.

We also found out from one of our store informers that Les, the manager, told the main office that he had no intention of pursuing the matter and what did *they* suggest? Main office didn't seem to care one way or the other as long as the perpetrators did things legally (which they did).

Later, Aimee called to say Les called her up to the office. The assistant manager and a witness were there. Aimee took it all in and decided to play it cool. Les wanted to know what Aimee's complaint were. He was ready for a long list and prepared to fill his note pad up.

Aimee had no complaints. She told us she felt she could've asked for a red carpet to be rolled out for her and management would've granted it.

Another informant conveyed to us that upper management is furious with Bill personally. This informant also said that certain "company" employees were voicing extremely derogatory comments about Aimee's dad. On the other hand, many employees were voicing cheers for Aimee's dad because he went to bat for them, and a couple of them even wanted a stack of extra flyers to slip into customer's grocery bags. Generally, though, Bill and I are not the most welcomed customers in the Woodland Park City Market at this time. So be it.

We've been in this town for 14 years and we know a great deal of people. The feedback we've received from them has been very encouraging in respect to the flyer. Yet, management would have the town believe that the public is against it and supportive of the store. I think that's called "blowing smoke" and "damage control." The correct term for it is "propaganda."

Management claimed that 26 people called in to voice support for the store. Our Advisors report more than that called in to support the flyer.

Well. . .the Raiders have done all they could to inform the public of the injustices. It's up to them now to bring pressure to bear on management. If they sit back, then the ongoing situation is on their shoulders. Public opinion is a powerful tool. . .but only if it's utilized.

In the mail today we received another cutting letter written by the razor-sharp pen of Mrs. Scissorhands. . .or is it Mrs. Freddy? This elderly woman is supposed to be a spiritual counselor but delights in cutting us to ribbons. She called No-Eyes an "old woman" and Many Heart a "young buck," and sarcastically wondered how I could learn *anything* from those two. She called Bill and I "babies who needed to get hurt in order to learn their lessons" and that "No-Eyes and Summer Rain had broken several Universal Laws."

This woman in New York seemed to delight in telling me the mean comments four of her friends had to say about Summer Rain and her books Was that supposed to add credence to her own warped perspective? She may like to know that, for every negative letter we receive, we get 2,000 that negate them. She's certainly welcome to her own opinion, but what's *really* eating away at her spiritual insides to make this "teacher" be so vicious and cruel? She seems to resent any spiritual teacher who is under the age of 70. From many of her comments, she gives clear evidence that she's not read all my books, where she would've gleaned enlightenment about who I am. She acts as though I've proclaimed myself as a great sage or Master. She doesn't comprehend that those first few No-Eyes' books represented only two years of my entire experiential life and were meant to recount my days with a beautiful Spirit of Light. She based her comments on the false premise that I knew nothing before I met No-Eyes and Many Heart, and that all my learning was confined to just those two years. She's completely in the dark about me and yet she cuts me to shreds. You'd better start behaving a mite more spiritual and begin living what you preach to others. Pull your razor claws in and learn how wonderful it feels to experience gentleness.

Another correspondent sent me a popular New Age "alien" map of the U.S., and how it will look after the changes. Oh dear, this map costs $18.00! My entire *Daybreak* book of maps didn't cost that much. What's so disturbing is that the projected configuration of this expensive map is grossly exaggerated to the point of being quite impossible when one gives a small measure of geologic logic to it. Oh well, as with all things, caveat emptor. I've finally become resigned to the ridiculous. I've finally come to realize that there are those who will always be gullible enough to believe anything —even the most preposterous information.

Received another monetary donation for Wellspring Mission today. What fun! I'm going to go buy Christmas toys for the little ones of our needy families. This new project of ours has given me more hours of pure joy and happiness than I've had in years. I can't even imagine how much more intense those feelings will be once we're settled and have our warehouse in full operation. It's almost too much "Happy" to look forward to. . .but I do. . .oh, how I *do*!

When Aimee came home tonight she said that her bakery boss made a comment to a customer that, "Aimee needs to get the lead out." Aimee should've responded by saying, "I could if I didn't have to do the work of two!" How is it that a company manager can so freely speak ill of a worker to a customer? Tomorrow morning she's taking this grievance to management.

Some people at the grocery store think Aimee is a "daddy's girl" and a complainer. Not so. It's a parent's responsibility to teach their young adult children to know their rights in society and the workplace. It's a parent's responsibility to teach their young adult children to stick up for themselves, so they'll be strong and exercise their warrior instincts for justice in the world. Nobody wants to see their children being made to sit back and silently be made into a slave of others, whether it's Big Business or another individual who's doing it. Aimee's not a daddy's girl, she's learning how to make her way in the world and fight for her individual rights as an equal human being.

Bill and I have decided to have Aimee quit working at the store if things don't improve. We will not have her working in a 1890's sweat shop and be exposed to constant ridicule. We love her far too much for that. If this happens our income will suffer, but there are principles more important than finances at work here.

I'm of the opinion we've done all we can for this town. I'm of the opinion our days of being a resident here are numbered. Soon we'll be moving on. And your guess as to where that will be is as good as mine right now. Spirit will lead us to wherever we're meant to be, for that location is about to be written upon the scroll of The Plan, and I prefer not to look upon the words until our destiny for its manifestation aligns to its prescribed time.

Tonight the Prayer Smoke will rise for the newborn boy of Hampton Road's office manager, Bridget Lewis. Tomorrow morning we'll receive the call that she finally gave birth. This week Bill and I will journey down Ute Pass to Manitou Springs to buy her little new warrior his first pair of moccasins.

11-26-91, Tuesday

This was a day I wished the telephone had never been invented. It rang constantly and, when it wasn't ringing, Bill was placing calls.

He and Jenny went into town early and when they came back, our business day erupted and shattered my atmosphere of sweet incense and Gregorian chants music. It was all downhill from there.

We'd received a call from Pete at Hampton Roads. Pete explained that he'd received a call from a woman in Divide, Colorado (just up the road from us) who'd ordered our children's book for her husband's birthday. The postal service mutilated the book and the man's special day is tomorrow! She needed to contact us for another copy.

Bill told Pete that we'd take care of it. Bill then called the lady and told her he'd be right out to personally deliver the replacement book. She couldn't believe it when he and Jenny pulled up in front of the Divide Feed and Grain Bin. Linda also had a friend who just relocated here from New York, who also wanted a signed book for a friend. Bill told her he'd bring it out at 10 o'clock tomorrow.

Linda said her husband's going to have the best birthday present of his life when he gets a surprise visit from Mary Summer Rain's "Bill" in the morning. Ahh, but Linda doesn't also know that Summer Rain will be arriving too! I love surprises.

Aimee had her meeting with the store manager and he was upset to hear what the bakery manager had said to a customer about Aimee. Complaints and problems were aired and considered, although my gut feeling is that management is playing a con game and only *appearing* to placate her. I have an ugly feeling that they're talking out both sides of their mouths and, quite soon, will pull some slight-of-hand maneuver to begin the process to eject her from the store.

I should've started this entry with the first call Bill made to Hampton Roads. Bob told Bill that Bridget had her baby—a boy.

The snow on the roof is dripping through the office ceiling onto our propane heater now. Calls were placed to the real estate property manager and calls came back from a new roofing company. This is not funny anymore, in fact, it never was.

We'd received a letter from a woman who said the A.R.E. couldn't get *Earthway* anymore. *What?*

Bill called Kassie at the A.R.E. to find out what the problem is. Kassie said they had 150 back-orders for *Earthway* that they had to refund because Pocket Books was out of stock—*Earthway* was out of print.

Bill asked Kassie who she talked to at Pocket and he called Jacqueline. Bill assumed a "book buyer" identity for the purpose of inquiring about the availability of *Earthway* copies. Jacqueline said the title was out of print. She said Pocket had 2,500 back-orders for the book and she tried to talk them into doing a reprint because of the demand. Pocket declined. They're preparing to publish the softcover trade edition in July of 1992. That's *eight* months of having *Earthway* unavailable to my readers! Unbelievable, just unbelievable!

Bill then tried calling my Pocket editor, Claire Zion, to complain. He got her secretary, who tried to say that the back-order figures were overblown hearsay. She didn't know what to say when Bill told her he'd gotten the figures from Pocket itself! This business is a royal headache. If Hampton Roads had that kind of back-order figure, they'd be on the phone to their printers in a flash, but I suppose Pocket doesn't consider 2,500 people important enough to go through the expense of even a small reprint.

Aimee's got EMT class after work tonight and then she's staying overnight at the fire station because she's on-call. We won't see her until tomorrow night, when she comes home from work.

When she called us this evening she didn't sound good. This Raider event and the stress from work has her upset. She's not eating and sounds like she's getting a cold. She's having an EMT test tonight and is nervous because she hasn't been able to concentrate on studying for it. If she can't handle the stress, we'll have her quit that store job. It's just not worth her health.

This evening we received a UPS delivery from A & A Periodicals (a book distributor) located in Colorado Springs. They'd ordered several cases of *Daybreak* and were returning eight damaged copies to Hampton Roads. . .so why did they send these books to Lodestar Press? *We* didn't publish the title!

So Bill had to call his contact person at A & A to have UPS pick them up from us, so the books can be sent back to the right publisher. Can't anyone do anything right anymore?

Well yes, I suppose they can. Hampton Roads sent us several copies of the *Soul Sounds* order form that they were beginning to send out to those on our mailing list. . .it looked great. I grinned and told Bill that maybe these flyers should be passed out at our post office next Saturday morning. That was a joke, of course.

Just before dinner, we received a call from Bill's brother in Traverse City, Michigan. Their mother was in the hospital. She'd fallen down the stairs and fractured her femur. In the morning she's being operated on. The problem is her heart, which hasn't been good. Her cardiologist is very concerned and had her placed in the ACU section so they can monitor her closer.

Jenny disappeared into the office this evening. I heard the computer printer tapping out page after page. When I went to investigate, Jenny had made three greeting cards and a calendar. When I told Bill what Jenny was doing, he grinned, "We're going to have to get her her own set-up. . .maybe she'll tap into NORAD and disarm all the nukes!" That was a joke, folks.

Earlier in the evening, Sarah had figured out how to run the game disks. She and Jenny were playing card games and, later, Jenny helped Mandy make a Thanksgiving card for her dad. Little Brains. They make us Old Fogies look like Stupeedos.

When Robin brought both local newspapers home tonight, one had a quarter-page notice written by the N. E. Teller County Fire Department as a disclaimer of any involvement with last Saturday's "handbill" distribution.

It's too bad the department had to spend money on that notice, but if the store management had checked out their facts before placing false blame, the fire department wouldn't have been even remotely implicated in our Raider activity.

I'm glad this day has come to a close. Tonight the Prayer Smoke will rise for Bill's mother. God bless and keep her.

11-27-91, Wednesday

This has been the Mother of All Days!

The day began beautifully. Bill called the hospital first thing and was told his mother was still in surgery. So far so good.

Bill, Jenny, and I drove out to the Divide Feed and Grain Bin where Bill went in to deliver the signed children's book. There were five people there. One, of course, was Frank (the Birthday Boy) who was completely blown away to meet Bill. They all talked for a few minutes before Bill casually said, "Oh! I left someone out in the truck!" He then peeked his head out the door and waved Jenny and me in.

When we walked through the door I was greeted by frozen faces and you could've heard a pin drop.

"Happy Birthday, Frank!" I said with a big smile as I went over to give him a long hug.

People had tears in their eyes and I was embarrassed because I knew they were caused by my presence. I gave big hugs to everyone and we talked for about an hour.

The woman, Becky, was there and was happy to receive her signed book. She'd pleaded with her boss to have the day off to meet Bill. Becky works in the college bookstore (or was it the college library?) and her boss had previously met me at one of the Mountains and Plains Booksellers Association conventions in Denver where I signed a book for her to give to Becky. So naturally her boss was very understanding as to why Becky wanted the day off.

Linda, the birthday man's wife, was just as surprised to see me as her husband was to see Bill. And their friend, also named Linda, was equally pleased. This Linda had met Aimee when she worked in a local western store. Aimee had asked her what made her move to Colorado and Linda was a little reticent to say that some Colorado author was the cause. She said it anyway.

Aimee grinned. "What's the author's name?"

Linda said, "Oh, you probably never heard of her."

"Maybe I have. What's the name?"

"Mary Summer Rain."

Aimee smiled wide. "She's my mom!"

And that was how Linda Creager first met Aimee.

When I hugged everyone for the last time, I looked into Frank's eyes. So warm they were. He said softly, "If you ever need anything. . .I'm here for you." I could see this was no idle statement. I looked at him for a moment longer.

"I'll remember that," I whispered back.

When we drove away we were all smiles. What fun it was to surprise those wonderful people.

Our next stop was the chiropractic office and then the grocery store to pick up last-minute items for our Thanksgiving dinner. While we were in the doctor's office, the receptionist gave us a message. We needed to get over to the grocery store before heading home. Oh-oh. This was not good.

We went straight to the bakery and saw Aimee carrying a stack of dinner rolls. When she saw us, tears began rolling down her cheeks.

"*Now* what?" Bill asked.

She reached in her apron pocket and pulled out a pink paper filled with complaints and reprimands. They were all contrived. They said she worked too slow and that she needed to speed up. This pink slip was given to her *on her "second" day of training!* Poor kid was an emotional basket case because she didn't understand it.

We saw red.

It was clear to us that this was management's first move to get rid of Aimee.

When I looked up at the smokey glass of the catwalk I saw we were being watched. When I looked back at Bill I didn't see a white man. I saw a warrior in full battle dress and paint. He said one thing to me.

"What do They say?" (meaning our Advisors).

The response from them was loud and clear. PULL HER OUT NOW! "Pull her out now!" I said. And I lifted the dinner rolls out of Aimee's arms and set them on the display table.

Bill strode over to the display case and called to the manager.

"Can we talk for a minute? Can you come over here so we can talk?"

"Well. . .well. . ." She wouldn't budge from the back of the bakery. Her eyes shifted up to the catwalk. She wanted help. They were *expecting* Aimee's dad to be upset for what they'd done to her.

Bill began to talk to her, but when she made a hand gesture to wave him off, he got irate then. At this point the warrior let loose with a verbal barrage of truths she needed to hear. Bill held up Aimee's pink slip so she could see it from so far away.

"*This* is BULLSHIT and you *know* it!"

Customers began gathering around to see the show.

"Aimee's a good, hard worker and *this* is UNFAIR! And you KNOW that!"

More customers had gathered.

"If you can't manage your people with these damn *hour cuts*, you shouldn't *be* a manager! This pink slip is BULLSHIT! I'm pulling Aimee *out* of this goddamn store!"

Then I waved my arm and pointed my finger at the manager. I shouted, "*You* are a *terrible* manager! *You* even *tell* your people that you're a BITCH to work for! We have to pull Aimee out of this damn store because you expect her to do the work of *two* people and then you write her up for being *slow*! You write her up on her SECOND day of TRAINING! This store is a *disgrace*!"

A gentleman customer came up beside me. "Give 'em hell, lady!" he cheered.

When Bill and I turned around, we were penned in by metal cages—people's carts were everywhere. We'd drawn quite an audience with our shouting. Well, we wouldn't have had to shout if the manager had been woman enough to come out and discuss it like an adult. It was her fault we had to shout to talk to her. We didn't have any intentions of broadcasting our personal problems to the entire store!

Bill, with pink slip in hand, picked his way through the carts and strode up the aisle toward the stairs to the office.

Upstairs, all the managers were watching through their window. When Bill arrived, the door was closed. He banged on it and was admitted.

There they were. All grouped together for safety in numbers. The manager, the assistant manager, and the cashier manager, and the "King," who heads up general merchandise. They all seemed to be expecting some violence from the warrior. Little do they know him, if that's what they thought.

"This goddamn *pink slip* is BULLSHIT and you KNOW it! You KNOW that Aimee's a good worker! What you're *pulling* is BULLSHIT and you know it! I'm pulling her *out* of this goddamn store! You haven't heard the *last* of this!"

Aimee had been standing beside her dad.

The store manager said, "Aimee's the employee here." He looked at her. "Does this represent your resignation then?"

"Yes," was all she said before turning on her heels and striding out the door and down the stairs.

As they were leaving the store, a couple store employees gave them the "thumbs up" sign and said, "*Yeah*, way to *go!*" And a couple more expressed regret that Aimee was gone.

Jenny and I met Bill and Aimee outside the store. We told Aimee to go home and calm down. She was concerned about our lost income now and we told her that we'd manage. Getting her out of that "Store From Hell" (as some employees were secretly calling it) was most important and we'd accomplished that. I told her that now she could concentrate on her EMT classes and spend a lot of time training with the police dispatcher.

Aimee left for home and we deliberated over our new dilemma. I had a grocery list that I still held in my hand. We needed to get those items for our Thanksgiving dinner and none of us wanted to give that store any of our money now.

"Let's go down to King Soopers," I suggested.

Bill glanced at his watch.

"We don't have time. The roofing man's coming to the house soon and we need to be there."

I looked over at Jenny and held out the list.

"Give Jenny the money and she'll go in."

Jenny just stood there.

"I'm not going back in that place!"

"Okay!" I said, taking the list, "we'll go in together then." I looked to Bill. "I think they'll call the police if you're seen back in there. You go get the wine."

He liked that idea.

It irked me to have to buy anything from that store. Jenny and I went about getting what we needed. We were being watched the entire time. When I pushed the cart past "the King," I said to Jenny, "this book's getting better 'n' better!"

Then we visited Robin in the deli.

"You hear what happened?" I asked. "You hear they gave Aimee a *pink slip* on her *second* day of training?" I hadn't said this too quietly either.

Robin caught my eye, put her head down as she busied herself and nodded. We were being watched was her message. Well, I *knew* that. It would appear that this was evidence that City Market customers who get verbal with their complaints. . .get watched.

Jenny and I left the deli so we wouldn't get Robin in trouble for being seen talking to us. Jenny took the cart through the checkout and the cashier said, "Gee, Jen, I hope your mom's okay." She could see how upset I was.

When we got home we talked at length to Aimee. We assured her that it was okay as far as her lost income for the family. She felt badly because she had such a good day at work yesterday, and said she really liked working in the bakery—especially since she was finally beginning to be trained for it. She was hurt at what they did to her. She reiterated that the store manager himself had complimented her on being a good worker in the past, and that she was one of the fastest cashiers he had when she worked the checkout. She just couldn't make any logic or sense out of being given a pink slip for being "slow" when she was just *learning* what to do! She got a firsthand lesson in company strong-arm tactics when they set their sights on getting rid of someone.

The more we talked, the more she understood and she began to feel more comfortable with what transpired. The only thing she really regretted was "signing" that pink slip. We informed her that she should've told management that the claims on it were false and that she was going to refuse to sign such a thing. She could've also demanded her attorney to be present. But she didn't know her rights and management sure didn't inform her of them. Well. . .she knows now, and what's done is done. We go forward from here. We have no intentions of making any more waves around City Market. We informed the public and we got Aimee out of there. From now on, Bill will take Jenny down to Colorado Springs to do her weekly grocery shopping at Cub Foods, as we used to do. The City Market case is closed.

Bill called the Michigan hospital again and found out that his mother came out of the operation with no complications. What a relief. We'll be glad when she can receive calls.

Our Norfolk attorney called to say that the court ruled in our favor—the case is going to a court trial. What great news! What a big coup that was for the Good Guys!

Later we were informed by our Advisors that a great battle went on over that ruling. The spirit forces fought a fierce confrontation that lasted for many days. We're so grateful for all the light warriors who fight for our causes.

While Bill had the attorney on the phone, he explained about the latest problem with Pocket Books and how totally disgusted we were that we were not only losing eight months of sale royalties, but our readers were being deprived of the book they want. John Hart told Bill to fax him our contract, and he'd see if we could do anything (which I doubt we can).

The roofer showed up and, while he and Bill were upstairs, Aimee came running down to say she'd just heard a call on her beeper for a medical emergency at an address near our home. There's only four houses on in our area, and one of them is ours. The call came from one of the houses right across the road out front.

Aimee grabbed her stethoscope and donned her fire department jacket. She was out the door and on her way. We weren't sure which house it was, but she was going to find it.

I grabbed our scanner and turned it on. Soon the radio sparked to life. The dispatcher said, "AIMEE IS ON THE SCENE." And when I heard that, my heart nearly burst with pride and love. Then another transmission came through. "AIMEE SAYS HOUSE HAS DARK WOOD AND IS ON CUL-DE-SAC."

While Bill was with the roofer, Jenny and I watched out the front window while listening to the scanner. The fire rescue truck relayed snowy, icy road conditions to the ambulance that was on its way.

Finally we saw the rescue truck pull around and we heard the dispatcher say, "AIMEE CAN SEE 780 NOW" (the number of the fire rescue vehicle). Shortly afterward, the ambulance arrived. We watched for a long time without hearing any more transmissions. Then we heard, "NEGATIVE TRANSPORT." They would not be taking the woman to the hospital. And the two vehicles pulled away.

When Aimee finally walked back home and came in, we all cheered her. She blushed, yet was totally within her destiny. She said the woman was an elderly visitor to the neighbor's house. She has emphysema and was alone when her oxygen tank emptied. The woman panicked and went into acute respiratory distress. When the woman saw Aimee come in with her fire jacket on and saw the stethoscope, she began to breath better when Aimee talked to her and calmed her down.

The lady who lives in the house works for social services and arrived behind the ambulance. The medical team administered their oxygen and the woman instructed Aimee how to use the special tanks she keeps in the house, so they can call Aimee over if it ever happens again. These were not the usual oxygen set-ups and Aimee was glad to learn how to operate them.

After the medical teams left the house, Aimee visited with

our neighbor and the patient. Our neighbor knew there were bad problems at the grocery store, because she'd gotten employees coming into social services. Our neighbor felt bad for Aimee and said that she'd keep her eyes open for a job for her. In the meantime, they'd keep our telephone number handy in case there was another medical emergency where the tanks needed to be switched.

Aimee felt so good that she was able to calm the woman down enough to breathe better. I couldn't believe how she took off when she heard that the call was right across the street. I was so proud of our tiny warrior I could've burst. She may have lost her job today, but destiny gave her a far better one to make up for it. Destiny. . .what a marvel it can be.

In the evening, we received calls from two store employees. Management was telling all the employees to write witness statements regarding everything they saw and heard Bill and Mary do and say. today. What the heck is that supposed to do? Prove we made threats or something? I bet they get a dozen different stories. We made damn sure neither of us said one thing that could be even remotely construed as a "threat." We're not *that* dumb. And I also bet those scared employees don't even know they have the right to refuse to write a statement.

I don't get it, I really don't. City Market always brags that "the customer is always right," and then when a customer becomes irate and gets vocal. . .well. . .he or she gets treated like a criminal. I wonder how they'd treat a little elderly nun that would shout at a manager for something? I'm sure she wouldn't be treated like we're being treated. So then, what's the *real* problem here? We had a valid complaint about valid injustices, and when we voiced them, the "customer is always right" policy went right out the door and proved to be false. Yes? We *were* customers today, were we not? Well, no matter, we hope to never step foot in that store again. And, I say, good riddance.

Tomorrow is Thanksgiving and we're going to celebrate to the hilt. We have so many blessings to be thankful for: we got Aimee out of the bakery from hell, we won the court ruling, we're having a good friend over to help us celebrate tomorrow, Bill's mom is okay, and we all have our health. What more could one ask for? God bless us. . .bless us one and all.

11-28-91, Thursday

Bill was up before the birds were. When I came down-stairs he was preparing the turkey.

Link arrived around 11 o'clock and was greeted by clear blue skies. She said Denver was foggy and grey. Since the snowstorm didn't make it today, the Christmas tree and lights didn't go up. That was fine with Bill because we had a wonderfully relaxing and enjoyable day. With all the family at home, it couldn't have been more perfect.

Aimee left at 6:30 for the fire station, to spend the night. It was her turn to be on-call. In the morning she's going to spend a few hours with the police dispatcher before coming home. Around 9:30 she called to say she was lonely. She's all by herself at the station. The other on-call firefighters live right in town, but Aimee lives too far, so, on her nights, she has to stay at the station and sometimes it can be lonely. She takes her medical books and spends the quiet time studying.

I'm grateful for the restful day we had. It was a rare gift to give thanks for.

11-29-91, Friday

It snowed all day and it was beautiful up here in the high country. While it snowed outside, it rained in the office. Bill figured it out. The snow on the roof above our bedroom is melting and running into the walls that slant down to our office below. Now we have two snow sleds on the office floor to catch the rain.

Bill tempted fate again. He drilled holes in the ceiling wood where the water was running. He was giving me fits and the girls were upset at him for taking such chances with water and electricity. He should've been electrocuted for what he did. Sometimes, with the things he does, he seems invin-cible. But each time I fear it will be one time too many.

Once the holes were made we got rid of the eight pans we had on the floor, but now we needed someone to shovel the three and a half feet of snow off that roof. Oh. . .no *way* was I going to let him do that!

He placed several calls to the real estate office and they, in turn, tried to locate someone to do the job. After several return calls back to us, no one was found and Bill had that determined glint in his eye. Luckily, our friend Bill called to say he'd received the journal manuscript and already had 300 pages scanned. He suggested I send him my next two manuscripts for him to do too. Astrologically, he sees a connection between us and all those who are involved with my books. He's going to call Bob on Monday to discuss how the spiritual aspects and physical mechanics can be merged to assist in manifesting The Plan.

Our friend, being well versed in psychology, understood the mind of my father, as was revealed in the early pages of the journal he was now reading and scanning.

Eventually our friend spoke to Jenny, Aimee, and Sarah in turn. They all think the world of Computer Bill. He connects with them in individualized ways that are unique to each, and they laugh and laugh while talking to him.

After we concluded our conversation, Bill and I went into town to photocopy my next two books to send to Bill. We took in the pictorial, *Whispered Wisdom—Portraits of Grandmother Earth,* and *Ancient Echoes—The Anasazi Book of Chants. Ancient Echoes* is not contracted for yet, but our friend wants to scan it onto a disk for when it is.

When we came home, I had a double stack of mail to process. After I became engrossed in responding to the letters, my concentration was broken by a commotion on the roof. . . yep, that Bad Boy had gone up on the icy heights when I wasn't looking.

I raced up the stairs, ran through our bedroom and climbed up the hidden stairs behind our wall paneling.

"What do you think you're doing?" I hollered, standing with my head and shoulders above the roof trap door.

Bill turned. "Get back inside!" he waved. "You're getting full of snow."

"You said you'd let the real estate people get somebody to do this!"

"I changed my mind. This can't wait. There's too much snow up here."

I stood half in and half out of the roof opening. I was furious he'd taken such a risk. I glanced at him and he laughed. "Will you get back down out of this snow! It's freezing out here!"

I climbed back down and entered our bedroom where Magic greeted me with a wagging tail. I vigorously rubbed her neck.

"Sometimes I think you've got more sense than somebody *else* we know around here."

Magic barked. Maybe that meant she agreed.

When the three came down from the roof, Jenny and I had our second turkey dinner ready on the table. We ate by candlelight. It was the first time in a long while that just the five of us were gathered for a family meal. Mandy was at her dad's, Robin was downtown shopping with her gentleman friend and Aimee was not at work—she was home for a real family dinner. The atmosphere was so warm and serene my anger at Bill melted like the wax on the flickering candles. We listened to Bill explain about the roof, but secretly, we were all thankful the mischief he'd gotten himself into had been uneventful. Later, the girls told me they'd gone up there to help their dad and. . .to help the Advisors keep watch over him.

Twice in one day he'd given fate perfect opportunities to strike a fatal blow. Twice today, fate was outmaneuvered. . . and outnumbered.

What irks me most when Bill tempts fate like this is what he says. When he does something dangerous he laughs, "Eh, if anything happens to me you get $50,000 for the land! Maybe I can get you your little cabin after all!"

Jesus, he *knows* that cabin would be *worthless* without *him* in it! God, I wish he wouldn't take such dangerous chances. His circle of protection must be incredible—just incredible.

When Robin came home tonight, she brought Aimee's check. She also informed us that Donna—the store baker— walked out on Thanksgiving. Oh well, the soap opera continues, but we're not players anymore. Thank God for favors large and small.

11-30-91, Saturday

Sarah's bird, Shadow, hasn't been feeling well, so Bill made an early run to town for antibiotics. We've had Shadow's cage on a footstool in front of our office WarmMorning propane heater for two days. He seemed to be a little more active this evening and I hope he completely recovers. If anything happens to that little fella, Sarah's going to be heartbroken.

Some evenings she takes him in our room to fly him while she studies and the little guy likes to land on her shoulder and hide behind the long hair covering the back of her neck. He'll sit back there and make whispered words in her ear. He's four years old and has been extremely healthy until this episode. I think he got a chill, even though Robin had made a full quilted cover for his cage, and we keep him by the woodstove all day during the winter. I hope the little guy keeps getting stronger.

Around 10 o'clock this morning, the family piled into the truck for a trip down to Colorado Springs. Our first stop was a western shop in Manitou Springs, where I bought baby moccasins for Bridget's new son. Then we headed over to King Sooper's where Jenny, Sarah, and I did the week's grocery shopping. Bill and Aimee headed over to Lorigs to pick up Aimee's fire department uniform that had been tailored for her.

When we returned home, Shadow wasn't fluffed up. He was eating his food. He began chirping as I worked on the mail. I talked to him while Magic curled up beneath my desk.

The evening was a quiet one. Bill was a little distant—I know he was concerned about the money. Suddenly losing Aimee's $1,100 a month income was going to severely affect our budget. I'm not worried because it does no good, and things always have a way of working out. I think Christmas is what's bothering Bill. I know he wanted this year to somewhat make up for last year's "bare bones" holiday, but we can only work with whatever we have. Maybe next year will be better.

When the shipment of our children's book arrives at the house next week we'll have to shell out $1,600 for the final payment of that reprint. I know Bill's going to wince at that now and may decide to give the book over to a publisher. Well? If we're not going to be able to pay for the reprints of it, then I suppose we'll have no choice in the matter. So maybe *Mountains, Meadows and Moonbeams* will be in bookstores next year—only time will tell.

Aimee's been having trouble with the pickup. We have to keep chains on the tires during this long season of winter mountain snow, but she still has a hard time climbing these inclines. The engine's so tired. It's going to have to push itself for a few more years though and I pray it has the energy to do so.

It's 4° out, yet the sky is filled with dancing lights and I hear my owl calling to me.

Two hours later (2:00 A.M.) —
I'd left the warm house to make my way through the untouched snow depths that lead into my sacred forest place.
So quiet were the white woods.
So sacred was the night.
Halfway to my secret wood, cougar appeared beside me. I

noticed his great paws left no trailing prints, yet a ghostly mist puffed from his mouth with each soft breath he exhaled.

Above, owl led our way.

When cougar and I reached our special place, I stared down at the ground. Someone had recently been there before me. The spot where I spread out my sacred bundle objects had been cleared down to bare earth. The clearing was circular and, as I stepped within the darkened area, I noticed the peripheral snowline had been blown in a circular fashion. It reminded me of the crop circles. It was that subliminal thought that confirmed who had so thoughtfully prepared my Prayertime sanctuary. My Starman was still around—watching out for me—still caring.

What transpired tonight was too sacred to write of. What I learned was meant to be revealed at a future time. But one aspect that brought warm tears down my face and swelled my heart was to learn the human identity of my cougar companion. I will not verbally voice his name—many will guess without my having to do so. Oh. . . to have the three of us together again in such a physical and touchable manner truly proves the magic of nature and the beauty of its incredible power. To have my spirit totems so near, to have cougar lay at my side, and to massage my fingers deep down into his coat was a feeling I cannot find words to define. To nuzzle my face to his and to hear the rumbled purr in response was far beyond my ability to describe. And owl, dear sweet owl, nestled down upon my lap and allowed me two feathers from each massive wing to have and to hold forever. . .my own proof of both my spirit totem's manifestation into physical reality.

If I am ridiculed or laughed at for writing of what occurred this night, my heart will only smile back and my soul will glow in remembered warmth, for no one—*no one*—can ever steal away the reality of it from my past. No one can change it with their cruel words of doubt and disbelief.

How truly honored I feel right now to have been allowed to know—to *feel*—what spirit totems *really* are. . .and the incredible power and peace they have to impart. No, no one can, or will, ever be able to take that from me.

December, 1991

This date marks the beginning of the last month of my shared journal entries. . .31 more nights of offering my readers a view through my life's window and letting them hear the sounds of my exposed soul. I wonder. . .I wonder how the offering will be received? Yet, in the end, it's not important—not really. What's meaningful is that I've done what was asked of me and, to me, that's all that ever matters.

And so. . .during this Cold Maker month, I will continue as I began. I will continue to write each night of my own private thoughts and experiences. I will continue to open my soul and offer its contents as a gift of tears to everyone who feels drawn to receive it. The gift is freely given. There are no regrets.

So then, the beginning of the end is at hand and, my soul sounds again, upon a blank page, turn into words written thereon.

This has been a magnificent Blue Day. The royal blue sky gave a clear and sharp backdrop to the sparkling white crystals that frosted the arms of pine and fir. A brilliant sun glistened the mountains and surrounded our home with the twinkling jewels of Cold Maker's regal robe.

Inside, the pitch in the burning pine snapped and popped in the woodstove. It was a good day.

I worked on answering the last of Saturday's letters and then signed some children's books that were ordered for Christmas. By the time I'd finished, Rocky Mountain Thunder was rolling through the house. The action at Mile Hi Stadium was echoed throughout the rooms of the house. Bill, Jenny, and Magic were deeply into the Bronco game and I joined the melee that was hard to ignore. We won.

After the game, I pulled back our deer tapestry and entered the hidden cupboard door in the paneling. I was shoving boxes out when curious kitty came over to see what was going on. Bill glanced over at the commotion.

"You *serious*?" he smiled hopefully.

"What does it look like? You think I'm pulling these Christmas boxes out of here for exercise? Com'on, let's get your tree up!"

I brought my cassette player in from the office and, while we listened to Christmas tapes, everyone joined in to set up and decorate the tree. Bill hung our pine wreath on the front door and I strung the boughs along the entryway stairs. By the time we were done, the living room had been transformed into a twinkling fairyland.

I don't know what tomorrow will bring, but tonight our home was filled with seven joyous hearts.

12-2-91, Monday

Bill dropped me off at Dr. Helland's this morning while he and Jenny went next door to Dr. Dave Powell's office for their chiropractic appointments. I was done first, so I walked over to the post office to pick up our mail before meeting them at Dr. Powell's.

While I was in the waiting room, Bill peeked his head out from behind one of the exam room doors and called me in. I took the stack of mail and the letter opener with me. When Dave came into the room, Bill grinned.

"Alright, Dave, I got her in here, now you can give her an adjustment too."

Dave turned to me with a wide white smile that swiftly faded to green.

I'd had my letter opener in my hand. It was held at a semithreatening angle.

"*Nobody* fools with *my* bones," I said softly. "I only let *one* person fool with my bones."

Dave stepped back and put up his hands.

"Whatever you say! Whatever you say is fine with me!" he laughed.

Bill was cracking up.

And I slipped my weapon back into its envelope scabbard.

Before we left for home, I bought our two mothers and my sister Christmas presents so we could ship them off.

Shortly after we began our heavy office day, the real estate company's home repairman came to check out our "rain" problem. It was definitely a problem. After we'd discussed what needed to be done, George Asbury told us about a simple device he'd invented to reduce radon gas infiltration into homes. This device also made fireplaces much more efficient by supplying a fresh feeder air vent which prevented cold rooms in houses heated by woodstoves. Technically, the idea was engineered from the simple law of physics that states a flame needs oxygen to breathe and that one can "control" where that oxygen comes from. He called his device F.R.A.T. which stands for "Fireplace Return Air Trap."

Bill expressed how uninformed his former customers were about the great need for a fresh air supply in their homes when he worked many years as a gas man. He told George of the frequent times when he'd be called to homes where the occupant's pets had died and the people were sick because of the lack of "make-up air" for their woodstoves or gas furnaces. Bill was impressed with George's simple solution and we tried to help him with ideas to market it. George said he knew nothing about that aspect of it, but was willing to talk to people who could help him get his invention into the public's hands. We suggested he contact Tom Martino who does a "New Products" segment every Friday on a Denver television news program. We also gave him the name of an organization in town that may be able to give him some good, solid leads. His device can save lives and we thought it was a shame that he was having a hard time getting it publicized. Locally, a few builders were interested, but that's as far as George got. I hope he goes further with it.

I finished answering the mail while Bill spent the rest of the afternoon on the phone. He'd called Bob for two reasons. We wanted to know if Computer Bill contacted him, and if he was receiving an acceptable number of pre-orders for *Soul Sounds*. The answer was yes to both.

In the mail we'd received a correspondent's gift check to Wellspring Mission, and we're going to use it to buy one of our recipients a much needed stove for her family. This is like being Santa all year long and there's no feeling in the world that can touch it.

Another correspondent's letter tore into us for the updated information letter she received from us. She's totally convinced that Summer Rain is only interested in "profit" now and that I no longer care about helping people. Oh well. . . all I could do was accept her opinion, while smiling as I thought about that new stove we were going to shop for.

We've got to make time for more things. We've got to get out of this office. Big John in Victor is waiting for us to visit him, we've got to get that stove and more warm winter clothes for our needy people. I want to buy more toys for their children too. Our days are so full and Bill's still in the office until late at night with his counselling calls. If I've said it once, I've said it a thousand times. "I wish we could clone ourselves."

After dinner, I was back in the office signing children's books, then I wrapped and packaged up the Christmas presents so Bill can mail them in the morning.

Finally I flicked off the office light and went into the living room to join Bill. I sat on a footstool in front of him and, while he watched a football game, I read some newspaper articles he'd marked for me. . .all the while he brushed my hair. He does that sometimes and it's so relaxing I somehow forget to tell him when to stop. From the living room we could hear the computer printer tap-tapping away in the office—Jenny was at it again.

By the time Bill's arm was ready to fall off, Aimee came up to me and said I had a fractured humerus that needed immediate attention. I was suddenly her accident victim. She splinted my arm up in no time, but I wasn't taken care of yet because now I had a sucking chest wound. . .then I needed CPR. . .then. . .

When the patient pretended to expire, prayers were said over the fatality and the equipment was packed away. Aimee, Bill, and I then sat and talked for three hours about medical emergencies and what Aimee still had an interest in learning as far as her firefighting work went. One aspect was HazMat (Hazardous Materials) and we were surprised that her fire training hadn't delved deeply into that subject.

Bill then began instructing Aimee about natural gas and propane and the lesson was interspersed with many helpful stories of his 24 years' worth of experiences with both.

We were about done with our discussion when Jenny came in with a pile of folded computer paper in her arms. She spread out the folded sheets to display her banner. It read: I WANT THE BRONCOS TO WIN THE DIVISION TITLE! Little Minx, I wouldn't begin to know how to make a banner like that.

It was a good day today. It was busy every moment, but each moment was good. Tomorrow I want to shop for that stove. Bill doesn't think we'll be able to fit it in. I hope we can manage it sometime this week.

My Prayer Smoke this night will be for a native elder who wrote me today. He's an AIM member who has a special request he asked me to help with. I will honor that request.

12-3-91, Tuesday

Another Blue Day gifted us with warm sunshine and laughing skies. Nature's joy spread out over all the land, and the mountains sang their hymn of gladness.

After I typed up last night's entry, Bill, Jenny, Aimee, and I took a trip down the pass to pick up a couple more Christmas gifts we needed to mail. One of these was for the crew at Hampton Roads. For them, we went to the Rocky Mountain Chocolate Factory in Old Colorado City, where the delicious smells that greeted us as we walked through the door brought visions of hot cocoa sipped before a crackling hearthfire.

Chocolate? you say, aghast and in shock? Summer Rain gave a gift of chocolate? Mmmm, yes! Moderation is the key to remember. A little treat now and again never hurt anyone —especially if one is conscientious about keeping the system in a balanced acid/alkaline state. Then the treats can be kept in perspective without causing an imbalance. We're not strict old killjoys and we don't expect others to be either—especially around the holidays.

So we had a great time looking at all the creamy varieties of the handmade goodies and decided on a special wrapped box that was nestled in a wooden chest. We chose a few additional pieces for ourselves and happily left the shop.

We delved into the stack of mail and book orders as soon as we got back home. I signed eight books. Our remaining stock is only 24, and it looks as though we'll just have enough to cover orders before our new shipment arrives this week. We cut it awfully close.

Two letters we received today informed me that they'd received the Hampton Road's pre-publication order form for *Soul Sounds* and that they'd not only called in their order, but wanted me to know what a very special gift I was giving to my readers by opening my soul to them. One of the correspondents also added that he thought the cover art for the book was extremely powerful and imagined it represented what was *in* the book.

These two letters gave me personal encouragement and helped to rest my mind about the diary I was going to open for everyone. The fact that these two people understood what I was giving, underscore the Advisors' reasons for wanting my private aspect shared. Of course, I realize that these people haven't *read* the diary yet and, after they do their opinion may reverse itself, but for now, it was comforting to receive these two kind letters, because it's scary to let others listen to one's soul sounds. It's scary to open oneself so completely. Yet, I know, warriors perform best when all their encumbrances are shed.

When Robin came home from work, Jenny presented her with two "Certificates of Award" for being the World's Best Pie Baker. We'd gobbled up all but two pieces of the cherry pie she'd baked for us while we were downtown today.

Then Robin told us about the store employees who were coming up to tell her how much they missed Aimee. She also informed us that Aimee's former bakery boss was given an order to attend a mandatory manager seminar or be fired. What does *that* tell you? And now more and more employees are asking each other if they sent in their union cards. If Aimee's situation served as the sacrifice catalyst to get these people moving and ready to stand up for their rights, then her example will have been for honor and well worthwhile. That, coupled with the flyers, did indeed move a mountain that everyone was too afraid to approach. We ended up sacrificing a good income to accomplish our goal this time, yet we've already been compensated through other means by seeing Aimee sleep and eat well now, and how excited she is to concentrate on her medical destiny. Money? Phooey! There are far greater riches in this world.

Aimee called late this evening from the Ambulance Barn where she'd just finished taking two important EMT exams. Her voice was smiling. She'd done well.

"*They* must've helped me out," she said.

I chastised her. "What makes you think you didn't do it all on your own? Aimee, you've got to have more confidence and trust in your own mind."

She sighed. "They didn't help me?"

"No. . .you did it all."

Silence.

"Aimee?"

"Thanks, mom. You made me feel so good."

"I didn't do anything, honey, *you* did it all. *You* made you feel good."

Then she told me she was on her way over to the fire station where they were going to vote on this year's officers. She didn't know when she'd be home so I told her to be careful on our icy roads. She'd taken the van so I wasn't too concerned. If she'd had the blue pickup I probably would wait up for her just to be sure. When your young adults live at home with you, you're naturally brought into their activities and have an extra measure of watchfulness over them. We're all so close. And that's exactly how they want it.

When Aimee did come home tonight, she proudly showed me her new, shiny Firefighter badge. I think, in her mind, that symbolized the "officialness" of her new volunteer work.

Aimee's new friend, Steve, hasn't called her back. He turned out to be engaged to a girl at college and, when he saw his fiancee over the Thanksgiving holiday, he was going to decide what to do. He wasn't sure about his former life decision. Now that he hasn't called here, Aimee says phooey!

Eric is due to show up around the 13th. Did Steve not work out because an opening was required during this time frame?

It just struck me that this diary has many developing sub-plots and mysteries that are leading up to a great ending.

Will we finally go to trial in Norfolk? Will it be a big public event? Will we win? Will we finally get to set foot on our land? Will Aimee end up with Eric after all? Will our Starborn friend end up giving us the energy device? Will those visions I get finally manifest into the physical? Will our Wellspring Mission be the large operation that was foreseen? Where will that be?

The trouble with all the above sub-plots is that the story's conclusion will most likely turn out to be a "cliff-hanger." STAY TUNED, FOLKS? TUNE IN NEXT WEEK? Nope. This journal ends on the last night of December and I'm afraid all the plots will be far from concluded. . .all the mysteries will be unsolved when the reader turns the final page. Ahh, but that's what makes life interesting, is it not? Tomorrow. What of tomorrow? Tomorrow will unfold just the way destiny and time want it to. They open all the doors we each choose to walk through. If I have my eye on tomorrow's dreams—what have I then seen of today?

I'm going to take advantage of the moment. Bill just recently kissed me goodnight and went up to bed. Maybe he'll still be awake. I feel the need to snuggle and listen to *his* heart sounds.

The curtain (book?) closes on another chapter.

Goodnight, folks. See you again tomorrow night.

12-4-91, Wednesday

Bill and Aimee went to the chiropractor this morning and they brought home a triple stack of mail. There were two boxes that Aimee brought in. One was the set of five small kitten figurines we'd ordered for Jenny's Christmas present and the other box was a set of my six books belonging to Mary Himes. She requested that they be autographed. Enclosed in the box was return postage and label—no problem.

Mary Himes is a good friend of Becky's (one of the people at the Divide Feed and Grain Bin where we went to surprise Frank Gonzales on his birthday), and Mary detailed how surprised the group was that day and hoped we didn't think they all were bumbling idiots for the way they acted. We never thought such a thing. We came away with the feeling we'd just met some very nice people.

Anyway, I signed the set of books and also the children's book Mary ordered. I boxed it all up and Robin took it back to the Post Office when she and Jenny later went into town.

In the mail I'd also received my Barnes & Noble book catalog. While I was browsing through the pages of literary goodies, my eyes widened with delight to see a large volume offered. The tome was entitled *Hazardous Chemicals Desk Reference.* We'd just discussed this subject with Aimee. How timely this was! I immediately ordered it for her for Christmas because the $79.95 volume was only $14.95!

While I worked on the mail, Bill called Bob to make sure he was going to be in the office on Friday.

"Why?" Bob asked. (He can be so suspicious, sometimes.)

"We're sending you something."

"What?" Bob said skeptically. Bill, upon hearing Bob's tone, played into it. "A letter bomb."

Bob laughed. "I'll call you Friday. . .if I'm still alive."

We didn't want Bob to know that our Christmas present would arrive on Friday, we just wanted to be sure he'd be there when it did. Bob also told Bill that Bridget had received the baby moccasins and was surprised to receive them. We were glad to hear they arrived safely.

Jan at C & M Printing called to say she expected our book shipment to be delivered on Friday. She needed directions to our house. Bill told her he was going to meet the driver in Woodland and to have him call us when he arrived. That was fine with her. This shipment will arrive just in time.

Since it didn't look like we'd have time to shop for the stove, Bill arranged for one to be delivered anonymously to the lady's house. That way we were still able to achieve our objective.

This evening, we received several large boxes of clothing from one of our correspondents. These, naturally, were for our needy families. It took me several hours to sort them out and they'll make some people very happy.

When Robin and Jenny returned home around suppertime, they brought in more mail. I browsed through it while watching the evening news. One large envelope contained material from an alleged "alien federation."

My Starman had previously discussed this group at length. It appears these "alien authors" are very, very human. I won't write more about them, for they are not exactly what one would call "user friendly." Yet I wonder how it is that not one of this group's followers has ever spoken face to face with one of the alien authors? My Starborn friend frequently comes right into our home and is a very touchable being. My friend once asked me what I noticed about this group's material? My answer was immediate.

"The material denigrates our government and various ethnic groups. They tend to incite fear and make people paranoid . . . untrusting of all authoritative aspects of society. The material is very politically oriented."

My friend had smiled at my words because they were accurate. Although there were some (very little) facts stated, the material gave off a racist and radical flavor, surrounding my perceptual sense with a black shadow that screamed BEWARE! I will not say more on this subject.

Late this evening Bill and I discussed this group's popular material. Our conversation shifted to the state of the economy, both now and where it was heading. He was deeply concerned that it would negatively affect our lawsuit settlement because, if the defendants couldn't pay for some reason, we weren't going to get settled on our land.

I told him not to be so concerned. I told him we'd get settled if we had to buy a *camper* and put it on just one acre of forest. That didn't go over well—it was not convincing.

"Where's everyone going to live?"

"We'll buy *two* campers. . .or *three*! I don't care anymore, just as long as it's ours and nobody can take it away. That's all I care about. That's the very rock bottom line."

He still was concerned, but hey, I'm not entertaining million dollar dreams here! If I had to sell every last thing we owned for us to fit into a little cabin, I'd do it in a minute and so would Bill. And we'd be as happy as two larks in a warm nest.

However, I don't want him to be so concerned about the money. I think we won't be able to swing another children's book reprint. We'll probably have to let it go out of print if we can't find a regular publisher to take it on. That'd be a shame too, because last week the lady at Moving Books distributor told Bill to be sure to let her know if we ever decided to distribute it nationally through bookstores. I guess she's had quite a few requests for it.

Nevertheless, I feel we've done our last reprint. We just don't have that kind of money.

I hate to keep yakking about money, but money is a big part of everyone's life. Everyone's hurting now and that includes us.

In this vein, I talked to a friend of mine the other night. We were on the subject of our slim savings, and he wondered if we couldn't (just once in a while) make personal use of a Wellspring donation here and there.

The idea was so unexpected coming from this individual that I was struck speechless for a few moments.

"Mary? You there?" he asked.

"I'm here," I said.

"Well? Who would know?"

"I would," I whispered. And my response was that he'd forgotten my nature or something, and he apologized for the suggestion.

After I hung up the receiver, I thought back on the time we'd received a clothing shipment and Jenny asked if she could keep a knitted hat. At that time I took a lot of care to explain why she couldn't act as if these donations were for us. She understood then. But this caller was an adult, and I still can't imagine what could've prompted his suggestion, other than caring about our finances. My God, he should've known I'd die of guilt if I ever did anything like that! Bill and I aren't Wellspring Mission. . .the *needy* are! And I'll be damned if we'll ever act like an Indian agent!

I didn't mean to get carried away and start ranting. I guess I got more than a little peeved, huh. I'm still known to do that now and again, yet this is *my* journal and I'm going to *get it all out* whenever I need to.

The Prayer Smoke rises tonight for Jenny. She's such a great help to us and we love her so much.

Some Prayertime will also be spent on those people who can't see the human propaganda and manipulation that smolders behind a fictitious alien facade.

12-5-91, Thursday

Bill's first call this morning was to John Hart, our Norfolk attorney, who said there was nothing we could do about *Earthway* being out of print for eight months. Then he informed us that our lawsuit defendants had submitted an appeal to the court ruling for a trial. Why did this not surprise us? I WANT MY NO-EYES BACK! *NOW!* How *dare* they fight to keep her from me! What do Schiffer and Walsworth hope to gain by prolonging it? Are they truly that hell-bent on keeping my lady hostage? And, of course, we all know why they're fighting to keep this from going to trial, don't we? A court trial would demand company records to be opened and sales figures and legal agreements to be shown. In arbitration a lot can remain hidden and undisclosed. What a tribulation this has been for so long—what a living hell. No wonder I'm getting grey.

Bill placed a happy call to Big John to tell him we'd be out to Victor on Saturday morning. We had to juggle some other appointments and activities, but we just didn't want to put off our visit any longer.

In the mail today I received "Birthday" cards! What a touching surprise those were because they were from my readers! How nice it was for them to remember me on my special day. Those kind thoughts really brightened my afternoon.

Jane from C & M Printing called to say that the book covers were still not dry enough to put the UV coating on. She said they plan to make the delivery on Monday instead of tomorrow. Bill told her "no problem as long as they did good quality control—we could wait." I bet we're going to be down to less than five books in stock when that shipment arrives. We're getting 500 delivered and when the last of those are gone it will be a sad day to see.

Jenny's been a closet computer addict and we never knew it. We can't seem to get her away from it in the evenings. Tonight she made a Christmas thank-you card for the gift money her Grandma sent her. Then, when Sarah showed her how to load the Hoyle card game disk, it was all over. She played Klondike (Solitaire) until Bill went to bed and she had to turn it off. It was a battle to get her to do that. Sometimes Jenny can be quite a challenge. When she wants to do something—all the heavenly powers can't keep her from it. That determined mind has been in operation since she was two years old and demanded to make her own bed and put her own toys away with the definitive voicing of two words: "ME DO!" At two years' of age that was cute. . .now it's not so funny. Her Virgo perfectionism won't allow anyone to help her with her housework because. . .they may not "do it right!"

When Aimee came home tonight she said she'd failed one of her review Practical sessions. I felt bad because I thought the scoring method was unfair to the individual. They had to work in "groups" and some in her group didn't perform well, consequently the entire group was scored on an overall rating of how they went about each medical step in caring for a medical emergency scenario that was given them. One was a hypothermia case and the other was an individual who was kicked by a horse. Aimee did well on the other aspects of the test that were scored individually. She needs eight hours of emergency room time, and eight hours of ambulance time to get in before she completes the course. On Sunday she's going to ride the night shift Ambulance A-1 Paramedics in Colorado Springs. After that she's going to try to arrange an eight-hour emergency room shift up in Woodland Park with Dr. Glanzer at our Medical Center.

Aimee is also dissatisfied with what she's learned about the heart—she wants to know more. She wants to be able to visualize exactly what's going on when she listens with her stethoscope. So Bill is going to call Dr. Tom Levy (our cardiologist friend who moved here because of the books), to see if he can manage a day when Aimee can shadow him and get all her questions asked to her satisfaction. She's got quite a full schedule right now. And in January, when her EMT course will be over, she's going to have to decide which path she wants to pursue. This evening I explained that, right now, she's a little fragmented because she's a firefighter, she's being trained as a police dispatcher and she's learning the emergency medical techniques. . .police, fire, medicine. She needs to choose one and go for it all the way.

She explained to me that the firefighting didn't feel like it was personally fulfilling. It was then that I smiled and drew her a sketch of a thin trail that led into a thick path. The firefighting was the thin trail that lead into the thick medical path of her destiny. She could then see how one interest was leading into the main one. The medical path is what she's shooting for. She wants to take each EMT level course until she finishes with Paramedic training. In the meantime, she wants to get a job in a hospital—preferably emergency room work. We give her a lot of credit for reaching out and grasping her destiny with a white-knuckled ferocity. She's of one mind and determined to carry it out until she's reached her goal. Yeah, Aimee!

While Aimee and I were discussing all of this, it was late at night. I'd been writing in my journal when she came home. The house was dark except for the mantle oil pots burning and the Christmas tree lights twinkling.

Suddenly, during our conversation, she snapped her head around to peer into the living room.

"I saw something move out of the corner of my eye," she said. "Are they here?"

"Three of them are," I smiled.

Her eyes widened with joy. "Can I meet them? Are they the children?"

She calls the smaller Starborn ones "the children."

"Yes, they're the little ones, but it's not up to me if you see them or not. You know that's their decision."

She stood up and faced the sunken living room. "Hey, you little guys, please let me see you."

Nothing manifested while she watched.

I felt sorry for her and wanted her to have an encounter.

"Aimee, go up the stairs to the front window. Lower the blind, switch off the Christmas doll, unplug her and stand at the top of the entry stairs."

She did as directed.

While she was doing that, the three little ones were scurrying back and forth, but she couldn't see them.

"Look over in the corner by my drum," I advised.

She peered through the tall plants to look at the drum.

I laughed because, as she turned and bent over the railing to peer into the shadowed darkness, I saw the outline of a Little One scurry behind her in an impish manner. Then he was gone. I called Aimee back to the kitchen and told her that they were having a great time playing with her. They were not going to fully manifest this night and I told her, "maybe next time."

She was disappointed but understood.

When we finally went to bed and I walked into our room, Bill was sound asleep with a ray of light in his face. Our paneling door was open about two inches and the light of the hidden stairs to the roof was on. How clever, I thought. They created a diversion for Aimee and me downstairs, while others were visiting Bill in our room. Actually, they don't need any light to see. The light was probably left on from the roofer who'd been here earlier today, but the paneling door is *always* shut and latched now. Bill would never go to bed with that door open, as it was when I went to bed. And he claims he never gets visited. . .ha. So I turned off the light to the roof trap door and closed and latched the paneling door. Sleep tight, Bill, sleep tight, your slumbering dreams tonight weren't even dreams.

12-6-91, Friday

Twenty minutes after Aimee and I went to bed last night, her emergency transmitter went off with a tone. A three-story structure was on fire down the pass in Green Mountain Falls. Their fire department called Aimee's for backup and she went in. It ended up that only one truck went down, but Aimee stayed at the station with the others in case more were needed. None were.

It was an incredibly busy day for us. Bill was on the phone all day and I processed the stack of mail and signed books. When we left the office at dinnertime, Bill laughed, "We really kicked butt today, didn't we."

I hugged him. "Yeah, we got it all cleaned up."

I received some more birthday cards and three gifts. One was beautifully handcrafted jewelry, one was a set of Frankincense and Myrrh essential oils, and one was tobacco wrapped in red cloth from a native elder. I was so touched by these gifts. I hope people can feel my appreciation when they think of me in this manner.

This evening Bill called Computer Bill and we were informed that my manuscript pages had all been scanned and that Jan already had run the first four hundred pages through Word Perfect. We were amazed that they'd had so much done already. When our friend asked me what I wanted for my birthday, I said, "nothing." There was no *way* I was going to say I wanted a thing! Besides, it seems that everything I do want is not for sale. I want world peace. . .pollution stopped and its effects reversed. . .the free energy device. . . food for everyone who's hungry. . .shelters for the homeless . . .and. . ..

After Robin came home from work, the lady who now

drives her Buick called to ask about a loud tapping noise that developed. The woman said the car's been running beautifully until now.

Robin never had any tapping noise in the engine and couldn't imagine what it could be from until, during the conversation, she found out the lady had been putting *unleaded* gas in. The Buick is a 1972 and always took regular gasoline. Now we hope the engine's not permanently damaged. The lady lives with a gentleman friend—you'd think he should've known better.

Woodland Park had their Parade of Lights celebration this evening and Aimee had to wear her Fire Department uniform and walk beside the fire trucks. Afterward, they gathered at the station for refreshments. She has a full day tomorrow so, for once, she managed to get to bed at a decent hour—hope her tone doesn't go off during the night again.

Buttercup, Jenny's little cat, sometimes reminds me of a gremlin the way she acts. This evening she suddenly decided to play Hunter and Prey with Magic. Guess who was the Hunter? With eyes big as a Hunter's Moon, she hid until the unsuspecting four-legged victim walked by, then she raised up on her hind feet and *ran* that way with front paws up to attack Magic's rump! Poor Magic. She doesn't care for the role of Prey, so she turned the tables on kitty and chased her around the house. Sometimes it's hard to tell which role they're each playing because they reverse them in mid-run.

But. . .then there are the times when Magic's sleeping or laying on the living room rug and kitty will creep up to give Magic's nose a sisterly nuzzle. In turn, Magic will do the same to Buttercup when she's resting. They love each other— that's plain to see—but there are times when kitty is in her growling, gremlin mood and Magic looks up at one of us as if to say, "Get me outta here!"

Bill just came downstairs. Hands on hips, he looked a little disgusted.

"Did you know our bedroom deck door was open about two inches?"

My mouth dropped. Then it closed into a little smirk.

He nodded. "Yeah. That's what I thought too. Can't you instruct your 'friends' to please close our doors when they're done visiting?"

"It wasn't open when I came to bed last night. Just the panel door was. That deck door couldn't have been open then, because our room would've been freezing when I came

in. Did you ask Jenny if she opened it for air upstairs today?"

"She said no. She even looked at me as if I'd lost it."

I smiled. "Then it's a mystery. Things around here are
getting weirder and weirder. The only reason that door could
be open would be because of our friends. Why they come to
an empty room is a mystery."

"Did Aimee take a nap in our room this afternoon?"

"No, she didn't have time."

"Well," he sighed with a grin, "please tell them to not
leave our doors open the next time you see them."

I grinned wide. "You tell them. Seems to me *you* were
the one with the friendly visitor last night."

He sighed. "Goodnight, honey, don't stay up too late."

Well. . .I wasn't planning on staying up late, unless I
have an unexpected visitor, that is. Oh God, what are people
going to think of all our goings-on? What a wacky house.
What a wacky family. Even the pets have weird behavior.
Know what though? I love it. Sometimes things get so weird
I smile to myself as thoughts of a modern-day Addams Family comes to mind—especially in *this* house. Yet, these happenings have been going on for so long now, I don't think
I'd know how to live a normal life. Methinks it'd be rather
bland tasting to our spiced up palates.

Although I do jest about it, things have intensified recently
and they don't normally do that without a very, very good
reason. I feel things building and sense the next few months
are going to be interesting—very interesting indeed.

Sarah's got something on her mind that she's afraid to tell
us. I think I know what it is. I feel she doesn't want to
move way over to Marble. I'll give her one more day to
approach one of us with it and then I'll help her voice it.

12-7-91, Saturday

It was a clear Blue Day and everyone in the family had
some place to go. Aimee had classes, Robin was getting
ready to take Jenny and Mandy downtown to do the week's
grocery shopping, and Sarah was coming with Bill and me to
visit John in Victor.

The drive took us 45 minutes and the mountain range beyond Cripple Creek never stood out with such stark clarity. It
seemed as though we could see all the way into Utah, it was
so clear.

We spent over two hours at Big John's visiting with him

and his friend. John was a veritable storehouse of stories and we listened with great interest as he told his tales of war experiences and Starborn encounters.

After we left Victor, our pass through Cripple Creek was somewhat impeded by the cars creeping along, with drivers impatient to find parking spaces, and people meandering across the streets to try their luck at the various casinos.

When we arrived home, we found a pile of mail that Robin had picked up for us. I began going through it while Bill processed the book orders and then began the time-consuming job of making address changes on our mailing list. The index cards have to be changed too. We'd received a large envelope of "returned" envelopes that went back to Hampton Roads from their *Soul Sounds* offer. What a job! It will be wonderful to have that mailing list on disk so we don't have to keep updating two record books. I might as well utilize this moment to request that all our correspondents who wish to be on our mailing list, please remember to think of us when you make out "change of address" postal cards. It would help us a lot to keep updated on a regular basis rather than be swamped with returned envelopes whenever Hampton Roads mails out an offer for one of my upcoming books and then find we've got two hundred addresses to change at once.

This evening, Bill called Dr. Tom Levy, our cardiologist friend, to ask him if he'd have any time available to help Aimee out. Tom was eager to do so and offered to assist in several ways. As soon as Aimee's finished with her medical classes we'll set something up. She's very excited about doing this.

One of the letters we received today was from the lady who addressed her prior letter to Rainbow. Today she apologized and said she felt great guilt for her childish reaction because the books have helped her and her family so much. She asked me if we could ever forgive her? Tomorrow I'm going to town to buy her a "We Forgive You" card. What's done is done and I don't want her to keep harboring guilt feelings inside—she needs to let them go. Our hurt over her letter has healed. . .so should her guilt about it once she receives our card. I hope it does.

My heart was on the ground when I opened and read a letter from Mr. Hobson of the University of Oklahoma's Department of English. They are going to invite 150 Native authors to a special function next year and their Native committee brought up my name. However, some committee members said I wasn't Native and there was a dispute among them.

Mr. Hobson was caught in the middle and needed a response from me. Am I a member of a tribe? Do I carry a "card?" What clan am I? Is there any Native organization that would vouch for me? Mr. Hobson explained that they couldn't include any non-Native authors, and that Ben Nighthorse Campbell was working on legislation to stop the "pretend Indians." Would I please respond to the committee for clarification.

Oh yes, I was fiercely compelled to respond, for although it made my heart shine to know some Native committee members went to bat for me, my heart was crying tears of sorrow because of those other members who opposed my nomination to attend. It's not that I feel left out that hurts me, because I would decline the offer to attend on the basis of leaving an opening for a "fullblood" author, my pain is caused by the basic principle of the thing.

I wish to share an excerpt of my response.

December 7, 1991

Dear Mr. Hobson,

First I would like to express my appreciation for all those kind committee members who honored me by recognizing my ethnic heritage. They are not alone in their assessment of me, for I've received hundreds of letters from native elders and AIM members who've read my six-book series. These letters have been extremely supportive of my efforts to bring the general public into a higher and greater awareness of the incredible beauty of the native culture and to enlighten them of the ongoing plights that still exist in society.

Yet, Mr. Hobson, I am one of the hundreds of people who can feel their native heart beating within them, yet cannot prove that nativeness with "papers" or ancestry. . .so then, now a "throwback" appears in the line that recognizes and deeply cherishes the sacredness of her blood, makes it a public matter and does something to enrich it—yet cannot be recognized for the red heart that beats strong within her breast.

A "pretend Indian?" Do you know how deeply that cuts one such as me? Especially when I cherish the native traditions so much? Do you know that I go out in 4° winter snows at night to offer my Prayer Smoke for the native People? That I try to help the native People as much as I can, both through my books and materially? That that is where my heart lies? Oh no, Mr. Hobson, I am no (author's name withheld), for she has been a disgrace. Please, never compare me to her.

. . .I am as an orphan who will never ever know who I am. But, in my heart, there beats a strong cadence that tells me who I am and that's enough for me.

You said you never read any of my books. That's okay, however, you should be aware that, in the Native chapter of my last book, Daybreak, I've openly chastised all those "white" and "pretend Indians" who are making money by allegedly teaching sacred native ways (sometimes improperly). I do not condone this practice as I see it as a terrible affront upon native culture and a taking-away of its high sacredness. I cry tears of sorrow to see authors such as (name withheld) pen the things she has and claim knowledge I know she doesn't have for the sake of notoriety and profit. Regardless, my goal has always been to bring a new heightened awareness to the public about the beautiful importance that the native people's culture has to offer and to wake the public up to current native plights around the country.

Mary Summer Rain is not a pseudonym. It was given to me in a vision and my native teacher called me by that name the first time I ever saw her. Later I made it my legal name because she performed a native Naming Ceremony for me. I now cherish that name because I know it is mine. I know it is all that I can hold sacred. . ..

Mr. Hobson, what happens to people like me? We're falling through the cracks. We who know who we are but cannot prove it to others and are being deeply hurt through discrimination that says, "You are not one of us!" But neither are we one of "them" either. Our hearts and spirits tell us who we are, but nobody can see those. Mr. Nighthorse Cambell is driving the arrows into our hearts by saying we're among the "pretend Indians" because we cannot prove otherwise. Do you know? Do you have any idea how much that hurts?

I thank you for thinking of me. I thank those committee members whose spirits can "feel" who I am. I thank them for bringing up my name, but clearly, if I cannot be accepted by all; I, like many others of my kind, must forever be cast aside and not brought into the sacred circle. We are the cast-outs, the camp pariahs, the non-entities. Yet to us—we are indeed native hearts.

Clearly, it would be for the best if you removed my name from consideration.

Many blessings to you, Mr. Hobson,

Mary Summer Rain

P.S. I think it's important to underscore the fact that, in

my books, I have publicly stated that I cannot prove my nativeness. Also, I've never gone about the country claiming to be a native teacher, I've never taught native ceremonies, I've never personally gone about publicizing myself. I'm basically shy and stay up in my mountains where my native spirit can best be felt. Am I not allowed to do that? Am I not allowed to write of my experiences that have dealt with my native soul and how deeply I feel it?

[End of response]

Tonight the Prayer Smoke rises for the purpose of the public's better understanding of the "who" of me. . .not for me alone, but for all those like me who are ethnic orphans nobody wants to claim.

12-8-91, Sunday

We had errands to do this morning, so Bill, Aimee and I went into Woodland. While Aimee and I went into Hallmark to look for the "forgive-you" card, Bill went over to Mail Boxes Etc. to photocopy the next 58 manuscript pages of this journal. One set was going to Bob to edit and one set to Bill to scan.

We were empty-handed when we met up with Bill because we could find no card. Aimee and I did get into mischief though. At the new Goodwill store, she spied a Christmas basket filled with artificial pine boughs, holly berries, and nuts. She pointed the arrangement out to me and I smiled. She took it off the shelf and handed it to me. We left the store with my two-dollar treasure.

When we arrived back home, Jenny was shouting in the living room. Magic was barking and running around. Football was on and Bill joined in the commotion while I snuggled down in my reading chair and tuned them all out. We won.

On the evening news, the big expected event at a Colorado Catholic Shrine was widely covered. A few week's ago, a woman claimed that the Virgin Mary appeared to her there and, on December 8th, would again appear to give another message. Since I knew it wasn't going to happen at this time, I'd forgotten all about it.

The cameras were rolling. The people flocked up the mountain to the shrine. Faces were turned to the sun in rapt attitudes. And the Lady didn't keep her appointment. Yet, according to some spectators who took pictures of the sun with their Polaroids—there she was in all her glory standing at the Gate of Heaven. However, the photos showed nothing but a normal sun and the messenger said she *was* given a message, yet no one else could see the Lady. Convenient, yes? Oh how the world is want to grab at each religious straw. How desperate its people have become.

This evening Bill drove Aimee to an EMT-IV's house in Woodland Park. Aimee's going down to Colorado Springs with this woman to ride the night shift with an ambulance crew. She wondered how much of Jenny's great baked chicken dinner she should eat. Aimee was concerned she might lose her dinner if they had a call to a bad scene. She ended up eating about half of it, mainly because she was so excited.

Sarah's bird is getting better. Kitty's getting worse—she rose up on two legs tonight and went after Aimee's legs when she walked by. Funny, kitty never tries that with me . . .I think she has a bright mind inside that furry little head of hers. We seem to have an unspoken understanding that says, "don't you *dare* fool with me!" But there are many nights when she's asleep on the couch that I go over and spend long moments watching her. She's so small and furry . . . so sweet. . .the innocence of that tiny four-legged brings forth a welling of great love from my heart, and I gently kiss her goodnight.

I had that talk with Sarah. I was right, she doesn't want to move away from Woodland Park. She said that she loves school, has great friends and really feels like she belongs here.

I assured her that it'd be a while before we were in any kind of position to make our "moving" decision and that it was possible we'd stay right around here. We talked at length about "living the moment," and about not ruining each moment's beauty or enjoyment of that beauty with concerns for tomorrow; for she feels guilt because she knows her mom's heart rests in another location. She doesn't want to be the one to hold me back or in any way interfere with my own joy in getting settled.

I told her that I understood and that, most of all, she needed to shed her guilt feelings that were ruining her beautiful days. I was convincing enough to see her make the necessary change in attitude. Now I needed to perform the same transformation within myself. I knew that there was no way we could move over to our preferred region if we only ended up with enough money for a small cabin. That scenario meant that we'd just move up into the mountains around here and, if the piece of property was right, I'd feel just as peaceful with it. Whatever Destiny has in mind for us will be accepted.

12-9-91, Monday

Jane, from C & M Press called early to say that she'd be bringing the book shipment down herself. She expected to get into Woodland around noon.

Then my former editor at Pocket Books finally returned Bill's week-old message to call us. Bill wanted to know why Pocket was letting *Earthway* stay out of stock for eight months. Claire said that just builds reader anticipation.

Phooey! Bill informed her that distributors and Pocket itself had thousands of back orders for the book and why can't they move up the date for the softcover edition?

Well, seems Pocket has done things this way for 50 years and they're a big successful company, Claire reminded Bill.

He reminded her back that it wasn't even logical for them to withhold *Earthway* from so many people who are looking high and low for it. Is Pocket in the business of selling books or playing Hide and Seek?

"Well, Bill, I'm sorry you're having a hard time *understanding* this," she said.

"It's not that I don't *understand*—it's that I don't *agree* with it! I find no *logic* in it."

"I'm sorry about that, but there's nothing I can do about it."

And so Pocket turns its back on thousands of people who have tried to obtain one copy of *Earthway*. And so Pocket will make them wait until July of '92 to provide the long-awaited trade copies. God, I hope this doesn't sour people on it. Well, let this be a secondhand lesson to struggling writers out there in Author Wanna-Be Land, don't set your sights on the Biggie Publishers who end up talking down to you and doing what they've been doing for 50 years—*raise* your sights to the smaller press companies who are open to change and will treat you with a decent measure of respect and not sarcasm.

When Aimee came home from her ambulance shift she was glowing with joy. They'd had four calls during the night and the two people she rode with were so considerate of her eagerness they let her take vitals on the patients and readily answered all her many questions. On the Evaluation Form they filled out, they wrote that Aimee had a good under- standing of what transpired and that she was welcome back at any time. She had so much energy flowing out of her I'm surprised all our plants weren't vibrating with the waves of it.

Eagerly she told us all about her night. She said they made Colorado Springs seem so small because they zipped from here to there in no time.

"How fast did you go?" the silly mother asked.

Her eyes lit up. "*Very* fast!"

Ahh, no wonder our little dynamo was so cranked up. Between the excitement of doing what she wants to do and the *speed*, it all fits her energy level. Finally there's a job that equals her mental and physical pace. No wonder she was bored to death standing behind a cash register for eight hours a day.

After she exhausted all the tales, she told me that one side of her throat was swollen. When I examined it there were the same sacs that Sarah used to get on her tonsils. I removed them and started her on antibiotics. She ate a man-sized breakfast and went to bed for most of the day.

Bill came home from town with a quadruple pile of mail. We got right on it because I had boxes of clothing to sort for Wellspring Mission.

Just as he began processing the book orders, Jane called to say she'd arrived in Woodland. When Bill found out how long it took her to get to Woodland from Thornton, I heard him say, "You must have a lead foot like Mary has! People used to call our blue pickup the Blue Streak!"

I don't know why he tells everyone that. Just because it doesn't take me long to get places he thinks I've no percep- tion of speed. Anyway, he left for town to connect with Jane, but he came back alone—with the van loaded down with 13 boxes containing 40 books in each.

Jenny helped him unload (he wouldn't let me) and as soon as they set the first one down on the office floor, I excitedly tore into it. What a surprise! The covers were so much more vibrant than the previous Walsworth books. Inside, the ink was blacker and I really liked the trimmed size—they'd had to trim the overall dimensions by a quarter inch all around. We were so pleased, as soon as all the boxes were unloaded, Bill called C & M and asked to speak to the supervisor. He told Michael, the production manager, that they'd done a great job. Michael was taken off guard by the compliment, not that this was the first great job they'd done, but because

it was a rarity to get complimented for it. I hadn't known
that. I hadn't known that it was now a rarity to thank another for a job well done.

By the way, our old stock had dwindled down to just two
books. That's cutting things a little close, yet that's exactly
how everything seems to go for us. . .always down to the
old wire.

I went back to my desk. Magic was sleeping beneath it.
Delving into the stacks of letters and cards, I was soon in
deep concentration.

More birthday cards arrived and they made me feel really
good. There were two small packages. One was from Sandy
and her mother in Seattle. They'd sent me a beautiful crystal
pendant. It was so delicate and dainty. It was just beautiful,
but I found the *words* in Sandy's letter to be just as beautiful, for she'd touched my heart with them.

The other package was from our friend, Charlie, in Minnesota. He'd sent me yet another Kitaro tape, which I loved
because of all the drums in it. Drums have always reached
into my soul to touch a sacredness dwelling there. Charlie
had also sent me a beautiful pair of earrings with beads,
feathers, suede, and a dove in the center. I wrote him right
back to inform him that he's spoiling me.

In one letter today a woman told me what we need to do.
We need to place all our problems on the spirit level where
"they" can take care of them. I think this lady is trying to
help, but doesn't have the whole picture. We *do* place our
problems on the spirit plane, but there are just as many battles "up there" going on over our problems as there are down
here on the physical level.

She also told us to *forget* about our problems after we
placed them on the spirit level. Well. . .that doesn't really
leave room for our taking responsibility for helping in their
resolutions if we did that. It's nice (and easy) to shove all
one's troubles onto another dimension and expect the spirit
helpers to fix everything, yet it's not exactly the spiritual
thing to do. One does not shove one's problems off on another and say, "*You* handle these!" No, no, it's *our* responsibility to *know* and keep abreast of what's transpiring with
our problems on *all* levels because there are usually things
we can do *here* to help them over *there* to bring about a
so-called "cooperative" resolution. The burden of one's problems must be shared by all in order to reach an effective and
positive outcome. It's everyone's individual responsibility to
be *responsible* and take an ever-active role in all facets of

their life. Never ship your problems off. . .face them head on!

We finished up the correspondence at 9:00 P.M. and I spent two more hours sorting clothes for our needy recipients.

Tonight my Prayer Smoke will rise for Charlie, Sandy, and her mother—not because of the gifts they sent, but because of what I felt from their hearts today.

12-10-91, Tuesday

The mail was light and it gave us time to finish up other office projects we had going.

Our Norfolk attorney called to tell us that they'd set the trial date. It's for June 1, 1992, in the Federal Court in Norfolk, Virginia. Six months isn't so long to wait, not after going through two years of agony over No-Eyes' captivity.

We're still waiting for the ruling on the defendant's arbitration appeal. We have confidence in our unseen warriors who are waging a fierce battle over this legal issue of ours. It will be a constant spiritual war until it's concluded.

We're hoping that this can be settled out of court. When I get those contracts back those first four books are going to have brand new jackets on them so my readers will know that No-Eyes has risen up from the ashes. And she will know how desperately I've fought to free her. No one can know the misery and heartache this has brought to me. I'd vowed to protect her essence and image with everything I had in me, yet the enemy came from within and struck a near-fatal blow. Donning itself, with Walsworth and Schiffer, spirited her away under cover of darkness. And so. . .when the moon is darkest on the first of June, I will reclaim She-Who-Was-Taken from me.

It won't be long now, No-Eyes, it won't be long before you're back in my arms again. You've entered the hearts of many—you've touched a million hearts—and they all want you back.

Goodnight, No-Eyes. I love you.

Tonight the Prayer Smoke rises for Rose in Seattle. She's a very special lady and I give thanks for her kind heart and the unconditional love she has shown us.

12-11-91, Wednesday

While Bill and I were busy at our desks today, he turned to me, "Do you realize this is the 11th of December and we've had no new snow this month?

"No, I hadn't realized that. We've still got a foot on the ground out there. It's still plenty white around here."

"I'd like a blanket of fresh snow for your birthday, tomorrow. I think that'd make a beautiful present from nature."

I smiled. "That was a really sweet thought, but I think it's a tall order." I glanced out our office window at the deep blue sky. "Yep, you're going to have to either sweet-talk Mother Nature or else have a powerful pow-wow with Cold Maker for that one."

He frowned. "That bad, huh?"

"That bad."

Then he grinned. "I've got friends Upstairs."

I grinned back. "Then you better not wait too much longer to get them on the horn."

We finished our office work just before dinner and, shortly afterward, all seven of us helped to stock the cord of wood that was dumped earlier in the day.

The evening was a peaceful one. We'd left only the Christmas tree lights on (and the oil pots on the mantle, of course), the logs in the woodstove were crackling and we curled up to watch one of our favorite videos. . .one of the ones I always end up crying from.

Just as the movie ended, Aimee turned on our outside floodlights, rolled up our front blinds and said, "Look! It's snowing!"

Big, beautiful snowflakes were falling through the light. We went to the window to see three inches had already accumulated. Oh, how it sparkled and glistened.

Bill wrapped his arms around me as we watched the swirling whiteness.

"Happy Birthday, honey. Mother Nature sent you her own gift. You'll have a sparkling world to wake up to in the morning."

"Somehow I feel the gift's not just for me. I think it's for us both."

He didn't respond to that thought, for he was deep into the precious moment of holding me and. . .admiring the gently falling snow.

12-12-91, Thursday

Shimmering rays of brilliance radiated down from the topaz gem that rested upon its velvety cloth of sky. . .sky blue as blueberry pie. And all around, around on the ground, the twinkling winks of countless diamonds blinked in sacred symmetry upon a bridal veil of winter white.

These and more presented themselves to Bill and me this morning as we journeyed down our snow-covered mountain road.

Tracks of the fox family trailed across the frozen pond we passed. White rabbits watched us from the brush along the roadside. Hawks lazily rode the air currents above.

This was going to be a good day.

Beginning one's birthday by going to the dentist wouldn't normally be one's destination of choice, but it didn't bother me in the least. This was a weekday and that meant another work day for us.

After my dental appointment, we checked out a sporting goods shop in town for an idea I had for Sarah's Christmas present. After she'd seen the Robin Hood film, she was total-ly absorbed with the time period (can't imagine why—that was tongue-in-cheek by the way) and became absolutely fas-cinated with archery. I'd done some archery when I was around ten years old, and remembered the hours and hours I'd spent alone aiming at the targets. Now that Sarah had excitedly expressed a strong interest in it, the idea grew into a Christmas gift.

The Woodland shop didn't have what I was looking for, so we'll have to try again when we all go down to Colorado Springs Saturday for our family day of Christmas shopping.

We dropped off some boxes of clothes and toys to some of our people and then headed home to work on the mail. In the afternoon, I took a break to shovel off the four inches of new snow on our front deck, so I could make space to spread out seed and nuts for my little critters. I filled the bird feeder and scattered bread pieces, nuts, and sunflower seeds on the deck and picnic table.

"Com'on Little Ones, come to my birthday party!" I called. And while I was putting out the food, snow toppled from pine and fir branches as the partygoers began to gather. My heart laughed with the feel of their anticipation.

When I returned to the office and turned on my type-writer, my monitor died. Bill called our IBM rep, and he said it'd be around $300 to replace it. Oh well. We packed it away in the box it came in two years ago and now I'm just using the machine as a regular typewriter. That's okay, I didn't need that fancy screen to do my work.

By the time Jenny called us for dinner, we were done in the office. We had a leisure dinner and then the lights went out as Jenny carried in the cake she'd baked. The birthday song was sung and I blew out all the candles (*not* 46 of them either).

Presents were presented then. Fresh flowers from Jenny, a new oil lamp from Aimee, three silk Victorian roses from Sarah, and an antique lace potpourri box from Mandy.

Then Bill and Sarah struggled to lift a very, very large box over to my chair. Carefully they set it down beside me. I went for the wrapping.

"*Don't!* Don't *touch* it yet!" Bill said. "You have to first tell us what it is."

I grinned. They know I always know. But this time they'd tried to fool me with the huge box that was *supposed* to be heavy. Bill thought I thought it was a wolf cub lamp I'd seen down in a Manitou shop. . .but that's not what it was. I didn't want to spoil their surprise when I'd first set eyes on the box so I'd said, "Oh! You got me a big basket!" And Bill had thought I thought it was a basket, but last night I had whispered in Sarah's ear. "It's not really a basket."

So now was the moment of truth when I had to "guess" what was in that box. I looked up at Bill.

"No. I don't want to say what it is. Just let me open it like a normal person."

"Nope. Guess."

"Oh, com'on."

"Guess," he said.

"Yeah, *guess,* Mary Summer Brain," Aimee urged with a big smile.

I sighed and then went for it. After all, it was *they* who were spoiling the surprise.

"You bought it in Cascade," I said to Bill.

He knew right away which shop I meant when I said that. It was an Indian shop where he'd bought my reindeer robe.

"Cascade? I'm afraid I didn't have *that* kind of money!"

I eyed him.

He was doing a great con job.

I grinned. "Can I *touch* the box now?"

"Might as well since you struck out. Guess you need a little extra help. Go ahead, but just pull the paper off the top."

I unwrapped the paper.

"You *did* get it in Cascade! Let me *see!*"

Everyone was laughing by then.

Inside the box, on the bottom, rested another reindeer robe. This one was larger than the one I had and I immediately wrapped it about my shoulders. It was perfect and so beautiful. The gift was from Bill and Robin.

I'm not going to go into the whys and reasons for the animal skins I have. They are not for public wear. They are more a part of me and who I am. Therefore, I have no inclination to explain them to anyone. So don't send me letters harping on their use.

As I was trying on the robe, Computer Bill called to wish me a happy birthday. He said that he and Jan had the journal and *Whispered Wisdom* all scanned and on disk. They'd been through WordPerfect and they'd printed out a hard copy of *Soul Sounds* for me to see. What a birthday gift *that* was! He said I should be receiving it tomorrow, and that copies had also been sent to Bob.

We talked for quite a while before I gave the receiver over to Bill. The two Bill's talked for an even longer time. When Bill hung up, he turned to me.

"Know what?"

"What?"

"Bill and Jan seem like angels sent from heaven."

I smiled. "Maybe they are."

I'm advised against going out to my sacred place in the woods tonight. The Wind Spirit is exceptionally active. The pine boughs are creaking outside and there is an eerie feel to the night. A few moments ago my pen halted when I heard wings fluttering behind my right shoulder. I will spend my Prayertime inside as advised. I will offer my smoke in thanksgiving for the many blessings I received this day that began with the presentation of Grandmother's nature gifts.

12-13-91, Friday

All through the night the Wind Spirit danced a mighty Mazurka. Trees swayed this way and that way, snow sounded like sleet as it was cast upon our bedroom window, and a great howling came down our chimneys.

Our bedroom window rattled so bad all night it was as though a great force was trying to gain entry. I got little sleep, for I'm used to the silent and still woods where no sound save an owl's hoot comes to my ears. Bill slept like a babe-in-arms because he'd stuffed in ear plugs—I can't use those horrible things because I need to hear every audible nuance of the house and woods at night. Unfortunately, the sounds last night were none that one had to listen for.

After Bill brought back the mail and I began working on it, he called me into the living room where he'd been stocking the woodstove.

"Come see the big bird on the front deck!"

Big bird?

I went to the front windows and there before me stood the grouse. His plumage was now grey with the beginning tips of white.

"Oh! It's that grouse I told you about. His winter feathers are coming in."

"Well I think he flew into the window. He look okay to you?"

I frowned when I heard that and watched big bird's behavior for a while.

"He seems fine."

"He's not stunned or anything?"

"No. In fact, he just flew up on the railing. He's watching the jays hog all the seed on the picnic table."

"Well tell him to get on over there before it's all gone."

I watched the grouse watch the jays.

"I think he prefers eating alone—or at least he'd like to eat in better company. Those jays are being really uncouth."

The grouse turned his eye to me. We communed for a bit, then I bid him a farewell. Just as I was about to turn away, he flew off.

The UPS man brought the disk and hard copy of *Soul Sounds*. He also brought a large envelope from Hampton Roads—more returned address changes. As if we didn't have enough to keep us busy.

The printed journal looked great and I placed the disk in my file. After our correspondence was done, it took us two more hours to make all the address corrections on our master mailing list and the file cards. What a job.

After dinner, Bill called Jan to thank her for all her computer work on my manuscripts. I finally got to talk to her and she's a real sweet lady. I'm glad we connected tonight.

This evening Bill and I discussed our shopping day tomorrow. We needed to revise—downscale—our previous list made before Aimee lost her job. We'd planned on getting each other a common gift—one for the family—a stereo VCR to replace our old one. Now that idea didn't fit the budget so we decided on a couple Wrangler flannel shirts for him and something small for me (which I'd find while shopping—probably a basket). The girls had some spending money saved up from Christmas gifts sent in cards from out-of-state family and friends, so they had ideas for each of their sisters.

Bill had called a few sporting goods stores today, and it doesn't look like an archery set is in the cards for Sarah this year. I got sticker-shock when Bill told me the price ranges he was given. Guess it's some art supplies for Sarah.

Aimee needs some medical equipment for her weekly ambulance runs as Third Rider. She needs a BP cuff, a new stethoscope, and medical pants that have pockets in the legs for scissors and other emergency items. The pants are nearly $50 and that's a lot. She'd received a vacation pay check from the grocery store, and she wants to use that for those supplies. Bill says he'll drop Sarah, Jenny, and me off at Target while he takes Aimee over to the surgical supply store.

I've already got Jenny's presents. While Robin took her downtown to do our grocery shopping today, I wrapped them and hid them in one of the cubbies behind the wall paneling—she'll never find them. Hope the little mice critters don't nibble off all the wrapping paper. When Aimee had all her shoes stored in that cubby they chewed up all her laces!

Well, well. . .a letter to the editor about our flyer finally appeared in one of our local papers. It was pro business. Yet the harsh things this man said to state his case "for the company" ended up backfiring (although I'm not sure how many people realized that). He'd said that profit always comes before employees, and that people who work in grocery stores get minimum wage because they're unskilled kids.

The writer of this piece was grossly uninformed because most of the store's employees are family providers—adults—and earn *eight* dollars an hour and above. If Aimee had been allowed to stay on as a cashier, next August she would've been making *11* dollars an hour!

The author of the letter stated that the situation at the store would've only been worse if it had a union—guess he didn't know that the "union" City Markets *weren't* making drastic manpower cuts like the Woodland non-union store was. I hate it when people spout off their mouths in an attempt to sound informed when they haven't even bothered to gather any hard facts. They only end up exposing their ignorance.

What we all found extremely interesting about this published letter was that it supported the *store's* side. . .and so does

the *store* support the *Ute Pass Courier* newspaper every week
with full page ads. Makes you turn a little green with disgust, doesn't it? Makes you wonder if any truth gets space in
small town newspapers—depending on who's paying its bills.
Scratch my back and I'll scratch yours. . . and we'll keep
your store looking mighty good.

This is what happens too, because in two issues of this
paper, there were separate photographs of the manager handing over donation checks for organizations. Do you know
what quite a few store employees thought about those photos?
Sorry. . .I can't repeat it, my publisher wouldn't take kindly
to me writing such explicit expressions.

But one can see the facade that's put up. Store pays big
bucks for ads. . .newspaper publishes pro-store letter about
the flyer, and Joe Good Guy photos. The End. Meanwhile,
back at the store (within) it's Bad News City and no one's
the wiser. Yes sir, that's small town politics and small town
reporting of small town businesses. Joe Manager at the store
goes country dancing with Jane Editor at the paper. . .they
do-see-do a bit and all gets settled over a shot an' a beer.
Hunky-dory it is, yessiree!

I wonder. . .I truly wonder how some folks in this town
can sleep at night. Well, it's real quiet out tonight. I'm going
to sleep as sound as kitty does. Tomorrow's a big family day
and I'm looking forward to it.

Goodnight Mrs. Calabash, wherever you are. Good grief, I
really dated myself with *that* one!

12-14-91, Saturday

Bill, Jenny, Aimee, Sarah, and I piled into the van at ten
o'clock. We picked up our mail and headed down the pass.

Our first stops were at two archery places and we were
singing the blues. These shops had no bows in our price
range. Next we went to Tuxalls, a police and firefighter's
supply store where we found Aimee's size-8 emergency medical pants, and a sweater.

As planned, Bill dropped Jenny, Sarah, and me off at Target's while he and Aimee drove to the surgical supply store,
where she bought her BP cuff, stethoscope, and trauma scissors. By the time Aimee appeared in Target looking for us,
we'd just started making our way to the door. The timing
was perfect.

From Target we went to the Citadel Mall where the traffic
was nearly gridlocked. Bill groaned. No way was he going

inside that mall. So after he found a great parking place, our girls and I took off to shop 'til we dropped.

Once inside the mall, I became aware of a constant buzzing. Wall to wall people. Moving masses of humanity. It was so crowded you had to move with the flow or be trampled. Thank God this was the only day we'd planned to go down from the mountain.

While we were sitting on a bench for a short rest, we people-watched. I said to the girls, "I think this must be what the inside of a bee's nest looks like." They thought that was a good comparison.

Finally, after three hours, we were all done and we headed out to the parking lot. There was Bill, happy as a lark, listening to his tapes. We told him how crazy it'd been inside, and he said it sounded like the usual Christmas "push an' shove" madhouse. It was.

By now it was dark out and we headed out of Colorado Springs. We stopped at the Red Rocks Pizza Hut for dinner and then pointed the van toward home. Before leaving Woodland Park, we picked up more mail at the post office. Tomorrow we'll work on it.

Overall it was a good day. I enjoyed an entire day out with the girls. We had a great time. And for once, we spent a day down in the city without getting culture shock or vibrational headaches.

Magic went crazy when we came home. We're not often all away at once like that and she didn't know who to greet first. God it's a great feeling to see one's little four-legged show such affection. We smothered her with love in return.

We're all pretty beat. When one spends most all of their days up in the quiet mountains, spending an entire day amidst heavy traffic and shoulder-to-shoulder crowds can be draining. None of us were actually drained—just relieved to be once again enveloped in the peaceful aura of our house in the quiet woods.

I'm thankful we made it through the wild traffic this day. We saw some incredibly foolish drivers. At one point it seemed we were in the middle of Dodge 'em Cars. What craziness.

12-15-91, Sunday

We processed the mail early because we'd decided to go back down to Colorado Springs to look for Sarah's archery gift. The three girls were going to stay home.

We ended up driving from end to end of the Springs with

no luck. Finally I remembered something else Sarah wanted and we headed back to the Radio Shack on Uintah. We walked in, spotted the item and we were done. I just wish Bill hadn't been so bent on getting the archery equipment— we would've saved a lot of time and unnecessary traffic hass-le.

On our way home, Bill expressed concern over what to get me for Christmas. We'd had a certain amount of cash set aside for everyone's gift and he was the last one to use from the "kitty."

"How much is left after all you girls have been shop-ping?"

"More than enough for me. In fact, we have extra to put toward bills. You can't spend more than we allotted for each person." He's been known to cheat.

"What do you want? I know you saw a lot of native things when we were in Joe and Monika's Manitou shop, but I can't remember which items you were drawn to."

I laughed. "That was before Aimee lost her job. We have a tight budget now, remember? Anyway, I saw a great basket in Ben Franklin and a stained glass hanging in Hallmark's. You can get them right in Woodland."

"A basket! I want to get you more than that!"

"Bill," I warned, "I'll be upset if you spend more than what we allotted. The girls and I did real well with the money when we shopped yesterday. We stayed within the budget and there's money left over for some bills, or for Jenny to use for groceries. You'll make us feel bad if you blow it by going overboard on me."

He didn't say any more.

One of Bill's greatest joys in life is buying me presents. Nothing pleases him more than going out and buying me things. He's always been that way, but I think this intensified after we had to sell off our possessions several times. Fre-quently he still apologizes for the hard life we've had. To me, that's just because of why we came and what we had to accomplish. . .it had nothing whatsoever to do with his ability to supply our needs, for he often worked two jobs to make ends meet—he was never afraid of hard work because provid-ing for his family was always his highest priority. Now he still derives great pleasure in buying me things he knows have caught my eye, but another *basket*? That's not *his* idea of a proper Christmas present.

When we returned home, the Bronco game was on and he got right into it. I spent time in the office signing books and wrapping presents that were purchased on Saturday. I didn't stay up tonight —I went to bed with my honey.

12-16-91, Monday

It was a heavy day for mail and Wellspring work. We'd received three shipments of clothing and food that needed to be sorted and repackaged. We worked on the mail first and cleaned it up by noon, then the donations were given our full attention. Bill and I worked like buzzing bees to finish in time to get it all distributed. We got back home just in time for Jenny's taco dinner.

In the evening, Bill and Jenny eagerly watched the Saints/ Raiders game. It was an important game because, if the Saints won—our Broncos would clinch the division title and Jenny's hopes would be realized. The Saints won and Jenny was beaming. She asked when the Bronco Division Champs tee shirts would be out and I laughed, "Probably tomorrow!"

I'd taken time out from some evening office work to watch the game with my two football fans. I sat beside Bill and, while he concentrated on the plays, I put cheese spread on his crackers and fed them to him. After all, he brushes my hair sometimes—I can fix his crackers for him. When he started shouting and telling the referees what they could do with their flags, I eased off the couch and faded from the room. He was done with his crackers anyway, so I know I wasn't missed. . .at least until I heard, "Where's my Mary?" and he came looking for her.

Tonight is not the night—nor tomorrow night, nor the next, but one night this week I feel a major ceremony will be performed out in the woods. I can feel its approach. I feel my three friends will be participating. Something has altered.

Tonight when we watched the evening news, scene after scene of homeless were shown sleeping on freezing park benches and eating in soup kitchens. My chest constricted and tears streamed down my face. I tried to hide my sorrow, but Bill caught me as I hurried toward the kitchen bathroom. When he asked me what was wrong, I could no longer contain the feelings and I sobbed into his chest.

"So many are hurting," was all I could manage to say.

He held me tight for a few moments then let me go cry by myself. He knows that's the way I prefer to release my empathy.

I'd done the same thing on Thanksgiving Day when Link

was over. After dinner we watched some news before we put the video in the VCR. When I saw all the homeless lined up for a turkey dinner, the tears began to build and, as hard as I tried to push them back, they wouldn't cooperate. I ended up leaving the room trying to stifle my sobs so nobody would know. But Bill knew and he followed me out to comfort me. I hope Link didn't feel uncomfortable. When I went back in the living room, no one mentioned it, but I think Bill told her the reason I'd left so abruptly.

This night the Prayer Smoke rises for those I cry for. May I one day be able to give more than my tears. I pray that our Wellspring Mission will not only be a touchable place, but also be a place that touches back. This is what I pray for.

12-17-91, Tuesday

For two reasons this was a rare day. One, we only had three letters in the mail and, two, both Bill and I were down in the dumps.

Some days the heaviness of our burden and our additional problems weigh on us.

It was not a good day.

Wild rabbits came around our deck at dusk and I fed them lettuce and alfalfa sprouts. That lightened my mood somewhat. . . until Bill said goodnight in a very tired and downcast voice.

It seems more and more of our days are like that, but it's so much worse when it hits us both at once.

It was not a good day.

12-18-91, Wednesday

Mail was heavy. We couldn't get to it because we had some clothing deliveries to make before we headed down to Colorado Springs for some business errands. While we were at Biz Mart, Bill spied my Christmas present. He was so excited. Not only was this item marked way down, but he'd talked the manager (who he knew) into lowering the price even more. When we left the store there was a roll-top desk in the back of the van and the driver had an ear-to-ear smile on his face. He'd been bad and gone over the allotted amount, but it was so good to see that smile. He was just beaming.

By the time we reorganized the office (he got my old desk), it was 9 P.M. All the while we were rearranging things, we listened intently to our scanner. . .Aimee was out on a house fire. After several hours, we were relieved to hear that it was out and the trucks were rolling back to the station. She came home at 10:30 and told us all about it. She'd been there for six hours.

UPS delivered late tonight. We'd received three packages, two from Hampton Roads. One of these contained more returned envelopes that we use to amend our mailing list, and the other package contained a dozen *Soul Sounds* posters. We all thought they looked great and appreciated the extra mile Bob went to do this for my readers.

The third package was from our friends, The Pruetts in South Fork, Colorado. They'd sent us piñon nuts to roast. What a clever gift! Can't wait to have the family gathered 'round for that homey project.

Tomorrow Bill and I will be going down to Manitou on more business errands. We'll pick up our mail on the way home and I hope we won't have too much because we still have today's to process.

The days when Bill can rest and put his feet up are few and far between. The days I can get out in the woods while it's still daylight are gone and my soul yearns for them to return.

Tonight the Prayer Smoke rises for two very special spirits whose shining lights reach us all the way from Michigan.

12-19-91, Thursday

One word describes this day. Hectic. Our mail was a triple dose and we had to make an unexpected trip back down to Colorado Springs. We didn't return until after dark and then we began to open letters, answer them and sign books.

We finally heard from Jeanne Jones again. It'd been quite a while since we heard from her and, at that time, she was headed out to California to try to interest some investors in the Redstone Castle for a Spiritual Center. Her efforts were a complete disappointment. She said she's given up on trying to solicit help from wealthy people, because they all wanted a piece of the pie or control. Jeanne's not given up though;

she's still got her sights set on that castle. Now she's shifted her approach a little. I give her so much credit. I know that if it's meant to be it will all come together. Jeanne may be in her seventies, but she's one young warrior at heart.

One letter today really frosted me. A lady said I'd cheapened myself and the books because of all the profanity, sex, and wine-drinking that was in them. God, she made me out to be a porno writer! She ranted about the little segment in the beginning of *Dreamwalker*, where my friend and I are in the RV joking about the teeny bathing suit she had for me. Then she railed about mentioning sections in *Phantoms Afoot* where Bill and I are lying together. For God's sake, we were sleeping in a cramped camper! Can't I mention a few moments of endearment between two people who've been happily married for 26 years? Oh God, lady, get out of my face and leave me alone. Take your hang-ups elsewhere. I think she's missing the boat. True love between married people is a very spiritual aspect. Yet she ranted as though my books were rife with orgies and drunken times. Geez, I didn't think it was possible for someone to be so critical as to completely twist beautiful expressions of love into something so ugly. I think I need to pray for this lady—still, her words did bother me.

Aimee spent all afternoon with Dr. Glanzer at the Woodland Park Emergency Center. She really enjoys doing that. The crew said she was welcome there whenever she had time to go in.

After she left the center, she went over to the fire station to participate in Apparatus Night, where they work on maintaining all the equipment, including the trucks.

When she finally came home, she told us about some of the patients that were cared for at the Emergency Center. Emergency medical work is definitely her forte.

I've been feeling nervous. My psyche has been picking up some strange vibrations and I've been uneasy the last few days. I can't seem to shake this knowing. I'm watchful.

Not tonight. Not tomorrow night. I think it's going to be Saturday night. If I'm not mistaken, there will be a full moon shining down on the mountains then. Yes. . .Saturday night will be the one.

My Prayertime tonight will be for Jeanne Jones. Her high project needs my prayers far more than someone consumed with a twisted perspective on love.

Goodnight Jeanne, the Force is still with you.

12-20-91, Friday

At 8:00 A.M. I was already in Dr. Helland's dental chair and by nine I was done. I'll be back again on Monday.

We picked up an armload of mail from the post office and headed home to begin our office day. While I was opening letters, Aimee came in and asked if I had a few minutes. She wanted to tell me about two dreams she had.

I put down the letter opener and gave her my full attention.

She looked concerned.

"I dreamed that you gathered us all together to tell us that you had to leave your body in two weeks. You're not going to die are you?"

I smiled. "I'm not planning on it, especially not in two weeks. I'm not done down here yet. Maybe the dream was referring to a spirit journey instead of the death you interpreted it as."

She shook her head.

"No, that's why it bothers me. You said that you had to leave your body in two weeks and that you'd be born again and write about it."

It came to mind that perhaps I'd have a near-death experience, but I've already had those and saw no import in that. Besides, this event was not foreseen to be in The Plan.

"Aimee," I softly began, "I think your dream represents your fears. Are you afraid I'll die?"

Tears welled in her big brown eyes.

"I don't know what I'd do if you or daddy died. What would I do? I love you both so much."

I leaned over and held her. I whispered words about being stronger than she thinks she is, and about how people carry on when they never believed they could. Then I underscored the fact that we had a lot more work to do yet and there was just no *way* I was going to check out before it was done.

"But you guys have been *through* so much. The problems keep coming, they never stop. You're both so tired."

"Aimee, nobody's life is free of problems, there's always irritations and obstacles to overcome."

"But it's so *stupid* that we're still waiting to be settled. I can *see* how much you want that. Daddy too, he's *sick* of the waiting. And don't tell me it's not the right *time* yet either. When *will* the right time be?"

Good question. Great question.

"I'm sorry, Aimee, but time has *everything* to do with it. I know you and daddy are sick of hearing that answer, but that *is* the answer. We've been advised that 1992 is our deadline year to get settled. Until the destined time is here, we have to accept the waiting period and live day to day."

She sighed.

"I had another dream," she said.

"I don't die, do I?"

She smiled. "No. You walked out in the woods to a place where the ground was like a circular clearing. It was night, yet bright. You were glowing. You went to meet another glowing person who was going to give you some information or answers. There were three people, no. . .beings with you. One in the middle of the circle was a real small one."

She'd seen my Sacred Prayer Ground. Saturday night. She'd tuned into tomorrow night. She saw it *all.* She'd psychically seen it all. I've never spoken details about my night walks, nor told anyone where I go, yet she'd been given a vision of the Sacred Prayer Circle.

"Aimee, you know I go out into the woods late at night."

"Yeah, but this was really *mystical,* mom. You and the other one were actually *glowing!*"

This could not be explained in a simple manner, but I could relate it to another similar aspect.

I sighed. "Do you remember the time daddy and I were sleeping one night and what he saw when he turned toward me?"

"He saw you glowing. He saw a gold light all around you."

"And what was that?"

"Your aura. . .don't play baby questions with me," she frowned.

"Was that a baby question?"

She rethought her statement. "No. What I saw in my dream was your aura—that other person's too." Then she was intensely pensive. "The dream was real, wasn't it? When you go out to your special place your aura shows."

I hesitated. "Sometimes, Aimee, sometimes it does."

"Can *you* see it?"

"Yes, when it's particularly bright, I can."

She was getting excited now. "Who were those others out there with you? Who was that little one? Who's the other person who glows like you did?"

I raised my brow. "Aimee."

Her shoulders slumped.

"Okay, I know it's part of your sacred Prayertime. I'm sorry I pried."

"Don't be sorry. I know you're naturally curious, but some things are best left to rest within The Silence where it belongs. Some things cannot be spoken of."

"And this is one of them," she underscored.

I nodded.

"What a bummer."

"Oh? Are you already forgetting that you don't *have* to hear about it?"

She smiled then. She smiled like she had a great secret.

"Yeah. . .I *saw.*"

The correspondence today included the beginning responses to the *Soul Sounds* poster readers received. The comments were so heartwarming. One lady cried when she saw it. A gentleman couldn't get over how powerful it was. Another said it was beautiful beyond words, and a woman said it took her breath away.

Way to go Carole. . .you made magic when you let spirit direct your colored pencils. It still amazes me that you do all your artwork with *pencils*!

In the mail we also received four jackets of the *Earthway* trade edition. Claire needs me to proof the wording and get back with her before January 2nd. Maybe that means they're thinking of publishing the softcover sooner, after all. That'd be nice.

Anyway, I need to tell her to remove the phrase that says I'm of Shoshone descent. I told them about saying things like that and I'm real finicky about it. They'll have to remove that statement because I can't prove it. I'll call her on Monday to have them delete that. I can't have Ben Nighthorse Campbell slapping a big fine on me for being a "pretend Indian," can I?

Goodnight.

12-21-91, Saturday

It was a beautiful Blue Day and I longed to spend some time out in the sunshine that made the snow sparkle like diamonds, but our stack of mail prevents my outing.

It's important to process each day's mail, otherwise, we'd get so bogged down we'd never catch up. Besides, I really couldn't enjoy a day out in the woods knowing I had a pile of correspondence to respond to. With the increased Wellspring work we've been doing, I have the feeling that something has to give way soon, and I expect it will be the mail. Priorities must take precedence, and now the needy and hun-gry *are* our priority. I've done all I can do in respect to bringing the Precepts to light. I've answered the questions and held high the wisdom of No-Eyes for all to see—the rest is up to each individual now.

Did I mention that I'd written my own "forgive you" card to the lady who apologized for writing to Rainbow? I never did find a card, so I wrote on a blank one.

Today she responded to that card. It made me happy to know her guilt has been lifted. We all do impetuous things that are later regretted. Holding grudges only magnifies the mistakes. Anyway, all is well now and life moves forward.

My psyche was still sparking during the day. It acted like an intermittent blip on a sonar screen that kept reminding me of something approaching. Whenever this happens, I'm watchful for minute signs that serve as forewarning indicators that identify the source. This time the indicators are not being recognized. It's as though something completely foreign approaches and our Advisors aren't giving me any clues. That in itself is unprecedented.

Aimee's words of yesterday haunted me today. Bill's mood was a black one. He's totally sick of our waiting. He always claims he wants to be settled because he knows that's what *I* want so badly, but I've been fine. Lately he's been dwelling on the fact that we're still renting and he worries that things will never work out for us. It's *him* that wants to be settled so bad and he can't live each day as it comes anymore. Each day appears to be an agonizing stretch into the next—each one like a neon sign that reads: YOU HAVE TO WAIT *ANOTHER* DAY!

I can't live like this.

I'm going out into the moonlit woods now. There are important things to do there and people to meet with. I'm going to wear my reindeer robe and take my medicine bundle. Maybe I'll come back. . . maybe I won't.

12-22-91, Sunday

The gathering at my Prayer Circle last night was a beautiful sight, for there were some in attendance whom I hadn't expected to appear. The ceremony was everything I knew it would be and my visitors all took part. Oh, what a *wonder* it was!

I'd been escorted back home by owl and cougar—so gentle they are—so wise and strong of being. And when I went to bed, it was with a restful heart, for my mind was then full of the knowing that everything was going to work out.

Perhaps Bill's spirit was there with us last night because he awoke this morning with a resolve to live for each moment.

He let me sleep in a little longer, and when I got up, we began our full day of delivering the rest of our goods before Christmas. This took the entire day and we were able to make it home just in time for dinner. Afterward, Bill surprised me by asking if we couldn't take the Christmas presents out of hiding and put them under the tree—he was actually in a holiday mood. I ran with the suggestion and we emptied the cubby behind the stairway paneling.

During the evening, I twice caught Aimee shaking her presents. She let out a squeal and giggled when I startled her at it. She's such a little minx. By Christmas she usually knows what all her gifts are. Between her psychic sense and her little girl curiosity, she rarely gets surprises. What can I say?. . .she's her mother's daughter.

For a couple of weeks now, Bill's been teasing about Santa bringing him his Blazer.

"Santa only has seven more shopping days left to get that Blazer. Only three shopping days left for my truck."

He's only joking because he knows darn well Santa's not bringing him any truck—even a toy one—so I tease him right back.

"Only three more shopping days left for Santa to put our land under the tree"; or, "Hope Santa has my first four book contracts under the tree on Christmas morning—right next to your Blazer!"

We get a good laugh about these little quips back an' forth. They help to ease our daily problems and moments of stress. Yet. . .I've had dreams that I dare not voice or pen— dreams that just may be real premonitions of a soon-to-be reality that might turn an ordinary day into a second Christmas. . .as a wondrous miracle. Such things happen, you know. Oh yes, miracles happen every day. Some would call them magic. I call them "gifts" from the Powers of Light. Cougar and owl are two such gifts, for they've come as my woodswalking companions to give comfort and deeper wisdom. In this mystical manner has my apprenticeship been greatly extended and deepened.

It's 2:00 A.M. Tonight my Prayer Smoke rises for my companions who participated in last night's woodland ceremony. I'm grateful for the wisdom each freely shared with me. May I always be worthy of their efforts and their love.

12-23-91, Monday

Began the day at Dr. Eric Helland's dental office. I gave him a signed copy of *Daybreak* and a *Soul Sounds* poster. Eric thought the poster was so striking he wanted me to sign it before he has it framed. I was surprised to hear that and it made me happy to know he liked it so much. He's doing a great job on my teeth and took a lot of extra time to get everything just right. I appreciate his expert efforts.

Our mail was packed like sardines in our mail box. It took so many hours to process it, I couldn't join Sarah for a woodswalk when she asked me to go with her. That's got to stop.

In the late afternoon, Robin brought home a second stack and I went back in the office to clean it up. One large envelope was from Schiffer Publishing, filled with forwarded letters they'd accumulated since *October*! I can't imagine why they let my readers' letters sit around for so long. It's a disgrace. When I responded to those poor people (who probably thought I didn't care enough to answer their letters) I explained that I'd just received them from Schiffer, and I apologized for the long delay in getting back with them.

Robin had also brought home a package from Ann Marie Eastburn and her husband Ted. Ann Marie is the artist who created the beautiful fairy and gnome art for my children's book and also the cover art for *Ancient Echoes*. The package contained two jars of homemade jelly. One was cactus jelly and the other was mesquite bean jelly. They smell delicious and I can't wait to taste them. We all thought that was so thoughtful for them to think of us around the holidays.

Before dinner we roasted the piñon nuts—tasted a little like cashews—and everyone loved them. We had so much I shared them with my four-legged relations who scampered up to the deck for seconds and thirds. . .and. . . .

I'm still feeling uneasy, but there's a second sensation that has appeared to blanket the edge of the uneasiness. . .acceptance. Whatever this is all about, I expect it won't be long in showing up. It's approach is nearly at our door. Knocking, knocking at my woodland door.

On the evening news tonight I watched in shock to see middle-class people vehemently protest the establishment of homeless shelters in their areas. I couldn't believe my eyes and ears. Oh Father! Why did you want us to come down to this apathetic place? So many are living in such misery, while others are turning their heads and closing their ears and hearts. Don't these comfortable people know what they'll be asked when they face You? Don't they know the question will be, "What did you do for your less fortunate brothers and sisters?"

Oh how I hurt for all the suffering I see. How can it be true that so many turn away from it? How can it be that they are not touched by the soulful sounds of hungry mouths and chattering teeth?

My Father, give me strength to endure amidst such chilling apathy, for it makes a great bleeding wound upon my heart. Help me to remain strong enough to once more tread upon the serpent that brings the vile darkness which poisons men's minds. Help me, Father, for I cannot do it without You. Only Your added strength can give me the power of the warrior You sent me to be. *You* are the *Force* of the charging buffalo within me.

Two correspondents' names will be whispered as the Prayer Smoke rises tonight. Nathan in Santa Fe and Joan in Michigan.

12-24-91, Tuesday

Skies clear and blue. Snow sparkling all around. It was a Colorado winter's day and the sun smiled down upon the Rockies. What glory to wake up to. What blessings.

While I typed up last night's journal entry, Bill went into town to pick up our mail. He returned with quite a lot, plus a package from Computer Bill. He'd sent me the second section of *Soul Sounds* on disk and the printed out pages. Also enclosed were the printed pages of *Ancient Echoes*, plus a disk for me and one for the publisher. That was really a surprise.

I worked on the mail while Bill prepared the turkey. We were supposed to have a Christmas goose, but. . .well, he does love his turkey dinners. So he did our Christmas dinner again this year.

Christmas eve day is our traditional day to celebrate because the Christ Child was born in the evening. We have our Christmas dinner on the 24th and then exchange presents afterward.

After the turkey was put in the oven, Bill and I had an absolute restful afternoon reading and listening to soft Christmas music in the living room with the woodstove crackling in the background. Robin had to work until dinner time. Jenny was playing around with the computer in the office. Aimee was napping in our room. And Sarah and Mandy were reading books in their own respective rooms upstairs. I can't recall ever having such a relaxing and tranquil afternoon.

As soon as Robin came home, we put dinner on the table. The candles were lit and Robin said the prayers. Dinner was delicious and we had a leisurely meal. It was so nice having all seven of us together.

Mandy and Sarah did the dishes while Jenny and Aimee cleared the food away and cleaned up the kitchen. The old folks retired to the living room where Bill proceeded to read us two letters to the editor that were published in our local paper about our flyer. Both letters tore apart last week's pro-company letter. Both letters were pro-union and pro-worker. We smiled and cheered as Bill read. Our little flyer sure did stir the stew in the kettle!

When dishes were done, presents were given out. We each took a turn opening one at a time. When I opened Robin and Mandy's gift to me, I squealed, "A basket! *Two* baskets!"

Bill shifted his eyes over to Robin.

"She's got a real *case* for baskets. How'd you know?"

I slid my gaze over at him. "Are you trying to say I'm a basket case?"

His palms came up as he laughed.

"Hey, *you* said that, not me."

After all the gifts were opened, Bill brought out one more and placed it in my lap.

"Merry Christmas, honey," he said.

"What's this?" I frowned. "You weren't supposed to get me anything more!"

He grinned his Little Boy grin. "I cheated." Then, "Bet you can't guess what it is."

I looked around at all the smiling faces.

"It's a framed stained glass," I announced with conviction.

"Nope."

"Yep."

"Nope."

"Yep-yep."

"Okay, smartie, how do you know?" he sighed.

"Because this is the gift wrap that Hallmark used this year and the size of this package has to mean. . ."

Bill threw his arms up and everyone began laughing as I tore off the paper.

"See?" I said, "a Hallmark box!" The stained glass was *The End of the Trail.* It was just beautiful.

Jenny presented me with the Savannah Gardens fragrance I like so much, and Aimee and Sarah gave me a miniature Victorian music box shaped like a heart.

It was a beautiful day. It was a Christmas filled with the warmth of loving family and friends. That alone was the most precious gift of all.

12-25-91, Wednesday

Robin and Mandy spent the day down in Colorado Springs with Robin's mother and sisters. We had another restful day. It was a strange feeling not to have any office work to do and I almost felt guilty having the entire day to ourselves.

In the afternoon, I stained two pine shelves that we'd given to Jenny for all her cat figurines.

We had a carbon copy of yesterday's dinner, but tonight it was just the five of us dining by candlelight. Magic and Buttercup shared in our holiday dinner by getting treats of turkey during the meal.

The evening was a quiet one, but I was restless with an inner sense of being bothered by something I could not name. When this happens, Bill perceives my distracted mood and he was upset that it came on Christmas night to disturb our peaceful atmosphere. I can't help that. I can't help the perceptions I receive and I wish he'd be a little more understanding of them at these times.

Once, when he allowed himself to be very open to psychic impressions and messages, it bothered him to such a degree that he said, "I don't know how you can operate being so open," and he voluntarily shut himself down, leaving me to bring in all the messages and advice. So now he sometimes forgets how the psychic impressions can affect one's daily life and moods. I can usually cover up my inner affectations from these sensings, but sometimes it shows anyway.

Another vision intruded upon my thoughts today. While I was staining Jenny's shelves, a clear visual flashed before my mind's eye. It was of a letter addressed to me here in Woodland Park and the postal clerk stamped it with MOVED - NO FORWARDING ADDRESS. That was all there was to the visual and it was puzzling. Clearly it represented a relocation for us, but there could only be a couple reasons why our mail wasn't being forwarded to a new address and I wasn't prepared to dwell on either of them. I let go of the vision's residual effects and continued the conversation I was having with Jenny while I worked on her shelves.

Sarah told me that she'd come to a realization over the last couple weeks. She said that she didn't really care where we lived as long as we were all together. She was ready to move to the Marble area whenever we were able to manage it.

At first I was skeptical of her words. I felt she was saying that because she didn't want anything to hold us back, but then I could feel a deeper level that the sentiments came from and I told her how much I appreciated her honesty.

All indicators point to a major move for us in 1992. Right now it all looks pretty shaky. However, I do know that, one way or the other, we will be making a move in '92. That year was given as our outside date—our deadline.

Merry Christmas, everyone.

12-26-91, Thursday

This morning was hectic with fancy footwork. Aimee had planned to go into town with Bill and me. He was going to drop me off at the dentist and then drop her off at the Emergency Center so she could finish her required emergency room hours for her State Certification Exam tomorrow.

Before breakfast, Aimee called her EMT instructor and while they were talking it came up that Aimee was doing her emergency room hours up here in Woodland Park. The instructor was taken aback because those hours can *only* be done at St. Francis or Penrose Hospital in Colorado Springs!

Aimee was all upset. She'd already put five hours in at our Emergency Center and was going to do the last five hours today. Her state exam is tomorrow and the ten hours of emergency room experience had to be done beforehand. She was devastated. Now she'd have to wait for the late January testing time.

When I came downstairs the atmosphere was like a heavy

wet blanket and Aimee was near tears with disappointment. I listened to the tale of woe and found it hard to believe she'd misunderstood her instructor.

"Well," I said, "seems to me you'd better get on the phone to see if St. Francis can accommodate an EMT trainee today."

Her eyes widened like an owl's before she ran to the phone. St. Francis already had three trainees booked for the emergency room today.

"Call Penrose," I said.

Penrose had no trainees and would be glad to have her come down. Aimee quickly gathered her equipment and stoked up the old pickup for a run down the pass. She was off for her ten hours of emergency room experience. And we were off to the dentist.

We spent the entire day in the office processing our ream of mail. Aimee called in twice to let us know how it was going. She'd made friends with a nurse and they'd gone to the cafeteria together. Aimee was enjoying her day.

When she arrived back home at 10:30 P.M., she told us about all the patients. One doctor went out of her way to answer Aimee's questions and take her to Radiology to explain the x-rays that were taken on patients that Aimee took vitals on. And one male nurse told another nurse that he'd been observing Aimee and that she was very sharp. This male nurse had Aimee do a patient assessment on a man who thought he had a dislocation in his hand. The nurse watched Aimee handle him and ask questions of the patient. Aimee's opinion was that there was no dislocation, and she explained why. . .she was right.

Now that her ten hours were squeezed in today—at the 11th hour—Bill will take her downtown tomorrow morning for the State Certification Exam. Those taking the test are given three hours to complete it. She's not at all nervous. I'm sure that's because she feels comfortable with the material.

Aimee sure has surprised us. We never realized that she had a real knack and aptitude for this medical work. She slipped into it like pulling on a kid glove. It's a perfect fit.

In January she's planning on taking the next course up from EMT. It's called EMT-IV, which allows the Emergency Medical Technician to begin intravenous lines in a patient. Aimee won't stop until she's a certified paramedic and is riding an ambulance. And all this from a young lady who graduated from. . .home schooling. Way to go, Aimee. We're so proud of you.

Received a letter today from a lady who amazed her dentist with a "great improvement" with her gum disease. . . she'd been doing Gateway Healing Treatments. That was great to hear, but she also said that she'd postponed surgery for her breast lump in favor of trying Gateway Healing on it. I immediately wrote her back to explain that her lump required routine monitoring and that true Earthway Healing was comprised of *all* healing methods—including the traditional modern ones of her physician. I also told her how to visualize her T-cells going into an Alert/Attack/Annihilate Mode for the breast lump. Programming the body's cells to do what you want is 90 percent of the battle.

Robin's going to resign from her job as employee representative at City Market, because her peers have been warned not to talk to her. No one comes to her with their problems anymore and she doesn't want the job unless she can help them out. She says there's a woman in her deli department that's pro-company and wants to be the rep. Robin's going to let her go for it because. . .it figures. She bent over backwards trying to help the employees who came to her, and now that they're all afraid to be seen talking to her, she has no use for the position and no longer cares to have it. She'd been the only employee representative that was truly pro-employee. I guess now they'll *all* be pro-company. Why bother? What a racket. I don't understand how employees can allow themselves to be so easily manipulated.

Robin took Mandy and Sarah to the show tonight. Jenny didn't want to see *Hook* because she had other plans. Robin had given Jenny a sewing machine for Christmas and Jenny spent the entire evening making small throw pillows with scrap material. This machine was one that one of Robin's sisters no longer wanted, and it'd been sitting down in Colorado Springs at her mother's house. When Robin's mother asked her if she knew anyone who could use it, she immediately thought of Jenny.

Jenny took sewing in school and seemed to have a talent for it. She'd made a down vest and a prairie skirt in the eighth grade. Last fall she had Robin help her make a jump suit. We never had a sewing machine of our own (except for my grandmother's old treadle) and Jenny always had to have assistance using Robin's. So now we hear new sounds coming from Jenny's loft. Rat-a-tat. Rat-a-tat. And we know she's busy at her new sewing machine.

How truly amazing it is that someone with a learning disability has a natural affinity for machines, while I have such an ingrained aversion to them. Jenny doesn't understand abstracts and I can't understand mechanical operating instructions.

What an interesting and paradoxical world this is.

Another vision came upon the screen of my mind's eye today. Bones. The bones that have no eyes, yet see. Bones that watch. Bones that have great power. I must make these Standing Shields of bones that clank in the wind. This is what the spirits are telling me. This is what I must do. It is time.

12-27-91, Friday

Sarah went with Bill to take Aimee down for her exam. They didn't return until dinner time because they'd stopped at a few stores. Aimee felt she did well on her test. She said she was done in an hour. I feel she did well too.

While they were gone, I did odds and ends around the house. Jenny's stained shelves were dry so I put them up for her. They look real cute with all her kitty figurines on them now.

Overall, it was an unremarkable day, except for the strong impression I received that I may not be publishing *Ancient Echoes* after all. The Anazazi Book of Chants may never see the light of day. The reasons were obscure, yet clear to me. And that's no paradox. I understand completely. I just wish this message would've been more timely because the manuscript has been put on disk already. I know that doesn't prevent me from deleting it from my series, but it certainly would've saved Jan and Bill a lot of computer time.

This strong impression came at a curious time, as I've been thinking of perhaps ending the books soon. Maybe I'll not publish the two novels, although quite a few of my correspondents keep asking me when *Ka of the Seventh Mesa* will be available. I don't know yet. Time will tell—it always does. Time is always the determining factor. Well, when folks see *Pinecones and Woodsmoke*, they'll know they've seen my final book. If *Ancient Echoes* or the two novels didn't precede it. . .they won't be forthcoming at all. Besides, with the *Ka of the Seventh Mesa* novel, I may have let too much out of the bag anyway.

Goodnight.

12-28-91, Saturday

Bill took Jenny down to King Soopers to do her grocery shopping. While they were gone, Aimee went into Woodland to pick up our mail. I dug into it as soon as she handed it to me. It took until 7:00 P.M. to finish it. I didn't want to leave any office work for tomorrow because I'd planned on going for a woodswalk with Sarah.

One correspondent's comment today really irritated me. She stated that "the poor were poor because that's their *karma*." She said "the poor *chose* that reality for themselves."

Oh really? Well, my friend, have I got a news flash for you! Your logic is all twisted in knots. Your reasoning is self-serving, in that it conveniently leaves you with no personal responsibility to help those in need. Your logic is designer logic, created for the sole purpose of easing your own moral conscience.

What ever happened to "visit the sick" and "feed the hungry" and "clothe the naked?" Huh? *Huh?* Jesus didn't look the other way. He didn't turn his eyes away from a hungry crowd of people—he *fed* them. "Whatsoever *you* do for these, the *least* of my brethren, you do for *me*."

I'm not trying to give a Christian slant to the truths, but dammit people, get that cockamamie "create your own reality" garbage out of your addled brains. Sure, folks' thoughts can affect their lives, but you tell me, who in their right mind says, "I *want* to be poor, hungry, and homeless?" And if they're *not* in their right minds and do say that, they need help too!

Think on this one. God places a homeless person in your path just to see what you'll do. He does this as a test. Do you show compassion or turn your head in disgust? Did you pass or fail said test? Ever give a thought to it perhaps being a possibility that *your* karma this time around is to *help* the needy and homeless? Ever give a moment's thought to the possibility that you're *creating* negative karma for yourself by *not* helping the poor?

For God's sake, the needy don't wish to be needy! I'm not talking about lazy welfare frauds here either. I'm talking about the truly needy individuals and families who want nothing more than a helping hand back up to self-sufficiency again. Have we become a cold, stone-hearted society that prefers to ignore the misery of the needy because it's personally uncomfortable to do otherwise? Oh, say it isn't so!

This correspondent also stated that, "God or the Powers That Be will care for the needy." Oh really? Are we *all* not

God's children who were given the responsibility to care for one another? How many angels have you seen lately coming down from on high to drop manna from heaven upon the homeless living under city bridges? My dear lady, don't you know that the angel is you? That God expects us to take care of one another? That the God Force that you expect to care for the needy is in *you?*

This woman's logic was incredible to me, because she even inferred that those people who come into the world as messengers get all their needs taken care of by God or their guides. Wrong. Nope. Wrong, wrong, wrong. The physical aspects are totally severed from the spiritual one. Did Moses or Jesus come upon the earth wearing robes of spun gold? Moses had such a devil of a time with Ramses that he had to call in the Big Guns and have the Angel of Death come to convince the stubborn pharaoh. Come on folks, get it together. Stop rationalizing your reasons for not having compassion for others. Stop playing mind games with yourself. I wouldn't doubt that, when God does come again, He'll enter as a ragged and hungry homeless person, and everyone who helps Him in some way will be gathered unto Him, while those who turn away and mumble, "well, that's *his* karma" or "he *chose* that reality" will *not* be gathered unto Him. Think on that one.

Do I sound like I'm preaching? Oh no, I'd never do that. What I'm doing is venting my spirit's anger at those who choose to be blind and deaf to all who are crying out to be fed and clothed. God does love all His children and it pains Him to see them suffer so. This much I know.

Amen, brothers and sisters. Amen.

12-29-91, Sunday

When Bill started the van this morning it sounded like a garbage truck trying to dump its load. I'm so disgusted with that Astrovan I could scream. He has to take it down to Team Chevrolet again to see if they can find out what's wrong. We should've gotten that full-sized Blazer instead of the van. The last thing we need now is more truck problems.

Robin gave us bad news this morning. City Market is again cutting her hours back. Now she'll only be working 26 hours a week. Deep depression. So Bill and I tried to project what our January income taxes would be. After paying that and our January rent, we'll have little left to our name. Great way to begin a new year.

These calculations didn't brighten our day any. We just looked at each other with the old "Well? What now?" look. After discussing the situation for several hours we decided the best course would be to wait out the rough seas and see how things looked when all was calm again. This, we've learned, has been the wisest choice to make in this situation—at least it has been for us.

Still, it bothered me to have more financial problems and I began to sort out my library shelves for the Goodwill. Aimee came down her loft stairs and watched me pull book after book and add them to the growing piles on the floor.

"Mom?" she said, "Are you having another mid-life crisis?"

I turned to her with a wide grin.

"That was funny. Why would you ask that?"

"Because every time you're really upset about something you sort out your library and give half of it away."

"I do?"

"Yes." I frowned as I looked down at the three piles of books.

"Yeah, guess I do. Go get me some boxes for the Goodwill."

When she came back with the boxes, she helped me pack them.

"Mom, I can go back to work again. I can find someth. . ."

"There *are* no decent-paying jobs in Woodland Park. Besides, your EMT-IV classes are coming up. That's more important. If our children's book orders don't drop off too much then that can carry us through. Those books have been paying our monthly living expenses since you were forced to quit work."

"Well yeah, but that was before Robin's hours were cut again. Mom. . ."

"We'll be okay, Aimee. All I want you to do is concentrate on your medical studies. You leave the finances for me and dad to work out."

"But. . ."

"Aimee?" I warned.

"Well, if all these books are any indication, you sure are upset."

"So let me work it off in my own way. Okay?"

"Okay, mom. I love you."

"I love you too, honey."

By the time I'd boxed up three-fourths of my books I felt better. I'd wanted to go for a sunny woodswalk with Sarah today, but things didn't turn out that way.

Two weeks ago, when Bill and Sarah were downtown at PetSmart they'd bought a new cage for her bird. Today she wanted to put him in his new home, so I helped her with the long project of arranging his "furniture and toys." After we'd accomplished that, she was at the computer and deeply involved in the Perils of Rosella game when I next went into the office. She was having such a good time I didn't want to take her away from it.

In the living room, Bill and Jenny were engrossed in a football game. I ended up sorting out more of my personal possessions and the stack of Goodwill boxes grew.

I don't know why I give my things away when I get down. Maybe it's the "giving" factor that helps to bring me back up. Before Aimee brought my idiosyncracy to my attention, I never realized I was doing it. All I know is that it works for me.

In the evening, Aimee and Sarah went to the show while Jenny stayed home with us to watch *Ghost Dad* on television. It was a quiet evening and everyone but me was in bed by 11 o'clock.

I just checked outside. The mountains are dark. The air is crisp, and the heavens are twinkling with brilliant lights. I'm going out to my special place in the woods. I have a great need to be in the quiet forest with my two wise companions. I also have the distinct feeling that my Starborn friend will also be there. His presence is strong.

I'm in a good frame of mind right now. Robin's bad news has been dealt with and I look to tomorrow as a brand new day. Now it's a brand new night—so beautiful and pristine— and I look forward to walking out into it, deeply inhaling the fragrant pine essence that so refreshes my soul.

Goodbye.

12-30-91, Monday

I awoke this morning with thoughts of my *Ancient Echoes* book on my mind. While Bill and the girls were in town, I took out the manuscript and reread it from beginning to end. And there I found something very peculiar. About two-thirds of the way through the manuscript I'd inadvertently shifted the tense from past to present. Where I'd previously written "was" I now had "is" and where I would've used "they" I used "we." I found this to be a curious discovery. As I thought about what this might mean, it came to me that I'd been so into my past that I maintained the old identity for a small span of time even while I was typing up the manuscript. I hadn't caught this shift in tense even when I proof-read it for typos. Now it stood out like an owl's screech at midnight.

I wonder if Computer Bill noticed the shift while scanning the manuscript, or if Jan took note of it while running it through Word Perfect? I also wonder what Bob will do about it if I do decide to publish the book? To me it represents a shift back into that lifetime.

I put the manuscript back in my file cabinet and thought no more about it except to smile, as I thought of our Advisors' clever ways of bringing things to our attention.

Bill returned with an armload of mail. Before I could dig into it, he said he had something to tell me.

"When I woke up this morning I saw you sitting in an old-time chair in the corner of our room. You wore some type of old fashioned white nightie."

"Was I old?"

"No, you looked just the way you do now."

"Did I say anything to you."

"No, you were just sitting there."

"But I was also asleep in bed with you."

"Yes. There were two of you. What does it mean?"

I smiled. "I would say my spirit's desperately trying to tell you that I'm not going to die anytime soon. That's why the spirit manifested wearing an old-style gown and appeared in an old-fashioned chair."

We discussed his psychic sighting until he was comfortable with it, then we concentrated on the mail, which took us all day to complete.

One of the letters I opened was a nasty complaint regarding some rude and curt responses I supposedly made to a few questions in *Daybreak*. Trouble was, this reader must not have read the introductory page of that book, where it explains that the responses come from several sources *other* than myself. The Advisors can be extremely sharp in their responses to some types of questions, as can No-Eyes. I think many readers forgot that I was not the only one answering the questions.

In this same vein, a few weeks ago, we'd received a similar letter wherein the correspondent thought one answer was unforgivably rude and sarcastic. Well, that particular answer came directly from the Advisor who "saw" the questioner as having a severe drinking problem. So then, the answer was directly to the point and didn't mince words about the overindulgence of martinis. Many people can be helped with the kid glove treatment, while many others have different needs.

The Advisors know the difference. By this example we see that responses that may, on the surface, appear sarcastic or rude—really aren't, because they were uniquely tailored for a specific individual.

In the early evening, while Bill was busy with a long consultation call, we received seven packages at our door. There were three from Bill and Jan which were filled with Christmas-wrapped computer gifts for each of us. What a wonderful surprise that was!

Three large boxes were clothing donations and I spent the entire evening sorting them for our needy recipients. I'm very grateful for the contributions we've been getting—so are our recipients!

The seventh package was from Hampton Roads. It contained more returned envelopes from their mailing.

Tonight, because it is fitting to do so, my Prayer Smoke will rise for two people who have turned cold hearts toward us. Their names will be whispered into the rising smoke. . . because *I* still care.

12-31-91, Tuesday

All morning we distributed the clothing I sorted yesterday. All afternoon we worked on the mail, revising our mailing list and taking care of business calls.

Carole Bourdo was in Mexico, so I spoke with her daughter, Lauri. I needed to know if Carole was going to have prints of the *Soul Sounds* art available to the public. If so, I wanted to state that on one of the last pages of the book.

The rest of the afternoon was taken up with our year-end bookkeeping. Bill had to close out his book order records and I closed out our general business expenses for the year. Before January 15th we'll have our income taxes paid and, hopefully, begin again to save for our cabin. I'd hoped to be settled somewhere by the time this journal ended, but that long-awaited-for goal will be reached in '92 if we have to sell all we own, including the van, to accomplish it.

This was a year that brought much heart pain from unexpected sources. Both Bill and I learned some invaluable lessons about relationships and, because of those, have gained a new depth of wisdom.

Our Starborn friends were much more active this year and the new year will prove to be even more involved as our destinies weave a more intricate and integrated pattern together.

Because of secrets revealed at my sacred ground gathering the other night, I now know where we'll be moving to. Odd how things work out, yet so inevitable in the end.

It's begun to snow. It hasn't snowed since my birthday. How appropriate it is for nature to bring a blanket of sparkling renewal to my mountains this New Year's Eve. This I read as a good omen.

I'm going to return to my place in the woods tonight. This eve marks the beginning of the end, for after tonight, no one will ever again hear the sounds of my soul—no one but owl. . .cougar. . .and me.

Postscript

I may be able to eliminate one of the cliff-hangers at the end of the journal. I know many of you are going to want to know how the situation with Aimee and Eric ended.

Young Eric called and talked to Bill. They set up a meeting with Aimee at our home. The encounter had a few false starts but Aimee found that she'd not held the destructive hate in her heart that she thought she had. What she discovered was that she was cleaving onto the "idea" of hate rather than true hatred. And that was a major realization for her to come to. She understood his reasonings for initially leaving her—he had to find himself before he knew where he was going—and she forgave him.

Eric stayed for dinner that evening and the two played on the computer until he had to leave. They needed a diversion to ease the discomfort they both felt with their first meeting after years of being apart.

Aimee says she wants to be friends with Eric and take a day at a time because they both realize they need to begin to get to know one another all over again, then see what develops.

Hampton Roads Publishing Company
publishes and distributes books on a variety of subjects,
including metaphysics, health, alternative/complementary medicine,
visionary fiction, and other related topics.

To order or receive a copy of our latest catalog, call toll-free,
(800) 766-8009, or send your name and address to:

Hampton Roads Publishing Company, Inc.
134 Burgess Lane
Charlottesville, VA 22902

Internet: www.hrpub.com
e-mail: hrpc@hrpub.com